DECEIVING BELLA

BOOK ELEVEN IN THE BODYGUARDS OF L.A. COUNTY SERIES

CATE BEAUMAN

Deceiving Bella

Visit Cate at www.catebeauman.com
Follow Cate on Twitter: @CateBeauman
Or visit her Facebook page: www.facebook.com/CateBeauman

First Print Edition: October 2016

Print ISBN-13: 978-1539333968
Print ISBN-10: 1539333965
eBook ISBN: 978-0997064117

Editor: Jennifer Stimson & the E-book Formatting Fairies
Proofreader: Editing by Kimberly Dawn
Cover: Demonza

Also By Cate Beauman

Bodyguards of L.A. County Series

Morgan's Hunter

Falling For Sarah

Hailey's Truth

Forever Alexa

Waiting For Wren

Justice For Abby

Saving Sophie

Reagan's Redemption

Answers For Julie

Finding Lyla

DEDICATION

To my favorite Life Coach Brenda Fahn. Without your great humor and wonderful wisdom, I'm quite certain Reed and Bella's story never would have been finished. Thank you for helping me find my way out of the dark.

ও CHAPTER ONE ৯

Clinton, Ohio
April 1995

BELLA DREW A HEART ON THE BACK OF A PALE PINK ENVELOPE while she sat at the small table tucked in the corner of her room. Smiling, she set down her lilac crayon, pleased that the shape of this heart hardly looked wobbly at all. She studied the assortment of stickers Mommy had given her to decorate her invitations with and picked the glittery fuchsia ones for the corners. Locking her ankles, she kicked her legs back and forth and hummed along with the music on the CD player, trying to ignore her parents shouting in the living room. "Here is my handle, here is my spout," she muttered, sealing the envelope closed with a puffy star sticker. "Tip me over and pour me out."

The yelling suddenly stopped, and footsteps stormed down the hall. Bella jumped when Mommy and Daddy's bedroom door slammed shut. Pausing, she listened to the quiet, then picked up the next envelope and smiled again when she recognized the letter '*M*.' "Mary Rose." She snatched up the sheet of silly smiley faces and put one right below Mommy's pretty handwriting, certain her best friend would love it.

"Bella Boop," Daddy called, giving a quick knock on her door.

"I'm in here."

The knob turned and Daddy walked in dressed in jeans and one of the grease smeared white T-shirts he always wore to work.

Bella picked up a sky-blue crayon. She paused as she met Daddy's gaze and realized his brown eyes were red, the way hers looked when she scraped her knees or got shots at the doctor's office and cried. "Are you and Mommy mad at each other?"

Daddy sat on the bed, wrinkling her Hello Kitty comforter with his weight. “No. We’re not mad at each other.”

“Mommy yelled at you. Did you leave the toilet seat up again?” She frowned, remembering the cold water she’d fallen into the other morning. “I don’t want my tushy to get wet again when I sit down.”

He closed his eyes as he laughed, but it wasn’t his regular laugh that always made her giggle. “No, I didn’t leave the seat up.”

“Good,” she said with a decisive nod and got back to work.

“What are you doing in here?” he asked.

“Coloring my invitations. Mommy said we can bring them with us to school in the morning. Everybody gets to have one—even the boys—so we don’t hurt anyone’s feelings.”

“That’s my girl.” He winked.

She handed over one of the envelopes in her finished pile for Daddy to admire. “This one is for Clara. See how it has a letter ‘*C*’? That’s how I know.”

“What’s this?” Daddy pointed to the next letter in Clara’s name.

“An ‘*L*.’”

“Smarty-pants.”

She grinned, always loving it when he called her that. “Clara’s going to be five too. Her mommy’s bringing brownies to school next week when it’s her birthday—just like you brought in the cupcakes for me to share yesterday. Everyone liked them. Pink frosting is the best kind.”

“With purple sprinkles, right?”

“Right.” She took the invitation back and continued decorating Mary Rose’s.

“I can’t believe my girl’s almost five. You’re not a baby anymore.”

“I’m a beautiful young lady now, right?”

He sighed. “Somehow you are. Not all that long ago, I was rocking you to sleep.”

“Beautiful young ladies have pierced ears and paint their nails.” She beamed at him, thrilled that she had both after a trip to the mall and a visit to the nail painter woman Mommy knew. “And young ladies go to kindergarten when the leaves fall off the trees, right after the summer is over.”

“I guess they do.” He blew out another breath. “Will you come sit with me for a couple of minutes?”

She hesitated as she glanced from the stickers to Daddy’s sad eyes. “Okay.”

He grabbed her under the armpits of her favorite Hello Kitty pajamas and boosted her up, settling her on his thigh. "Here we go." He wrapped his arms around her and hugged her tight.

She returned his embrace, breathing in the familiar oil smell of the garage where he fixed cars. "Is your tummy sick?"

"No, baby." He played his hand through the curls Mommy had made at the end of her long ponytail this morning.

"Did you get a boo-boo at work?" She picked up his stained black fingers, checking for a cut.

"No, honey." He clenched his jaw. "I have to go on a trip."

She gasped her excitement and clapped. Daddy always took her on the best adventures. "Can I come?"

He shook his head. "Not this time."

"We could get ice cream at the Dairy Stop," she said in a singsong voice, hoping that would convince him to change his mind.

"I wish we could, Bella. I have to go on this trip by myself."

She pressed her cheek to his chest. "I don't want you to go unless I get to come too. I always come too, Daddy."

His fingers moved through her hair again. "I know."

"You can stay right here with me." She leaned forward and picked up her favorite book from the pile on the nightstand. "We can read instead."

He nuzzled his chin on top of her head, keeping her close.

She clung to him as her stomach started to hurt. Daddy never went away. He and Mommy always read her books together and took turns bringing her to school after breakfast. "Will you come back soon?"

He shook his head. "Not for a long time. Not till you're an even bigger young lady."

Her lips trembled as her eyes filled. "But I'll miss you so much."

"I'll miss you too. I'll think of you every day."

"Daddy." She sniffled. "I want you to stay."

"I have something for you." He grabbed something from behind his back she hadn't noticed when he walked in and held up a small snow globe.

She took the delicate glass and studied the pretty two-story house surrounded by pine trees in the center—much bigger than the home she lived in now. "It's so nice."

"When you look at it, you can think of me."

"You'll live in there?"

He looked at the ceiling as he swallowed. "Something like that."

She stared at the lights on in the cheerful home as the snow fell to the ground. "Will you come out for my party in a couple of days and sing 'Happy Birthday'?"

"I can't."

Her shoulders sagged. "But you can come out at night and read to me and tuck me in?"

He shook his head.

Her lips trembled again, and she blinked as tears fell.

"Don't cry, Bella." He wiped her cheeks with his thumbs, like he always did. "If there was any other way... If I could be sure you and your mom would be safe, I'd take you with me."

"We could call the policemans. They'll make us safe."

"That's an idea." He swiped another tear away. "How about I tuck you in and we'll read?"

She nodded. "Can I sleep with this?" She gestured to the globe.

"How about we put it right next to you on the table? I don't want it to break and cut you."

"All right." She leaned over and set it next to her lamp. "There."

Daddy stood, lifting her with him, and pulled back her covers, then settled her in bed. "Here we go." He tucked the blankets around her and read the story she and Mommy had picked out at the library.

She giggled when the silly puppy got into mischief and yawned, struggling to keep her eyes open as Daddy turned to the last page.

"The end."

"That's a good one." She yawned again. "Maybe we can get a doggy like the girl in the book."

"Someday."

"I love doggies."

"I know you do."

She rubbed her tired eyes. "Let's read it some more."

"You need to get some rest." Daddy stood from his chair. "Snuggle up."

She rolled on her side and nestled her cheek on the pillow. "Night-night, Daddy. I love you."

"I love you too." He knelt down and hugged her tight, his breath shuddering in and out next to her ear. "I love you, Bella." Clearing his throat, he eased back and smiled. "I love you."

She smiled too. "I'll see you in the morning."

He shut his eyes, swallowing several times. "Okay." Standing again, he turned off her light. "Bye, baby."

"Bye, Daddy."

ଓ CHAPTER TWO ଓ

Los Angeles, California
March 2016

REED TOOK THE STAIRS IN TWOS, BRINGING ONE OF THE LAST storage containers to his new master bathroom. He set the plastic on the granite countertop and turned in the doorway, glancing around at the half-dozen boxes in his bedroom and the bed-frame lying in pieces on the solid wood floor. Now appeared to be as good a time as any to put things to rights.

Grabbing the safety blade from his back jeans pocket, he went after the tape on the small box labeled 'Hangers' as his phone started ringing. He paused, looking at Joey's face filling the screen, and debated whether or not he wanted to answer. Sighing, he pressed *talk*. "Yeah."

"It's moving day," Joey boomed in his New York accent.

"Thank God."

"You officially out of your mother's place?"

"Finally."

"She's a good lady."

"No man wants to live with his mother, Joe, even temporarily."

Joey chuckled. "How's it going?"

"Not too bad. I'm pretty much moved in." He swiped at his dripping brow with his forearm. "Sweaty work, though."

"Shoulda stayed in the Big Apple. It's colder than shit here."

"I like that I'm wearing shorts." He lifted the hem of his white T-shirt and wiped at the perspiration more thoroughly, going after the drops tickling his temples.

"Sunshine'll get boring after a while. You'll get twitchy sooner or later."

He doubted it. He'd been in LA for almost seven months and liked it just fine. "What's up?"

"Big stuff. Fuckin' big stuff, buddy, that's what. You're never gonna guess what just happened."

Wincing, he held the phone away from his ear as his former partner got louder. "With you, that could be just about anything."

"You better believe it. I'd be losing my touch if I couldn't keep you on your toes."

Reed grunted his agreement as he grabbed a bunch of the hangers and walked to the closet, waiting for Joey to swing around to his 'big news.'

"So, twenty minutes ago, I'm at Walter Hodds's funeral, and I get the break we've been looking for."

Reed thought of the US Marshal they'd worked with occasionally over the last several years—a good guy gone too soon. "That was today?"

"Yeah, I told you I was going when I talked to you on Monday."

"I forgot. I hope you gave his wife my condolences."

"I took care of it. It was like a greeting card: heartfelt, fucking poetic."

Joey rarely spoke a sentence without some sort of expletive in it. "I bet."

"You're going to go crazy when you hear the rest. I'm telling you, this is our big break, buddy. We can blow our investigation wide open with this one."

"Last time I checked, I wasn't looking for any big breaks, and we don't have an investigation. You keep forgetting I'm not a cop anymore." He went back for another handful of hangers, glancing out the windows at the palm trees blowing in the breeze.

"Once a cop, always a cop."

He slammed more hooks on the rod. "Nope."

"So, I'm at Walt's funeral—the thing afterward—the reception or whatever," Joey went on despite Reed's denial. "We're at his house and I spill a fuckin' glass of red wine down my pants."

Reed rolled his eyes. Joey had huge hands to go along with his linebacker-size. "What a surprise."

"Melanie grabs my arm and we start toward the bathroom, 'cept the line's a mile long. We decide to try the master bathroom 'cause I can't wait forever, you know? I look like I pissed myself. We go in, kinda close the door, and I take off my pants while Melanie tries to figure out how she's gonna get the mess out of my clothes without staining the white washcloths Walt's missus keeps on the towel rack. One thing leads to another and I'm kissing Mel's neck, giving her a little grope—getting fresh."

Reed attacked the tape on the box holding his shoes. "At a *funeral*?"

"Hey, nobody wants to feel alive more than when they're among the dead."

"Jesus," he scoffed, shaking his head.

"That's what Melanie said."

"So, we're making out, and we hear these guys as they walk into the bedroom. I got a fuckin' boner and someone's coming."

Reed laughed. Had it really been almost a year since he'd sat in an unmarked car, listening to one of Joey's insane stories?

"I grab my pants and Mel's hand and yank her into the shower stall with me—quietly close the curtain and pray that no one finds me with my pecker hanging out of my boxers."

Reed cringed. "I don't need to know this."

"Ends up that it's Peter Salada from FBI and Corey Upshaw from the Marshals. I'd recognize their voices anywhere."

Reed frowned as he tossed a pair of flip-flops next to his boxing shoes. "What were they doing in Walter's bedroom?"

"That's what I wanted to know. Of course it piqued my interest, so I'm listening real close when I hear Upshaw telling Salada how he was with Walter at some diner downtown when Walter fell out of his chair dead. They were talking and the poor bastard just croaked."

Reed grunted again as he went after the tape on the next box.

"This is where it gets good, buddy, real good. Right before Walter bit it, he was telling Upshaw how he was worrying about one of his former witnesses who left WITSEC several years ago. Walter had been trying to track him down to check in with him. Nicoli Fuckin' Caparelli."

Reed froze when he heard the name.

"You listening to me, boss? *Nicoli Caparelli.* All these years we were working with Walt and he knows Nicoli Caparelli. Never said a damn thing. Those Marshals. I'm tellin' you."

Reed relaxed his jaw and set down the box cutter. "Why are you telling me this?"

"Why am I telling you this? Why am I *telling* you this?" Joey laughed incredulously. "Did we not spend almost a decade of our *lives* trying to take down the Caparellis?"

Reed clenched his jaw again. "We're out of it."

"Bullshit. You and I both know their organization is growing stronger every day, and Alfeo's gonna be out of the big house in less than three-and-a-half months."

Reed felt his nostrils flare as he gripped the side of the cardboard. "Not my problem."

"Right. Not your problem. Upshaw mentioned two different identities Nicoli used while he was in the program, and you can bet your sweet ass they're branded on my brain. He's more than likely still using one of them."

"Hopefully Upshaw finds Nicoli before his brother does, or he's a dead man."

"Upshaw's going to do a search—do Walter one last solid and make sure his old witness is safe and sound."

There was a long silence, and Reed knew where this was going.

Joey said, "We could find him first—"

"No."

"Reed—"

"*No*," he said, giving a bad-tempered push to the box in front of him before he turned away.

"We can do this, man."

"Do what exactly? What are we going to do, Joey? NYPD shut down our unit; the investigation's closed."

"So what? When has that ever stopped us?"

"There's no 'us' anymore." He paced to the bathroom and back. "We're finished with this."

"Since when does Mad Dog McKinley let a little red tape get in the way? We'll work the angles."

He shook his head. "You're Vice now and I'm close protection. In another state. Across the country."

"After what they did to your pops, to your grandpops and uncle? We've got the information. Let's see what we can do with it, where we can make this go."

Reed had come to terms with the fact that he would never pay the Caparellis back for slaughtering his family—or he was trying to come to terms. "I've let it go, Joe—"

"Bull."

"I've let it go," he repeated. His marrow-deep craving for revenge, for justice had ruled his every thought and move for the last decade, eating him alive until there was nothing left of him but a shell of who he'd once been. "We've both got a couple of ugly scars that say we're done." He gave the box another solid shove, no longer interested in settling in, and walked downstairs, stopping in his tracks as he stared at the huge-ass dog standing in the middle of his empty living room. "Uh, I've gotta go."

"Reed—"

"I'll call you later." He hung up, eyeing the fawn-colored Great Dane as he shoved his phone in his back pocket, noting the pink bandana tied around the animal's neck and her color-coordinated nails. Why were people so *weird* around here? "Nice doggy," he said from the last step. "Nice—"

"Lucy," someone hissed in a whisper outside Reed's half-open front door. "Lucy, come *here*."

He held out his hand, hoping the dog would give him a sniff instead of turn him into a snack. His shoulders relaxed when the sweet-eyed animal stepped closer and licked his fingers.

"Lucy—"

"Your dog's in here," Reed called.

A black-haired goddess peeked her head around the door. "I'm so sorry." She stepped all the way inside wearing a pale blue above-the-knee spaghetti-strap sundress.

Reed's gaze trailed over amazing features: sun-kissed skin, big brown eyes, high cheekbones, full, glossy lips, mile-long toned legs. Lucy's owner was spectacular. "It's no problem." He stroked his hand along the dog.

High-heeled sandals slapped against the polished wood floor as the beauty moved closer and perfume, something expensive and sexy, filled his nose. "Lucy doesn't usually do stuff like this. Never, actually."

"I guess that's what I get for leaving my door open."

She flashed him a hesitant smile. "Still, it's rude." She cleared her throat as she extended her hand. "I'm Bella."

He gripped her soft skin. "Reed."

"Reed," she repeated before she let him go. "I'm your neighbor. The next building over—first unit closest on your end." She pointed to the condo he could just make out from his current angle at the window. Barely thirty feet separated their properties.

"Good to know." He went back to petting the dog that was now leaning her weight against the top of his thigh. "Lucy's a big girl."

"Yes, but she's sweet—very gentle. She's just finished her training as a therapy dog."

He studied his new neighbor again, noting that her legs were every man's dream, even if she was relatively short: five-four, five-five at the most. Lucy had to outweigh her by a good fifty or sixty pounds—maybe more. "How old?"

"Uh, she's just about one."

Reed's eyes went huge. "She's a *puppy*?"

She flashed him a grin, far less hesitant with her smile this time. "If you can believe it, I used to be able to hold her in my palms. They grow fast." She stepped closer, stroking the pup with a perfectly manicured hand. "We should get out of your way. I'm sorry again for just barging in."

He shrugged. "It's no big deal."

"Come on, Lucy." She turned toward the exit. "Let's go home." Bella stopped and looked over her shoulder, her cascade of shiny hair following her movements. "Welcome to the neighborhood, by the way."

"Thanks."

"Knock. Knock." Wren Campbell gave a quick rap of her knuckles to the doorframe and walked in, hugely pregnant yet professionally sleek in heels and a dress, before Bella could make it out the door. "It's a full house in here."

Reed barely held back a sigh as he glanced at the notebook and measuring tape Wren held. He'd been hoping she'd forgotten about their afternoon interior design consultation she'd bullied him into when they bumped into each other at Ethan Cooke Security last week. "Hey, Wren."

"Hey." She grinned and bent at the waist. "Lucy. Hi, sweetie."

Lucy abandoned Bella and hurried over to Wren.

Reed shoved his hands in his pockets while Wren cooed and made kissy noises at the dog. "It looks like you've already met my neighbors."

Wren gave Lucy a thorough petting. "It's a small world, really. You work for Ethan, and Bella's one of my best friends."

Bella blinked as she looked at Reed. "You work for Ethan?"

He nodded as he rocked back on his heels. The day just kept getting more and more interesting.

"Reed's one of my brother's lean, mean fighting machines." She grinned, sending him a saucy wink as she closed the distance between herself and Bella. "I didn't realize I was going to run into you."

Bella enveloped her in a hug. "Lucy decided to stop in without an invitation." She sent Reed a quick apologetic smile before she returned her attention to her pal. "Will I see you at yoga tomorrow?"

"You might have to roll me around the studio, but I'll be there with the rest of you girls."

Bella laughed. "You look amazing."

Wren shook her head. "I've got this pregnancy mask thing going on." She gestured to her face.

"Melasma," Bella said as she touched Wren's cheeks and forehead with gentle fingers. "It's a temporary condition. Keep up with the sunblock. If you come by my office, I'll show you a few tricks with concealer. And we can do a facial." Bella's phone dinged, and she peeked at the screen and dismissed it.

"Will it help with this horrible pigmentation?"

"Not really, but it will feel great."

"Sold."

Bella and Wren grinned at each other.

"I'm booked tomorrow," Bella continued, "but if you come in around eight, before we open, I'll get you taken care of."

"I'll be there."

Reed cleared his throat, hoping the girl talk going on in his living room was just about finished. Pregnancy and facials had been covered. He feared cramps, placentas, or something equally as horrifying might be next.

Wren and Bella looked at him.

"I should go," Bella said. "Reed, it was nice to meet you. Wren, I'll see you tomorrow." She tossed them a wave and left with her huge dog.

"Well." Wren settled her hand on her belly as she looked from Reed to his empty apartment. "It looks like we've got some work to do in here."

"I'm renting, so I really don't need an interior decorator."

Wren blinked and smiled politely. "Of course you do. This place will be a masterpiece by the time I'm finished." She narrowed her eyes as she studied him. "Masculine. Intense. Basic. I'm seeing brown leather couches for this room here, maybe strong, muted tones for accents."

He rubbed at the back of his neck, in way over his head. "Uh—"

"I'll just take some measurements and come by the office with my mock-ups."

How was he supposed to say no to his boss's sister and one of his coworkers' wives? This was clearly a woman serious about design. "Sounds great."

"This is a wonderful complex. I know Bella loves living here."

He could still smell his new neighbor's perfume wafting on the air. "She does your makeup?"

"Sometimes." Wren got to work with her tape measure by the window. "She's a medical aesthetician."

He had no idea what that was. "Huh."

"She's gorgeous and smart." She turned with her pad and pen in hand. "And single. Are you interested?"

Ethan's sister was also direct. "Uh," was all he said as he held her gaze, not liking the twinkle that had come into her eyes. Bella with the big dog was phenomenal...and definitely not his type. She looked like she'd stepped out of a magazine. Her hair and makeup were perfect—Beverly Hills all the way. He liked someone with a little more grit. Someone who could kick his ass in the boxing ring. "I'm going to get the rest of my stuff from my truck."

Wren grinned. "Sure."

He scratched his head, growing more uncomfortable by the second.

"I'll be out of your way in just a few minutes," she said.

He hoped so. "Take your time." He walked outside into the perpetual California sunshine, glancing toward Bella's condo and the white VW convertible Bug in her designated parking spot. "Definitely not my type."

Bella shut herself inside and leaned against the door as she slid her feet from her Jimmy Choos, no longer concerned about Lucy booking it into her sexy new neighbor's home without an invitation. Maybe he had killer blue eyes and broad shoulders to die for, but that was the least of her problems right now. She set her purse, the latest design from the Abby Harris line, on her entryway table and pulled her phone from the front pocket, nibbling her lip as she read the text she'd received moments ago while she spoke to Wren.

Give me a call when you can.

She sighed, not so sure she wanted to talk to Jed. Once or twice a month, her PI texted her a similar message—courtesy updates that always got her hopes up but never led anywhere. "Not this time. Not today," she assured herself as she searched her contact list for his private line. Five months ago, she'd finally decided to move forward and track down her father after so many years. Now that Mom was gone, she needed to find him, to know why he left them without any explanations.

Taking a deep breath, she selected Jed's number, pretending her heart rate hadn't just kicked up a notch as she listened to the ringing in her ear.

"Hey, Bella."

"Hey." She swallowed, loosening the tightness in her throat. "I just got your text."

"Thanks for giving me a call. I'm happy to report that I actually have some good news. I think we've got him. It took some digging, but I think I found your father."

"You found him," she mumbled, hurrying over to the couch and settling herself on the biscuit-colored cushion before her legs had a chance to give out. "Are you sure?"

"I had to dig pretty deep—bend a few rules—but I've got him. He likes to stay off the map—no driver's license—only a picture ID from Nebraska. He rents his home, pays cash for most everything. I found a bank account he opened about nine months ago. There's been some recent activity."

She gripped the phone in one hand and extended her opposite arm to the coffee table, tracing the chunky white candle in frantic circles. "You're sure it's him?"

"As sure as I can be without swabbing for DNA. There wasn't much of a paper trail to follow, but his age fits. The picture you gave me of the two of you matches up fairly well if you add about twenty years."

She gained her feet and sat just as quickly, realizing her knees had indeed turned to Jell-O. "You saw him? You saw my dad?"

"Yeah, at his house—"

"You went to Nebraska?"

"No. He's in California—up in Reseda. That's where I found the bank account."

"Reseda?"

"About an hour north of the Palisades. I'll email his information."

She blinked rapidly as tears filled her eyes. She'd been waiting for this, wanting this for so long, and now it was happening. "I don't know how to thank you."

"I'm glad I could give you a hand."

She nodded to no one. "Thank you, Jed. Are you sure I can't pay you?"

"A friend of Ethan's is a friend of mine. Maybe we can grab a drink sometime."

Jed was handsome but not necessarily the *GQ*-type she was typically attracted to. But he'd just found her father. "Sure. That would be nice."

"I'll send the information over now."

"I appreciate it."

"Bye."

"Bye." Hanging up, she dropped her phone and pressed her face into her trembling hands. "Oh my God." Nearly twenty-one years. She'd waited over two decades.

Her phone dinged, startling her. She opened Jed's email, studying the address. "Reseda," she whispered, absently petting Lucy as her puppy sniffed at Bella's hair. "He's in Reseda, Lucy. For months he's been so close, and I had no idea." She buried her face in the dog's short, soft coat, taking the comfort her best friend offered as she tried to believe that this was actually real.

☙ Chapter Three ❧

BELLA SAT IN HER CAR, GRIPPING THE STEERING WHEEL WHILE she stared at the white ranch-style house to her left. She bobbed her leg up and down as heat blasted from the vents, warming her chilly skin despite the balmy seventy degrees on the other side of the window. The sun shined bright and the trees swayed in the breeze while a young couple strolled down the sidewalk in the rougher section of town. Life moved on around her, yet Bella was stuck in the past as her tired eyes stayed glued to the small home where her father currently lived.

For much of last night, she'd lain awake, unable to shut down her mind. Her thoughts had raced, remembering Daddy taking her to the library or the park and reading with her before bed. Her happy childhood had ended the morning she pulled back her Hello Kitty covers and realized Dad was gone. Days later, Mom had strapped Bella into her booster seat in the old Honda hatchback, pulling a tiny U-Haul behind them as they left Ohio. And nothing had ever been the same. There had never been any explanations, just that Dad had to go. He'd ripped her life apart and she wanted answers.

She reached for the door handle and snatched her hand back, clutching the steering wheel again. "What are you doing?" she muttered, unable to make herself move. Was she really going to knock on his door? What would she say? *"Hey, I'm your daughter. Where the hell have you been?"*

She shook her head and turned over the ignition, then shut it off just as quickly. No matter what, she needed to see her father. Steeling herself, she tossed her sunglasses on the passenger seat and got out, smoothing her purple knee-length dress as she walked up the steps to the painted black door.

With a deep breath, she balled her fist, hesitating, then knocked, closing her eyes momentarily as her stomach began to roil. Long moments passed in pure torture while she waited, watching the curtain in the window to her right move before the door finally opened to a man blinking, clearly surprised.

"Bella."

"Daddy," she heard herself whisper as she stared into brown eyes so much like her own. He looked different—older, yet so much the same. His once black hair was mostly gray, and he had crow's feet and a few deep wrinkles among the numerous fine lines. She remembered him being much taller, more muscular, but this was definitely him.

"Bella," he repeated.

She opened her mouth and closed it, nodding when she couldn't find her words.

He looked around, sliding his gaze from left to right as the strong scent of cigarette smoke wafted from the house.

"I found you," she finally said, waiting for him to smile or pull her close in a hug, the way she'd fantasized their reunion more times than she could count. "I, um, I wanted to see you." She shifted in her strappy heels as each second passing became more and more awkward. "I was wondering... Where have you... Can I come in?"

He held her gaze, then finally stepped back and opened the door wider.

"Thank you." She walked inside, glancing around the dim space at the dark emerald curtains closed over the windows and the cheap, simple furnishings in the small living room area. There were no pictures on the yellowed walls, no décor to speak of at all, nothing that made this house a home.

"I have some Diet Coke or coffee if you want some."

She crossed her arms, rubbing them warm as she watched him shove his hands in his pockets and pull them out again. "No. Thank you."

"Do you wanna sit down?" He gestured to the lumpy couch. "Or we could go out to the back porch and get a little fresh air?"

The suffocating stench of cigarette smoke wasn't helping her raw stomach. "The porch would be fine."

"Sure." He grabbed a can of soda off the coffee table, along with a pack of cigarettes, and walked down a short hallway to the back of the house. "I've got a little table and chairs out here."

"Great." Stepping out onto the small concrete slab, she pulled out one of the two plastic seats, gripping her fingers together as she sat and rested her arms on the glass patio table. She tried to ignore the fact that he kept glancing at his watch and decided that small talk might help break the ice, like it always did when she consulted with a new client. "So, how long have you been here in Reseda?"

"A while." He flicked the flame to life on a pink Bic and puffed on a cigarette until the tip burned orange.

"Nice," she said as he took another deep drag. He hadn't smoked when she'd been little. Mom hadn't either, but that had changed too. "You're killing yourself slowly." She gestured to the plume of smoke he expelled.

He smiled. "I'm not too worried about it." He sipped his soft drink, then fiddled with the can. "You're beautiful."

She looked down at her hands as he made an effort to converse—and a compliment at that. "Thank you."

"You look so much like your mother."

Mom stopped being lovely a decade after Dad walked out the door. Too many plastic surgeries along with the overuse of Botox and fillers had ruined Kelly Colby's stunning natural beauty. "She's gone. She died last year."

"I know."

Her gaze snapped to his. "How do you know?"

He shrugged.

She expelled a long, quiet breath. Did he have no regrets about walking away?

"What happened to her?" he asked.

"She had a chronic condition." And that was all she planned to say about her mother's death.

"What are you doing here, Bella?"

Her eyes sharpened on his. What was she doing here? This just kept getting better. "I thought you might like to see me." *The way I've so desperately wanted to see you*. "You're the only family I have left."

"What about her brother? Did he ever stop being a bastard?"

Had Dad always been so matter-of-fact, so harsh? She remembered a quiet, sweet man who wiped away her tears when she cried and let her style his hair with her pink Barbie brush. "I don't speak to anyone in Ohio."

"I'll take that as a no, then."

"I haven't seen Uncle Dane since we left." She traced the edge of her polished nail with her opposite thumb. "I thought you would be happy that I came."

He sucked in more smoke before crushing out the cigarette in the heaping ashtray. “You shouldn’t be here.”

She huffed out a quiet laugh. “I’m sorry I came.” She stood and sat just as quickly, knowing she probably wouldn’t see him again once she walked out his door. “Did you love us at all?”

“I thought about you every day.”

Not exactly a confession of love or remorse. “Then why did you go? Why did you leave us?”

“It was the right thing to do.”

Would he say that if he knew how she and Mom had lived, if he knew that his fiancée had reduced herself to a whore? “You and Mom were going to get married. I have the ring in my jewelry box.” The only piece of jewelry she’d kept from Mom’s extensive collection.

He chuckled. “It wasn’t much of a ring.”

“She talked about you before she died.”

Dad paused with the soda can at his lips.

“She said she never loved anyone the way she loved you.” She stared at him as he drank, as if she’d said nothing of importance. “This was a mistake. I’m sorry I bothered you.” She rushed to her feet and started back through his house.

“Bella.”

She kept walking, in a hurry to be gone.

“Isabella.”

She stopped as the firmness in his tone registered, but she refused to turn and meet his eyes. “What?”

“You being here. This isn’t a good idea.”

“I agree. That’s why I’m leaving.” She opened the front door.

“I made a lot of mistakes when I was younger—”

She whirled in the doorway. “What does that have to do with now?”

“Everything.”

She shook her head and walked outside.

He hurried after her down the steps and short path to the street. “It was good to see you, to see that you’re grown and beautiful and doing okay.”

“Yeah.” She reached into her purse, grabbing a business card. “If you’re ever down in the Palisades.” Not that she expected him to look her up.

He took it, running his thumb over her name. “Your own business.”

"I contract with a dermatologist. I have an office in her building."

"I'm glad you came."

She wasn't, but she nodded as she grabbed for the door handle and got behind the wheel. She turned over the ignition as she shoved her sunglasses in place, looking at the man who could have been any other stranger—except they shared the same brown eyes. No longer cold, she wanted the top down, but settled for rolling down the windows instead. She put the car in drive and pulled away from the curb, glancing in her rearview mirror as he stared after her.

"God," she shuddered out as she followed the GPS's directions back through town. That couldn't have been any more of a disaster. Technically, he could have slammed the door in her face, but for the most part he had—just more painfully, dragging out a moment in time she wished she could take back. It would have been so much better to have the memories of a man who'd cared and loved her...or maybe he never had.

Her eyes filled as she found her way to the 405 and punched the gas, eager for speed and the wind blowing through her hair. As the Volkswagen ate up the miles, her mind raced, remembering the night Dad had told her he needed to go away. She could recall only snatches of their last evening together: a book about a dog, the smell of the garage on his shirt, the long hug before he said good-bye.

"I thought about you every day."

"Right." But he might have been telling the truth. Shaking her head, she dismissed the idea as nothing more than her desperate need to believe that there'd been something more to his quick departure than simply flaking on his family. It happened all the time, right? Men and women walked out—gave up, caring little that they left a mess behind.

"Exit in one mile," the GPS reminded her.

She focused on the road, realizing she'd lost track of time as she merged right and took exit 57, impatient to get home. Lucy would likely be in full-pout mode because she hadn't been invited along, but that's what the beach was for. They were going to walk until the ebb and flow of the ocean waves soothed the sickness in her heart... after she took a shower and washed away the stink of cigarette smoke.

Her phone rang and she dug through her purse, glancing at the readout, not recognizing the number. She pressed *talk* anyway, hoping Ms. Sanderson wasn't experiencing some sort of complication after yesterday's chemical peel. "Hello?"

"Bella, it's—it's Dad."

Not Ms. Sanderson or any of her other clients. For the second time in one day, she had no idea what to say.

"Hello?" he prompted her.

"Yes. I'm here."

"I don't like the way we left things. You caught me off guard."

She appreciated his honesty. "I'm sorry about that."

"It's probably not a good idea, but maybe we could go out for lunch sometime."

He wanted to have lunch. Dad wanted to sit down and enjoy a meal together. "Uh, sure." She eased on the brake as she came to a red light. "When?"

"I don't know."

"What are you doing tomorrow?" she blurted out, afraid that if she didn't make plans now, he would change his mind.

"Nothing much."

"We could go to lunch or do brunch."

"All right. We'll meet somewhere."

"Or I can come by and we'll go together."

"It would be better if we meet up. I prefer using taxis."

Why didn't he have a car? He'd driven just fine when she'd been a child. They'd driven all over western Ohio, picking up automotive parts for the garage he'd worked at, always stopping for ice cream when they got back to town. "It's no trouble for me to pick you up."

"No. There's a place that serves a good lunch in Van Nuys. I'll text you the address. They have excellent sandwiches. I like a good grilled cheese."

She smiled sadly. "I remember. What time?"

"One o'clock, maybe two?"

"How about we meet at two?"

"I'll see you then," he said.

"Okay. Bye."

"Bye."

She hung up and pulled into her sweet little neighborhood, starting toward her building down the road. Nothing about today was turning out the way she'd anticipated. Apparently she was having grilled cheese with Dad tomorrow when she'd fully expected never to see him again.

Reed dropped the kickstand in place and took off his helmet as he kicked his leg over his Ducati. He took two steps toward the house, frowned, and turned back to the bike when a streak on the polished black paint caught his attention. Using the edge of his T-shirt, he wiped away the smudge, then made his way to his front door. The sun was warm, the breeze just right—a perfect evening for a long ride. It was too damn bad he wasn't in a better mood. His latest conversation with Mom was still pissing him off. He'd stopped by only to grab the sunglasses he'd forgotten yesterday, not to listen to her crap.

"You're different, Reed—cold. I was always afraid your father would have ended up the same way if he'd lived long enough to see retirement."

It was no secret Mom hated that he'd followed in Dad's footsteps—and he couldn't necessarily blame her, but did she realize she insulted her husband's memory and the sacrifices he'd made every time she brought him up like that?

He unlocked his door and stepped inside, pulling off his backpack, then the leather jacket he wore whenever he took the motorcycle out for a spin. Muttering a curse, he tossed the bag on the floor and hung up his coat with far less care than usual, unable to shake off the sting of Mom's words. Maybe he was hard. Maybe he'd turned into a cynical son of a bitch somewhere along the way. But he was alive, wasn't he? And despite what Mom thought, he didn't need a woman in his life to help him with his problems or smooth out his rough spots.

Shaking his head, he kicked off his sneakers and headed upstairs, taking a quick shower. He was securing a towel around his hips when his phone started ringing on the counter. Groaning, he glanced at the readout and turned away for his deodorant, waiting for Joey's call to go to voicemail. He didn't want to chat with his old partner in crime today, especially after his little go-round with Mom.

The ringtone started again less than thirty seconds after it stopped. "Son of a bitch." He yanked it up. "Why do I talk to you more now than when I was in New York?"

"What can I say? I miss you, man."

Surprisingly, he missed Joey too, but not enough to go back. "Tell me what I have to do to get rid of you for twenty-four—no—forty-eight hours."

"You can go check a few leads."

"I told you no."

"I had Leo, that PI I work with sometimes, compile lists for me so I didn't have to run anything through my home or work computers. I don't want nobody figuring out what we're up to."

Reed closed his eyes and let his head fall forward in a moment of defeat. "We're not up to anything."

"I didn't give Leo any specifics—physical descriptions or whatnot. Just told him to get me names, so the lists are a little long—people we'll definitely be able to eliminate once we get a good look at them."

Reed held the phone with his cheek and shoulder as he made quick work of rolling on his deodorant. "Joe—"

"You've got several possibilities right there in LA and the surrounding areas," Joey continued.

Reed jammed the cap in place and set the stick down with a snap. "No."

"If I'm remembering right, there's eight, maybe nine Tim Wolcotts and the rest are Vincent Pescoes."

He clenched his jaw, staring at his blue eyes flashing with temper in the foggy reflection. "This is bullshit and a waste of our time. What about all of the other Vincents and Tims out there? You really think our guy's just sitting here somewhere in California?"

"I'm giving you twelve, more like fifteen names. We're not exactly looking for John Smith, buddy."

Reed turned away from the mirror, leaning against the counter. "We might as well be. Eight or nine Tim Wolcotts and potentially seven Vincent Pescoes? And that's one state."

"Nationwide there aren't a huge number. Several states don't have a hit on either name. I'm gonna check the few here in the five boroughs, although something tells me our boy isn't stupid enough to hang around his old haunts when his family wants to blow his head off. We got a Tim in Montana—"

"I am *not* flying to Montana."

"Take a fuckin' pill. I'm gonna go myself next week when I have three days."

Reed flared his nostrils. "Why? Why won't you let this go?"

"Why are you walking away so easy?"

"You're kidding me, right?" He paced into the bedroom and back. "Explain this one to me. Say we find him. Say we find Nicoli Caparelli aka Vincent Pescoe aka Tim Wolcott or whoever the hell he is. What do we do with it? What the hell good does knowing where he is do us, especially when we have no jurisdiction and I don't have a *badge*?"

"Let's find the guy first. We'll figure out the rest later because, buddy, I do wear a badge. You're forgetting that."

Reed mimed bringing the barrel of a gun to his temple and pulling the trigger before he dropped his towel and went to his chest of drawers, grabbing boxers, then a pair of black gym shorts. He pulled on a white Ethan Cooke Security T-shirt next, intending to beat the hell out of a punching bag since he couldn't get at Joey. "Why are you doing this, Joe?"

"The same reason I know you're gonna check the addresses I send you. It's in your blood. It's in mine. You wanna keep Alfeo in prison?"

He gritted his teeth. All the years of hard work he and Joey had put in. All the risks of deep cover and the "leads" that had gotten them absolutely nowhere, then they get a carrot like this dangling in front of their noses. Nicoli Caparelli was their only hope of bringing down a notorious crime family and keeping a cold-blooded killer where he belonged. "Yeah, I want to keep him in prison."

"Then let's find his fuckin' brother. If we don't get something on Alfeo now, we both know we never will."

He sighed. "Send me the addresses." He hung up and tossed his phone on the bed, where he intended for it to stay. For the next two hours, he was unavailable. Grabbing his gym bag, he walked downstairs and outside, stopping when Lucy ran his way through the small side yard separating the properties, accessorized with a purple bandana around her neck and the same pink paint on her nails.

"Lucy!" Bella shouted, scrambling around the side of her house, barefoot and beautiful with an apron tied over a simple white sundress. She'd pulled her hair back in a French braid, leaving her stunning face unframed.

"Hey," he said.

"Hi." She smiled, pressing a hand to her chest while she held a spatula in the other. "Lucy scared me half to death. I don't know why she keeps doing this, running after you the way she does."

"She likes me. Don't you, girl?" He crouched down, accepting the puppy's kisses on the cheek while he gave her sides a good rub.

"She definitely has a puppy crush."

"I don't mind saying hello."

"She can't just run off, though. I don't want her wandering out by the cars."

He stood, glancing toward the white smoke coming from the back of her house. "What are you grilling?"

She glanced over her shoulder in the same direction. "Just a couple pieces of chicken, which are going to burn if I don't get back."

Why did seeing Bella all tidy and domestic stir his libido? "I'll let you go."

"Okay. Bye. Come on, Lucy."

Lucy didn't budge from her spot next to Reed.

"Lucy. Right *now*."

Lucy stayed glued to his side.

"I can follow you around back," he said.

"That would be great."

He fell into step beside Bella, breathing her in as they walked to her deck.

"Lucy's well-trained—or I thought she was. Maybe we need another class." She hurried to the grill and flipped the two chicken breasts with an expert hand.

"Looks good."

"It's simple—lemon pepper. The best I can do for now."

He peeked into her cozy kitchen through the open French doors: granite countertops similar to his, white wood cabinets—again much like his, but the upscale cooking gadgets set here and there and thriving plants scattered about gave her place a homey feel. Bella was certainly classy all the way.

"Thanks for walking Lucy back."

"No problem."

"Do you want to stay?"

He frowned. "Do you always invite strangers to dinner?"

She smiled. "I guess I don't think of you as a stranger. She pointed to the Ethan Cooke Security insignia on his T-shirt. "Plus, Lucy can be vicious, so I don't worry about it too much."

He raised his brow as he looked at the puppy wagging her tail and staring at him with adoring eyes. "Right."

Bella leaned against the wooden railing. "Wren and I were chatting during her appointment yesterday morning. She mentioned that you happen to be the very same Reed who helped Chase save Julie's life."

He shrugged, not interested in being anyone's hero. "I was on duty." He hadn't been, but he'd been in the office when his coworker realized his girlfriend was in trouble. Brothers helped brothers. End of story.

Her smile dimmed. "Modest."

His shoulders jerked again.

"She almost died."

"Luckily, we got to her in time."

"Yes." She stood straight and gave the meat a small poke with the spatula. "What do you say? Want a piece of chicken?"

"I can't."

"Maybe some other time."

"I'll definitely take a rain check." But not anytime soon. Bella with the big brown eyes was dangerous territory.

"Sure. I'll see you around."

"See ya." He gave Lucy one last pat and turned to leave.

"You're antisocial, Reed. A grumpy hermit. When was the last time you had dinner with a pretty girl?"

He fisted his hands as one of his mother's searing potshots burned his ass. He turned back as Bella was sliding the chicken on a platter. "Can I change my mind?"

She beamed at him. "Of course."

He set his bag on one of the lounge chairs. "I can take that for you." Their fingers brushed as he accepted the heavy dish.

"Thanks. Come on in." She stepped into the kitchen, gesturing for him to follow.

He looked around at the open concept layout identical to his condo's, but the similarities stopped there. High-end furnishings decorated this space. Thick candles on fancy holders burned throughout the room, and Top 40 music played low on the large-screen TV. Pictures—some of her posing with friends or maybe family members—filled frames on tables and hung among the prints of flowers and seascapes on the walls. Bella clearly did well for herself. "Nice digs."

"Thank you. I love it. I had a few visions in my head. Wren helped me pull them together, and this is what we came up with."

"Nice," he repeated as he set the platter on the table.

"Thanks. Do you like wine?"

He preferred beer. "Sure."

"I think I have some iced tea, or there's water if you'd rather have that."

"Wine is fine."

"Great." She moved to a cupboard and stood on her tiptoes, making her calves bunch as she grabbed two glasses. "White will probably go best with the chicken."

"Perfect." He crossed his arms and uncrossed them just as quickly, aware that his body language was often perceived as standoffish. For a decade, keeping people at a distance had kept him alive. Now it made him an asshole.

"I made a corn salad with this and threw together some greens," she said as she opened the bottle. "I wasn't expecting company, so we're going humble tonight."

"You won't hear me complaining. I was going to grab a burger on my way home from the gym."

She poured two glasses and handed him one.

"Thanks."

"You're welcome." She brought an extra plate and silverware to the table. "Where do you work out?"

"Rusty's over in Santa Monica. It's a little place—kind of rough."

"Oh." She sipped her chardonnay on her way back by the island, then reached in the fridge for the corn and small side salad and brought them over, placing them next to the chicken.

"You're into yoga?" he asked.

"I am. I try to go every day. I think we're ready." She pulled on the apron strings and lifted the stylish smock over her head, giving him a better look at all of her smooth skin and the slightest tease of cleavage before she turned to hang the apron inside the pantry door.

He took a deep drink of his wine, doing his best to ignore the fact that his neighbor was one perfect package. Every inch of Bella appeared to be toned and polished.

She turned back, sending him a friendly smile. "Ready for dinner?"

"Yeah." The faster they ate, the sooner he could leave. Goddess-like or not, he had no intention of getting mixed up with Bella. The last thing he needed right now was a romantic hassle. Sitting across from her at the small table, he served himself a hearty portion as Bella helped herself to her own. "This looks amazing."

"I hope you like it." She cut a bite of chicken and sampled with a considering nod. "Not bad."

He followed her lead, enjoying the hints of lemon and pepper melding with the meat. "I'd say it's better than not bad."

She shook her head. "I'm not a great cook...yet, but I want to be. I'm thinking about taking a few classes."

"Cooking classes?"

"Sure. It's never too late to learn new things."

He helped himself to the corn salad and discovered it to be out-of-this-world delicious. "True."

"And they're supposed to be a lot of fun. I'm looking forward to it, actually." She chewed a small spear of asparagus and swallowed. "So tell me about yourself, Reed. Let's start with your last name."

"McKinley."

"Reed McKinley." She nodded, then sipped more wine.

"And you?"

"Colby. How long have you been working for Ethan?"

"Give or take six months."

"And before that, what did you do?"

"Cop. NYPD." He wiped his mouth. "What about you?"

"I've been in California for about a year now."

He went after his salad. "Where were you before?"

"All over but mostly Vegas."

He'd been expecting some high-end place like Napa Valley. It wouldn't have surprised him to hear that her family had a mansion up in The Hills. "Huh. How did you meet Wren?"

"I do a lot of work with Abby Quinn at her downtown Stowers House location—the shelter she helped start. I also work with Sarah on occasion if she needs help with makeup at her photo shoots. They introduced me to everyone else in the Ethan Cooke Security family."

"Wren said you're a...I don't know what that was she said you are."

She grinned, lighting up her amazing face. "I'm a medical aesthetician."

"There's the title but I still have no idea what that is."

She laughed. "Skin care. I work with Dr. Huberty—a dermatologist—just a couple miles away from here. I do all kinds of stuff: facials, makeup consults, body sculpting, laser treatments."

He paused mid-cut into his chicken. "Laser treatments?"

"Sure. I'm a laser technician as well—skin correction."

He got back to work, thoroughly enjoying his meal. "What do you do with your lasers?"

"Vein reduction, hair removal. I take off tattoos and do acne reduction therapies. I can even whiten teeth." She flashed her pretty pearly whites at him.

He helped himself to more of the corn salad. "And how do you body sculpt someone?"

She grinned again. "Long story short: I hook my clients up to machines that freeze fat in problem areas. The cold temperatures kill the fat cells and the body absorbs them."

"Huh. You must do well in this town."

"It was a slow start, but Sarah and Abby have been great about sending people my way. They got me in with Dr. Huberty when her former aesthetician went on maternity leave. She decided she didn't want to come back to work, and Dr. Huberty wanted to offer more treatment options, which I'm qualified to do. Luckily, my appointment book stays pretty full." She curled her leg beneath her. "Chase and Collin go overseas a lot for work. What about you?"

"Nah. I deal more with the private sector details—keep a low profile." And he would for several more months to come until he could be sure he was in the clear. His cover had been blown. Keeping his face out of the public eye was for his own good. "Mostly megarich businessmen and women who don't want to get kidnapped and held for ransom when they stop for a cup of coffee."

"I imagine that could ruin their day." She set down her fork after clearing her plate. "I haven't seen you at any of Ethan and Sarah's parties."

He shrugged. "I work a lot." Just the way he liked it.

She made a sound in her throat as she nodded.

He set down his silverware, not sure what to say now that their meals were gone. They'd pretty much small-talked it out. The only thing left on the topic docket was the weather, which spoke for itself.

"I'm afraid I don't have any dessert to offer you."

"This was great as-is."

"Any big plans for the rest of the weekend?"

He shook his head. "I'm working tomorrow morning. You?"

"No. Just lunch out and probably a walk on the beach afterward."

"Sounds like a good way to spend a Sunday." When was the last time he'd let himself relax?

"It is." She pulled his dirty plate on top of hers.

He pushed back his chair and stood, picking up the dishes, and brought them to the sink. "I should get out of your way."

"Only if you want to. Lucy and I are thinking of binge-watching something on Netflix."

He looked around, seeing that he was leaving her with very little to clean up. That was acceptable, right? "Yeah. I'll probably try to get in a workout."

She stood, bringing the remains of the corn salad to the island. "Have fun."

"Thanks for dinner."

"You're welcome."

"Night." He walked to the French doors, gave Lucy a good-bye pat, and stepped outside into the fading light.

"Good night."

He tossed a last look into Bella's cozy home, realizing he wasn't sorry he'd stayed. It was hard to go wrong with easy conversation and good food.

☙ Chapter Four ❧

Bella sat in the stop-and-go traffic on Highway 1 with the convertible top down, singing along with Ed Sheeran on the radio. Today the weather was glorious—the perfect opportunity to enjoy Mother Nature's beauty. Smiling, she savored the warm breeze playing with her hair as she accelerated again, loving the way the late-afternoon sun felt on her skin.

She'd left Dad at the restaurant almost two hours ago, still surprised that they'd had a fairly nice time. Talk of her work and home in the Palisades dominated much of their sixty or so minutes together. Dad hadn't seemed interested in bringing up the past or sharing much about himself other than the couple of tidbits she'd been able to weasel out of him while they ate their grilled cheeses and soup. He'd kept to his work as a mechanic over the years, but never married or had more children—not even a dog or cat. And that was about it. Now she couldn't help but wonder if their meal and conversation was a one-time interaction, some sort of obligatory gesture so he would be able to tell himself he'd tried, or if Dad would reach out to her again.

She thought of him all alone for the last two decades, finding the idea incredibly sad. Her life with Mom had been a series of ups and downs—mostly downs—but they'd had each other for the most part. Now she had so many wonderful people in her life. And Lucy.

She grinned as she glanced over at Lucy's currently unoccupied seat, completely in love with her sweet pup. She'd always wanted animals. Mom and Dad had promised her a puppy for her sixth birthday, but that never happened. Last year, she'd finally gifted herself the Great Dane of her dreams—the perfect twenty-fifth birthday present. Lucy had been her biggest joy and best friend since the moment she brought her home. And her best friend was bound to mope when she smelled the ocean breeze on Bella's hair. Her puppy was a champion sulker when she didn't get her shot at chasing the seagulls. The sun was just hinting at turning toward the horizon for the day, the perfect time to walk the beach—something she and Lucy did almost every night.

She merged over a lane as she got closer to her neighborhood, waiting for her chance to turn left as Reed pulled in from the opposite direction, taking a right on his sleek motorcycle. Her neighbor was a hottie. There was no doubt about it. Striking eyes and a strong, solid chin set in one heck of a face. A great, muscular build worthy of second and third glances. Quiet. Intense. And the motorcycle certainly added a healthy hint of bad boy, but he was too rough around the edges for her. She preferred suits and ties, maybe a pair of glasses—intellectual, sophisticated. But that didn't mean they couldn't be friends, especially when he lived so close.

She saw her shot at a left and took it, darting onto the quiet street. Driving down the road, she pulled into her spot as Reed took off his helmet, still sitting on the monster machine that was probably a great time to ride. "Hey, there," she called as she pulled her keys from the ignition.

"Hey." He kicked his long leg over in the blinding sunshine and faced her.

She got out and shut her door, walking over to his property line. With her sunglasses and her hand shielding the worst of the sun's rays, she realized he was wearing slacks and a tie beneath his leather jacket: a mouthwatering combination. "How was work?"

"Four a.m. flight to San Francisco, a couple hours in a breakfast meeting, and another flight back."

She wrinkled her nose. "Sounds exciting."

"Not really."

She settled her purse more comfortably on her shoulder. "Lucy and I are going to walk the beach."

He unzipped his jacket and loosened the knot at his collar. "You really dig the water."

She smiled. "I love it."

"Why?"

She frowned. No one had ever asked her that before. Everyone loved the beach, didn't they? "It's beautiful and relaxing, and I love to watch Lucy chase the birds. She kind of looks like a big, awkward moose when she runs." She chuckled, but he didn't smile back the way she'd expected him to. Wow, he was serious. "Wanna come?" she asked on a whim, trying to figure out why she was in such eager pursuit of his friendship. Maybe it was because Reed McKinley seemed to be a rare and refreshing member of the male species. Most men fell all over themselves trying to get her attention, often seeing nothing more than her looks. This man standing in front of her didn't seem to care one way or the other. She liked it.

"To the beach?"

"Yeah."

"I think I'll pass. I'm not much for sand in my socks."

"That's why they make sandals." She shrugged, finding herself slightly disappointed after such an enjoyable meal last night—or at least, she'd thought so. "Well, I'll see you then."

"Yeah. See you around." He turned toward his house.

She shook her head and made her way to her door, glancing over her shoulder as she watched him shut himself inside.

Reed bobbed his leg up and down as he sat on his front step, waiting for Bella. He still wasn't exactly sure *why* he was sitting there, but minutes after he turned down her invitation for a walk on the beach, he found himself hurrying with his shower, then throwing on gym shorts, a T-shirt, and a pair of flip-flops, hoping he hadn't been too late to catch his neighbor before she left. He wasn't a big fan of the sand, and the salt often irritated his skin, but here he was anyway when he should have been calling it an early night.

San Francisco this morning. Then he spent the rest of the day chasing down Joey's leads. He wasn't ready to call them *their* leads because as far as he was concerned, this was a long shot. He and Joey no longer sat in parked cars running surveillance. They didn't risk their lives by wiring up and making deals with the scum of the earth, hoping to gain access to the higher-ups in the elusive Caparelli crime family. Months ago, the jig had ended in a hail of gunfire with him and Joey nearly bleeding out on some filthy warehouse floor, but taking a look at Joey's information couldn't hurt, especially with several hundred miles separating him from the violence in New York.

Satisfying Joey's curiosity—and his, if he was willing to admit it—was nothing more than a professional courtesy. They weren't having a whole lot of luck anyway. For hours today, he'd driven around the Los Angeles area, systematically crossing names off the long list. A year ago, they would have narrowed down their man in a fraction of the time, but without access to a DMV database, he was stuck doing this the old-fashioned way. Technically, Ethan could give him a hand, but then there would be questions, and he wasn't supplying answers to his new boss. Eventually Joey would realize...

He came to attention when Bella opened her front door, wearing a curve-hugging white tank top and flowing blue tie-dyed skirt that showed hints of her golden skin every time she took a step. Christ Almighty, she was a sight as the breeze played with her sun hat and teased strands of her long, glossy hair. Never in his life had he seen anything like her.

His eyes wandered to Lucy's bandana, which matched Bella's dress, and he remembered right then and there that this woman was not what he was used to. She'd changed her outfit to take a walk. Technically he had too, but he sure as hell didn't look better than he had before.

She locked her door and glanced up, smiling when Lucy started trotting his way. "Off to the gym?"

That was his out. All he had to do was say yes. "Not if you're still looking for company."

She beamed. "Definitely. Come on." She started toward her Barbie car.

"How about we take my truck? Lucy can hop in the back."

Bella hesitated. "Do you think that's a good idea?"

He shrugged. "We'll all have a little more room that way."

"Sure. We can try it." She changed directions and moved to his black F-150 Limited as he dropped the tailgate.

"Do you think she'll be okay up here?"

"I think she'll love it."

She exhaled a deep breath and nodded. "Okay, Lucy. Up you go." She tapped the back of the bed.

Lucy looked at her, wagging her tail.

"She's never ridden in anything but the car."

"Maybe this isn't going to work."

"Of course it will." Bella crawled up into the back. "She just needs to see that it's okay. Come on, Lucy."

Lucy jumped up in a semi-graceful leap.

"That's my girl." Bella grinned as she bent down to give the puppy a kiss and pet her side. "Now lie down."

Lucy did as she was asked.

"Stay down just like that. I don't want you getting hurt." She moved to the edge.

"Need a hand?"

"If you're willing to give one."

He reached up, grabbing her around her waist as Bella settled her hands on his shoulders. Lifting her, he set her on the ground.

She smiled at him, standing inches away, giving him a close-up of her flawless skin and a solid whiff of her perfume. "Thanks."

"No problem." Clenching his jaw, he watched her walk to the passenger side. This was such a bad idea. Now that it was too late to change his mind, he could count a million reasons why he should have stayed inside. He didn't do stuff like this—take nights off and walk on beaches with women and their dogs. They would keep their evening short—a quick stroll, Lucy would chase a couple of birds, and then they could go. The next time his mother gave him crap about being a bitter ex-cop with no life, he'd be able to tell her he'd been in the company of a gorgeous woman not once but three times. He slid his sunglasses in place and hurried to the driver's seat, buckling up. "So, am I heading any place special or should we go to the main beach?"

"Lucy and I have the perfect spot. It's pretty quiet. I'll give you directions." She looked back at the puppy lying where she'd been told to stay.

"She'll be fine."

"I know."

He backed up and came to the set of lights leading out of the development.

"You'll want to take a right."

He waited for a lull in the traffic and they were off.

"It doesn't take long—just ten or fifteen minutes, and it's totally worth it."

He made a sound in his throat as the wind blew through the open windows, sending her intoxicating scent his way. Bad idea, he reminded himself as she chatted away, telling him to turn here, then there.

"This is it." She pointed out his window, grinning. "Paradise."

There was barely anyone on the beach as he took a free spot among the parking spaces. He stared out at the horizon, captivated by the sparkle of the sun on the water and the waves crashing to the sand.

"Perfect," she said and got out, walking to the back.

Reed locked up and put down the tailgate.

"Come on, Lucy," Bella encouraged the dog.

Lucy didn't need any more convincing. She was out of the back and in the sand before Reed could turn around.

Bella laughed. "And she's off chasing her gulls."

He watched Lucy run like an awkward moose, just as Bella had described. "She really goes after them."

"It's her favorite thing. She sleeps like the dead after."

"Has she ever caught one?"

Bella's eyes filled with horror as they met his. "Of course not. I wouldn't let her do it if I thought she actually had a chance."

He returned his attention to Lucy. "That's a lot of activity for such a big animal."

"She's not so big."

He looked at Bella as if she were crazy. "Just another Chihuahua."

She grinned as she pulled off her sandals and stepped into the sand. "She looks like any other dog to me."

He followed her lead, holding his shoes in one hand. It had been years since he and his cousin had done this very thing. Now Kurt was gone.

They kept a slow pace, strolling in silence as the breeze plastered their clothes to their bodies and the constant sound of waves hypnotized, lulling Reed into relaxing by degrees.

"Thanks for coming with me tonight. It's nice having company."

He looked at her, staring at the fading light playing off her eyes. "The water smells better than a bunch of sweaty guys."

"Your gym." Her brow creased ever so slightly as she held his gaze. "What do you do for fun?"

"Work and box."

"Sounds...like a good time."

"I like it."

"Do you smile?"

He frowned. "Huh?"

"I was wondering if you ever smile—or laugh. I haven't seen you do either since we met."

He sent her an exaggerated grin.

She laughed.

He smiled for real this time, finding her laughter infectious.

"You *do* smile. I wasn't sure if you had some sort of facial paralysis we hadn't discussed yet."

He grinned.

"You should do that more often." She hooked her arm through his.

He almost missed a step as the warmth of her skin met his, surprised by her casual gesture. He wasn't used to people being so touchy-feely. "I do it plenty."

"I'll have to take your word for it."

How was it possible she smelled even better now that they stood so close? It had to be her hair. "I don't know what to say to that."

She stopped abruptly. "Are you seeing anyone?"

He studied her, not sure that he liked where this was going. "No. You interested?"

She shook her head. "You're not really my type."

He tried to ignore the direct hit to his ego. "You're not mine either."

Another smile warmed her face. "I think we could be great friends, and I like projects—love them, actually."

His frown returned. "And that means..."

"It means I like you. And I love that you don't seem to have any interest in getting into my pants."

Years of concealing any and all facial expressions kept his eyes from popping wide. "Wow." He ran his hand through his hair, speechless once again. "Okay."

She laughed. "I'm a big fan of honesty—putting it right out there."

He chuckled as he settled his sunglasses on top of his head. "Clearly."

They started walking again.

"There's something about you that feels...safe."

He raised his brow, taken aback. He'd been called many things, but this was a first. "Safe?"

She nodded. "Safe. It's a good thing, but you're pretty serious. We need to lighten you up. You need to play more."

"I play plenty. I box."

She scoffed, "Beating someone's face in can't lead you down the road to happiness."

Her side brushed his with every step. He imagined he should ease away, break their connection, but he liked the way she felt, that she trusted him. "There's more to boxing than beating someone's face in."

She looked at him as if she wasn't so sure.

"I'll have to show you—" He glanced over his shoulder when he realized they hadn't seen Lucy for a while and laughed as the dog lay on her back in the sand with her front paws in the air. "What is she doing?"

"Sunbathing."

He laughed again, shaking his head. "I've never seen anything like that." His eyes met Bella's as she stared at him. "What?"

"You have a great laugh."

To his surprise, he was having a great time. It shocked him further that he liked Bella as much as she seemed to like him. Being here with her was exactly what he'd needed. "How long do you want to stay?"

"The sun sets soon. It's the best part."

The sand wasn't bothering him much, and he couldn't remember the last time his shoulders felt so loose. "I don't have a blanket."

"We can sit on our shoes." She tossed hers down. "We can plunk ourselves right here."

Lucy rolled to her side, stood, and ran their way.

He shrugged, dropping his flip-flops to the ground. "I guess this is as good a place as any."

"It'll be spectacular." She took his hand, pulling him down next to her. "You won't regret it."

"We'll have to remember a blanket next time."

She smiled. "You want to come back?"

He stared ahead, petting Lucy when she curled up next to him, breathing in Bella with each inhalation. "I could see myself doing this again."

She gave his shoulder a bump. "Good. You can be my beach buddy."

He nodded, liking the idea. "Yeah, sure."

"Great."

"Great." He crossed his ankles in the sand, his foot brushing Bella's as they settled in to enjoy the show. It had been too damn long since he watched a sunset.

☙ Chapter Five ❧

Reed glanced at the time on his dashboard clock while he sat in his truck, hoping to catch a glimpse of the next man on Joey's long list. He'd gotten up early on his only day off, fully intending to eliminate a few more names before the day was over. If he could get a good look at three or four potential Nicoli Caparelli candidates—especially on a weekday, when most people worked—he would consider his endeavor a success. He had a Tim Wolcott to check out in Simi Valley, another in Thousand Oaks. Then he had to drive his ass all the way up to Bakersfield to see if he could set eyes on one of their Vincent Pescoe possibilities. But he needed this guy to cooperate first.

It was tempting to move things along, knock on the door, and pretend he was at the wrong address, but that wouldn't play as well on a Tuesday morning as it had on Sunday afternoon. His party-sized bag of Fritos and shocked surprise that he'd somehow ended up at the wrong place for his buddy's poker game did the job forty-eight hours ago, but it wouldn't serve him well now. People tended to be more guarded Monday through Friday, and he wasn't taking any risks.

Today he was prepared to spend plenty of time sitting behind the wheel, chasing down dead ends. Patience was always a virtue in this line of work. Surveillance was a constant waiting game, and he missed it. He and Joey had spent hours—sometimes days—parked along the busy streets of Brooklyn, hoping for their big break. More often than not, they didn't get jack shit, but sometimes they hit pay dirt. It was all about the big score, the unexpected link in the chain that brought about the next clue.

Stifling a yawn, he rolled down his window as the late-morning sunshine beat through the glass, baking his left side. He fiddled through the radio stations, looking for sports talk instead of the music he was currently listening to, and stopped abruptly, powering off the unit, when a cab pulled into Vincent Pescoe's driveway. "Here we go. Here we go," he muttered, waiting to see what happened next.

Moments later, a tall man with a solid frame and salt-and-pepper hair stepped outside, locking the door behind him.

"Son of a bitch," he whispered, yanking up the surveillance camera he'd borrowed from the office. He adjusted the lens and zoomed in to snap several shots. The guy definitely fit the bill. Olive complexion, right age and build—certainly a possible first-generation Italian American. He grabbed up the last picture the media had captured of Nicoli Caparelli twenty-seven years ago, before he vanished into WITSEC, trying to compare the image to the man getting into the back of the cab, but it was impossible to tell if this was who he and Joey were looking for.

Reed waited until the lime-green vehicle drove up the street and pulled into the steady flow of traffic before he followed. It wouldn't be hard to keep his eye on such a vividly painted car, but if this Vincent Pescoe had spent nearly thirty years hiding, he would be well-versed in spotting a tail.

He gunned it through one stoplight, trailed at a distance through another, then drove on even when the cab turned into the plaza adjacent to North Medical Center. He was forced to go through one more intersection before he could turn around and pull into the gas station across the street from the large hospital complex where he'd watched Vincent get out. Parking in the first available space, he went into the convenience store for good measure, grabbing a small bag of salted nuts and a bottled water, then went back out, sitting for over an hour before the familiar cab pulled up in front of one of the buildings and Vincent settled himself inside.

He followed the vehicle the two short blocks back to Darby Avenue, watched Vincent get out, then drove on, heading toward the 405 and Palisades instead of northwest to Simi Valley. This lead was promising. They might actually have something here. He wanted to call Joey right then and there, but he needed to be sure—or surer than he was right now.

Pushing the speed limit, he made it home ten minutes faster than the GPS's original estimated time frame. Instead of heading upstairs to his desk, he sat at the counter on a rickety barstool he'd picked up at a discount store and made himself as comfortable as he could while he imported the images into his laptop. Waiting impatient seconds, he found the best shot of the bunch and leaned closer, scrutinizing the man's face.

When he still wasn't certain, he typed *Nicoli Caparelli* into Google Images and glanced at the dozen surveillance photos the FBI had captured back in his mafia days. In two of the pictures, Nicoli stood next to Patrizio Caparelli, Nicoli's father and boss of the Caparelli crime family. In almost every other shot, he walked next to his brother, Alfeo Caparelli, current Caparelli Godfather and inmate at Lewisburg Penitentiary…for the next one hundred six days.

He took one of the full-on shots, courtesy of the Feds, and dragged it next to the photo he'd snapped this morning. The familiar rush of excitement started flowing through his veins when he compared Vincent Pescoe's and Nicoli Caparelli's noses, mouths, and jawlines. "There you are, you bastard." He yanked up his phone and dialed Joey's number, listening to his heart thunder as he composed an email while waiting for his partner to answer.

"Yeah."

"We've got him."

"What?"

"We've got him."

"Are you sure?"

He hit *send* on the email. "Take a look for yourself."

Seconds passed in tense silence. "Holy fuck. Holy *fuck*!" Joey's incredulous laugh filled Reed's ear. "We've got him."

Reed felt himself smile before it disappeared. "I'll go up this weekend and make sure—get a close-up, walk by him or something. Get actual eyes on him instead of a lens."

"This is him, Reed."

He stared at the pictures again. "You know I want to be one hundred percent certain. I was parked a good twenty-five, thirty yards from his place."

"You get your positive ID, buddy."

He stood and paced, unable to be still. "If this really is Nicoli, what the hell's next?"

"I haven't gotten that far. He's a gold mine of information—the key to bringing down the Caparellis once and for all. We all know the Feds never put the squeeze on him the way they could have—should have."

"I guess that's where we come in." And he was more than willing to do his part. Decades ago, the FBI made a deal with the devil—Nicoli's testimony against his brother for the brutal slayings of a Caparelli mob man, his pregnant wife, and their toddler. Nicoli spilled the beans in court, then walked away scot-free even though he'd played just as big a part in the same murders Alfeo got locked away for. And that's all Nicoli had shared: details about a gruesome winter night in the late 1980s—the tip of the iceberg for one of the most powerful crime families ever to exist. Now they just had to figure out how they were going to use the knowledge Nicoli aka Vincent Pescoe had to their advantage.

"Unreal. Unreal, man." Joey laughed again. "This is so big, I'm still trying to wrap my head around it. Think on it for the afternoon, and I'll do the same. We'll come up with something."

"We always do. I'll catch up with you later."

"Good work, buddy."

"Thanks." He hung up and closed his laptop, ready to go upstairs and pound on a punching bag. Some of his best ideas came to him when he imagined he was ramming his fists into Alfeo Caparelli's face.

ꟹ Chapter Six ꟹ

BELLA GOT OUT OF HER CAR IN THE POURING RAIN AS LIGHTENing flashed in the distance and thunder boomed seconds later. Her umbrella kept her dry for the most part as she raced around to Lucy's side in the gusting winds, but she was eager to get inside on such a miserable night. "Go to the house, Luce. I'll be right there."

Lucy wasted no time following Bella's directions and ran to the door.

"Good girl," she called, starting Lucy's way but stopping when she caught a movement out of the corner of her eye. She frowned, realizing it was Reed stepping from his front door with no protection from the downpour. Within moments, his gray Nike T-shirt was plastered to his tough build and his jeans dotted from the huge drops falling from the sky. "What are you doing out here?"

"Getting soaked."

She quickened her pace on the sidewalk connecting their driveways and offered him shelter from Mother Nature's wrath, caught off guard by the devastating combination of Reed's vivid blue eyes and long eyelashes gone spiky from the rain. "Tell me you're not going out in this." She raised her voice, competing with the pounding water on the umbrella's fabric canopy. "I could barely see the cars in front of me on my drive home, and there's still a little daylight left."

"I need to get to the barber." He swiped his hand through his light brown hair, darker now that it was wet.

She tore her gaze away from the hypnotizing effect of his baby blues and studied his neat modern Caesar cut. "You look fine to me."

He shook his head. "I'm getting shaggy. And I won't have another chance for a cleanup until Saturday. Waiting four more days is too long. I'm leaving for Seattle in the morning."

"More business meetings?"

"Bingo. And I've heard rumors of a hostile takeover while we're there, so that should be interesting."

"Maybe you'll see a little action—stuffy CEOs losing their tempers and crawling over the tables to get at each other." She wiggled her eyebrows, imagining sexy, intense Reed taking control of the situation.

He grimaced. "I'm more of the mind that no action is good action. Action tends to mean lots of paperwork."

Her smile turned into a wince as thunder cracked overhead and the wind picked up again. "You can't get a trim up in Washington?"

He shook his head. "I'm on the clock the entire time. Can't leave my principal."

"You know there are flash flood warnings?" She looked down at the water racing over her exposed toes in her heeled sandals. "The news was saying a couple of cars have already been washed away."

"I guess I'll have to be extra careful, then." He jiggled his keys in his hand. "I should get going—"

"I can do it if you want."

He lifted his eyebrow.

"I'm not licensed for hair, but I used to do my neighbor's in Las Vegas all the time, and he never complained. I trim my own." She stood on her tiptoes and brushed her fingers through his soft layers, making certain she wasn't offering help she couldn't deliver. "You're short and mostly clean. I can fix you up easy enough."

"Are you sure?"

"Of course. It'll take ten minutes. Fifteen if I screw up and have to shave you bald."

A smile ghosted his mouth. "This is where I'm supposed to laugh, right?"

She chuckled. "Come on. Trust me." She grabbed his hand and walked with him to her front door, where Lucy waited beneath the overhang.

"Hey, girl." Reed gave her a solid rub while Bella twisted the key in the lock.

"Come on in," she said, pushing open the door.

"Thanks."

She waited for Lucy and Reed to move inside and collapsed the umbrella, leaving it out of the worst of the rain. Stepping out of her heels, she flexed her toes and sighed. "Better."

"I bet." Reed swiped at his dripping hair as he gave his shoes several wipes on the rug. "Are you sure about this?"

"Yeah. Definitely." She set down her purse. "Let me change real quick—get out of my work clothes—and we'll start."

"I appreciate it."

"I'm happy to help." Hurrying upstairs, she exchanged her pencil skirt and blouse for skinny jeans and a pale sage cashmere sweater to chase away the evening chill, then walked to the bathroom for the canvas organizer she kept beneath the sink and snagged a towel too, taking her supplies with her downstairs.

Reed turned from the grouping of pictures on one of her living room walls. "You have a lot of friends."

"I'm very lucky."

"Do you own stock in companies that specialize in wedding gifts and baby toys?"

She grinned as she stepped closer, looking at the shots of her posing with brides and grooms and mothers-to-be. "I don't, but that's a good idea." She looked from the photographs to him and handed him the towel. "Here. Dry off some."

"Thanks." He rubbed at his muscled forearms, neck, and face.

"I wish I had a shirt to offer you."

"This is fine." He swiped at his arms once more and balled the Egyptian cotton in his hand.

She glanced at the pictures again. "Why don't I ever see you at any of these functions?" She pointed to a shot of her smiling with Reagan and Shane after their simple yet lovely ceremony early last winter. "Don't you like your coworkers?"

"I like them fine. I'm on duty a lot."

She frowned. "We're going to fix that. You're my new project, remember?"

"How could I forget?"

They smiled at each other.

"Does it count that I was in Europe for some follow-up training when Reagan and Shane got hitched?"

"Since you can't be in two places at once, it does, but think of all the gatherings you've missed since then. You've been here for months, and Friday was the first time I saw you. There's more to life than boxing gloves and those bodyguard earbuds."

He grinned. "Bodyguard earbuds?" He pursed his lips and nodded. "I like the jargon."

She laughed. "You know those things the Secret Service wear—and you guys?" She gestured to her ear and the wire that would disappear under her collar.

He flashed her another smile. “Yeah, I know what you’re talking about.”

“Well, what do you call it, then?” She gave him a playful shove to the arm, knowing he was teasing her.

“An earpiece and microphone.”

She rolled her eyes. “That’s pretty boring. For some reason, I thought they would have a cooler name.”

“Like what?”

“Like...I have no idea, but something much less dull.”

He chuckled. “Some parts of what I do are. The movies make it look action-packed, but it’s a lot of waiting around and assessing situations before they can turn into problems.”

“I think I like Hollywood’s version better.”

“If my life were a Hollywood movie, with all of the action those guys see, I would never get out of the office. Remember the paperwork?”

She laughed again. “Right.”

“It truly sucks.”

“I bet. Should we get started?” She gestured to the kitchen.

“After you.”

She walked in front of him, hurrying to the table to pull out a chair. “Does this work?”

“Yeah, it’s fine.” He sat down.

She immediately draped him with the black cover, wanting to get to his hair while it was still wet. “So, what are we doing here, exactly?”

“Just a cleanup, especially on my neck.”

“Sure.” She grabbed the sheers and took her place by his side, sliding her fingers though his short hair and stopped. “Oops.”

His shoulders tensed. “What?”

“Just kidding. A little haircutting humor.”

He tilted his head up, meeting her eyes. “A comedian.”

She laughed as he smiled. “I haven’t even started cutting yet.” She gave him a bump. “Try to relax. I promise you’re in good hands.”

“Chop away.”

“Thanks.” She combed her fingers through his hair once more, using small snips to freshen up his look. Silent seconds ticked by as she breathed in the masculine scent that was Reed. He didn’t seem to wear cologne or use any fancy shampoos, but he smelled good just the same. “So, how was your day?”

“Not too shabby.”

She worked her way around his head, finding his cut a breeze to clean up. He easily could have gone another week without any problems. "What did you do?"

"Worked a little. Boxed."

"Fascinating."

"I could make up something about stopping a bank robbery in progress or rescuing a cat from a tree."

She smiled. "The truth is fine, thanks."

"What about you?"

"It was pretty much a normal day at the office—a second-session tattoo removal, a microdermabrasion, two stretch mark reductions, the usual stuff."

"What's the tattoo of? The one you're taking off?"

"A woman's name. Genevieve. The relationship didn't work out."

He winced. "Ouch."

"Triple ouch. Tattoo removal is *not* a pain-free procedure, nor is it cheap—and he went pretty ornate with *Genevieve*. Hopefully next time he'll pick a woman with a shorter name or abstain from getting himself tatted up altogether."

He laughed.

She grinned, loving that sound. Did he have any idea how gorgeous he was when he smiled like that? She picked up the clippers off the table and let her knees rest against his as she leaned in and gently lifted his chin, evening out his sideburns. She swallowed, feeling his breath on her skin and his eyes studying her face. Licking her lips, she met his gaze. "You better hope I get this part right, or you'll have to tilt your head for the next four days."

He sent her another one of his pulse-pounding smiles. "You'll have to help me decide if I should lean more to the left or right."

Oh, this cutie had the potential to be trouble. Her eyes darted to his mouth mere inches from hers as his five o'clock shadow tormented her sensitized fingers. She took a step back and a steadying breath. It was a good thing they were just friends—currently the only relationship status she was interested in. "The goal is straight." She nudged his head slightly higher and narrowed her eyes, scrutinizing. "I think we've achieved success." She let him go and removed the guard from the clippers. "Let me just get your neck, and you should be good to go." Moving behind him, she cleaned up the few hairs that needed to be banished. "There."

"That was pretty quick."

She shook powder into her hand and dusted it along his skin, then gave him a wipe with the towel. "And not a bald patch anywhere to be seen."

"Bonus."

She slid her fingers through his hair again, making certain everything was even, and started massaging, unable to resist as she noted the rigid set of his body.

He tensed, then groaned. "What are you *doing*?"

"I used to have this hairstylist who would give me a scalp massage when she washed my hair. I would die and go to heaven every time. It's a great addition to any haircut." She transitioned to his neck, then a little lower, frowning at the knots she discovered along his trapezius muscles. "Jeez, you're tight through here." She went after the trigger points with firm, stroking movements.

Another grumble escaped his throat as he let his head fall forward. "You never have to stop doing that."

"You know, Julie's a massage therapist."

"Feels like you are, too."

"My clients receive brief massages with certain treatments."

"This works just fine for me."

She shook her head, even though his eyes were closed. "You need deep tissue. Julie does yoga more than massage these days, but I bet she would hook you up if you asked." She moved along the contours of his rock-hard shoulders, pretty darn certain that Reed had to look like a god with his shirt off. "I'd suggest an hour, even ninety minutes on a table."

He grunted.

"Seriously."

"Maybe sometime." He sighed. "You two should go into business together—you and Julie."

"It's crossed my mind. But I love where I'm at now, what I do now." She kneaded a final time and ended with a soothing effleurage technique before taking off his cape and shaking it out.

He stood, rolling his neck. "That is hands down the *best* haircut I've ever had."

"Thanks. I—" Her cell phone rang on the table, and she glanced at the readout, recognizing Dad's number. "Um, hold on one second."

"Sure," he said, continuing with his neck rolls. "Where's your broom?"

"In the closet." She pointed to the door in the corner of the kitchen and pressed *talk*. "Hello?"

"Bella, it's Dad."

Would she ever get used to hearing his voice? "Hi."

"Hi."

Awkward silence filled the line, making her more nervous than she already was. She'd prepared herself for the very real possibility that their lunch date in Van Nuys was the last she would see of him—a defense mechanism against hurt and disappointment—but here he was, calling again. "I was thinking about you today," she said, hoping to get things started. Holding up a finger to Reed, she moved to the living room as he cleaned up the hair on her floor.

"It was nice having lunch on Sunday."

"Yes, it was."

"Damn good grilled cheese."

She smiled, trying to relax. "I agree."

"Maybe we could do it again."

She fiddled with a book on the built-in shelf, pulling it out and pushing it back. "I would like that."

"How about dinner?"

"I'm pretty fond of dinner."

He chuckled. "I could take you out for seafood or a steak or whatever it is that you like to eat."

She thought of his tiny house and lack of transportation. Expensive meals weren't a good idea, nor were they necessary. "I could always bring something over. We could eat in."

"I don't have much in the way of pots and pans or nice dishes. I'd like to take you out."

She sighed quietly. "All right. I would love it."

"Does Saturday work?"

He was reaching out, making a real effort. "I happen to be free Saturday night. It'll take me a little while to get up to you with the traffic—"

"I'll make the reservation for seven. We can meet."

She stopped herself from offering to pick him up. He clearly didn't like her coming to his home. "Sure."

"I'll find someplace nice—unless you have a preference."

"Whatever you want. I like a little adventure."

"Great. I'll call you tomorrow."

"I have clients until five, so text or leave a message if you don't get ahold of me. I'll call you back when I can."

"Sounds good. I'll see you Saturday."

"See you Saturday."

"Bye."

"Bye." She hung up and pressed the phone to her chin, smiling and closing her eyes. Dad wanted to see her, to get to know her as much as she wanted to know him. She turned back, remembering Reed was still in the kitchen, and hurried to take the dustpan he'd just finished emptying into the trash. "Sorry. I needed to take that."

"No problem." He pulled out his wallet. "What do I owe you?"

"Nothing."

"I have to pay you something."

She shook her head. "That's what friends are for."

"You've fed me and taken me to the beach, and now you've cut my hair. The friend balance is off."

"How about a ride on that fancy motorcycle of yours sometime?"

He shoved his wallet back in his pocket. "You like motorcycles?"

"I don't know. I've never been on one, but it looks fun."

"It is. Whenever you want."

She beamed, thrilled with the idea of a new adventure. "Great."

"Catch me on a day when you're not busy and I'm actually home, and we'll ride up the coast or something."

"Deal." She put the broom and dustpan back and glanced outside where the rain still poured. "I'm going to heat up some butternut squash soup. I bought it at the little gourmet grocery down the street on my lunch break yesterday. I could make us paninis if you want to stay."

"That sounds good, but I have a couple of reports Ethan needs, and I still haven't packed."

She nodded. "Some other time."

"Let me know about the bike ride."

"I will." She walked him to the door, pretty sure she'd imagined the electricity buzzing between them before, because there was nothing sparking now. "Safe travels, and good luck with the hostile takeover."

"Thanks. And again for the hair. Bye."

"Bye." She watched him jog over to his house, tossed him a wave, and shut the door, looking back at Lucy. "Two unexpected surprises in one night. You saw your boyfriend, and Dad wants to have dinner on Saturday."

Lucy wagged her tail.

"It's great, huh?" She bent down and hugged her girl. "What do you say I put this stuff away and we have some dinner?"

Lucy licked her cheek.

"Thanks. We'll snuggle up after and watch something on TV."

She went to the kitchen and finished cleaning up, always eager to put things back to rights. Her mind kept wandering to the moment when she'd held Reed's chin in her hand, staring into his eyes. "It's perfectly normal to be attracted to a gorgeous man," she rationalized to Lucy as the puppy stared at her from her cozy bed in the corner of the room. "Right?"

Lucy wagged her tail again.

"Exactly. You'd have to be dead not to notice that our neighbor's a hunk." She gave a decisive nod, feeling better about the entire situation. "Let's have our dinner." She moved to the fridge and got out the makings for soup and a pesto chicken Panini.

Reed sat at his desk, staring at the ideas he'd jotted down after his round with the punching bag a couple of hours ago. His thoughts had sounded good at the time; now most of them had a solid line drawn through the middle. Strategies to force Nicoli Caparelli into talking didn't matter much until he and Joey had their positive ID. It didn't make a whole lot of sense for them to establish some long, drawn-out plan if the man he'd followed today wasn't even their guy. Making one hundred percent certain that *this* Vincent Pescoe was a one-time Caparelli mobster needed to happen first, but that would have to wait until he could find some free time later in the week.

He came to attention when Bella's voice carried through his open window as she stepped onto her back deck with Lucy. The puppy headed for the grass in her tiny backyard while Bella crossed her arms, rubbing them roughly on the unseasonably chilly night.

He'd opened his windows shortly after he got back from her place, finding the brisk breeze blowing in soothing. It was odd not hearing the constant drone of traffic or honking horns. And he liked this view much better than the one he'd glanced out at in Manhattan—when he'd been home long enough to see it. Bella Colby in snug designer jeans and a stylish sweater, all for a simple night at home alone.

He looked back at his legal pad, then the new file he'd created for Vincent Pescoe. There weren't many details yet, just an address and this morning's picture of the man he was mostly certain was an older

Nicoli Caparelli. Flipping to another tab and the image he still had open, he studied the infamous Caparelli brothers. Although Alfeo currently sat in a prison cell, none of the Caparellis had paid for their long list of crimes—not the way they should have. Back in the eighties and nineties, law enforcement had decimated La Cosa Nostra, the five mafia families of New York, but somehow the Caparellis dodged the majority of the RICO charges that devastated the other families so thoroughly. Slippery, corrupt, so powerful that the federal prosecutor's accusations never stuck, even when the evidence was there.

The FBI's days of going gangbusters on the mafia were over, but that didn't mean he and Joey couldn't figure a new equation. They'd never had an inside man to help them before—or not anyone on the same caliber as Nicoli Caparelli. Walter Hodds and the Marshals had done their job well, keeping their most compelling witness hidden. Nicoli's testimony had put his father away for the rest of his life when he made the jury believe that Patrizio ordered his sons to carry out the deadly hit on one of his men. His brother had gotten a measly twenty-six years due to a technicality when it should have been a death sentence. But Alfeo "Alfie" Caparelli had yet to pay for the murders of two police officers and an FBI Senior Special Agent. Reed had every intention of settling that score.

He tore his gaze from the images of his enemies and stared at Bella as she crouched down to pet her puppy. Why was he so distracted by the bombshell talking to her dog on her back porch? He had a job to focus on, Mafiosi to take down. Nothing had ever gotten in the way of that before. Because he hadn't let it.

Closing his laptop, he stood, watching Bella gain her feet and glance toward his window. Their gazes locked, holding through the glass. He clenched his jaw, remembering her conversation as she made a date with another man.

"I was thinking about you today."

Foolishly, he'd been thinking about her. He could still remember the way her legs felt pressed against his while she held his chin and licked her sinful lips. He'd regretted turning down her invitation for soup, sandwiches, and conversation. But now he was glad he had.

She smiled and sent him a quick wave, then went inside and shut off the light to the porch.

He turned away, thanking his lucky stars that it was bound to be a good four or five days before they bumped into each other again. They'd only just met, yet he found himself drawn to her. They had *nothing* in common. She wasn't his type, and she'd made it clear he wasn't hers either, but that didn't mean he was stupid enough to believe that they didn't share a mutual attraction.

He walked down the hall toward his home gym. He'd already worked out today, but maybe another round with the punching bags couldn't hurt. For years, boxing had been his lifeline, giving him an outlet for the pent-up anger that seemed to come with the endless frustrations of his career. He wasn't so angry anymore. He wasn't sure what he was, but boxing was something he knew and understood—one of the only things he understood. Bella Colby was kind and funny, but beyond that she was a mystery. And that was exactly the way she was going to stay. If she wanted to have dinner every now and then or take a walk on the beach, that was fine, but otherwise he had every intention of giving them both plenty of space.

ᴄᴙ Chapter Seven ᴙᴐ

BELLA SAT ACROSS FROM DAD IN NORTH BASIN COUNTRY CLUB'S upscale dining room. She stabbed spinach, leeks, and the other half of the seared sea scallop she'd sampled moments ago and bit in, finding her dish to be perfectly prepared. "This is really good. How about yours?"

Dad nodded. "I enjoy a good lobster tail every now and again."

She went after more of the wilted spinach. "And to think we used to beg Mom for pigs in a blanket."

He smiled. "I still like pigs in a blanket, but I can never get the dough cooked around the hotdogs without burning the rest."

She couldn't remember the last time she'd eaten crescent rolls and processed meat. "Mom was an expert."

"She was."

She sipped her wine and set it back down, trying to think of ways to keep the conversation going. They'd had several long, uncomfortable pauses over the last hour. She glanced around at the other patrons, wondering if she and Dad appeared as cozy and happy as everyone else enjoying their evening meals. Clearing her throat, she focused on Dad again. "You know, I would love to cook for you, maybe have you down to my house one of these days."

Dad paused with another bite on his fork before he brought it to his mouth.

"It's only an hour or so away, depending on traffic," she rushed on when he didn't appear to be excited about the idea. "I would love to introduce you to Lucy."

"You can bring Lucy up to see me. We'll meet at the park or something."

Why didn't he want to come to the Palisades? "Sure, but I would love for you to see where I live. I could take you to my office and show you around. I'll make you a home-cooked meal. Lucy and I have an amazing beach spot too."

"Maybe."

Definitely not the enthusiastic yes she'd hoped for. "It's something to think about."

"I'll do that." He shook his head and chuckled. "I still can't believe you have a Great Dane."

She nodded, grinning and grabbing her phone. Although she'd shared a few pictures with him on Sunday, she found another, showing off her pretty girl once again. "She's beautiful."

He smiled. "She's a big one."

Bella shrugged. "I guess. She's smart and gentle and has a sweet personality. The kids at the children's hospital love her. I do a rotation one Saturday a month in the oncology unit and thought it would be fun to get Lucy involved."

Dad frowned. "I didn't realize you have a medical degree."

She let loose a small laugh. "I wish, but no, I don't." She swiped at one of the tendrils she'd left free from her French twist to complement the halter neckline of her black wide-leg jumpsuit. Slowly, she found herself relaxing as she and Dad fell into an easier rhythm. "I consult with the pediatric patients and their parents about their skin care needs. Chemo treatments can dry out their little bodies and wreak havoc on their systems. I do an assessment and come up with a plan to keep them moisturized and as comfortable as possible. And the kids really dig the little facials I give them."

"That sounds like a great thing. Your mom raised you right."

By the time Bella had turned eleven, she'd been raising herself and oftentimes her mother as well, but she nodded anyway. What good did it do to tell Dad that the Kelly Colby he'd left behind had ceased to be the same woman who'd made them waffles on Sunday mornings? "I love the kids, and I love giving back."

"I'm proud of you."

How long had it been since she'd heard those four simple words, and why did they hurt and lift her spirit all at the same time? She dropped her gaze from his and stared at the flame dancing on their tea light. "Thank you."

Dad set down his fork and patted his belly.

She glanced at his plate. He'd hardly eaten anything at all. "Are you finished?"

"Yeah. I had a snack before we came."

"Oh." She forked up another bite of greens and seafood, then set down her silverware, not wanting to be rude.

"Don't be afraid to eat."

"I'm full," she fibbed. "But I'll take this with me. I'll have it for lunch tomorrow."

"Good idea. Do you want a peek at the dessert menu?"

She studied Dad, dressed in his cheap mint-colored golf shirt and khaki slacks. The decades had flown by, and Dad had grown tired and old. He would be sixty-five in August, but he easily could have been mistaken for someone five to ten years his senior. Neither of her parents had aged well. "No, thanks. I need to be heading back to LA before it gets too late." She scrutinized his pasty complexion. "Are you feeling all right?"

"Never better." Dad raised his hand, signaling for the check.

She nodded, but as their evening was coming to an end, she realized that the pedestal she'd held her father on all these years had been distorted by fond memories and the complete adoration of a five-year-old girl. No one was perfect, but she'd built him up to be exactly that, whether he'd abandoned them or not. Dad was no different than her or any other flawed human being. Foolishly, she'd hoped their reunion would bring her peace and a sense of the normalcy she'd craved but had gone without for so long. Instead, she found herself shaken and a little sad that every time they met up, her happy illusions slipped further away. "That's good."

The waitress brought over the bill and set it in the center of the table.

Bella made a grab for it.

"I've got it." Dad snagged it before she could.

"Are you sure? You paid for lunch."

"I'm retired, but that doesn't mean I'm destitute."

"I know."

"A father likes to treat his daughter to a nice meal." He pulled out a bank card—probably the one Jed had used to track him down—and handed it off to the waitress.

"I'll run your card and box up your meals," the waitress said.

"Just hers."

"Sure." She walked off with Bella's dish.

Bella looked at Dad's full plate again. "You could make a lobster salad for lunch with your leftovers."

"I'm all set."

"Okay."

He picked up his phone. "I should call for a cab."

She shook her head. "I'm driving you home. It's the least I can do."

"That's not necessary."

"Yes, it is. I insist."

"Bella—"

"I insist, Dad." This not being welcome at his house was foolishness. If he was embarrassed, he was going to have to get over it. His zip code and lack of square footage mattered little to her. "I'm taking you home." She pushed back from her chair as he signed the bill, considering the debate over.

"All right."

They stepped out into the fresh air, and he lit a cigarette.

Bella opened her mouth to scold but closed it again. It wasn't her job to be a nag. She planned to help him change his ways subtly—less soda and cigarettes, more fruits and vegetables. But they needed to get to know each other better first. She waited several steps away for him to finish, then kept the top down in the car for the ride home.

"Nice night."

"It is. I love feeling the wind in my hair."

Dad nodded.

The silence stretched out again as the miles passed by. She slid him a glance and gripped the wheel tighter. "So, I'm going to a wedding next weekend. Would you like to come? You can be my plus one."

"That sounds nice, Bella, but I like to keep to myself."

That hadn't changed. Dad had always been quiet—a family man who'd done his job and come home to his fiancée and daughter. "I thought I would ask." And it shamed her when she realized she was relieved that he'd turned her down. Although she was happy to have him back in her life, she found their visits exhausting.

"You should bring a real date. A beautiful young woman like you shouldn't have any trouble finding someone who would like to go along."

"I'm not interested in dating right now."

He looked at her. "Someone break your heart?"

"More like bruised. But I'm over it. I go out occasionally, but I haven't found anyone that I feel that click with." She shrugged, immediately dismissing any thoughts of Reed that tried to sneak into her mind. "There's no rush."

"No, there's not. You're young."

"Exactly." She turned down his street and into his driveway, then shut off the headlights and unfastened her seat belt. "Home sweet home."

"You don't have to get out."

"Of course I do." She opened her door. "I'll walk you to your door."

"Only if you want to." Dad scanned the dark as he got out—a habit of his she'd forgotten but remembered as soon as she saw him do it.

"I don't think we're going to get mugged in the driveway."

"You can never be too careful."

"I suppose that's true." She waited for him to come around to her side. Taking a chance, she grabbed his hand.

He hesitated, then secured her fingers in his big palm as they took the steps to his house. They stood in the porch light.

She smiled at him. "Thank you for dinner."

"You're welcome."

"I've—I've missed you."

"I missed you too. You've always been such a smart, pretty girl. I'm proud that you grew up kind and that I can say you're mine."

Her eyes filled as she smiled again and hugged him.

He wrapped his arms around her.

She closed her eyes and held on, embracing him as she'd wanted to for so long. "I love you, Daddy." She eased back and kissed his cheek. "I'll see you soon."

"Good night, Bella Boop."

She grinned. This was their new beginning. He'd been gone, but he was here now—and trying.

"Go get in your car. I want to see that you get back on the road safely."

"Okay." She gave him another kiss on the cheek. "Let's do this again soon."

He nodded. "We will."

She walked to her car and got in, waving after she backed out, struggling with a myriad of emotions. As she made her way through town and to the 405 on-ramp, she was tempted to call Abby or Wren so she could talk to someone about this huge development in her life, but she didn't reach for her phone even though she had an hour to kill on the interstate.

Long ago, she'd learned the hard way that some things were better left her secret. She'd worked tirelessly for everything she had now, always eager to leave her past behind. But it was right here in her face again. The moment Jed called her and told her he'd found Dad, she'd been forced to take it all back out and remember everything she'd rather have forgotten.

In Kansas City, Nashville, Albuquerque, and the million other places she'd lived, people had known about her broken home and figured out, eventually, who her mother had been. Here in LA, she got to be anyone she wanted—who she'd always needed to be. If her friends knew the truth, they might look at her differently—the crushing disapproval she'd recognized when people realized she was the daughter of a one-time stripper turned prostitute.

Reed sat parked three houses down from Vincent Pescoe's residence, hoping to catch a glimpse of his man. His eyes had been glued to the property for close to two hours, but so far, no dice. Someone was home. The lights were on in the living room, but it was impossible to see what was going on inside with the curtains drawn over the windows.

He tapped his fingers on the steering wheel and blew out a long breath, struggling with a sense of restlessness. Typically he didn't mind the endless waiting. He and Joey had done it for years, but everything was different now. He no longer had twenty-four hours a day to sit idle and hope for his big break. They were running short on days to keep Alfeo Caparelli locked away.

They'd already missed out on a good chunk of time while Reed had been on duty in Seattle. If he didn't get them something to work with soon, they were going to have a serious problem. Finding Nicoli was only the beginning. Getting him to cooperate was going to be a whole nother matter. But they had to make absolutely certain this was him first.

His gaze wandered to the door handle as he thought about getting out and knocking on the door, but Vincent wasn't likely to answer. It was late—close to nine. Reed could be anyone—someone from a Caparelli hit team sent to pop a bullet in the back of Vincent's brain—the deadly price for being a traitor. Shaking his head, he stared straight ahead. Now wasn't the time to get stupid and screw everything up. The last thing he wanted to do was spook their one and only promising lead and send the guy running.

He perked up when a car turned down Darby Avenue and pulled

into Vincent's residence. "Here we go," he said, yanking up the camera as he relished the familiar rush of excitement. Ruthlessly, he turned off his emotions, focusing only on the job as the vehicle's headlights switched off, throwing the driveway into darkness. He zoomed in, but it was impossible to see who sat in the VW convertible.

A woman got out of the driver's seat and stood in the shadows as a man came around to the front of the car. They clasped hands and walked up the steps, standing in the porch light. He tightened his focus on Vincent's face, lit up by the naked light bulb only inches away, while his date kept her back to Reed.

"Got you, bastard. We've definitely got you," he whispered, his heart pounding with his certainty that this was indeed their man as he leaned in closer to the windshield and captured several crisp shots of Nicoli Caparelli.

Now he wanted a peek at the woman. If she would just turn her head a little more to the left...

As if she heard what he said, she hugged Vincent and rested her head on his chest, giving Reed a full-on look at her stunning face.

He fumbled the camera and yanked it back, staring at Bella Colby cradled in one of America's most dangerous mobsters' arms. "No way," he muttered as he absorbed the slap of shock. "No fucking way."

Adjusting the lens once again, his mind raced, trying to reject what he was seeing, but the lighting was hitting her just right, leaving him no doubts that this was his neighbor. He zoomed in as far as the camera allowed, studying her fancy updo and stylish outfit as she eased away and kissed Vincent's cheek. How the hell was this happening? *Why* was this happening? This was Bella's Saturday night date?

Vincent Pescoe had to have thirty, maybe even forty years on her. He was old enough to be her... He swallowed, watching Vincent and Bella smile at each other, and his confusion vanished into perfect clarity. Her big brown eyes. Vincent Pescoe's brown eyes. "Son of a bitch."

Keeping his finger on the shutter button, he captured every move Bella made until she backed out of the drive, waved, and headed toward the interstate.

He tossed the camera on the passenger seat and secured his safety belt, ready to turn over his engine, but he was forced to wait as Vincent stared in his direction. He wouldn't be able to come back here again in his truck. Reed had little doubt that he was making the man suspicious. Vincent Pescoe aka Nicoli Caparelli was bound to know exactly who was coming and going on his street and which vehicles didn't belong. Bobbing his leg up and down, Reed watched five minutes tick by on the dashboard, certain Vincent was giving Bella plenty of time to get on her way. If he believed people were tailing him, he wouldn't want them following her as well.

Finally, Vincent went inside and shut off the porch light, then the lights in his living room. Reed wasted no time heading south on the 405. Bella would beat him home. She had a good ten minutes on him at least, but that didn't mean he couldn't knock on her door. He didn't have an excuse in mind, but he would ask her for sugar if he had to. Wasn't that some sort of clichéd neighborly line? He wanted another look at her eyes. They haunted him in his sleep, but another peek while he was fully awake couldn't hurt. There was nothing wrong with corroborating a theory several times.

He puffed out an incredulous laugh as he replayed his night. This was a curve ball he hadn't seen coming. Never in his wildest dreams had he believed he would work a case for seven years, come up with jack shit for the DA, then hand in his badge, move to LA, and not only find Nicoli Caparelli but also discover his *daughter* living in the next condo over.

Before long, he was making his way down Sunset Boulevard. As he drove closer to home, he spotted Bella getting gas at the plaza less than a mile from their development. Grinning his triumph, he slowed down and waited his turn to make the left into their neighborhood. Minutes ticked by before Bella finally pulled into her driveway. Reed got out of the truck as if he'd just returned home himself. "Hey, stranger."

Closing her door, she sent him one of her gorgeous smiles. "Hi. Welcome back."

"Thanks." He walked through the grass, meeting her halfway and staring at her in the light from the streetlamp. She looked good—damn good in her pretty black outfit. Usually she wore her hair down, but tonight's updo showed off the delicate line of her neck.

"How was Seattle?"

"Relatively boring."

"No hostile takeovers?"

He made himself smile as he held her gaze, breathing in Bella's usual scent. "Lucky for me, things stayed friendly."

"Less paperwork."

"Right." He didn't want to talk about work. He wanted to ask her about Nicoli Caparelli and find out what she knew about his mafia life. "How was dinner?"

She frowned. "How did you know I went to dinner?"

"Those look like leftovers." He pointed to the Styrofoam container she held in her hand.

"Oh. Yeah." She chuckled. "Scallops. It was really good."

"Where'd you go?"

"To the North Basin Country Club—just outside of Reseda."

"Huh. I've never been. I don't golf, so I doubt I can get in."

"It's open to the public."

He kept waiting, hoping she would say something more about whom she'd dined with, but she didn't. "Good to know."

"Yeah."

He shoved his hands in his pockets, sensing that their conversation was quickly coming to an end. "I guess I'll see you later."

She nodded, smiling. "Good night."

He started toward his door and stopped. "Don't forget about that bike ride."

"I won't." She let herself into the house, waved, then closed the door.

"Damn," he muttered when he circled back to the truck for his camera and went inside, hurrying upstairs to get a look at the shots he'd taken. His shoulders tensed as he sandwiched an image of Bella between a current photo of Vincent Pescoe and a younger Nicoli Caparelli. "Holy shit."

Why hadn't he picked up on this sooner? Their eyes were exactly the same—minus the mascara Bella always wore and the deep lines Nicoli now had. And their chins.

He'd been obsessed with the Caparellis since he turned thirteen, studying every detail about the family he could get his hands on. Nicoli had been a handsome man in his younger days. He'd passed on his black hair and dark eyes to his child—classic Italian traits. Reed grabbed his cell phone and found Joey's number as he searched the web for more information about his neighbor.

"Hello?"

"I'm one hundred percent sure we've found Nicoli Caparelli."

"And that's a damn good thing, 'cause it's almost one in the fucking a.m. here."

He winced as he glanced at the time in the corner of his screen.

"Sorry."

"Hold on." Joey cleared the sleep from his throat as he muttered something to Melanie and rustled the sheets, getting out of bed. "Okay. Talk to me."

"You can circle Reseda, California, on your map, because he's definitely our guy."

"Yes! This is huge. *Huge*."

"It gets better."

"Lay it on me, buddy."

"Is there any possible way Alfeo has another kid, other than Matty?"

"No, not that we know of. We've never heard of nobody else, and Lewisburg doesn't allow conjugals. Why?"

"Just covering all the bases." Even though he already had the answers, he was still struggling to wrap his mind around this latest development. He sent off the picture of Bella along with her professional bio he found on the Pacific Palisades Dermatology and Skin Care Associates website. "Take a look at your email."

Joey tapped keys in the background and whistled low through his teeth. "Well, hello, beautiful. Who the hell is this? Your new California chick?"

"Nicoli's daughter."

"*What*? What the hell are you talking about? How do you know he has a daughter?"

"Take a look at her eyes and chin. Search for one of the pictures of Nicoli before he got old." He heard more taps on the computer keys.

"Holy shit. The resemblance is right on."

"She's my neighbor."

"*What*?"

"That, my friend, is Isabella Colby. She lives right next door."

"Get the fuck out."

"We've had dinner and she's cut my hair."

"You've been dining with a mafia daughter?"

"Apparently."

"You gonna ask her about her pops?"

"I don't know what I'm going to do yet, but knocking on her door and asking her to tell me about her killer family probably won't go over well."

"So be smooth about it. We've got our in, Reed. Take advantage of it."

He stared out at the high-end patio furniture on her deck and the fancy little grill. It wasn't every day an opportunity like this fell into his lap. "I told her I would take her out on my bike."

"See? There you go. Take her out on the fuckin' bike. Do whatever you have to do to get her to talk."

Sweet, funny Bella was his in. And she wasn't being square with anyone. What would Ethan or Jerrod or any of his coworkers say if they knew their wives' girlfriend was the daughter of a mafia man? "I'll see what she's doing tomorrow."

"You get her to trust you, maybe you can get her pops to trust you too."

Bella did trust him. He glanced out at her fancy furniture again and squashed any stirrings of guilt. Getting Nicoli to confide in him was a long shot, but he had to try. Bella's family was due a little payback. "That's the plan."

"You be careful, buddy. If this goes sour, you're a dead man. Nicoli Caparelli might go by another name, but something tells me he won't hesitate to end you if he has to."

"I guess we'll have to end him first. Get me everything you can on Isabella Colby. You have her work address and now her home address as well. We'll see what we can do with that."

"I'll call you sometime tomorrow."

"Talk to you then." Reed hung up and stared at the pictures on his screen, wrestling with an odd sense of betrayal. Long ago, he'd learned that nothing and no one were ever what they seemed to be. Apparently, his neighbor was no exception. Beautiful Bella Colby was going to help him bring down the most powerful crime family still in existence. She just didn't know it yet.

☙ Chapter Eight ❧

Reed's phone rang, waking him out of a deep sleep. Groaning, he rolled to his side, keeping his eyes closed to the brilliant sunshine boring in through the windows as he felt around on the floor for the damn thing. His fingers finally made contact with the plastic edge and he yanked it up, silencing his obnoxious ringtone for Joey. This no-furniture thing was getting old. Next time he was at the office, he was going to look at the mock-ups Wren dropped by a few days ago. "Yeah."

"Rise and shine, Sleeping Beauty."

He blinked against the bright light and turned his head, glancing at the alarm clock across the room on the edge of his desk. Barely seven thirty. "Is this payback for waking you up?"

"Nah, that's just a bonus. Make yourself some coffee 'cause I sent some stuff your way."

He tossed back the covers and sat up, scrubbing at his face and yawning loudly.

"Jesus, you're losing your touch. What happened to up at five and off to work?"

He stumbled out of bed, tripping over the pair of shoes he hadn't bothered to put away before he'd called it a night. "I have the day off."

"That never stopped you before. California's making you soft."

"Bull. I slept like crap—couldn't shut off my mind with everything that's going on," he said on his way down the stairs to the kitchen.

"I hear ya. Do you have that coffee yet?"

"No." He opened the cupboard door and grabbed one of the two mugs he owned, shoving it under his Keurig and pressing the button. "How about you tell me what you've got while I get something going in my cup? Then I'll take a look at what you sent me."

"Sure thing. The hottie next door is definitely hiding something."

Reed glanced toward Bella's house, frowning despite what he'd seen for himself last night. Something about all of this wasn't adding up for him. At no point over the last few days had he ever gotten the impression that Bella wasn't on the complete up and up. His instincts were rarely wrong, but he had two scars to remind him that he wasn't immune to the occasional blip.

"What do you want first?" Joey asked.

He yawned again. "Surprise me."

"I'll keep it routine since you're half-asleep."

"I appreciate it."

"Isabella Raine Colby. Born April twentieth, 1990 in Clinton, Ohio. Mother's name is Kelly Colby. Interestingly enough, there's no father listed on her birth certificate."

"Very interesting." He walked over to the fridge and grabbed the creamer, waiting for the coffee to stop its teasing trickle into his cup.

"Mother's deceased. Died late December 2014. Death certificate says cirrhosis of the liver."

"Alcoholic, maybe?"

"Could've been."

"There's a couple of different addresses on an old credit report Leo was able to dig up. Looks like Isabella and her mother lived in Kentucky, Nashville, Kansas City, Albuquerque, but stayed in Las Vegas the longest."

He snagged the mug, dumped creamer in, and headed back upstairs, wanting to be able to follow along with Joey as they looked over the documents. Two sets of eyes were always better than one.

"I took a minute to pull up the website for their old address—luxury apartment complex not far from the Strip. And somewhere around here I thought I saw that payments were made to a private school."

Reed took his seat at the desk and opened his laptop, typing in his user name and password to access his emails. "What did Mom Colby do to make such a fine living?"

"I haven't found that one out yet. There's no track record of her employment. But one thing I do know is beautiful Bella's got herself an interesting banking history."

"What does that mean?" He opened the "Colby Bank Records" document and scanned the spreadsheet. Bella had made several sizeable deposits to her Nevada savings account last year: eighty-three thousand here, twenty-five grand there, an eighteen-thousand-dollar chunk of change at one point, and a few other large amounts after that. "All in January 2015 except for the one deposit on February first."

"Adds up to about two hundred thousand."

"Did you find a paper trail to go along with this? Maybe some of it's a life insurance payoff from her mother's estate. The timing fits."

"Leo couldn't find a policy or any records along those lines. Nothing we have matches anything like that."

He rubbed at his jaw, trying to find some sort of pattern, but nothing made sense. "A couple days after the last transaction, she closed the account and opened a new one in Los Angeles."

"Definitely makes you wonder, boss," Joey said, tapping on a table in the background, a habit Reed had long since gotten used to. "Especially after I looked into her last few filings with the IRS. She does okay, but she's not wealthy by any means. In 2012 through 2014, she pulled in right around twenty-five to thirty a year. Between 2008 and 2011, she was making chump change—fifteen or so. When she moved to LA and hooked up with the dermatologist, things started getting better. Last year, she made sixty-eight. This year she's filing quarterly and is on pace to hit eighty-nine."

Reed glanced at her California savings account, noting that Bella had never touched a dime of the two hundred thousand after the initial deposit. "She's gotta carry some serious debt, then. She has expensive taste."

"Nope. One credit card with a current balance of one hundred fifty bucks."

Reed thought of Bella's high-end furnishings, designer clothes, and sporty little Volkswagen. Something wasn't adding up. "She must be taking something in on the side—something she's not reporting—because she's A-plus all the way. Everything I've seen is top end. Top, top end, Joe. Sixty-eight thousand sounds great, but when you compare what she has to what she's bringing in, it's way off, especially in an expensive area like the Palisades."

"Since we're keeping things interesting, I'll point out that Bella's move to California coincides with Vincent Pescoe opening his account in Reseda a couple weeks later."

"You're thinking he asked her to hold on to some of his money."

"You're thinking it too, boss. They meet up in Vegas, he deposits some cash, and they head out of town—her to the Palisades, him to Reseda. Maybe Daddy passes her several grand to thank her for her help, tells her to set herself up nice and pretty."

Reed sipped at his coffee, barely tasting his favorite hazelnut blend as he focused on the Bella Colby puzzle. "It makes sense. Sort of."

"Sort of?"

"Sort of," he repeated as he continued mulling it all over. He and Joey had been at this long enough to know that pigeonholing theories too early on in an investigation could lead them down the wrong path. Alfeo's release date didn't leave them any room for screw-ups. Time was not on their side in this scenario. "I'm trying to see this from all the angles—keep an open mind."

"You got it, buddy."

"What else do we have?"

"Vincent Pescoe's got himself a small savings—'bout fifteen hundred, nothing remarkable that would raise any brows."

"Why keep a large sum when your daughter can do it for you?"

"Exactly." Joey gave another tap to the table or desk—whatever it was he was sitting in front of. "Leo was able to find a non-driver's ID card issued to Vincent by Nebraska's DMV."

Reed searched for the new documents Joey must have just opened. "When?"

"About four or five years ago with a couple of eight-year renewals in Nebraska with an ID card issued in Wisconsin before that. I'm thinking our boy worked under the table after he told the Feds to kiss his ass, 'cause we've got nothin' after that—no addresses on file other than the ones he put down on the paperwork to get his picture identification."

"What about a Social Security number? WITSEC would have given him new ones along with his identities. But I'm not seeing anything." He scanned through sheet after sheet.

"Leo couldn't find nothin'. Me neither, 'cept for the credit line he opened in Clinton, Ohio, back in 1989, but there's nothing before or after."

Vincent Pescoe had lived like a ghost for the last twenty years. He'd stopped off in Wisconsin and Nebraska at some point to collect an ID, but he could have lived anywhere after he grabbed what he needed. "Do you know how lucky we are that we found him?"

"I'm going to church tomorrow, 'cause this is pretty much a fuckin' miracle."

Chuckling, Reed clicked back over to Bella's California savings account, staring at the balance. "We certainly have more questions than answers."

"I guess you better start digging."

He glanced up, catching a movement in his peripheral vision as Bella walked out on her back porch, wearing a fancy mid-thigh navy-blue robe. Her silky black hair glistened in the sun as she sat in one of the loungers, cupping a mug in her hands, while Lucy followed her, taking her spot at Bella's side. His sexy neighbor appeared to have just rolled out of bed, yet she looked like a flawless picture in a magazine. "What about her phone records?"

"I haven't been able to get my hands on those yet. It's gonna be tough without a warrant. I have some favors I can call in."

"Just keep it discreet."

"No, I'm gonna shout it from the rooftop. Maybe I can get my ass fired and take another couple of bullets while I'm at it."

Reed took another sip of his coffee, unconcerned by Joey's offended tone. "For less than eight hours on the job, we're off to a great start. Leo does good work."

"Yes, he does."

"We need more."

"And we'll get it. You do what you can on your end and I'll do the same on mine."

Reed glanced out at Bella again. "I should probably get started."

"Let me know how it goes."

"You'll be the first." He hung up and swallowed the last of his coffee as he stared at her basking in the sun. Today was the beginning, his and Joey's shot at actually building a case against Alfeo Caparelli. They'd waited a long time for this. He wasn't about to waste another second. Setting down his cup, he opened his window and crouched in front of the screen. "Morning."

Bella looked up, shielding her eyes with her hand. "Good morning."

"What are you up to today?"

"Right now, I'm drinking a cup of decaffeinated coffee."

He wrinkled his nose. "Decaffeinated?"

"I like the taste, but I don't like feeling jittery all day. Did you sleep well?"

He'd thought about her all night, replaying her embrace with her mobster father a million times. "Like a baby."

"Good."

"Wanna take a ride today?"

She smiled. "Sure. I need to shower first and feed Lucy her breakfast."

"Take your time. How about we leave around ten? I'll take you up the coast. We can stop off at this little place I know and have lunch."

She nodded. "That sounds great, but I can't be gone too long. Lucy will get offended."

"We'll probably be three hours, four at the most, if that works for you."

"Definitely. I'll make it up to her with a long walk tonight." She stood, giving him a good look at her excellent legs. "I guess I should get moving. I'll see you in a little while."

"See ya." His friendly smile vanished as she turned away and started inside. Here he was, back to the lying and secrets—a part of his life he thought he'd left behind, but clearly that wasn't the case.

Shoving away any regrets, he walked down the hall to the spare room he used as his gym and grabbed an old, ratty blanket they could bring along for their beach date. It had been a long time since he'd planned anything even remotely special for a woman, but he was willing to try if it got him the results he was after. People talked more when they were relaxed. Bella loved to be by the water, so that's where he was going to take her.

With a loose plan in place, he readied himself for the day with a shower and shave, dressing in jeans and one of his many white Ethan Cooke Security T-shirts. A bagel was next on the agenda, which he smooshed into a sandwich of bread and cream cheese. Then he went to the closet, pulling out his helmet along with the extra he kept on hand for occasions just like this. Bella was going to need a leather jacket for the ride, but nothing he had would fit her well.

A knock sounded at the door. He turned, opening it, and smiled as Bella stood in front of him, dressed in snug jeans and a simple white sleeveless shirt that she'd paired with Vans sneakers. Her hair was French-braided and her makeup and jewelry were in place, but this was the most relaxed he'd seen her. "Hey," he said.

"Hi."

Already, her subtle scent wafted his way, teasing his senses. "Come on in."

"Thanks." She stepped inside, and her smile faded as her gaze tracked around his empty living room. "Wow, Reed, I like what you've done with the place. It looks so different since the last time I was here."

He grinned, shutting the door behind her. "I haven't had a chance to study Wren's plans yet. I keep forgetting them at the office."

"If you were thinking about being comfortable while you live here, you might want to get on that."

"It's on the agenda for this week. Wren said she came up with three or four different ideas. Maybe you can give them a once-over and see what you think."

"I would love to. Wren and I had such a good time working on my house."

He imagined that asking Bella how she'd paid for everything wouldn't be a great way to start off their day. "You did a nice job."

She smiled. "Thanks."

"So, I was trying to figure out what we're going to do about a jacket for you."

"Do I need one? It's warm outside already."

"If we dump, you'll want something on."

"Dump?"

"Tip over, which we won't do," he added quickly when her eyes widened. "Better safe than sorry, though." He walked over to the closet. "I've got a couple of options." He pulled out both hangers with her choices on them.

She blinked as she stared at them. "They're pretty big."

"Yeah. I've probably got a good sixty pounds on you."

"Well, let's take a look." She tugged the first off the hanger and put it on, lifting her brow as the hem hung to her thighs and her hands were lost in the sleeves. "What do you think?"

He chuckled. "I think it would make life easier if you had a jacket of your own."

"True. But I don't." She took off their first attempt.

He pulled the second off the hanger himself and helped her into it, zipping the zipper and easing her braid free from the back of the collar. "A little better."

She nodded. "A little."

"It's not a fashion statement, but it'll keep you safe."

"That's the most important thing."

"We're going to need this too." He grabbed the backpack he'd folded the old blanket into. "You'll have to wear this."

"Sure. Do you mind if I throw in my purse?"

"Go for it. Just leave your sunglasses out. And let's get this adjusted." He sunk the open-face helmet down on her head and fiddled with the strap, his knuckles brushing her baby-soft skin with every movement. “Is that comfortable?”

“Feels fine.”

“I think we’re ready to go.”

Excitement filled her eyes as she smiled. “I can’t wait.”

“Let’s do it, then.” He locked up, and they walked out to the bike. “There are a couple of rules, though.”

“All right.”

“When I turn, I want you to lean with me—nothing crazy, just follow my lead.”

She nodded.

“When we stop, keep your feet in your spot. I’ll get on first.” He zipped his jacket, shoved his sunglasses in place as Bella did the same, put on his helmet, then kicked his leg over and took his seat. “Okay. Go ahead and hop on.”

She climbed on behind him. “Um, where should I hold on?”

He could sense her rigid posture as her thighs barely brushed his hips. “There’s a spot behind you if you want.”

She moved to settle in.

“Are you comfortable?”

“Yeah. Sure.”

“That doesn’t sound very convincing.”

“No, this is fine.”

He reached behind him and took her hands, settling her arms around his waist. “Let’s try this.”

“Better,” she said closer to his ear.

“You sure?”

“Much.”

She felt good nestled up against him. It was a damn shame that Bella was not only not his type but also a Caparelli. “Then let’s go.” He drove off toward the main road and pulled into traffic, taking a detour around the block, giving Bella a chance to get used to the feeling of turning.

She stiffened, gripping him tight as they went right.

“Relax, Bella. Just lean with me.”

“Sorry.”

“You’re doing fine.”

He waited at the light, and they took the next right and another. By the time they made it into their fourth turn, she was moving with him, and seemed to be ready to go. “Are you feeling good about this?”

“Definitely.”

"If you change your mind at any time, just let me know."

"I won't change my mind."

He accelerated from their spot at the intersection and they started their journey north, driving for almost an hour on Highway 1 with the Pacific for the view to their left and the canyons to the right. Somewhere along the way, Bella had fully relaxed, her arms going loose on his waist and her head occasionally resting on his back. He spotted the sign for Louie's Seafood Shack and smiled, slowing and parking by the desolate patch of beach. He put his feet down, set the kickstand, and killed the engine. "How are you doing back there?"

She sat up, breaking their connection. "I love this. *Love* it."

"Good. Go ahead and get off first."

She climbed down and grinned as their eyes met. "This is one of the best times I've ever had."

He took off his helmet and unclipped hers. "It doesn't take much to impress you."

She took hers off, holding it against the side of her body with one arm. "Look at this *view*. What more could you ask for?"

He stared out at the waves rushing the sand, and caught hints of Bella's perfume on the wind. "It's great. I've driven up here a couple of times."

"I'm glad you brought me with you." She took his hand and squeezed. "Thank you."

He glanced down at her fingers clasped around his and struggled to keep his jaw from clenching. It was hard not to be affected by her friendliness and constant need to touch. "You're welcome. How about some lunch?" He pulled his hand free, gesturing to the refurbished lifeguard tower turned seafood stand. "It's kind of a dive, but they have amazing clams."

"I've never tried fried clams."

"Then you're in for a treat." He walked with her over to the window, studying her out of the corner of his eye as she read the menu. Bella had high-end taste, but there was nothing about her that appeared to be high-maintenance. He'd half expected her to turn up her nose at his lunch idea, yet here she stood, ready and enthusiastic to try something new. Why didn't anything about this woman add up?

They ordered two plates with sides of fries and made their way to the sand, protecting their food from the birds while they took turns removing their socks and shoes and Bella her jacket.

"I brought a blanket if you want to eat closer to the water."

"Perfect." She led them to a quiet spot five or six feet from the surf and pulled out the blanket. Sitting, she buried her feet in the sand. "Mmm. Paradise."

"Wait till you try your lunch." He lifted a fried clam to her lips.

She bit in and her brow winged up. "Wow."

He loved that she liked it. "Yeah?"

She grabbed his wrist and snagged the rest of the bite from his fingers. "So good. They don't even need the tartar sauce." She swallowed. "What a charming little spot."

"It'll get crowded as the weather warms up."

"I don't see how it couldn't." She sighed and closed her eyes as the wind rushed over their faces. "I don't know how I lived without this for most of my life."

"The clams?"

She grinned, meeting his gaze. "The water."

"Vegas is pretty landlocked, huh?"

"No ocean to be seen." She popped another piece in her mouth.

"You grew up there?"

"Mmm, we settled in when I was eleven. We moved around some before that."

He sampled a crispy fry. "Brothers and sisters?"

"Just me. What about you?"

"Only child, but my cousins lived right down the road—my mom's family."

She narrowed her eyes, studying him.

"What?" he asked.

"Sometimes I catch a hint of an accent, but I can't place it."

"I'm originally from New York, but my mom and I moved to a tiny town outside of Fargo after my dad died. On the Minnesota side of the city—if that's what you want to call the place."

The light vanished from her eyes. "I'm sorry about your dad. How old were you when he passed away?"

He wanted to correct her. His father had been murdered—hunted down and shot like a dog—along with his grandfather and uncle. "Five—a couple days before my sixth birthday."

She made a pained sound in her throat as she touched his arm, her eyes radiating compassion. "It's tough losing a parent so young." She gripped his hand in hers. "I'm sorry for your loss."

"Thanks." He removed his hand from hers, reaching for his soft drink. He didn't want Bella's sympathy. Her regrets didn't make his family any less dead. "It was a long time ago."

She reached for a french fry.

"What about your family?" he asked. "Do your parents live close by?"

"My mom died last year."

"Sorry to hear that. That must be tough for your father."

She paused with a bite at her lips. "Yeah."

He didn't miss her hesitation. "He's still in Vegas?"

"Uh, no. California."

He could sense that she wanted to drop the subject as her posture grew rigid, but he wasn't ready to let it go. "It's great that he has you."

"We see each other occasionally." She wiped her hands on a napkin and stood. "I'm going to use the bathroom."

He'd struck some sort of nerve. "I'll be right here."

"Go ahead and finish those up." She gestured to her meal. "I'm finished."

"Are you sure?"

"Yeah. I'll just be a minute."

"Take your time." He watched her walk away, bringing her shoes with her but forgetting her purse. He waited for the door to close behind her before he wiped his fingers on a napkin and unzipped the backpack. Glancing over his shoulder once more, he reached for her trendy little bag and opened the snap, peeking inside. Keys, lip gloss, a small tube of something or other, wallet, and phone. Not much to work with.

He grabbed her wallet, noting the twenty and five she carried in cash, the change in the small pocket, her California license, the one credit card Joey had tracked down, and her bank card, but nothing of any significance. Shoving the wallet back among her things, he eyed her phone. That's what he wanted access to—her contacts, but he didn't dare risk it, especially when she probably had a password. At a dead end, he put everything back exactly the way he'd found it and zipped the backpack. At some point, he would find an opportunity to get what he was after. He and Bella were going to start spending a lot of time together.

Bella stood in front of the mirror in the tiny beachside bathroom, pushing the flyaway hairs back into her braid. She wished she hadn't forgotten her purse in Reed's bag; her lips could use a little gloss, but that would have to wait. Leaning closer, she fixed her simple teardrop earrings, lining the silver tips up straight, the way they were supposed to hang, then frowned at her reflection. Not everything had to be perfect today. Her only focus needed to be on having fun: cool new experiences, good company, and amazing food. She could do without Reed's twenty questions where her family was concerned, but it made sense that he would ask. They were still getting to know each other—and most people were proud to talk about their moms and dads. But most people didn't have parents like hers.

Sighing, she shoved her negative thoughts away and tried to focus on the present. Reality and complicated family issues were for later. Right now was for the beach. She slid her sunglasses back in place and opened the door, taking off her shoes and starting Reed's way. He'd taken off his jacket while she'd been gone and was currently leaning back on his hands, his impressive triceps bunching in his snug T-shirt while the wind played with his hair. From a distance, he appeared to be the picture of calm, but there was an unwavering intensity in his eyes that led her to believe he was always on guard.

He turned his head and smiled.

"Man, that's a lethal grin," she murmured and smiled back, sending him a quick wave.

"Lucy's missing out on some serious fun." He gestured to a couple of seagulls dive-bombing a family trying to enjoy their lunch. "Oops. There goes the kid's hot dog."

She laughed as she took her spot next to Reed. "Poor guy."

"I wonder how many meals they steal in a given day?"

"More than a few, I'm sure." She sighed, crossing her ankles as the breeze rushed up to meet her. "The wind feels good."

"It does. The sun's hot."

"Mmm. These are the days you burn and don't even realize it until it's too late." She looked at him. "You're wearing sunblock?"

"Nah."

She frowned, sitting up straight. "Why aren't you wearing sunblock?"

He shrugged. "I forgot to put some on."

"You're risking sun damage and skin cancer." She unzipped the backpack and reached in her purse for the small tube of sunscreen she always kept handy.

He grinned. "You carry that stuff with you?"

"Of course. Do you know how many cases of melanoma Dr. Huberty and I see every month? I just referred someone over to her on Thursday." She took his hand, squirting a small glob in his palm. "Lather up, buddy. You're not getting cancerous growths on my watch."

He chuckled. "Is this part of the Reed McKinley Project?"

"You bet. Your face is way too pretty to be getting sliced and diced."

"Pretty?" He frowned this time as he rubbed the lotion on his arms and the majority of his face. "I'm not pretty."

She rolled her eyes. "Handsome, then. You missed a few spots." She faced him and leaned in, spreading out the streaks along his nose, then went to work on his forehead.

He closed his eyes beneath his tinted shades and let loose a breath. "Feels good."

"Touch is very therapeutic."

He grunted his response.

"This is an all-natural product fortified with green tea and antioxidants. It's great for your skin."

"I'll take your word for it."

She dabbed a pea-sized drop on her index fingers and traced his ears.

He opened his eyes, meeting hers through amber lenses.

She swallowed, finding the power of his stare both mesmerizing and unsettling. "Most people forget their ears—men especially, which is unfortunate. I had a client lose an entire portion of his helix."

"I'm not up on my anatomy."

"This part here." She outlined the upper area of his cartilage as her gaze wandered to his mouth. "Uh, are you finished with your lunch? Because you should protect your lips as well."

He snagged a fry from the paper plate, bit in, and held the other half up to her mouth.

She smiled and took it. "These are so *good*. I wonder what seasoning they use?"

"We could ask."

She shook her head, applying a light coat of product to his lips as their eyes locked again, then finished by protecting her own. "I can't see myself making french fries anytime soon."

"They're the food of champions."

"Grease is horrible for the complexion."

"I've never seen skin as flawless as yours." He skimmed his knuckles along her cheek. "It's like porcelain."

Butterflies danced in her stomach, even though she was certain Reed wasn't trying to put the moves on her.

"How do you keep it so soft?" he asked.

"Product and treatments." She inched away. "And I try to eat well and drink a ton of water. My face is my advertisement to the world."

"You can't be hurting for business, then." He sat up, snatching another fry. "One more?"

"I can't resist." She popped one last fried potato in her mouth. "I don't think I mentioned it, but I'm officially signing up for the cooking classes I was telling you about."

"No kidding."

"Yup. I've decided I'm taking the plunge. I can't decide if I want to do the block of four or six lessons."

"Is it a daytime thing?"

She shook her head. "No, it's on Tuesday nights for the four or six weeks. The first one starts this week. It's a dessert workshop."

"Sounds great."

"Mmm." She wiggled her eyebrows. "I'm pretty excited. I'm going to see if one of my friends wants to sign up with me."

He perked up. "Are you looking for a partner?"

She frowned. "You want to take a cooking class?"

He shrugged. "Guys can cook."

"Of course they can. I just didn't realize you had any interest."

"I'm willing to try it out—broaden my horizons, especially since it's on my night off." He stood. "Want to walk?"

"Sure." They started down the beach, and she took his hand, loving how easy it was to be around him.

He hesitated a step, then held her hand more firmly in his.

"Are you serious about the classes?"

"Yeah."

"Huh." She nibbled her lip as she thought of the course offerings she'd perused last night.

"What?"

"We could—we could save twenty-five percent if we sign up for the couples' classes. No one needs to know we're just neighbors."

"I'm all for bending the rules a little—especially for a twenty-five percent discount."

She smiled. "It's dishonest..."

"I don't think they'll be pulling us aside and quizzing us on which side of the bed you sleep on."

She laughed. "I have the paperwork at home—or I can download it, anyway. I think this could be seriously fun."

"We get to eat everything we make?"

"Yup," she said with a definitive nod.

"I don't see how it couldn't be."

They moved closer to the water, getting their toes wet in the surf.

"Describe your perfect day," she blurted out, wanting to know him better.

He looked at her. "My perfect day?"

"Yeah."

"Uh, waking up late and maybe hitting the gym."

She sent him a pained look. "*That's* your perfect day?"

"It sounds pretty good to me."

Shaking her head, she chuckled. "To each his own."

He smiled. "What's wrong with that? What's yours?"

"I liked your idea about waking up late, but instead of punching someone in the face, I would have a lazy breakfast and spend the afternoon at the beach. I missed the lazy breakfast today, but lunch was good—and spending time with you. You're a good guy, Reed." She bumped his arm and smiled. "I'm glad you're my buddy."

"Thanks." He bumped her back.

She breathed deep as she stared out at the endless shades of blue, savoring the beauty. "Right about now I feel wonderfully happy. I love embracing these little miracle moments because they're so rare."

"Life's pretty complicated."

She thought of her dad and the confusing emotions she'd struggled with since she knocked on his door. "It can be."

The water rushed up and soaked them to their ankles. Reed pulled her back with him as he stepped clear of the surf. "I think the tide's starting to come in."

"Looks like it." She expelled a long breath, realizing her perfect moment was over. "As much as I hate to say it, I need to head home. Lucy's probably lonely."

"Let's get our stuff." He started back toward the blanket.

"Wait." She stopped him with a tug on his hand.

"What's up?"

"I wanted to— Thanks for today. I can't remember the last time I've had this much fun."

"Me neither." He gave her fingers a squeeze. "We'll have to take a look at the cooking class stuff when we get home."

She nodded. "We can fill it out online and make sure we get our spot. Tuesday, we're making molten lava cake."

"Definitely a good plan if we want to eat molten lava cake."

They walked back and grabbed their stuff, then headed home.

Reed typed up the details and his impressions after his afternoon at the beach with Bella, adding them to the new folder he'd created for the Nicoli Caparelli investigation. Their bike ride along the coast and fried clam picnic had turned into a shrimp dinner at her place while they filled out the forms for their Tuesday night cooking classes. For the next six weeks, he was guaranteed a three-hour block of Bella's time.

Sighing his satisfaction, he sat back in his chair. His first official day of Operation Caparelli Takedown was in the books and it didn't appear that his neighbor suspected a thing. If all went well, she never would. Despite who she was and the secrets she kept, he couldn't help but like her. She was easy on the eyes and fun to be around, which worked to his advantage. The more real he could be with her, the better all of this would play out. Bella wanted his friendship, and for the time being, he could get on board with befriending a mafia daughter. He and Joey were down to mere months. He planned to make every second count.

☙ Chapter Nine ❧

Reed was pulling on a clean pair of jeans when he heard the knock on his front door. Muttering a curse, he grabbed a shirt from his drawer and snagged his favorite sneakers off the floor, then hurried downstairs. "Just a sec," he called as he yanked the dark gray T-shirt over his head and opened the door. "Hey."

Bella sent him a small smile. "Hi."

"Sorry I'm running a little behind." He sank his feet into his Nikes. "The traffic sucked, but I wanted to grab a quick shower before we left."

"That's okay. We should still make it with plenty of time."

He breathed in her familiar scent as he tracked his gaze down her white and black polka-dot shirt, snug navy-blue pants, and black heels. Not exactly relaxed. "Are you wearing that to class?"

"Sure. It's a simple wrap blouse and ankle pants." She glanced down at herself. "I'm just coming from work myself. Do you think I should change?"

"No. You look good." And she did—beautiful with some of her hair clipped back in a barrette and the ends curled.

"I like wearing heels so I'm taller, but maybe I should do something with sneakers instead."

He shook his head. "You're fine like that."

"You think?"

"I'm positive." He snagged his keys and sunglasses off the counter and shut the door. "Should we go cook?"

She gave him a decisive nod. "Absolutely."

He locked up, ready to get their evening started. Bella would be in her element—relaxed, happy, and distracted: the perfect time to slip in a question here and there while keeping things casual. "How about the truck?"

"Yeah, that's fine."

As they headed to the driveway, he looked at the downstairs lights on in Bella's place despite the sun still making its way toward the horizon. "Is Lucy upset that you're leaving her?"

"She's fine. We stopped off on the way home and got her a cookie at Paws."

He shrugged, shaking his head. "I'm not sure what that is."

"It's the pet bakery on Sunset. Everyone loves when she comes in for a visit."

He raised his brow. "A pet bakery?"

"Yes, a pet bakery. There's nothing wrong with pampering your pets."

He scratched his head, certain he'd never heard of anything so foolish. But this was the same woman who painted her dog's nails. "I guess that's what the owners at Paws are counting on."

She frowned. "Lucy's my family. She's all I have."

He reached for her door handle. "What about your dad?"

"I mean, locally she's all the family I have."

He nodded, but there was something here—as if it hadn't crossed her mind to include or consider her father. He would have to dig around until she told him about it. Luckily, they had the next three hours to get the ball rolling. "You said he's in California?"

"Reseda—about an hour away."

"That's not too far."

She got in. "No. It makes it easy to spend time together."

That's what he was hoping for. He shut her door and hustled around to his side, getting in and buckling up. "Ready?" he asked, wiggling his eyebrows.

A smile ghosted her mouth as she studied him. "You're excited."

"Of course I am. Who doesn't like cake?"

Chuckling, she shook her head. "We'll have a good time."

"I don't see how we couldn't." He turned over the ignition and drove through the neighborhood to the main road, pulling into traffic with the green light. As one mile turned into two, he glanced Bella's way. Usually she was bubbly and chatty, but tonight she stared out her window with her arms crossed at her chest. He frowned, realizing she didn't seem excited about their plans at all, and she was the one who'd been gung-ho about the cooking classes in the first place. "Is everything okay?"

"Yeah. It's been a long day."

He narrowed his eyes beneath his shades when she didn't bother to look at him. Something was definitely up. "Do you want to talk about it?"

She shook her head, blinking rapidly as she bit her bottom lip.

His frown returned when he recognized that she was trying not to cry. "Hey, what's up?"

She swallowed and cleared her throat, crossing her arms tighter. "I, um, I lost a patient today."

He stopped for a red light. "Someone *died*?"

She nodded as she finally met his gaze. "Yes."

"At your office?"

"No. One of the girls I work with at the children's hospital lost her battle with cancer." Her eyes welled again as she pressed her trembling lips together.

He started to reach for her hand but stopped himself, leaving it on the steering wheel instead, never quite sure what to do with women and their tears. "I'm sorry."

A tear spilled over as she closed her eyes. "She was only eight."

Death was nothing new to him. For years, he'd witnessed the ugliness and brutality human beings inflicted on one another. Long ago, he'd learned to turn off the sorrow and focus on the hows and whys of an investigation, but any time a kid died, it was rough. "That's tough."

"I saw her a couple weeks ago. She was doing so well, getting ready to go home. Her doctors thought she was going to beat it. We were all so hopeful." She wiped at her cheeks as she expelled a shaky breath. "I'm afraid I'm not going to be very good company tonight."

"That's okay." He pulled into the Culinary Arts Center parking lot and took a spot, killing the engine. "We can go home if you want."

She shook her head. "We paid for the class and you're looking forward to it." Another tear slid down her cheek. "I just need a minute and I'll be all right."

Clenching his jaw, he stared at her sagging shoulders and hands white-knuckled in her lap, watching her battle to shore herself up. He turned toward the window, trying to ignore her hitching breaths as he reminded himself that this wasn't his problem. There was nothing he could do for her. He wasn't a damn counselor. His gaze slid her way again and he got out, swearing under his breath as he walked around to her side, opening her door.

"I'm sorry about this," she choked out, staring straight ahead. "I found out a couple of hours ago. I thought I was handling it. The call was so unexpected..."

He sighed, reaching out to her, then pushed his glasses on top of his head instead, craving to touch and comfort, knowing he was on the verge of crossing the forbidden line into emotional involvement. "Come on out."

She shook her head. "I'm not quite ready."

He leaned in and released her seat belt. "Come on out, Bella. Get some fresh air."

She stepped onto the blacktop, meeting his gaze with devastated eyes, then looked down as the dam broke and she started crying quietly.

Gritting his teeth, he tugged her against him.

She cushioned her forehead in the crook of his neck and gripped the sides of his shirt, sniffling as her shoulders shook.

Closing his eyes, aching for her, he wrapped his arms around her, tightening his hold when she settled her cheek against his chest and returned his embrace. "I'm sorry for your loss, that you've had a tough day," he said quietly next to her ear.

"She was such a sweet girl. I've worked with her for about five months. I wanted her to be okay. I want all of them to be okay. They're children—little boys and girls who should be playing with their friends instead of lying in hospital beds."

Before he knew what was doing, he found his palm pressed to her back, gently stroking up and down her blouse. "How about we do dessert another night?"

"But your chocolate lava cake."

He eased her slightly away, startled by the effect her big brown eyes had on him, by how much he needed to make this better for her. "We can have that anytime. Let's go home and get Lucy. We'll take a walk on the beach."

Her face crumpled again.

"Or not," he said quickly. "We don't have to."

"That sounds wonderful." She sniffled. "Actually, pretty perfect." She smiled even as her eyes still radiated with sorrow. "Sweet and kind."

He didn't know he could be sweet and kind, wasn't sure when the last time was that he'd tried. "Here." He lifted the hem of his shirt and dabbed at her cheeks. "Let's go."

She nodded. "Thank you."

"That's what friends are for." That's all this was, he assured himself as she got in. Friends for now, doing whatever needed to be done, playing whatever angle was necessary for the investigation. "Go ahead and buckle up."

She nodded again.

He shut her inside and started around to his side, wondering what in the hell his problem was. He'd never done anything like this before, but as he opened his door and met Bella's teary-eyed gaze, his instincts told him that this was right, so he went along with it, letting his gut lead the way. Reaching out, he took her hand. "Maybe we can grab an ice cream too."

"Okay."

He gave her fingers a squeeze, then put the truck in reverse. "Let's go get your girl."

Bella held Reed's hand as they walked in the sand, eating ice cream cones under the stars. The warmth of his palm pressed to hers and the pounding waves rushing the beach soothed her after such a horrible day.

"How's the ice cream?"

She swiped another taste, enjoying the melding of sweet vanilla and salty ribbons of caramel. "Really good. I'll definitely be ordering caramel chunk again."

"I could take your word for it, but I like to judge for myself."

She stopped and held the cone up to his lips.

He gripped her wrist, bringing the treat closer, and pulled a healthy sample into his mouth. "Mmm. That *is* good."

Her eyes widened as he helped himself to more. "You just ate the whole thing."

He smiled through his mouthful, his gaze mischievous as he held hers. "You're such an exaggerator. There's plenty left."

She examined the deep dip in her enormous scoop of ice cream. "I didn't realize you had such a big mouth."

He laughed, sliding some of her blowing hair away from her cheek. "Here. Have some of mine."

"I know what chocolate swirl tastes like," she said with a lift of her chin, feigning insult, as she started turning away.

He laughed again, pulling on her hand until she faced him. "Have some anyway."

She sampled far more politely than he had.

"So?"

"It tastes like chocolate swirl." Her serious expression dissolved into a smile.

He chuckled, giving her fingers a squeeze as they started walking again with Lucy leading the way. "You have some of your spunk back."

"Thanks to you." She leaned against him, resting her head on his strong arm, enjoying their easy connection.

"Do you know when they're having the funeral?"

"Sunday." She sighed as the dread of having to say good-bye to someone so young hurt her heart. "The whole family is wonderful—just so kind. I hate that this is happening to them."

"It's nice that you offer your time to the hospital."

"I love it. I wanted to be a doctor—a pediatrician, but it didn't work out."

"How come?"

Shrugging, she thought of the two backbreaking years when she'd worked forty hours a week to make ends meet while trying to keep up with a full load of pre-med courses. "Sometimes life chooses another path for you. Doing what I do now is mine."

"It sounds like you're good at it."

"I want to be the best at everything I try."

"Why?"

"I don't know." She jerked her shoulders. "I guess so people will know I was worth the investment, that I wasn't a waste of their time."

Reed made a sound in his throat as he finished off his cone. "Do you think you'll still make it to the wedding on Saturday?"

"I wouldn't miss it—Julie and Chase's special day."

"Do you want to drive over together?"

She stopped. "You're going?"

"Sure. Why not?"

She smiled, truly delighted. "Reed, this is great." She handed him the rest of her dessert, too full to finish.

He took it, licking at the drips before they could fall. "So you'll be my date?"

"Sure. I have plans that afternoon, but we can head over around five-ish if that works for you."

"Five-ish, it is." His phone rang, playing several notes of "Sexy and I Know It" before he silenced the ringtone and shoved it back in his pocket.

"Wait. Take that back out."

He stiffened.

"Come on. Let's see."

Rolling his eyes, he grabbed it, holding it out to her.

She laughed as she stared at a handsome bearded man with huge broad shoulders, flipping Reed off in the picture. "That's what I thought I saw." She laughed again. "Who on earth is this?"

"That's Joey, my ex-partner and best friend."

"He looks like quite a character."

He grinned. "That's definitely a word for him. He insisted this song be his ringtone. I haven't gotten around to changing it yet, but I need to."

She chuckled as they continued their stroll and Reed finished off the rest of her ice cream. "What is it that you and Joey did for the NYPD?"

"We were special unit detectives. Joe and I worked deep cover in a secret operation for seven years."

"Sounds exciting."

He bobbed his head from side to side. "It had its moments."

"I take it the secret operation's over."

"For the most part." He turned them around, starting them toward his truck. "This way, Lucy."

Lucy followed at Reed's side.

"We should head back," he said. "I don't know about you, but I have to get up early—another flight in the morning."

She wrinkled her nose. "San Francisco?"

"How'd you guess?"

"That must get old."

He shrugged. "At least we're staying for three days this time—big convention."

"Any more hostile takeovers to worry about?"

"Nah. I'll be doing a lot of sitting and standing around."

"Looking tough and intimidating the whole time."

He huffed out a cocky laugh. "Of course."

She smiled, loving that Reed was relaxing more and more around her. "Don't you like working the big premieres and stuff?"

"I'm keeping a low profile for a while. Joey and I had some complications in New York."

Frowning, she slowed her pace. "Like what?"

"Our cover was blown. Staying away from countrywide broadcasts is a good thing for the time being."

She stopped. "Are you in danger?"

"No. And I'd like to keep it that way."

She studied him, worrying for her new friend.

"I'm fine, Bella. It's just a precaution. Why invite trouble if it's not knocking on your door?"

She nodded, but she was going to be keeping an eye on him.

Reed's phone rang again, playing the same ringtone.

"Do you need to get that?"

"Nah. I'll call him later. He can complain about his day after I get home."

She grinned as they approached the pickup. "Lucy, come."

Lucy trotted over.

"Up you go."

Lucy hopped in and lay in her spot up by the cab.

Reed secured the gate. "She's got that one down."

"She'll forever see your truck as one of her beach mobiles."

They got in and drove back to their neighborhood in silence as the breeze blew through the window. Bella glanced Reed's way, studying his profile in the play of shadows. He wasn't Mr. *GQ*, but he comforted heartbroken women in parking lots, which was far more important than nice suits and silk ties.

He pulled down their road, then into his driveway. "Home sweet home."

"Here we are." She got out as he shut off the engine.

Reed followed her, letting down the back for Lucy. "Out you go, Luce."

Lucy jumped down and headed toward the house.

"And she's off for the door," he said.

She smiled. "Have fun on your trip." Reaching around him, she pulled his phone out of his back pocket and put her number in his contact list. "If you find yourself falling asleep, don't be afraid to call. We'll chat and I'll keep you awake."

He smiled. "You may be sorry you did that." Taking the phone back, he held it up. "Smile."

She bent down and hugged Lucy, grinning up at him.

He pressed the button and glanced at the shot. "That should do it. And no middle finger."

"I'm not a middle finger kind of girl."

"Classy Bella."

Is that how he saw her? That worked for her. Better than trashy

Bella and her prostitute mom. "Thanks again for everything, for being just what I needed tonight."

"No problem."

She nodded, snagging her bottom lip with her teeth. Typically, she ended an evening out with friends with a hug, but as she thought of the way he'd held her tight, letting her rest her head on his solid chest, it didn't seem like a good idea. For the first time since she'd dumped Linc, she felt the click she'd mentioned to Dad. She wasn't so sure she wanted that type of click with Reed—not when she was enjoying the simplicity they had going on between them. "Good night."

"Night."

She let Lucy and herself inside, waved, and shut the door, turning to her puppy. "I don't know about him, Lucy."

Lucy wagged her tail.

She crouched down, giving Lucy a good rub. "He's pretty cute, huh?"

Lucy gave her a kiss.

"Aw, thank you." She hugged her and pressed a kiss to her neck. "I'm going to go put on my pajamas, and we'll have a cup of tea. You and I are going to have a long conversation about our buddy next door."

Reed locked up for the night and kicked off his shoes as he dialed Joey's number.

"How was the chocolate cake, Chef McKinley?"

"We didn't get around to cooking," he said as he went upstairs and flipped on the light in his bedroom. "We went to the beach for ice cream instead."

"Sounds like a date."

"It wasn't a date." He sat in his ratty office chair and opened his laptop. "She was upset. One of the kids she works with at the children's hospital died today."

The line stayed silent.

"What?"

"Nothing."

"She was crying." He rushed up from his seat and began pacing as tension started squeezing his shoulders. "What was I supposed to do, grab her hand, yank her into a cooking class, and drill her about her father?"

"She's a beauty, boss. Those kinda looks are dangerous for any man."

Tonight her tears had been lethal weapons. "I'm not worried about it. We have a job to do."

"If you're not worried, I'm not worried."

"Let's keep it that way." Why was this bothering him—Joey's insinuations; his inability to take Bella's hand and drag her into a class and question her about her father? Not even a year ago, he would have been able to overlook her heartache. The job would have come first, but tonight his objectivity had been compromised by an unfamiliar need to soothe and comfort.

"I got the phone records," Joey said.

He clenched his fingers around the phone, already knowing Joey had something he wasn't going to like. "And?"

"And your dream neighbor's in deep. She definitely has ties to the mafia. Right in fuckin' Bensonhurst. You'd think she'd be a little more careful, ya know?"

Reed sat again, trying to equate teary-eyed Bella with the organized crime, and couldn't. "What the hell are you talking about?"

"I was looking through the phone numbers. A Brooklyn number kept popping out at me, so I checked on it."

"What did you get, Joe?"

"She's frequently in contact with a woman named Luisa De Vitis."

"Should that ring a bell?"

"Mrs. De Vitis uses her maiden name for business. Asante—"

"Asante? As in Dino Asante, Patrizio's consigliere?"

"You got it, boss."

He walked to the window, staring out at Bella's pretty porch. "What the fuck?"

"Luisa's running her own beauty place in Bensonhurst. Small—upscale. Looks like they're just about to open a new building."

"If Bella's in contact with Nicoli's old people, how is she not dead? Killing Bella would be the next best thing to Nicoli."

"Maybe Nicoli made some sort of deal with them. He might've paid them off or something."

He shook his head. "That doesn't sit right. Alfeo would've taken the money and had her murdered anyway. He wants revenge. That's no secret. I'm sure the contract on his little brother extends to Nicoli's daughter as well." Clenching his jaw, he turned away from the cozy scene outside. "Let's keep a monitor on that."

"You've got it. So what's next with the bombshell?"

"We're going to a wedding on Saturday."

"Things are moving right along."

"Yeah. Just the way we want." He closed his eyes, trying to forget the way Bella felt wrapped in his arms. "I've gotta go. Keep me up to date on any more calls."

"Sure thing."

He hung up and flung the phone on his bed, finding the rage that had consumed him for a decade rushing back to haunt him. "Goddamn." He'd had a taste of a normal life. For a couple of months, he'd found a little peace. Now he was stuck in the thick of it all again. Bella was playing with fire by keeping in contact with the people in her father's old life—or maybe current life—and for the time being, there was nothing he could do to stop it.

☙ CHAPTER TEN ❧

BELLA GAVE A FINAL STIR TO THE HOMEMADE YOGURT DIP SHE was whipping up and poured it into the circular platter, being careful not to make a mess. Carrot sticks, broccoli florets, and grape tomatoes were doled into the small trays in an alternating pattern before she grabbed a spoon for the fruit salad she'd made and took the plastic wrap off the black bean brownies Lyla had shared a recipe for. Stepping back, she appraised her presentation in the center of the kitchen table and nodded. "I think that's it. We're ready for the girls," she said to Lucy as she gathered the prep bowls and rinsed them in the sink.

Lucy stood, wagging her tail.

Drying her hands on a clean towel, she glanced at the clock. "They should be here any minute." She bent down and straightened Lucy's handkerchief, anticipating a fun, therapeutic afternoon for two of her favorite people. "Thanks for being a good sport about the nail polish remover. Painting your nails is one of their favorite things to do." She kissed Lucy's neck. "You're a good girl." She kissed her again. "The best."

A car pulled up, and two doors slammed. Bella smiled and walked to the open front door, waving to Emilia's aunt as she started backing out of the driveway. Her smile turned into a grin when she spotted her buddies running toward the house. She stepped out into the warm midmorning sunshine and hurried to meet them, crouching down and holding out her arms, eager for their hugs. "And who are these two beauties?"

"Bella!"

The girls moved faster, stepping into her embrace.

She gripped them tight and kissed both of their cheeks, finding the moment all the more special after losing Angela just a couple of days ago. Her dreams of changing lives through medicine had vanished when she couldn't keep up with her classes, but being a support system for children in need of a little extra TLC was something she could do and loved to be a part of. "You two look wonderful." She kissed them again, noting that Bianca's hair was starting to grow in ever so slightly, and Emilia's suture line where her hand had once been was looking better among the massive scaring covering most of her body, some of the worst of it on her face. "I've missed my *girls*." She hugged the six-year-olds for a second time. "How are you doing?"

"My hair's coming back." Bianca pointed to her bald head. "But it's probably gonna go away when I have another treatment."

Bella nodded, not wanting to give Bianca false hope. "Probably, but it won't stay gone forever."

"Sometimes I think it will."

"It won't. I promise." She slid her hand over Bianca's peach fuzz. "Lucy has a couple of cool bandanas for you. They match hers."

Bianca's eyes lit up. "Really?"

She nodded. "Really."

"I'm going to have another surgery on my neck." Emilia pointed above her tracheostomy tube, where the contracture to her skin was still debilitating. "They're going to give me more of a chin, and I'm gonna be able to move my head better, maybe like I could before I got burned."

"That sounds wonderful." She took Emilia's hand, giving a gentle squeeze. "Lucy helped me pick out a couple of hair bows for you."

She smiled. "Lucy's a good girl."

"Yes, she is." She glanced over toward Reed's place when he walked outside in a sleeveless T-shirt and sweat shorts, carrying car washing supplies in a bucket. Her pulse kicked up a beat as her gaze traveled over his well-muscled arms, remembering how good they felt wrapped around her. She focused on his face instead and the lenses of his sunglasses as she smiled and stood up. "Hey, neighbor."

The girls looked his way.

He put down his stuff and walked over. "Hi."

She caught whiffs of his shampoo as the breeze blew his damp hair. "How was your trip?"

"Pretty good." He crossed his arms and uncrossed them just as quickly. "What do you have going on over here?"

"Some girl time with my very special friends. Reed, this is Bianca and Emilia."

He held out his hand, giving each of them a handshake. "It's nice to meet you."

She smiled, finding him more than a little irresistible when both of the girls grinned. "Girls, Reed is my next-door neighbor and friend."

"Are you gonna wash your truck?" Emilia wanted to know.

"You bet. It's a beautiful day."

"We're gonna have facials and eat snacks and listen to music," Emilia added.

"Sounds like quite a party."

Bianca looked at Bella. "Can we paint Lucy's nails?"

"I think her feelings would be hurt if you didn't. I bought a couple of new colors you can choose from. She's waiting for you." She gestured to the doorway where Lucy patiently sat. "Should we go say hi?"

Emilia beamed. "It's one of my favorite parts."

Bella took both of the girls' hands as she looked at Reed. "I'll see you tonight?"

"Yeah. Five o'clock, right?"

She nodded. "Five o'clock."

"Have fun."

"We plan to." She walked with Bianca and Emilia to the house, ready for her afternoon of pampering and pleasantries with the girls.

Reed rinsed the suds from his truck, glancing toward Bella's place as peals of laughter carried through her open French doors. Apparently facials, snacks, and music equated to a damn good time. He could imagine that was exactly the case with his neighbor in charge. Bella seemed to have fun no matter what she did.

He brought the hose around to the front of the vehicle, giving the grill and headlights a good spray, trying to get a bead on Bella Colby. They'd spent several hours together over the last couple weeks, yet nothing about her made any sense. She was nice—incredibly kind. Not even an hour ago, he'd watched her from his kitchen window, crouching down in cutoff shorts and a simple pink T-shirt, embracing two little girls, kissing their cheeks and talking to them while her eyes lit up with unmistakable delight.

So what was up with the phone calls? Why the hell was she in contact with Luisa Asante, daughter of one of the Caparelli family's most notorious captains turned consigliere? Rumors painted Dino Asante as a brutal bastard who wasn't afraid to take care of his boss's business—he'd just never gotten caught. And by all accounts, Bella was friendly with them. Joey had tracked three more calls to and from Bensonhurst while Reed had been away in San Francisco.

He shut off the water with a bad-tempered twist, staring at the drops falling to the ground as he struggled to figure everything out. She was high-end, living well beyond her means, but she had no debt, which wasn't jibing, especially when she didn't rely on the money in her savings account. She kept dangerous mafia ties, yet welcomed ill and disfigured children into her home for skin treatments and dog pampering parties. Lucy's painted nails now made sense. Bella didn't spend time on her puppy's paws. The little girls she helped did.

How could this woman possibly be related to some of the most violent gangsters ever to walk the streets of Brooklyn? And why the hell couldn't he get her off his mind? Ever since Tuesday night, he'd been thinking about the smell of her hair and the way her smiles made her impossibly more beautiful—details that had nothing to do with the investigation.

The long hug in the parking lot and walk along the beach had been messing with his head, which he had every intention of remedying on their "date" to Julie and Chase's wedding. Bella wasn't his girlfriend or lover. She was a means to an end. Tonight, he was going to turn up the heat. It was time to start working toward the answers he and Joey needed. By the time he dropped her off, he planned to have them.

Chapter Eleven

Bella tapped her foot in time with the music playing in the ballroom while she waited in line at the bar. The party was going strong, with several couples living it up on the dance floor now that the dinner plates had been taken away and the vanilla cream wedding cake served.

"What can I get you?" the older woman asked from behind the counter when the patron in front of Bella walked off with his beverage of choice.

"Uh, just a water, please—the biggest glass you have, if you don't mind."

"Sure thing, honey."

Moments later, the bartender was back, shoving a pint glass full of ice water and lemon into her hand. "Here you go."

"Thanks." She dropped a five in the tip jar and took a long drink, craving something other than the champagne she'd consumed during the toasts to the bride and groom. Turning to escape the chaos, she bumped into Abby. "Oh, my gosh. I'm so sorry."

Abby grinned, dressed like some sort of sexy fertility goddess in her stylish spaghetti-strap frock. "No problem." She gave Bella a hug, her sweet baby belly getting in the way. "It's crazy around here."

"Just a little." They stepped off to the side, out of the main flow of guests wandering about. "Are you having a good time?"

"Of course. The new Mr. and Mrs. Rider know how to throw a party. And Julie looks amazing."

She glanced toward the beautiful bride in her lace gown with a sweetheart neckline, grinning up at her husband while they slow-danced despite the tempo of the DJ's current song choice. "She does."

"And you're looking pretty fine yourself." Abby took a step back, nodding her approval. "Whoever designed that little number has mad skills."

Bella laughed as she looked down at the curve-hugging mid-thigh-length black dress. "That Abigail Quinn is pure genius."

Abby grinned.

"How does Baby Quinn like weddings?" She touched Abby's belly.

"She seems to dig it." Another smile lit up her face. "I think she has rhythm already."

"It's never too early for rhythm."

Abby laughed. "So where's your date?"

"Reed's not my date." She spotted him across the room, looking all tough and handsome in his black slacks and tie. Long ago, he'd lost the suit jacket and rolled his sleeves halfway up his muscled forearms, giving her plenty of opportunities to pretend that she didn't notice how broad his shoulders were in a simple white button-down. "We just rode over together."

"Well, that's a bummer."

She looked at Abby with surprise. "You think?"

"Sure. Reed's a hottie—kinda tortured and intense, but Jerrod says he's a really good guy. They worked together in New York."

She frowned. "Jerrod was a police officer?"

"No, a US Marshal, but Reed, Jerrod, and Shane crossed paths a few times—interagency stuff, I guess. That's all Jerrod will say about it."

She remembered Reed talking about special investigations and his cover being blown. "Maybe it's better that way."

"Probably. You never know with this bunch." Abby rolled her eyes and gasped. "I forgot to tell you those tops you wanted came in."

"Oh, really?" She wiggled her eyebrows, thinking of the latest Abigail Quinn designs she would be adding to her wardrobe.

"They arrived Wednesday, I think. I meant to call you… Pregnancy brain is a real thing."

Bella grinned. "It's no big deal. What do I owe you?"

"I was thinking of another one of those moisturizing facial treatments like we did last time, and that insane shoulder rub thing you do." Abby moaned.

"You've got it. Whenever you want. We can do a morning session before work or an evening. Or I can always come to you if that's better."

"Let me look at my calendar and I'll email or text you."

"Perfect."

Abby settled her hands on her belly. "The little lady and I are going to head to the bathroom before we embarrass ourselves."

Bella laughed. "Have fun tonight."

"You too." She watched Abby walk off with a slight waddle and glanced Reed's way, realizing he was staring at her as he nursed a beer and talked to Jerrod and Shane. The dim lighting was hitting him just right, accentuating the hints of dark stubble along his jaw. God, he was pretty.

Smiling, she tossed him a wave, set down her drink, and headed in the opposite direction. It wouldn't hurt for them to take five—or even a thirty-minute break from one another. Everyone was getting the wrong idea. Maybe she'd caught *herself* getting the wrong idea when he buttered a roll for her during dinner. He'd slipped it on her plate mid-conversation, and she'd picked it up, muttering her thanks as she'd bitten in—as if they did stuff like that all the time, as if that was normal.

It was such a simple thing, yet it somehow screamed intimacy; it shouted click as it had the other night after their walk on the beach. And she wasn't so sure she wanted that with anyone anytime soon. Single was working well for her. She was in no rush to get into another relationship... And why was Reed suddenly synonymous with *boyfriend*? They were simply neighbors who'd agreed to drive over to the wedding together—nothing more than carpooling buddies, saving the environment and enjoying each other's company. Why did it have to be anything more than that?

"Hey."

She stopped, closing her eyes and wincing before she turned to Reed with a smile. "Hi."

"Where are you off to?"

"Uh, I was thinking about a walk," she decided on the spot. "Along one of the paths." She gestured to the windows and the massive gardens that were part of the resort property.

His brow furrowed as he held her gaze. "Are you okay?"

"Yeah. Yes. Fine."

"Want some company?"

She definitely did *not* want another stroll in the moonlight with Reed McKinley—at least not right now, but how could she say no? "Sure."

"Great." He offered her his arm.

"Great." She slipped hers through his and they started down the hall, slowing when they spotted the photo booth tucked in the corner.

Reed frowned. “Is that a photographer and photo booth station?”

She smiled as she studied several different props set out on a small table. “They’re pretty popular at weddings these days.” Her eyes stopped on a bright fuchsia feather boa and foolish top hat. “Pictures or a walk?”

He sent her a pained look. “Tell me you’re kidding.”

Grinning, she shook her head. This was something he needed. “Oh, I’m perfectly serious. We would consider this little adventure part of the Reed McKinley Project.”

“You get a row of six—one for you to keep and one for the bride and groom,” the booth attendant said. “Go ahead and get creative with it.”

Reed sighed as he stared at her.

Her worries of clicks and moonlit walks vanished as the potential for some serious fun overshadowed the rest. “Don’t let the dark side win, Reed,” she whispered, taking his hands and walking backward as she pulled him closer to the booth. “Come play with me.”

He sighed again, smiling this time. “All right. Let’s make it count.” He grabbed a fedora and Bella a pair of huge glasses along with the feather boa.

They stepped in front of the camera, where the man waited for them.

Bella closed the space between her and Reed, fixing his tie.

Chuckling, he shook his head. “You know you look absolutely ridiculous.”

“Of course, Mr. PI.” She tossed him an exaggerated wink as she touched the rim of his hat.

“Go ahead and smile,” the photographer said.

They held each other’s gazes, grinning.

“Let’s close our eyes and pick the next thing,” Bella suggested as they headed back to the table full of goodies. “It’ll be more exciting that way.”

Reed ended up with boing-y, glittery pink hearts that stuck up a good six inches on a headband and Bella a sign that said “Kiss Me.”

She held up the heart, feigning shock with her hand covering her open mouth as Reed leaned in and pressed a kiss to her cheek.

They both laughed.

This was great. This was *fun*. This was two friends being silly with photography.

They held an empty picture frame next and smiled, crossing their eyes.

For another, Bella wore cat ears and Reed floppy dog ears. He acted as if he growled, holding up his hands like claws while she stared at him sweetly and laced her fingers, begging him not to attack.

For another they went prop-free, sticking out their tongues.

"What about a real one for the last shot?" Reed suggested.

"Sure." They wrapped their arms around each other's waists and grinned.

"Nice," the photographer said with a nod of approval. "Some of the best we've had tonight." He printed off two strips, put one in the stack for Julie and Chase, and handed the other to Bella.

"Let's see what we've got," Reed said, leaning in closer as they both looked at them.

Bella laughed. "They should have something like this at every wedding." She glanced up, her gaze landing on Sarah and Wren looking their way.

Wren sent her a saucy smile.

Bella gave her friends a tiny shake of her head, barely suppressing a groan. Everyone definitely had the wrong idea. Next girls' night, she was going to set the record straight. She studied the pictures of herself and Reed again and saw friends—and potential lovers. She frowned. "I'm, uh, I'm going to use the restroom."

"Sure. I'll meet you back in the ballroom—unless you're still thinking about a walk."

"No," she said quickly. "No. I'll be in shortly." She handed him the strip of pictures. "Can you hang on to these for a minute?"

"Yeah." He took them and walked off.

Hurrying into the bathroom, she shut herself in a stall, trying to convince herself that everything was status quo. Buddies and energy savers. That was all.

Reed leaned against the bar, sipping at a bottled water instead of a beer as he scrutinized the pictures he and Bella had just taken. Dog ears and fedoras. Had he lost his damn mind? Yet he smiled at the photo of himself and Bella crossing their eyes and grinning while they held the ugly gold picture frame together. He couldn't remember the last time he'd behaved so foolishly or let himself have a little fun.

And every one of these shots was exactly that. Except for the last one, in which he wrapped his arm around Bella.

Sighing, he stared at the two of them holding each other close like any couple might. They'd been here for nearly three hours and he had yet to do his job. What was it about Bella, the magic she possessed, that made him forget his purpose? One look into those pretty brown eyes of hers and he completely lost his edge. Luckily, the night was still young. He and Bella had shared a few laughs. Now it was time to get to work—

"What have you got there?" Jerrod asked, stopping off for a water of his own.

Reed stood up straight. "Pictures from the photo booth."

"That was a pretty good idea." Jerrod glanced at the strip in Reed's hand. "You two seem to be hitting it off."

"She lives next door."

"Just neighbors?"

"Just neighbors," he confirmed with a nod, debating once again whether or not he should mention what was going on with the Caparelli investigation, but he decided to keep it to himself for now—until he and Joey had more to work with.

"Well, here's trouble standing in the corner." Abby walked over, smiling.

Reed smiled back. "Hey, Abby."

"If you don't mind, I'm going to grab my husband." She tugged on Jerrod's tie. "Come on, big guy, you owe me a dance."

"That's my cue." He took Abby's hand, and they wandered off.

"Have fun." Chuckling, he looked up. His smile vanished as he zeroed in on Bella across the room. Nobody had a right to be that damn *gorgeous*. Tonight, she'd done some fancy thing with her hair, pulling her soft, glossy locks up in a loose twist. And the black strapless dress she wore clung in all the right places, teasing his libido.

She grinned, throwing her head back and laughing at something Morgan said.

Rubbing at his neck, he took a deep drink of water. Joey was right; a woman that beautiful was dangerous. But he could be pretty lethal himself. And now was as good a time as any to get down to business and prove to himself that Bella Colby didn't hold any power over him.

Bella made her way back toward their table.

He set down his water and slipped the strip of pictures into his pocket as he started in her direction. "How about a dance?"

"Sure."

Taking her hand, he weaved through the other couples to the center of the floor and settled his arms around her waist, wanting to keep things casual and friendly—exactly what she would be expecting and just what he needed to get their evening back on track. "Are you having a good time?"

She steepled her fingers behind his neck. "I am."

"I don't think I told you how beautiful you look tonight." When she'd knocked on his door several hours ago to catch a ride, he'd been speechless.

She sent him a small smile. "Thank you."

He opened his mouth to move their conversation along in another direction, but he heard her quiet sigh as her gaze left his to look over his shoulder. There was something in her eyes—hints of sadness that hadn't been there before. "What's wrong?"

"Nothing."

"Bull."

She shrugged. "I guess I keep thinking about tomorrow."

"The funeral."

She nodded. "Yeah."

He touched his forehead to hers, almost offering to go with her, but he couldn't bring himself to take advantage of such a terrible situation. There were some lines he wasn't willing to cross for information. "The girls you had over today, they're sisters?"

She shook her head. "Friends. They play together fairly often."

"I heard a lot of laughter coming through your French doors."

She smiled, her eyes brightening as she did. "They're great."

"The girl with the burns—"

"Emilia."

"You met her at the hospital?"

"No. Abby introduced us through one of the Stowers House programs for abused children."

"I've never seen anyone burnt like that—in person, I mean."

"Two years ago, her father doused her and her mother with gasoline and set them on fire."

He winced. "Jesus, that's awful."

"Emilia's mother died. She lives with her aunt now."

"And the bastard?"

"He's in prison."

He felt his nostrils flare. Prison wasn't enough of a punishment for some assholes. “She has a tough road ahead.”

Bella nodded. “Emilia will need several more surgeries. Now that her scars are mature, they’ll start releasing the contracture around her neck.”

“You’re not speaking my language.”

“The doctors will reconstruct her neck and chin where her skin has tightened up. The goal will be to give her a more normal appearance and better range of motion.”

“Christ, that’s tough.”

“It is. Her aunt told me today when she picked the girls up that they’ve been having a lot of trouble with Emilia’s left foot again. She might lose it—probably most of her leg. She’s had several issues with ulceration.”

He shook his head, thinking of how small the child had been in Bella’s arms. Someone so young shouldn’t have to go through that. “What’s her long-term prognosis?”

“She’ll never look like a typical little girl. Her father robbed her of that. Prosthetics are a good possibility for her hand and leg, but unfortunately, she’ll always have some degree of disfigurement.”

“That really sucks.”

“Yes, but that’s why I love working with her on her makeup skills—little tricks that help as much as they can. I want people to be able to look past her burns and see that she’s beautiful. I want them to see what I see—who she is in here.” She touched her hand to her heart.

He swallowed as he stared into her eyes, finding himself captivated by her compassion.

“Emilia’s more than a victim of domestic violence. Despite everything she’s been through, she’s smart and has so much love to give—so much to offer. I want to have Kylee and Olivia over the next time she visits. Emilia will be starting back to school soon. She’ll be a year behind her peers. She’s embarrassed by her appearance and how she’s ended up in the situation she’s in, but I want a couple of the kids to know her story and welcome her. If Kyle and Olivia accept her, the other children will too—be her allies and support system in a world that’s not always so nice.”

“You’re amazing,” he said before he thought to stop himself.

“I’m just trying to help.”

“You’re amazing,” he repeated as he pulled her closer and pressed his cheek to her hair, breathing in her shampoo as he slid his hands up and down her sides. What was she doing to him—with her words, with her kindness? He closed his eyes as she wrapped herself more tightly around him and nestled her forehead in the crook of his neck, just as she had the other night.

He looked around at all of the other couples, spotting Chase and Julie dancing as he slowly turned with Bella. She was so soft and her breath warm on his skin as they clung to one another. His pulse pounded a fast beat, and he suddenly, desperately wished Joey had never overheard Salada and Upshaw talking about Nicoli Caparelli, that Bella could just be Bella and he could just be Reed. But that wasn't the way things were. The woman in his arms was tied to the mafia—the men who'd killed his family.

The song ended and he stepped back, holding her gaze.

"I'm ready to go home," she said, turning away and heading toward the exit, not waiting for his response.

He stood where he was, taking a moment to get himself together. This wasn't the way the evening was supposed to have gone. Why the hell hadn't he just pulled up a seat next to hers at their table and asked for two cups of coffee? Glancing up, he watched her disappear down the hall and hurried after her, not entirely sure she would wait for him for a ride home. "Bella."

She kept her pace fast and steady as she reached the main entryway.

"Bella." He sidled up next to her. "Are you sure you want to go?"

"Yeah. Lucy probably needs a potty break."

He hit the unlock button on the key fob as they walked through the parking lot. They got in the truck, neither of them speaking on the quick drive home. Tense, silent minutes passed before he finally pulled into his driveway.

"Good night." Bella got out and shut her door before he could turn off the ignition.

He rushed out and around to her side. "Bella."

She stopped but didn't turn. "Lucy's waiting."

They were on boggy ground and they both knew it. She'd been just as affected by their dance as he had—by whatever had passed between them. "If you need anything tomorrow, let me know."

She nodded. "Good night," she repeated.

If he were someone else, if Bella was someone else, they wouldn't be ending their evening here on the lawn. "Good night." He went inside and directly upstairs, turned on his laptop, and began composing his notes and impressions after their "date"—not that he had much more than a sentence or two to add.

This was a surveillance operation and deep cover mission of sorts—and he was failing miserably at doing what needed to be done. Sighing and sitting back, he pulled the pictures out of his pocket, staring at himself and Bella. “Damn,” he whispered as he set the strip down and stood, glancing at his phone before walking to his gym instead of calling Joey. He didn’t want to hear his partner’s shit when he had to confess that his night with Bella brought nothing new to the table. He needed to get a fucking grip, to remember what this whole thing was supposed to be about, because he was in big damn trouble where Bella Colby was concerned.

ꟲ Chapter Twelve ꟳ

BELLA LET HERSELF INSIDE AND SLID HER FEET FROM HER BLACK pumps as Lucy ran over to greet her. "Hi, sweetie." Sniffling, she walked to the coffee table and plucked a tissue from the box, blowing her nose before she bent down to hug her girl. "I'm so glad you're here." She nuzzled her cheek against her puppy's soft coat and closed her eyes. She'd done so well, holding herself together at the service while she did what she could to offer Angela's grieving family comfort and a few kind words, but once she'd gotten into her car for the half-hour drive home, she'd fallen apart.

Angela was gone—another victim of cancer. At moments like this, when her stomach was sick and her heart broken, she wondered why she kept going back to see the kids month after month and let herself get more and more attached. She'd attended two other funerals during the eight months she'd been working at the hospital. Unfortunately, they wouldn't be the last. Some of the cure rates were getting better, but they weren't good enough—not even close.

More than once over the past few days, she'd contemplated calling the patient care coordinators she worked with to tell them her schedule was just too busy to continue with her volunteering, but then she would miss out on all of those sweet smiling faces and precious hugs. Making a difference wasn't always easy, but helping in the limited ways that she could was important. Wiping at her nose again, she eased away from Lucy. "I need to change."

Lucy followed her upstairs, keeping close by her side.

"You're my girl." She petted her best friend, forever grateful that Lucy understood what she needed so well. "I don't know what I would do without my pretty girl." She took off her simple black dress and hung it up, hoping to get one more wear out of it before it had to go to the dry cleaners.

Glancing toward the sun shining bright through the windows, she walked over to her chest of drawers. Shorts were certainly an option today, but she pulled on yoga pants and a tank top instead, then tied her hair back in a ponytail, planning to do as little as possible for the rest of the afternoon. "Let's go downstairs. We can try a movie or something."

Lucy followed, staying close as she had on the way up.

"I'm thinking we should go for something funny. Maybe a romantic comedy, or straight-up comedy would work too." At this point, it didn't particularly matter. She just wanted to stop thinking about the small white casket and the graveside portrait of the smiling, healthy little girl that had been captured on a sunny vacation day only weeks before Angela's entire life had changed.

Snagging the box of tissues and the remote, she plunked herself down on the couch as someone knocked on the door. Sighing, she rested her head against the cushion, debating whether or not to answer, then gained her feet, twisting the knob when she heard Reed calling her name. She stared at him dressed casually in black mesh athletic shorts, a light gray Under Armour T-shirt, and his baseball cap worn backward, giving her a good look at his bold blue eyes and the stubble on his jaw he hadn't bothered shaving.

"Hey."

Her lip started wobbling as all of the emotions she'd been trying to tuck away flooded to the surface again. Despite things being strained between them after the wedding last night, she was glad to see him now. "Hi."

"Rough day?"

She nodded, fighting back her tears.

"Do you want company or would you rather be alone?"

She opened the door wider as a tear fell down her cheek.

He stepped inside and held open his arms.

She walked into them and closed her eyes, letting her head rest on his chest as he folded himself around her. He smelled good, like laundry soap and Reed. He felt even better, his tough body holding her close.

"How are you doing?"

"That was awful." She pressed her face into his shirt as her voice broke. "Awful."

He rubbed his hand up and down her back. "I bet." He exhaled a long breath. "Do you want to get out of here for a while—maybe take a walk?"

"No, not right now. I kind of feel like lying around."

He eased her back some, sending her a sympathetic smile. "Want a friend?"

She stared into his kind gaze and nodded. Today wasn't the day to analyze her feelings or the heat that had snapped between them while they danced. Apparently, Reed had decided the same thing or he probably wouldn't be here. "Only if you're not busy."

"I'm free for the rest of the afternoon."

"I was thinking about binge-watching *The Office*."

"If Michael and Dwight can't cheer you up..."

She smiled. "It's a great show."

"I never had much of a chance to watch it, but the couple of episodes I've seen were great."

Her eyes widened. "You didn't watch *The Office* when it was on the TV?"

He shook his head. "I was pretty caught up in my work."

She scoffed, rolling her eyes. "You've been missing out." She took his hand, pulling him with her to the couch. "Today's the day, my friend. Consider this another step in the right direction as we fix this serious, serious problem."

"Not watching *The Office* is a serious, serious problem?"

"Yes." She gave him a gentle shove to the cushion. "Sit right there while I get us set up."

He chuckled. "You're the boss."

She grabbed the remote and turned on Netflix, finding their silly banter just what she needed—a beautiful distraction. "Should we start from the beginning or watch random episodes?"

"Sounds like we should start from the beginning."

"I was hoping you would say that." She went to season one, episode one. "Do you want anything to eat or drink?"

"I wouldn't mind some water."

"I'll get us a couple of glasses. Ice?"

"Sure."

"I'll be right back." She went to the kitchen, stopping at the cupboard for glasses, then moved to the fridge for a lemon and the pitcher of filtered water. Absently, she grabbed a knife and cutting board from the drawer, gasping when the bracelet she'd been wearing caught on the drawer pull and snapped.

She stared in horror as the colored noodles Angela had painted and strung as a present for Bella fell to the tile floor and shattered.

"Oh, no. No." She scrambled down on her hands and knees, picking up the pieces, grabbing a red penne that had rolled halfway under the stove. The noodle cracked in her fingers, and she started crying.

"Is everything okay in here?" Reed asked as he walked in.

She nodded, sitting back on her haunches and staring at the mess instead of looking up at him.

"Bella." He crouched down, tilting her chin up until their eyes met.

"I broke Angela's bracelet." She shuddered out a breath and sucked in another as she held open her palm, showing him the crumbled remains. "She made it for me, and it's broken."

"Maybe we can fix it."

"I don't know. I don't think so. She can't make me another one."

"We'll see what we can do." He transferred the pieces from her hands to his and set them on the counter. "Come on." He took her hand and helped her to her feet. "Let's do something else for a while."

She swiped at her cheeks. "What about your water?"

"We'll get some later." He walked with her to the couch, sat down, and settled himself across the length of the cushions, pulling her down so she lay on her side in front of him. Taking off his hat, he tossed it onto the coffee table and hooked his arm around her waist. "Let's see what we've got here." He pressed *play* on the remote, and the iconic music from *The Office* filled the living room as he tightened his hold around her and pulled her back, securing her feet in place with his leg. "How's this?"

"Good." But she struggled to focus on the theme song, then the opening scenes of the pilot episode as his breath heated her neck and her heart raced. Their relationship was supposed to be simple. Why did this feel so complicated? On impulse, she rolled over, facing him.

"You okay?" he asked.

"I don't know." She stared into his eyes mere inches from her own as their bodies lay tangled together. "What are we doing?"

"Watching *The Office*."

Was that all this was: walking beaches, attending weddings, snuggling on couches? Were they really just friends? Because last night and right now... Testing herself and him, she touched his cheek, trailing hesitant fingers along the rigid set of his jaw.

He reached up, grabbing her wrist, halting her movements. "Bella—"

She swallowed as his unsteady breaths mingled with hers. "What are we doing?"

He held her arm tighter. “We’re watching TV.”

She gave a small shake of her head when he loosened his grip and their fingers found their way to each other’s, lacing together. This was more than beach buddies and the Reed McKinley Project. Easing forward, she pressed her lips to his.

He jerked back, breaking their connection, his breath steaming out in torrents as he let his forehead rest against hers. “We can’t.”

“Reed,” she whispered, closing her eyes when his hand left hers to slide along her arm and into her hair, freeing her long locks from the elastic.

“We can’t,” he said again, even as he pulled her to him.

She closed the mere centimeters separating them, capturing his mouth despite his weak protests.

He stiffened, going perfectly still before he groaned and yanked her against him, diving in and teasing her tongue with his.

She moaned, engulfed by flames as he cupped her cheeks and took her deeper, rolling and lying mostly on top of her. Her hands found their way beneath his shirt, sliding over the hot skin and firm muscles of his back, giving as good as she got.

He nipped her bottom lip and plundered until she thought she might perish from the inferno. “Bella. Bella,” he panted out, pulling away. “This isn’t what I’m looking for. I’m not looking for this.” He sat up, untangling himself from her.

She nodded and fought her way up to sitting as well. “I’m sorry.”

“It’s okay.” He scrubbed at his face and blew out a long breath. “It’s all right.” He looked at her.

She swallowed, realizing she was as frightened by what had just happened as she was turned on. The intensity... “I don’t know why I did that.”

“Probably because you’re a little raw after today and we’ve been dancing around this for a while.”

She crossed her arms. “Last night...things got a little...heavy.”

“We’d both be lying if we said there wasn’t an attraction...” He blew out another breath and stood, pacing away and back. “Look, I don’t want this to be weird. I like spending time with you. I like that we’re friends.”

“Me too.” She uncrossed her arms and played the pad of her index finger over her thumbnail, still tasting Reed on her tongue. “We could—we could chalk the whole thing up to curiosity. That’s pretty normal, right? Being curious is perfectly natural in a situation like ours."

"Yeah." He jammed his fingers through his hair. "Yeah, definitely." He sat again, holding her gaze.

"And now that we've gotten that little make-out session out of the way, it never has to happen again."

"Right. I couldn't have said it better. Does that work for you?"

She nodded, relieved. She didn't want this—anything so all-consuming. She couldn't handle it right now—didn't even want to try. Clearly, Reed didn't either. "You're a great kisser, but you're still not my type."

He grinned. "Right back at ya."

She returned his smile. "Just friends?" She held out her hand to him.

He shook it. "Just friends."

"Exactly the way we were ten minutes ago before I lost my mind?"

"Perfect."

"Are we—should we sit up or lie down?"

"Nothing that just happened has to change anything." He pulled her back down into his arms, lying with her the way he had before she rolled to face him. "How about we focus on *The Office*?"

"Sounds great." And it truly did. She rewound the episode to the beginning and let herself relax against him. The line had been crossed, then redrawn, putting their relationship into a comfortable category they both understood and could live with. She was snuggled up with her buddy on a day when she felt sad and out of sorts, and she was watching one of her favorite shows. It couldn't have been any better.

Reed chuckled and Bella laughed while the final minutes of episode five played on Bella's big screen. Lucy's tags jingled on her collar as she moved on her bed in the corner, pulling Reed's focus away from Michael Scott's latest shenanigans to his current situation. Somehow during the last two-and-a-half hours, he'd rolled farther onto his back. Now that he was paying full attention, he realized that Bella lay more on him than the cushions—and her head rested in the crook of his shoulder instead of on the pillow they'd been sharing when they started their binge-watching marathon.

The credits rolled. He leaned forward, snatching up the remote from the coffee table, and pressed *pause*. "I don't know about you, but

I could use a glass of water."

Bella sat up and stretched. "I'll get it."

He sat up too, rolling his neck, loosening a couple of kinks. "I can get it. Cue up the next one if you want."

"Is this okay? Are you bored?"

They'd shared one hell of a lip lock, then spent the afternoon snuggled up on her couch. Boredom wasn't a word he would use to describe his day. "No way." He stood. "Need anything?"

"I'll take a water too if you don't mind." She glanced at the clock across the room and gaped. "It's almost *five*?"

He glimpsed at his watch. "Looks like it."

"I guess we should be thinking about dinner. Do you want to stay?"

He studied her, ignoring the sexy, sleepy look in her eyes, wanting to make sure they were one hundred percent okay after their epic blunder in judgment. So far, there didn't appear to be any lingering awkwardness between them. "Sure."

"I don't have a whole lot. I didn't make it to the store."

"So we'll order in." He started toward the kitchen, finding himself surprisingly at ease after they'd attacked each other on her couch. Bella Colby looked good, felt great, and tasted even better. Luckily, kissing her had been as much a gift as a huge mistake.

Things had gotten complicated; their mutual attraction and curiosity had clouded his objectivity since the beginning, but their brief make-out session took the edge off and cleared the air. When he'd knocked on her door earlier this afternoon, he'd fully intended to talk to her about the post-wedding awkwardness. Never in a million years would he have guessed that practically eating her alive would have allowed everything to work itself out.

The last twenty-four hours had afforded him a new clarity. Instead of sleeping last night, he'd had plenty of time to think. His conclusion: he'd gone about this investigation entirely wrong. For seven years, he and Joey had hung around bastards who would just as soon kill them as talk to them. Early on, he and Joe had learned to keep their guards up and maintain a professional distance. But that wasn't going to work with Bella. She wasn't a brutal Mafioso. The Bella Colby he was getting to know was a sweet, touchy-feely woman with ties to a life he needed access to. And that's where the adjustments came in. Playing the friend card was giving him access to everything he needed, so why fight it? Was there an attraction between them? Sure. Had he been ready to rip off her clothes before he remembered to put on the brakes? Absolutely. Did he want to do it again? Hell, yeah. But neither of them was interested in traveling down that road. So all in all, things were good.

Perhaps he'd been a little shaky over the last couple weeks while he got his bearings, but they were moving right along. He had full access to her house. She trusted him with her thoughts and tears. Right this minute, he could get at most anything he wanted—case in point: the small, neat stack of bills in the wooden organizer on the desk built into the kitchen counter he was glancing at. Electric, cell phone, water. Nothing earth-shattering. But here he was, unassuming, looking his fill. And on Tuesday, when she wasn't so upset, he would start up with the questions again and work his way to the ultimate goal: a meet and greet with Nicoli Caparelli.

Everything was going to be fine, just a little different. He was still on the fence as to whether he would share his new philosophy with Joey. His partner had said to do whatever needed to be done to get them their information, and he was, but that didn't mean Joe would like his new approach. At the end of the day, he didn't have to. Joey just needed to trust him and go with the flow.

Grabbing the two glasses Bella had set on the counter earlier, he turned to the refrigerator, adding ice. He paused, glancing at the little girl he didn't recognize on her freezer door. "Who's the kid on your fridge?"

"That's Emilia."

He frowned. "The girl with the burns?"

"Yeah."

He stared now. She'd been adorable with a pretty smile and dimples in her cheeks. "She was cute."

"She still is." Bella walked into the room with her hair pulled back with the tie he'd tugged from her soft, glossy locks while he'd fought his need for her and lost. "She gave that to me yesterday along with a drawing."

"I thought you said she got burnt a couple of years ago."

"She did. That was the last school picture taken before her father hurt her. She's not ready to take or share photos of herself the way she is now. The psychologist is working with her on that."

He pulled the three-by-five photo free of the magnet as a wave of sympathy flooded him. "It's a damn shame."

She smiled at him, her eyes full of understanding. "She's doing well. She's strong."

"You do good things, Bella. Helping her. I'm glad she has you."

"Me too." She took his hand, giving it a squeeze. "They're doing amazing things with reconstructive surgery. Her doctors still have so much they can do to help her. They have to take it slow, though."

"Is she going to come back to the house again?"

Bella nodded.

He wanted to be a part of something, to make a difference the way Bella was determined to—and not because of the investigation. "Can I hang out with you guys?"

Holding his gaze, she exhaled a quiet breath.

He frowned. "What?"

"Nothing."

"Did I say something wrong?"

"No. You definitely didn't say anything wrong."

"So, I can come hang out?"

She smiled. "Yes." She took the glasses and poured them water, then put Emilia's picture back on the fridge. "Let's order in some Chinese."

"What do you like?"

"There are these insanely delicious mixed vegetables and brown rice."

He grimaced. "I was thinking more like kung pao chicken and egg-rolls or beef teriyaki—stuff like that."

"We can order that too. But I'd like wonton soup and my veggies. I'll share."

"You don't have to," he said, sending her a grin.

She grinned back. "Yes, I do. You'll be amazed at how good they taste. And I'm eating some of that teriyaki."

"All right. I'll take a few pieces of broccoli on the side."

"And carrots and bamboo shoots and mushrooms. Come on." She gestured with her head. "We'll order in and start another episode." She turned her back as she opened a drawer and pulled out a folder with alphabetized takeout options.

Everything in the drawer was set in its very own space. "Let's do it." He studied her tidy house and need for organization, then let his eyes trail up her excellent body, pausing on her firm ass. There was a huge part of him that was hungrier for her than he was Chinese, but that wasn't what this was all about. Today they were pals chilling on a Sunday afternoon, but he was always going to be a detective. No matter what, the job came first.

☙ Chapter Thirteen ❧

BELLA GRINNED AS SHE SPOONED THE PUMPKIN PUREE SHE'D blended onto the doughy disks Reed was making with the circular cookie cutter. She breathed deep, catching hints of the garlic and chili powder they'd added to the mixture, loving everything about their very first cooking class. For the last hour and a half, she and Reed had been working side by side, laughing and having fun while they created the first course of their three-course meal. "This is going to taste *amazing*. I can already tell."

"I can't wait to try it." He folded one of the circles into a half-moon shape, covering the small glob of pumpkin. "I'll have to let you know how they were."

She grinned, relieved that everything seemed completely normal between them. They hadn't seen each other since he left Sunday evening after Chinese food and another episode of *The Office*. When he'd knocked on her door to pick her up for tonight's class, she'd been afraid something might be different, but so far so good. If the apron tied around his snug black T-shirt accentuated his delicious build and made him look like some tough, sexy chef, she hardly noticed... sort of. "I'm willing to fight you for my share."

He chuckled.

"I can't believe we're actually doing this. Just think, we're forever going to know how to make pumpkin raviolis."

"That's a big thing for you."

"It is." She folded a piece over the pumpkin, being careful to line up the edges. "I love trying new things—learning."

"That's a big thing too."

"What?"

"Perfection." He gestured to her exacting movements as she worked.

"I like things to be right—orderly."

"I never give it a whole lot of thought."

"I guess I've always been this way." She shrugged. "Who knows? Maybe it's some coping method to compensate for a traumatic childhood."

"Did you have a traumatic childhood?" he asked, looking at her as he folded another piece of dough over the orange blob in the middle.

She dropped her gaze to the table, focusing on the task at hand, not quite sure how she wanted to answer. Her childhood wasn't something she talked about. Ever. Life with Kelly Colby hadn't been a storybook by any means. Campouts in strip club dressing rooms when she'd been a little girl and lonely nights spent by herself during her teenage years often came to mind when she thought of where she came from. Her mother's profession had afforded her everything she could have ever wanted except a responsible parent. "No more than anyone else, I guess."

"You guess?"

She jerked her shoulders. "I imagine we all have things we wish could have been different."

"My eleven o'clock curfew was a pretty big bone of contention between me and my mom. It's hard to be cool when you have to be home before midnight."

She let out a scoffing laugh. "I bet."

He flopped another disk end to end.

Wincing, she struggled not to reach over and fix the misshapen piece.

"You can hardly help yourself, huh?"

She smiled as he did. "It's a little messy."

"And it's going to taste just as good whether the ends line up perfectly or if it's a little lopsided."

"All right. Fine. I can fly by the seat of my pants." She tossed one of the disks end to end and moved on to the next, but kept staring at the one she'd just made.

"Tick, tick, tick," Reed whispered next to her ear as he came up behind her and wrapped his arms around her waist. "She's gonna blow."

She laughed, turning in his embrace and swatting at his shoulder. "Don't tease me about my neuroses."

Chuckling, he tucked a loose strand of her hair behind her ear. "I happen to like your neuroses."

She brushed away some flour on his apron, thrilled that Reed was so relaxed and playful tonight. She'd worried their kiss would ultimately erode their precious new friendship, but somehow she'd never felt closer to him. Reed's guard had come down and she adored this sweet, funny man who had finally let her into his world. "Then you won't mind if I fix those a little bit."

"You can do whatever you want. I'm just messing with you." He let her go with a wink.

She turned to face the less-than-perfect raviolis on their workspace and puffed out a breath as she rolled her eyes. "I'm leaving them like that, even if it's going to drive me crazy. Just to prove you wrong."

He grinned. "I dare you to try."

"I never walk away from a dare."

"Sounds serious."

"You better believe it." She smiled again and moved on to the next ravioli as Reed did. "So, now that we've gotten the jokes out of the way, tell me about your day. How was it?"

"Not bad. I'm being reassigned to a family-type deal, so I'll have fairly regular hours for a while."

"Why is Ethan reassigning you?"

"Because one of the newbies can do what I'm doing."

"What are you going to be doing now?"

"There's a kid who's been receiving some threats—stalker-type stuff."

"Oh. How old?"

"Sadie's sixteen."

She shook her head. "That must be so scary."

"Yeah. The threats seem valid. They're pretty disturbing, so Tyson and I are going to be keeping our eye on things while the police try to sort stuff out."

"Are you going to help them with the investigation?"

He shook his head. "That's not really my thing anymore. If something pops out at me, I'll mention it, but for now, I'll be keeping my eyes and ears open for anything I don't like."

"Like what?"

He shrugged. "People loitering around the house or school. A tail when she's in the car. Stuff like that."

"You'll, uh, you'll be staying with the family?"

"Nah. I lucked out and got the day shift. I'll be going to school with her and softball practices. Tyson has the overnights."

She expelled the quiet breath she didn't realize she'd been holding. Now that she had Reed in her life, she hated the idea of him being assigned to a position that would take him away for long periods. Whom would she cook or watch *The Office* with if he left? "When do you start?"

"Tomorrow." He gave her arm a couple of gentle bumps with his elbow. "No more five a.m. flights. I'll meet her at the house at eight and go back to high school until we get this situation figured out."

"Is the person threatening her another student?"

He shook his head. "They're not certain at this point, but I am. This is much more sophisticated than kid stuff. A couple of PIs Ethan works with are on this too."

"Jed?"

He looked at her. "Yeah. You know Jed?"

She shrugged. "We've talked a few times."

He folded the last of the dough over. "He's a good guy."

"Yes, he is."

"So how was *your* day?"

"Good. Busy. I'm going out of town next Thursday, so I'm trying to squeeze in a bunch of my clients before I leave."

"Where you going?"

"To New York."

He stopped making the small fork indentations along the sides of the dough. "Yeah? How come?"

"Some business stuff I have to do."

"Okay, class," their instructor interrupted. "It looks like everyone's finishing up. We're going to get our water boiling and start on the brown butter."

"Do you want the water or the butter?" Bella asked.

"I'll get the water. You'll have to tell me more about your trip while we eat."

"Sure." She focused on the instructor and got to work with the butter and sage.

Reed put four raviolis on Bella's plate, then did the same to his own as he impatiently waited for her to spoon the brown sage butter over their dishes. She wiped at each plate with exacting motions, clearing away any drops, when all he wanted to do was sit down, talk to her, and eat as a bonus.

"That looks great, Bella," Paul, their instructor, said as he stopped by their station. "Fantastic presentation."

She beamed. "Thank you. But Reed placed the raviolis, so I can't take all of the credit."

"Nicely done, Reed."

Reed tossed a friendly enough smile at the man who looked more like a clichéd California beach boy than a chef. He couldn't help but notice that the guy kept checking Bella out. "Thanks."

Bella added a few pine nuts and fresh shavings of Parmesan to the mix as Paul walked away. "There." She set down the block of cheese. "I think that takes care of it."

He crossed his arms and uncrossed them again, forever mindful of his body language. "Should we eat before they get cold?"

"Definitely." She grabbed their plates and walked over to the tiny table set for two.

He followed, taking his seat as Bella did.

"I can't wait to try this. It looks *so* good."

He smiled as her eyes sparkled. There was nothing quite as beautiful as Bella when she was excited. "It does."

"Ready?"

"Sure." He cut one in half, blew on the steaming bite, and put it in his mouth, surprised by how amazing the flavors played together. "Wow." He nodded his approval. "Wow."

"Mmm." She closed her eyes as she chewed slowly. "Oh, my gosh, Reed." She moaned and opened her eyes, smiling. "We made this. We made something that tastes like heaven."

He ate more, trying to forget that she'd made the very same sound while his tongue tangled with hers when he pinned her down on the couch. "This is great."

She grinned. "Do you feel accomplished?"

He would after he got the details of her trip to New York. So far, his new approach to things was working well. Bella was happy; he was relaxed. They were having a great time. "Cooking is a skill I can always use."

"I can't wait until next week's class. Soup, steak, crème brûlée." She glanced over her shoulder toward Beach Boy Paul. "He already knows how to make all of this stuff. I wonder if he's married?"

Reed paused as he cut into his next ravioli, then kept going, unable to tell if Bella was kidding. Either way, it annoyed him that he felt a quick flash of jealousy. "You could go ask him for his number, but then our couple's discount might be in jeopardy."

She wrinkled her nose. "That's an unfortunate little detail."

He swallowed, finding that this bite didn't go down quite as easily. "If you're interested, we can just confess."

"He's cute, but I would be using him only for his culinary skills." She grinned.

He made himself smile back, realizing he was more worried about Bella and the damn chef than he was the objective of the cooking classes in the first place. "So, you were telling me about New York."

"Yes." Her eyes lit up again. "My friend Luisa is opening a medical spa—a bigger one, I should say. It's a pretty big move. I'm excited for her."

"What part of New York?"

"The city. Brooklyn." She wiggled her eyebrows. "I can't wait. We took a class in Arizona for our laser certification. We hit it off from the first day and ended up rooming together. We talk all the time—share marketing ideas. And she's needed a shoulder with all of the stresses of moving to the new location."

"Sounds nice that you two have each other."

She nodded. "She's one of my best friends."

"You met in Arizona?"

"Yeah, about three years ago." She cut another bite.

"When did you say you leave?"

"Next Thursday. I'll be back on Sunday."

"Short trip."

"I don't want to miss too many days at work. Two days away from the office is plenty."

"I imagine you'll have a good time. Two single girls on the town."

She smiled, shaking her head. "Luisa's married and has a little boy. I'm not anticipating anything particularly wild going on while I'm there."

He ate more of his ravioli as Bella sipped her water. Why did he believe her? Why did this make more sense to him than Bella making calls to Luisa Asante for some sort of mafia dealings? She was meeting up with a friend to wish her well in her business. Could it really be that simple? "Sounds like fun either way."

"I'm so excited."

"I'm looking forward to hearing all of the details when you get back."

"I'm looking forward to telling you all about it."

"Can't wait." He winked and sat back, watching Bella dive into her next pumpkin-filled ravioli.

Reed sat with his ankles crossed on his desk, glancing at the notes he'd typed up as he spoke to Joey and fiddled with a pen. "It could be a coincidence," he said after letting Joey in on Bella's explanation for her calls to Bensonhurst and her upcoming trip.

"I don't know, boss. It seems like a cover to me."

"I checked out Luisa's website. She's opening another spa, so it's not complete horseshit."

"I don't know," Joey repeated.

"What don't you know, Joe?"

"None of this makes any sense. Beautiful Bella's father is Nicoli Caparelli and she just randomly meets the daughter of Dino Asante in Arizona for some class? It's too neat—a little too perfect, if you ask me."

"You're absolutely right. I couldn't agree more, but there's one thing we can't overlook: women aren't welcome in the life."

"They might be if their Godfather *uncle* is in prison and their father is one of the last ties to the most powerful mafia family ever to walk the streets of Brooklyn."

"She wasn't nervous or evasive about anything she said tonight." He'd detected something when he poked and prodded about her childhood, but not about New York. "I can tell when she's trying to be. This seems aboveboard."

"*Seems* is the key word. The fuckin' mafia's all about pretenses. A restaurant that holds illegal gaming in the back. Nightclubs where they do their business in plain sight."

Reed dropped his feet to the floor and sat up straight, becoming more annoyed. "Those days are over. They don't do that shit anymore. That's how they all got busted the first time around."

"You're right. They don't. They've gotten smarter—sneakier. Maybe they're moving some of the business through the women now. We can't put anything past them."

Reed stood now, restless. "It's not adding up for me."

"Women and the mafia?"

"Any of it. Bella being a part of the life. She's so damn sweet—down-in-the-bones kind."

"Sounds like you're losing your ability to see things clearly."

"Bullshit." He punctuated the word with a point of his finger to the air. "If anything, I'm seeing things *more* clearly."

"I told you that kind of beauty was dangerous."

He flared his nostrils as he paced back and forth. "Is that what you think this is about? I live in Los Angeles, for Christ's sake. You think I'm not surrounded by beautiful women everywhere I go? You should see my coworkers' wives. Every damn one of them is worth another look. Bella's more than a fucking pretty face."

Joey laughed humorlessly. "I wish you could hear yourself, boss, 'cause you're toast—objectivity gone."

Why wouldn't Joey *listen* to him? "Did she tell me about her trip to Brooklyn?"

"She would have to tell you something. She's leaving for four days and you're neighbors."

"Bella could have told me anything she wanted. As far as she knows, there would be no way for me to check her story. We're getting what we need. You just focus on things on your end and I'll take care of Bella out here."

"Whatever you say, boss. I'll have Leo look into the school in Arizona and Bella and Luisa's attendance dates."

"Fine."

"I'll let you go."

"Good night." He hung up and shook his head, clenching his jaw. Why the hell was Joey being such a tool about all of this? He was getting the job done. Not as fast as either of them wanted, but they were moving in the right direction. His partner was forgetting that he too wanted Alfeo Caparelli served up on a platter. It was damn insulting that his abilities were being questioned.

He looked toward his desk, glancing at the notes on his computer screen, and walked over, slamming the lid closed. He'd had enough of all of this for tonight.

☙ Chapter Fourteen ❧

Bella walked inside with Lucy at her side after another long day. She closed the door and huffed out an amused laugh when Lucy made a beeline for the dog bed and lay down with a long sigh. "Busy day, huh?" She slipped her feet out of her pumps and wiggled her toes. "This, sweet girl, is why I don't go out of town very often. It's not worth trying to cram everyone in before I leave." She walked over to her puppy, crouching down and petting her as she looked at the clock, noting that it was well after seven. "And I have a feeling it's going to be the same way when I get back. Good thing I have such a great assistant." She kissed Lucy's nose. "Let me change and we'll think about dinner. What do you say?"

Lucy gave her a kiss.

"You're the best." Standing again, she glanced out the window when she heard a vehicle slow as it drove by, but it was her other neighbor Mr. Clausen—not Reed. She ignored the flicker of disappointment and turned away. They didn't have to see each other every day, but she wanted to hear about his first day on his new assignment. She'd picked up extra lamb chops at the market just in case he wanted to join her, but it looked like she would be preparing herself dinner and tomorrow's lunch instead.

"I'll be right back," she said and headed upstairs, stopping halfway up the staircase when her cell phone started ringing. "I almost made it." Hurrying back down, she grabbed her phone off the entryway table and glanced at the readout. *North Medical Center*. Frowning, she pressed *talk*. "Hello?"

"Yes, good evening. Is this Isabella Colby?"

"Yes, this is Isabella."

"Ms. Colby, my name is Regina. I'm with Patient Services at North Medical Center. I'm calling because we need someone to come pick up your father."

Her frown deepened. "My father? I don't understand."

"Mr. Pescoe was brought in by ambulance this evening—"

"Ambulance?" Confusion quickly turned into fear. "Is he all right?"

"He needs someone to bring him home and stay with him. He gave us your number."

"What happened?"

"I'm afraid our privacy laws prohibit me from disclosing that without Mr. Pescoe's consent."

"Okay. All right," she said, nodding to no one as she jammed her feet back into her powder-blue pumps. "I, um, I'll be there as soon as I can."

"If you'll come to Patient Services on the first floor, right next to the emergency department, and ask for Regina, we'll get everything figured out."

She grabbed her purse and keys with a trembling hand. "It's going to take me about an hour—probably longer with the traffic. I'm down in the Palisades."

"That's fine. I'll see you when you get here."

"Thank you." She hung up and opened the front door. "Lucy, I have to go." She locked up and hurried to the car, searching for her friend and occasional dog sitter's number in her contact list as she sat in the driver's seat. She paused on Reed's information and kept scrolling. It would be easier all the way around if he could help her out with Lucy, but then she would have to explain her current situation, and that wasn't something she had any intention of doing. She selected Jenny's number and listened to it ring as she turned over the ignition.

"Hello?" Jenny answered in her Kentucky drawl.

"Jenny, it's Bella Colby." She backed up, holding the phone with her shoulder.

"Hi, Bella."

"Hi. I'm having a little bit of an emergency." She gunned it down the road and pulled out into the small break in traffic. "I know this is short notice, but is there any way you and Faith could come stay with Lucy?"

"Sure, we can do that."

"You still have the key I gave you?"

"It's on my keychain."

She exhaled a deep breath of relief. "Good. Okay, that's great. Um, Lucy will need two-and-a-half cups of kibble tonight, and you'll just have to take her out by the house to go potty. Unfortunately, she'll have to wait until tomorrow to walk on the beach."

"I'm sure she'll understand."

"I might have to stay overnight." It was best to put that out there now, since she had no idea what was going on. "Can you stay at my house tonight?"

"Yeah. Faithy has her playgroup tomorrow afternoon, but I have the day off, so we can be flexible."

"You're a lifesaver. There's food in the fridge. Help yourself to anything you'd like. And don't forget Lucy will get another two-and-a-half cups in the morning."

"I remember."

That's why she loved having Jenny look after Lucy. She never worried about Lucy's care. "I really appreciate this."

"I hope everything works out for you."

"Thank you. Just give me a call if you need anything. And Reed McKinley lives right next door now. He works with Shane."

"I know who Reed is. He's been over to Reagan and Shane's a few times."

"Okay. I've gotta go. Thanks again, Jenny."

"You're welcome."

"Oh, there's a fifty on my dresser. Go ahead and grab it."

"I don't need money."

"Please take it."

The line stayed silent.

"Buy something for Faith from me and Lucy. Please."

"All right."

"Bye, Jenny."

"Bye."

She ended the call and tossed her phone on the passenger seat, focusing on the stream of cars as she merged onto the 405. Glancing at the dashboard clock, she punched the gas, hoping to eat up some of the miles. The typical hour-long drive was taking forever and she still had a good forty minutes to go. She gripped the wheel and nibbled her bottom lip, worrying about Dad. Had he fallen and broken something or maybe hit his head? Had he forgotten about a cigarette and burnt himself? Whatever was going on, it was serious enough for him to give the hospital staff her name and number. For years, she'd imagined him to be invincible, but she couldn't ignore the fact that he was getting older. Dad hadn't always been there for her, but she had every intention of being there for him. That was the only way they were going to be able to move on with this new chapter they were writing. Now if she could just get to him...

Minutes passed like hours as the traffic slowed the closer she came to her exit. "Come on. Come on," she muttered as she inched her way to the off-ramp. Finally she made it and sped through downtown Reseda, growing more impatient by the moment. She sat through one stoplight then another two before taking the right into the medical complex that was less than a block from Dad's house.

Pulling into a spot in Emergency Parking, she hurried toward the entrance, almost forgetting to arm her car. She hit the button on her key fob and ran more than walked into the building, searching for the Patient Services sign. "There." Yanking open the door, she moved quickly to the front desk.

"Good evening." The pretty woman with beautiful ebony skin smiled at her.

"Good evening. I'm Isabella Colby. I'm supposed to meet Regina here. She called me about my father, Vincent Pescoe."

"Yes. Hold on just a moment." The woman picked up a phone. "Regina, Isabella Colby's here. Okay." She set the phone in the cradle. "Regina will be right with you."

"Thank you." She crossed her arms, rubbing them warm, wishing she'd thought to grab a cardigan or light jacket to cover her bare shoulders. Her breezy blue sundress was no match for the air conditioning pumping through the vents.

Moments later, a woman with long red hair opened the door and smiled. "Isabella?"

She tried to smile. "Yes."

"I'm Regina. Come on back and we'll go see your father."

"He's going to be okay?"

"I'm sure he'll be happy to see you."

Her stomach lurched when Regina didn't answer her question with any sort of reassuring confirmation.

They walked into a curtained-off space in the ER where Dad lay on a bed, pale and thinner than he'd been the last time they saw each other. But where were the casts or bandages? "Dad?" she said quietly.

He opened his eyes. "Bella."

She hurried over to him and took his hand. "What happened? Are you okay?"

"I'm sorry they called you all the way up here."

"I'm glad they did." She squeezed his fingers. "What's going on?"

"I'm a little run-down."

She studied his pallid complexion, sending him a sympathetic smile. "You must have picked up a flu bug—"

"No."

"No?" She shook her head, still trying to piece together the vague details of his hospital visit.

"I have cancer, Bella."

"Oh." She sat in the chair next to the bed, afraid she would fall if she didn't. "Oh," she said again, pressing his knuckles to her cheek, fighting to keep her composure as her world began to crumble. "What—what kind of cancer?"

"Colon."

She nodded, barely hearing him over the thundering of her heart. "You found out today?"

"No. I've known for a while."

She looked at Regina, hoping for a better explanation, but she already knew Regina wasn't able to tell her anything that Dad didn't want her to know. "Daddy—"

"I'm ready to go home."

"Okay." Her gaze wandered to Regina again. "We're good to leave?"

"Yes, your father will need to take it easy for the rest of the evening and the next several days. He has a mild concussion and was prescribed a dose of pain medicine to ease any discomfort."

She looked at Dad. "What happened?"

"I got a little dizzy and fell. Smacked my head on the floor. Cracked it open a little."

She swallowed a new wave of fear. "You passed out?"

"Just a dizzy spell."

She sighed quietly as her shoulders grew heavy with the burden of worry. "Okay. Let's go home." She helped him up and grabbed his paperwork, then walked with him to the car as her mind raced with a million questions she wanted to ask right now, but he needed to get into bed and rest. "We could go to the Palisades," she said as she settled behind the wheel. "You could come home with me and stay. I can give you a hand for as long as you need."

He shook his head. "I like my own bed. I'm ready to get in it."

She nodded. "Okay." She drove the half block to his house and pulled into the driveway, watching his gaze track around their surroundings despite the nasty bump and small row of stitches on the back of his scalp. "Ready?"

"Yeah." He got out, struggling a bit.

She walked around to his side and wrapped her arm around his waist as they took the three stairs to the door.

"I'm all right, Bella." He gave her hand a reassuring pat, then twisted the key in the lock, welcoming her inside.

She stepped into the overpowering scent of cigarette smoke and stopped, staring at the overflowing ashtrays on the kitchen table, coffee table, and counter. That certainly wasn't helping his situation. Instead of scolding, she followed him back to his bedroom. "Can I get you anything?"

"No."

"I'll bring you some water just in case."

"I guess I wouldn't mind a Coke."

"I'll get you some water." She walked down the hall to the living room, opening windows to let in some fresh air before she went to the kitchen, peeking in cupboards, noting the packaged junk food. Finally she found a cup and filled it with tap water when she realized Dad didn't own a filtering pitcher. She opened the refrigerator again, scoffing at the contents on his shelves—soda and condiments. "No wonder you're sick." Shaking her head, she hurried back down the hallway and knocked on the doorframe. "Are you settled in?"

Dad pulled up his covers. "Yes. You can go home."

"No, I can't."

"I'm fine."

His coloring told her different. "I'll camp out on your couch tonight."

"It's better if you go."

She shook her head.

"You need to close the windows and lock them," he said. "Shut the curtains too."

"I will after we get a little fresh air."

"You need to go home tomorrow."

"We'll figure out tomorrow when it gets here. We can talk everything through." The urge to ask him for all of the information came rushing back. Not knowing was torture, but he was tired. "Good night, Daddy." She kissed his forehead. "If you need anything, just call."

"Okay." He closed his eyes.

She studied him for another moment before she shut off the light and walked out, closing his door most of the way. Leaving him to sleep, she went down to the living room, locking her arms across her chest and leaning against the window frame as she stared out into the dark.

"I have to go on a trip."

"Will you come back soon?"

"Not for a long time. Not till you're an even bigger young lady."

"But I'll miss you so much."

"I'll miss you too. I'll think of you every day."

"Daddy, I want you to stay."

She closed her eyes, wishing there was some way to forget the memories that kept coming back to haunt her. Why did he have to go? Why did he leave her? Did he have any idea that nothing had been warm or safe or *right* after that night? Right now, she felt exactly the same as she had when she woke up that next morning: small, scared, confused, empty.

She turned away from the window, looking for something to do, needing to distance herself from the fear and pain. She glanced around at Dad's messy house, eager to make things right. Hurrying to the closet, she searched for cleaning supplies, finding very few. Using what she had available to her, she dumped ashtrays, chased the dust away, and deep-cleaned the kitchen and bathroom, pausing in the hallway when she spotted the blood and chunk of Dad's hair where he must have collapsed.

Swallowing, she wiped up the mess and put things back, organizing the cramped closet space. "Better," she whispered, glancing at the clock, realizing she'd killed a couple of hours, but there were many more before the sun rose again. She walked to the windows and shut them before she secured the locks and pulled the curtains over the glass the way Dad seemed to prefer.

It was late. Time to try to get a little rest whether she was tired or not. She grabbed a blanket from a second closet and settled on the couch, making do with the corner pillow to cushion her head, wishing she'd thought to grab her laptop before she left the Palisades. She needed to research, to find out exactly what they could do for Dad. She would contact one of the oncologists she was friendly with at the children's hospital... Her phone rang and she glanced at the readout. Reed. Her thumb hovered over *talk*. She wanted so badly to hear his voice, but she silenced the ringtone and set the cell phone down on the coffee table instead. She couldn't talk to him right now, not when she craved his hugs and strong arms wrapped around her. If they spoke she would start crying and tell him everything. He would offer to come be with her. It frightened her to know she would accept.

She didn't want to cry, and she didn't want to tell him what she wouldn't mention if her world wasn't turning upside down. They were friends, growing closer every day, but that didn't mean she wanted to let him into this part of her life. Her relationship with Dad was so complicated. She had no plans to explain it to anyone anytime soon.

She would call him back tomorrow, when she was more composed. She would also go to the store and buy Dad some food, and they would talk about the plan of action for his diagnosis. If it was best, she would insist he come stay with her. But for now, she would curl up under her blanket and worry.

She settled more comfortably under the thin cotton and stared at the ceiling as the small fan turned in a slow circle. Eventually, her eyes drooped closed and she slept.

Reed took a right into the neighborhood with two cups of soup and sandwiches from the gourmet grocer Bella seemed to like so much. It was getting late and she'd probably already eaten, but it didn't hurt to stop by and make sure. Maybe they could catch another episode of *The Office* and she could nibble on one of the brownies he'd grabbed to go with their meal. It was starting to become a habit—needing to see Bella at the end of a long day, wanting to have dinner with her and listen to her laugh or watch her smile. Whatever it took to move the investigation along...

He slowed, frowning as he pulled into his driveway, staring at the car he didn't recognize parked in Bella's spot. The lights were on in her living room and the blue glow from the television shined through the windows, but her Volkswagen was gone. He grabbed the grocery sack and walked to the mailbox, checking out the license plate on the Toyota Corolla, noting that the vehicle was registered here in California. Absently, he collected his mail, caring little about what was in the pile as he let himself into his house, setting his dinner for two on the counter.

Bella hadn't mentioned anything about having plans this evening while they'd been at class yesterday night, but that didn't mean something hadn't changed. She was most likely out with a girlfriend or maybe even a date. They weren't exclusive by any means. Bella was free to come and go as she pleased—free to see whomever she wanted. But he was still curious.

Reaching into the bag, he pulled out one of the sandwiches and turned toward the window, spotting Lucy walking around in the side yard. He moved closer to the glass, frowning again when he spotted a pretty blonde with a baby in her arms. "Jenny." Opening the door, he went outside, petting Lucy when the puppy ran up to him. "Hey, girl." He crouched down, giving her a good rub on the sides. "Hey. Where's your mom?" He looked up as Jenny walked closer. "Hi."

"Hi."

He stood, catching a hint of her southern drawl in just one syllable. "I'm Reed McKinley. Bella's neighbor. I work with Shane."

She smiled. "I know who you are. You've been to the house for dinner."

He smiled back at Regan and Shane's adopted daughter—or practically adopted daughter. She'd been living with them since their return from Kentucky. "It's dark. I wasn't sure how well you could see. I didn't want to make you uncomfortable."

"You're not."

"Where's Bella?"

"I'm not sure exactly. She called me a couple of hours ago, sayin' there was some sort of emergency."

His shoulders tensed. "Is she okay?"

"I'm thinkin' so. I'm pretty sure she's not the one havin' the emergency." She shrugged. "Maybe a friend or somethin'. She sounded real upset, though."

"Huh. Maybe I'll give her a call."

"I guess it couldn't hurt. You can tell her Lucy's fine."

Faith cooed and gurgled as she grinned, holding out her hand to Reed.

He stepped closer, touching the baby's soft knuckles. "Hi."

Faith smiled as she gripped his index finger.

He grinned. "She's getting big."

"She's seven-and-a-half months now. My girl's growin' up on me."

Jenny was a kid herself—seventeen or eighteen. "She looks just like you."

Jenny beamed. "Thank you."

"I'm going to head in and see if I can get ahold of Bella. Let me know if you need anything."

"Faith and I are gonna spend the night, more than likely."

He didn't like this at all—not knowing what was going on and worrying. "Good night."

"Good night. Lucy, come on inside now."

He shut himself in the house, making certain Lucy followed Jenny's directions, then took out his phone and found Bella's gorgeous face in his contacts. He selected her image and listened to several rings, rubbing at the back of his neck when she didn't pick up.

"This is Bella. Leave me a message and I'll get back to you."

"Hey, Bella. It's Reed. I just bumped into Jenny outside the house. Lucy's fine, but I'm wondering about you. Give me a call. Bye." He hung up and sat down, starting to eat, confident that Bella would call him back any minute.

But she didn't. He glanced at the clock on the microwave several times, watching ten minutes turn into twenty. Eventually, he tossed the wrapper into the trash and put the rest of their uneaten meal in the fridge.

Taking the phone with him upstairs, he changed into sweat shorts and put himself through a workout with the bags. By the time he'd finished, an hour and a half had passed since he'd reached out to Bella. Why wasn't she calling him? She didn't owe him any explanations, but he wanted one anyway.

He rubbed at his jaw, then settled his hands on his hips, still cooling down after one hell of a set. Something wasn't right. This wasn't like Bella. She wouldn't leave him hanging this way. He wiped his forehead with his arm and dropped it as another thought occurred to him. What if she couldn't call? What if the Caparellis had her? Had Alfeo decided tonight was the night for revenge? Had she gone up to see her dad and run into some sort of threat from the mob? He yanked up his phone and ran down the steps, ready to go to Reseda despite the fact that he was shirtless and dripping sweat. He stopped with his hand on the doorknob and swore. "What the hell is *wrong* with you? Get a grip."

Shaking his head, he took a seat on the rickety barstool. This was ridiculous. If Joey could see him right now, he'd shit a brick. Scrubbing at his face, he clenched his jaw. His partner was right: he was losing his cool. Just because he was approaching this investigation differently didn't mean he didn't have to keep his head on straight. Bella would call when she could. If she wanted to.

He went back upstairs to the bathroom and showered, then headed to the bedroom, more restless than he cared to admit. Getting into bed, he set the phone on the pillow by his side and lay back, steepling his fingers behind his head as he stared at the ceiling. His gaze wandered to his clock on the desk. "Eleven." Eleven o'clock and there was still no word.

"Fuck it." Picking up the phone, he dialed again, and got her voicemail for the second time. "What the hell?" He waited for the beep. "Hey, Bella. It's Reed again. I haven't heard from you, so my detective's imagination is working overtime. I'm hoping you're okay. Give me a call when you get this no matter what time and put me out of my misery. Bye." He hung up, certain he would hear her voice any second now.

By one, he was up and pacing, debating whether or not to sit his ass in the truck and ride up to Reseda after all. If she was even there.

His phone beeped with a text, and he hurried over to the bed, glancing at the screen as he sat down with a swift wave of relief.

Sorry to keep you in suspense. I turned off the ringer, fell asleep, and just now realized you called again. Everything's fine.

"Son of a bitch." He set down the phone and closed his eyes. "Son of a bitch," he repeated. The lines were definitely blurring where Bella was concerned. He kept forgetting that their friendship was a ruse to get to Nicoli. "Son of a bitch," he said for a third time as he lay back, trying to pinpoint the exact moment when he'd let his emotions get in the way.

☙ Chapter Fifteen ❧

Bella blinked as she stared at the thin beam of sunlight blazing in through the emerald-green curtains, trying to figure out where she was. She sat up with a start, remembering that she was at Dad's. She snatched her cell phone off the coffee table and sighed as she noted the time. "Eight fifteen. Damn." Somehow she'd fallen back to sleep after she texted Reed in the wee hours of the morning. Now it was time to get up and deal with today.

Sighing, she took a moment to stretch her aching back, then dialed the number for Tonya, the office assistant she and Dr. Huberty shared. Unfortunately, there was bound to be some backlash for making last-minute changes to her schedule. Her intention had been to take care of this hours ago, but the emotional aftermath of last night's bombshell had gotten the better of her, and she'd slept surprisingly deeply.

"Hello?"

"Good morning, Tonya. This is Bella."

"Hi, Bella. How are you?"

"I'm all right." Gaining her feet, she grabbed her purse and walked to the tiny bathroom, turning on the light and wincing as she studied her disheveled hair and tired raccoon eyes in the mirror. "I hate to do this to you on such short notice, but I'm going to have to cancel my day. I'm hoping you might be able to call today's clients and let them know."

"Of course I can handle that for you. I'll get right on it. Are you okay?"

"Yes. I've had something come up that couldn't be put off," she said as she slid her fingers through her long, tangled locks, smoothing them down the best she could. "I can make up appointments Saturday if anyone wants to schedule then. I'll also make myself available Sunday if that works better. Please tell them I'm sorry."

"I'm sure they'll understand."

Most would; some wouldn't. "Thank you."

"We'll see you tomorrow?"

"Yes. I'll be there for sure."

"Okay. See you tomorrow."

"Bye." She set the phone on the counter and dug through her small bag, pulling a cleansing wipe from the trial-size pack she kept handy and the tiny tube of sunblock she hadn't touched since the day at the beach with Reed—the only tricks she had up her sleeve for this morning's impromptu beauty regimen. Making quick work of cleaning her face and protecting her skin from the sun's damaging rays, she did what she could with her rumpled dress next, smoothing out the worst of the wrinkles. She switched off the light in the bathroom, not particularly concerned about her vanity—not when she had much bigger problems to contend with.

Her mind raced with today's new agenda: grocery shopping, a long conversation with Dad to figure out what was going on with his diagnosis, and a phone call or two to her oncologist friends for their thoughts on Dad's treatment plan. But Dad needed good, quality food first. She tiptoed her way down the hall to his room, opening his door and peering in. He was still sleeping. She went back to the living room, searching for and eventually finding a pad of paper and pen, writing him a quick note.

Went to the grocery store. Call if you need anything.

Hurrying to his bedroom, she set the note on his side table.

Dad rushed up on the mattress, gripping her wrist with painful pressure.

She gasped, stifling a scream. "It's just—it's just me."

He sighed, and his shoulders relaxed as he let her go. "Sorry."

"It's okay." She rubbed at her throbbing skin where his fingers had left marks. Dad still looked pale, much like he had last night, but there was nothing wrong with his strength. "I didn't mean to frighten you."

"You didn't."

She swallowed and took a step back, still shaken by the flash of violence she'd seen in his eyes. "I'm going to the grocery store to get us some breakfast."

"You don't have to."

"Yes, I do. I'm hungry." She wasn't, but he didn't need to know that. "Are you feeling well enough for me to go, or should I stay?"

He touched cautious fingers to his injury. "I'm fine."

"Okay. I'll be back soon."

"You should go home."

"I'll be back soon," she repeated and left, making her way to the nearest store to fill a cart with fruits, vegetables, and several other nutritious items he would need to help his body heal. They were going to fight this disease and win. Changing his diet was a major first step.

She made quick work of chore number one and was back at the house in less than an hour, bringing in bags and putting stuff away. Setting the next bag on the counter, she reached in and stopped when she realized the patio door was open and the smell of fresh cigarette smoke was wafting her way. "Dad?" Sighing, she grabbed one of the vegetable juices she'd picked up at the juice bar and brought it outside, squinting in the bright sunshine.

He looked at her with dark circles under his eyes, holding a can of soda in one hand and a cigarette in the other.

"What are you doing?" She snatched the beverage from his grip and slapped the juice down in front of him. "Try this instead. You need to start eating better. You need to take care of yourself. Your cupboards are full of junk."

He blew out a long stream of smoke. "That juice isn't going to help me much."

"Of course it is. Vitamins and minerals are exactly what you need. Not this." She jiggled the can. "I'm filling your fridge with good food, and I'm tossing away all of the crap—"

"I'm dying, Bella."

"No." She shook her head. "A cancer diagnosis isn't necessarily a death sentence."

"Mine is."

Her frustration grew along with her fear. Dad sounded like he'd already thrown in the towel. "Daddy—"

"I've got about six months if I'm lucky."

"You don't know that."

"Yes, I do."

Her hand holding the can fell to her side, the cold, dark drops splashing from the cement to her legs barely registering. "The doctors—they told you that?"

"Yeah." He sucked on the cigarette.

She sat down, staring at the table as she struggled to grasp what Dad was saying. "How long have you known?"

"A while. I had cancer a couple years ago. I beat it with surgery and chemo, but it came back. I'm not going through all that again."

Her gaze flew to his, recognizing the finality in his voice, seeing the acceptance in his eyes. "You can't just give up. We could get a second opinion."

"I've had two already. It's too late, Bella."

"No. No, it's not." She shook her head adamantly this time. "I know several oncologists—"

"There's nothing anyone can do."

She stood slowly, making certain her legs would support her as her heart raced and fear pumped through her veins. "I'm going to—I'll make us some breakfast." She didn't want to eat. She could barely tolerate the idea of food, but she had to do *something* before this utter sense of helplessness drove her mad.

"I don't have much of an appetite."

"You can eat what you want. And you need your antibiotic."

He tamped out his cigarette. "I don't see much of a point."

"I need you for as long as I get to have you," she choked out over the emotions strangling her throat. "That's the point." She turned toward the house.

"I have to go to my regular doctor today. They need to take a look at my head and check my blood."

She closed her eyes, summoning some strength, and turned back. "I'll drive you."

"I can take a taxi. You have a job."

"I canceled my day."

"Bella—"

"I'm here, Dad. I'm not going anywhere."

"That's what worries me."

She frowned, absorbing the hurt. "I'm sorry that makes you unhappy."

"It doesn't make me unhappy. When I hugged you good-bye all those years ago, I accepted that I would never see you again. Having my beautiful daughter standing on my porch makes me luckier than I have a right to be."

She nodded as her eyes welled. "I'll get us some breakfast." She walked down to the kitchen and stopped at the counter, her shoulders slumping as she gripped the cheap laminate edge, fighting to keep her breathing steady. How was this happening? How could Dad be dying when she'd only just found him again?

She allowed herself the indulgence of one tear, dashing it away as quickly as it fell, then stood straight. Crying would do nothing for her right now. Dad needed her to keep it together. She absently rubbed at the growing ache in her temples, ignoring the dull shooting pains radiating in her head as she cooked them both a plate of scrambled eggs and toast. She added grapes and strawberries to a bowl, not sure how much Dad would be able to tolerate. Picking up their dishes, she pasted on a smile and brought their morning meal to the back porch. "Here you go," she said as she set Dad's plate in front of him.

"This looks good."

"I hope you like it." She took her seat and forced herself to chew and swallow several bites of egg and toast in the tense silence. "I want you to come stay with me."

"No."

"I can help you—"

"No."

She set down her silverware with an impatient clatter. "Why?"

"I like my doctors here. I'm right down the street from the hospital."

"You're alone."

He shrugged. "I like being alone."

"We had friends in Ohio. We used to have barbeques with the neighbors."

"That was a lifetime ago."

"I love those memories. I don't have many with you. I was little, but I remember our garden and going for bike rides in the park. You and Mom were happy. Then everything changed."

"And I'm sorry for it."

She wanted more than that—an actual explanation, but now wasn't the time. "When's your appointment?"

"One."

"We'll be able to have lunch first." She wiped her mouth with a napkin. "I'd like to talk to my friends about your case. The oncologists I know."

"I'm not going to spend what time I have left pumped full of chemicals, feeling worse, just to die anyway."

She stared down at her lap, trying to accept that Dad's mind was made up. "Then what can I do for you?"

"Nothing."

She exhaled a biting breath.

"Get together with me for dinner sometimes—or lunch. Be my daughter."

She met his gaze again. "I'm coming to see you every week. I'm going to bring you food."

"Bella—"

"You'll feel better if you eat well."

Sighing, he sat back.

"I want you here." She took his hand, staring into his eyes. "Maybe that's selfish, but I want you here. I just found you."

He squeezed her fingers. "I'll try to eat better."

She nodded.

"I feel good today. I'm fine except for a little bit of a headache."

"I'll get you some pain reliever. I'm going to cook you up some meals and put them in the freezer. I'll take you to your appointment."

"Then you need to go home."

"Okay." She took his barely -touched plate and went to the kitchen, doling out over-the-counter pain relievers for Dad and two for herself. Her head was pounding.

Reed drove home in the truck, wishing he'd gone with his first instinct and taken the motorcycle when he pulled out of his driveway this morning. The sun shined bright and the wind felt good blowing in through the windows—an experience always better on his bike. But he couldn't complain. Not even an hour ago, thunder and lightning had filled the sky, canceling Sadie's afternoon softball practice. When she told him she wanted to go directly home after the last bell rang in the hallowed halls of Beverly Hills High, he hadn't wasted any time arguing. He'd considered it a hell of a bonus when they pulled through the gates at the James' property and he spotted Tyson's sweet little ride parked in its place for the night shift. After quickly briefing his buddy on the status of their principal's day and the lack of threats against her, he'd cut out early—a rare but beautiful thing.

He was tired after his long night of pacing the bedroom floor, but not even his shitty three hours of sleep was going to keep him away from the gym today. All he needed to do was stop by the house and grab his bag, and he was off to Santa Monica for a solid workout in the ring with Rusty or one of the other guys. How long had it been since he'd sparred? Three weeks? A month? Pretty much since he'd met Bella. He'd have been lying if he said he regretted his dinners and walks on the beach with his gorgeous neighbor, but that didn't mean he wasn't looking forward to throwing a few punches at someone who would actually hit him back.

Smiling at the idea of taking full advantage of his free afternoon, he turned into the quiet neighborhood, then into his driveway, surprised to see Bella's car parked in hers and Jenny getting ready to leave. Bella worked until five Monday through Friday—often later with her upcoming trip right around the corner. He killed the engine and got out as Jenny settled Faith in her car seat. "Hey."

She smiled. "Hi."

"How's it going?"

"Good. Bella looks awful, though—real pale." Worry filled Jenny's pretty eyes as she glanced up from securing the buckle across her daughter's chest. "She says she's fine—a little tired—but maybe you could check on her later."

"Sure. I just need to grab something from the house." He gestured to his condo. "I'll stop in before I head out again."

"Thanks." She closed the baby in the back and walked around to the driver's side. "Faithy has her play date, so I'm gonna get goin'."

"Have fun."

"Thanks."

He tossed Jenny a wave as he hurried to unlock his door, not bothering to shut it behind him when he ran upstairs and changed into navy-blue mesh shorts and a ratty white sleeveless top. Grabbing his bag, he threw in his boxing shoes and a towel he snagged from the bathroom before he sank his feet into his Nikes and headed back outside toward the side yard connecting his and Bella's properties.

He glanced at his watch, trying to figure his schedule. He would pop his head in and make sure Bella was all set. She could catch a nap if she wanted, and he would grab them some dinner on his way back from the gym. Maybe they could take a walk on the beach and she could tell him about the emergency that kept her away all night. He stopped at her door and rapped his knuckles against the solid wood.

Lucy barked.

He frowned. Never had he heard Bella's sweet puppy bark—unless she was chasing her seagulls. "Bella," he called, knocking a second time, his shoulders tensing when Lucy sent up another din and

Bella didn't answer.

Something was off. He twisted the doorknob, muttering a curse when it opened. Locks were the first line of defense against the criminal element, but people rarely took advantage of them.

Lucy hurried over to him, whining and panting instead of greeting him with kisses and her tail wagging.

He crouched down in front of the agitated pup, his eyes darting around the house, his ears straining as he listened for any movements in the eerie silence. "What's going on, huh, girl?"

Lucy whined again and ran toward the downstairs bathroom.

He gained his feet, following on high alert, stopping outside the partially closed door as Lucy whined inside. "Bella?"

She didn't answer.

He eased open the door and his heart rushed into his throat as Bella lay curled in a ball on the floor. "Shit. Bella." He hurried over to her, crouching and checking for a pulse.

"I'm fine," she croaked out, keeping her eyes closed. "I have a migraine."

She was sheet-white. "You're not fine."

"I'll be okay in a little while."

It frightened him to see her down for the count when she was usually so full of energy. "Do we need to go to the hospital?"

"No. I get these sometimes. Not very often. I have medicine upstairs in the bathroom."

"Can you stand up?"

"Yes, but I don't want to."

"Come on up." He reached underneath her and settled her in his arms, breathing in the overpowering stench of cigarette smoke as he lifted her carefully.

She groaned, resting her head on his shoulder. "I can't promise I'm not going to throw up."

"We'll deal with it. Come on. Let's get you in bed." He brought her upstairs, grimacing with each inhale. "Christ, you stink."

"I know. It's making me even more nauseated than I already am."

He brought her through the master bedroom decorated with dark furnishings and different shades of white to the bathroom while Lucy followed close behind. "How about a shower?"

"I can't."

"One of my friends used to get these pretty bad like you. She would take a hot shower and it would help."

"I can't, Reed."

He set her on the toilet seat and glanced around at candles and plants in her luxurious setup, but he wasn't seeing what he needed to help Bella out. "Stay right here."

She held her face in her hands. "Okay."

He hustled over to his place, grabbing the crappy, cheap barstool from his kitchen, then hurried back to her house and upstairs. "I'm back," he said as he walked in, finding Bella sitting exactly where he'd left her, except now she hugged Lucy and rested her forehead on the puppy's soft coat.

Bella lifted her head, blinking in the light shining in through the privacy glass above the bathtub. "What are you doing with that?"

"Putting it in the shower. Since neither of us are up for hopping in together, I thought this was the best alternative." He set the stool in the tub and turned on the water, adjusting the temperature to almost hot before he turned to her. "Take off your dress."

She closed her eyes again, settling her head back on Lucy. "I just want to lie down."

He moved over to her, cringing as he breathed her in. "You smell, Bella. Awful."

"Thanks."

"Lift up your arms."

Groaning, she did as he asked.

He pulled the wrinkled blue sundress over her head, leaving a sheer white strapless bra and panty set behind. Sweet Jesus, she was spectacular. "Come on." He lifted her again, checking the water, and settled her on the stool so that her back was to the spray while he stood on the plush bathmat, avoiding the worst of the spray.

She gasped, her eyes flying open as the water rained down her body. "It's hot."

"Too hot?"

"Almost."

"Then it's perfect." He grabbed the shampoo and dumped some in her hair, the familiar scent filling his nose as he rubbed gently at her scalp and tried to ignore the fact that her wet, perky breasts were every man's fantasy. "I bet after we get the stink off you, you'll start feeling better."

"I hope so."

"Let's rinse." He tipped her head back into the stream.

"Dizzy," she moaned as she gripped his forearm and leaned forward, vomiting—dry heaving, mostly.

He winced, realizing his sudden movements had been too abrupt. "Sorry. Jesus, I'm so sorry, Bella."

She opened her mouth, filling it with water, and spit it out. "It's okay."

Damn, she was in rough shape. "Can you sit up a little so I can get the rest of the soap out?"

"Yeah." She let the water soak her head.

"Better." He slid his fingers through her soft, thick hair, chasing away the last of the suds.

"I want to get out."

"Just one more minute." He grabbed the body wash next, lathering the liquid in his hands and rubbing them around on her arms, shoulders, what he could get of her back and stomach, then her legs, making certain to be gentle, pretending he didn't notice how slippery smooth her skin felt against his palms. "You *have* to smell better now. I don't see how you couldn't."

He made sure the bubbles were washed away, then shut off the water. Grabbing two towels, he wrapped one around her body as best he could and settled the other on her head before picking her back up and bringing her into her bed with Lucy following closely. "Let's get you in here."

"Okay."

He set her down at the foot of the mattress and pulled back the white comforter and sheet set. "Where are your pajamas?"

"In the top drawer."

He opened the drawer to more panties, bras, and sinful spaghetti-strapped nighties. He lifted out a dark purple camisole. "These are your pajamas?"

"Yes."

"You don't have any sweat shorts or long T-shirts?"

"No."

Why didn't that surprise him? He snagged a pair of flossy black panties. "Can you handle this on your own?"

"Yes."

And thank God for it. Her underwear left little to the imagination, especially now that it was soaked through and she was cold. He was all for being good and honorable, but stripping Bella down to bare skin and not being able to touch and taste was bound to be torture. "I'll get your medicine. Where is it?"

"In the cabinet."

He walked off, leaving her to change, and went to the medicine cabinet. Opening it, he noted Band-Aids and pain reliever, cotton swabs and birth control pills, several missing from the pack in accordance with the days of the month. Then he found the medicine. He read the directions and the warnings not to drive or drink alcohol, then shook one into his hand. "Are you dressed?"

"Yes."

He grabbed a paper cup, filled it with water, and went back in.

Bella lay on her side beneath the covers, looking a little better than she had when he found her on the floor. "Here you go."

She took the pill and drank the water. "Thank you."

"You're welcome." He sat down next to her, tucking her wet hair behind her ear. "You smell good—like you."

A small smile touched her lips as she took his hand, holding it in hers against the pillow. "Thank goodness."

He laced their fingers, stroking her wrist with his thumb. "You have some color in your cheeks."

"The throbbing isn't quite as bad—or the nausea."

"Good. Do you want to try eating something?"

"No. The medicine knocks me out."

"What about Lucy? Is she all set?"

"She might need some dinner. And if you can take her out real quick."

"How about I take her for a walk?"

"You don't have to."

"But I can. It'll be good for her. She's worried about you." He was too. As he stared into Bella's glassy eyes and felt the warmth of her hand in his, he realized his trip to Santa Monica wasn't going to happen after all. He kept waiting for the flickers of irritation or the sense of burden he'd so often felt in New York when something got in the way of his rare moments of free time. Instead he smiled at her, wanting nothing more than for her to feel better. "It'll be good for her to get out of the house."

"But she's my girl."

"I'll take care of Lucy. You take care of you."

"Thank you," she said again and closed her eyes.

He wanted to ask her what was going on in her life: where had she gone, why had she smelled like she spent the night in some grody bar, but she was drifting off. "I'll check on you later."

"'Kay."

He stood. "Come on, Lucy."

Lucy stayed where she was by the bed.

"It's okay. She's going to be all right. Let's go to the beach, Lucy."

Lucy's ears perked up.

"Do you want to walk on the beach?"

Lucy stood.

"That's a girl. Come on."

He walked with her downstairs and grabbed Bella's keys off the entryway table, pausing when he spotted her cell phone sticking out of her purse. There it was; the chance he'd been waiting for was finally presenting itself. He picked it up, slid his finger on the screen, swearing when he was prompted to put in a pin. He gave Bella's birthdate a shot, felt the phone vibrate with a warning that he had nine more shots to get it right, and glanced Lucy's way as she stared up at him.

Her tail wagged and she pressed her weight against his leg.

He shoved the phone in his pocket, looking away from the trust and adoration he saw in the puppy's eyes. "This is my job, and you're a freaking dog, so we're both going to pretend that you're not making me feel guilty."

This didn't have to be a big deal. He would bring the phone with him, see what he could do about the password, take a gander through her contacts, and have it back before Bella was the wiser. Walking to the closet, he snagged the leash and stopped with his hand on the doorknob. What if Bella needed him? What if she woke up while he was gone, feeling worse than she already did, and couldn't get ahold of him?

"Son of a bitch. Give me a second." He ran upstairs to the bedroom and pulled the phone back out of his pocket, settling it next to Bella's side as she slept deeply. He'd never been one to care much about procedure and protocol. His goal had always been to secure the information he needed, but this was about Bella's safety.

Sighing, he brushed his fingers through her hair, then left with Lucy, locking up behind him and making sure the volume on his phone was loud enough to hear in case she called. "Come on, Luce. Let's go chase your seagulls."

☙ Chapter Sixteen ❧

Reed exhaled short, quick breaths in time with his jab-backstep-jab combination to the heavy bag. He dodged to the right and again to the left, as if an opponent threw a series of punches at him, then paused when he thought he heard someone knocking on his front door. He walked over to the window and looked down, catching sight of Lucy's back half and her wagging tail past the roof's overhang. Chuckling, he pulled off his gloves and hurried downstairs, opening the door and smiling at Bella. "Hey."

"Hi." Her gaze trailed up his sweat-soaked muscle shirt. "It looks like I'm interrupting your workout."

"Nah, I was just finishing up." He swiped his arm across his dripping forehead as he breathed in her familiar scent. "How are you feeling?"

"Much better. Thank you for everything you did yesterday."

"No problem. You look good." And she did—damn good in her snug, knee-length navy-blue skirt, matching heels, and white blousy sleeveless top. She'd added loose curls to her silky black hair. "A little tired, though."

"It's been a long couple of days."

His gaze sharpened on hers, not missing the flash of unhappiness in her pretty baby browns or the weariness in her voice. "Wanna talk about it?"

She let out a small, humorless laugh. "No."

"Wanna come in?" He stepped back, opening the door wider with his invitation.

She smiled. "Sure." She took two steps inside and stopped, lifting her eyebrow as she looked from the empty space to him. "Reed—"

"I know. You love what I've done with the place."

Chuckling, she shook her head. "Do you hear that?"

He frowned. "What?"

"The echo. Our voices echo, Reed."

He grinned. "But not for long. I remembered to grab Wren's plans when I was downtown the other day." He pointed to the binder on the counter as he walked to the paper towel roll and ripped one off, wiping his face. "Do you wanna take a look at what she came up with while I clean up real quick? You can let me know what you think."

"Sure. How do you feel about grabbing something to eat and going to the beach after?"

"Yeah, definitely. Just give me a couple of minutes and I'll be right back."

"Take your time," she said as she opened the fancy little book with *Campbell Interiors* scrolled across the front.

Reed made quick work of the shower, changing into jeans and a plain white T-shirt to go along with his flip-flops. He slid his fingers through his hair, smoothing it down as he walked downstairs. "So, what do you think?"

"I think options one and three are close contenders."

He stepped up behind her, his body brushing hers as he leaned his hip against the counter. "One and three?"

"They seem the most you."

"The most me. And what does that mean? The most me?"

She shrugged as she tilted her head, looking up at him. "I don't know. They're kind of simple—understated—but they still have a warmth about them."

"Huh." He studied the first option, then turned to the third. "I like this big-screen TV and these sink-in couches."

"They look comfy."

"What do you say I go with three?"

"I think you should think on it—make sure. Decide in the morning after you've taken one last look."

He'd already made up his mind. "But I like the couches."

"It's up to you. This is your house."

"For now."

She frowned as she turned to face him. "You're not staying?"

Why did he like her concern when it came to the location of his living arrangements? "Would you miss me if I left?" he asked, wiggling his eyebrows.

"Yes."

He grinned, far more pleased than he should have been. "Yeah?"

"Of course." She gave a gentle bump to his arm with her elbow.

"You're my beach buddy and dinner partner. And who would I cook with?"

He smiled again. "I don't see myself going anywhere for a while, but I also can't see myself staying forever."

The crease in her brow returned. "Will you go back to New York?"

"No. I mean living here in the condo. I'm renting for now."

"Me too."

"I thought you owned," he fibbed, knowing her financial situation as well as his own.

She shook her head.

"Who's your landlord?"

"Dr. Huberty. Her tenant moved out a few days after I took the job at her office."

"Perfect timing."

"Agreed."

He closed the book. "Wanna get out of here?"

"In a minute." She surprised him with a hug. "Really, thanks for yesterday, Reed."

Closing his eyes, he wrapped his arms around her, holding her head to his chest with his hand. This was the Bella he'd missed yesterday—kind, sweet, affectionate. "You were in a tough spot."

"I was, and you took care of me." She eased away enough to hold his gaze but not break their connection. "I want to take you to Malcoms."

"Malcoms?"

"The best burgers you'll ever eat. It's greasy—definitely guy food. And I'm buying."

His fingers found their way into the ends of her hair. "Only if you want to."

"You showered and washed me while I puked. Buying you dinner is the least I can do."

"It wasn't that big of a deal." Although he'd paid the price for being a decent human being last night with several dreams about Bella and her silky underwear. "Friendship isn't always pretty."

She grinned. "No, it's not. But I would do the same thing for you."

"You would?"

She nodded. "In a heartbeat."

And he knew she meant it. "Thanks."

"You're welcome." She broke their connection, then took his hand. "Let's go. I'm going to feed you."

"You won't hear me complain." They walked out and he locked up. "Lucy, we're going to the beach."

Lucy ran to his truck and jumped in the back.

He and Bella laughed.

"I guess she knows the drill." Bella stopped by the bed, shutting the tailgate. "Lie down, sweetie."

Lucy did as she was asked.

Bella took her seat as Reed shut his door and turned over the engine.

He buckled his seat belt, waiting for Bella to do the same, then pulled out of the driveway and started toward the main road. "So, I've heard of these burgers now that I think about it. Everybody at the office swears by them."

"Mmm. I can't wait for you to try one. I'm kind of excited that you're a Malcoms virgin—that I get to experience this with you for the first time."

Laughing, he pulled out into traffic, making his way through rush hour. "A Malcoms virgin," he repeated, shaking his head. Was there anyone more adorable than Bella?

She grinned. "It's a pretty big moment and *way* better than any first sexual experience."

"Yours wasn't any good, huh?"

"It certainly wasn't the sex of my dreams. What about you, Casanova?"

He tossed her a quick look, then focused on the traffic. "I'd probably be exaggerating if I told you I lasted longer than two minutes."

She threw her head back, laughing.

Damn, she was beautiful with her eyes bright and the wind blowing through her hair. "They were two great minutes, though."

"I bet."

He'd wanted this when she'd been sick and helpless—her vivacity, the way they laughed together, the way he could be easy in her presence. "My ego demands that I brag about my current staying power and the fact that I'm a hell of a lot better in the sack now than I was several years ago."

"Of course you are, Stud." She sent him a playful wink.

He grinned, catching sight of the Malcoms sign a couple of blocks down the road. "Are you sure you want to eat there?"

"Definitely."

"What about the whole 'grease is bad for your complexion and your face is your billboard to the world' thing?"

"I'm going to have grilled chicken."

"Ah," he said with a scowl. "That's so *boring*, Bella."

She shook her head, smiling. "They're really good. I'll let you try some...after I'm finished with a large majority of my sandwich. The last time you had a bite of my food, you practically ate the whole thing."

"She's still an over-exaggerator, folks," he yelled out the window as cars rushed by.

She swatted at his arm. "I'm totally not. You ate most of my ice cream the other night."

He huffed out a breath, feigning his insult. "Not even close."

"You're clearly bad with details."

"I never forget a detail." He went through another set of lights, just making the yellow before it turned red. "We're almost there."

"I know." Grinning, she rubbed her hands together.

His phone started ringing, and he peeked at the readout. "It's my mom."

"Go ahead and answer."

"Hello?"

"Reed, it's Mom."

They hadn't spoken much since their ridiculous argument about his love life. "What's up?"

"Are you working?"

"No, I changed assignments, so I'm pretty much locked into normal hours right now, which I like." He looked over at Bella and smiled.

"That's good to hear. I'm wondering if you might be able to do me a favor?"

"Yeah. Sure."

"My bridge group is meeting for an impromptu get-together. I'm hoping you might be able to come stay with Aunt Bonnie."

"Right now?"

"I know it's short notice..."

Mom rarely had a chance to get out on her own. She asked for favors even less. He sighed as he looked at Bella. "Mom, can you hold on?"

"Sure, honey."

Bella sat up in her seat. "Is everything okay?"

"I'm going to have to take a rain check on dinner."

"Oh. Okay."

"I need to give my mom a hand with my aunt."

"Sure. We'll go do that first. We can eat later."

He shook his head. He didn't want her coming with him. There would be questions—and his mother was bound to get the wrong idea. He never brought women home with him. No one had ever been important enough. And he was already struggling to keep Bella in the friend zone. The last thing he needed was to send his mother mixed signals when she was so desperate for a daughter-in-law and grandchildren. "I should probably take you home."

She blinked, her eyes full of surprise. "Oh."

"Reed," Mom said. "Is that a woman?"

Ah, shit. "Yeah."

"I didn't realize I was interrupting a date."

"I'm not on a date."

"But you're with a woman."

"It happens occasionally."

"Who is she?"

He rolled his eyes. "No one."

"But you're with a woman."

"Mom, she's no one. I'll be over as soon as I can."

"Reed—"

"I'll be over soon." He hung up and stopped at the next set of lights. "Sorry to cut tonight short."

"It's fine."

He could tell by her clipped tone that it wasn't. "We can try again tomorrow." He looked her way when she didn't respond.

"Is your aunt sick?"

He pulled a u-ey and started back toward the condos. "She has dementia."

"I'm sorry."

He shrugged away her apology. Regrets never changed anything. "My mom moved out here after my cousin died last year. Aunt Bonnie's my dad's sister-in-law, but Mom takes care of her. I try to give her a hand when I can."

"We could take her to the beach—pack up a couple of chairs and get some fresh air. I would love to meet everyone."

He shook his head again. "That's not a good idea. She gets pretty confused. A lot of the time she doesn't know who I am." His phone rang again. Mom. "Son of a bitch," he muttered as he answered. "Hello?"

"Honey, I've changed my mind. I'm staying in. You have fun."

"I'm already on my way. I'm dropping Bella off and I'll be over."

"Bella. What a beautiful name."

Damn, he wasn't going to hear the end of this one for a long time. The fifty questions would start as soon as he walked through her door. "Mom—"

"Bring her with you."

"Mom, I have to go. The traffic's bad." He hung up. "Jesus. Talk about getting the wrong idea."

Bella sent him a small smile and looked out her window.

He stopped at the lights by their development, waiting his turn to go right. "We'll try tomorrow?"

"I'm busy tomorrow."

"Okay. Then Sunday."

"I already have a commitment."

Her voice had definitely gone cool. "Bella, I'm sorry." He pulled up in front of her house.

"Don't worry about it." She got out.

"Bella—"

"I'll see you around." She walked to the back and put down the gate. "Lucy, come on."

What the hell? "Bella," he called through the open passenger side window as she started toward her house. He got out of the truck, hurrying after her. "What's your deal?"

She whirled. "You're the detective. I'll let you figure it out." She sent him a chilly smile and closed the distance between herself and her door.

He followed. "You're really getting upset because I'm putting burgers and the beach on hold to help my mother?"

She gaped at him. "That's what you think?"

He rubbed at the back of his neck, well aware that every time he opened his mouth, he was making this worse. "Clearly I don't know what I'm thinking."

"I didn't realize our friendship was such an embarrassment to you." She jammed her key in the lock.

"*What*? It's not. My mom thinks we're dating."

"Well, God forbid."

"No. It's not—"

She opened her door. "Good night, Reed."

He snagged her by the arm before she could shut him out. "Do you want to come with me?"

"Ten minutes ago: yes. Now: no."

He sighed. "Just get in the truck."

Temper flashed in her eyes as she yanked away from him. "You get in the truck and drive away."

"Christ, you're stubborn."

"Lucy, bite him," she said primly, raising her chin as she held his gaze, but the heat was gone, replaced by a well-guarded vulnerability.

Lucy wagged her tail.

"We're going to have to work on that command," Bella added.

There was something here—something painful. Anger was often a balm for raw wounds. "I'm sorry." He reached for her hand. "I didn't mean to hurt your feelings. But you don't know my mother."

"You should appreciate your family."

"I do. It's just—if I bring you over there, she's going to start thinking wedding bells and baby showers."

"And then she'll see that we're just friends."

"Do you want to come?"

"Not if you're going to be uncomfortable having me there."

There it was again—the lack of confidence he wasn't aware she possessed. He'd genuinely hurt her. "No. I won't be." He lifted her knuckles to his lips. "I'm sorry, Bella. The *last* thing you are is an embarrassment to me. It's not just my mom. Aunt Bonnie's usually a little extra agitated at night. Sometimes people with dementia have more trouble in the evenings."

Her eyes softened, and she brought his palm to her cheek.

He sighed, realizing his latest series of mistakes—inviting her to Aunt Bonnie's place, kissing her soft skin, rushing after her and panicking a little when he'd thought she was kicking him to the curb, letting himself become more and more deeply involved.

"Should I leave Lucy? She's a therapy dog, and dementia patients often respond well to animals."

"So let's bring her along."

She smiled at him. "I'm sorry for overreacting."

He shrugged. "The last few minutes probably weren't either of our finest moments."

She laughed and hugged him.

He returned her embrace and settled his cheek on top of her hair, cursing himself for a fool for ever believing he would walk away from this double life he was living unscathed. "We're good?"

"We're good." She eased back. "Let's go give your mom a hand."

"I'm ready if you are." He settled his arm around her shoulders, walked with her to the truck, and opened her door. Damn, he was in trouble.

Bella stared out the window as Reed drove them toward his family home. She nibbled her bottom lip and closed her eyes with an inner cringe as she replayed the last several minutes of their evening together. Everything had started out fine: fun, jokes, laughter—typical stuff now that Reed had let his guard down. Shockingly, it was *she* who had almost ruined their night.

His words had surprised and hurt her—a small slap in the face when he told his mom that she was "no one." Her knee-jerk reaction had been to push him away and pretend that it didn't matter whether or not he wanted to introduce her to his mother and aunt. She could only be sorry for her nasty behavior and ashamed that her insecurities had gotten the better of her.

Sighing quietly, she watched the miles race by. She was supposed to be over all of this. Los Angeles had given her a freedom she'd never felt in Las Vegas—or not after her "best friend" Liza had broadcast to the student body of Stiles Preparatory Academy that her mother was a prostitute.

Not long after they arrived in Sin City, Kelly Colby had hung up her glittery pasties and platform heels to make a pretty penny as a high-end call girl. Mom had been choosy about her clients, only accepting handsome, wealthy businessmen who knew how to treat a beautiful woman right. Mom's exception had been Liza's married father—whom Bella and Liza had walked in on one unfortunate afternoon in the middle of their ninth-grade year.

From that moment on, the secret Bella had tried so hard to hide had become fodder for five hundred other students' jokes: lewd pictures and notes with disgusting propositions shoved through the slots of her locker, whispers and disapproving stares from judgmental mothers afraid that their husbands would fall victim next. Her nightmare until she'd transferred out to a public school and tried to get lost in the crowds.

Eventually things had settled down. After some time, she'd found new friends, but she'd constantly looked over her shoulder, waiting for someone to recognize her as "the daughter of that whore." Even after she'd moved out of her mother's high-rise apartment on her eighteenth birthday, she'd worried, always hating to be judged and looked down upon for something she'd never had any control over. She loathed that Reed's perceived slight had brought her back to that place where she'd questioned who she was and wondered whether she was good enough in his eyes.

"We're just about there."

She sat up, paying closer attention to their surroundings when he turned down a quiet residential road, slowed again, and pulled into a well-maintained driveway. Grinning, she studied the adorable pale yellow ranch with vivid flowers planted in window boxes and lights blazing bright beyond the glass. It was hard to hang on to her melancholy mood when she stared at such a sweet, cheery scene. "Look at this. I *love* it, Reed. It's so charming."

"It's my aunt's place—was my cousin's."

Her smile vanished when she recognized the strain in his voice. "What happened to him?"

"He committed suicide. Shot himself."

Her heart went out to him, unable to imagine such a horrid loss. "I'm sorry."

He exhaled a long breath. "I wish I would've known he was struggling so much. I would have tried to help him. We were pretty close growing up. My uncle's death really messed him up."

"I'm sorry," she said again, taking his hand and squeezing.

"Thanks." He squeezed back and pulled away, reaching for the door handle.

"For tonight too," she rushed on, grabbing hold of his wrist before he could get out. "My behavior—"

"I thought we decided we were okay."

"We are. I just—"

"Don't worry about it, Bella." He slid a lock of her wavy hair through his fingers, sending her a reassuring smile. "Don't worry about it."

She nodded, exhaling a quiet breath of her own as they both got out.

He met her at the back, letting down the gate for Lucy. "Come on out, Luce."

Lucy jumped down, hurrying toward the bushes in the backyard.

"Lucy," Bella called.

"She's all right. She can't hurt anything."

"Are you sure?"

"Yeah, she's fine. Let her sniff around a little."

The front door opened and a tall, pretty woman with shoulder-length brown hair stepped outside wearing jeans and a simple black top. "Honey, you didn't have to come." She stopped, blinking her blue eyes at Bella, her face lighting up with a smile. "Sweetheart, look at you." She made a delighted sound in her throat as she wrapped Bella up in a warm hug. "Reed, she's absolutely *gorgeous*."

"Mom, this is Bella Colby, who happens to be pretty easy on the eyes." He shoved his hands in his pockets and rocked back on his heels, winking at her.

Bella chuckled as she drew away, any nerves she'd had about meeting his family immediately vanishing. "Mrs. McKinley—"

"Linda. You call me Linda." She pulled her back for another quick embrace. "I can't tell you how happy I am to meet you. Reed never brings anyone home."

"Never?"

Linda shook her head. "Not once."

"Never," Bella repeated, meeting his gaze as hers twinkled with mischief. "Well, I'm happy to be the first."

"That makes two of us." Linda smiled again. "How did you and Reed meet?"

"We're neighbors."

"What a great way to start a relationship." Linda made another wistful sound as she clasped her hands, looking from Bella to Reed. "I can already tell you two are perfect for each other."

Reed closed his eyes, letting his head hang. "Jesus, Mom."

"What? A mother knows when she's met the woman who's going to help her son make beautiful grandbabies."

As Reed muttered an expletive and pressed his fingers to his forehead, Bella laughed. "Thank you for welcoming me to your home, Linda."

"I'm sorry I interrupted your evening, but now that you're here, I'm glad I did. Come on inside..." Linda gasped as Lucy wandered over from around the corner of the house. "What on earth?"

"This is Lucy."

Linda chuckled, giving Lucy a gentle pat. "She's *huge*."

"She's big, but she's very sweet. Lucy's a certified therapy dog."

"Bonnie's just going to love her. Come with me, sweetie." Linda wrapped her arm around Bella's shoulders, leading her to the door with Reed and Lucy following behind. "She's been in and out of it today, so we'll have to see how this goes."

They walked into a cozy living room decorated simply with southern California style in mind. A middle-aged woman with short blond hair rocked in a chair while she stared at the TV.

"Bonnie, we have company."

Bonnie glanced over, her brown eyes meeting Bella's through thick prescription lenses before they widened when she spotted Lucy. "Oh my." She laughed. "Who is this big love?"

Lucy made a beeline to Bonnie, sitting down next to her, accepting the affection Bonnie gave lavishly with hugs and gentle petting to her side.

"That's Lucy, and this is Reed's girlfriend, Bella."

Bonnie frowned. "Reed's girlfriend?"

Reed opened his mouth and closed it again when Bella shook her head, assuring him with her subtle gesture that his mother's assumptions didn't bother her any. She crouched down next to Bonnie and smiled. "Reed told us all about you, Aunt Bonnie. We've been wanting to come say hi."

"Well, I'm sure glad you did." She hugged Lucy again. "She's a good girl."

Bella stroked Lucy's back the way she knew her puppy liked best. "She's very special."

"How old is she?"

"One."

"*One*?"

"Lucy's still little."

"Honey, there's nothing little about her."

Bella grinned. "She's my baby."

Bonnie chuckled, patting Bella's hand. "Aren't you a precious, precious woman?"

"Thank you."

"Bonnie, I'm going to go play some cards with the girls down the road," Linda said, walking over to the opposite side of Bonnie's chair. "Reed and Bella are going to stay here with you."

Concern replaced the pleasure in Bonnie's eyes. "You're going to leave me?"

"Just for a little bit."

Bonnie gripped Linda's arm. "Where are you going to go?"

"Just down the street."

Bonnie rushed to her feet. "I can't stay here alone."

"I'll only be gone for a little while. You're going to stay with Reed."

"Reed?"

"Hey, Aunt Bonnie." Reed sent her a wave, keeping his distance over by the couch.

Bonnie stepped back, the calm, kind woman of moments ago now breathing hard and clinging to Linda. "I can't—I don't know him."

Bella heard Reed's quiet sigh as she gained her feet, stepping closer to Bonnie. "Aunt Bonnie, I love to do hair." She cautiously touched her hand to Bonnie's arm. "Do you think maybe I could do your hair while you pet Lucy?"

Bonnie tore her terrified gaze from Reed and focused on Bella. "I'm going to the beauty shop?"

"You are." Bella nodded, sending Bonnie a reassuring smile. "The beauty shop right here in your own home."

"Where should I sit?"

"How about right back in your chair? I know Lucy likes to keep close."

"Okay." Bonnie sat again.

"I'll, uh, I'll go get her brush and a few other things," Linda whispered.

Bella looked at Reed, noting that his jaw was clenched and his arms crossed.

"I guess she doesn't know me tonight," he said.

What should she say? She'd never been in a situation like this before. "I guess not."

"Here we go." Linda came back with a brush, rollers, and other assorted hair items in a small basket. "I'm not exactly sure what you need."

"I'll make something work."

"I can't tell you how much I appreciate this." She took Bella's hand. "Thank you."

"Everything's going to be fine here. Go have fun."

"I will." Linda gave her a hug, then walked over to her son. "She's a keeper, Reed."

"Bella's a good *friend*."

"Don't say things like that." She gave him a pat on his cheek. "You'll break my heart."

Smiling, he uncrossed his arms and wrapped them around his mother. "Go kick some butt at bridge."

She hugged him back. "I'll be about an hour—maybe two, but no longer than that."

"I don't want you worrying about the time."

"That's probably easier said than done. Bye." She kissed Reed and closed the door behind her.

He sighed and rubbed at the back of his neck as he looked from the entryway to Bella. "Do you want anything to eat or drink?"

"Maybe some water."

"Sure. Aunt Bonnie, do you want a drink?"

"No," she snapped.

"I'll be right back." He walked off.

Bella stared after him. Why was he so cool and tense? She hadn't seen him like this since they first met. Did he not get along with his family? His mother was wonderful and warm; his poor aunt a little lost, but they were here for him to cherish and love. Not everyone was so lucky. She focused on the woman in front of her, staring at the TV. "Aunt Bonnie, what should we do with your hair?"

"I don't know."

"How about some curls?"

"That might be nice."

"I'll set some rollers and you can take them out in the morning."

"That's just fine."

Reed brought back a glass for her. "Here you go."

"Thanks." Bella took the water and put it on the small table close to Bonnie, snagging him by the elbow before he could walk away. "Are you okay?"

"Yeah," he said, sliding his free hand through his hair, his jerky movements telling her a different story.

"Reed, what's going on?"

"I didn't realize how much worse things were getting." He gestured to his aunt.

"I'm sorry. I hate that I keep saying that. I wish there was something I could do."

"You're doing it. I sure as hell can't curl her hair." He smiled.

She smiled back.

"I'm at the beauty shop?" Aunt Bonnie asked.

"You are." Bella got to work on Bonnie's hair, brushing for several minutes in soothing strokes as the TV blared with another game show and Reed sat in a chair, bobbing his leg up and down while he looked from the television to his watch. She was securing the last roller in place when Bonnie turned her head and looked at her nephew.

"Mason."

Reed sat up.

"Mason, come on over here, honey."

He looked at Bella as he stood. "Mason was my uncle."

"Mason." Bonnie reached out her hand for his.

Reed took hers.

"Come on down here now. Come look me in the eyes and let me see your handsome face."

He settled on his knees in front of her.

"Did you have a good day at work?"

"I did."

"Did you catch a bad guy or two?"

"I caught three."

Bonnie grinned. "Do you remember when we met?"

"I do."

"The song playing on the jukebox in that old diner while you bought me a Coke."

He smiled. "'My Girl' by The Temptations."

"'I got sunshine,'" Bonnie started to sing and stopped. "'I got sunshine,'" she said again, then blinked. "I don't—I don't know what's next."

"'I got sunshine on a cloudy day,'" Reed sang in a surprisingly smooth voice, giving her hands a gentle squeeze.

Bonnie laughed. "That's right. I remember now. 'When it's cold outside,'" she joined in.

Bella stared, her heart melting as Reed sang through the whole song. Last night he'd been tender and sweet, helping her when she felt awful. Now, this... It wasn't every day a grown man was willing to shower his nauseated neighbor or serenade his ill aunt while pretending to be her dead husband.

Bonnie laughed again when they finished and cupped his cheeks. "Well, Reed, what on earth are you doing here?"

He grinned. "I came to see you."

"Well, you're a good boy."

"Thanks." He kissed her cheek. "It's almost time for bed, Aunt Bonnie."

"I know it is. And tomorrow I'm gonna have a pretty head of curls." She touched her hand to the curlers.

"You are." He kissed her cheek a second time and stood, looking at

Bella. "She likes 'My Girl.'"

Her pulse pounded as she nodded. Every day she discovered something new she liked about him and found more irresistible. "You're a good man." Closing the distance between them, she pressed her mouth to his and eased away.

He clenched his jaw and lifted his hand, hesitating before he slid his knuckles along her cheek. "Come here," he said quietly, dangerously, tugging her closer and kissing her, drawing out the simple meeting of lips with a quick glide of his tongue.

"Oh, young love," Bonnie said. "It's always so nice to see young love."

Bella didn't know that this was love. This was certainly a strong, strong like. And this time, she didn't shy away from the click she always tried to ignore.

"When's the wedding?"

"Not for a while," Reed said, never missing a beat or taking his eyes off Bella's.

"I hope you'll consider me for a bridesmaid," Bonnie said.

"Of course," Bella answered, slightly breathless from the intensity of his gaze.

"I should probably be heading off to bed." Bonnie stood.

"I'll—I can go with her." Bella held his stare a moment longer and walked off, following Bonnie to her room with Lucy close behind.

☙ Chapter Seventeen ❧

Bella let the warm breeze caress her skin as Reed drove them home from Aunt Bonnie's. It wasn't particularly late—only nine. Dinner and a walk on the beach were still an option, especially on a Friday night, but Reed hadn't mentioned any sort of desire to stop off at Malcoms for a burger. He hadn't said much of anything since their little...kiss thing in his aunt's living room. By the time she'd finished helping Bonnie settle into bed, Linda had come home. She'd spoken with Reed's mother at length, answering several of her eager questions, but Reed had kept quiet, sitting on the couch, making it hard for her to concentrate every time their eyes met across the room.

Something had changed tonight. It was hard to pinpoint exactly what, but something was undeniably different between them. Maybe their relationship had been evolving all along. From the beginning, they'd assured one another that they weren't each other's type—and in many ways that was still true. They had different outlooks on life. Reed tended to be a little more cynical than she was, but somewhere along the way, his sense of humor and kindness had become more important.

In months past, she'd dabbled in dating, refusing to take the opposite sex too seriously. She'd convinced herself she wasn't looking for anything long-term or for any major commitments, but for the first time in a long time, the idea of settling into something warm and cozy with the right man was appealing. Now she needed to figure out what Reed was thinking.

She slid him a glance, noting his rigid posture and hands gripping the steering wheel tight. Sighing, she sat up straight, hating the tense silence. "So, thanks for taking me with you."

He looked her way, then back at the road. "Thanks for coming."

She swiped several strands of her hair behind her ear, turning her body more in his direction, eager to keep their conversation going. "I had a good time."

"I'm glad. Aunt Bonnie likes you."

"She likes Lucy."

He grinned and his shoulders relaxed. "She was digging you more than she was me—until she thought I was Uncle Mason."

"She seems fairly young for such an advanced condition."

"She is. Fifty-nine, I think. Or something right around there. Every time I see her, she's a little worse."

She wanted to reach for his hand, but didn't, not quite sure where they stood. "That can't be easy."

"I'd say the hardest part is knowing Mom has to deal with it every day when Aunt Bonnie's less and less the person she used to be."

"Does she know about your cousin?"

"I'm not sure. Sometimes she might, but most of the time I don't think so, which is a good thing as far as I'm concerned."

"It's sad."

"He did it in a hotel room in Utah when he was away on business—shot himself. Even though he was in a horrible place emotionally, he made sure she wouldn't be the one to find him."

"I'm so sorry, Reed."

He jerked his shoulders. "My aunt's had a lot of problems since my uncle died. She had a nervous breakdown after he was killed and never really came back from it. It was hard for the doctors to pinpoint what was going on for quite a while. At first they thought some of the memory loss and mood swings were a result of the trauma—until things kept getting worse. Neither Mom nor I knew how bad it was until we came out for Kurt's funeral."

"Kurt's your cousin?"

He nodded. "Aunt Bonnie's always been sort of off—a little fruity. Or at least, for as long as I can remember, but the dementia's gotten pretty intense. I wish Kurt would have picked up the phone—told us what was going on."

"Sometimes it's hard to ask for help."

He made a sound in his throat. "It's a damn shame, because he was a great guy."

She nodded her sympathy instead of apologizing again. "Your uncle was a cop?"

"Yeah. So was my dad. My grandfather was FBI."

"Crime fighting runs in the family."

"I guess it stopped with me."

"Are you sorry you gave it up?"

"No. I miss police work—a lot of the stuff Joey and I used to do, but sometimes the universe sends signs that it's time to throw in the towel."

"Your blown cover?"

"Yeah."

She nodded, wanting to tell him she was glad that the universe had sent him her way, but this didn't seem like the right time. "I want to help your mother—set up a day for her to come over to the office and I'll give her a facial. Probably my green tea treatment. It's very soothing: neck and shoulder massage and these great new under-eye gels that my clients are going crazy over. Maybe I'll add some hot stones too."

"I'm sure she would dig it."

"I like her."

"She definitely loves you. Now if I'll only buy a ring and get down on one knee, her life will be complete."

She laughed. "I thought she was eager for beautiful grandchildren."

He winced. "She did mention that, huh?" He cringed again. "Sorry about that."

She grinned. "I thought it was sweet."

"I did warn you."

"I'm flattered that she thinks I'm good enough for her son. Mothers can be touchy about those things."

He eased off the gas and pulled into their neighborhood, maintaining a slower speed on the quiet streets. "She'll meet us at the church tomorrow if we tell her to."

She laughed. "I want to go over with you again."

He turned into his driveway. "If tonight's visit didn't scare you off, who am I to stop you?"

She chuckled as she unbuckled her belt. "Not even a little."

He shut off the engine and killed the lights. "How about we go over again in a couple of weeks?"

"Definitely. We can give your mom a break and let Aunt Bonnie love on Lucy. I can bring over some sample product and give her a little facial too."

"Yeah, sure. They're working on getting a part-time nurse to help." He opened his door.

"I hope it works out."

"I'll just keep giving her a hand until it does."

Following his lead, she opened her door and got out. "Do you want to come over? We can make sandwiches and watch the next episode of *The Office*."

"Sounds good, but I think I'm going to pass tonight."

She nodded, sensing the tension rushing back with her invitation. He always came over. Tonight was supposed to be like the last time—when they'd made that simple little mistake and kissed each other crazy on her couch. They'd brushed it off and carried on as if nothing had ever happened. That's how this was supposed to go too. "All right." She sent him a cautious smile and let Lucy out of the back. "I guess I'll see you soon."

"See ya."

That was it? She felt herself frown as she stared after him, then started through the side yard toward her house. Stopping, she puffed out a breath and turned. "Reed?"

"Yeah?" he said, turning back.

"Tonight...I hope I didn't make you uncomfortable. With the kiss and—"

"Nah, it's no big deal." He walked her way, closing the distance between them until she could make out his handsome features in the street lamp. "We're friends."

Whatever was going on between them was getting harder to fit into the "just friends" category, but that's where he seemed to want to keep them, so that's where they would stay. Eventually, the heat snapping between them could end only one way. She wasn't foolish enough to believe otherwise—neither was Reed. But for now, leaving things status quo worked just fine. "Exactly. I know I can be a little overly affectionate sometimes..."

He shook his head. "You're perfect."

It was her turn to shake her head. "I am by no means perfect."

He smiled. "I like you just the way you are."

She returned his smile. "Thanks." She glanced down at the grass, sliding her hair behind her ears before she met his gaze. "I probably won't see you much until I get back from New York, so I wanted to make sure we were okay."

"That's coming right up."

"Yeah. Thursday. I'm pretty booked up with appointments next week—trying to make up for missing yesterday. And tomorrow night,

I have plans."

"We're still on for cooking class though, right?"

"I wouldn't miss it."

"It looks like I'll see you Tuesday—" He glanced over his shoulder toward the houses across the street when they both heard a quick click and hiss. His gaze snapped to hers.

"The sprinklers," they said in unison.

Before Bella could react, she heard the familiar click—but much closer—and was beaned right in the face by a rush of water. Squealing, she blocked the frigid stream with her arms.

"Come on." Reed grabbed her hand and they ran, laughing as they did what they could to dodge the torrents pelting them on their journey to her door. "Well, shit," he said as he gave his arms a solid shake, sending drops flying through the air.

She grinned, staring at him as water continued dripping off him despite his efforts. "I guess it's that time of year again."

"A little warning wouldn't have sucked."

"They usually send an email when they're going to fire up the sprinklers."

"I guess they forgot."

"Apparently." She chuckled. "Want a towel?"

He tossed a baleful look over his shoulder at the steady back-and-forth motion of the water. "That would be great."

She unlocked the door, following Lucy and Reed inside. "Towels first. Then I need to get Lucy her dinner," she said as she moved toward the downstairs bathroom. "My poor girl is probably starving."

"How about you get us something to dry off with and I'll put food in her bowl?"

"You've got a deal." She shivered in the air conditioning as she opened the small linen closet and grabbed hand towels for herself and Reed. She started back out and stopped when she spotted her blue silk robe hanging on the drying rack. Making quick work of changing out of her soggy clothes, she wrapped her bra-and-panty-clad body in one of her favorite pieces from the Abigail Quinn line, happy to be warm again. She hurried back through the living room and turned on the stereo on her way to the kitchen. "This is the best I can do unless I go upstairs for something bigger." She handed off the soft cotton, smiling as Lucy dug into her evening meal.

"This is fine." He took it from her and wiped his face and arms. "Looks like you changed."

"Lucky for me, I washed some laundry this morning before work." She blotted at the drops remaining on her cheeks and forehead. "I have a black one upstairs if you want to borrow it." She sent him a teasing wink.

"It's just like that?"

"Yup. And equally as comfortable. Abby's a genius."

"Tempting, but I think I'll pass."

Chuckling, she set down the towel and walked to the fridge, opening the door. "Are you sure you don't want a sandwich or something? I have turkey and a little ham."

"Yeah, all right. Why not?"

"If you'll grab us the bread and a couple of plates, I have a salad in here too." She pulled sandwich makings and condiments from the shelves and turned as Reed met her back at the island.

"I saw two loaves, so I grabbed this whole grain."

"Perfect." Their fingers touched as he handed it to her and she smiled. "Somehow you're still dripping." She stood on her tiptoes and combed her fingers through his hair, brushing at the drops.

"Don't." He stepped away and turned.

She blinked her surprise, staring at his back.

"I'm sorry," he said, but he didn't face her. Instead he walked to the French doors and looked out, his shoulders as rigid now as they were on the drive home.

Unsure of what to do—of what was going on—she opened the bread and pulled out four pieces. "I, um, I guess I'll make us turkey."

"We're friends," he said, turning.

She set down the Dijon mustard, holding his chilly gaze. "I know."

"This thing that we keep doing. I can't afford complications."

She nodded, trying to keep up with his scattered thoughts. Minutes ago everything was fine. Now it wasn't.

"I'm going to go." He hurried through the kitchen to the living room.

She followed, terribly afraid she was losing her new friend. "But what about your sandwich?"

"We'll talk tomorrow." He opened the door and quickly shut it behind him.

She stood where she was, listening to the music that suddenly seemed too loud in the silence. What had just happened? What did she do to make him so upset?

Lucy pressed her weight against Bella's side.

"We should—let's clean up." Turkey on nice, thick whole grain sounded wonderful five minutes ago. Now she wasn't hungry. Moving back to the kitchen, she started gathering items and putting them in the fridge while her mind raced. What complications had Reed been talking about? Was she pushing him— She gasped, whirling around when someone knocked on her French doors.

Reed stood by the glass, his shirt plastered to him.

She took a step toward the door, paused, then hurried to let him in. "What—"

"I'm sorry," he said, wrapping her up in a hug. "I'm sorry, Bella."

She returned his embrace, closing her eyes as she held on. "It's okay." She eased away. "Please tell me what's going on. You're too important to me to ruin our friendship, but I don't know what I did wrong."

Clenching his jaw, he sighed. "You didn't do anything."

"I must have done something."

"Bella." He paced away and back, jamming his fingers through his hair. "I'm not looking for a relationship."

"I know. I didn't think I was, either."

He shook his head. "I can't be with you."

She ignored the sting of his words. "All right."

"We should probably spend some time apart."

Her throat clogged as tears filled her eyes. "Oh."

"You can't keep *touching* me." He stopped in front of her, reaching for her, then dropped his hand. "You can't kiss me anymore."

She nodded, realizing they weren't fighting. He was fighting himself. "Okay."

"It messes with my head." He grabbed hold of her belt and yanked her against him. "Everything about you messes with my head."

She swallowed, staring into the heat radiating in his eyes. "I don't know what—"

He trailed the pad of his finger down her neck, stopping on her rapid pulse point. "I keep telling myself I'm okay with the way things are. We're friends. That's enough."

She gripped his wrists as their breath mingled. "Things are good—"

He shook his head.

She frowned. "What are you saying?"

He moved his hands, tracing the outline of her robe. "Hell if I know. I have no idea what I'm doing anymore."

She let her palms wander up his muscular arms. "You're confused."

"No. I've never been confused about how much I want you." He leaned in and nipped her bottom lip.

She whimpered as heady anticipation rushed through her belly.

He tangled his fingers in her long locks and tugged. "Do you want this?"

"Yes," she whispered against his lips. "I want you."

He groaned and his mouth was on hers, diving deep—all flash and fire as he pressed her back against the counter.

Her hands were in his hair, then running down his firm chest before sliding under his wet shirt.

"Christ, I have to have you." He parted her robe and sent it to the floor as he went after her neck and jaw with teeth and tongue. "I have to have you, Bella."

"Upstairs." She walked him backward. "Upstairs." She gripped his butt.

He moaned and turned in the living room, stopping and pushing her up against the wall, cupping her breasts and teasing her nipples with several strokes of his thumbs through the silky barrier.

She purred her satisfaction, letting her head fall back, enjoying the sensations as she went after the snap on his jeans. "Let's go upstairs."

He clutched her ass and yanked them fire to fire. "In a second."

She tugged his pants, fighting them down past his hips and thighs, and reached for him, gripping him in her hand.

"God," he hissed next to her ear as a flick of his wrists sent her panties to the area rug. "How about the couch? It's closer."

She throbbed for him, ready to explode just from wanting. "The couch. Yes, the couch."

Holding her gaze, he lifted her up. "I need to be inside you." He sank her down onto him, and a grumble erupted in his throat.

She clutched at his shoulders and moaned, welcoming the way he filled her so perfectly.

"How about right here?"

She wrapped her legs around him and opened her mouth to tell him he could have her wherever he wanted her, but her words dissolved into a cry of ecstasy as he pounded himself inside her.

He gripped her hips, angling himself deeper, kissing her wildly, until she stiffened with another orgasm and he let himself go.

She clung to him, shuddering, as their gasps for air filled the room.

"That was really..."

"Fast."

"Intense."

"We didn't make it to the bed...or the couch."

She shook her head. "Not quite, but I'm not complaining."

He grinned.

She stared into his eyes as she caressed his cheek, well aware that he was holding himself so he stayed nestled inside her. "We weren't exactly responsible."

"No, not exactly."

"I'm on the pill."

"I know. I saw yesterday when I was getting your medication."

"I'm always safe. Condoms. I have some in my nightstand drawer."

"I'm big on protection. Always use it." He glanced down at their current situation. "There's a first time for everything."

She smiled.

He smiled back before it faded and he rested his forehead against hers, sliding his fingers through her hair. "What are we doing, Bella?"

Hadn't she asked him that just the other day? "I don't know. Do you regret this?"

"No." He kissed her, cupping her cheeks and gliding his tongue over hers tenderly. "Not at all."

Her heart stuttered. "How do you feel about going upstairs?"

He pulled himself free of her. "I think I like the idea of doing this horizontal."

She nodded, staring into his eyes as he lifted her in his arms, much like he had last night, but tonight everything was wonderfully different.

Reed carried Bella upstairs, smiling when she let loose a long satisfied sigh and rested her head on his shoulder. "Oh, yeah?" he asked.

"Mmm," she said, snuggling closer. "I was just thinking about how happy I am that it's sprinkler season again."

He laughed. "That played a pretty integral part in the way things turned out tonight, huh?"

She sighed again and nodded. "I'll never think of that click and hiss in quite the same way." Grinning as he chuckled, she pulled his mouth to hers, kissing him, making that little sound in her throat that drove him crazy.

He stopped in the hallway, taking them both deeper into the kiss, hungry for her taste, eager to touch her all over again. This wasn't supposed to be happening. He wasn't supposed to feel this way about Nicoli Caparelli's daughter. In less than a month's time, he'd managed to break every single rule of a deep cover operation. Tonight's infraction was considered the worst of the worst—and he didn't care. As he breathed in Bella's shampoo and felt her skin pressed to his, nothing else mattered.

"Take me to bed, Reed." She drew away enough to stare into his eyes. "I want you in my bed."

"I'm not going to argue with that." He walked to her room, pausing for her to switch on the dim overhead light, and set her on her feet by the bed. He let his hands trail down her body, looking his fill at the mostly naked woman he couldn't get enough of. "You're so damn beautiful."

She smiled. "You're not half-bad yourself, handsome."

"No." He cradled her face, wanting her to see he meant what he said. "Everything about you is beautiful, Bella. Everything."

Her eyes went soft as she leaned her cheek into his palm. "Thank you."

He kissed her again, needing her in a way he'd never needed anyone. "How do you feel about us ditching the rest of our clothes?"

She grinned. "I definitely think we should." She lifted his shirt over his head, and her smile vanished as her gaze wandered from the indented circular scar below his collarbone to the one on the right side of his waist. "Reed."

"Occupational hazards."

"Bullets," she whispered, gently stroking both of his healed wounds, then added a kiss to the ugly puckered crater inches away from his heart. "Your blown cover."

He closed his eyes, absorbing the warmth of her tender gesture. "He was a bad shot."

"Good enough to hurt you." She pressed her lips to his marred skin again, then to his neck and chin as the pads of her fingers wandered over his body.

He steamed out a long breath as he palmed her breasts through silky fabric, watching her nipples respond to his featherlight teasing.

"Mmm." She snagged her lip with her teeth.

He held her gaze, tracing her firm, sensitive peaks, then reached around to work the clasp free and let her bra join his shirt on the floor. "God, Bella," he whispered, bringing his mouth to her breast.

She brushed her fingers through his hair and moaned.

"You taste so good," he said, giving her other breast equal attention, circling his tongue around her nipple and gently tugging.

She sighed, trailing her hands up and down his back.

He eased her onto the bed, kissing a trail down her stomach and hips, making goose bumps appear as he explored her soft skin the way he should have done the first time around.

"That feels good."

"Good." He lay on his side next to her and slid his fingers down her thigh and back up, touching her the way he'd yearned to for weeks, making her arch and moan. Dipping into her wet warmth, he pushed deeper, playing her until her muscles clenched and shuddered. He kissed her, continuing his work, knowing she was close by the way her hips jerked with his movements.

"Reed," she gasped, staring into his eyes. "Reed."

He kept his pace steady, drawing out her pleasure, watching her eyes go blind as she fell over the edge.

Her cry was quiet, stunned—sexy as hell.

He took her up again, fast, relentlessly, finding a primal satisfaction in her husky scream.

"No more. No more," she begged, breathless and flushed, squeezing his hand with her firm thighs. "Your turn. It's your turn. Let's take off your pants."

He fought his damp jeans and boxers down his legs.

"Much better." She gripped him in her hand, and he sucked in a breath through his teeth as she stroked him.

The teasing was torture. He had to have her right now. "Come here." He pulled her against him and rolled, pressing her into the mattress. "How's this?"

She smiled. "Good."

"I'm thinking we should go for great."

"I'm all for great."

He grinned and kissed her, sliding inside her, their twin gasps filling the air. Clasping her fingers, he pushed their hands up and under the pillows as they moved together, her hips rocking in time with his lazy thrusts, until her breathing grew unsteady. She urged him to move faster, but this time he was in no hurry.

"Reed. Please."

"Are you ready?"

"Yes," she choked out. "Yes."

He picked up his pace, kissing her deeply as he took them both over, swallowing her moans as her fingers clutched at his. He rested his head in the crook of her neck, inhaling her high-end perfume as he fought for his breath.

She stroked her hands along his sides. "You said we were going for great, but I kinda think we made it to fantastic."

He lifted his head, grinning. "They're both acceptable adjectives."

She laughed. "And to think I was looking forward to Malcoms tonight. Who knew I should have been looking forward to this?" Wiggling her eyebrows, she nipped at his ear.

He smiled, twisting a long lock of her hair around his finger. "We certainly changed things."

"Is that a problem?"

He stared into her eyes—Nicoli's eyes—and thought of Joey, of what he was going to have to do to make this entire situation right. "Not for me."

"Good." She brushed her fingers through his hair, then moved to trace his ears. "Why did you walk out on me tonight?"

He sighed and kissed her shoulder. "Because I'm an idiot."

She shook her head. "No, you're not." She pulled his hand to her lips and kissed his knuckles. "You're not, but why did you go?"

He sighed again, trying to figure out what in the hell he was supposed to say. He couldn't exactly tell her he'd walked away because his partner wouldn't understand or that closing the door in her face had been his last-ditch effort at pretending he wasn't crazy about her. How could he possibly share with her that the whole reason this thing had started in the first place was that he needed to get to her father? "A lot of reasons."

She frowned. "Oh."

"But none of them matter more than this—lying right here with you."

She smiled, blinking as her baby browns grew dewy. "Aww."

He loved the way he could read her emotions just by looking in her eyes. "When I moved to LA, my goal was to focus on me for a while and get my head screwed on straight. I was pretty messed up after the investigation fell apart. I was never looking for this, Bella. When I met you—I didn't expect things to happen this way."

"I like that we're here. That we were friends first before we took this step."

"Me too." He kissed her forehead, then her temples, and moved until they were facing each other on their sides.

"Are you going to sleep over?"

"I want to, but tomorrow's an early day." And he had something he needed to take care of before things went any further. "We could camp out tomorrow, though."

"Sounds good. We'll get dinner."

"Dinner with a side of Bella." He nipped at her neck and growled. "That's quite an offer."

She chuckled. "It'll have to be a little later, though. I have two clients coming in for makeup appointments since I missed yesterday. Luckily, one will be in and out in fifteen minutes."

"That's fine. I'll have some time to get my workout in."

"You do that, Stud." Smiling mischievously, she slid her hand down his chiseled abs and veered off to the wound above his hip. "I'm glad you're back in high school again instead of doing deep cover."

He smiled, but he didn't want to talk about this—not when he was still in the game. "You know, we never got around to sandwiches."

"We should eat."

"And then I need to get home."

"Okay."

Neither of them moved.

Bella let her hand wander lower. "We could have sex again, eat after, and *then* you could go home."

"I like the way you think."

They laughed and rolled across the bed.

Reed let himself into his house sometime after two. Sandwiches hadn't turned out to be much of a priority for him and Bella after all. He smiled, thinking of how they'd gotten out of bed several times to make their dinner, only to fall back to the mattress and exhaust one another all over again. It had been damn tempting to shut off her bedroom light and snuggle up for the last few hours of the morning, but he'd pulled on his cold, damp clothes and headed next door instead, settling for the torturous smell of Bella on his skin and her taste on his tongue rather than the soft, warm woman tucked under her covers.

Yawning, he switched on the small lamp on the desk and glanced at his computer, feeling the tension tightening his shoulders as he picked up his cell phone. The simple pleasure of being wrapped up in Bella vanished as reality rushed back to greet him. He wasted no time dialing despite the early hour: five a.m. in New York, so Joey wouldn't be able to bitch all that much.

"Hello?"

"It's Reed," he said, rubbing at the back of his neck.

"What the hell? We've gotta talk about this calling in the fucking early morning hours—"

"I'm out," he interrupted, needing to get this over with.

"*What*?"

"I said I'm out. I'm not doing this to Bella anymore."

"You gotta be *fuckin'* kidding me. What about Nicoli Caparelli?"

Reed began pacing, the gritty edge of Joey's shocked disappointment not lost on him. He'd expected no less, but actually hearing it ate at him as much as lying to Bella did. "I don't care."

"What about Bensonhurst or the fact that Alfeo will be out running the streets again in just a few weeks?"

"That's not my problem anymore. That's why I gave up my badge."

The line hung heavy with silence.

"You're sleeping with her. You're literally in bed with the mafia."

Rage flooded his veins at the invasion of his privacy. What he had with Bella was supposed to be his alone—just theirs. "That's none of your business."

"It is when your dick's doing your thinking. What the hell happened to Mad Dog McKinley?"

"He died the night we almost did."

Joey laughed humorlessly in his ear.

"I don't want to be that guy anymore, Joe." He sat down, wearily resting his forehead in his hand. "I want what I have here. I want her. For the first time in my life, I'm doing what's right for me. Bella's right for me. I'm not interested in living for revenge or to avenge."

"Well, I guess that's that. She still goin' to Bensonhurst?"

He felt his nostrils flare as he clenched his jaw. "That's the plan. Luisa's her friend."

"Right. You go ahead and keep telling yourself that."

"Damn it, Joe, I want you to be happy for me."

"You know I want nothing less than your happiness. You're like my brother."

"So let's leave it there."

"This isn't about me, boss. It's about you. Are *you* gonna be able to be happy knowing what you know? You don't have her whole story—not even close. I know you, Reed, better than anyone else on this fuckin' planet. You're gonna wonder about her and her father. You'll try to let it go, but you'll pick at it until it festers and eats you up. I don't see how that won't come between the two of you."

He gained his feet, wanting to deny everything Joey was saying. "She didn't kill my family."

"No, but her family did. You're walking dangerous ground. Take a few days and think on what I've said, then give me a call." He hung up.

"Damn it." He threw down his phone, afraid that Joey was right. No matter how much he cared for Bella or how happy he was when they were together, the past and unanswered questions would always be in his face.

☙ Chapter Eighteen ❧

BELLA GLANCED AT THE CLOCK AS SHE PACKAGED UP THE LEFTover chicken, wild rice, and roasted veggies she'd made for herself and Dad's simple dinner. It was almost eight thirty, more than time for her to be heading home. "Are you sure you're going to be okay while I'm gone?"

Dad looked up from his spot at the small kitchen table, dressed in sweatpants and an old grease-stained T-shirt. "Bella, I'm a grown man."

But he was sick—stage four, the oncologist from the children's hospital had confirmed for her today. It had been a week since Dad's news shattered her world. For days, she'd been waiting with a sense of false hope while Dr. Jahensen went through Dad's files. Finally, on her way up to Reseda this evening, he'd gotten back to her with his opinion. Now that the diagnosis was undeniable, she was struggling with the idea that their only course of action was keeping Dad comfortable and enjoying the time they had left together.

On Sunday, she'd taken a few hours to come visit him while Reed went to the gym. Tonight, she was doing the same. Every time she knocked on Dad's door, she couldn't help but notice that he seemed a little thinner and weaker. She glanced at the vegetable juice in his hand instead of the soda—a step in the right direction, but her small interventions were hardly enough.

Dr. Jahensen had lifted her spirits some when he told her Dad's labs looked great considering his prognosis. It was highly unlikely he would get better, but he was certainly holding his own. She had every intention of keeping Dad as healthy as possible for as long as she could. "I know. I just don't like leaving you when you need me the most."

"You'll be gone for four days. Your business is important. I'm not going to stand in the way of your career."

"I'm not traveling for my business," she said as she washed the last of the dishes in hot, soapy water. "I'm helping a friend with hers."

"New Hampshire's not that far away."

She sent him a wry smile, drying the glass bowl and putting it in the cupboard. "It's across the country. And I'm going to New York."

Dad moved to take a sip of his beet, carrot, and kale concoction and set it back down. "I thought you said New Hampshire."

"Nope. My friend lives in Brooklyn."

Dad stood in a rush. "Brooklyn?"

Bella stared at him, blinking her surprise. "Yeah, Dad. Brooklyn. We talked about this on Sunday."

"You never said anything about Brooklyn. I don't want you going."

She gaped, shaking her head, trying to figure out what in the world was going on. "What?"

"You should stay here."

She frowned, growing afraid that something hadn't gone quite as well as he'd let on at his latest checkup earlier this afternoon. "I thought you said you were feeling fine."

"I am. I just—the city can be a dangerous place."

Her shoulders relaxed a little. "Dad, I live in Los Angeles and spent years in Vegas before that. I know how to take care of myself."

"Brooklyn is different."

She raised her eyebrow as she got back to work, wringing out the dishcloth and wiping the counters. "You're an expert on Brooklyn?"

"I liked the idea of my daughter in New Hampshire—where there's trees and mountains—little towns and stuff. That's all."

"Well, maybe I'll get a chance to visit someday." She grabbed the Tupperware and put it in the fridge. "If you need me to stay because of your health, I will. But I'm going if you're just being an overprotective father."

He sat down again. "I just—I want you to call me every day."

"Of course." She walked over and kissed the top of his head. "I was planning on it anyway."

"You take care of yourself. Be careful. Keep to yourself—don't be telling people your life story. Less is more."

She laughed. "I don't typically talk about my past—mostly about work or Lucy. I'm going to help my friend, go to a grand opening party, and come home." She pulled a piece of paper from her purse. "I'm leaving this number with you. If you need anything, I want you to call him. Tell him you're my father and he'll give you a hand." She hesitated and handed over the sheet.

"Reed McKinley." Dad looked at her. "And who's Reed McKinley?"

She smiled sadly as the protective light came into his eyes. Was this what it would have been like if Dad had been around when she'd been a teenager? She'd debated long and hard when she wrote down Reed's number, but she couldn't leave without knowing Dad would have someone to contact if he needed help. There would be plenty of explaining to do when she got home, but it would be worth it to know Dad wouldn't be alone if there was another emergency. "He's my friend."

"Friend?"

"We've been dating, I guess."

"How do you not know if you're dating?"

Another small smile touched her lips, and she rolled her eyes at his third-degree. "He's my neighbor. We hang out a lot. Things sort of evolved from there."

"Is he good to you?"

She grinned as she thought of the last five days—since they changed everything: long walks on the beach, cozy candlelight dinners on her back porch, sexy evenings in bed where they drove each other crazy more than they slept. "He's very good to me."

"Is he the one?"

She swallowed, alarmed when her first instinct wasn't to dismiss the idea as ludicrous. "I don't know."

"You didn't say no."

She kissed him again. "I need to get home. My flight leaves early tomorrow. I'm glad you're drinking your juice."

He shrugged. "It's not too bad. I have more energy."

She beamed. "That's great. I want you to try to eat the food I've put away for you for the next few days."

"I'll see what I can do." He stood and pulled her close in a long hug. "You be careful, Isabella."

"I will." She held on to him. "I love you."

"I love you too. I want a call every day." He drew her away and held her gaze. "Every day."

"Promise," she said with a decisive nod.

"Go see this Reed McKinley."

"Call him if you need anything."

He grumbled his agreement.

"Bye, Daddy." She blew him a kiss at the door and left, content that

Dad was hanging in there and that she was going home to Reed.

She got behind the wheel and drove toward the 405, nibbling her lip and worrying some, knowing he would be waiting for her by now. She and Reed were officially spending every free moment they had together. This would be the second time in less than a week that she would walk through her front door stinking like cigarette smoke—like the day he'd helped her shower and change.

On Sunday, he'd given her a hug and asked her where she'd been. She'd simply told him she'd had some things to do. Reed wasn't a fool. She saw the questions in his eyes, but he hadn't asked her anything further. Eventually, she would have to tell him her story, but she didn't have to do it yet.

Not once since her ninth grade year had she voluntarily offered up any information about her family. How did one broach such a conversation? *Reed, let's sit down so I can tell you about my father who abandoned me days before my fifth birthday and my prostitute mother who was more interested in the men who paid her for sex and gave her expensive gifts than she'd been in raising her daughter.*

Groaning, she pressed her hand to her stomach as the thought made her sick. Everything was going so well between them. She was fairly sure her confession wouldn't change things...but she couldn't be certain. Sooner rather than later, she was going to have to spill the beans, but for now she just wanted to pretend she was Isabella Colby from any other normal family. Nothing would be quite the same once he knew the truth.

Reed lay on Bella's couch, watching TV and petting Lucy while she rested her head on the cushion from her spot close by on the floor. He flipped through the channels and glanced at his watch—like he'd done several times over the last few minutes. It was getting late for a weeknight, especially when Bella had a plane to catch first thing in the morning. Flat tires and being stranded somewhere on the interstate had crossed his mind more than once over the last little while, but Bella was a capable, independent woman, and she carried a cell phone. He wasn't about to turn into that guy who had to know where his girlfriend was at every minute of the day, particularly when his very responsible girlfriend had covered all her bases by telling him she was going to be home much later than usual.

Now, if she didn't call in the next half hour or so, he might think about sending off a text to make sure she was okay. He was an ex-cop, after all. He couldn't just ignore violent crime facts and statistics, specifically those pertaining to beautiful women out on their own well after dark. Bella didn't even have her dog with her... The tension coiling in the back of his neck vanished, and he let loose a long breath when he heard her car pull in the driveway. "Sounds like your mom's home."

Lucy was already on her feet and her tail wagging as she hurried to the door.

Moments later, Bella stepped inside and grinned. "There's my girl." She set her purse on the entryway table and crouched down, hugging and giving Lucy a kiss as her puppy's tail moved double-time. "Did you have fun with Reed?" She gained her feet and looked at him, smiling. "Hi, handsome."

Damn, she took his breath away. She'd added curls to her hair this morning. And no one wore a sundress and high-heeled sandals quite like Isabella Colby. He sat up and returned her smile. "Hi. You got some of that for me?" Winking, he opened his arms, welcoming her to come join him.

"I do, but let me go shower first." She flashed him one of her best grins, but he didn't miss the way her gaze momentarily left his as she swiped her hair behind her ear. "It'll just take a second."

"There's no rush." He stayed where he was, scrubbing his hands over his face as she hurried upstairs. Why did he already know she was keeping a wide berth because she reeked of cigarette smoke? Currently, he couldn't smell her, but he had little doubt that she would stink if he pulled her close or that she'd been in Reseda for the last several hours. As soon as she'd rolled over in his arms this morning and mentioned she would be late tonight, he'd known where she would go. She'd avoided his gaze then too.

It was unfortunate he couldn't pretend that something about this entire situation wasn't quite on the up and up. It was a damn shame he was a trained fucking lie detector, because he wanted nothing more than to move on with Bella in ignorant bliss instead of questioning why she went to visit her father hours before her plane left for New York. And now he sounded like Joey. "Son of a bitch," he said wearily, rubbing at his jaw again.

The last five days had been perfect, everything he never thought he could have or knew he wanted. Bella was warm and sweet—even more so now that they were closely connected. He'd been lost in her, savoring the gift of true intimacy, reveling in the fact that Bella had stripped herself bare in every way that mattered. If only he could give Bella back everything she was giving him, but he was afraid he would never be able to let his guard down—at least, not when she felt the need to keep her father a secret. Why *would* she keep Vincent Pescoe a secret if there was nothing to hide?

"You're gonna wonder about her and her father. You'll try to let it go, but you'll pick at it until it festers and eats you up."

He shut off the TV and stood, trying to forget his last conversation with Joey. Even as he climbed the steps and caught the nasty scent of stale smoke lingering in the hallway, he didn't regret choosing Bella over the investigation. They had a mess on their hands, whether she knew it or not, but he was willing to fight his way through the doubts and deceptions to keep her in his life. He wanted her to tell him about Vincent—needed her to, and eventually she would. Maybe she just needed more time.

Sighing, he followed the sound of the shower running in the bathroom and pulled off his clothes, stepping into the spray and wrapping his arms around Bella as she washed shampoo from her hair.

Gasping, she whirled. "You scared me."

"Sorry."

She rinsed her hair completely and kissed him. "That's okay." She pressed her lips to his again and locked her arms around the back of his neck. "How was your day?"

"Good. Pretty much the same as yesterday, although there was a food fight in second lunch, so that caused quite a stir. And Sadie's friend Marnie might be sleeping with Tommy, but the girls aren't sure. They were hoping to find out in a text after school today."

She grinned. "Sounds pretty intense."

He groaned out a laugh as he looked to the ceiling. "I liked high school once upon a time, but I can't say I'm glad to be back. It's different from when we were kids—or when I was, anyway. I've got a few years on you."

"Not that many."

"Six."

"Not that many," she repeated, pulling herself closer and letting her breasts rest against his chest. "You were a jock, huh?"

He frowned as his hands automatically started sliding up her waist, loving the way her wet skin felt beneath his palms. "How'd you know?"

"I can tell. What was your sport?"

"Football and baseball."

She raised her brow. "Two?"

"I'm an overachiever."

"Oh, don't I know it." She nipped his chin as she purred in her throat.

He grinned. This right here was worth everything—sharing moments exactly like this.

"Were you good?"

"All things considered, yeah. I was offered a full ride to any Big Ten school I wanted for football."

She blinked. "Really? And which did you choose?"

"None of them. I went to New York instead."

"To protect and serve."

"Something like that. It was easier to get into the police academy and some of the other law enforcement stuff I wanted to be a part of if I went to school in the city."

"You're an honorable man."

"I'm just me."

"And you're all mine." She kissed him.

He grabbed the soap and reached around her, washing her back as she stared into his eyes. "How was *your* day?"

"Good. Busy. I can't wait to get back from New York so I can resume some sort of normal schedule at work."

He moved his hands to her front, sliding slippery fingers over smooth, perky peaks. "How was tonight?"

She snagged her bottom lip with her teeth and made that little whimper in her throat that begged him to eat her alive. "Fine."

He teased her nipples as they pebbled against his skin. "Did you have late clients?"

"No." Her gaze left his as she dropped her arms from around him and turned, reaching for the bottle of conditioner.

He could have Bella right now. All he had to do was shut his mouth and slip inside her wet heat. Hot, steamy shower sex was so much simpler, but he was choosing a different path tonight. "So, where'd you go?"

She worked the cream rinse through her hair. "I had dinner with my dad."

He waited for her to say something more or turn and face him again, but she did neither. "That's nice."

"Yeah."

"You don't talk about him much."

She jerked her shoulders. "What do you want me to say?"

"I don't know. He's your dad." He captured her by the wrist and made her face him as his frustration grew. "What does he do for work?"

"He was a mechanic. Now he's retired." She rinsed her hair, holding his gaze as the water sluiced down long inches of silky black and the tension grew between them. "Did you eat?"

He swallowed, absorbing the swift disappointment. She wasn't going to tell him anything. "Yeah. I made a sandwich."

"Do you want anything else?"

Just answers. He shook his head. "No, I'm good."

Something moved through her eyes—apology, regret. He couldn't be sure as she wrapped her arms around his waist, holding on tight. "I'm going to miss you this weekend."

Clenching his jaw, he returned her embrace, closing his eyes as he settled his cheek on top of her head. "I'll miss you too." And he would.

"If you let me finish up in here, we could light some candles and open a bottle of wine." She drew away, looking into his eyes. "I kind of feel like ravishing you."

"Really?"

"I can't seem to get enough of you." She gained her tiptoes and tugged on his ear with her lips, then her teeth. "I was thinking about riding you," she whispered. "Then maybe you could ride me afterward."

He kissed her hungrily. "How about we just get started in here?"

"Tempting." She stroked his erection. "But I want you in my bed. I love taking advantage of you on silk sheets."

He debated for about thirty seconds whether he was going to let her have her way with him or cave to instant gratification and take her against the shower wall. "I'll get out and light a few candles."

"Give me five minutes and I'll be in to join you." She smiled at him.

He smiled back, marveling that the sexy tigress with the sly eyes was his. "Try and make it four."

She grinned. "Four it is."

He stepped from the tub, and his smile faded as he breathed in the misty scent of cigarette smoke and secrets. Grabbing a towel, he wrapped it around his waist and left the bathroom, assuring himself that he was fine with the way things were.

☙ Chapter Nineteen ❧

PLANES RUMBLED OVERHEAD AS REED AND BELLA WALKED through the early morning madness at LAX. He wheeled her carry-on behind him and tightened his grip on her hand as they weaved their way among harried travelers in a rush to make it to their destinations. Even at six thirty a.m., Los Angeles International was a zoo.

A woman struggling with two cranky toddlers knocked into Bella as she passed by. Then a man easily twice Bella's size plowed into her, sending her into Reed's side.

"Whoa, take it easy, buddy." Reed frowned, wrapping a protective arm around her.

"Sorry about that," the guy called over his shoulder and continued down the long hall.

"Geez." She chuckled as she met Reed's gaze.

"Luckily, this is your stop right here." He guided her out of the worst of the traffic as they approached the terminal checkpoint.

"Thank goodness." She set her laptop case on her luggage. "I was starting to fear for my life."

"You don't have to do that, baby," he joked, playing Mr. Cool as he pulled her against him and laced his fingers behind her waist. "Consider me your personal bodyguard."

"My hero." Batting her lashes, she mirrored his loose hold, dressed as casually as he'd ever seen her in snug capri jeans and a simple white sleeveless top. She'd tossed her hair into a ponytail and shoved her feet into her Vans sneakers instead of her typical high heels, but she was no less stunning in her laid-back attire.

He chuckled and nuzzled his face next to her ear. "You always smell so good."

She wrapped her arms tighter around him. "You always smell like you."

He lifted his head, staring into her eyes. "I hope that's a good thing."

She nodded and kissed him. "It's perfect."

He let his hands wander up and down her sides, always eager to feel her under his palms. "You're going to call me when you land?"

"Mmm. As soon as we start taxiing to the gate."

"Maybe you can get a little rest—ask for a pillow and catch a few Z's." He touched a gentle finger to the dark circles she hadn't been able to erase completely with the concealer stuff she used.

She grinned. "I'm starting to think a couple days apart might not be such a bad thing. We can actually get some sleep."

Silky sheet sex had turned into floor sex. Then they'd ended up back in the shower before they fell asleep an hour before the alarm went off. He smiled and hooked his thumbs through her belt loops. "Today's going to suck, but every second of last night and this morning was totally worth it."

"Agreed." She winked and nipped at his chin.

He glanced at the departing flights screen. "You should get going." But he didn't want her to. He wanted her to stay right here in LA, where he wouldn't have to worry about her...or wonder.

"I have an hour until I need to board."

His gaze wandered toward the line, noting that it wasn't too bad. "I want you to be careful. Stay off the subways at night."

She slid her hands up his arms, stopping and resting them on his triceps. "I will."

"I want you to have fun."

"I'll do that too."

"Make sure Luisa's watching out for you."

She shook her head. "I can watch out for myself."

"I know you can."

Sighing, she smiled. "I'm going to miss you, but I'm really looking forward to helping her. It's exciting to think of her dreams coming true. And I get to be there to see it—to be a part of her big moment. She's worked so hard for this."

Why was it so easy to believe her? Why did this trip seem like nothing more than a friend helping a friend? He needed answers. Eventually, Bella was going to have to tell him about her father, but for now he wanted to focus on Reed and Bella the couple—on how good they were together. On how right everything felt for the first time in his life. "Sometimes I think you're too good for me."

She shook her head again. "I think we make each other happy."

He rested his forehead against hers. "I'll pick you up on Sunday."

She nodded, her soft skin rubbing against his. "You and Lucy will be all right?"

"She's going to hang out at the Cooke Compound for a few hours while I'm at work. Then we're going to go chase some seagulls, grab an ice cream or two—"

"No people food. "

He rolled his eyes. "So we'll just chase seagulls."

She laughed.

He glanced at the departure screen again. "You should go, Bella."

"Okay." She let herself settle against him.

He tightened his hold around her, savoring the feeling of her cheek pressed to his chest the way he liked best. "Let me know when you get in."

"I will." She drew away.

"See you in a few days."

"See you." She kissed him and gave him another long hug. "Bye."

"Bye." He watched her walk toward the back of the line, certain he was the biggest of fools for already missing her. "Bella?"

She turned.

He closed the distance between them and captured her cheeks, kissing her deep and sliding his tongue against hers.

She moaned.

He eased away, touching his lips to the tip of her nose, then her temples. "See you."

She nodded and got on with the process of handing over her ID and ticket. Moments later, she stood on her tiptoes, waving to him through the new rows of people.

He smiled and waved back, watching her turn and disappear among the chaos of travelers getting their items ready to be x-rayed. Sighing, he started back the way he'd come. Everything was going to be fine. Bella was going to go see her friend in Brooklyn, and he was going home to Lucy. In three days, he would pick up his girl, and they would get back to their lives.

Bella stood among the huge crowds at Luisa's grand opening event, slightly overwhelmed by the insane turnout. Body Bliss was one hopping place—everything she'd hoped it would be for her friend. Platters of classic Italian hors d'oeuvres were constantly being replenished as she and Luisa filled out dozens of gift certificates for assorted laser treatment options, massage therapy sessions, and microdermabrasion/chemical peel packages. The new Bensonhurst location was off to one heck of a start.

"Rumor has it you're in need of a water."

Bella glanced up from her spot behind the desk, smiling at the older man she knew to be Luisa's father. "I am." She accepted the plastic bottle and took a long sip, subtly adjusting the hem of her above-the-knee strapless white dress, wishing she'd chosen something more comfortable to wear, like yoga pants and a workout top. She was certainly getting her exercise today. "Thank you."

Mr. Asante's gaze tracked around the full room. "I should be thanking you. Luisa tells me all of this wouldn't have been possible without the support of her good friend from Los Angeles."

Bella's smile returned, charmed by his strong Brooklyn accent and the kindness in his eyes. There was something about Luisa's father that reminded her so much of her own. "I'm happy I could be here to help."

"In my experience, loyalty's a rare trait. Luisa's lucky to have found it in you."

"I love her very much."

He nodded. "Do you like a good joke?"

She blinked at his rapid change of subject and grinned, sensing a mischievous streak. "I'm always up for a laugh."

"Ugh, not the jokes, Pops," Luisa groaned as she hurried over, rolling her brown eyes and kissing her father's cheek. She was dressed similarly in a white sundress of her own.

"What? Bella's never heard this one before. I can guarantee it."

Luisa groaned a second time. "Let me be as good a friend to Bella as she's been to me. Spare her your idea of comic relief." Luisa smiled her pretty smile as she glanced from her dad to Bella—a petite version of the man who had given her life.

"A daughter should respect her father." He tapped Luisa's nose with one of his big, beefy fingers.

"I do, Pops." She hooked her arm around Bella's shoulders. "I'm taking Bella away for a few minutes to introduce her around, since she's been a slave behind the desk for most of the afternoon."

"Wait just a minute now." Mr. Asante took Bella's hand and

brought it to his lips. "It was nice to meet you."

She grinned. "You too, Mr. Asante."

"That's Dino."

"Dino," she said with a nod.

"Have fun, Bella."

"Thank you."

Luisa huffed out a breath as she pulled Bella into the crowd. "My pops is such a flirt."

"He's very sweet."

"That's one word for—"

"Luisa." A handsome man with an olive complexion and solid build signaled her over with a wave of his hand.

"Oh, Matty's here. Come on over and meet him."

Bella sized up Luisa's pal as another one of her many successful friends—expensive golf shirt, designer slacks, thousand-dollar Italian shoes. "Sure."

Luisa zigzagged them through the throngs.

"Tell me about these package deals you have here." He tapped his finger on one of the flyers Bella had copied just this morning, before the madness began.

"I want you to meet someone first. Matty, this is my good friend Bella."

Matty smiled, flashing his straight white teeth as he held out his hand. "It's good to meet you, Bella."

She accepted his greeting, surprised to find herself preferring Reed's calloused palms over Matty's smooth grip. Not all that long ago, this was the type of man who would have made her heart go pitty-pat. "And you."

He frowned. "You're not from around here. I don't hear any New York in your voice."

She grinned. "I'm from Los Angeles."

"Bella and I went to school together in Phoenix."

"You're in the beauty profession too?"

"I am."

"Luisa," someone shouted from across the room.

"Oh, shoot." Luisa sighed. "I better go see what's what."

"Bella can help me with this menu." Matty moved closer to her side. "I want to pick something out for my girl over there." He gestured to the bleach blonde with fake boobs wearing too much makeup and an overly tight shirt.

"She's lovely," Bella fibbed.

"What would be a good surprise for her?"

They were both jostled by a group of kids running around.

"It's crowded in here. How 'bout we go outside, and you can help me pick out somethin' nice for my girl."

"I would love to." Grabbing a pen with the Body Bliss logo printed on it, she stepped out onto the sidewalk with him and sat down at one of the tables belonging to the restaurant next door.

"Hey, Matty," someone called from down the block, sending him a wave.

Matty waved back, then at another man farther down the street.

"We're in the city, yet everyone knows you."

He shrugged. "You grow up around here, people know who you are."

She smiled, liking the idea of something so quaint despite the urban setting. "So, are you looking for a beauty enhancement treatment or more of a pampering session for your girlfriend?"

He shrugged again. "Beats the hell out of me."

She laughed. "Luisa offers a great variety of services. My suggestion would be to go with something more along the lines of a pampering session. If..." She waited for Matty to supply his lover's name.

"Carissa."

"If Carissa enjoys herself, she'll probably inquire about the other options that interest her."

Matty nodded, tipping back in his chair and lacing his hands behind his head. "Sounds like a good plan."

"What does Carissa do for a living?"

"She works for an advertising firm in Manhattan."

"Stressful."

"I guess it can be."

"What about this hot stone facial followed by a firming vitamin C mask? It's very relaxing. Luisa includes a hand, neck, and shoulder massage as well, which is a great way to finish a treatment."

He sat up, reading what Bella pointed at. "Sure."

"Great." She circled the selection with the pen. "I'll also suggest the back facial. Basically, she'll be in heaven for close to two hours." She added an asterisk by the follow-up treatment.

"That's what you recommend, huh?" He held her gaze, scrutinizing.

"I do," she assured with a decisive nod. "My own clients love both options."

"I'll take your word for it, Beautiful Bella from Los Angeles, especially since you're Italian. That counts around here in Bensonhurst."

She sat up straighter, tucking loose strands of hair that had long since fallen free from her updo behind her ear. "I'm afraid I'm not Italian."

He frowned. "You look like you got Italian in your blood to me."

She shook her head apologetically. "Both of my parents are of English descent, but that doesn't mean something didn't sneak in somewhere."

He laughed, a big bold sound as he threw his head back. "We'll go with that." He hooked his arm around her shoulders, affectionately tugging her against him. "Italian that snuck in there somewhere. You're all right, Beautiful Bella."

"Thank you." Chuckling, she slid him the piece of paper. "This is for you. If you tell Luisa to set you up with a gift card, Carissa will thank you a million times over. And Luisa too."

He nodded, folding it and tucking it in his pocket. "Should we go back into the chaos?"

"Sure."

They stood and started toward the front door as Dino came out, popping a fat cigar in his mouth.

"Jesus, Dino." Matty shook his head with a pained look on his face. "Why you gonna light that thing up?"

"I'm going to go sit on over there at the table and give it a smoke—enjoy a little peace and quiet."

"Looks like a dick." Matty shook his head again. "Never understood why anyone would want to smoke something that looks like a dick."

Bella struggled to suppress a laugh when Dino swore and tossed the cigar in the trash as she and Matty walked back inside.

"There you are." Luisa took Bella's hand. "You wanna help me behind the desk again? I'm getting swamped."

"Absolutely. Success looks good on you, friend."

"You're a lifesaver." Luisa kissed her cheek. "How about you give up your space in LA and come work with me?"

She smiled. "Aren't you sweet to offer."

"I'm only half joking."

Bella thought of Reed and her life in Los Angeles. "I would miss my palm trees."

"I guess I'll have to use you while I've got you." She pulled on her hand. "Come on."

Reed sang along with the music playing on Bella's stereo, absently mumbling the lyrics more than enunciating the words as he focused on the task at hand. He grabbed the last sack of groceries off the floor and snagged a box from the environmentally friendly shopping bag, setting the package on the counter when he realized it was tampons—not food.

He'd spotted the item on the small list Bella had running on the fridge and took a chance with the selection, fairly certain this was the brand he'd seen under the sink upstairs. The whole absorbency and flow thing had thrown him for a bit of a loop, so he'd settled for the variety pack, figuring Bella would end up with what she needed one way or the other. Typically he was happy to leave lady business to the ladies. He'd never bought a woman feminine products before. Apparently, there truly was a first time for everything.

He'd guessed on a couple of other items too—creamy peanut butter versus crunchy and organic low-fat yogurt instead of regular. Bella didn't seem like the crunchy peanut butter type, and in his mind it was logical to go with the organic option until he knew otherwise, but he was starting to learn what she liked.

He picked up the cans of black beans and opened the cupboard, staring at his protein powder sitting next to Bella's cereal, then glanced over his shoulder at the basket of dirty clothes in need of a wash—a combination of his stuff and hers. For the most part, he and Bella were cohabitating. Occasionally, he went back to his place for another outfit, but more and more of his things were becoming mixed up with hers. The sudden realization that he was pretty much living with a woman should have freaked him the hell out, but as he looked at Lucy snoring on her dog bed in the late afternoon light, he smiled.

A year ago, he never would have fathomed himself here. For so long, he'd been ruled by anger and his need for revenge. Then Bella walked into his life and changed everything, lighting up his entire world. For now, all of this was his: the sweet, gorgeous woman, the adorable dog, a cozy home, friends, and a job that wasn't half-bad. It was still early stages where he and Bella were concerned, but he was pretty sure he was planning on keeping her—keeping it all.

Not even New York was turning out to be a problem. Admittedly, he'd had a few bad moments when he feared her trip might somehow drive a wedge between them, but everything was working out fine. Bella was helping Luisa; it truly was that simple.

He grinned, thinking of how she spared him no detail of her adventure every time she called. Thursday and Friday night, they'd talked for a good two or three hours, sharing the events of their days. And this morning when his phone rang at four, she'd bubbled with nervous excitement, chattering on about this afternoon's big event. He imagined he should have been annoyed with the interruption to his sleep, but he'd been too happy to hear her voice to care. Ideally, she would be checking in again soon. And tomorrow she was coming home.

His phone on the counter dinged with a text, and he chuckled. "How about that? I bet this is her right now."

Lucy opened one eye and closed it again.

His smile disappeared when he glanced at the screen. Joey. They hadn't spoken in over a week. Reed had never bothered to call his ex-partner back after their disagreement. He wasn't entirely interested in what Joey had to say, particularly where Bella was concerned.

Take a look at your email when you have a chance.

Clenching his jaw, he steamed out a long breath, mostly certain he didn't want to. "Shit," he muttered, opening his laptop and shoving his hand through his hair as he turned away. "Shit," he repeated and whirled back, knowing it was better just to get it over with. He clicked over to his inbox and selected the message from Joey, opening the attachments.

He swallowed, staring at Bella sitting at a sidewalk table with Mateo "Matty" Caparelli, grinning at him as he grinned at her. His heart pounded as his gaze trailed over her hair pulled back in a sexy twist and the flirty white dress Reed had watched her pack three nights ago, trying to believe what he was seeing.

Clicking on the next series of images, he watched a sickening scene play out through Joey's rapid-shot photography: Bella writing something down as she spoke with her cousin, laughing and smiling the entire time before she handed off a piece of paper for Matty to shove in his pocket.

"Damn you," he mumbled, his stomach roiling as he stopped on the last picture: Bella, Matty Caparelli, and Dino Asante all huddled up together outside Body Bliss's grand opening. There was no distress on her face; Bella seemed perfectly comfortable—totally at ease as she stood among ruthless killers. Just part of the family. And that's what made this all the viler: they *were* her family, and he'd fallen for it, deluding himself with the notion that none of it had mattered.

His phone rang, and he answered before the first note ended on Joey's obnoxious ringtone. "Yeah."

"Did you get it?"

"Yeah," he said again.

"She's been making calls to Reseda every day too—right before she calls you, she calls her dad. I'm sorry, man."

He wanted there to be another explanation. He needed for there to be, but the truth was staring him right in the face. "Got it." He hung up and slammed the laptop closed, his breath heaving as he looked from the laundry basket to the tampons on the counter, picking them up and chucking them across the room. "Fuck!" It was all a lie. The life he wanted so badly had never existed in the first place. "Fuck it all!"

Lucy rolled over and stood, whining as she gave a cautious wag of her tail.

"I'll be back later." He left Bella's dog staring after him as he grabbed his helmet and went outside, getting on his Ducati, needing a ride to clear his head.

He gunned it out of the neighborhood and started up the coast, trying to figure out what in the hell he was supposed to do next.

☙ Chapter Twenty ❧

BELLA SAT IN THE SMALL DINER SITUATED IN THE SAME PLAZA AS her hotel, listening to the deep rumble of massive jets taking off and descending for their arrival at JFK International. Early tomorrow morning, she would be on one of those planes, heading back to California. And she couldn't wait. It had been fun exploring New York City and seeing Luisa again, but all she wanted was to get home to Lucy and Reed. Knowing that they were waiting for her back at the condo made her smile as she calculated her waitress's tip for the grilled chicken salad she'd ordered for her evening meal.

She sighed her contentment as she signed her name to the credit card slip, then glanced at her phone, trying to decide whether she should cave and call Reed right now or wait twenty minutes until she was in her pajamas and snuggled up in her temporary bed. Now was definitely as good a time as any.

She stood from her booth, far more comfortable in the blouse, blue jeans, and heel combination she'd changed into after the party, and grabbed her purse, hooking it over her shoulder, city-style, as she started toward the exit. As she reached up to push open the door, she stopped, doing a double take when she spotted the bearded linebacker-sized man sitting at a corner table.

Their eyes met, and he smiled politely, sending her a quick nod as he looked back at his newspaper.

"Joey," she said quietly, certain the stranger tucked in the dimly lit space couldn't possibly be Reed's buddy, but she skirted her way around several tables, stopping in front of his. "Excuse me."

He looked up.

She grinned, positive that this guy was indeed Reed's former partner. "You're Joey, right?"

He frowned.

She shook her head, realizing he had to think she was some sort of stalker nut job. "I'm Bella Colby, Reed McKinley's girlfriend."

"Reed?"

She nodded. "I've seen your picture on his cell phone. You have the 'Sexy and I Know It' ringtone."

A smile lit up his surprisingly handsome face. "Well, whad'ya know." He held out his hand. "Bella, I'm Joey Holmes."

She laughed her delight as she shook his big hand. "Reed is never going to believe this. *I* can't believe this."

"You're tellin' me. Small world."

"It really is."

"How about a seat?" He gestured to the empty chair across from him.

"Are you sure I'm not interrupting?"

"Are you kidding? You're Reed's girl. Sit."

"Thank you." She made herself comfortable, setting her purse on the table.

"Can I buy you something to eat? Maybe get you something to drink?"

"Oh, no, thank you," she said, pressing her hand to her full stomach. "I just finished my dinner."

He leaned back in his seat, crossing his huge arms—a gesture so similar to one of Reed's, she found herself smiling again. "You Los Angeles bound?"

She nodded. "Tomorrow morning. How about you? Are you flying in or out?"

"In. I had some business to take care of out west. Thought I'd have a bite to eat before I try to get through all of the fuckin' traffic." He winced. "Sorry about that."

"That's fine." She touched his arm, wanting him to be at ease as they got to know each other. "I'm still shocked that this is really happening. I feel like I should call Reed right now. He's bound to think I made the whole thing up."

He chuckled. "You talk to him today?"

"Early this morning." She tucked her hair behind her ear and wrinkled her nose. "I kind of called him at four."

He sent her a grin. "Reed's called me *plenty* of times after midnight. We'll consider it karma. She always has a way of paying people back."

Bella laughed. "Yes, she does."

Joey sat further forward, lacing his fingers on the table. "So what brought you out this way—business or pleasure?"

"Both. I was helping my friend open her new medical spa over in Brooklyn—Body Bliss." She pulled out one of Luisa's business cards. "If you're ever down in the Bensonhurst area, you should check it out."

Joey took the card, tracing his thumb around the edges. "Body Bliss. Not sure that sounds like my kinda place."

She grinned. "You might be surprised. Luisa just hired an amazing massage therapist. She gave me a quick shoulder rub this afternoon." She rolled her eyes, groaning with the memory. "Pure heaven."

He picked up his coffee. "You know, Reed told me you were a beauty—and very kind."

Her heart melted a little. "Thank you."

The waitress brought a water over for Bella.

"Thank you," she said again.

"I was thinking about a piece of pie." He pointed to the cherry a la mode on the stand-up menu sandwiched between the ketchup and sugar packets. "I really can't interest you in some dessert?"

"I don't think I could eat another bite."

"You sure? Cause then I can tell Mad Dog I had dinner with his girl. Might make him jealous," he said with a wink.

She felt her brow wing up. "Mad Dog?"

"Hell, yeah. Mad Dog McKinley. He was like a damn bulldog when we were on a case—didn't stop until he had all the answers. Nothing got in his way."

Why did his words feel like they had some sort of double meaning? "You two worked undercover together."

He nodded. "For seven years. We were beat cops together for three years before that."

"It's nice that you keep in touch."

"Reed's very important to me. He's family."

She nodded, trying to figure out if she'd just imagined the sudden edge inflecting his tone. "I know he feels the same way about you." She touched his arm again, hoping to put him at ease. It was sweet that he cared so deeply for Reed. She liked him all the better for his protective streak. "He's lucky to have such a good friend."

He gave her fingers a friendly pat before he broke contact by reaching for his coffee. "Reed mentioned something about you having a big-ass dog."

"Lucy." She found a selfie Reed had taken of the three of them at the ocean the other night—her snuggled up in his arms while they sat on a blanket in the sand with Lucy by their side. "Here she is."

Joey took her phone, examining the screen. "Looks like a nice little family."

She loved that he thought so. "We try to get to the beach as often as we can. It's kind of our special place. Reed's a big fan of stopping off for ice cream."

"He looks happy—happier than I've seen him." Joey handed her back the phone.

She smiled, staring at the picture again as her finger automatically touched Reed's handsome face. "He's the best. My life hasn't been the same since Lucy walked through his front door." She winced, catching herself being completely sappy. "Sorry."

"You're fine. I've wanted this for him. He deserves nothing but the best."

She swallowed, realizing that Joey was staring at her, scrutinizing and measuring despite his relaxed body language and their easy conversation. Sitting up straighter, she put her phone in her purse, reminding herself that Reed had come off as pretty intense the first time they talked as well. She met his gaze again, smiling, imagining how terrifying it must have been for suspects to meet up with Reed and Joey in an interrogation room. "So, do you think you'll get out to LA anytime soon?"

"It depends. I've got a couple of cases I'm working on. The road to justice can take me anywhere."

"Well, I hope it leads you to California."

"You never know." He sipped his coffee. "Reed tells me you're in the beauty industry."

"Skin care. I'm a medical aesthetician. Like my friend Luisa." She gestured to the business card again.

"Huh. That must be a good business out there with Hollywood and all."

"I find that people are image-conscious wherever I go. Luisa's books are full for the next three months, which is really great."

"And you work at a hospital? I thought Reed said something about that."

"No. I have my own office. I share space and consult with a dermatologist. I volunteer my services at one of the children's hospitals."

"A good lady."

She shrugged. "I just like helping. The kids go through so much. So do their families. It's the least I can do."

Joey's phone vibrated with a text.

He took it out of his pocket, glancing at the screen. "My girlfriend."

"I bet she's looking forward to having you home."

"I'd like to think so."

She nodded, sensing that their conversation was winding down. "I should probably let you go."

"I'm hoping the traffic's died down some." He reached into his wallet and tossed a few dollars on the table. "Can I give you a ride anywhere?"

"I'm actually staying right here at the hotel." She stood.

He gained his feet, towering over her. "It was nice to meet you, Bella Colby." He held out his hand again for another shake.

"I feel like I should hug you."

He opened his arms. "I'm all for hugging."

Laughing, she stepped into his embrace.

He gave her a friendly squeeze. "Take good care of my buddy."

"I will." She drew away and walked out with him. "Bye, Joey."

"See ya, Bella."

She waved as he started toward his car, and she walked to the hotel, looking forward to telling Reed about her day and the unexpected surprise she'd found at the diner.

Reed tapped his fingers on his desk, staring at Bella's personal information he'd accessed well over an hour ago. He wasn't exactly sure of what he was doing; he and Joey had gone through every note and file with a fine-tooth comb, but here he sat anyway, scrutinizing each page again. Maybe he was in search of the one clue that would finally make all of this make sense—or maybe he was a fucking idiot, secretly holding out hope that Bella's phone records, credit history, and banking transactions would paint an entirely different picture than the one he'd seen today.

Shaking his head, he shoved his computer away. The truth had been staring him in the face all along; he just never wanted to believe it. From day one, the evidence hadn't stacked up in his neighbor's favor, but he'd slapped on his blinders and pretended otherwise.

His motorcycle ride up the coast was supposed to have cleared his mind. When that didn't work, the long session with the punching bags was supposed to have helped him sweat away the worst of the disgust and anger, but he was still as sick now as he'd been when he walked out on Lucy earlier this afternoon. Eventually, he was going to have to come to terms with the fact that Isabella Colby wasn't who he wanted her to be. She was a criminal just like the rest of her family.

Sighing, he picked up the photo booth pictures from the night of Julie and Chase's wedding, studying the stunning woman standing next to him in every shot. She wasn't real. The sweetheart with the big brown eyes was a lie. He stared at the last picture in the series of six—the one where they held each other close and grinned. Clenching his jaw, he tossed the strip facedown on the desk and looked at Lucy curled up on the posh puppy mattress he'd dragged over from Bella's place. After his workout and shower, he'd walked next door, grabbing what Lucy would need till morning, and got the hell out of Bella's space. He hadn't been able to stand the classy, cozy atmosphere of her living room, let alone cover up in her sheets and smell her shampoo on the pillows for the rest of the night.

"Fuck," he groaned wearily, settling his face in his hands and flinching when his phone started ringing. He glanced at Bella's amazing face filling the screen, letting it ring three times, then four, muttering another swear as he picked up. "Hello?"

"Hey."

He closed his eyes as her friendly voice washed over him. "I wasn't sure if I was going to hear from you. It's pretty late."

"I know. I can't sleep. I'm still on California time. Plus, I wanted to talk to you. How was your day?"

She asked him that every night, but did she really care? Who the hell was this woman he shared his life with? "Good."

"Just good?"

"Yeah, I took the bike out for a while, but other than that, nothing much is going on."

"Well, things are pretty exciting up here."

He thought of her sitting at the café table with her cousin. "I believe it."

"I ran into your friend."

He frowned, struggling to focus on the here and now. "My friend?"

"Joey—"

He rushed to his feet. "You saw Joey?"

She laughed. "Pretty crazy, huh? We were at the same diner—the one by my hotel. He'd just gotten in from a flight and stopped off for a meal to avoid the worst of rush hour."

Jesus, this whole investigation was turning into a disaster. Clearly he wasn't the only one screwing up on the job. "You guys *talked*?"

"Of course we did, silly. I recognized him from that picture on your cell phone."

He started pacing. "What about?"

"You, mostly. We both agreed you're pretty amazing."

He rolled his eyes to the ceiling, wishing with every fiber of his being that he could get his hands around his ex-partner's neck. "I can't believe you saw Joey."

"We were both shocked. I definitely surprised him, but I'm glad I got a chance to meet him. He's very nice. And I love that you two have some of the same mannerisms."

He blinked, slightly horrified by the idea. Joe was his best friend, but he couldn't imagine how they were anything alike. "No, we don't."

"Yes, you do." She chuckled. "The arm crossing and intense stares. You two must have made quite a pair in the interrogation room—kinda scary."

He rubbed at the back of this neck.

"I'm wondering if I should start calling you Mad Dog?"

Her voice was full of fun. Last night—or even eight hours ago—he would have laughed at her teasing, but nothing about this situation was funny. "I thought I'd left that nickname behind." Or he'd tried. Wasn't there a saying about how the more things changed, the more they stayed the same?

"You know what else I was thinking about?"

He stopped in front of the window, staring blindly out the glass. "No."

"About how much I can't wait for tomorrow. I want to come home, Reed. I want to see you. If I could hop on another flight right now, I think I might."

He clenched his jaw, pressing his forehead to the pane, pretending that her words weren't a fucking knife to his heart. He wanted her to be the woman who cried over sick kids. He longed for her to be the woman who smiled into his eyes while they talked after making love. He *needed* her to be all of those things so badly, it nearly killed him to know she wasn't—or that wasn't all she was. "That sounds good." He took a steeling breath, needing to play this out, knowing what he had to do. A couple of hours on the bike might not have made anything better, but as he remembered the pictures of her sliding Matty Caparelli information, the goal was crystal clear. "How was the party?"

"Great. Luisa introduced me to so *many* people. She has a lot of friends and family. My head's still spinning." She chuckled. "We booked her full for a good three months, and if I ever have to fill out another gift card in my life..."

"Good for her."

"I would officially call today a success."

How could she not? Help a friend, aid and abet the mob, all while fooling her ex-cop lover. "I bet. You'll have to tell me about the people you met."

"Sure."

There was a long pause when he had nothing else to say—or nothing else he wanted to.

"Reed, is everything okay?"

"Yeah."

"You sound different—tense, maybe even a little sad."

He stood straight, surprised that she could read him so easily, even with hundreds of miles separating them. "I'm just tired." He scrubbed a hand over his jaw. "Bella..."

"Hmm?"

"I can't—I don't think I'm going to be able to pick you up tomorrow."

"Oh."

He heard the disappointment in the one syllable. "Something came up with work."

"Okay. I'll grab a cab or...I'll figure something out."

"I'm sorry." She had no idea how much he meant it.

"It's fine. Work happens. It sounds like you could use a shoulder rub after you get home, though, and I happen to be a trained professional."

Why was she pretending? Why couldn't she just be a fucking viper like her father, uncle, and cousin? They didn't mess around with pretenses. They were scum-of-the-earth sleezeballs and didn't care who knew it. "Nah. I'll be fine."

"Do you think you'll be around for dinner? I could make us something nice. We can eat out on the deck...or in bed."

He whirled away from his view of her cozy backyard setup. "I don't know."

"I guess we'll play it by ear."

"Yeah."

"I should probably try to get some sleep. I miss you."

He flared his nostrils, because despite what he saw today and knew her to be, he missed her too. “I’ll see you tomorrow.”

“Okay. Bye.”

“Bye.” Hanging up, he looked at Lucy looking at him and walked away, ready for another round with the punching bags. He’d made huge mistakes ignoring the obvious. Now he had to fix them.

☙ Chapter Twenty-One ❧

REED PULLED INTO THE FIRST SPOT HE CAME ACROSS IN THE parking garage and glanced at the dashboard clock as he shut off the engine. Surprisingly, he was twenty minutes early when he should have been late. It wasn't until the last second that he'd decided to grab his keys and head to LAX. For most of the morning, he'd gone back and forth, debating how he wanted to play the new game: meet Bella in a public place and ideally avoid any serious PDA or wait until later in the afternoon and catch her alone at the house. For better or worse, he'd chosen the airport. Now he was ready to get the whole thing over with.

With time to kill, he picked up his phone, finding and selecting Joey's number from his contact list. It had been tempting to give his former partner a call last night and rip him a new asshole. God knew he'd been angry enough, but the last few weeks had already put a strain on their friendship. Bitching out Joe for something that wasn't entirely his fault wouldn't have done either of them any good.

"I was waiting to hear from you," Joey said.

"What the hell were you thinking?"

"I was tailing her. I didn't know she was gonna fuckin' recognize me. How the fuck was I supposed to know that?"

"Since when are you careless?"

"Like I said, I didn't know she had any idea who I was. I was sitting in the darkest corner in a crowded freakin' restaurant."

"You followed her the entire weekend?"

"She was here, wasn't she?"

He wanted to stay pissed at Joey for being the voice of reason all along—for following through with the investigation and ruining his pretty new life with the truth. But he couldn't—not when his friend had presented him with evidence he could no longer ignore. "What did you get?"

"Not much of anything until yesterday. Friday she and her buddy ran errands and spent their afternoon at Body Bliss, blowing up balloons and stuff, getting the place ready. Friday night they stayed in—had a little backyard barbeque and played with Luisa's kid."

Reed made a sound in his throat, remembering that Bella had told him pretty much the same thing.

"Saturday was definitely the day," Joey continued. "Dino *and* Matty. There were other wise guys inside too—Carlo Lamberti, Felipio Rossi, their wives and kids. Things've gotta be patched up in the family. Maybe Nicoli's coming back to Brooklyn after Alfeo gets out."

Reed shook his head even though the same thought had occurred to him at some point during his sleepless night. "Alfeo hates his brother. *Loathes* him, Joe. He sent him away for close to thirty years."

"Well, he doesn't hate his niece. I didn't see any sort of tension between Matty and Bella when they were yakking it up outside."

He rubbed at his jaw. "I don't know, man. If Nicoli's in the clear, why is he living like he's still hiding?"

"Beats the hell out of me."

"None of this makes *sense*." He yanked off the seat belt still holding him in place, seething with frustration. "They'll kill Nicoli but not his daughter?"

"I don't know what to tell you on that front, but I get why you got distracted—why you fell for Bella. I didn't at first... I'm sorry about that."

Sighing wearily, Reed rested his head against the seat, shrugging away the worst of the pain. "It doesn't matter."

"Yes, it does. She's fucking gorgeous and she seems genuinely nice."

He steamed out a long breath. "I'm supposed to be able to look past that."

"Not with this one. A couple bats of those big brown eyes and any guy's a goner. Can't say I didn't fall in love a little myself. And she's definitely into you. Bad apple or not, that came across perfectly clear."

Reed pressed his forehead to the steering wheel with the agony of his problem. How the hell had he let this happen—falling for his enemy? "I know I've gone about this thing all wrong, but I want us to keep going with the investigation. I want to take them down."

Joey muttered a curse.

"What? I thought that's what you wanted. You sent me the pictures, right?"

"I sent them because I want you to be careful—to see what you're dealing with. No matter how she feels about you or how kind she comes across, she's in this thing."

"Of course she is." But he didn't want her to be. He would give just about anything for her not to be. "Goddamn, if I could just *ask* her—convince her to confess."

"Don't let her make you stupid."

"I'm not stupid."

"No, you're not, but she's still got you."

"No, she doesn't."

"Yes, she does. I can hear it in your voice. This is eating you up."

"I need answers. This morning I went through some of her stuff at the house—older check registers and other things I could find along those lines, peeked in her closets and whatnot."

"And?"

"And there's nothing." He gave an edgy pound of his fist to the center console. "Maybe we can get her to flip, and we'll do what we can to get her a deal."

"Then what? You guys gonna ride off into the WITSEC sunset?"

"No. We're finished. She and I are over."

"I don't know about this one, Reed. I don't think this is a good idea. You're too close. If she finds out what we're trying to do, you're dead."

He huffed out another breath, growing more impatient with himself when he couldn't equate Bella with bodily harm. "She wouldn't hurt me."

"That doesn't mean her pops will give it a second thought. He's an hour up the road. The fact that she's hanging out with a cop in the first place is dicey—surprising."

"Ex-cop."

"Give me a break. Like that matters. You might be close protection now, but the stakes are higher all the way around because of who you were."

"Bella knows who I am—who I used to be—and it's never made a difference."

"Bullshit. She doesn't know anything. You haven't been straight with her from the beginning."

And he regretted it. Even after the way everything had shaken down, he was sorry he'd never been able to give her all of the pieces. "Maybe, but I need us to finish this. Once and for all, let's finish this."

"Reed—"

"Help me, Joe." He winced, hearing the hints of desperation in his own voice.

Joey sighed in his ear. "You got it, boss. What's the plan?"

"I'm at the airport. I'm picking her up."

"Then what?"

Wasn't that the question he'd been asking himself all night? He'd spent nearly a decade lying and pretending, doing whatever needed to be done to bring a case to a close, but he didn't know if he had it in him to pull this one off. "Hell if I know."

"I don't see you getting very far without carrying on with your relationship."

And that was the part that was going to destroy him. Longing and hate were a dangerous mix. "Yeah."

"Can you handle it?"

"Looks like I'm going to have to."

"Be careful."

"I will." He glanced at his watch, noting that his time was just about up. "I have to go."

"Let me know how it goes."

"I'll call you later." Hanging up, he got out of the truck and started toward the American Airlines terminals, sliding his sunglasses on top of his head as he stepped inside. He smiled politely at a woman as their gazes met across the hall and lowered his aviators back in place, afraid for the first time ever that he wouldn't be able to conceal his emotions the way he'd been able to for years. Whether Bella knew it or not, nothing was the same between them anymore. In an unfortunate moment of clarity, all of that had ended. So how in the hell was he supposed to ignore what he saw yesterday and move forward with a relationship that he would have walked away from in any other situation?

He shoved his hands in his pockets and stood back among the crowds as Bella's plane was announced and passengers exited to the left of the security gates. He scanned dozens of travelers, eventually spotting Bella decked out in strappy sandals and a pretty pink spaghetti-strap sundress. She'd added curls to her hair and clipped it back, leaving her stunning face unframed. "Goddamn," he muttered, rocking back on his heels. She took his breath away, like a kick to the throat—that hadn't changed. He tracked her with his gaze while she pulled her carry-on behind her and talked on the phone, oblivious to the long stares of many men and envious women. Stepping in her direction, he opened his mouth to call her name and stopped, fisting his hands at his sides when her perfume wafted his way and he had to fight the urge to snag her by the arm and pull her against him.

Son of a bitch, he wasn't ready for this—not even close. If he let her see him now, he would mess everything up. And that wasn't an option. He finally had what he and Joey had needed all along: his surefire way into the Caparelli crime family. Now that there were no doubts about Bella's involvement, nothing else mattered anymore. Nothing else should have mattered in the first place.

Taking a deep breath, he focused on his mission and followed her outside, keeping his distance as she helped an older woman get into the shuttle heading toward the Palisades. When the van pulled away from the curb, he hurried to his truck, catching up with the vehicle on the interstate. He tailed them in the same lane, careful to keep several car lengths behind them as they moved closer to the condos.

Eventually Hooper's Shuttle Service turned into their development and dropped Bella off. Reed came in the back entrance, stopping down the street as Bella let herself into her house, then came outside with Lucy, bending down numerous times to give the puppy hugs and kisses. She sat on one of the cushy deck chairs, holding her phone in her hand while Lucy wandered around in the grass.

His phone dinged with a text.

I'm home. Can't wait to see you.

He stared at the words for several seconds, then dialed her number, ready to move this along as he listened to the phone ring.

"Hey, handsome. I hope I didn't disturb you at work."

He swallowed. Her smooth voice affected him as powerfully as seeing her for the first time had. "Nah, you're fine."

"You went grocery shopping," she said as she stood, following the puppy back inside, shutting the French doors behind her. "Thank you."

"You're welcome." He settled his head against the rest, hearing the stiffness in his own words. Clearing his throat, he reminded himself that there was a game to play and he was off to a rough start. "Lucy must be glad you're home."

"She seems to be. I promised her a long walk on the beach later." Bella came back outside, locking up the front door and getting into her car. "You sound tired again."

"A little, but I'm fine." He turned over the engine as she backed out of the driveway. "What are you up to today?"

"I have a few errands to run." She drove down the road, hitting the light into the main flow of traffic just right.

He followed. "Yeah? Like what?"

"Just a couple of stops here and there. Do you think you'll be home for dinner?"

He didn't have to be. He could say that work would be keeping him busy for as long as he needed the excuse, but he was going to have to stand face-to-face with Bella eventually. Tonight seemed like as good a time as any. "Yeah, I'll be home."

"Great. What time do you want to eat?"

"How about six?"

"Six, it is. I'll make something special. How do you feel about chicken?"

"I feel fine about it."

"All right. I'll see you later, then."

"See ya."

"Bye."

"Bye." He hung up, trailing her in the busy Sunday morning traffic. It didn't surprise him any when they merged onto the 405, heading toward Reseda. Bella probably had all kinds of things to tell her father. Eventually, she was going to tell him too. He was done fucking around with all of this. Bella had the answers that were going to help him keep her uncle locked away.

Bella packaged up Dad's meals for the upcoming week while he sat in his favorite chair, watching TV, still clad in a T-shirt and pajama pants despite the fact that it was late afternoon. Her impromptu midmorning trip to Reseda had turned out to be a wonderful opportunity to share the adventures of her long weekend away, run a few errands on Dad's behalf, and gauge his health for herself. For days, she'd been forced to take Dad at his word when he'd assured her over the phone that he was doing fine, but in reality his weight had dropped again. He was losing instead of maintaining—not at all what she wanted to see.

Looking his way, she sighed, consumed by a fresh wave of guilt as she studied his big hands growing bonier every time she visited. As much as she'd enjoyed her visit in New York, she wondered if she should have stayed in LA where she was needed most. Dad seemed happy enough and his energy levels appeared to be okay, but they weren't great either. He'd joined her at the table for lunch, chatting for a solid thirty minutes before he'd been ready to settle back in his recliner to rest. At this point, they were both doing what they could to keep him at his best, but it was obvious they were losing the battle.

Tucking her terrifying thoughts away, she focused on her current chores, putting the Tupperware containers in the freezer, then wiping the counters clean. "Dad, do you want any tea?"

"Huh?" he said, jerking his head off his chest as he opened his drooping eyelids.

"Do you want a cup of tea? I found a new herbal mix that's supposed to be good for your immune system."

"No. I'm still full from my sandwich."

He'd eaten half of his grilled cheese and tried a sip or two of the roasted tomato soup she'd prepared. At least there was something nourishing in his system. "I can make it anyway and set it close by, just in case you change your mind."

"I'll probably stick with my juice." He gestured to the container on the side table. "This new one with the beets is pretty tasty."

"Okay. Great." She dried her hands on the cloth and walked over to where he sat, resting her butt on the arm of his chair, smiling as she scrutinized his pale complexion.

He stared back at her. "You should go—get home to your life."

She glanced at her watch, torn between staying in Reseda and leaving. Dad wasn't the only one on her mind. Reed was worrying her too. Their last couple of conversations had been off. He'd seemed out of sorts and tired. She hoped his new assignment hadn't taken a turn for the worse. On Thursday and Friday night, he'd sounded fine—Saturday morning too, but she imagined a lot could go wrong with a stalker case in a short amount of time. "I have a little while yet."

"Do you have plans with Reed?"

She felt herself smile. "Yes. I'm making us dinner."

"Good. Go home to him. Have a nice meal. Be twenty-five. I'm going to take a little nap—" He aimed the remote at the television to shut it off when Channel Four started a segment on Brooklyn. He turned up the volume and settled the remote back on his lap.

"...was shot in the head, reminiscent of the old mafia days right here in this section of the city. Rocco Bastoni's freedom from Allenwood Penitentiary lasted less than seventy-two hours after serving twenty-three years. The former Caparelli associate was brutally gunned down outside his home on the South Side tonight..." The reporter continued his coverage as pictures of a man named Alfeo Caparelli, the rumored Caparelli crime boss, were flashed on the screen before the live footage cut back to police cars and yellow tape in the Bensonhurst neighborhood.

"Damn fool," Dad muttered, shutting off the TV.

"You know, I don't think that was too far from where I was staying. I'm pretty sure Luisa's shop is a block or two down from there."

"What'd you say her last name was again?"

"De Vitis."

"Huh. Don't know that one."

She grinned. "Why would you?"

He shrugged. "I wouldn't."

"It's scary to think I was there just yesterday."

"I'm glad you're home. From what I hear, Bensonhurst is quite a place—not a place for my daughter."

"I don't see myself going back anytime soon."

"Good." He took her hand and kissed it. "Go home, Bella. Thanks for driving all the way up here and making me something delicious."

She kissed his forehead. "You're welcome. Are you sure you don't need me to come to your doctor's appointment tomorrow?"

"No, I'm doing fine."

"You'll call me and let me know how everything goes?"

"I told you I would."

She hesitated, then stood, getting the hint loud and clear that he wanted his space. "I'll come up on Saturday."

"Only if it works for your schedule."

She hated that she would have to wait another six days before she could see him again. "It does."

He got out of his chair and hugged her. "Thanks for coming."

She held on tight, startled again by how much less of him there was to wrap her arms around. He'd been strong and muscular—not nearly as built as Reed, but robust and healthy once upon a time. "You're welcome."

He walked her to the door. "Have a good week."

"I will." She stepped outside, noting the way he leaned against the doorframe for support. "Daddy, are you sure you don't want to come stay with me? I could bring you to your appointments and cook for you—"

He shook his head. "I'm not helpless."

"I know you're not."

"I like my house."

She nodded. "Okay. Call me tomorrow."

"See you soon, Bella Boop."

She smiled. "All right."

"Drive carefully," he called as she got into the car.

"I will." She turned over the engine and backed up, waving before she started on her way. Glancing in her rearview mirror, she gripped the steering wheel tight, wishing he would come home with her to the Palisades, but every time she brought it up, he immediately shot her down. She hoped everything would go well with his appointment tomorrow. And they were going to start talking every day whether he liked the idea or not. If he was going to insist on living an hour away, she was going to insist that he check in. That wasn't too much to ask.

With a decisive nod, she considered the matter settled and glanced at the clock, smiling as her mind wandered to Reed. He would be home in an hour and a half. If she was lucky, the traffic would cooperate and she'd shave a little time off her drive. Then she would take a quick shower, grill up some chicken, and mix up an easy cucumber salad. Tonight was going to be about simplicity and reconnecting. She'd missed him so much.

It should have scared her some that Reed was quickly becoming such a huge part of her life—vital—but it didn't. For once, she was letting her heart lead, trusting that Reed would take care with her. In ninety minutes or less, she would be snuggled up in his arms, and everything was going to feel right again. He was going to tell her his troubles over a glass of wine or maybe while they enjoyed an ice cream at the beach. It didn't matter which, as long as they were together.

Reed glanced at his watch as he sat on Bella's couch, bobbing his leg up and down while he flipped through her channel lineup. If he was pegging things right, she would be home any minute now, and for the first time since this morning, he felt like he was ready to do whatever needed to be done to get the ball rolling again. He'd had plenty of time to prepare. For much of the afternoon, he'd followed her around Reseda, watching her go from the grocery store to the pharmacy, then to the local Home Depot before she finally parked in her father's driveway. More than once, he'd scratched his head, trying to figure out what her normal, everyday errands had to do with Nicoli Caparelli and the mafia. The dots weren't connecting. No matter how he and Joey theorized and tried to make something stick, nothing was aligning. After ninety minutes of sitting idle half a block from Vincent's place, he'd called it a day, figuring that a round in the ring at Rusty's would serve him better than waiting for some unlikely event to happen on Darby Avenue.

A car drove down the street and stopped, pulling into Bella's spot. He turned his head, looking out the window as she grabbed her purse from the passenger seat and got out. Shutting off the television, he stood, shoving his hands in his pockets as Lucy rushed to the door.

Moments later, Bella let herself inside, absently greeting Lucy as she grinned at Reed. "Hey, you."

Damn, she made his heart skip a beat just from being in the same room. No amount of preparation or training was ever going to change that. "Hey."

She laughed and launched herself at him, wrapping him up in a tight hug. "I *missed* you."

He made himself return her embrace, closing his eyes and clutching at her dress as he nuzzled her temple with his chin and breathed in the scent of her perfume and cigarette smoke.

"It's so good to be home—to see you." She pressed her palms to his cheeks, pulling his mouth to hers for a noisy kiss.

He gripped her shoulders, fighting the urge to yank away when his first instinct was to tell her this couldn't happen anymore. Remembering his role, he slid his hands down her baby-soft skin, letting the moment play out.

She eased back, smiling into his eyes as she hooked her arms around the back of his neck and swayed slowly in a dance. "I missed you."

He followed her lead as his fingers found their way into her hair—like they always did. "I missed you too."

"Thank you for taking care of Lucy."

"You're welcome."

"How was your day?"

This felt normal—like any other day when they talked and held each other close. But it wasn't. "Not too bad."

"Yeah?"

"Yeah."

"Then why do you seem so unhappy?" She stopped their dance. "I heard it in your voice the last couple of times we talked, and I can see it in your eyes right now."

He stood taller, startled that she was reading him so easily when he was trying like hell to play this through. "I'm fine."

Shaking her head, she caressed soothing fingers along his neck. "No, you're not. What's going on, Reed?"

He clenched his jaw, sensing her genuine concern. Here stood the kind, sweet woman he knew Bella to be. And that's where everything stopped making sense. Isabella Colby his girlfriend didn't add up with Isabella Colby the mafia accessory. "Nothing."

She sighed quietly. "Is everything going okay with your assignment? Sadie's safe?"

"Yeah. There hasn't been any new activity. She's fine. I'm fine."

She held his gaze as if she wasn't so sure.

"I'm good, Bella." He pressed his mouth to hers, remembering too late that he wasn't supposed to make the first move. "Really."

"Okay." She stood on her tiptoes, touching her lips to his—once, twice, making that sound in her throat as she opened her mouth and teased his tongue with hers.

Christ, she was sinful—her taste, the way her breasts pressed against him as she hugged herself closer. He fought himself, only giving her back what he had to until her hands wandered down to his hips and over his ass. Then he couldn't take it anymore—fighting what he knew he shouldn't want but did. He groaned, cupping her face and plundering, surrendering to his weakness for her before he pulled back, his breath steaming out in torrents. "You stink, Bella," he blurted out, grabbing hold of any thought that didn't involve him pulling her down to the area rug and finishing what they started. "Like cigarettes."

She nodded. "I know. I need a shower."

"Where do you go? Why do you smell like a chimney so often these days?"

Her gaze left his, darting to the floor. "My dad smokes."

He clenched his jaw, waiting for something more. "You met up with him?"

Nodding again, she turned away. "Let me go shower real quick."

He snagged her by the wrist, growing more frustrated as she continued to evade. "What's the big mystery?"

She whirled around. "What?"

"I don't get it. Why's your father such a secret?" He heard the edginess in his tone and couldn't make himself care if this was the wrong approach.

"He's not."

"You don't talk about him."

She jerked her shoulders. "What is it that you want to hear?"

"I don't know. Something. Anything." He crossed his arms and uncrossed them just as quickly. "You got pretty pissed when I wouldn't bring you to meet my family. You won't even talk about yours."

She stared at him, blinking, clearly surprised. "I didn't—I'm sorry."

He jerked his shoulders this time. "I just don't get it."

Her gaze wandered to the floor again, staying there. "Not everyone is proud of where they come from. I don't like to talk about my past."

"Why?"

She swallowed. "It's complicated."

"So uncomplicate it. Tell me about it."

Finally she made eye contact again. "Reed—"

"It's hard to have a relationship when you don't trust me."

A look of horror washed over her face. "I do trust you. I can't think of anyone I trust more. I just...I've worked really hard to get to where I am."

"What does that have to do with anything? With you and me?"

"Everything."

He shook his head, refusing to take that as her answer.

"You're important," she said, "more important than anyone has been in a long time."

"Good, because the feeling's mutual." Why not be honest when he could?

She turned away, fiddling with the lampshade, her posture rigid as the tension in the room grew thicker by the second. "I'm sorry that I've given you the impression I don't trust you." She glanced over her shoulder, looking at him with such anguish in her eyes, he faltered in his resolve to get his answers no matter the cost.

Sighing, he walked up behind her and wrapped his arms around her waist. Clearly this method wasn't getting him where he needed to go, so he would try something different—something better. "I know you do. Come here." He pulled her onto his lap as he sat on the couch.

"I just want to understand." He kissed the top of her head, never speaking truer words. "I want to know all of you, Bella."

She blinked back tears. "It's hard for me to talk about my parents."

He slid his knuckles along her jaw. Why were her tears so damn lethal? When would his kneejerk reaction always to believe her catch up with the facts at hand? Even after the pictures and mounting evidence, he was a sucker for Isabella Colby. "How about we wait until you're ready?"

She closed her eyes and rested her forehead against his. "Thank you."

He combed his fingers through her hair. "I can't help you if I don't know how."

"You're so good to me." She adjusted the way she sat on his lap, straddling his thighs. "How did I get so lucky?"

He trailed his palms up and down her back. "I want to help you, Bella. Whatever's going on, I want to help."

A tear slid down her cheek.

This was real—her pain. No matter what, he couldn't stand seeing her hurting. "Don't cry."

"I'm trying not to. I just—I'm sorry."

"It's okay." He caught a fresh drop with his thumb. "We're going to make everything all right."

She traced his ears, the way she did when they lay in bed after making love. "I want to believe you."

"You can believe me."

Her gaze darted from his eyes to his lips. She moved in, her mouth meeting his, taking him on a slow, sweet journey.

He fought to remember the pictures of her smiling at Matty Caparelli, even as he played his tongue against hers and wrapped his arms around her.

"Be with me, Reed. I missed you."

"I—"

"Be with me." She went after his jaw and neck with teasing nibbles.

"Bella." He gripped her hips, pulling her closer. "Bella."

"I need you."

His phone dinged with a text, saving his sorry ass. "I have to check this. I'm on call tonight."

"Okay."

He untangled himself and stood, desperate to be free of Bella as he pulled his phone from his back pocket and stared at Joey's message.

How's it going?

He was rock hard and making out with the woman he was supposed to be emotionally distancing himself from. By his estimation, things weren't going great.

"Is everything okay?"

He looked up from Joey's message, staring at gorgeous brown eyes and lush lips swollen from his. "I'm going to have to take a rain check on tonight."

"Oh." She stood, fixing her dress.

"I'm backup for a couple of the guys," he lied without qualm.

She nodded.

"We'll do dinner tomorrow night."

She nodded again.

He shoved his phone back in his pocket and closed the distance between them, taking her hands—the only thing he dared to do. "I'm sorry I have to cancel."

"I'm sorry I messed up our evening."

"You didn't." He gave her fingers a squeeze. "Everything's fine, Bella. We're fine."

"Okay."

He gave her a peck and headed for the door. "I'll text you and let you know what's going on."

"Do you think you'll be back?"

"It's hard to say," he lied yet again. "I might be late. I want you to get some sleep tonight."

"Be careful."

"I will." He walked out, swearing under his breath as he started toward his truck. What the hell was his deal? This wasn't going to work until he got his fucking emotions in check and his head on straight. He dialed Joey as he got behind the wheel.

"So?"

He backed up, waving at Bella as she stood in her doorway. "I can't do— I need a couple days to figure this out."

"So take them."

He drove away, his heart pounding as he glanced back in his rearview mirror. "You were right, Joe. She's got me. I thought I was going to be able to— I don't know if I can walk away from her."

"I know, buddy. Give yourself some time and we'll see how you want to proceed."

"This is our shot at taking them down, but as soon as I see her...as soon as I touch her...there's something about her..."

"Take some time, Reed."

"All right. I'll talk to you later." He set the phone down and took a left out of the neighborhood, needing to figure out how he was going to pull this off when what he wanted and what was reality weren't the same thing.

☙ Chapter Twenty-Two ❧

Bella stifled a yawn as she drove the five miles home after her quick stop off at the deli for tonight's easy dinner. The week had been a zoo of extended office hours and missed lunches in her attempt to make up appointments after her long weekend away. From sunup to sundown, she'd been busy. And she still had one more day to go. Lucky for her, the last client on today's books canceled. She'd used the opportunity to duck out as quickly as possible. New product needed to be ordered, a couple of phone calls needed to be made, but tonight was for her and Reed.

They hadn't seen each other since Sunday. Between her insane schedule and his, there hadn't been time. Monday, Tuesday, and Wednesday night, she'd waited up, hoping to catch him as he rolled in from one of the extra duties he'd taken on to give Ethan a hand, but she'd fallen asleep every dang time.

They'd been forced to rely on their cell phones, catching up while he drove from one assignment to the next or when she was in between clients, but that wasn't good enough. For the next couple of hours, they were going to bring a little normalcy back to their lives. Reed was bound to be as tired as she was, but they needed a simple dinner and ice cream at the beach. Although everything had sounded fine each time they spoke, she still didn't like the way they'd left things Sunday evening.

Reed had assured her things were good, but nothing felt okay. For days, she'd been walking around with a heavy weight on her shoulders, waiting for her opportunity to fix the mess she'd made by keeping her secrets. When he confronted her about the stench of cigarette smoke on her clothes and asked questions about Dad, he'd taken her completely by surprise. The idea of telling him everything had seemed scary—terrifying. He'd wanted answers right then and there, and she hadn't been prepared to give them. But she was now.

Tonight, she was determined to share the ugly details of her past.

The thought of baring her soul was still frightening, but Reed was right. If they were going to move forward with their relationship, she needed to move beyond the fear that he was going to judge her and walk away. This evening was going to come down to trust—and there was no one she trusted more than the man who'd captured her heart. Besides, everyone had a past—skeletons they weren't necessarily proud of. Reed likely had one or two of his own. "This is going to be good. Everything's going to be okay. Right, Luce?"

Lucy gave her a kiss on the cheek from the passenger seat.

"Exactly." She stopped at the red light and waited her turn to pull into the neighborhood, then drove down the street, grinning when she spotted both of Reed's vehicles in the driveway and the lights on upstairs in his gym. "He's home."

Lucy's ears perked up.

"Let's put you inside and I'll go get him. It'll be nice to see him again, huh? Maybe we can have a sleepover."

She got out, grabbing the deli bag from the back seat, then opened Lucy's side and let the puppy into the house. "I'll be right back." She closed the door and walked over to Reed's, testing the doorknob and smiling when she found it unlocked. Stepping inside, she glanced at the ceiling as the floor above creaked and music played. "Reed," she called, setting their dinner on the counter and starting upstairs.

He didn't answer as Nine Inch Nails' gritty rock blared throughout the second story.

She moved down the hall, stopping in the doorway, watching him hit the heavy bag with several solid punches. The bag swayed and he maneuvered around it before offering up another series of blows, his powerful muscles bunching and flexing as his naked upper body glistened with sweat.

He paused, looking at her, and stepped back from the bag.

She grinned, turning down the music. "Hi, there, handsome."

He sent her a small smile. "Hey."

"Looks like I caught you in the middle of your workout."

"Yeah." He pulled off his gloves and grabbed his water bottle from the weight bench, drinking deep.

"Did you eat?"

He shook his head. "Not yet."

"Perfect." She stepped farther into the room, picking up on the chill blowing her way despite the heat in his gym space. "I bought us soup and sandwiches from the deli—tomato basil and turkey pitas."

He put his gloves on and got back to work. "I'll grab something later. I'm not quite finished in here."

She frowned, staring at him. "Are you coming over tonight?"

He jerked his shoulders. "I don't know. I'll have to see."

"Reed." She took a chance and got in his way. "What's wrong?"

"Nothing. It's been a busy week." He settled his hands on his hips, taking several deep breaths. "I'm tired and a little grumpy."

She moved closer, hesitating, then wrapped her arms around his waist, hoping a hug would help with his mood.

"I'm sweaty."

"I see that."

"Your dress is going to get dirty."

"It'll wash." She smiled again, wanting to soothe away whatever was bothering him. "Did something happen at work?"

"No." He took off his gloves, tossing them to the floor. "I guess I have a bug up my ass."

"How about we walk the beach? That always helps me when I'm feeling mad at the world."

He shrugged again, holding her gaze, but he didn't return her embrace the way he usually did.

"I've missed you this week."

"Busy weeks happen."

"Luckily, this one's almost over."

"Yeah."

"Come on. Shower up and walk by the water with me." She stood on her tiptoes to press a kiss to his lips.

He evaded her mouth. "I'm hot, Bella, and you're hanging on me."

She stepped away, absorbing the rush of hurt. "Did I do something to upset you?"

He blew out a breath and turned away, grabbing a towel and wiping his forehead and temples. "No."

"Clearly I did."

He faced her again, rubbing the ratty cotton over his chiseled chest and abs. "I said everything's fine."

"I thought you were big on full disclosure."

His gaze whipped to hers and he tossed out a humorless laugh.

She swallowed with the cruelty of his meaning. "This is about Sunday—because I wasn't ready to tell you about my dad."

He drank from his water bottle again, saying nothing, only staring at her.

"You said you understood. It's painful to bring it up—"

"We all have pain."

She pressed her hand to her racing heart, blinking rapidly as her eyes filled. What was happening here? Where was the man who'd been kind and accepting just a few days ago? She'd been ready to tell him everything—to share her deepest shames and fears. "What's wrong with you?"

"Nothing."

She crossed her arms, hugging herself. "If this isn't—if this isn't working for you anymore..."

"It's working just fine."

She studied his rigid posture, the disdain she saw in his cold blue eyes. "I don't understand what's going on."

"Nothing's going on," he snapped. "Why does everything have to be a big thing with you? We both have stuff to do. We don't have to see each other every second—check in with each other every second. That bullshit's for high school."

She nodded. "I'll let you get back to your punching bag." She turned toward the door.

He sighed. "Bella."

She turned back, waiting for him to say something—to explain. "What's changed?"

"I thought we just covered that."

"Right. I don't know what this is all about, but I think we should spend some time apart." She cleared her throat when her voice broke. "We'll give each other a little space." Turning, she left, hurrying downstairs and across the side yard to her own house. She shut the door and locked it behind her, leaning against the solid wood. "What was that?" She dashed at her cheeks and sat on the couch.

Lucy stood from her bed, walking to Bella.

"I don't know what happened." She ran a trembling hand down Lucy's soft coat as her mind raced, still trying to catch up with the last few minutes. Who was that horrid, nasty man? "That was awful." She hugged Lucy. "He was really awful, Luce." And she would be damned if she was going to sit around and let him ruin what was left of her night. "Come on." She stood on legs that weren't quite steady. "Let's go to the beach."

Grabbing Lucy's leash, she stepped outside and locked up, turning toward the driveway as Lucy made her way to Reed's truck. Her throat grew tight as she shook her head. "The car, sweetie. It's just you and me." She opened the passenger side door, waiting for Lucy to hop in, and left as quickly as she'd come home, trying to figure out how everything could have gone so wrong in less than a week's time.

Reed stood with his hands on his hips, listening to Bella hurry down the stairs and close the door behind her as she left. She didn't bother slamming it as he thought she might, nor did she tell him to fuck off moments ago when he'd so plainly deserved it. "Son of a bitch," he muttered, knowing he'd hurt her—that he'd been cruel—and he was only half-sorry. The wounded woman with tears in her eyes broke his heart. The mafia daughter who kept secrets: not so much. It was unfortunate they were one and the same.

His four days away were supposed to have made some sort of difference. Somehow his mind was supposed to have been clearer after intentionally keeping his distance with short phone conversations and picking up a few extra duties to avoid coming home, but he was right back where he started. This morning, he'd assured himself he was ready to see her again. When he told her at lunchtime that he didn't have plans for the evening, he knew she would come by. Dinner with Bella hadn't seemed like an awful idea. And he'd been prepared to walk the beach and eat ice cream while they held hands. Maybe somewhere deep down, he'd hoped she would finally confess everything, and he would be able to find a way to look past the worst of it. Then Joey called while he was on his way home from dropping Sadie off with Tyson. There'd been another murder in Bensonhurst, another Caparelli associate gunned down days after his release from prison.

This wasn't their way. The Caparellis didn't drop bodies in the streets. Their enemies simply vanished, never to be seen again by friends or family alike. Or at least, that's how it had been done when Sony Caparelli and his son Patrizio had been in charge. Alfeo appeared to be a different beast entirely. He was known to be ruthless but lacked the cool composure and finesse the generations before him possessed. Clearly Matty was following in his old man's footsteps.

It wasn't hard to see what was going on. The old timers were being killed off—anyone who could testify to Alfeo's past crimes was being exterminated while he had the cover of his prison jumpsuit as an alibi. Alfeo had been put away for three murders but was spared life in prison and even the death sentence due to a technicality—or a bribe.

Mateo "Matty" Caparelli was more than likely ordering his hit teams to take care of anyone who could cause problems. So what was Bella's role? What exactly did she do for the Caparellis? Things were heating up in Brooklyn again, and she'd been in contact with Luisa and her father every day this week. Nicoli had clearly wormed his way back into the mafia trenches.

Reed's opportunity was here. For a decade, this was what he'd worked so hard for: to end them once and for all. But maybe he didn't want that anymore. Months ago, he'd walked away, living with the knowledge that he would never destroy the men who had so quickly decimated his family. He'd turned in his badge and started over, carving out an entirely new life for himself. Maybe that was good enough. He hoped that's what his dad would have wanted for him. But what about Bella? How was he going to leave behind the one person who made him a better man?

He heard her voice outside and stepped closer to the window as she moved toward her car with Lucy. She was so damn beautiful with the wind teasing her hair and the sun shining on her golden skin. He swallowed regret and ignored the ever-present sense of longing as they got in the convertible and drove away. He knew where she was headed. All he had to do was get on his bike and go to the beach and find her, but he stayed where he was, unable to make himself do it—not for himself or for the investigation.

He was no longer Mad Dog McKinley. At this point, he didn't want to be. But who was he without Isabella Colby? That was the question that scared him the most.

ଓ Chapter Twenty-Three ଔ

Bella woke with a start when her phone started ringing on the bedside table. Half-asleep and mostly confused, she glanced at the bright green lights of her alarm clock, realizing it was well after one in the morning. "Yes," she answered, clearing her throat when her word came out as a croak. "Hello?" she tried again.

"Isabella Colby?"

She sat up, her stomach immediately sinking as she remembered another conversation starting much the same way. "Yes, this is Isabella."

"Ms. Colby, this is Francis up at North Medical Center. Your father was brought in by ambulance about an hour ago. He's been admitted and asked us to give you a call."

She rushed out of bed, turning on the light and blinding herself as she stumbled over to her dresser for a change of clothes. "He's been admitted?"

"Yes."

She yanked on the first pair of jeans she pulled from the drawer. "What happened? Did he hit his head again?"

"No, ma'am. He woke up feeling unwell and called for an ambulance. The doctors are running some tests now, but they're planning on keeping him for a couple of days. He's a little run-down and weak."

Sighing, she closed her eyes. Just a few hours ago, Dad had told her he was fine when she called to check on him. "Thank you. I'll be there as soon as I can."

"He's stable and in good hands."

Francis's reassurances did little to soothe her already fraying nerves. "Thanks." She hung up, pressing her hand to her heart as her breathing rushed out in shudders. "I have to go," she said to Lucy, struggling with tears as she took off her camisole and replaced it with a bra and short-sleeve T-shirt she grabbed at random. "Dad needs me." She picked up her phone again and stared at Reed's contact information, her finger hovering over his handsome face. He was right next door but he couldn't help her. He didn't *want* to help her. Somehow their relationship was over. She'd needed time to figure things out—time he hadn't been willing to give, but she couldn't worry about that right now. "Jenny," she whispered. She found her friend's number, nibbling her lip as she sent the call through.

"Hello?"

She winced, hating that she was waking a single, working mother in the middle of the night. "Jenny, it's Bella."

"Bella?"

She pressed her fingers to her temple, her guilt compounding when Faith started crying in the background. "I'm so sorry to call you—"

"Is everything okay?"

"No. I'm afraid I have another emergency." She swallowed as a ball of emotion tried to choke her. "I'm hoping you'll be able to come over and let Lucy out before you go to work."

"Of course. I'll have to swing by around six thirty. I have an early shift."

"That's fine. I don't know how to thank you."

"You don't have to. You're my friend."

She blinked back another wave of tears. "Thank you, Jenny."

"I'll give her breakfast too."

"That would be great. I'll be home in time for work but... I'm so grateful for your help. I'm sorry for waking Faith."

"It's all right. Don't worry about anything. I'll take good care of Lucy."

"You're the best. There's a twenty on the entryway table. Go ahead and grab it."

"I don't—"

"You'll hurt my feelings if you don't take it."

"All right.

"Bye, Jenny."

"Bye."

She hung up and bent down, kissing Lucy's head. "I'll be back later. Get some more sleep." Hurrying downstairs, she put money on the table, went out to the car, and took off, making excellent time on Sunset Boulevard, then the 405 in the light traffic. She pushed her speed to eighty-five, hoping the highway patrol was busy watching another stretch of road. She needed to get to Dad and find out what was going on. Forty-five minutes later, the GPS barked out directions Bella didn't need as she got off the exit and made her way through Reseda to the hospital. Parking in the first available spot she could find, she ran inside, stopping at the admittance desk. "Good morning. My father, Vincent Pescoe, was brought in by ambulance a little while ago."

The woman tapped a few buttons on her keyboard. "It looks like they just took him up to his room. They have him settled in on the fourth floor."

"Thank you." She beelined it to the elevator, impatiently pressing the number 4 when the doors took forever to close. Moments later, she stepped out into the oncology unit and headed for the nurses' station.

The woman sitting behind the desk smiled. "Good morning."

Bella did her best to smile back. "Good morning. My father, Vincent Pescoe, was brought up a few minutes ago."

"Yes. Visiting hours are at eight."

She shook her head. "I have to work today. I need to see him now. They called me up here from the Palisades."

"That must have been the admittance clerk. She should know our procedures."

"But I'm here now."

"I'm sorry—"

"Please," her voice broke. "I drove over an hour. I just need to see that he's okay and I'll go." She dashed at a tear as it fell.

Sympathy filled the woman's eyes. "I can sneak you in real quick. Your father needs his rest."

She nodded, sniffling, trying desperately to pull herself back together. "He's going to be okay?"

"They've started a round of antibiotics."

She nodded again, even though she wasn't sure what the antibiotics were for. "Okay. That's good."

"Here." The nurse plucked a tissue from a box.

"Thank you." She blew her nose. "Thank you," she repeated, perilously close to losing it again.

"Let's take you down."

"I appreciate it." She walked behind the nurse.

They stopped in front of room 420. "Here we are."

"I'll be quick."

"Just make sure he rests."

She nodded and took a deep breath before she stepped into Dad's room.

He opened his eyes in the blue light glowing from the television. "Bella, I thought you would come by after work."

She shook her head, walking over to his bed and taking his hand as she sat on the edge of the mattress. "I needed to come now and make sure you're okay. You told me you were okay, Dad."

"I've got an infection. The doctors gave me some medicine on Monday—"

"Monday?" She touched the back of her fingers to his forehead and cheeks. He was burning up. "You didn't tell me anything about this."

"I had some sniffles. They turned into a touch of pneumonia."

"*Pneumonia*? Daddy," she scolded, trying her best not to get too frustrated with his lack of disclosure.

"That's what they're saying." He shrugged. "I was taking the pills."

"So what happened tonight?"

"I got a little lightheaded again and fell, but I didn't crack anything open this time."

She frowned when he smiled. "You're not taking this very seriously."

"I'm going to be fine. They're giving me some pretty potent stuff." He gestured to the liquid dripping down the IV tubing. "They want to keep me here for a couple of days."

"It sounds like they should." She fussed with his pillow. "We're going to start you on probiotics as soon as we get you home. We'll need to get your healthy bacteria back to where it should be."

"Bella." He gripped her hand tighter. "They ran some new tests."

Butterflies immediately fluttered in her belly as she stared into his eyes. She could already tell she didn't want to hear what he had to say. "Okay."

"Some of the tumors are getting bigger. They're spreading."

She swallowed as her pulse began to pound. "What does that mean, exactly? Are they shortening your time frame?"

"No. It means they said I should start expecting to have a few more bad days mixed in with the good."

"Oh." She brought his hand to her cheek as she pressed her lips together to keep them from trembling. "Oh," she said again, when she couldn't think of anything else to say.

"I'm going to enjoy my good days. Having you here makes every day better, Isabella." He winked.

She made herself smile. "We'll focus on the good, then."

He yawned. "I think I'm ready to close my eyes for a while."

"I want you to." She kissed his forehead. "Get some sleep. I'll stay—"

He shook his head. "Go home to bed."

"I'm going to sit for a few minutes."

"For a few minutes."

"Just a couple," she assured him as she settled in the chair next to his bed, keeping her hand tucked in his. Slowly Dad dozed off while she stared out the window, watching the night fade into day. She was exhausted. Her body begged her to sleep, but she focused on his big, bony hand swallowing hers. She didn't have endless moments with him to take for granted. He wasn't going to be here much longer.

She glanced from the IV drip to the hospital bed, then finally at her watch. Unfortunately, she had to go. She stood and kissed Dad's cheek, knowing she had to get home and ready for work. Looking his way one last time, she closed the door behind her and stopped by the nurses' station, where the same woman still sat. "If there are any changes with my father's condition, please call me right away."

"I'll do that."

"If you can, let him know I'll be back tonight after work."

"As soon as he wakes up, I'll tell him."

"Thank you." She got in the elevator when she wanted nothing more than to stay, but she had clients and a dog waiting for her an hour down the road.

Reed brushed his fingers through his wet hair as he walked downstairs, yawning loudly. He was starting to wonder why he bothered getting into bed every night when he barely slept anymore. For hours, he'd tossed and turned, catching a few minutes of shut-eye here and there, but mostly he'd stared at the ceiling, thinking about the way he'd handled things with Bella yesterday.

It bothered him that he'd caused her pain, that he'd allowed his frustrations to become an excuse to be careless and unkind. Bella meant too much to him to have treated her the way he had. Not all that long ago, he'd used his anger and intimidation tactics to get information—that's how the mafia crowd rolled, but that wasn't going to work with Bella—nor did he want it to. She owed him plenty of explanations. Waiting patiently for her to give him the answers he needed wasn't getting him anywhere, but neither was being a dick.

At some point last night, he'd realized he couldn't back off the investigation, nor could he walk away from Bella. Both were too important to him. He wanted to take down the Caparellis. They deserved to rot in hell, but most of all, he needed to know who Bella was. He meant what he'd said when he told her he was going to help her no matter what, but first he needed to know exactly what they were dealing with.

Basically, he and Bella needed to talk.

Sighing, he walked to the Keurig, set a mug beneath the spout, and pressed the *brew* button as he tried to figure out what his next step should be. He contemplated grabbing Bella breakfast and stopping by her office, waving a white flag, but then he remembered the tears in her eyes when she'd told him they should take a break. An egg burrito and his attempt at making light of a bad situation probably wasn't the best idea. Maybe the beach and ice cream would be better—their special thing...

The car slowing and pulling up at Bella's place caught his attention. He frowned as he glanced at the clock, then out the window, watching Jenny rushing toward Bella's front door, dressed in nursing scrubs. "Shit." Bella had been keeping early hours this last week, but she always brought Lucy with her. Bella's Volkswagen was gone from the driveway, and Jenny was on puppy patrol—not a good sign.

The fact that Bella was clearly having issues again and she hadn't bothered calling when he was right next door wasn't lost on him. He abandoned his hazelnut brew and walked outside.

Jenny looked at him as Lucy ran over from the side yard. "Hey, Reed."

He absently petted the puppy. "Where's Bella?"

"She had another emergency. She called me in the middle of the night—real upset again. She thought she'd be home for work, but I'm not so sure since it's almost six forty-five." She looked at her watch. "I mean, seven. Come on, Lucy. Do your thing."

Her gaze kept wandering to her car. Apparently, Jenny was running behind. "Do you have Faith with you?"

"No, I wouldn't leave her by herself. Reagan's got her."

"I can keep Lucy with me."

"I haven't fed her breakfast," she said, glancing at her watch for the second time.

"I can take care of it."

She hesitated, looking from her vehicle to Lucy. "I don't know. I should have been here sooner, but Faithy was givin' me a fit with her oatmeal. We both had to change."

"I'll take care of Lucy."

"That's real nice of you. Thank you. Tell Bella I hope she's feelin' better."

"I will."

"Bye." Jenny got in the Toyota and took off.

He sighed, looking at Lucy. "Where'd your mom go, Luce?"

The puppy wagged her tail and leaned against him.

"Let's get you some breakfast." He walked to Bella's, opening the door Jenny had left ajar, and stepped into the cozy space he hadn't been in since Sunday. It smelled like her: perfume, shampoo, and the scent that was simply Bella. "Want some grub?"

Lucy hurried over to her bowl in the kitchen.

He chuckled, following behind. "You definitely have a healthy appetite, and you actually seem to understand every word I'm saying, which is kinda weird." He scooped food into her bowl from the half-empty container and glanced at the new list started on the fridge, noting that Bella already jotted down that Lucy needed more kibble. She'd been busy—work was crazy for her right now, but she was still as organized as ever. There were several things written down that she needed to do, stuff they would have divided between the two of them just a few days ago, but he'd left her to deal with life on her own—something he wasn't particularly proud of. He'd handled this entire situation poorly, losing his cool like a complete jackass. But then again, he'd never been crazy about a woman whose family had killed his.

Walking over to the cupboard, he grabbed a cup and set it under the Keurig, like he'd done at his own house just minutes ago, then reached in the refrigerator for milk and snagged a spoon from the drawer, pausing when he recognized how easy it was to make himself at home. For a little while, this had been theirs. So much had changed, yet this place was exactly the same: lush green plants thriving in their pots, candles burned down a little more than they had been before, a toy waiting to be wrapped with cheerful paper—the small glimpses of Bella's life he'd been a part of for too short a time.

He scrubbed at his jaw and leaned against the counter, waiting for Lucy to finish up while he debated whether he wanted to be here when Bella got back. Maybe she needed some space, or maybe she would walk through the door the same way she had last time—pale, sick, and exhausted.

They had their problems. He and Bella were certainly at a crossroads, but he couldn't just leave her. He didn't *want* to leave her—at least not until he knew everything was okay. Perhaps now was as good a time as any to ask her what exactly was going on. He'd avoided that option all along, hoping she would share voluntarily, but maybe it was time to lay everything out on the table and go from there. Making his decision, he sat down at the table with his coffee and stared out the window as the sun made its way up for the day.

☙ Chapter Twenty-Four ❧

BELLA CLUTCHED THE STEERING WHEEL AS SHE SAT IN HER driveway, staring at her house through the windshield. She needed to get out of the car and go inside, but she didn't want to. Sitting here like this seemed better—easier. Unlike anywhere else in her life, she had complete control when she was in the driver's seat. At this point, not a whole lot seemed to be up to her, certainly not anything of importance. Dad's health was rapidly declining despite their best efforts, and Reed was gone.

Taking a deep breath, she unfastened her seat belt and got out, far from ready to face the day. She walked to the door and twisted her key in the lock, stepping into the entryway, where Lucy waited to greet her. A rush of emotions swamped her as she crouched down, wrapping her arms around her puppy. "You're here. I'm so glad you're here." Pressing her face into soft fur, she surrendered to the horrid sense of helplessness and fear she'd been forced to endure since early this morning. She let her tears fall, purging the worst of the dread, cherishing the silent support of her best friend.

Lucy let loose a sympathetic whine.

"It's going to be okay." She stroked Lucy's sides as she clung to her. "Everything's going to be all right," she reassured the dog, even when she didn't believe it. Sniffling, she kissed her puppy on the neck. "You give the best hugs." She kissed her again and lifted her head, rushing to her feet when she realized Reed was standing in the kitchen, watching her. Their gazes locked, and she took a step in retreat when her first instinct was to run to him. "What are you doing here?"

"I saw Jenny."

She swallowed, refusing to acknowledge the way the sexy scruff along his jaw and his tired eyes made her pulse pound. "You should go."

"We need to talk."

She shook her head even as she yearned for him to pull her against him and make everything okay again. "Please go." She turned and hurried upstairs, huffing out an exasperated breath when Reed's footsteps followed close behind. "I don't have time for this right now."

"You'll have to make time."

She tossed a glare over her shoulder, welcoming the heady rush of anger that consumed her as she walked into the bathroom and turned on the shower. For the first time in twelve hours, she wasn't afraid—she wasn't in pain. Riding high on her fury, she yanked her shirt over her head, hoping that getting naked would help Reed take the hint that she wasn't doing this today.

He reached around her and twisted off the faucet.

She turned it back on. "I have to go to work."

He shut it off again. "I want you to tell me what's going on."

Narrowing her eyes for the second time, she went after the front clasp on her bra.

He grabbed her wrist, halting her movements. "Tell me what's going on, Bella."

Her breath rushed in and out as she held his gaze, fighting to suppress the raw emotions bubbling just below the surface.

"Please." He loosened his grip on her arm and brought her hand to his lips, kissing her knuckles. "Please."

The flash of rage vanished as they stared at each other, leaving her as vulnerable as she'd been moments before. She pulled away from him and moved toward the bedroom, stopping and clutching at the doorframe when he caught her with two gentle hands on her waist.

"Please, Bella," he said next to her ear.

She stood rigid, squeezing her eyes shut as he caressed his thumbs along her skin. "He's—he's dying," she choked out, unable to keep her secrets any longer.

"Who?"

"My father."

"What?" He turned her to face him.

"He has colon cancer." She sniffled and wiped her cheeks.

"People survive that."

She shook her head. "He's stage four. They gave him six months, but I'm afraid he might not last that long. He's getting weaker. They admitted him this morning with pneumonia."

He sighed as sympathy filled his eyes. "Why didn't you tell me?"

"Because I didn't want anyone to know."

"*Why?*"

She shrugged. "I just...I didn't."

"You didn't have to deal with this alone."

"Yes."

He shook his head. "No."

She nodded and covered her face with her hands, crying quietly with the relief of finally being able to say everything out loud. "Every time I visit him, he looks worse—paler, thinner. I've been trying so hard to keep him healthy with juices and good food, but it's not helping. I thought the extra measures were going to let me keep him longer..."

"Come here." He took her hand and walked with her to the bed. "Sit down."

She slumped down to the mattress, her energy completely gone.

He pulled her against him, settling her head on his shoulder. "You could have told me."

"I found out a couple weeks ago." She grabbed a tissue and wiped her nose. "Even though I've known his diagnosis, I think today is the first day I've really let myself accept that he doesn't have much time." She sucked in a breath. "I just found him again and I'm going to lose him."

He frowned. "What do you mean, you just found him?"

She stared at him as more tears fell, understanding that there was no turning back. Reed wanted all the answers.

"*Tell* me, Bella." He took her hand, giving her fingers a squeeze as compassion and frustration warred in his eyes. "I need to know who you are. All of you. No matter what. So I can help."

She thought of last night, of how he'd treated her, and pulled away.

"Bella—"

She stood as her insecurities came rushing back—her fears that he wouldn't understand. "Do you really care who I am?"

"Of course I do." He gained his feet. "You know I do."

She shook her head. "No, I don't. Yesterday—"

"I was a prick."

She turned away, walking over to the dresser, fiddling with a leaf on her favorite ivy plant. "You hurt me."

"I know. I'm sorry."

"I don't date jerks."

"Good." He walked up behind her, wrapping his arms around her shoulders, and pressed a kiss to the top of her head. "You deserve so much better than the bullshit I dished out."

She turned in his embrace, studying him cautiously.

"I'm sorry I hurt you—that I made you cry. It kills me that you're trying to decide if you can trust me."

She stared into his eyes, seeing the regret, hearing it in his voice, knowing he meant what he said. "I don't know what to do anymore. About anything. I thought we were building something—"

"We are." He cupped her face in his hands. "We are," he said with more determination.

Her body sagged against him in defeat.

He brought her closer. "Please trust me. Please tell me about your family. Tell me about your dad."

His gentleness was her undoing. She cocooned herself in his warmth, taking the comfort he offered. "He's all I have left. I lost my mom last year. I finally have him back..."

"Did you two have a disagreement?"

She shook her head. "He left us when I was four—a couple days before my fifth birthday."

He eased her away. "He left?"

"Yes." She looked down at the floor, hating the familiar sense of shame, even when she knew it wasn't her fault. "He walked into my bedroom one night while I was decorating invitations for my party and told me he had to go away. The next morning I woke up and he was gone."

"Your dad left you and your mom?"

She nodded.

"He didn't call or—"

"I never saw him again until a few weeks ago. Jed found him for me—"

"Ethan's PI? Jed Hoffman."

She nodded her confirmation. "It took Jed a few months to track him down."

"Here. Come sit with me." They walked over to the bed. Reed surprised her when he eased her onto the edge of the mattress as he stood on his knees on the floor in front of her, sandwiching his body between her thighs so she sat eye-level with him. He settled his hands on her hips, giving her his full attention. "How's this?"

"Nice." She sent him a small smile. "Warm and safe."

"Good." He tucked her hair behind her ear and kissed her. "When did Jed find your dad?"

"The same day you and I met. I was standing in your living room, talking to Wren, when I got the text to call him."

He sighed. "I remember that."

"I'm glad I asked him to help me." She toyed with the arm of his T-shirt as she spoke. "I hate to think of Dad going through all of this alone."

"When he left, where did he go?"

"I don't know. He's never said." She shrugged, her gesture casual even as her eyes welled with the pain of remembering. "Mom said he gave her some money when he told her he was leaving. I remember them fighting that night. They never spoke again."

He wiped her tears. "What happened to you and your mom?"

"We moved around a lot. She tried waitressing and telemarketing but it didn't pay the bills. Mom didn't have much of an education—just her high school diploma. She had just started cosmetology classes when she met my dad. She got pregnant right away. She was barely twenty."

"So she did some telemarketing?"

"Um, for a little while." She focused on the sleeve of his shirt again, knowing she wasn't going to be able to avoid the rest much longer. "Then she tended bar."

He nodded.

She flicked him a glance, then stared back at the white cotton. "And danced."

"Danced? Like an instructor?"

"Uh, like a stripper." She blew out a long, shaky breath as she closed her eyes, waiting for Reed to say something, to judge her.

"Hey."

She opened her eyes, refusing to meet his.

"Hey." He lifted her chin. "Nothing you tell me is going to change anything between us—the way I feel about you."

Her bottom lip trembled. "I'm not so sure."

"I am."

She nodded, needing to believe him. "She was beautiful. The manager at the bar she worked at convinced her that she would make more money taking off her clothes than pouring drinks. I guess he was right."

"How old were you?"

"Six—maybe seven. I would go with her and sleep in the dressing room in a sleeping bag. The other women would keep an eye on me when she was on stage. They liked to put makeup on me and do my hair. It wasn't too bad."

"Sounds like your mom was doing the best she could."

Bella shrugged away Reed's excuses for her mother. Dancing might have started out as a way to pay the rent, but there was no excuse for the rest. "Mom liked to move—Indiana, Louisville, Nashville, where we stayed for three years, until I was eleven. We lived pretty well. I had nice clothes, went to good schools."

"Exotic dancers can make some pretty great coin."

He was being so kind—a good listener. "It wasn't enough for her. Nothing was ever good enough. She always wanted more."

"What do you mean?"

"We moved to Las Vegas and she changed."

"How?"

She traced his ears the way she often did, finding it impossible to keep her hands still. "Sometimes I think she did the stuff she did because she wanted to pay my dad back for leaving us."

"What did she do?"

"She started drinking a lot and pretty much checked out in the motherhood department."

"She left you?"

"No. Or not technically, anyway. Sometimes I wish she would have." She rolled her eyes at herself because she'd had more than most. "I had everything any teenager could ever dream of—credit cards, braces, more clothes than I could ever need, endless freedom. I hated all of it."

"Why?"

"Because it always felt tainted."

"How come?"

She gripped his shoulders as her heart beat faster and her stomach grew queasy. "God, I hate this."

He pulled her closer. "You can tell me."

More tears fell as her composure crumbled. "I don't want to."

"I'm not going anywhere," he reassured her quietly. "Why did you hate it?"

She swallowed, staring into his eyes, wanting to see the exact moment everything changed between them. "Because she was a prostitute."

He pressed a gentle kiss to her lips. "Okay."

She started crying when he let it be as simple as that. "No, it's not.

She called herself an escort, but it's still the same thing."

"Your mom was an escort."

"Why are you being so good about this? My mother was a prostitute."

"Bella, I was a cop. I saw that stuff all the time."

"You didn't see it with me. You didn't live my life."

"No, I didn't."

She pushed away from him and stood, needing some space. "I made good grades, went to a private school, lived in a luxury apartment because my mother sold her body to rich men. That doesn't bother you?"

"It bothers me because it hurt you, but who your mother was has nothing to do with who you are. It doesn't have anything to do with us."

"You're kinder to her than I ever was. There were so many days I resented her, had no respect for her because she had no respect for herself. She let herself die of hepatitis C. The pills the doctors prescribed made her gain weight, so she refused to take them."

"I'm sorry."

"I needed her. For so long, I needed her." She sighed, shaking her head, because it didn't matter anymore. "I would have killed for her to have cared about my homework or to have asked me what I wanted for dinner the way she used to. I just wanted for us to be a normal family. I had that for a little while."

"Before your dad left."

She nodded. "Sometimes I think I'm still looking for that, the feelings that used to come with that: warmth, safety, home."

"Come here." He wrapped her up in a hug, pressing a long kiss to her temple. "I'm sorry you went through all of that."

"I just—it makes me feel ashamed. And I feel ashamed that I'm ashamed. She was such a good mom when I was little. I remember our garden and Dad taking me to the park. They read to me every night." A smile ghosted her mouth. "He used to let me brush his hair with my Barbie brush."

"He sounds like a good guy."

"He is. I love him so much. I've missed him for so long."

"He never saw you in Vegas?"

"No."

"Do you have any other family?"

"An uncle."

His arms gripped her tighter as he slid his hand through her hair. "Do you keep in contact with him?"

"No. He's my mother's brother. He made it clear a long time ago that my mother was trash and he wanted nothing to do with either of us."

"What about your dad's side?"

She shook her head. "We never knew any of his family. He told my mother his parents died." She rested her hands on his hips. "I know I was named after my grandmother. I remember once he told me she was the only good one out of the whole lousy bunch." She tried to smile. "He said I should be proud of my name."

"It's a beautiful name." He smiled at her, kissing her again. "Thank you for trusting me, for telling me. I know this wasn't easy for you."

"Thank you for listening—for being so understanding."

"I want to help you. I want to meet your father and do whatever I can to make this easier for you."

She nibbled her lip. "I don't know."

"Let me be here for you, Bella."

She sighed.

"Let me help you."

She'd never let anyone share her burdens. The idea of having Reed by her side felt good. "I'm going to see him tonight after work—bring him something to eat."

"I'll drive. You're exhausted. Why don't you call in and get some rest today?"

She shook her head. "It's more work to cancel than it is to just go in and do what I need to do."

"Are you sure?"

"Definitely," she said with a decisive nod.

"All right. Then I'll pick him up some food before we go. What does he like to eat?"

"I've been feeding him a lot of fruits and vegetables, but probably something easier on his stomach. Maybe some soup."

"Consider it taken care of."

She wrapped her arms tighter around him. "Thank you, Reed."

"You're welcome."

"I'm going to go take a shower. I have to get to work. I'm already running late."

"Okay."

She walked into the bathroom, feeling lighter despite everything that had happened over the last several hours. She and Reed had a tough night, but today he'd been exactly what she needed.

Reed waited until he heard Bella step into the shower before he pulled his phone from his pocket and selected Joey's number.

"'Lo?" Joe said, answering on the second ring.

Reed rolled his eyes, listening to the noisy sounds of the precinct in the background. He didn't have to be sitting at the desk across from his old partner to know that Joey was tackling a police report with his two-finger typing method. Joe had never been much of a conversationalist when he was concentrating on the keyboard. "Working hard?"

"Fuckin' scumbags. If they would just do the right thing, I wouldn't be sitting here doing this."

He glanced toward the bathroom again and turned away, wrestling with the guilt of betraying Bella for the benefit of his job. "I'm meeting Nicoli Caparelli tonight."

"*What*?"

He winced, holding the phone away from his ear when Joey's booming voice ticked up several more notches.

"What?" Joey repeated, much quieter this time. "How the fuck did you manage that?"

"Bella's taking me to see him. He's sick—dying of cancer." He sat on the edge of the bed, sliding his fingers through his hair, hating that this was his priority when Bella was in so much pain.

"He's dying?"

He nodded, despite the fact that Joey couldn't see him. "She told me this morning. Colon cancer. He's got less than six months."

"She just found out?"

"No. She's known for a few weeks."

"And she's just sharing the news?"

He rubbed at his jaw, restless, struggling with the idea of breaking Bella's confidence. Her shame and grief—the things she'd shared with him—were supposed to have stayed between the two of them. "He left her. When she was four. One night, he told her he was leaving. She woke up the next morning and he was gone."

"Where'd he go?"

"She doesn't know. She just found him again."

"You believe her?"

"Yeah, I do. I think she's in the dark. I don't think she has any idea about Nicoli's life."

The line stayed silent.

He stood and started pacing. "Look, I know I've screwed this up. On every level I've fucked this up, but my gut's screaming at me, Joe." He puffed out a long breath when Joey still said nothing. "You weren't here. You didn't see her eyes, hear the agony in her voice." It still ripped him apart that there hadn't been anything more he could do for her than listen. "You don't have to trust me on this one. Right now, I'm having a hard time trusting myself, but I can't shake the feeling. This makes more sense than anything else."

"Because you want it to?"

"Maybe." He sat again and gained his feet just as quickly. "No. This fits—her phone calls to Reseda every day, driving up to check on him. She went to the grocery store for him on Sunday. That didn't make sense at the time, but it does now."

"What about the pictures?"

"I don't know. I don't know, Joe. But the woman who cried in my arms this morning isn't a mobster." He fiddled with the ivy leaf Bella had touched several minutes ago.

"I don't know what I'm supposed to say."

"I don't either. I get the position I've put you in. We both know I'm fucking crazy about her, but my eyes are open. They're wide open." He moved away from the dresser, standing by the window. "She hired one of Ethan's PIs to track down her father."

"You gonna corroborate?"

"No. I don't want anyone knowing we're sniffing around. If I ask questions, he'll ask questions. We both know how that goes."

"Yeah."

He sighed.

"Go see him. Get some impressions."

What else could he do at this point? He and Joe finally had something to work with. Bella had given him a glimpse into her past—who she knew her father to be—but it still wasn't the answers he needed. "That's the plan. He's in the hospital with pneumonia. We're bringing him dinner."

"Sounds like we're running out of time."

It certainly wasn't on their side. Nicoli was dying and Alfeo was counting down the days until he was free from his cell. "It's working against us." The shower shut off. "I should go. I've gotta get to work."

"Call me later."

"I will." He hung up and shoved his phone away, resenting that the Caparellis ruled his life once again. Giving a quick knock on the bathroom door, he walked in, finding Bella standing in front of the mirror, wrapped in a towel and brushing her hair. "How are you doing?"

"Better."

He hooked his arms around her waist, meeting her gaze in the foggy glass. "I have to go to work."

"We both do."

"You're going to be okay?"

She nodded.

"You'll call if you need anything?"

She turned and faced him, lacing her fingers at the back of his neck. "I'll be fine."

"I want you to let me know if you're not."

"Okay."

He kissed her, letting himself get lost in her taste, in the way her soft skin felt beneath his palms as he cradled her face and took them both deeper. For just a second, he wanted to pretend that the investigation didn't exist, that there weren't still too many questions unanswered. Bella needed this moment—he did too.

She eased away, smiling at him. "I think that will get me through till tonight."

He smiled back. "Call me if you need me."

"I will." She stood on her tiptoes, pressing another kiss to his lips. "Be safe today."

"I plan on it." He stepped back, breaking their contact when he wanted to stay. "See you tonight."

"Bye."

He left her to get ready and hurried downstairs, needing to get over to the Hills to pick up Sadie. At this point, he was stuck leading a double life, but that didn't mean he couldn't be here for Bella when she needed him the most.

☙ CHAPTER TWENTY-FIVE ❧

BELLA PRESSED THE BUTTON FOR THE FOURTH FLOOR AS SHE stepped into the elevator with Reed by her side. She smiled when the doors slid closed and he hooked his arm around her shoulders, pulling her back against his chest.

"How are you doing?" he asked next to her ear.

"Good." She rested her palms on the warm skin of his forearm and leaned into his embrace, finding his cozy hold comforting. "I'm a little nervous, I guess."

He hugged her closer, settling his chin on top of her head. "Everything's going to be okay."

She nodded, even as jittery anticipation and pure exhaustion wreaked havoc on her system. She was officially running on fumes after a night of minimal sleep and her nine-hour day. Her jam-packed schedule had passed in a blur of worry and second-guesses while she thought about Dad and replayed her morning conversation with Reed a million times. Despite the fact that she was still getting used to the idea of Reed knowing her secrets, it felt good to have everything out in the open. She'd never allowed herself to be so vulnerable, but that wasn't what currently had her on edge.

Reed and Dad were about to meet for the first time. She nibbled her lip, wondering how that was going to go. Dad tended to be overprotective, and she hadn't exactly mentioned that she was bringing along another visitor, particularly the man she was sleeping with. She hoped everything was going to turn out fine. Reed was an important part of her life, equally as important to her as Dad. She wanted the two people she adored most to know each other.

"Hey." He jostled her gently. "You're tensing up on me again."

"I'm trying not to." She inhaled deeply, then exhaled, consciously relaxing her shoulders. "Dad's dinner smells good."

"I think he's going to like it." He gestured to the bag he held in his opposite hand. "The woman at the deli said they make the best chicken stew around."

"I'm sure he'll love it, but he doesn't eat a whole lot anymore."

"Then he'll enjoy what he can handle." He nuzzled her neck. "I bought some for us too."

Smiling, she turned enough so she could meet his gaze and clasp her hands around his waist. "You did?"

"Mmm-hmm." He let his forehead rest against her temple. "Sandwiches too. And maybe a couple of brownies."

Her heart melted. "That's very sweet."

"I put everything in the fridge while you took Lucy out to go potty before we left. I figured we would chow down when we got home."

"Sounds perfect." She let her fingers slide through his hair, savoring this moment when everything felt warm and perfectly safe. "Thank you. For dinner. For coming with me. For being here."

He lifted his head and kissed her. "There's nowhere else I want to be."

The elevator dinged and the door opened. Bella let loose a small sigh as they broke their connection and stepped out, walking to the nurses' station. "Good evening," she said to the nurse sitting behind the desk—a different woman than the one who had been there this morning. "I'm Bella Colby. I'm here to see my father, Vincent Pescoe, in room four twenty."

The nurse glanced at the duty board over her shoulder and turned back. "Go on down, honey."

"Thank you."

Reed took her hand as they started down the hall. "Can I ask you a question?"

"Sure."

"Your dad's last name is Pescoe, right?"

She tossed him a curious glance. "Yeah."

"Why isn't yours?"

"He wanted me to have Mom's." She shrugged. "I don't know why, exactly, but I have to admit I like Colby better."

He smiled. "Isabella Colby has a nice ring to it."

She grinned. "I happen to agree." They stopped outside his door, and she took a deep breath as her nerves came rushing back. "I guess we're here."

He tucked her hair behind her ear. "It's going to be fine."

She nodded. "Are you ready?"

"Yeah. Let's do this."

She pushed down on the door handle and stepped inside, frowning as she studied Dad's ghostly complexion while he slept. He looked worse now than he had before. "Daddy?"

He opened his eyes. "Bella." He tried sitting up some as he looked at Reed.

"How are you feeling?"

He pressed the button on the bed, turning off the TV. "A little better."

"I brought someone to meet you," she said as she glanced back at Reed. "We brought you some dinner."

He cleared his throat. "I'm not much good for company."

"I know. We won't stay long." She walked over to him and kissed his forehead, then pressed her hands to his cheeks, relieved to find him cool to the touch. "Your fever's gone."

"It broke this afternoon. They say the drugs are helping this time around."

"Good." She scrutinized the mostly empty bag of antibiotics hanging on the IV pole, then gave her attention back to Dad. "Did they run any more tests?"

"Just some blood work."

She smoothed his blankets across his chest. "Have you been eating and drinking?"

"A little."

"Good." She touched his cheeks again, wanting to be certain he was indeed on the mend.

He took her hand. "I'm doing fine."

She nodded. "I want you to meet Reed."

"Reed McKinley." Dad studied him with sharp eyes.

"That's me." He stepped forward and shook Dad's hand. "It's nice to meet you, Mr. Pescoe."

"Call me Vinny since my daughter's willing to call you her boyfriend."

"Vinny," Reed said with a small nod.

"Bella talks about you—says you treat her well."

"I try."

"Good." He sat up taller, the protective light still shining in his eyes. "You'll want to keep that up."

"Reed's very good to me," she soothed with a pat on Dad's arm, wanting to move things along in a more positive direction. "He picked up dinner for you—chicken stew. Do you think you're up for it?"

Dad glanced toward the bag in Reed's hand with interest. "I could probably try a bit."

"Supposedly it's the best around." Reed pulled out the small to-go container and set it on the tray.

Dad rolled the mini table closer. "Smells great."

Bella ripped the spoon and napkin from the plastic baggy and handed them over. "This might help with your energy."

He took a small sample and nodded. "This is damn good."

She beamed, happy to see Dad eating something. And the worst of the tension in the room seemed to have subsided. "Enjoy it."

"Go ahead and have a seat," Dad invited.

Reed took one of the two chairs, sitting next to Bella.

"So, Reed McKinley, what is it that you do to make a living?"

"Close protection. I'm a bodyguard."

Dad paused with a chunk of carrot on his spoon. "Really? And who do you guard?"

"Wealthy businessmen and women, celebrities."

Bella hooked her arm through Reed's and leaned against him. "Right now, he's handling a stalker case for a teenage girl."

"Like she's being followed or whatnot?"

"Pretty much," Reed confirmed. "She's received some disturbing notes—has been tailed three or four times, which means I'm back in high school for the time being."

Dad grinned. "Well, how about that?"

"It's been an experience. If I ever have a daughter, I'm locking her up until she's thirty and throwing away the key."

Dad laughed.

Bella blinked her surprise, smiling her delight. It had been years since she'd heard one of Dad's full-out laughs. She grinned at Reed, thanking him for such an exceptional gift.

He winked and took her hand, lacing their fingers.

Several minutes passed with easy conversation—mostly pointless small talk. By the time Dad finished half of his dinner, he looked tired again. Setting the spoon down, he gave a satisfied pat to his belly. "I think that was enough for me."

Bella lifted her head off Reed's shoulder. "We should probably be thinking about heading out so you can rest." She stood and gathered the trash, handing it to Reed when he reached for it.

"I wish I had the energy for you to stay longer."

"Next time."

"Thank you for coming and bringing me something delicious."

"You're welcome." She fixed his covers again. "If you need anything, please call me or have the nurses call me. Anytime, day or night."

"They're thinking I'll be able to go home on Sunday."

"That's great." She poured more water into his cup from the small pitcher—just in case he needed it after she left. "I'll be here to get you."

He shook his head. "You have things to do. A life to live."

"I'll be here to get you," she repeated, refusing to argue with him. "I'll pick up some groceries and put some meals in the fridge for you as well."

"I'm under the weather, not helpless."

She suppressed a sigh of frustration. Why did Dad have to be so stubborn? "I know that, but the last thing we want is for you to go to the store and catch more germs. Give yourself some time to recover." She kissed him. "I'll see you tomorrow."

"No. I'll see you on Sunday. Tomorrow you go to lunch with your friends or do something with Reed. Take Lucy to the beach."

She frowned. "But my whole day's free."

"And you need your rest too. You're tired, Bella." He touched gentle fingers to the dark circles under her eyes. "A father knows when his daughter needs a break. Don't make me tell the nurses you aren't welcome in my room."

She gaped. "Daddy—"

He tossed her a stern look, assuring her that he wasn't kidding. "Don't make me tell them, Isabella."

"Okay. Fine." She huffed out a breath. "But I'm going to call."

He rested his head against the pillow and turned on the TV, his hint that he wanted them to go. "You can call."

"Bella, we should head out. It was nice to meet you, Vinny." Reed extended his hand again.

"And you. Take care of my little girl."

"I will."

She leaned over, hugging Dad tight. "I'll see you Sunday."

He returned her embrace. "See you then."

They walked out into the hall, hand in hand, and started back the way they came, passing the nurses' station.

"I'm sorry Dad was a little intense."

He shrugged. "He's your dad. I didn't expect anything less."

"You made him laugh."

"I'm a part-time comedian."

"No." She stopped, wanting Reed to understand. "I haven't heard him laugh like that since I was a little girl. I forgot what that sounded like."

He exhaled a deep breath as he held her gaze.

"Almost twenty-one years."

"That's a long time."

She nodded as her eyes grew misty. "Yeah."

He brought her knuckles to his lips. "Let's go home."

She nodded again as the elevator doors opened and they stepped inside. "You're coming over tonight?"

"Yeah, I'll come over for a little while." He wrapped his arm around her as the doors slid shut, much like he had on their ascent to the oncology floor.

She relaxed against him, and for the first time in nearly a week, her world felt like it was finally starting to settle again.

Reed twisted the key in his front door and let himself into his place while he waited for Joey to pick up his phone. He glanced toward the second-story lights shining bright in Bella's house, knowing he had to be quick.

"How'd it go?" Joey answered on the third ring.

"Good. Better than expected." Hurrying upstairs, he stripped out of his jeans and T-shirt. He grabbed his favorite pair of ratty gray sweat shorts and put them on, then threw his laptop in its case—his excuse for coming over to his condo so he could call Joey. "He's in rough shape, though—definitely dying."

"That bad?"

"It's not good." Vincent Pescoe did *not* look like Nicoli Caparelli. Cancer had been unkind to the one-time mobster—to the point that Reed had second-guessed himself a couple of times while he'd studied Bella's father from his chair in room four twenty. The frail, thin man lying in the bed was a startling contrast to who he'd been in his glory days. "We don't have a lot of time."

"Sounds like we should be bringing in Skylar on this. We've done the preliminary work. If we're going to make something happen, it's now or never."

He'd been thinking the same thing on the hour-long drive home. Reaching out to their FBI contact and Reed's longtime friend was the next step. "I'll give her a call."

"Let me know what she says."

"I'll send you a text." He shouldered the computer bag, shut off the bedroom light, and headed downstairs. "I need to get back to Bella. She's had a long day."

"How are things going between you two?"

"They're going. I believe her, Joe. I can't help but believe her. If we could just explain the pictures..." He hated that the connection was still there—still plaguing him, still making him question and doubt. He locked up and started across the side yard.

"Hopefully Caparelli will be able to clue you in on what the hell's going on."

"If he'll even talk to me."

"You brought him dinner. You're sleeping with his daughter. He'll talk to you. Maybe to tell you to fuck off, but he'll definitely have something to say."

He grunted his response, again on the same page as his partner. Things were finally happening—moving in the direction he and Joey had worked so damn hard for. How ironic was it that now that he had bedside access to one of the top dogs in the Caparelli crime family, the only thing he was worried about and focused on was Isabella Colby. Tomorrow he would have his answers when he paid Vinny another visit—or the one that mattered the most. Bella was either part of the life or she wasn't. If nothing else came out of meeting with Nicoli, he needed to know that. "Let's hope he loves his daughter enough to do the right thing."

"Let me know what Skylar says."

"Will do." He hung up and stepped inside Bella's entryway, satisfied when he heard the water running through the pipes. She was still in the shower. Securing the locks for the night, he moved into the kitchen, searching through his contact list for Skylar Grayson's number. He sent the call through and waited, his heart kicking up a beat, knowing that Skylar would make this case or break it. And he had to hope like hell she was up for keeping this between the three of them. Vincent Pescoe was in no shape to run. If word got out that Vincent Pescoe was Nicoli Caparelli, he wouldn't be able to hide fast enough.

"Special Agent Grayson."

"Skylar, it's Reed McKinley."

"Reed McKinley. I swear I've heard that name before."

He smiled as he opened the refrigerator, pulling out the container of chicken stew he'd put away for later. "I have something big. Can I trust you with it?"

"How big?"

He grabbed two bowls next. "As big as it gets."

"Yeah, you can trust me with it."

He dumped soup into the dishes and popped them in the microwave, setting the cooking time to three minutes. "I found Nicoli Caparelli."

"Nicoli Caparelli."

"The one and only."

"And how did you do that?"

He leaned against the counter, keeping his ears trained and his eyes on the stairwell across the room. "It doesn't matter."

"I thought you gave up police work, bodyguard."

"You didn't expect me to get out of the game entirely. Now that I don't have all those pesky rules and procedures to follow, it's more fun."

"Where is he?"

"I have an in."

"Which is?"

"I can talk to him tomorrow."

"And what will you two be talking about?"

He glanced at the ceiling as the water shut off upstairs. "About how he's going to help keep Alfeo locked away for the rest of his miserable days."

"And why do you think he won't just kill you, ditch your body, and take off?"

"Because he's sick. Dying. He's got a couple months left." The line stayed silent and he knew he had her. "Think of all of those prison letters and phone calls we tried to decipher over the years. You've got two dead mafia men on your hands, and you know the orders are coming from the Godfather himself while he sits in his cell. Do you think that's going to stop?"

"We've got a statute of limitations."

Bella's footsteps moved from the bathroom to the bedroom. "Not on murder. Not on class A felonies. And we both know Alfeo has plenty of those under his belt."

"No, we don't. Nothing we can prove or we would have done it already."

"That's where Nicoli's going to come in. We just need something to stick, something solid little brother might be able to hand over, and Alfeo's done."

"You see what you can come up with and we'll talk."

He shook his head, even though Skylar was hundreds of miles away in Manhattan. "We'll talk and I'll see what I can come up with."

"I'll talk to my supervisor."

"Wrong." He ignored the beeping microwave, knowing he was running out of time. "We'll keep this to ourselves until I get something worth mentioning. I want to know you're in once I do. Whatever it takes, we're moving forward with keeping that son of a bitch in prison and protecting Nicoli while we're doing it."

"I'm in. That bastard killed my grandfather's partner."

"Yeah. I've heard something about that. I'll get back to you tomorrow."

"Bye." The ball was rolling now. Tomorrow he needed to go see Vinny Pescoe and let him know who he was, but for now, he planned to take care of the woman upstairs. Bella was absolute toast. He opened the microwave and pulled out steaming bowls, muttering a curse when he burned his fingers on the scalding crockery. "Damn," he swore again, diminishing the pain with several shakes of his hand. Glancing around, he grabbed one of the oversized cutting boards, used it as a makeshift tray for their dinner, and started up the stairs. He paused in the doorway, studying Bella as she sat on the bed with her back to him, wrapped in a towel with her wet hair cascading down her shoulders. A small box was tucked by her side, and she held something in her hands. "What have you got there?"

"A snow globe."

"Huh." He set the cutting board on the dresser and sat next to her, studying the two-story house surrounded by pine trees in the center of the glass.

"Dad gave this to me the night he told me he was leaving. He said I could think of him when I looked at it." She turned it, stirring up the white flecks with her movements. "For a long time I thought he lived in there." She smiled sadly as she continued to stare. "I would read to this thing, talk to it. More than once I begged him to come back out."

He touched her arm, stroking his fingers along her soft skin, overtaken by a wave of sympathy for the little girl who'd wished for her father, for the woman who still suffered from the aftermath of a less than ideal childhood. "He adores you."

Her gaze locked on his.

"You can see it all over his face—the pride, how much he loves you."

She smiled. "That's nice to hear." She turned toward the box, taking out a picture. "This was my normal—what I've been looking for ever since it went away."

He took the photo from her, studying the four-by-six shot: pretty preschool Bella Colby with a striking woman and her handsome mafia father sitting together on a picnic blanket in a small backyard. Summer was in full bloom in the photograph—ripe gardens thriving. Here he had no trouble recognizing Nicoli Caparelli. "You look a lot like your mom. She was beautiful."

"In this picture, she was my mom—garden planter, cupcake baker, the woman who would walk me to the library for story time and take me to school. She taught me to read when I was four. She always told me I was going to have more than she did. Smart, pretty girls could have it all. Then she stopped telling me—stopped caring."

He tucked her hair behind her ear. "I'm sorry, Bella."

Her shoulders lifted in a small shrug. "I wanted her to believe in herself. I wanted her to be strong."

"Some people aren't." He pulled her against him. "Maybe that's why you are—because she couldn't be."

She held his gaze, her eyes soft, her guard completely down as she cupped his cheeks in her hands and kissed him. There was no heat, no attempt to deepen the gentle meeting of lips. "How do you know what to say? How do you know how to take away the worst of the pain?"

"I'm just telling you what I see—what I know to be true. You're so strong, Bella."

"I never wanted anyone to know, but I'm glad you do. I'm so glad I get to share this part of myself with you." She kissed him again and rested her head in the crook of his neck as she grabbed another photo. "This was the last picture we took together. Christmas 1994."

"Your dad was a pretty handsome guy."

"I only have a couple of pictures of him. He didn't like to be photographed. Kind of like you, but not for the same reasons." She smiled.

He glanced from the grinning, sweet little girl decked out in a red velvet dress to the gorgeous woman she'd become, smiling even though he and Nicoli Caparelli were wary of picture taking for *exactly* the same reason. "Yeah."

She took the photos back and put them in the box. "Sometimes I like to bring this stuff out and remember. Not very often, though."

"Because it makes you sad."

She nodded.

"Bella," he whispered as he pressed his head to hers. "I wish I could make everything better."

"In this case you can't."

"I'm sorry about that."

"It's okay."

It wasn't, but they could only focus on now. "How about some dinner? I heated up the soup."

"I should probably get dressed." She walked to her drawer and grabbed a black nighty and panty set. She let her towel fall, and pulled flossy black up her firm thigh, and settled the swatch on slim hips. The camisole was next—silky fabric slipping over taut breasts that begged to be tasted, then her sexy stomach.

He swallowed a ball of lust, wanting her, but he couldn't be with her. Not until he had the answers. He cleared his throat and stood, pulling back the covers. "You wanna eat in bed?"

Her gaze flew to his. "You're staying here?"

He didn't have to—he could say no, but this was where he wanted to be. "If that's okay."

"It's more than okay. I've missed having you in my bed." She plopped down on the mattress and rested her head against the pillows, moaning. "This feels so *good*."

Damn, she was killing him. Abandoning his plans for a late meal, he got in bed beside her. "Are you sure you don't want to eat?"

"I'm too tired for food." She pulled the covers over them and snuggled up against him.

"You should eat." Although he wasn't particularly hungry, either, with so much weighing on his mind.

"I'll have something in the morning."

"Or we can have a snack if we wake up later."

"Mmm." She looked at him with her big, sleepy eyes. "Thank you for today."

He brushed her hair back from her forehead. "You're welcome. Thanks for letting me sleep over."

"I like having you here." She settled her head in the crook of his arm as she hooked her leg around one of his.

He shut off the light and hugged her closer, breathing her in, loving the way her body felt pressed to his. It had been over a week since they'd lain together like this. Ideally, tomorrow he would be here just like this again. If there was any justice in the world, Nicoli Caparelli would help him put the pieces together once and for all and give him back the most important part of his life.

☙ Chapter Twenty-Six ❧

Reed rode the elevator to the fourth floor, waiting impatiently as the bright red numbers counted off his ascent. The door finally slid open and he got off, stopping at the nurses' station.

"Good afternoon." The nurse smiled.

He sent the woman his best grin. "Good afternoon. I'm here to see Vinny Pescoe in room four twenty." He gestured to the two cups of coffee he held in his hands.

"I don't think Mr. Pescoe is expecting visitors today."

"Yeah." He smiled again. "Bella, his daughter, promised to stay away today and do something for herself, but I told her I would come check on him." He shrugged. "Technicalities."

The nurse chuckled. "That's very sweet of you. Go ahead."

"Thanks." He walked to Vinny's room and knocked.

"Yeah. Come in."

He used his forearm to press down on the handle and pushed open the door, watching Vinny frown as their eyes met.

"Reed. What are you doing here?"

He was glad to see Vinny had a little color in his cheeks. He didn't want his visit to cause some sort of setback. "I thought I would bring you some coffee."

His frown deepened. "You drove an hour to bring me coffee? Did Bella put you up to this?"

He shook his head, setting one of the cups on the tray by Vinny's bed. "Nah. I wanted to talk to you."

"Sounds serious." He turned off the TV. "You here to ask for her hand in marriage?"

He choked on his sip of hazelnut java. He was prepared for just about anything today, but Bella and marriage hadn't been on his mind. "No. We haven't been dating for that long. We're not moving that fast."

"She likes you. I like that you make her smile."

He studied the sickly man taking a testing sip of his coffee, trying to see him as the ruthless bastard he knew Nicoli Caparelli to be instead of the adoring father. "She's an amazing, beautiful woman."

"You're smart to see that." Vinny tapped his finger to his temple. "Don't ever forget it."

He sat in the same chair he had last night. "I won't."

Vinny set down his cup. "So what's this about, then?"

Time to cut to the chase. "Vinny, I'm a former undercover detective with NYPD's Special Organized Crime Unit."

He saw the quick flash of surprise and watched Vinny mask it expertly with a look at his paper cup and another drink. "So the bodyguard thing's a bunch of BS?"

He shook his head. "I did deep cover for seven years, infiltrating and working my way up into the Caparelli crime family—got myself shot and decided I would give close protection a try."

Vinny met his gaze again. "This is all interesting, but why are you telling me?"

"Because I know you're Nicoli Caparelli, and I want your help."

Vinny smiled. "I hate to burst your bubble, but you've got the wrong guy. I have no idea what you're talking about."

He set his cup on the floor next to him and pushed his chair closer to the bed. Vinny aka Nicoli was good—smooth. "Alfeo gets out in a little over two months."

Vinny's frown returned. "Who?"

He pushed himself closer again. Nice didn't appear to be working. "Let's cut the shit here, Vinny. I worked with Walter Hodds from the Marshals. I know Peter Salada and Terry Upshaw are hoping to find you before your big brother does."

Vinny's eyes changed, going flat—killer cold. Here was the ruthless Mafioso. "What do you want?"

"I want you to help me keep Alfeo behind bars. I want something that will extend his sentence and ideally send your nephew away too."

"I'm gonna tell you like I told Salada and Upshaw when they came knocking on my door a couple weeks ago. Get the hell out of here."

He shook his head. "I found you, Vinny. So did your daughter with the help of a PI. It took a little digging on both counts, but we found you nonetheless."

His nostrils flared as he sat up. "You leave Bella out of this."

He brought himself closer, until his knees touched the side of the bed. "What's her role? What does she know about your life?"

"Not a goddamn thing, you bastard." His hands shook now—maybe fear, probably rage. "I left her so douchebag assholes like you would never connect the two of us."

He wanted so desperately to believe him, but he needed more. "Then what was she doing with Matty and Dino last Saturday afternoon?"

"What?" His breath wheezed out, his cheeks growing pinker.

"Last Saturday in Brooklyn."

"You're a fucking liar." He pointed, punctuation his last word.

Reed took out his cell phone and pulled up the pictures, handing it over to Vinny, watching his face register the surprise—and there was no disguising the ripe fear in his eyes. "Did you send her to New York?"

Vinny grabbed Reed by the collar of his T-shirt, yanking them face-to-face. "Listen here, you little fucker, I don't know what my daughter was doing with these two pricks, but I'm telling you she has no idea who I am, no idea I had any part in the life. This is some sick coincidence. They would kill her if they knew she had my blood coursing through her veins." He gave a nasty jerk to Reed's shirt. "They would let her die slowly."

He freed himself from Vinny's death grip, keeping eye contact the entire time. "So help me put them away."

"Don't you dare use Bella as a way to get me to cooperate. They have no idea I have a daughter. I vanished off the face of the earth in 1989. I haven't been seen since."

"I'm looking right at you, Vinny. Salada and Upshaw were looking right at you, knocking on your front door. If I found you, it's only a matter of time before someone else does too."

"By then I'll be in the ground, so it won't make much of a difference anyway."

"Bella won't be. Bella has her whole life ahead of her. How long do you think it will take to connect her to you?"

"No one can connect her to me."

"Too many people know your identity: a marshal, two detectives, two FBI agents. Stuff leaks. We both know it." He pulled one of his old cards from his pocket, wrote his new number on it, and handed it over, grabbing his coffee as he stood. "You think about how you want this to go for Bella. What kind of life are you planning on leaving for her?"

"You stay away from her. You stay far fucking away," he spat, pointing again. "Don't think I'm not well enough to get out of this bed, hunt you down, and end you."

He had no doubt Vinny meant it. The deadly look in his eyes was one more than a few men had most likely seen before they took their last breath, but he refused to be intimidated. "You'll have to end me, because I'm not going anywhere. I cared about Bella before I knew she had anything to do with you. And having me close, knowing every move she makes, is probably a good thing, because they'll come, Vinny. Don't be stupid enough to believe otherwise. It's not a matter of if. It's when." He walked out and down the hall, lifting his half cup of coffee to the nurse at the desk, giving her a small smile as he realized his hand wasn't quite steady. Adrenaline was surging through his blood.

He pushed the button for the elevator and stepped in, shoving his hand in his pocket as he stared at the bright red numbers on his descent. Bella wasn't a Caparelli. He let his head rest against the wall and his shoulders relax as he allowed himself to believe what he'd known in his gut. The look in Vinny's eyes, his reactions left Reed positive that Bella knew absolutely nothing about the mafia. Nicoli Caparelli might have been a skilled liar and killer among other things, but Reed recognized when a man was telling the truth. He never should have doubted that Bella was too.

He glanced at his watch, eager to get home. Now that he was convinced of her innocence, he couldn't get there fast enough.

The elevator stopped on the ground floor and he got out, waiting until he was back in his truck before he dialed Joey.

"So, how'd it go?"

"He called me a little fucker and he's definitely stronger than he looks."

"That well?"

He grinned. "Bella's not involved, Joe."

"What was his explanation for the pictures?"

"He didn't have one, but when he saw her sitting next to Matty Caparelli, I thought his eyes were going to pop out of his head."

"And you bought it?"

"One hundred percent." His light mood lessened as the reality of the situation sank in. "He was afraid for her. He knows they'll kill her if they ever find out who she is."

"We'll have to keep that from happening. I guess congratulations are in order, boss. Your girl's not a mafia princess after all."

He chuckled. "Thank God."

"What's the next step?"

"Going home. Seeing Bella. I left Vinny my card. We'll see what he wants to do with it—"

"Hold on," Joey interrupted as a small commotion erupted in the background and someone muttered something to Joey that Reed couldn't understand. "Shit," he said, giving Reed his attention again.

Reed's shoulders grew tense. "What?"

"Word's filtering down that another murder just happened over in Bensonhurst. Mob hit. They're pretty sure it's Caparelli-related."

"Looks like my meeting with Vinny happened at just the right time—a little incentive to remember that he could be next."

"The guys dying are the ones he helped put away when he took down Alfeo."

"That's not lost on me."

"I'm gonna get out of here and head down to the scene—see what I can figure out."

"Call me when you know something."

"You got it."

"Bye." Hanging up, he turned over the ignition. He didn't want to think about mafia murders or Nicoli Caparelli for the rest of the day. He was stopping off at the farmers' market for flowers. Then he was going home. He didn't know where he stood with Nicoli Caparelli, but he was ready to pick up with Bella right where they left off at the airport.

Reed stuck his key in Bella's front door and muttered a curse when he realized she'd left it unlocked again. They were going to have to work on that, even if she did have Lucy with her all of the time. Dogs were excellent crime deterrents, but deadbolts *and* a barking Great Dane were even better. He shut himself inside and secured the lock, then walked through the living room, frowning when the house seemed too quiet. "Bella?" He moved toward the stairs and stopped when he caught a glimpse of her through the French doors. He started her way, trailing his gaze over her dark pink tank top and denim short shorts as she sat on the back porch. She'd pulled her hair back in a ponytail and left her feet bare, the perfect complements to her relaxed Saturday attire.

Smiling, he watched her scoop soil into a pot while she said something to Lucy. She was so pretty, so tidy, even among the mess she was making. And she was his. By some crazy twist of fate, beautiful Bella Colby had chosen to be with him. Thanking his lucky stars, he opened the door, catching the scent of her perfume melding with the earthy dirt.

She turned her head and smiled. "Hey, handsome."

Damn, she made his heart race. "Hey." He pulled a big bouquet of sunny daisies from behind his back.

Surprise brightened her face as she glanced from the flowers to him. "You brought daisies."

"Just for you."

"Aww." She stood and wrapped her arms around him, careful not to touch his white T-shirt with her dirty gardening gloves. "Reed." She studied the bright white blooms with their bold yellow centers. "Thank you."

He would have to remember to bring her flowers regularly. There was nothing better than watching Bella's eyes go soft. "I wasn't sure what you liked."

"This. Anything." She pulled off her gloves and kissed him. "I need to get a vase." She walked into the kitchen and opened the cupboard below the sink, selecting a simple clear globe from her half-dozen options.

He studied her firm legs and excellent ass as she straightened again and filled the glass halfway with water, ready to take from her what he hadn't dared.

"I can't believe you brought me flowers."

He plunked the stems in the bowl—flimsy plastic covering and all—and took the vase from her hands, setting it on the counter.

"Wait."

He shook his head. "We can deal with these later. They're not going anywhere." He pulled her against him and kissed her, instantly teasing her tongue with his. "I need to taste you." He nipped her bottom lip and dove deep again.

She made a sound in her throat as she stood on her tiptoes and hooked her arms around the back of his neck.

He savored her flavor—the way she wanted him as much as he wanted her. Scooping her up, he walked through the living room and brought her upstairs. "We have something we need to do."

"Take a nap?" she asked playfully.

"We'll probably need one afterward."

She smiled, wiggling her eyebrows. "I like the way you think."

"I thought you might." He moved through the master suite and laid her down in the center of the bed, kissing her some more, certain he would be happy never to stop.

She tilted her chin, giving him better access to her neck as his mouth moved along her jaw. "Good day at the gym?"

He lifted her shirt over her head and went after the front clasp on her bra. "The best."

Her hands wandered over his back. "I guess so."

He palmed her breasts, clenching his jaw when she whimpered and arched. "I need to be with you."

She yanked off his shirt and went after the snap on his pants. "Great idea."

"It's been awhile." He unfastened the button on her shorts and tugged at her panties, sliding them off her legs.

"Over a week."

"Too long." He looked his fill at the naked woman who drove him absolutely insane just from wanting. "Christ, you're stunning."

"Thanks." She fought his jeans and boxers over his hips and off. "Mmm. Come on in, big boy."

"I plan to." He teased her nipples with his lips and tongue and trailed openmouthed kisses down her stomach, nibbling at her hips and thighs before settling between her legs. "In just a minute."

Her chest rose and fell with her unsteady breathing as she sat up on her elbows and held his gaze. "What are you thinking about doing down there?"

He traced soft skin. "I was thinking about making you come a couple of times—and making myself crazy in the process." He dipped two fingers inside.

She closed her eyes and moaned.

He swept his fingers in her wet warmth, finding the spot that always got her off. "If you're okay with that."

She sucked in a sharp breath, her stomach shuddering. "More than."

He went to work, adding his mouth, lapping, suckling, watching her build, his eyes locking on hers.

"Oh, God," she whispered as her brow furrowed slightly and her mouth opened with her panting breaths. "Reed." She bit her bottom lip and moaned, rocking her hips with the back-and-forth rhythm of his tongue. "Reed." Her fingers found their way into his hair, clutching as she teetered on the edge. He increased his pressure, moved faster, feeling her throbbing against him as her eyes went blind and her head fell back on the pillow with her long, loud cry.

He wanted her to go again, to bring her as much pleasure as she brought him simply from watching her climax. He played her some more as she thrashed and bucked, calling out to him mindlessly as she tensed and gasped, falling on a stunned scream.

"God, I need you. I need you." She reached down for him. "I can't take it anymore."

Neither could he. He crawled back up the length of her body, kissing her belly and breasts, then shoved her knees to her shoulders, driving himself inside. He groaned as she whimpered and gripped his wrists. She was wetter, tighter. "You feel so good." He thrust hard, flesh slapping against flesh, taking the edge off, but this wasn't how he wanted to finish. He let her legs go and settled himself on top of her. "Like this."

She nodded, her cheeks pink, her eyes darker and dazed.

"I want to be with you like this, Bella," he panted out, slowing his pace to lazy thrusts. They moved together, clasping hands, kissing tenderly, while he waited for her to climb again. Minutes passed, but there was no hurry. There was only Bella. Eventually she tensed, and he let himself fall with her, swallowing her cries as he emptied himself into her.

"Wow." Her breath rushed in and out next to his ear. "I think you should go to the gym every Saturday afternoon if you're going to come home like this."

He grinned, brushing damp locks away from her forehead, ignoring the fact that he'd lied about today's destination. "I thought about you the whole drive home."

She kissed him as she stroked her fingers along his spine. "I think about you all the time."

He smiled again, staring down at the most important person in his life. "That's a pretty good thing, because I've never felt about anyone the way I do you." And it felt so damn good to be able to say so, finally to be able to let his guard down and give her all of the pieces.

Her eyes grew misty as she blinked up at him. "You're on quite a roll."

"I love being with you." He kissed her forehead. "I'm so glad Lucy walked through my front door all those weeks ago."

"Reed," she whispered, nuzzling his cheek with hers.

"I want to cook you dinner." He wanted to be all the things he'd been too afraid to be when he didn't know who she was.

"Really?"

He nodded.

"What are you going to feed me?"

"Fish. It's a New England recipe and one of the only things I know how to make well."

She grinned. "You know how to make raviolis and steak and crème brûlée."

"This dish is even better." He winked and kissed her again. "I have to go to the store and pick up a few things."

"I'll come with you if you want, but I might have to sit in the cart. My legs are still trembling."

He chuckled, settling his face in the crook of her neck as she wrapped him up in a hug.

☙ Chapter Twenty-Seven ❧

Bella finished the last bite of her cracker-crumb-topped cod and set down her fork with a smile. "That, Mr. McKinley, was amazing."

He smiled back, sipping the white wine they'd picked up to go along with the roasted broccoli and fish. "Joey's mom would make this for us when she invited us over every couple of months. She's from Maine, so this is pretty traditional New England fare."

"You'll have to let Joey's mother know your West Coast girlfriend approves."

He took her hand, playing with her fingers as he held her gaze. "I'll do that."

She covered his hand with her free one, sandwiching his between hers. "Thank you for dinner."

"You're welcome."

She looked to the daisies she'd finally taken out of the plastic wrapper and arranged when they came back from the market. "And the flowers add a nice touch of spring to the room."

"As soon as I saw them, I had to get them. They made me think of you."

Would she ever get used to this sweet man? Tonight, he was different somehow. More in tune, maybe? More present? She couldn't quite put her finger on exactly what it was, but she would happily take it.

"You're probably more suited for roses or those calla lily things," he continued. "They're fancier—kind of like you, but the daisies seemed warm and friendly, which is also like you."

Her heart stuttered in her chest. How had she lucked out to find herself a man who put that much thought into which flowers suited her best? "I think I like being friendly more than I like being fancy."

"I'd say you're a good combination of both."

She stood, walked over to his chair, and settled herself in his lap, staring into his eyes as she hooked her arms around the back of his shoulders. "You better be careful, Reed. If you keep this up, you're going to make me fall in love with you."

He returned her embrace, locking his hands at her waist. "Oh, yeah?"

"Mmm-hmm." She snuggled closer. "Is that going to be a problem?"

He shook his head. "Not for me."

"That's good to know." He'd stolen her heart long ago, but there was no rush in sharing the news. Things were good between them—perfect. She kissed him and sighed, her bubble of contentment bursting when she looked around at the small mess they'd made with their dinner preparations.

"What?"

"I have some cleaning up to do. On the porch too." She stood from his lap and walked to the French doors, staring out at the dirt crumbles and freshly potted plants still needing water. "I should probably start out there."

Reed walked up behind her and settled his hands on her hips. "I distracted you."

"You did." She grinned as she lifted her head to look at him. "But in the most amazing way."

He grinned back, playing with her hair. "I'm thinking it was a good plan."

She laughed. "The best."

He smiled again, glancing out the panes of glass. "It looks like you planted basil. I don't know much about the rest."

"Come on out with me." She took his hand, and they stepped outside with Lucy following behind. "This plant here that kind of looks like a pine tree is rosemary." She broke off a tiny twig and held it up to his nose. "It smells really good."

He sniffed. "It does."

"It'll taste great with pork or chicken—all kinds of stuff, really. This one's thyme." She pointed. "And I'm trying my hand at some lavender." She touched her finger to one of the pretty purple flowers.

"Do you eat it?"

"You can, but you can also use it for aromatherapy and to make scrubs and salves. Julie does a lot of stuff with that. She's going to teach me how to make some of her more popular products. She doesn't carry them anymore since she's so busy with her yoga classes. I might make up a few batches and we'll sell them under her license."

"You two could make a killing together."

"Life isn't all about money. We both love what we do."

"That's pretty important."

"It's vital. Do you love what you do?"

He shrugged. "I'm starting to. For the first time in a long time, I feel like my life is settling into place—every part of it."

Her stomach fluttered, catching his meaning clearly enough. "Balance is key."

"You might have something there."

She laughed. "I definitely do."

He glanced around at the garden trowel, gloves, and general mess she'd made. "What can I do to help out here?"

"You could sweep up this extra soil."

"Done."

They tidied up and watered the herbs she was growing in stylish yet practical buckets. "I haven't done anything like this in so long."

He pushed the last of the excess dirt to the grass with the broom. "Since your mom?"

"Since my mom and dad. We had a big garden—all kinds of fruits and veggies." She blinked as a memory she'd completely forgotten about rushed back to her. "We had raspberry bushes. I would help Mom make jam and we would give it out for the holidays. I want that back—the little pieces that meant so much. I can recreate them for myself."

"So we'll make sure you get them back. This is a good first step. This year, you're trying your hand at herbs. Maybe next year you can add on."

She shook her head. "I want a house before I start my garden. Something small and homey with two or three bedrooms and enough space for a few garden beds out back."

"It's pretty expensive around here."

"That's why I'm saving." She shrugged. "For someday, but this is fine for now. I'm content with my herbs and Lucy and this cute little place. You're not too bad either."

He grinned. "Should we go clean up the kitchen?"

"Yes." They went back inside. "Then I think we should shower up and finish the second season of *The Office*."

"Sounds like a plan. Let's get to these dishes."

She grabbed the dish soap and squirted some into the hot stream of water as he gathered the dirty baking sheets. She'd missed this over the last week and a half—their easy teamwork. They'd had some rough days, but tonight the future looked bright again. She planned to treasure every moment of this amazing new life she and Reed were building together.

Reed stepped out of the shower while Bella finished rinsing the conditioner from her hair and hurried toward his phone on the counter as it went into its third ring. Typically, he would have let it go to voicemail, but not now, not with everything that was going on. "Hello?"

"They took out Dino Asante," Joey boomed in his ear.

"*What*?" He grabbed a towel off the bar and wrapped it around his waist in a half-assed manner as he closed the bathroom door behind him and stepped into the bedroom. "Are you serious?"

"Does it sound like I'm kidding?"

He shook his head in disbelief. "This is *crazy*. What the fuck is going on out there?"

"Beats the hell out of me."

"Dino." He sat on the edge of the bed, trying to wrap his mind around the idea of Alfeo ordering a hit on his father's longtime consigliere and the man who'd raised his son for him while he'd been locked away. "He ran the organization until Matty was old enough to take over. He's Alfeo's closest friend."

"Apparently there's no longer any loyalty in the family."

He rubbed the towel through his hair and wiped at the drops running down his face. "I just—I don't even know what to say."

"One by one, they're taking them down. Alfeo's not fucking around. He wants a clean slate when he gets out of prison."

"But Dino's been with him all along."

"Takin' them all down," Joey repeated.

He moved the towel over his chest and abs. "How'd they do him?"

"Bullet behind the ear as he reached down to open his driver's side door."

"Jesus. No one's safe."

"That's the message they're sending loud and clear."

He sighed, scrubbing his hand over his jaw. "Bella will probably get a call from Luisa."

"Let's hope she doesn't think about coming out for the funeral. Things aren't good around here."

He sat up straighter, his muscles clenching, barely able to tolerate the thought of Bella back in Bensonhurst, especially now that he knew exactly what the stakes were. "I'll find a way to make sure she doesn't."

"You hear from Vinny yet?"

"No. Not yet." He glanced at the bedside clock as the shower shut off in the next room. It had been four hours since he left Vinny to stew over his choices. "Once this hits the headlines, he'll have another reason to pick up the phone."

"The media's already got their teeth in this one. It's making the news all over the city. I'm watching it right now." Joey exhaled a long breath. "I have to admit, I don't mind being out of the game. I like going home to my girl every night and not looking over my shoulder the way we used to. Cause that's what we'd be doing right now if we were still mixed up in this."

They *were* still mixed up in this, but it was different—better, safer. "It works for me too."

Bella smiled at him as she opened the door and stepped into the room, wrapped in a towel.

He winked at her. "I'm going to let you go."

"Let me know when Vinny bites."

"If he does, you'll be the first."

"He'll bite. They blew Dino away. Everyone's running scared. Something tells me Vinny's looking over *his* shoulder."

"I have to imagine you're right. I'll talk to you later."

"Bye."

"Bye." He hung up and set his phone on the bed. "Sorry I had to cut our shower short."

"That's okay." She slid another one of her silky nighties over her sinful body, and pulled on sexy panties. "Is everything all right?"

"Yeah." He stood, wanting to hug her, to tell her that her friend's father was dead, but he sent her a reassuring smile instead. "Joe was just checking in."

"I think your buddy misses you."

"Probably—" His phone rang again.

"Aren't you popular tonight."

"Lucky me," he said as he studied the number he didn't recognize.

She walked over to him and gained her tiptoes, pressing a kiss to his cheek. "I'll get *The Office* ready for us."

"Sounds good. I'll be right there."

"Okay." She left the room with Lucy following behind.

He waited for Bella's feet to hit the stairs before bringing the phone to his ear. "Hello?"

"Come with Bella tomorrow when she picks me up," Vinny snapped. "We're going to talk." The line went dead.

He frowned, sighing as he looked at the screen, then put a call through to Joey.

"Yeah, boss."

"I'm meeting him tomorrow."

"Well, how about that?"

"I'll talk to you later. Bella's waiting for me."

"Bye."

He put on a pair of boxers and went downstairs as Bella poured them glasses of lemon water then put some strawberries and grapes in a bowl.

"I thought we could have some dessert."

"Sure. Why not?" He took the bowl and walked into the living room as she carried their drinks. "Did you end up calling your dad today?"

"Yes. A few minutes after you left for the gym." She sat next to him on the couch.

He crossed his ankles on the coffee table, loathing himself for playing games with her—for asking her questions he already knew the answers to. "How's he doing?"

"Pretty good. They officially think he's well enough to go home tomorrow."

He hooked his arm around her shoulders. "That's awesome."

"It is." She snuggled in, resting her body against his. "They said his labs are better."

"I want to go with you."

She shook her head. "You don't have to. I usually cook for him and visit for a while. Then I come home."

"I can give you a hand—run errands or whatever."

She stared at him. "Are you sure?"

He nodded. "We're in this together, remember?"

She smiled. "I'm still getting used to that."

"Get used to it." He tucked her damp hair behind her ear. "We'll get him hooked up with food and meals for a few days."

Grinning, she grabbed a strawberry and brought it to his lips. "You're too good to me."

"Not even close." Plucking up a grape from the bowl, he fed it to her. "How about *The Office*?"

She pressed *play* and settled back against him.

He laced their fingers, hating that there was no way around the lying, that he was stuck living a double life, but he couldn't tell her what was going on. In the long run, all of this was going to keep her safe when Vinny helped him keep Alfeo where he belonged. Deceiving Bella was the last thing he'd ever wanted to do, but at this point, it was his only choice.

☙ Chapter Twenty-Eight ❧

"I can't believe he was murdered," Bella said, looking at Reed as he drove them north on the 405. "He was such a nice man—funny, very jovial. Luisa's absolutely devastated."

He reached for her hand, giving her fingers a gentle squeeze. "It's tough. I'm sorry Luisa's going through such a hard time."

"I feel bad that the media's making this so much worse. How can they say such horrible things about Mr. Asante?" She huffed out a breath, still as angry as she was heartbroken for her friend. "The charming man I met wasn't some gangster. There's no way he's a mafia man—or rumored mafia man." She rolled her eyes.

Reed made a sound in his throat as he changed lanes, moving past a slower vehicle.

"The funeral's on Saturday." She nibbled her lip. "I'm thinking about going."

His gaze left the road, meeting hers through his amber-tinted lenses. "That's a long trip."

"I know, but Luisa needs me."

"What about your dad? Do you think this is a good time to be leaving him?"

"No." She sighed, shaking her head. "He needs me too—more."

"We can send flowers. And she can talk to you on the phone anytime she wants."

That was hardly enough, but it would have to do. Her traveling days were over for the foreseeable future. She would never be able to forgive herself if something happened to Dad while she was gone. As it was, she'd barely given any thought to his homecoming, which was completely unacceptable. "I wish there was more I could do to help."

"I know you do." He kissed her fingers.

"Have you ever heard of the people the news was talking about—the Caparelli crime family?"

"Everyone in New York law enforcement has heard of the Caparelli crime family, Bella. They're one of the original five families of La Cosa Nostra."

She shrugged. "I don't know what that is—La Cosa Nostra?"

"It's Italian for Our Little Thing. They're organized crime. Most of the families lost a lot of traction after the Feds indicted them in the eighties. All of the bosses were put away when they were convicted on RICO statutes—except for Patrizio Caparelli. They couldn't get much to stick on him."

"How come?"

"Bribes, threats. They're powerful, brutal—extremely dangerous. The Caparellis are the most ruthless of the bunch."

"So what's a consigliere, then? The thing they're saying Mr. Asante might have been?"

"Uh, it's kind of like an advisor to the boss of the family. They're a pretty big deal—usually well-respected."

"And a boss is the same thing as a Godfather?"

"Right. They're the head honcho of each family. If what they're alleging is true, Dino would have been Patrizio's advisor. Eventually, Patrizio ended up going to prison for orchestrating a hit that killed a man who worked for the family."

"So what happened to the Caparellis after that?"

"Other people in the organization took over."

She rested her head on the back of the seat, trying to take it all in. "RICO statutes, bosses, shootings. It's hard to believe that stuff is real."

"Oh, it's real."

"I still don't see how Luisa's family could have anything to do with that. They're good people."

"We'll have to see what shakes out in the investigation."

She nodded and glanced over her shoulder, smiling despite her mood as she looked at Lucy lying in the bed of the truck with her ears flapping and her face tilted up to the sun. "She's having the time of her life."

"Of course she is. The wind's blowing in her face; she's smelling all kinds of new smells: doggie paradise."

She laughed.

He merged over, taking the Reseda exit. "What do you think your dad's going to think of her?"

"I think he'll love her. Everybody adores Lucy."

"But there's no bias there," he teased.

She grinned. "Not even a little."

He made it through one green light, then another, and turned in to North Medical Center. "I bet he's ready to get out of here."

"It's always nice to be home. I wish he would come stay with me. He keeps turning down my offer, but I think it would be good for him."

He pulled into a parking spot and turned off the ignition. "It's probably good for him to have a sense of independence for as long as he can."

She felt herself frown. "I never thought about it like that, but you're right. I guess I'm being selfish—"

"You are *not* selfish, Bella."

"Sometimes."

He shook his head. "Nope."

She smiled. "Of course I am. We all are."

He shook his head again as he unbuckled his belt and tugged her closer. "You're perfect."

"No."

"You're perfect," he said softly as he leaned in and kissed her.

She wrapped her arms around him. "I'm glad you think so. And I like when you wear your hat like this." She touched the rim at the back of his head. "It's sexy."

"Oh, really," he said, wiggling his brow.

"Mmm-hmm."

"I'll have to keep that in mind."

Who knew that ball caps worn backward, sleeveless T-shirts, and athletic shorts would be the attire that sent her pulse into a frenzy? "I think you should."

He snagged her bottom lip playfully, then drew away. "Do you want to go spring your father from this place?"

"I imagine he would like nothing more."

"I'll wait here with Lucy."

"Thanks." She kissed him this time. "I'll be back soon."

"Call me when you come down and I'll pull up to the front."

"You're the best." She walked toward the entrance in far better spirits than she'd been in when she'd gotten the call from Luisa half an hour after she'd woken up this morning.

Reed filled a glass with water at Vinny's kitchen sink, studying the slightly pathetic digs of a man who'd once belonged to a family worth millions. He breathed in the remnants of stale cigarette smoke on his way back to the tiny living room, understanding perfectly why Bella reeked every time she came home from Reseda. Stopping by the couch, he lifted his brow, watching Bella tuck Vinny in on the threadbare cushions with a blanket.

"Here we go," she said. "How's that?"

"Fine, but I'm feeling much better. The medicine did the trick."

"I'm glad to hear it." She touched his forehead and cheeks with the back of her hand, then glanced at her watch. "You'll need another pill before Reed and I leave."

"And I'll happily take it." Vinny settled more comfortably against his pillows. "I don't like feeling like shit."

"Good. I'm going to pick you up some probiotics while I'm out. We need to get your healthy bacteria back in balance." She bent down again, tucking the blanket more securely around Vinny's legs.

Vinny frowned. "Bella, I'm fine."

"I know, but I want to make sure your feet stay warm."

"Bella." Reed snagged her by the elbow and nudged her back, even though he couldn't necessarily blame her for playing mother hen. Vinny was home, but he wasn't looking so hot. "He's good."

She wrinkled her nose. "I'm hovering."

He held up his thumb and index finger an inch apart. "A little bit." Smiling, he winked and held out the glass to her. "One glass of water—no ice."

She grinned, taking it from him, and set it on the coffee table. "Thanks."

"No problem."

"I guess we should probably think about heading to the store—"

"Reed can stay here with me and Lucy. We'll play a round of cards." Vinny eyed him—as he had several times since they'd picked him up half an hour ago. "I could use the company."

Bella looked at Reed. "Does that work for you?"

"Yeah. Definitely. Lucy and I'll help hold down the fort."

"All right, then." She tucked her hair behind her ear. "Um, Dad, is there anything specific you want?"

"The juices go down easy."

She nodded. "I'll pick some of those up."

"That's a big help."

"You know I don't mind." She kissed Vinny on the forehead, then closed the distance between her and Reed, settling her hands on his waist. "I'll be back soon."

"We'll be fine here." He handed over the keys to the truck.

She stood on her tiptoes and kissed him. "Have fun."

He slid his palms down her arms, lacing their fingers before he let her go. "We will."

Bella grabbed her purse and headed for the door. "Oh, can you open some of the windows for a little fresh air?"

"Sure."

"See you soon." She closed the door behind her.

Vinny yanked the blanket off himself as he sat up. "You've got one hell of a nerve touching my daughter like that."

"I'm pretty sure she touched me first." He made quick work of opening the living room windows, then settled himself in the chair next to the couch, paying close attention to where Vinny kept his hands. He was mostly sure Vinny wasn't planning on pulling a gun from beneath the cushions, but he couldn't be one hundred percent certain. "I already told you I'm not going anywhere."

"You're a bastard."

"You've mentioned that."

Vinny narrowed his eyes. "A cool son of a bitch. I bet you were real good at your job."

"The alternative was death, so it paid to make a solid effort at keeping a level head."

"How do I know you're not playing my little girl?"

"You don't. But I'm not. You'll have to trust me."

Vinny let out a scoffing laugh. "I don't see that happening." He grabbed the deck of cards off the side table and slapped them down on the table. "Remind me again why I'm not putting a bullet in your head."

Reed scooted closer and started shuffling. "Because I care about Bella, and I'm going to be here to keep an eye on her after you're gone." He met Vinny's hostile gaze as he dealt them each ten cards. "You said you wanted to see me today. I hope you're planning on doing more than trying to intimidate me. Game's gin rummy, by the way."

"You mention one word about any of this to her and I *will* end you. I promise you that. Any arrangement you and I make is over the second you open your mouth to Bella."

"I don't want her involved in this any more than you do. I'm confident we can get this done without her ever knowing anything about it."

Vinny looked at his cards. "They took out Dino."

He followed Vinny's lead, noting that he didn't have much of a hand to work with. "I saw it on the news. Bella was asking questions. She's friends with Dino's daughter."

A look of horror filled Vinny's eyes as his gaze whipped to Reed's. "What the hell are you talking about?"

"Luisa, the woman she went to visit in Bensonhurst. That's Dino's daughter."

He shook his head. "Bella said her friend's last name is De Vitis."

"Luisa Asante De Vitis."

"Son of a bitch." He sat back against the cushions. "What did you say to her?"

"I told her the truth. She wanted to know about the Caparellis from someone with a law enforcement background. I kept it vague but truthful."

"They'll kill her if they find her."

"We'll have to make sure they don't. Who knows about Bella?"

"Walter Hodds did."

"What about Salada and Upshaw?"

He shook his head. "They didn't mention anything when they darkened my doorstep, so I'm assuming no. Walter promised he would never say anything—kept tabs on her for me through the years."

Reed wondered if Walter had ever mentioned that Bella's childhood had been less than ideal. "You trusted him to do that?"

"We had an agreement. He would keep my daughter safe and I would make sure I didn't have to hurt his family." He picked up a card from the draw pile and set one down. "Although threats were never necessary with Walter. He was always good to me."

Reed picked up a two of diamonds for his run. "You disappeared on him."

He shrugged. "Bella was mostly grown and doing fine. It was better if I vanished."

"It's quite a coincidence you two live an hour away from one another."

"True coincidences are a rare thing."

Picking up a card, he set another down, not paying all that much attention to the game. He and Vinny both new gin rummy was nothing more than a prop while they felt each other out. "You followed her."

"I'm dying. I needed to see her again."

"But not reach out to her."

"Like I said, she's dead if they ever link her to me."

Reed shook his head. "I'm not going to let that happen. I'll take my last breath before they touch her."

Vinny held his stare, scrutinizing. "I almost believe you."

Reed set his cards facedown. "Let's clear something up right here and now, Vinny. I'm a straight shooter. I won't promise things I can't deliver. I won't lie to you."

"Just to my daughter."

He clenched his jaw. "I don't have any more choice in that decision than you do, but my relationship with Bella is one hundred percent real. She's all that matters—the only thing I want out of this whole deal. Taking down Alfeo's just a bonus."

Vinny studied him again. "Why?"

He sat back, relaxing some as their conversation found an easier rhythm. "I'll be assuring Bella's safety."

Vinny's eyebrow winged up. "You're doing all this for my daughter?"

That hadn't been the original plan, but protecting Bella had quickly become more important than paying Alfeo back. "He killed my family."

Vinny's eyes sharpened on his.

"I was the kid in the back seat of the sedan leaving the Mets game when your brother's hit team came along and blew my father and grandfather's brains out. While they were taking care of that, another team knocked on my uncle's door and did the same thing to him in front of his wife."

"Well, Jesus Christ. How old were you?"

"Five. I've been waiting twenty-six years for this. Hopefully you're going to help me."

Vinny set down his cards and sipped his water. "I don't know what I have to give you."

"You give me everything you've got and we'll see what we can make stick."

"It's been a long damn time."

"You gave the Feds enough to lock your brother up for the 1989 murders."

"That's the deal we made. That should have put him away for life. It did my father." He shook his head. "Slick bastard."

"Which means there's all kinds of things you haven't shared. And we won't have to worry about double jeopardy."

"It's been a long time," Vinny repeated.

"There's no statute of limitations on class A felonies in New York. You tell me everything you can and my friends and I will take care of the rest."

"Friends?"

"My former partner and a FBI Special Agent—her grandfather and mine were partners. She's my good friend."

"I don't like friends."

"Joe's pretty much my brother, and I played with Skylar when we were kids. They're both solid. I wouldn't bring them in if I wasn't absolutely certain."

"If I'm doing this, I'm working with you—and only you."

"We can play it that way, but we need someone on the outside if we're going to get an indictment. I don't have a badge anymore."

"So I'm just supposed to spill my guts about anything and everything?"

He nodded, petting Lucy when she came to sit by his side. "Pretty much. I also want you to look at the letters Alfeo's written over the years and listen to phone calls the penitentiary's recorded. We think they're coded, but we've never been able to figure anything out."

"If he's smart, which he is, he didn't say much—at least, not in writing."

That's not what he wanted to hear. "We know he's been running the organization from inside. We need proof of his activities—leads we can follow. Something that's going to help us get to Matty as well."

"Is he allowed visitors?"

"Yeah."

"Then that's when he does his business. He wouldn't have written anything down."

"I want you to look anyway. What about the recordings? Could there be something there?" He glanced toward the windows when Bella pulled up in the driveway.

He nodded. "Maybe."

The familiar rush of excitement was coming back. "I'll email Skylar and have her send stuff our way."

"Where will we meet?"

"Here—maybe once a week or something."

"I don't know how many weeks I have left."

"Then twice or three times until we get what we need."

"What about Bella?"

"I'll take care of that."

"Don't you hurt her." He pointed at him, the protective father back.

"I'm not planning on it. This thing here," he gestured between himself and Vinny, "has nothing do to with what she and I have."

Vinny shook his head, letting loose a humorless laugh. "You're a fool if you believe that."

He needed to believe that this would never come between them.

The door opened, and she walked in with a bulging cloth bag. "Hi."

Reed smiled. "Hey."

"There's another bag in the truck. This one's heavy or I would have brought that one too."

Reed stood. "I'll go grab it."

"Thanks." Bella started toward the kitchen.

"Between you and me," Vinny muttered, subtly mimicking the firing of a gun at Reed.

He walked out the door and grabbed the second bag. They were heading in the right direction. He could do without the threats, but he was willing to put up with just about anything if Vinny was going to give him what he needed.

❧ Chapter Twenty-Nine ☙

REED SAT ON ONE OF THE CUSHY LOUNGE CHAIRS ON BELLA'S back porch, finally accessing his email account after one hell of a long day. He'd been waiting hours for this opportunity—since Skylar's text came through earlier this morning—but getting a moment alone to take a peek at the files she sent over had been impossible. Sadie had been his priority until four thirty. Then Bella had pulled into her driveway just as he'd tried to sneak over to his place right after he got home.

He glanced toward the French doors, watching Bella dump kibble into Lucy's bowl while she talked on the phone. Now appeared to be his moment. He clicked on the first attachment, waited for it to load, then scrolled through a dozen letters written in Alfeo Caparelli's handwriting. Stopping randomly, he scanned one of Alfeo's many correspondences to his mother—mostly bitching about lumpy pillows and cartons of milk that tasted like cardboard. Reed had read through these before—dozens of times in New York—trying to find some sort of code among the words that would have given him and Joey insight into the Caparellis' world and helped them take the fuckers down, but as he stared at Alfeo's chicken scratch, he remembered his conversation with Vinny yesterday. Perhaps there was nothing here—no clues to the Godfather's biddings. Maybe Alfeo really was just a miserable bastard, unhappy with his less-than-stellar prison accommodations. That was something he needed to figure out once and for all.

He grabbed his phone from his pocket and shot off a text.

Got what we were waiting for. Can you meet tomorrow around six?

His phone dinged with Vinny's reply.

I'll be here.

"Hey, you." Bella smiled as she stepped outside, carrying a glass of lemon water.

"Hey." He shut the laptop and set his phone screen-side down on the cushion as Bella sat next to him, handing him the glass. "Thanks."

"You're welcome." She kissed his cheek. "What are you doing out here?"

He hooked his arm around her shoulders. "Catching up on a little work."

"Do you need some space?"

He had what he needed for his meeting with Vinny. That was good enough for now. "Nah. I can be done for the day."

She settled more comfortably against his side. "Dinner's ready whenever we are."

"I love your Cobb salads. The shrimp is a nice addition. Thanks for making them."

"You're welcome. How was your day?"

"Not too bad." He sniffed her neck. "You smell good. Look good too." He loved when Bella changed into sexy short shorts and simple tees after work.

"Thanks." She played with his fingers. "How are things going with Sadie's case?"

"They've been better. Tyson intercepted another letter last night."

Bella looked at him, the concern in her eyes clear. "How's she doing with that?"

"She doesn't know."

She nodded. "Could he—could he hurt you?"

"No. Probably not," he amended, finding it imperative to be honest with Bella any chance he could. "All I can do is keep my eyes open and communicate everything with Tyson."

"I hate that this is happening to her—and you. I worry."

"You don't have to worry." He pressed his lips to her temple. "Every time he writes, it gives us more insight into who he is—helps us build a solid profile of who we're looking for. Hopefully one of these times, he'll make a mistake." He kissed her again. "They all make mistakes eventually."

"That's not very reassuring."

"I'm being careful. I want you being careful too—keep the doors locked when I'm not home." He wasn't concerned about Sadie's stalker focusing on Bella, but the Caparellis were an entirely different story. It didn't hurt to make her aware of potential threats in the only way he could. "I want you paying attention to your surroundings."

She nodded again, her shoulders stiffening.

"I'm not saying he's coming after you, Bella. Those are things you should be doing anyway, but when you're dealing with a whack job, nothing is entirely out of the question. Because I handle Sadie's protection, it makes me a bit of a target, which can make anyone I'm close to a target too. If you see anything suspicious, I want you to tell me about it right away."

She swallowed as her fingers tightened on his.

"Hey." He snuggled her closer. "There's no immediate danger, but I feel better saying that out loud. It's something to keep an eye out for, but it's nothing I want on your mind all the time. If I was still doing police work, I would say the same thing. I'm sure all the employees at Ethan Cooke Security have had a similar conversations with their significant others. If you're going to be in a relationship with someone who does what I do, that's a standard precaution."

"All right." She licked her lips as she sat up more. "Let's talk about something different."

"Okay. Like what?"

"Mmm, how about ice cream and a walk on the beach after class tomorrow night?"

Shit. "Cooking class."

She frowned. "You forgot."

He sighed, pissed at himself for getting so caught up in Alfeo's letters that Bella's favorite night slipped his mind. "I did." He picked up his phone. "Let me see if I can rearrange some things."

"No." She set her hand on his. "It's fine."

His guilt compounded when she smiled at him with her eyes full of understanding. She was being good about his screw-up. If there had been any other opportunity for him to meet up with Vinny this week, he would have changed the schedule, but there wasn't. "Can someone else go with you and fill in for me?"

"I'm sure I can find someone. I'll ask around at yoga tomorrow morning."

"I'm sorry, Bella."

"Don't worry about it. It's fine." She lifted his hand, pressing his palm to her cheek. "Truly. Hopefully you can make it to the next one."

He *would* make the next one. The investigation wasn't going to interfere with his and Bella's life. This was the first and last time he would allow that to happen. "Definitely." He played his fingers through her hair. "This week is going to be pretty busy. Sadie has an away game and I told Ethan I might be able to cover a couple of evening shifts, but I'm free Friday night. Will you be my date? I'll take you to dinner and we can have ice cream for dessert."

"You've got a deal."

He smiled and stood, pulling her to her feet. "How about we go inside and I'll set the table?"

"I think that sounds like a great idea."

He grabbed his laptop and phone, then hooked his arm around her shoulders again. "Come on."

☙ CHAPTER THIRTY ❧

BELLA'S PHONE RANG AS SHE CARRIED HER BROWN RICE SPRING rolls from her cooking station to the table set for two. She set down her plate and glanced at the screen, grinning at the picture of Reed's gorgeous face. "Hello, there, handsome."

"Hey. How's class?"

"Good. Fun. I'm just about to bite into a freshly made spring roll."

"Man, that sounds good."

She dipped the first fried wonton wrapper into the peanut sauce she'd whipped up and sampled, moaning as the melding of pork, shrimp, and herbs hit her tongue. "Oh, my gosh."

"That good?"

"Mmm. Even better."

"And what does... Who did you end up bringing?"

"Actually, I'm on my own. Everyone was busy."

Reed muttered a curse. "Bella, I'm sorry."

She shrugged as she took another bite. "It's not that big a deal. Chef filled in during the couple of spots when I needed an extra hand."

He sighed. "I wish I was there."

"Me too, but it didn't work out this time."

"Next week."

"Next week when your schedule's better," she agreed, wiping her fingers on a napkin. "I'm saving you your half. Do you think you'll be home before I'm in bed?"

"I hope so. I'm going to try to be."

"I'll wait up." Eyeing another spring roll, she picked it up and bit in, unable to resist. "How was your day?"

"Okay. Sadie broke up with her boyfriend after biology class, so that got a little intense."

She smiled, imagining Reed standing around the hallowed halls of high school, dealing with teenage drama. "Uh-oh."

"Apparently he was cheating on her."

Her smile vanished. "That's awful."

"Yeah, it wasn't good. He begged me not to punch him, and she spent most of third period in the bathroom crying, which made for an interesting situation from a security standpoint."

She couldn't help but grin. "I bet, but I'm sure they'll work everything out and be back together again by the time you walk into school tomorrow."

"I don't know. It was with some cheerleader—sounds like it was going on behind her back for quite a while."

"Ouch. I've been there and it's no fun. Hopefully she won't waste too many tears on a toad."

"Who was stupid enough to cheat on you? Dumb jock."

"He wasn't a jock. Linc was a financial analyst. Although technically I was the other woman and had no idea."

"*What*? How have I not heard this story?"

"I guess it never came up."

"I'm going to need details."

She glanced around at the other couples enjoying their appetizer course. Talking to Reed on the phone instead of having him here wasn't ideal, but it wasn't such a bad alternative. "It's pretty boring—pretty pathetic."

"I need deets, Bella."

Chuckling, she rolled her eyes. "We'd been dating for a couple of months. I went to the mall to pick him out a gift for his birthday and saw him with a woman. At first, I thought maybe she was a sister or a friend, and then they kissed. Turns out he'd been engaged to her for two years and he was seeing *another* woman on the side besides me."

"Jesus. I'm sorry."

"I'm not. Breaking up with him was pretty much the catalyst that helped me realize I was ready for some big changes. Mom had died a few weeks before that, so it wasn't hard to pack up and leave Vegas behind—finally go after a fresh start."

"I kinda feel like I should track the guy down and thank him for being so damn stupid."

She laughed. "I'm happy—the happiest I've ever been. That's all the revenge I need."

"Sounds good to me."

Bella glanced toward the front of the room when Chef Paul spoke to the class. "Oops. I have to go. It's time for the next dish."

"I'll let you go, then."

"Okay."

"Hey, Bella?"

"Yeah?"

"Later on, you're mine."

Butterflies fluttered through her belly with the rush of anticipation. "I can't wait."

"Have fun."

"I will. Bye." She shoved her phone in the back pocket of her jeans and put Reed's portion of the meal in a container, wishing he was there with her, but that wasn't how things were. Work was busy for him right now. Being a bodyguard wasn't a typical nine-to-five career. If they were going to be together, she would have to get used to that. And she was willing to make sacrifices if it meant keeping Reed in her life. Tonight, she planned to wait up for him, and Friday they were going out on a date. That was more than good enough.

Chef walked over. "Are you ready for the next step, Bella?"

She smiled. "I am."

"I'll work with you."

"That'll be great. Thanks."

Reed hung up, clenching his jaw as he thought of Bella sitting by herself at their cooking class. He'd messed up big-time putting the investigation first, especially when it was getting him nowhere. So far, he and Vinny were coming up empty. Two fucking hours and eighteen years of letters later, and they had nothing. Alfeo Caparelli had bitched endlessly, cursed his rat brother's name several times, and vowed revenge, but that was all he and Vinny had taken away from his rants.

They needed something rock solid the DA would give a second glance—something the Caparellis' high-powered attorneys wouldn't be able to reduce down to time served or get dismissed entirely. At this point, he and Vinny were off to a rough start. He steamed out a long breath and looked over his shoulder at Vinny, keeping his distance on the edge of the back patio while he filled his lungs with smoke. "Are you ready to get back to it?"

"Yeah." Vinny tamped out his cigarette. "For what it's worth."

Reed moved closer, eager to get on with it. "Hopefully the last four years of correspondence will give us something."

"I doubt it." He shrugged. "Alfeo's a smart man. I haven't been in the life for over two decades. My wits aren't as sharp as my brother's when it comes to breaking the law—or at least, not anymore. After Bella came along, I knew I didn't want any further part in organized crime."

Reed shoved his hands in his pockets, trying to stay patient and keep his shitty mood in check. Vinny was talking. They were building a tenuous rapport. In the long run, that was going to serve him better than Alfeo's damn letters. "That couldn't have been easy."

"Anything's easy once you set your mind to it." He jerked his shoulders again. "I was never the criminal my brother was. For a long while I tried to be, but he was always better: brutal, cunning—a cut from my father's cloth."

"And you?"

"I loved the hell out of my mother and brother. Still love my mother—God rest her soul."

"And your brother?"

"He'll kill my daughter if he gets a chance. What do you think?"

"Let's go see what we can do to make sure that never happens."

Vinny stood, gripping the chair as he struggled with his balance.

Reed rushed forward but stopped himself from reaching out, knowing that his attempts to help wouldn't be appreciated. Vinny's color looked better than it had Sunday afternoon, but his weight wasn't good. He was wasting away to nothing—dying before Reed's eyes—but he still had his pride. "Are you all set there?"

"I'm fine." He started down the hall toward the kitchen table. "I'll go through what's left. Then I can look at everything again. Maybe I missed something."

He followed Vinny, making sure he made it to his seat without passing out. "I'm going to contact my old informant in Bensonhurst—see if he'll talk to me," Reed said.

"Who is it?"

He shook his head as he sat down. "I can't say."

Vinny frowned. "What do you mean, you can't say?"

"I have an obligation to protect the people who take care of me. He's been hooking me up with information for a long time."

"Alfeo's gonna reign with an iron fist—make sure people realize he hasn't lost his touch, hence the bodies they're finding in the streets.

You don't need your informant for that. I can tell you that."

Reed nodded. There were probably very few people who knew the inner workings of the Caparellis or Alfeo's mindset better than Vinny.

"I don't like that you're involving more people."

"It's one person—someone I've worked with before. I'll keep in contact with him on a burner phone. I know how to be careful, what questions to ask. I'll have Joey send him a package from a dummy Manhattan address so no one knows I'm communicating from LA."

"I don't like it."

"It's a piece of paper with my name and a phone number on it—a few hundred dollars in cash to help him remember how much he likes to talk. He's the one who has everything to lose if he gets caught."

Vinny held his gaze for several seconds, then picked up the next letter Reed had printed out after his quick trip to the office this morning. "Let's get back to it."

An hour later, Vinny read the last of Alfeo's written words out loud and set down the paper. He took off his glasses and rubbed his eyes. "Nothing."

"Damn it." Reed pushed back in his seat and stood, pacing to the window and back as his frustration grew.

"Like I said, he's smart. Careful." Vinny picked up the sheet of paper again. "I told you these weren't going to do you any good."

He scrubbed at his jaw. "Yeah, you did."

"I can also tell that he's only going to get more cautious the closer he gets to June."

Reed stopped by his chair, too restless to sit down. "What does that mean?"

"I'll bet you he's stopped talking on the phone."

"A couple months ago. He hasn't made a call since."

"And he won't. He's not gonna say anything to anyone that might get his ass in trouble."

"But there might be something in the recordings we do have, right?"

"Could be. I know the Feds got all excited when they busted up the families with their RICO statutes all those years ago, but what you need to understand is that they taught everyone how to work smarter. The Caparellis have kept the organization small and sealed tight. Law enforcement hasn't been able to get at them the way they have the other families because Alfeo's suspicious—extra paranoid. I imagine he and Dino raised Matty to be the same way."

"I want us to listen to the recordings," Reed said.

"So, where are they?"

"Skylar's working on getting them. Copying a file full of papers is one thing. Sneaking out recordings is entirely different."

"Tell her to hurry. Time isn't on my side."

"I know. She'll get them. And I'll see what my informant can do as well."

"I'm telling you, Alfeo's going to button up and keep quiet. Matty knows what he needs to do for the time being—keep things running smoothly until his pops is out of a cell. It's just a waiting game at this point."

Reed sighed and looked at his watch. "I need to get out of here." If he was lucky, he would get home before Bella was asleep. "Go ahead and keep these." He gestured to the letters. "Read them over again if you want."

"I'll take care of it tomorrow. Let me know when you want to meet again."

"You'll be the first. I'll text you when Skylar sends me what we need." He gathered his laptop and walked to his truck, then drove to the discount store a couple of miles from Vinny's house for a throw-away phone. Within minutes, he was back on the road and merging onto the 405. Tomorrow he would have to wire money out to Joey and pay him back for getting the ball rolling with the Caparelli Captain who'd kept him in the loop for the last five years. They needed to move this investigation along before Vinny couldn't help them any-more. Swearing, he dialed Skylar.

"Special Agent Grayson."

"I knew you'd be up."

"Sleep is for the dead."

"I need those recordings."

"I'm working on it now."

"There's nothing in the letters."

"You're sure he's being straight with you?"

"I'm positive. He wants Alfeo to stay right where he belongs."

"I'll have them to you by tomorrow morning—tomorrow after-noon at the latest."

"I'll be looking for them."

"Keep an eye out for my text." Skylar hung up.

He set down his phone, well-used to her abrupt endings, and fo-cused on the road instead of his irritation that they were once again at a dead end. An hour later, he pulled into his driveway and hurried into his house, showering off the stink of Vinny's place before he went next door. He walked quietly up the stairs and stopped in the doorway, staring at Bella asleep with a magazine open on her chest and the bedside lamp on.

Lucy stirred, giving a lazy thump of her tail.

"Hey, girl." He petted her, then shut off the light as he set the copy of *Cosmo* on the side table before sliding into bed with Bella.

She rolled over and snuggled against him. "You're home."

He kissed the top of her head. "Go back to sleep."

"I tried to wait up."

"I know you did." He wrapped his arms around her soft, warm body, needing the connection, wanting to feel her close to him, to breathe her in.

"I missed you."

"I missed you too. Go back to sleep, Bella."

"'Kay."

He stared into the dark long after her breathing had grown deep, hoping that they were going to find what they needed and end this sooner rather than later.

CHAPTER THIRTY-ONE

REED SAT ACROSS FROM VINNY AT THE SMALL KITCHEN TABLE, much like he had forty-eight hours ago, but tonight they were listening to Alfeo's gritty smoker's voice as he spoke to Dino Asante or Matty Caparelli on the prison telephone. Twenty-five years of recorded conversations was far less tedious to get through than the letters had been, but they weren't making any progress with the investigation. Vinny had identified a few minor gimmicks—some gambling and bookmaking activities—but this certainly wasn't their big break. Reed let his head fall back and scrubbed his hands over his face as Alfeo went on and on about getting a good haircut and a decent meatball sub when he got out in June.

"You getting bored?"

Reed sat up straight. "No, I'm getting pissed. What the hell is this—"

Vinny's phone rang at his side, interrupting the beginnings of Reed's rant. He glanced at the readout and held up his hand. "It's Bella."

Reed paused the recording.

"Hello?" Vinny smiled. "I'm doing fine. Watching a little TV. What are you up to? Huh. Never heard of that. Sounds nice. Yes, I'm drinking my juice." He scrunched up his nose. "The ones I'm drinking now are fine. We don't have to add more kale and spinach to the mix. You don't have to come up. Make plans with Reed." Vinny's gaze met his. "How about Sunday, then? Your birthday's soon." He looked at Reed again. "I'm going to worry about it. Twenty-six is a big deal. We'll talk about it when I see you on Sunday. Okay. I love you too. Bye." He hung up.

Reed stood, needing a break. "Let's take five."

"She's home by herself tonight. Said she's cooking something called a galette."

He paced to the window and back, restless. "Yeah. It's like a pie without a top on it."

Vinny raised his brow at him.

"What? That's what she told me when I asked her about it this morning. She's using a couple of different berries." And he wished he was with her right now, helping Bella in the kitchen.

Vinny laced his fingers on the table. "Her birthday's right around the corner."

"I know."

"You're an old man compared to her."

He frowned. "I'm thirty-one—almost thirty-two. It's not that big a deal."

"Old."

"Didn't you have two decades on Bella's mother?"

Vinny bobbed his head from side to side. "Touché. You want kids?"

Reed shoved a hand through his hair. He liked it better when he was asking the questions. "Yeah. Someday."

"What are you doing for my daughter's special day?"

He leaned against the back of the recliner, crossing his arms. "I imagine she'll want to spend it with you."

"Probably. It's the last we'll get together."

His heart hurt for Bella as he studied the sickly man whose clothes had long since gone baggy on his fragile frame. "So we'll make sure it's good. I've already picked something out for her."

"She needs cupcakes—vanilla with pink frosting and purple sprinkles. Her mom used to make those for her."

Reed nodded, making a mental note to take care of Vinny's request.

"We'll have a party for her on Sunday. Come up here with her."

"Okay. I'll get the cupcakes and bring them with us." He stood and walked the half-dozen steps to the table, sitting down again. "Let's finish this. I want to go home and help Bella eat the dessert she's making."

"You tell her you're working?"

Bella thought he was picking up an extra shift to help Ethan out, but Tyson had taken over Sadie's protection at one so he could get up here to Reseda. "I am, aren't I?" He clenched his jaw and rubbed at the back of his neck, growing more uncomfortable with his half truths.

"The lying isn't easy."

"It used to be. Before Bella, I didn't have any problems saying whatever needed to be said."

Vinny stared at him. "Maybe you're not such a bastard after all."

He smiled. "I guess that's a compliment."

Vinny grinned and picked up his juice. "Let's hear the rest of this bullshit."

Tapping the mouse on his laptop, Reed sat back, listening to the last hour of Alfeo and Matty's mindless chatter. He steamed out a breath, muttering a swear as he glanced at the screen, realizing there were only seven minutes and twenty-eight seconds left of their conversation. This was all there was. This was the last they would get, and they had nothing to work with.

"Dino's looking into that thing with Chops," Matty said.

Vinny and Reed both perked up, knowing that was the nickname Alfeo had given Nicoli Caparelli.

"And?" Alfeo asked.

"And I'm still waiting for more details."

"I want to know when you have them. If Chops has got a chops of his own... Well, that's something."

Vinny rushed to his feet. "They know about Bella."

Reed frowned. "What? How do you know?"

Vinny pointed to the screen. "He just said it."

He struggled to keep his heart rate steady as he watched the color leave Vinny's cheeks and the pulse pound in his throat. This was the first time he'd seen the man lose his cool. "Vinny—"

"They fucking know about Bella."

He shook his head. "I don't—"

"Play it back," Vinny said, making a whirling motion with his finger.

He backed up the recording an entire minute, listening through the same exchange he heard moments ago.

"See? Right there." Vinny pointed at the screen again. "'If Chops has got a chops of his own."

Reed let it play through, hanging on every word.

"It's early stages yet, Pops," Matty continued. "We'll have to see what we see."

"I like the idea. I like it a lot."

Matty chuckled. "I should go. I'll be back to see you next week."

"Face-to-face. Without the glass. A father likes to hug his son."

"Without the glass," Matty assured him.

"See you soon."

The conversation ended, and Vinny paced this time.

Reed played the conversation back through his mind as he watched Vinny stop by the windows, peek out the curtain, and move away. "It doesn't sound like they know anything," Reed said.

"The fact that they're asking questions means they know something." Vinny lit a cigarette and puffed deep—once, twice. "They fucking know something.'"

Reed glanced at the date of the last conversation. "The recording is from February twentieth. They don't know about Bella, Vinny. Matty was sitting right next to her in Bensonhurst just a couple weeks ago. They wouldn't have let her get on a plane back to LA if they knew who she was."

"They know something," Vinny repeated.

"How?"

He jerked his shoulders. "Beats the hell out of me. Walter must've said something." He sat on the couch with a heavy thump. "That bastard opened his mouth."

He still wasn't seeing it the same way Vinny was. "Are you sure you're not focusing on something that isn't there? Walt was a good guy. Why would he say something when he'd kept quiet for so many years?"

"I'm positive. And who knows?"

"I'll look into it."

Vinny puffed out a plume of smoke and scoffed, "How are you gonna look into it?"

Reed grabbed his phone off the table and called Joey.

"Yeah, boss."

"Hey. Do you remember the day you called me from Walt's funeral telling me about Upshaw and Salada talking in the bedroom?"

"Yeah. How could I forget?"

He settled in the recliner close to Vinny. "What did they say?"

"You know what they said. They talked about tracking down Nicoli to check in on him. Walt was concerned with Alfeo's release on the horizon."

"Upshaw was at the diner with Walt when he died?"

"Fell over dead," Joe reminded him.

"I need for you to find out what Upshaw and Walter discussed that day. Vinny's thinking Walt might have said something about Bella."

"Yeah, I'll get right on that one, buddy."

He felt his nostrils flair. "Joe—"

"How the fuck am I supposed to do that? I can't just go up and ask. I was never supposed to hear that conversation in the first place."

"Figure something out. I need this."

"Okay. It'll probably take a couple of days while I figure my angle."

"Fine. Just get it as soon as you can."

"You know I will."

"Thanks. I'll talk to you later." He hung up, looking at Vinny. "Joe's going to look into it."

He pressed his fingers to his temple. "And that's supposed to reassure me?"

"It reassures me."

Vinny narrowed his eyes. "You're taking this news real casual."

He stood again, not liking Vinny's insinuation. "I'd say I'm approaching it cautiously."

He took a final puff on his cigarette and tamped it out in the full ashtray. "Do you know what they'll do to that little girl if they find her?"

Reed swallowed, not even wanting to think about it. "We're looking into this because you think there's something worth looking into, but I worked with Walt, Vinny. He never mentioned you. Joe and I had no idea Bella was your daughter until I saw her hugging you on your front porch, and I've been obsessed with the Caparellis for a long damn time. Matty talked to her for several minutes in Brooklyn and let her live. I'll call my informant later." He walked to the table and glanced at his notes, reading the miserly bits of information they were able to come up with in regard to crimes discussed in the recordings. "At this point, I'm not all that concerned about Bella's identity being revealed, but this"—he tapped the mostly empty legal pad—"this is shit. We need more. What do you have on your brother that's going to keep him locked away?"

Vinny picked up his Bic and lit another cigarette. "Don't you think I would tell you if I had something?"

"You have something. You have all kinds of things. You were a mafia bastard for the first thirty-nine years of your life. Letters and recordings didn't get us anything. We can cross that off our list, so let's talk murder. For decades, people disappeared. Who did the killing?"

"Me, on occasion. Dino if we were in a pinch. But mostly Alfeo. Almost always, it was Alfeo. He liked it. My father liked to use him to send a message directly from the Caparellis: you piss off a Caparelli, you die by a Caparelli. How the fuck's that gonna help us now?"

It was going to help them plenty. "What did you do with the bodies?"

"Buried them."

He nodded, grabbing the pad of paper and a pen, sitting in the recliner again. "How'd you do them?"

"A pop to the back of the head. Alfeo liked to get 'em in the forehead so they knew it was coming."

"Where did you bury them?"

"In a big field. A couple other places too."

"How?"

He frowned, exhaling another plume of smoke. "What do you mean, how?"

"Did you chop 'em up?"

He shook his head. "No. Most of the time we zipped them up and dropped them in a hole we dug."

He frowned. "Zipped them up?"

"In body bags."

"You weren't worried about the cops?"

Vinny raised his brow. "We owned the fucking cops. Fucking dirty pigs."

He bristled, thinking of his dad and Joey. "Not all of us are dirty."

"No. But there were enough in those days that we didn't worry much about getting locked up. It wasn't until the Feds stepped in..."

Reed went back to the table and pulled up Google Maps. "You buried them in Brooklyn?"

"Some. Most."

"How many?" Reed brought his computer over to the couch, sitting next to him.

"It's hard to say. Maybe twenty—more like thirty."

Reed's eyes popped wide. "You and your brother killed thirty people?"

"No. I did six. Dino a couple. Alfie did the rest."

"Where'd the cleanup teams take them?"

"We didn't use cleanup teams. Alfie liked to bury them himself—take care of his own work from start to finish: order them to a sit-down, talk to 'em for a while, then blow their brains out. He got a hell of a kick out of them walking on eggshells, wondering if Alfie was gonna whack 'em or have a meeting. When he whacked 'em, which was most of the time, I helped him clean it up—usually Dino too. We buried them and moved on. Didn't talk about it again."

"So you've buried thirty bodies?"

"I guess so."

He put the computer on Vinny's lap. "Where?"

Vinny stared at the screen. "Who the hell knows on this thing? I hate computers."

He zoomed in the map. "This is Brooklyn."

Vinny squinted. "I haven't been back since the Marshals took me out of there."

He reached forward, grabbing Vinny's glasses off the coffee table. "You buried them in Brooklyn, right?"

Vinny put them on. "Yeah."

"So then they're still there."

"Yeah."

"So let's find them."

"Everything looks so different."

"Not that different. The neighborhoods are still a lot alike. There are different people living in them, but the structures haven't necessarily changed much."

"Over by the railroad yard." He pointed to the southern end of the city. "In this big field here. And this looks like one of the places here on Cropsey Avenue. I think. But these buildings weren't there then."

Reed focused on the huge field, immediately dismissing any place that they wouldn't be able to gain access to. Two to three hundred yards worth of trees and grass was a beautiful thing. "How many are buried here—that Alfeo did?"

He shrugged. "I don't know."

"Give me an idea. Four, ten, fifteen."

"Maybe like fifteen or twenty."

That was an excellent number. The odds of finding the remains of someone Alfeo killed were high. "You put them in bags?"

"I told you we did."

"Always?"

"Every damn time. Wrapped them in plastic first. Kept the smell down—plus we'd heard about dogs sniffing out bodies, so we thought that might help if anybody got nosy. Fucking hard work getting them in there, though—messy after Alfie finished with them, but it made for easy moving, and we didn't have to worry about leaving anything behind in the trunk."

"What does that mean—after Alfie finished with them?"

"He was a cruel son of a bitch. Liked to torture them before he killed them—cut off their hands."

"While they were alive?"

He nodded. "They weren't alive much longer after. Liked to shove money in their mouths—sometimes up their ass. A symbol of their disrespect and greed."

He winced. "Jesus. Did he wear gloves?"

"No."

His excitement started to build. DNA was a long shot, but it wasn't impossible. "Where did you guys stash your guns?"

"Dino and I would toss them in the water, but Alfeo always used the same one—said he liked it the best." He shook his head. "Cocky bastard."

Was he really hearing this? "Alfeo used the same firearm for every murder?"

"Every one."

"The same pistol he used the night you guys took out that family?"

Vinny cleared his throat. "Yeah."

This was big. This was fucking huge—exactly what they needed. If they could locate and link a bullet to Alfeo's gun that would still be locked away in evidence somewhere, this would be endgame. "Where would the bodies be?"

"It's hard to say. That's not exactly a small place, which was the point. We liked spots where not many people wanted to go—mud up to the ankles most of the time. Probably somewhere around here." He pointed to an area about fifty yards from the water. "Or maybe it was over here. Somewhere around there, I'm thinking."

"This is good. Real good, Vinny. Where else?"

He shook his head. "I don't know."

He tore his gaze from the computer and potential gravesites to look Vinny in the eye. "How do you not know? I would think you would remember something like that."

"It doesn't look the same. I told you, I hate these fucking computers."

"I want a list of everyone you guys killed. I want everyone Alfeo did. Focus on that." He slammed the laptop closed. "You get it to me and I'll see if I can get us some sort of map of the location." Skylar wouldn't be able to get a team together to go looking for remains without something more solid to work with.

Vinny tamped out his cigarette. "Not on Sunday. Sunday is for Bella."

"Agreed. We're going to move on this." It appeared that this was going to be their only shot—and it was still a long one. But it was good. Finding bodies was always very good.

"What now?"

He took the laptop from Vinny and walked over to the table. "You start working on that list—every detail you can remember about each murder, and I'll contact my informant and see what he can figure out about Nicoli having a child."

"He got your package?"

"Yeah. He signed for it this morning."

"I don't want you saying anything to him about Bella."

"Let me do my job, Vinny."

"You didn't do such a hot job the first time around—getting yourself shot."

"If it doesn't kill you, it makes you smarter," he said, touching his hand to the small crater in his chest beneath his shirt.

"Let's hope to God you're right."

He gathered his papers and stacked them. "You just think about where we're going to find the bodies, and I'll be back on Sunday with Bella."

Vinny nodded, his movements jerky.

"I'm not going to let anything happen to her. Trust me."

"Are you in love with my daughter?"

"Yes." What was the point in denying it? He grabbed his laptop case and shoved the computer inside, the remaining items next. "I want to get home to her before she goes to bed. I've barely seen her this week." And he missed her—was so damn sick of the lying. "I'll see you Sunday."

"Okay."

Reed locked up behind him, looking around as he got in the truck while the sun moved closer to the horizon. He needed to call Skylar and Joey, let them in on the latest development, but that would have to wait a bit yet. The drive back to the Palisades would give him plenty of time to get everything taken care of. Right now, he was eager to find out if there was something to Alfeo's cryptic comments about Nicoli's potential child. He dug through his wallet for the number he hadn't touched in almost a year and dialed on the burner phone before backing out of the driveway.

"Hello?"

"It's Reed."

Silence filled the line.

He turned onto the busy street, heading toward the interstate. "I need information."

"I'd heard rumors you were dead."

"I'm talking, so I guess not."

"Things are too dangerous."

He blew through one green light, then a yellow. "You know I pay for information. You got my envelope this morning."

"That's not enough this time. I want a guarantee that you'll get me out of here after I get you what you need."

"We've worked together long enough for you to know that I don't promise anything I can't guarantee."

"Find a way to guarantee me my safety. Everybody's dying around here."

He made it through the next traffic light and merged onto the 405. "Let me make some calls and I'll see what I can do. You're going to have to be able to get me something big—something I can use—if you want a deal with the Feds."

"What do you want?"

"I want to know what Matty's up to. What are he and Alfeo planning once Alfeo's out?"

"How the hell am I supposed to get you that without ending up like Dino? Nobody's saying nothin'. Everybody's on guard—keeping their mouths shut."

He moved into the left lane, kicking his speed up to eighty-five, craving home and Bella. "Try anyway. I heard rumors that Nicoli Caparelli has a kid."

"I haven't heard that one."

His shoulders relaxed slightly. His informant was one of the higher-ups—certainly not part of Alfeo's inner circle, but he had his pulse on the family. "Check it out anyway."

"I'll do what I can, but it's gonna take time."

"You get me something good that shows the Feds you're not fucking around—look into my inquiry into the kid, and I'll do my best to get you that deal."

"I want payment too. A grand for this kind of information."

"I'll give you six hundred when you deliver something I can use."

"Seven hundred."

"Fine. Watch your back. You don't do me much good dead."

"I'll call you back on this number."

"No, I'll call you next week."

"That's not the way we've always done things."

"It's the way we're going to do them now." He hung up. When his informant used to deal with him, he dealt with Mad Dog. Every day, more pieces of Mad Dog McKinley slipped away, but he would have to find that part of himself again. At some point in the near future, he had no doubt that he would be heading back to the mean streets of Bensonhurst. He wanted this over quickly, but his gut told him things were just getting started.

Bella combed her fingers through her damp hair as she walked downstairs toward the kitchen. She hit the light switch along the way and stopped in front of the island, studying the golden crust and pretty berry center of her first-ever attempt at a galette. "Not bad," she muttered, currently as impressed with her culinary efforts as she'd been when she pulled her creation out of the oven nearly two hours ago. Now if only she could eat it. She glanced at the clock and sighed. It was well past eight and Reed still wasn't home. She'd waited for him, stalling with a long walk on the beach and then a shower, wanting to share the results of her cooking adventure with her partner in crime, but things didn't appear to be working out that way tonight. "I guess I'm diving in alone," she said to Lucy, taking one plate from the cupboard when she'd hoped to be grabbing two.

Lucy thumped her tail halfheartedly on her bed, not bothering to open her eyes.

"Those seagulls get you every time, huh?" She chuckled as she cut herself a small slice and paused mid-transfer to the plate when she heard a key twisting in the lock and Reed walking through the front door. Grinning, she abandoned her treat and hurried into the living room. "Hey, there, handsome."

He smiled, toeing off his shoes. "Hey."

"Welcome home."

"Thanks." He set down his laptop bag and closed the distance between them, wrapping her up in a tight hug.

She returned his embrace, grimacing as she breathed in the nasty scent of cigarette smoke. "Yikes, you smell like you've been at my dad's."

He shook his head, still keeping her close, running his fingers through her hair. "A bar."

She frowned as she moved her hands up and down his back. "You were at a bar?"

"On duty. Not drinking." He wandered his palms along her sides, stroking. "God, I love when you wear your nighties."

She eased away enough to look him in the eyes, slightly concerned by his tired tone and unusual greeting. Reed hugged her all the time, but this was different—sort of desperate. "Is everything okay?"

"Yeah." He kissed her. "It's been a long day—a long week."

She nodded her agreement. "I've heard a rumor that tomorrow's Friday."

He groaned, resting his forehead against hers. "And you're all mine. Our date—just you and me."

"I like the sound of that."

He sniffed the air. "Something smells good in here—besides you."

"Dessert—the galette I told you about this morning."

"Right."

"You want some?" she asked, wiggling her eyebrows.

"Try and stop me." He nipped her chin. "But I should shower first."

She wrinkled her nose. "I'm not going to argue with you."

He grinned. "I'll be right back."

"Okay." She went to the kitchen, her brow furrowing slightly as the stink on Reed's clothes trailed behind her. She hoped wherever he'd been tonight and whomever he'd been with weren't going to be a regular thing. Working in a smoky environment wasn't good for his health. She shrugged away her concern and cut Reed a large slice, then grabbed the vanilla ice cream from the freezer, scooping two decent-sized helpings to finish off the presentation of their desserts.

Moments later, Reed hustled into the kitchen, wrapping his arms around her waist and nuzzling her neck, smelling much better.

"That was quick." She turned to face him, realizing he'd come downstairs boxer-clad. "Are you a superhero or something?"

He smiled. "No, I just missed you."

"I missed you too." She smiled back, tracing her fingers along his excellent pecs. "Tell me all about your day."

He sighed. "There's not a whole lot to tell—just lots of running around." He glanced over her shoulder. "But it looks like it's about to end pretty well. Dessert with my girl. Couldn't be better."

She studied him, noting that he didn't look quite so tired anymore. "That was an excellent answer."

He chuckled. "How about we grab these plates and you can tell me about *your* day? In bed."

She lifted her brow. "Okay."

He picked up their plates. "Or we could sit down at the table and eat this right now."

She laughed. "Let's sit at the table."

He grinned. "I'm a sucker for sugar and instant gratification."

She laughed again. "Clearly." She pulled out his chair for him. "Have a seat. Enjoy."

He sat down, setting her plate at her usual spot. "This looks so *good*."

She loved that he loved her cooking. "Go ahead."

He cut into the berries and piecrust, sampling a huge bite. "*Man*, this is killer." He groaned, closing his eyes as he chewed. "A-plus, Bella."

"I'm glad you like it."

"Like's not a strong enough word," he said through another mouthful, giving her a thumbs-up.

Grinning, she sampled a bite of her own, enjoying the combination of tart berries, sweet ice cream, and flaky crust. "I'm turning into a chef." She beamed at the idea.

"Yeah, you are." He ate more. "So, how was work?"

"Not much happened. But I talked to Emilia's aunt this afternoon."

"How's she doing?"

"She's fighting another infection right above her knee. Keeping that leg isn't looking good."

He shook his head. "That sucks."

"Yes, it does." She stabbed a strawberry, sliding it around in the melted ice cream. "She's been pretty down in the dumps, so she and Bianca are coming over sometime in the next couple of weeks."

He got up, pouring them glasses of water. "I get to hang out with you guys, right?"

"If you want to."

He came back, setting one in front of her. "I totally want to."

"Thanks." She gestured to her glass. "I was going to have Kylee and Olivia over, but Olivia's pretty booked up with ballet for the next little while, so they'll come next time. I think it would be best to have a two-to-two ratio to make sure everyone feels comfortable."

He nodded, taking his seat again. "Makes sense."

"I talked to Abby and Sarah too." She popped a blueberry in her mouth. "Abby has a fashion show next Friday that she's inviting us to—a fundraising event for the Stowers House locations—and Sarah's putting together a party the weekend after."

"Huh."

"I was thinking we could make an appearance. I know that's not your thing—"

He paused with another bite on his fork. "But it's yours. We can go."

"To both? Are you sure?"

"Yeah, it's no problem." He scraped up the remains of his dessert. "Bella, this is really great."

"Thanks. I think my dad would love it."

"Have you talked to him today?"

She nodded, setting down her fork. She'd had all the sweets she could handle. "I called him tonight. I'm going to go up on Sunday."

He took her hand, kissing her knuckles. "How do you feel about a tagalong?"

She snagged her lip with her teeth when he nibbled the tip of her index finger. "You know you don't have to come."

"I want to. He's a nice guy, and you're my girl." He winked.

She smiled, liking it when he called her his girl. "We would love to have you."

"Sounds like it's settled, then." He stood, stacking their plates.

"We'll probably do what we did last time—I'll go to the store and you can keep Dad company."

"Yeah. Definitely. I'll make sure we're locked up." He rinsed the plates and put them in the dishwasher, then headed off to check the doors while Bella wrapped the remains of their dessert and set it in the fridge. "Ready?" he asked, holding out his hand.

"I am." She laced their fingers. "Come on, Lucy. Let's go to bed."

Reluctantly, Lucy got up, following behind.

"You took her to the beach."

She grinned. "How could you tell?"

He shrugged. "Just a guess."

She leaned against him as they climbed the stairs. "I like having you home at night."

"I *like* being home at night." He kissed her forehead as they walked down the hall and into the bedroom.

Bella moved to the bed, pulling back the covers. "Have you ever given any consideration to bringing the rest of your stuff over here and just staying?"

He stared at her across the mattress.

She swallowed, worrying that she'd just crossed some dreaded early relationship line. "I don't want to make you uncomfortable or rush you into anything you're not ready for." Settling in, she pulled up the covers and grabbed her magazine, afraid she had.

He got in next to her. "Is that what you want? To move in together?"

"We don't have to." She jerked her shoulders, turning the pages randomly, not daring to look at him. "It's pretty sudden."

"Hey." He tilted her chin his way. "Is that what you want?"

"It kind of makes sense. You're over here all the time anyway, and most of your stuff is in my closets and drawers."

"What about my boxing stuff?"

She nibbled her lip as she thought of the guest room she'd painstakingly decorated that would have to be taken apart for Reed's punching bags. "Boxing's pretty important to you."

"It's been my lifeline for years." He kissed her. "How about I keep my place for a while so you can keep your guest room and I can keep my gym?"

She nodded. "That makes sense. If only I had one more bedroom. I'm just afraid my dad might need the one I've got."

"That's a logical thought." He kissed her again. "I love staying here with you. I love waking up right next to you. Maybe we should consider a place with a third bedroom."

She sighed. "I want my own house."

"We'll have to keep saving."

"Are we going to buy a place together?"

He shrugged. "Why not?"

She held his gaze, liking the idea. "We'll keep the topic open for discussion."

"Sounds like a plan." He snuggled her against him and grabbed the men's fitness magazine from his side table.

She settled back, tucked cozy in his arms, breathing in his familiar soapy scent as she stared at her favorite ivy plant, then at Lucy asleep on her bed. She closed her eyes, savoring this perfect moment—a rare flash in time she wanted to remember and hold close. "Reed?"

"Hmm?"

"I was content—really happy before we met." She turned to look at him. "Then Lucy barged through your front door. Nothing's the same."

"Is that okay?"

She nodded. "I don't know how anything could be better. I just wanted you to know that."

He kissed her. "I like where we're at too."

She rested her head against his shoulder and turned the page, wondering how the guy next door had somehow become "the one."

☙ Chapter Thirty-Two ❧

Bella got out of Reed's truck and let down the gate for Lucy as she studied Dad's sad little house in the afternoon sunshine. "This place would be so cute with some flowers out front—maybe a couple of cheery pots by the steps."

Reed stepped up next to her, sliding his hands in his jeans pockets as his gaze tracked over the property. "Flowers would definitely add something, but I don't think Vinny's up to taking care of them."

She nodded, smiling sadly. "You're right. I guess sometimes it's easier to focus on silly little things that don't really matter."

He met her gaze with eyes full of understanding as he skimmed his knuckles along her cheek. "They would make a nice addition."

She leaned into his touch. "I'm just thankful Dad made it through the week without another visit to the hospital."

He hugged her. "That's a great thing."

She returned his embrace, realizing how on edge she'd been since last Sunday, constantly waiting for someone to call her from North Medical Center. "Yes, it is."

"Hopefully we'll have another week just like it."

"We'll cross our fingers." She eased away. "We should get inside."

"I'll be right there."

"Okay." She walked up the steps with Lucy following and knocked.

Dad peeked out the side window and opened the door. "Hi."

"Hi." She smiled even as she noted that he'd lost more weight and hugged him, barely suppressing a sigh as she felt his ribs through his shirt. "It's so good to see you."

"You're as beautiful as always." He stepped back and frowned. "There's not much to those shorts, though."

She glanced down at her adorable new off-the-shoulder chiffon blouse and ripped short shorts, all from the Abby Quinn Summer Collection. "There's nothing wrong with my shorts. This happens to be a very fashionable outfit. In fact, I'm going to the designer's fashion show this Friday night."

His frown returned. "A father doesn't want to see his daughter's butt hanging out of her clothes."

She scoffed, "You can*not* see my butt hanging out of my clothes." She looked over her shoulder at her backside. "There are a good three or four inches of denim keeping the world from seeing my derrière."

"What happened to wearing those shorts that stop at the knees?"

She rolled her eyes. "Daddy, these are fine." She stepped inside and stopped, staring at the half-dozen pink and purple balloons tied to one of the kitchen chairs. "Balloons."

"It's your birthday on Wednesday, isn't it?"

"Yes, but you didn't have to do that."

"Of course I did."

Reed walked in, carrying a small stack of boxes as he gently kicked the door closed with his foot.

Her eyes welled as she recognized the pale blue box from her favorite gourmet bakery and a present wrapped in pretty paper. "What did you two do?"

Reed set the packages on the table. "I believe they call this a birthday party."

She looked from her sweet, sickly father to the gorgeous man she absolutely adored. "You two didn't have to do this."

"Maybe we wanted to." He pressed a kiss to her lips.

"Thank you." She hugged him, then walked to Dad. "Thank you."

"You're welcome." He wrapped his arms around her. "It's nothing fancy. Just some cake and a couple of gifts."

"That's plenty. Perfect."

He moved to the table and pulled out her chair. "How about you take a seat and I'll go get your present."

"You didn't have to get me anything."

"I'm your dad, right?"

"Yes."

"Dads have presents for their daughter's birthdays."

Not when they left. Not when they handed them snow globes and disappeared for twenty-one years. But she nodded, watching him walk back to the bedroom, noting that his jeans were cinched tight with a belt, and his shirt hung baggier than the last time she'd seen him wearing it. Sighing, she took her seat and stared at the floor.

Reed crouched down next to her. "What's wrong?"

She swallowed, fighting the sudden emotions choking her. "I'm not sure." How could she put into words how touched she was by such a lovely surprise or explain how much it broke her heart to know that this was her last birthday with her father?

He tucked her hair behind her ear. "He's doing okay today."

She nodded, knowing that was what she needed to focus on. They had today. She would worry about tomorrow later.

"Here we go." Dad came back, a little more breathless, moving slower, as he carried a thin black box with him.

She blinked her eyes dry, determined to be strong. These moments weren't just hers. They were Dad's too. "That looks very interesting."

Dad grinned as he took the chair next to hers. "I didn't get it wrapped."

"That's okay."

He handed it to her.

"Thank you."

"You haven't opened it yet."

She smiled. "I mean for the thought."

"Open it up."

She flipped open the lid and stared at the delicate silver and diamond bracelet with an ornate B-shaped clasp. "Daddy, this is stunning." And expensive.

"As soon as I saw it, I knew you had to have it."

She wanted to give it back as much as she wanted to treasure it. He couldn't afford to shower her with such lavish gifts. But how could she possibly refuse when his eyes were so bright with pride? "It's truly beautiful." She stood, hugging him and holding on tight. "I love it. Thank you."

He gripped her hard. "I have a lot to make up for."

She shook her head and squeezed her eyes shut, struggling not to cry. She didn't want to do this—have this conversation while she opened her presents. "You're here now. That's all that matters."

"I wasn't for a long time."

"You're here now." She drew away and sat down, gently taking her new jewelry from the box, considering the topic closed. "Will you help me put this on?"

He nodded. "Sure."

She held out her wrist while he fastened the clasp in place.

"That should do it. You're all set."

She touched the cool silver against her skin as the diamonds caught the light. "So, what do you think? How does it look?"

He took her hand, gently twisting it from side to side. "Like it belongs there. Gorgeous and classy like my daughter."

She leaned forward and kissed his cheek. "Thank you, Daddy."

He captured her jaw in his hand. "You're a good girl. I love you very much."

She covered his hand with hers. "I love you too."

"Let's see what Reed got for you."

She nodded. "We should definitely see what Reed got for me."

Reed slid the gift in front of her. "Go ahead and find out."

She tore at the silver-swirled paper and opened the robe-sized box, gasping. "Is this what I think it is?"

"It's custom-made."

She pulled the black leather jacket from the tissue paper. "Reed, this is *amazing*."

"Abby gave me a hand with the sizing. Now you'll be comfortable on our rides."

She stood and slid it on, feeling the soft leather against her skin. "This is perfect." Leaning down, she cupped his cheeks. "I love it. Thank you."

"You're welcome." He kissed her again. "I'm taking you to the b-e-a-c-h later." He gestured to Lucy as he spelled. "Ice cream and a walk after a nice ride."

Grinning, she wiggled her eyebrows. "I can't wait." She put the jacket back in the box, wanting to keep the scent of stale cigarettes off her new clothing.

Reed kissed her forehead and stood. "What do you say we break out a couple of sweet treats?"

She looked at Dad and saw that he was starting to tire out already. "I'm game. I'm particularly intrigued by that little box." She pointed to the small package on top of the bakery box.

"This one's for Lucy."

She frowned. "For Lucy?"

"This is a party, right? I stopped off at Paws last night."

She grinned, remembering that it wasn't all that long ago when he'd given her a hard time for buying things at a pet bakery. "You went to Paws for our girl?"

He shrugged. "I didn't want her feelings getting hurt." He pulled out a cookie decorated like a cupcake.

She laughed when Lucy hurried to the table and grabbed her

treat. "I think she's pretty excited." She stood and pressed a noisy kiss to Reed's lips. "You make my heart happy."

He tugged gently on her hair. "Right back at ya. Now for your special treat." He opened the bigger bakery box, pulling out a cupcake with pink frosting and purple sprinkles. "These are for you."

She laughed again, truly delighted. "Just like Mom made."

"You were so excited the day I walked you to preschool and you shared those with your friends." Dad smiled. "You told me they were better than the cake your pal brought in for her birthday a few days earlier."

She wished she remembered, wanting to hold close any memories she could get. "I did?"

He nodded. "You were always proud of your mom's baking."

"She made delicious things." Or she had. Somewhere along the way, Mom had let her culinary magic disappear. "Do you remember her raspberry jam?"

Nodding, Dad grinned. "I've never tasted better. That was a prime patch of bushes we had in our backyard, and your mom knew what to do with them. She always had a gift in the kitchen. I told her she should go to school for her baking instead of hair."

She studied his eyes, watching them light up as he talked about Mom. "You never stopped loving her," she said out loud when it was a thought she meant to keep to herself.

He looked down at the table. "You get only one love of your life."

She wanted to tell him that he'd wasted a precious gift—that Mom had been there the whole time, yearning for him the way he'd clearly yearned for her.

Reed stuck a white candle in the top of her cupcake. "Should we light it?"

She nodded. Now wasn't the time to stir up old wounds. "Sure."

Reed and Dad sang "Happy Birthday," and they started on their cupcakes.

Bella stared at the two bites Dad had taken. "There's one left over. Dad, you should keep it and have it for dessert tonight."

"I'm good." He patted his belly. "You go ahead and take it with you."

"Are you sure?"

"Positive."

She glanced at her watch. "I still need to get to the store for you."

He shook his head. "I went myself."

She blinked. "You did?"

"I needed a break from the house. I grabbed one of those electric carts and got my juices and a couple other things—plus your balloons."

She wasn't sure how much she liked the idea of him out among the germs. "Can I cook something for you?"

"I'm liking soup the most right now. I have a few cartons of that organic stuff in the fridge."

"Okay."

"I think I might sit down and put on a movie."

His color was starting to look a little off. "You should. Maybe catch a nap."

"I might." Dad stood and walked to his favorite chair, sitting down and covering himself with a blanket.

She knelt down next to him. "I want you to consider coming and staying with me. I know you like to do your own thing, but it's something to think about."

He nodded. "I'll think about it."

It surprised her that he didn't immediately refuse. "Thank you for such a special afternoon." She kissed his cheek.

"You're welcome."

"Call me if you need anything."

"I will."

"I love you, Daddy."

"I love you too."

Reed grabbed the box with her new jacket in it and tossed the wrapping paper in the trash. "Are you ready?"

She couldn't leave fast enough today, but she also wanted to stay. Dad needed her. "Yeah." She gave her attention back to Dad. "I'll see if I can get up here sometime this week."

"You have a life, Bella." He patted her hand. "The weekends are nice."

"Okay. I'll see you Saturday or Sunday. Lucy, come on."

Lucy got up from the opposite side of Dad's chair and walked to Reed.

He opened the door. "Come on, girl. Let's get in the truck. Thanks for having me up, Vinny."

"Thanks for grabbing the cupcakes. It's handy that Bella left your number for me."

"Call anytime."

"Thank you."

"Bye, Daddy." Bella made sure the door was locked and stepped out, settling in the truck and buckling up as Reed shut Lucy in the back.

He got in and looked at her, studying her through the amber tint of his lenses. "What's up?"

"Nothing," she said, shaking her head. "I had a nice time."

He raised his brow.

If he kept looking at her, she was going to burst into tears. "I had a nice time," she repeated.

"Okay." He fastened his seat belt and turned over the ignition. "Let's go home."

She nodded and stared out the window for the hour drive back to the Palisades.

Reed glanced Bella's way when one of her favorite songs started playing on the radio. Typically, she turned up Justin Timberlake's fun, funky beat and they sang along, but today she stared out the window on their silent drive home. "How's it going over there?"

"Good," she said, folding her arms tighter across her chest.

He lifted his eyebrow. Bella was a terrible liar. "Should we stop off and grab something to eat for later?"

She shook her head. "I'm still full from my cupcake."

He clenching his jaw and focused on the road. This afternoon hadn't turned out quite like he'd hoped. In hindsight, he wasn't sure what else he'd been expecting. Celebrating a birthday with a dying loved one didn't exactly rate high on the fun-o-meter. "We could get grilled chicken sandwiches from Malcoms. I know how much you like those."

"No, thanks."

He slowed as they approached a red light and merged into the right lane, turning toward the beach. He'd wanted to take her out on the bike and drive this way later, but Bella needed her favorite spot now. Having her party had been for Vinny as much as Bella—Vinny wouldn't get another chance to sing "Happy Birthday" to his daughter—but they weren't in Reseda anymore. No matter the intention, today's focus hadn't been entirely on Bella; that was going to change right now.

She turned, finally looking at him. "What are we doing?"

"Going for a walk."

"We don't have to."

"Sure we do." He pulled into a parking spot at the surprisingly quiet beach and got out. He let down the back for Lucy, then opened Bella's door, extending his hand. "Come on. Walk with me for a little while."

She laced their fingers and pulled off her sandals as they approached the sand.

He grinned when Lucy ran away, barking and chasing her gulls. "And she's off."

Bella sent him a small smile. "There she goes."

He took off his flip-flops, studying her troubled eyes through the light tint of her sunglasses. Today had done a number on her. Things weren't good when Lucy couldn't make her laugh. "Ready?"

"Yeah."

He said nothing for several minutes, keeping their pace lazy, letting the endless breeze and rush of waves work their magic. Eventually, her fingers relaxed against his, and he pulled her closer, hooking his arm around her shoulders. "Do you want to talk about it?"

She shrugged. "It's been a long day—a great day," she added quickly.

He stopped, facing her. "I'm sorry this afternoon upset you."

She shook her head adamantly. "It didn't."

"Bella—"

"It didn't," she repeated. "You made everything so special. The jacket's wonderful. And the bracelet." Her bottom lip trembled before she turned away and covered her face with her hands, crying quietly.

"Hey." He pulled her back around, wrapping her up in a hug. "Today was tough," he said close to her ear.

She pressed her forehead to his chest, sucking in several unsteady breaths. "I tried so hard to focus on the good things—on how much thought you and Dad put into my party..." She clutched at the sides of his shirt when her voice broke again. "I'm just so sad."

"Of course you are." He slid his hands up and down her back. "There's nothing easy about what you're going through, Bella."

"I'll be twenty-six on Wednesday and I've spent five birthdays with my dad. Today was it. We don't get another one together."

He kissed the top of her head. "I'm sorry."

"I just—I couldn't..." She shook her head.

"What?" he encouraged her, playing with her hair.

"I couldn't stop thinking about—what would it have been like if he never left us?" She lifted her head, meeting his gaze. "Why did he leave us, Reed? He loved her."

He stared into her devastated eyes, hating that he knew exactly why Vinny had left his family behind and couldn't tell her. "Have you asked him?"

"Sort of." She dashed at her cheeks. "No."

"Come here." He sat down, crisscrossing his legs and settling her on his lap so she straddled him. "Maybe you should ask him. Get some answers—some closure."

"I know I should." She lifted her shoulders in a jerky shrug. "Lately, I can't seem to take my mind off my mom and dad and our little house. She was so good to us—so happy. For a little while, we were all happy." She lost her composure again. "I never get to have that back."

"No, you don't." He captured her hands in his, kissing her knuckles, wanting so badly to take away her pain. "But you get to keep the memories the three of you made."

"I don't have that many. I was so little." She closed her eyes, crying harder. "He looks worse every time I see him. I'm going to lose him soon."

He pulled her closer, not sure what to say, so he held her tight.

She returned his embrace, settling her head in the crook of his neck as she sucked in more shaky breaths. "I don't know how I'm going to handle it when I have to say good-bye."

"You're going to hurt and grieve, and I'm going to be right by your side while you work through the worst of it." He kissed her. "The days will suck for a while, but they'll pass, and things will get a little easier."

She sniffled. "You always make me feel so much better."

"Good."

She sat up, cupping his face. "What would I do without you?"

He'd wondered the same thing about her more than a few times. They'd been together mere months, but he knew his life no longer made sense without her. "I'm thinking we should never find out."

"Agreed." She kissed him. "I can't imagine not having you in my life."

God, did he love the hell out of this amazing woman. "I'm not going anywhere."

She nodded and kissed him again. "I want to think about something else for a while. Do something else—be happy on this beautiful day."

"So let's keep walking."

"I don't know. You look pretty sexy with your hair blowing in the wind like that."

He lifted his head higher, catching more of the breeze. "Even sexier, right?"

She grinned. "Definitely." Her smile faded as she pushed herself forward in his lap, bringing them fire to fire. "You know what else is pretty sexy?"

He slid his palms up and down her thighs. "What?"

"You buying our puppy a cookie at the bakery even though you think it's silly—just to make me happy."

"Hey, I aim to please."

"Oh, I know." She trailed her fingers down his chest and abs, staring at him with teasing eyes. "That thing you do to me with your tongue pleases me plenty."

He felt himself go rock hard. Taking her hand, he rubbed her palm against him, making himself crazy in the process. "This is what you do to me." He snagged her bottom lip with his teeth. "What do you think we should do about it?"

"I have some pretty good ideas." She nipped at his chin. "I want you."

He went after her neck. "It's your special day."

She smiled and pulled his face to hers, capturing his mouth in a hungry kiss. "I need you, Reed."

He dove in again. "Who am I to deny the birthday girl what she wants?" Ready to explode, he scrambled to his feet, bringing her with him in the process. "We should go home so I can do all kinds of things to you."

"The tongue thing, right?"

He gripped her ass, giving it a good squeeze. "Try to stop me. Come on, Lucy," he called, then ran with Bella to the truck, grinning as she laughed in his arms.

☙ Chapter Thirty-Three ❧

"So, what do you think?" Reed asked, sitting next to Vinny at the kitchen table, watching him study the detailed aerial map of Brooklyn's south end.

"This spot." Vinny nodded, tapping his finger on a grassy area approximately two hundred yards from the Coney Island Creek—the same location he'd pointed to on the laptop last Thursday. "I'm positive this is a spot."

"On a scale of one to ten, with ten being absolutely certain."

"I'd say nine."

The excitement was back—the old juices that stirred when he knew an investigation was heading in the right direction. They were getting somewhere. It was too damn bad he'd had to wait so long to show Vinny the map Skylar overnighted last Friday, but his schedule hadn't allowed for anything different. "Good." He picked up Vinny's list of murder victims, scanning both sides of the paper. "Who's buried there?"

Vinny jerked his shoulders. "Hell if I know."

Frowning, he tore his gaze away from the insane number of names—men he'd first read about when he'd been a teenager—and looked at Vinny again. "How do you not know? You wrote all of this." He gestured to the page. "You killed them—buried them—didn't you?"

"I'm not a fucking serial killer. It's not like I ditched a body and went back to check it out again. I was getting rid of assholes before I got caught."

He nodded. "All right. Fine." *Who* wasn't as important as *where* at this point. The anthropologists could make positive IDs with DNA if worse came to worst. "How many bodies are buried there?"

He shrugged again. "Probably one. Maybe two. A couple of guys got whacked at the same time. We tossed them close together, but I don't know if they're here."

Reed circled the area with a red pen, wrote the possible body count for that site, and took a picture, texting it to Skylar with a message.

Here.

He set down his phone and gave his attention back to Vinny and the map. They were rolling right along, but they needed more—lots more. "Where else?"

"Uh." Vinny pushed his glasses farther up on the bridge of his nose, scrutinizing the two-foot-by-two-foot image. "Maybe here or over here. Or maybe this spot."

The uncertainty in Vinny's voice wasn't lost on Reed as Vinny pointed to areas a good fifty to one hundred yards apart. "Take your time and think about it."

Vinny moved the map closer and shook his head. "I'm not sure. Looking at stuff on a picture isn't the same as being there in person."

"There has to be some way to remember. We can't dig up the whole field." He glanced at his watch, clenching his jaw as time ticked away. He'd gotten to Reseda twenty minutes ago, and Bella was expecting him at cooking class in an hour. He shouldn't have come at all tonight, but he needed these bodies. They needed this break if they were going to make something happen with the investigation. The long stretches between visits with Vinny weren't working; they'd lost five days this time around. "A landmark. Something that looks familiar."

"There are trees, bushes, and more trees and bushes. It's green on green."

Reed scrubbed his hands over his face as his frustration grew. Things were starting to fizzle before they even began. "I'm not gonna lie, Vinny. You kinda suck at this."

Vinny glared. "It's not like we put flags in the ground to call attention to the places where we left the bastards to rot. We dug holes and dumped them in when it was dark."

"Think back—"

"We did this over years, Reed. Years and years of whacking people when my father gave us the orders to do so."

He steamed out a breath, well aware that being an ass wasn't getting them anywhere. "I know. Try to think back to just one or two. Something specific that might have caught your attention when you were there that night."

Vinny nodded and looked at the map again. "Maybe this little spot here by this grouping of trees."

Reed sat up taller, hopeful that they were back on track. "What makes you point it out?"

"I remember losing my boot. It had been raining the day before—got stuck up to my knees. Alfie and Dino had to pull me out. The suction took my damn boot."

"And you think it was here?"

"Yeah. But here's another clump of trees too."

He rubbed at his tense neck muscles. "Let's talk about the scale again—one to ten. How positive?"

"Five—six."

"And this was one of Alfeo's hits?"

"More than likely. The odds are in our favor."

He nodded, circling the two potential spots by the groupings of trees and added question marks, then sent off the text, not bothering with another message. Skylar would get the idea, and he was trying to keep things vague on his personal phone.

"This damn thing's not doing me any good," Vinny said as he slapped at the map and sat back in his chair. "It would be easier if I could go there. Looking at a twenty-five-year-old picture doesn't do me much good. It doesn't look the same as standing there."

Reed shook his head as he stared at Vinny's bony shoulders accentuated in his T-shirt and the yellowish tinge to his skin. "You can't travel."

Vinny's spine snapped straight. "I can do whatever I want."

How the hell would they slip that one by Bella? "Let's see what Skylar and her supervisor can come up with."

Vinny sipped at his juice. "What's the plan?"

"Skylar talked to him last Thursday night—after she and I got off the phone. Now that we have the map, they're waiting on us to get them something to work with. They'll take an evidence response team out tomorrow—probably start with dogs. See if they can pick up on a scent. Maybe bring in ground radar."

"They better dig fast, cause they won't be able to keep stuff under wraps for long. Alfeo's got eyes everywhere around there."

"They'll go in small—keep it discreet."

"What's your informant coming up with?"

"Nothing. He has no idea what Alfeo and Matty's plans are, and he's never heard of Nicoli having a child."

"A call wouldn't have hurt."

"I'm trying to keep calls to a minimum. The less there is to trace between the two of us, the better."

Vinny nodded.

"I would have called if there was a problem."

"I figured." Vinny stood, holding onto the back of his chair for several seconds before he started over to his recliner. "Your snitch better watch his back if he plans to live a long life. Everyone in the organization has their antennae up with Alfeo's release date so close. I can guarantee you that."

"It's tense in Bensonhurst." He folded the papers Vinny had written up and put them in his laptop case. "I want more, Vinny. We need more bodies. As many as we can find." He glanced at his watch again and winced. "I've gotta go. Bella and I have cooking class in forty-five minutes."

Vinny covered himself with a blanket. "So go. Don't disappoint her."

He was doing his best to juggle both ends of his life, and he was currently screwing up the most important one. "I'll lock up. Keep thinking. Try to remember. Look at the map every now and again and see if something pops into your mind."

"I will."

He set Vinny's juice on the side table next to him and locked the door. Hurrying to his truck, he dialed Bella's number as he turned the key in the ignition and backed up.

"Hello?"

"Hey. I just wanted to let you know I'm on my way."

"You have plenty of time. Are we meeting at the house?"

He flared his nostrils as he glanced at the dashboard clock. "Uh, I should probably meet you there. I'm on the road now but I'll be a couple minutes late—maybe ten or fifteen."

"I'll get us started. Just be safe."

"I will. See you soon."

"Okay. Bye."

"Bye." He hung up, waiting at a stoplight. If Vinny was closer, things would be a hell of a lot easier. If Vinny was healthy, they could do this differently, but neither was the case. He accelerated and merged onto the 405, swearing when he came to a dead stop at the end of the on-ramp. Taillights glowed bright for as far as he could see.

"You've gotta be fucking kidding me," he muttered again as he closed his eyes and settled his head on the seat cushion. At this rate, he was going to be more than a couple of minutes late. He wasn't making it anywhere anytime soon.

Bella hunched over her prep table, piping lemon mousse curd onto shortbread crusts. She squeezed the bag gently, moving her arms in careful swirling motions, making certain that each golden peak had a perfect point. Satisfied with the results, she focused on the next tart, trying to ignore the fact that everyone else was cleaning up and Reed still wasn't there. He'd texted over an hour ago, letting her know he was stuck in one doozy of a traffic jam, but he'd missed the majority of their cooking session. Again.

"Those look great." Chef Paul stopped by her table. "Really beautiful, Bella."

Smiling, she stood straight, scrutinizing her work. "Thank you."

"You have a real talent in the kitchen." He crossed his arms and leaned his hip against the shiny metal. "I hope you'll consider taking more classes. My advanced courses start next month."

"I've actually been giving it a lot of thought." She wiped the hairs tickling her forehead back toward her ponytail with her arm. "I'm having a lot of fun."

"Spots are filling up fast, but I can make sure we keep one open for you."

Smiling again, she nodded, never quite able to tell if Chef Paul was being friendly or flirty. His golden surfer guy looks were certainly appealing, but he wasn't Reed. "Thanks. Can I let you know in the next week or two? I have some stuff going on that's making it hard for me to give you a definite yes right now."

"Of course. Consider a spot yours if you want one."

"I appreciate it."

"Reed's been absent the last couple of sessions. Is, uh"—he cleared his throat as he stood tall again—"is he no longer joining you?"

"He said he was coming." She glanced at her watch and struggled with another wave of disappointment. "I'm sure he'll be—"

The front door opened and Reed hurried in, rushing over to their cooking station. "I'm here. I'm sorry, Bella."

"Welcome, Reed." Chef sent him a polite nod and walked off.

"I'm sorry," he repeated as he put on his apron. "The traffic was awful—some sort of rollover. It was down to one lane." He hooked his arms around her waist, pulling her close and kissing her.

She wrinkled her nose and stepped back. "You smell like cigarettes again."

"I know. My principal smokes."

She frowned. "The same person as last week—the one from the bar?"

He nodded. "Yeah."

Why did that annoy her? "It's not good for you to be breathing that stuff in. You should talk to Ethan."

"I try to keep my distance, but we can't tell our clientele they can't smoke."

"I don't see why not. He's hurting your health." She heard the testiness in her own voice and turned, getting back to work, piping the last of the curd onto the star-shaped cookie centers.

"What are you making?"

"Tonight we created summer fare. Herb-grilled chicken breasts, an infused fruit salad, greens, and these tarts." Not that he'd been there to help her with anything. She set down the bag and grabbed the bowl of raspberries and blueberries, adding one of each to the desserts, reminding herself that Reed didn't have a typical job. He didn't have regular hours, but he was trying. "I saved it in some dishes."

"You didn't eat?"

"No. I thought we would eat together when you got here." She finished her presentation with a bit of lemon rind.

"Hey." He turned her to face him, nudging her close with a pull on her apron strings. "I'm sorry about tonight."

She shrugged. "It's fine."

He shook his head and hooked his arms around her waist. "No, it's not. I'm not a big fan of breaking promises." He kissed her. "Work has been a lot lately."

She settled her hands on his chest. "This is what you do. I'm trying to get used to that."

"It sucks right now."

"Yes, it does, but we don't have a lot of time together, so I don't want to be mad at you when we do."

"But you are mad."

She shook her head, then nodded. "Yes, I am. Or at least, a little."

He rested his forehead against hers. "Things will get better."

She nodded, exhaling a long breath.

"And tomorrow, I'm yours. Just yours, Bella. On your birthday." He rubbed her nose with his, then lifted his head. "I'm sorry."

"It's okay." And everything was, now that they'd talked about it. She held up one of the tarts, seeing the regret lingering in his eyes. "Want to try?"

"What about dinner?"

"We'll spoil our appetite a little."

He took a bite, groaning and nodding the way he did when he genuinely liked something. "Really good. You should make these for Sarah's party next weekend."

"That's a good idea." She popped the rest in her mouth and rolled her eyes, loving the complementary flavors of tart lemon and buttery sugar cookie. "I'm definitely making these."

He cupped her cheeks. "Thank you for being so understanding. It's not easy."

She gripped his wrists. "I want you. I want us."

"So do I."

"Then we can make anything work."

He hugged her, holding on tight. "Should we take our dinner to the beach? We can eat in the back of the truck and listen to the waves." He leaned close to her ear. "Maybe we can make out a little."

She smiled. "Definitely."

"Let's clean up and we'll go eat by the water."

"Okay."

Chapter Thirty-Four

Music pumped through the stereo speakers while Bella chopped fresh vegetables for a huge salad. She smiled, glancing Reed's way as he stood on the deck, keeping his eye on their filets cooking on the grill. For once, they were home on a weeknight, and she planned to enjoy every second of their time together. The fact that he'd spoiled her with a quart of her favorite triple chocolate chunk ice cream and a gorgeous bouquet of mixed flowers was an excellent bonus. She wiggled her hips to DNCE's "Cake by the Ocean" beat and tossed red peppers and cucumbers into the bowl of greens.

Reed opened the door, popping his head inside. "We're probably five, maybe six minutes out."

She shimmied again. "Okay."

He walked in and yanked her around, pulling her against him as he gyrated his hips.

She laughed, surprised by his agile rhythm. "I knew you could sing, but you dance too?"

"I couldn't tell you all my secrets right away, baby." He spun her and settled his hands on her waist, bringing her back against him. "Every relationship should have a little mystery."

She laughed again, hooking her arms around his neck as she followed his lead. "Well, I like your moves."

"I've got all kinds of moves you haven't seen yet." He glanced toward their bedroom and winked as he flashed her a cocky smile.

She grinned, relishing the rush of tingles in her belly, knowing that Reed could and would deliver on his sexy declaration. "As much as I would love to dance here all night—in the kitchen and upstairs—I think our dinner's going to burn."

"Shit. I'll be right back." He hurried outside, closing the door behind him, and opened the grill.

She chuckled, studying her gorgeous man saving their steaks, ogling his amazing ass. She'd developed quite a thing for jeans, T-shirts, and bare feet. Looking at Lucy, she smiled. "I love him," she whispered. "He's pretty much the perfect guy."

Lucy wagged her tail.

"I know you agree. You were the one to barge through his front door. Did I ever thank you for that?"

Lucy stared at her, moving her tail faster.

"You're the best." She focused on the salad again, grabbing a carrot stick from the cutting board as Reed's cell phone started ringing in the living room. "Your phone," she hollered, but he didn't move from his spot on the porch. She ran to his phone and glanced at the screen as she picked it up off the coffee table. *Skylar G.* "Hello?"

The line stayed silent.

Bella frowned and pressed her hand to her opposite ear. "Hello?"

"Um, yes, is Reed there?"

"Sure." She hurried over to the stereo and turned it down. "Hold on. He's outside."

"Thanks."

She walked back through the kitchen and opened the door.

He turned. "What's—"

"Your phone was ringing," she said as she handed it over.

"Oh. Thanks."

She nodded, sending him a small smile as she went inside and closed the door. Heading back to the cutting board, she chopped the carrots, trying to focus on the vegetables instead of the mystery woman Reed was talking to. Skylar G. was clearly a friend; her name and number were programed into his phone. So why hadn't Skylar responded when Bella answered?

Her gaze slid Reed's way as he chatted and paced back and forth. That had happened in Las Vegas too. On a couple of occasions, she'd picked up Linc's phone and someone hung up. She frowned, shocked by where her thoughts were going. Reed was *not* Linc. Most men didn't have girlfriends and fiancées stashed around the city. It wasn't fair to put them in the same slot.

She glanced his way again as he hung up and shoved his phone in his pocket, hating that even as she told herself she was being silly, she couldn't entirely dismiss her doubts.

Moments later, he walked in with the steaks. "Ready to eat?"

"Sure." She met his gaze, then looked toward the cupboards as an ember of distrust tried to hold firm. Admonishing herself again, she moved to the shelf where she kept the plates and grabbed two.

He came up behind her. "That was Skylar Grayson. She's a long-time family friend. Our grandfathers worked together when I was a little boy. We keep in touch."

She turned to face him. "Okay."

"She's also in law enforcement. We worked together a few times in New York."

"It's fine, Reed." Or she wanted it to be.

He took the plates from her and set them on the table. "Then why are you looking at me like you're trying to decide if my story's bull-shit?"

She shrugged. "I guess it's a kneejerk thing."

He settled his hands on her shoulders, sliding his palms along her arms. "I would never, *ever* cheat on you, Bella. That guy out in Vegas might be a dumbass, but I could never do something like that to you."

She nodded, overcome with guilt for letting herself travel down that road when Reed had never given her a reason to. "I'm sorry."

He shook his head and cupped her cheeks. "I don't want anyone but you."

"The feeling's mutual." She kissed him and wrapped him up in a hug. "I'm sorry."

"You don't have to be. No more apologizing."

She nodded. "Do you want to sit down and have some dinner?"

"Heck, yeah. I'm starving. Let's eat."

She stared at him as he put a plate on the table for each of them. Reed had brought her flowers and a delicious treat to help her celebrate her birthday, but being able to trust the man she loved completely was the ultimate gift.

Reed snuggled Bella on the couch while they watched another episode of *The Office*. They were well into season three, but tonight, he was having a hard time following the storyline. His mind was too focused on New York after Skylar's latest phone call. Big things were happening. Big, frustrating things. This morning, the ground radar team had detected a body in the initial location Vinny pointed out. After hours of digging—first with a backhoe and then by hand—they'd unearthed several dozen buckets of mud and a partial mandible—a somewhat decent first day but not nearly good enough, especially when they'd come up empty at the groupings of trees Vinny guessed at.

Bella laughed, bringing him back to the moment. He concentrated on the show again, catching the last couple of minutes before the credits rolled. "Dwight's an idiot."

She chuckled and turned her head, looking up at him. "But he's funny."

He wrapped his arms tighter around her as he stared into her beautiful eyes, realizing that he was letting the investigation take priority when this evening was supposed to be about Bella. There were things to do—calls to make, a text to send off to Vinny—but Bella turned twenty-six only once. "I'm pretty sure I would knock Michael out, and Dwight wouldn't be far behind."

She grinned. "Do you want to watch another episode or do something else?"

He opened his mouth to answer as Joey's ringtone filled the room. Wincing, he grabbed his phone off the coffee table and silenced it. "I'm sorry. I can talk to him tomorrow."

"It's fine." She kissed him. "How about you see what your pal wants and I'll go up and take my shower?"

"Are you sure?"

"Yup," she said with a decisive nod.

"I'll be up in just a second."

"Okay." She stood and made a grab for their ice cream bowls.

"I'll get those."

"Thanks." She started upstairs.

He waited until he heard her footsteps in the hallway, then answered. "Hey."

"I talked to Upshaw."

He frowned. He hadn't expected their conversation to start like this. He'd assumed Joey was calling for an update on the dig. "Just now?"

"Just now, buddy. I dumped him in a cab five minutes ago—took him out for my own version of a pub crawl and got him shit-faced over a few rounds."

He stood, bringing the dishes to the sink. "So?"

"The Marshals had a security breach mid-February—Manhattan's WITSEC branch. Someone hacked into the computers."

He rinsed the bowls and put them in the dishwasher. "Do they know who?"

"Doesn't sound like it."

"What information were they looking for? What did they get?"

"Upshaw has no idea. Apparently, it was on a need-to-know basis and Upshaw didn't. He hadn't heard anything about it until Walt mentioned it."

"Sounds like Walt was on the need-to-know list."

"Ding ding, buddy."

He leaned against the counter, using his shoulder to hold his phone as he crossed his arms. "What else?"

"Walt's house was broken into less than a week later. Perps messed up the house some—went through his home office, the bedrooms, et cetera. Didn't steal anything, but they did try to access his personal computer."

Reed scrubbed at his jaw, not liking where this was going. "He was the target."

"Sounds like. Upshaw said Walt didn't report the break-in."

"Interesting. What's your gut saying—you think this was Caparelli-related? Do you think they got to him?"

"Could be. Timing's right. Alfeo's getting out. They're blowing witnesses' brains out. Maybe they're thinking they want Nicoli too. Upshaw said Walt was a mess after the break-in—real nervous, lost some weight, asked Upshaw to keep an eye on the family if anything ever happened to him. Then he drops dead. The guy was in great shape. His death was stress-related."

Reed made a sound in his throat as he remembered Vinny's comments about Walter opening his mouth to the mafia and Matty telling his father about Dino looking into something concerning Nicoli Caparelli on the prison recordings. "Do you think Walt wanted Upshaw's help tracking down Nicoli so he could hand him over to Alfeo?"

"Could be. If they threatened his family, I'd say definitely."

"Do you think that's what happened?"

"I couldn't tell ya."

He narrowed his eyes. "What was your impression on Upshaw? Do you think he and Salada intend to turn Vinny over?"

"I don't think Upshaw has any clue that Walt was heading that way. Hell, neither do we. We're guessing here—on all of this. We know there was a breach. We know Walt had a break-in. We know he asked Upshaw to help him track down Nicoli to make sure Nicoli was safe a couple minutes before he keeled over. Those are the facts we can be one hundred percent certain of."

Reed nodded. "Bella has to be in the clear, though. Matty didn't mess with her in Brooklyn."

"Seems about right to me. Upshaw didn't say anything about Walt mentioning that Nicoli has a daughter. I didn't want to touch that one too much—give anyone any reason to believe he does."

He closed his eyes with the rush of relief. Bella was safe—or, at this point, they had fairly good reason to believe she was.

"I'll keep my ears open, though. Upshaw's a lightweight, so you let me know if we need anything else."

"I will."

"How'd the dig go?"

"Not great. They hit the water table at four feet—filled the whole damn hole. They brought in some pumps but it's fucking mud the rest of the way down. Skylar said evidence response is having a hell of a time. It's like quicksand. So far, they have half a mandible and muck up to their kneecaps."

"How the fuck's that even possible? I thought Vinny said they were in bags."

"Not this guy. Whoever he is, he's definitely not in a bag—or at least not all of him. Who knows what they'll find when they get back to it tomorrow."

"And the locations by the trees?"

"They're no good. There's nothing there. The dogs didn't alert and ground radar didn't pick up anything."

"Shit."

Reed rubbed at the back of his neck as the weight of their problems settled on his shoulders. "We need more. Even if they find the rest of the skull, it doesn't mean it'll do us any good. It sure as hell isn't likely they'll find a bullet if there was one left behind at all. And for all we know, this was one of Dino or Nicoli's hits." He shook his head. "I need to talk to Vinny—make something happen."

"Bring him to New York."

He laughed scoffingly. "Give me a break, Joe."

"What?"

"He can't handle it. He's skin and bones and light-headed most of the time. How the hell would he walk through all of that brush and mud to find what we're looking for?"

"We'd figure something out."

He shook his head again. "Not gonna happen. We'll have to take another look at the map. I'll have him go through each murder with me—step by step. See if that sparks something." The shower shut off upstairs. "I need to go. It's Bella's birthday."

"Keep me in the loop."

"I will. We've gotta come up with something."

"We will, boss. We always do."

He nodded. "I'll talk to you later."

"Tell Bella I said happy birthday."

"Sure thing."

He glanced toward the ceiling, listening to Bella walking around as he located Vinny's number in his contact information.

We need to talk. I'm coming up tomorrow.

He wasn't sure how in the hell he was going to make that happen, but he was going to have to. He shoved his phone away and checked the locks, then went upstairs. From the sounds of Joe's conversation with Upshaw, they could cautiously put Vinny's concerns about Bella aside. Tomorrow was for Bella's father and the investigation. Right now was for the birthday girl.

Bella stepped out of the bathroom with her long hair dripping and a towel wrapped around her as he walked into the room. "How's Joey?"

"Good." He closed the distance between them and hooked his arms around her waist. "He told me to tell you happy birthday."

She smiled. "Aw, isn't he sweet?"

He shrugged, twisting her glossy, wet locks around his fingers. "He's okay."

She grinned. "I like you better."

"Yeah?"

She nodded. "You're my very favorite person."

Nodding, he raised his brow. "Your *very* favorite person?"

"Mmm. Very favorite." She played with the button on his jeans.

"What do you say we lose the towel?" He yanked on the hem and sent it to the floor, trailing his gaze over her sensational body. "God, I love looking at you."

She took his hands and pressed them to her breasts. "I love it when you touch me."

He used his thumbs to tease her nipples into points and went after her chin with gentle nibbles. "What's the birthday girl looking for tonight?"

She pulled his shirt up and off. "What have you got?"

He slid his palms down the sides of her waist. "Anything you want."

She unzipped his jeans and tugged his pants, crouching to help him step out the rest of his clothes. "You said something about moves I haven't seen before." Her breath heated his erection as she spoke.

"I did."

She touched him, sliding her palm against him.

He steamed out a breath as cool fingers wrapped around him.

"Feel good?"

"Yeah."

"How about this?" She put him in her mouth.

He groaned, gripping her hair. "Bella."

She pleasured him with her clever lips and tongue until his toes curled and his stomach muscles trembled.

"Bella. You're about to end this right here."

She eased away, still working him with her hand. "That's not such a bad thing."

"It is when I haven't had my turn." He helped her to her feet. "Come here." He sat on the edge of the pretty armless chair tucked in the corner of the room and brought her down on his lap so she straddled his legs and they both faced the mirror on Bella's half-closed closet door. Palming her breasts, he watched her snag her bottom lip with her teeth as she closed her eyes. "Let's do this for a little bit," he said.

"Okay."

"It's different." He kissed her neck.

"Yes."

"We're both going to watch as you take me in." He lifted her up and sank her down on him, sucking in a sharp breath as she gasped. "How's that?"

"Very good."

"Your cheeks are pink."

"You make me hot."

He went back to her breasts, then trailed his hand between her thighs, playing with her.

She closed her eyes and let her head fall back on his chest.

"Watch, Bella. Watch what I'm doing to you."

She opened her eyes as he moved his fingers in circles and her hips rocked slowly.

"Does it feel good?"

"Yes."

He nipped her shoulder and increased the pressure of his fingers against her.

She moaned and jerked. "I'm going to—"

"I know." He stroked her the way he knew she liked best and sent her flying.

Her eyes went wide, holding his gaze in the glass as she called out.

"How about one more?"

"I want to face you. I want to see you."

"You can see me now." He continued his teasing, waiting, waiting, and sent her over again.

"Reed. Reed."

Damn, he loved that, listening to her pant out his name. "How do you want to finish?"

"Kissing you."

"Turn around."

She stood and turned, capturing his mouth as she sat down and took him in deep. "Like this. Just like this, but my feet are barely touching the floor."

He smiled. "I'll do the work." He stroked her back and kissed her neck, then gripped her ass, thrusting her up and down on him.

She whimpered and whispered his name next to his ear as she clutched at his shoulders. "I'm ready." She met his gaze. "I'm ready."

He moved her faster.

She kissed him with abandon as their moans mingled and they fell over the edge together.

He hugged her close, stroking her damp skin as she rested her head on his shoulder. He caught a glimpse of her strong, beautiful body entwined with his in the mirror. "Happy birthday, Bella."

She sat up and smiled into his eyes. "Flowers, ice cream, and amazing sex. I think this might be my best one yet."

He stood, walking with her to the bed, and fell with her to the mattress. "Maybe we should try that again and really make sure."

She laughed. "I'm up for that."

Chapter Thirty-Five

Bella's eyes flew open when her cell phone started ringing in the dark. Already on high alert, she tugged herself free of Reed's hold and sat up, yanking her phone off the bedside table. "Hello?"

"Bella, it's Dad."

She swiped her hair out of her face as she blinked away the fog of a deep sleep. "Is everything okay?"

Reed sat up on his side.

"I wanted to let you know that I'm at the hospital. They're running some tests."

She glanced at the time and hurried to her feet. One fifteen. "Why? What tests are they doing?"

"I was having a hard time breathing. They have me on some oxygen. I'm feeling a lot better."

She pressed her hand to her heart, still groggy but scared nonetheless. "I'll be right there."

"You don't have to—"

"I'm coming. I'll be there as soon as I can."

"I'm in the ER for now. I'm not sure if they're going to admit me."

"Okay, I'll find you. I'll see you in an hour. Bye, Daddy." She hung up and turned on the light, blinding herself and Reed in the process.

"Jesus," Reed said, shielding his eyes.

"Sorry."

"It's okay." He scrubbed his hands over his face. "What's going on?"

"Dad's in the emergency room. He's having trouble breathing." She rushed over to her chest of drawers, grabbing jeans, a bra, panties, and a T-shirt. She whirled and slammed into Lucy on her way back to the bed. "I'm sorry, sweetie."

Reed was up, pulling on boxers, jeans, and a shirt from the drawers on his side of the room.

"What are you doing?" she asked.

"Getting dressed so I can come with you."

"No. I don't know how long I'll be." Her hands weren't quite steady as she slid her panties on and secured her bra in place. "I might have to call in to work." She pulled her shirt over her head and tugged her pants up her legs, fighting with the snap.

Reed walked over to where she stood, capturing her hands in his. "I'm coming with you. You're not going through any more of this on your own." He kissed her knuckles and let her go, securing the button for her.

Her adrenaline was pumping—and the fear—as they did every time she got a call in the middle of the night. "He said he couldn't breathe well. He called me at one o'clock in the morning. Even though he said he doesn't need me there, I know he wants me to come."

"Let's go see what the doctors have to say."

She nodded, struggling to keep her emotions in check. "We didn't make it through the week. It hasn't even been two since his last admittance. He's getting worse so much faster than I was expecting."

He cupped her cheeks, stroking her skin with his thumbs. "I'm going to be here with you every step of the way."

She gripped his wrists as a tear escaped. "Thank you."

"Don't thank me, Bella," he said gently, kissing her lips. "I don't need or want to be thanked."

"I'm thankful anyway. One part of my life is so good, Reed. You're so good. We're so good. And then there's my dad. It's like my heart's half-broken."

He sighed, holding her gaze with eyes full of understanding. "I'm so sorry you're going through this, but I'm right here."

Sniffling, she nodded again.

"Get your purse and we'll go."

She glanced at Lucy curled up on her bed once again. "What about our girl?"

"She's okay for now. If it doesn't look like we'll make it back before breakfast, we can have Jenny come over, or she can give Shane the key and he'll come take care of her."

Another tear fell as relief warred with worry. It felt so good to have a partner, someone she could depend on to help her through the rough spots. "All right. I want to keep the light on for her."

"We can do that."

"And some music." She walked over to the clock radio and switched it on, filling the room with the relaxing music she liked to wake up to.

"Ready?"

She wasn't, but she needed to be. "Yes."

"Let's go." He took her hand, and they grabbed their flip-flops, then hurried to Reed's truck, driving toward Reseda for another long wait at the hospital.

Reed snuggled Bella on his lap while he stared at the ugly curtain cordoning off Vinny's cramped space from the rest of the ER. He slid his fingers through her soft hair in long, soothing strokes, listening to her deep breathing as she dozed off in his arms. They'd been waiting a solid hour and a half for the doctor to come back with an update, but Vinny's ongoing medical issues had taken a back seat when multiple car accident victims started rolling into the trauma rooms shortly after he and Bella arrived. He stifled a yawn and shook away the trance-like state of exhaustion as he studied Vinny sleeping while a tube forced oxygen up his nose. The Caparellis' youngest son was quickly losing his battle with cancer, and the investigation was in grave danger of falling apart. He clenched his jaw, hating that his focus was on keeping Alfeo in prison when Vinny's declining health was breaking Bella's heart. But as he breathed in her shampoo and felt her soft skin against his cheek, he knew that moving forward with Operation Caparelli Takedown needed to happen.

The more he thought about the final minutes of the prison recordings and Upshaw's conversation with Joey, he didn't like either. There were too many question marks where Bella's safety was concerned. On the surface, she appeared to be in the clear, but there would never be any way of knowing whether the mafia had compromised Walt before his death or if Walt had taken Nicoli Caparelli's secret to the grave. The only way to make sure Bella never had to worry about the Caparellis was to destroy them once and for all—and that started with keeping Alfeo right where he was, with Vinny's help. Vincent Pescoe was the key to his brother's demise. Now they needed him to live long enough to ensure his daughter a long, happy life.

The doctor poked his head in. "I'll be right with you folks."

"Thanks." Reed kissed Bella's forehead and rubbed her back. "Bella."

"Hmm?" She stirred, blinking up at him as she rested her head on his shoulder. "What's going on?"

"The doctor's about to come in."

"Oh." She tucked her hair behind her ear as she sat up. "Oh," she said again, taking his hand.

The doctor pushed the curtain to the side and stepped in, nodding politely as he slid it closed behind him. "I'm sorry for the long wait. We've been busy tonight."

"Sounds like it," Reed commented as he laced his fingers with Bella's, noting her rigid posture. For a little while, she'd been able to relax, but she was strung tight again already.

Vinny opened his eyes and cleared his throat. "You got some results?"

The tall, studious-looking fifty-something nodded as he took a seat on the exam stool. "Mr. Pescoe, I've gone over your blood work and latest scans."

"How's everything look?"

"We're seeing some fluid buildup in your right lung—a condition called pleural effusion."

Bella gripped Reed's fingers tight. "Will that go away?"

"At this point, it's hard to say. Right now, we're not seeing any major inflammation or infection, which is a positive sign. We'll keep an eye on the situation and hope things move in the right direction without any need for intervention."

Bella nodded, looking at Reed with hopeful eyes. "That sounds good," she whispered. "Right, that sounds good?"

He swallowed, giving her fingers a squeeze, wanting to reassure her, but it was more than clear that nothing about Vinny's situation was "good" anymore.

The doctor cleared his throat. "Unfortunately, this morning's scan is also showing us several areas of concern that I want to discuss. Mr. Pescoe, we're seeing new tumor growth, particularly on the liver, kidneys, and lungs. There are also indications that the cancer is spreading to your bones."

Bella blinked rapidly as shock and utter devastation played over her face.

Reed pulled her back against him, kissing the top of her head and wrapping her up tight, hoping his strong hold did something to ease some of her pain as her breath shuddered in and out against his neck.

"Your oncologist will discuss your results further when she comes in for her rounds later today," the doctor continued, "but I didn't want to leave you in the dark."

"I appreciate it."

"What are we—what happens now?" Bella dashed at her cheeks as she sat up again.

"For now, we're going to keep your father here with us and monitor his lungs and oxygen levels—probably for the next forty-eight to seventy-two hours. If all stays well, we can send him home after that." The doctor stood. "I wish I had better news for you."

"Thank you, doctor," Vinny said.

"We'll get you transferred to a room shortly."

"I'll be here waiting."

The doctor smiled and left.

Bella took a deep breath and gained her feet, walking to sit next to Vinny on the bed. "It, um, it sounds like we're going to get you settled in here."

Vinny took her hand. "I could use some coffee—a good cup with some cream and a little sugar."

"I should ask—make sure that's okay."

"I'm stuck here for the next little while, and I'd like a little caffeine. It's not like it's going to hurt me any."

She frowned. "Don't say that. That's not funny."

"Sorry."

She stood, walking back to Reed. "Do you want anything?"

He gained his feet and closed the distance between them, recognizing that she was trying her damnedest not to fall apart. "How about a second coffee—hazelnut if they have it."

She nodded.

He cupped her cheeks. "Get yourself a tea. Take your time." He kissed her tenderly, hurting for her as she stared at him with tears pooling in her shattered eyes. "I'll stay here until you get back."

Closing her eyes, she gripped his wrists, taking several deep breaths.

"We're going to get through this," he muttered for only her to hear. "You and me together, Bella."

Her head bobbed again.

"Go get a tea."

"I'll be back."

"Okay."

She looked at Vinny, then walked out of the curtained space, closing it behind her.

"Goddamn, those eyes of hers have always been my weak spot," Vinny said. "I never could raise my voice at her and never thought to raise a hand."

He recognized the same anguish in Vinny's eyes that he saw in Bella's. Vinny was putting on a brave front, but this couldn't be easy for him as a father or as a man facing his mortality. "She's going to be okay. I'm going to make sure of it."

"I'm counting on you, Reed. That should be tough for me to say, but my little girl loves you." He sat up in bed, motioning him closer. "What's the news from New York? Your text said you wanted to talk."

He debated whether or not to say anything, but how could he not? "They found a body at the first spot you pointed out," he said quietly, glancing around the small space, well aware that this was not a secure location.

"That's good, right?"

He nodded, trying to work from an optimistic perspective when there wasn't a whole lot of positive news to share. "It's a start."

Vinny frowned. "A start?"

He crossed his arms as he settled his hip on the bed's safety bar. "The water table's high. There's a lot of mud in the hole. They didn't find a body bag."

"Don't bullshit me, Reed," Vinny hissed in a nasty whisper. "They don't have anything."

"They have part of a mandible." He gestured to his lower jaw.

"Is that gonna get the job done?"

He sighed. "At this point, no."

"What about by the trees?"

He shook his head. "There was nothing there."

Vinny's eyes grew wide with surprise. "What do you mean, there was nothing there?"

"They tried dogs and ground radar."

"At both places?"

"Both places. We'll have to look at the map again when you're up to it."

"I told you that map doesn't do me any good. We need to go."

Reed let out a scoffing laugh, much like he had when Joey suggested the same thing, and walked back to the chair. The idea was appealing—could potentially solve all their problems—but it was also incredibly risky, bordering on stupid. "Look at you, Vinny. How are we going to go? How am I supposed to take you across the country and trudge through the mud when you can't breathe lying in a bed?"

"I can do anything I want." He motioned Reed close again.

Reed complied, moving back to the bed.

"This would put Alfeo away—keep him locked up?"

"If we can find bodies and prove it was him, he'll never get out again."

"This is how I get to make sure my little girl is safe—"

Vinny's little girl would lose her shit if she had half a clue that Reed was even considering the thought of traveling with her ill father. "I can't take you to New York, Vinny."

"Didn't you tell me just a few days ago that eventually they would find her, that things had a way of leaking? Did you not say it wasn't a matter of if but when?"

He pressed his fingers to his mouth and blew out. "Yeah, I did." Because most of the time, it was true.

"This is the last thing I have to give her," he said, his voice growing harsh again. "You find a way to get me to New York."

Reed looked at the ceiling and shook his head adamantly. "What are we supposed to tell Bella?"

"We'll figure that out after you figure out how you're getting me on a damn plane. Today."

"*Today*?" He paced away and back. "Fuck, Vinny—"

Bella slid the curtain to the side and walked in. "Your waitress is here."

Reed turned, making sure he was smiling. "Great."

"Dad, your cream and sugar coffee. Reed, by some miracle, they had your hazelnut. And I got myself a decaffeinated tea."

"Thank you." Vinny took the cup from Bella. "Now you should go home."

Bella frowned. "No. I want to make sure you get settled in."

"It could be awhile." He took a sip. "You have to work in a few hours. So does Reed."

Bella looked at Reed. "Why don't you leave me here—"

"I want you to go home, Bella," Vinny interrupted. "Exhausting yourself isn't going to change one damn thing. You can't visit me if you're sick. You go get some sleep and go to work."

"All right."

"I don't want to see you until this weekend—Sunday afternoon."

She gaped. "But—"

"You have your friend's fashion show tomorrow night that I know you've been looking forward to. You're going to go to that, then you're going to do something fun for yourself on Saturday, and I'll see you Sunday."

She shook her head. "Daddy—"

"Don't make me put my foot down. I called you because something was wrong. Don't make me regret that decision. Don't make me hesitate if something comes up next time."

"But you're"—her voice broke and she looked down—"it's getting worse."

Vinny lifted her chin, holding her gaze. "And you camping out by my bed isn't going to change that. It makes me feel good knowing you're out living your life—gives me some peace. I'll look forward to your phone calls telling me all about it."

"All right." She dashed at her cheeks. "I won't come back until Sunday."

"I want your promise."

She hesitated.

"Promise me, Isabella."

"I'm going to call every day."

"You can call twice a day if you want."

"I don't like it, but I promise." She kissed his forehead.

"Sunday will be here before you know it. Now take Reed and go home."

"If you need anything—"

"You'll be the first to know."

"I'm going to go make sure the desk has my number."

"Good idea."

She walked out from behind the curtain.

Vinny looked at Reed. "I just bought you till Sunday. You get us on a plane to New York this afternoon."

Clenching his jaw, Reed stared at the oxygen tubing. "What about the doctors—"

"I'll check myself out—refuse care."

Reed closed his eyes. This had disaster written all over it. "Vinny—"

Vinny yanked him close, gripping his arm. "You get me on a fucking plane. I'm running out of time. I can feel myself dying, damn it. You get me on a plane."

And that was that. Vinny was dying and Bella needed them both to do what they could to keep her safe. "All right. I'll make it happen."

"Call me with the details."

"I've gotta go." He walked out, trying to smile as Bella forced one of her own. "Let's get home and back to bed for a couple of hours." He had a hell of a lot of planning to do after Bella fell back to sleep.

Bella splashed water on her face in the master bathroom as she tried her best to pull herself together after another troubling couple of hours in the ER. Sniffling, she shut off the water and grabbed a towel from the bar, pressing her face into the soft cotton as she fought another staggering wave of fear. Dad was in bad shape—far worse than she ever could have imagined. She'd been foolishly hopeful when the doctor mentioned the currently benign fluid buildup in Dad's lung. Then he'd dropped one heck of a bombshell...

"Bella," Reed called, knocking on the door.

"Um, I was just changing. I'll be right out." She took a deep breath and blotted at the remaining drops on her skin, then opened the door to Reed stripped down to his boxers.

Sighing, he held open his arms. "Come here."

Hearing the sympathy in his voice, seeing the compassion radiating from his eyes, she shook her head. "I can't."

He frowned. "Why?"

"Because I'll start crying," she choked out, her composure already lost.

He walked to her and wrapped her up. "This has been a tough one."

She nodded, clinging to him and crying harder.

"Come snuggle with me." He picked her up and carried her to their bed, settling them both in the center of the mattress. He adjusted their pillows and nudged her down with him, holding her close as they stared into each other's eyes. "Do you want to talk about it?"

"I don't know what to— He's so sick. I thought we were going to have more time."

He took her hand and pressed her knuckles to his lips. "He's doing what he can to hang in there."

"I know." She traced his ear, finding the familiar gesture comforting. "I think I'm going to break my promise and go see him—"

"No."

Her hand paused against his skin as she frowned at the sharpness of his tone. "But—"

"You can't, Bella," he said, gentling his voice as he took her hand again. "This is what he wants. He wants to think of you out being happy—laughing with your friends or walking the beach with Lucy. That's what you'll be doing while he's still here with us, and that's what you'll be doing long after he's gone. I think he needs to know you're living your life—that you're going to be okay."

More tears fell as he spoke. "I feel like we're wasting the time he and I have left."

He shook his head. "Not if what he's asking of you makes him happy and gives him peace. The best gift you can give your dad right now is going to Abby's fashion show tomorrow night and watching Lucy chase her gulls this weekend. Call him, tell him about all of the adventures you're having—the ones he can't have anymore."

She exhaled a long, shaky breath. "I didn't think about it like that."

"That's what you've got me for." He winked and kissed her forehead, then turned off the light and covered them with the blankets. "Get some sleep."

"Okay." She moved so she rested her head on his chest, listening to his steady heart beating while she stared into the dark. Eventually her eyes drooped closed, and finally she slept.

☙ Chapter Thirty-Six ❧

"Morning," Reed said to Shane and Jerrod as they filed into Ethan's office. He shut the door behind them and waited for his buddies to snag their designated coffees from the cup holder and take their seats. "Thanks for coming in early."

"Thanks for picking up coffee." Ethan gestured to his cup and took another sip.

Reed nodded, figuring that grabbing Starbucks on his way downtown had been the least he could do when he'd pulled everyone away from their families a good hour earlier than usual. "I appreciate you and Tyson finagling things to cover Sadie for me."

"No problem." Ethan sat back in his chair, settling his foot on his opposite knee. "So, what's up?"

Reed exhaled a long breath, not quite sure where to start. At five, he'd eased himself away from Bella, leaving her in bed to sleep while he called Joey and Skylar, then sent texts off to his coworkers, setting into motion their insane new Operation Caparelli Takedown strategy. By six forty-five, he'd been on the road, heading toward Ethan Cooke Security, eager to make things happen. "Too damn much." He opened the file folder he'd brought with him and pulled out a picture of Nicoli Caparelli in his glory days, imagining that this would get their conversation moving along.

"Is that Nicoli Caparelli?" Shane asked, frowning.

"Yeah."

"Why do you have a picture of Nicoli Caparelli?"

"It's no secret—at least not in this room—that I worked in NYPD's Special Organized Crime Unit, or that we were focused on taking down the last stronghold of La Cosa Nostra." He nodded toward the picture he still held. "A couple months ago, my former partner, Joey Holmes, got a lead on the potential identities Nicoli was using during his years in WITSEC—before he abandoned the program. Long story short: Joe gave me some lists, I checked them out, and we found him."

Jerrod, a former US Marshal and WITSEC handler, frowned this time. "A Marshal leaked Nicoli's identities?"

Reed shook his head. "Joey overheard a conversation at Walter Hodds's funeral. Alfeo Caparelli's set for release in June. Walt wanted to locate Nicoli before his brother could—check on him, make sure he was okay."

"No one should have been talking about him in the first place."

"Agreed. But they were, and now Nicoli's talking to me. I've been working with him—feeding information to Special Agent Skylar Grayson with the goal of keeping Alfeo in prison."

Shane shook his head, huffing out an incredulous laugh. "You've been working with Nicoli Caparelli? The fucking mafia legend?"

"Yeah."

"How the hell did you pull that one off without getting yourself killed?"

He clenched his jaw and rubbed at the back of his neck. "He's Bella's father."

Shane smile vanished.

"She has no idea," Reed added quickly, noting the surprise in all three men's eyes. "She knows nothing about any of this. When Bella and I met, *I* had no idea she was Nicoli's daughter." He sat down and stood again, too restless to be still. "Nicoli goes by the alias Vincent Pescoe—the identity he was using when Bella was born. He left just before her fifth birthday, hoping to keep her away from anything that could touch her from his former life."

"Well, son of a bitch," Shane muttered.

"He's sick. End-stage cancer," Reed continued. "It's fucking everywhere—tumors in his lungs, kidneys, liver. Bella and I were with him at the hospital for a couple hours early this morning. He doesn't have much time left." He picked up his coffee and set it back down, thinking better of adding a jolt of caffeine to his system when he was already keyed up.

"So, what's the plan?" Jerrod wanted to know.

"We're in the middle of making some adjustments now." He went after his neck again, rubbing at the painful knots. "Vinny and I spent a couple days checking out Alfeo's old correspondence—reading through letters and listening to prison recordings. There's nothing there—a lot of bitching and a few small-time schemes, but nothing the DA's going to touch. Since that's not getting us anywhere, we're going after bodies. Vinny identified a large field by Coney Island Creek—the Caparellis' private fucking dumping ground. We're hoping for some trace evidence, maybe a bullet that we can link back to Alfeo's gun."

"It's a long shot," Ethan said.

Reed nodded. "But it's not impossible, especially when the dumbass used the same gun for every murder—the very same nine-millimeter he used for the 1989 hits he was sent away for. It's still locked up in evidence somewhere for easy comparison. We just need to get the crime lab something to work with."

"Cocky bastard," Jerrod added.

Reed nodded again. "Vinny's sentiments exactly."

"Why are you bringing us in on this now?" Ethan wanted to know.

"Because I'm worried about Bella." He started pacing, needing to rid himself of the pent-up energy he'd been forced to hold on to while he did what he could to comfort Bella throughout the night and this morning. "There are too many questions—too many variables and loose ends that I can't tie up." He made eye contact with all three men and went back for another lap to the huge wall of windows. "There was a security breach at the Manhattan WITSEC branch in February. A couple days later, Walter Hodds has a break-in. A couple weeks after that, he's acting off—nervous, asking his buddy to look after his family if something should ever happen to him. Then he drops dead from a stress-induced heart attack. Alfeo and Matty mentioned some stuff in the last prison recording that led Vinny to believe they know Nicoli has a child. I don't like it."

Shane muttered another curse.

"Exactly." He pointed to his friend, winding up all over again. "We're dealing with a lot of unknowns—nothing's for certain, but I still don't like it. They'll kill her if they ever—" He shook his head, not wanting to think about it. "Basically we need bodies and something that's going to keep Alfeo locked away." He scrubbed his hands over his face. "But we're not getting very far. Vinny's having a hard time locating what we need on the map Skylar sent out. He wants me to take him to New York today." He finally sat down and rubbed at his tired eyes. "He thinks it's our only shot, and I agree."

"What can we do?" Ethan asked.

"I need Tyson to cover me until I can get this figured out."

"Consider it done," Ethan said.

"I talked to him about it when I spoke to him on my way down here this morning—left it vague but he got the gist."

"I'll follow up when we're finished here."

Reed nodded. "Thanks."

"We'll keep Bella covered while you're gone," Jerrod added.

Reed shook his head, even though he wanted to say yes. "She can't know about any of this. I've been lying to her." He gained his feet again and shoved his hands in his pockets. "I lie to her more than I tell her the fucking truth."

"It's a tough spot." Ethan stood, giving Reed a supportive slap on the shoulder.

"I keep hoping this thing will *end* already. In a perfect world, we'll locate something compelling enough for the DA to bring before the grand jury, Alfeo will stay where he belongs, my informant will get me something on Matty, and this will all go away without Bella ever knowing anything about it."

All three of his friends winced simultaneously.

He looked to the ceiling as he shook his head, well aware that his hopes were a long shot. "We've pulled it off so far."

"A tough spot," Ethan repeated. "But it sounds like we need to get you to New York—on business." He hit the button for Collin's extension.

"Yeah?"

"Can you come in here?"

"I'll be right there." Moments later, Collin walked in, looking at everyone as he shut the door. "What's up?"

"Do you still have access to your friend's jet?" Ethan asked.

"If I ask real nice and buy him a bottle of his favorite imported vodka."

Reed finally understood what was going on. Collin had a pilot's license and access to a plane. "I'll buy your buddy a case if you can get me to New York."

"I'll ask him—"

"Today."

"Today?"

Reed explained the situation to Collin, showing him pictures and the map of the area they would focus on in Brooklyn.

"Jesus," Collin said. "There's never a dull moment around here."

Ethan pulled another sip from his cup. "We're lucky like that."

"When would we be back?"

"Saturday night at the latest," Reed said. "I have to deliver Vinny back to his place before Bella realizes he's been gone."

"Yeah. I'll see what I can do."

"Thanks." Reed blew out a long, slow breath, feeling some of the tension draining from his shoulders. "What am I going to do about Bella?"

"She's coming to Abby's fundraiser tomorrow night?" Jerrod asked.

"Yeah. I'm supposed to go with her." He was going to have to cancel on her. Again.

"She works all day tomorrow, right?"

"Yeah."

"I'll have Abby invite her over to the house before the party," Jerrod said.

"I appreciate it. I'm just concerned she's going to decide to head up to Vinny's before we can get back."

"I'll make sure Reagan and I are busy Saturday," Shane added. "We usually keep an eye on Faith for Jenny while she's working. Bella can do it."

"At my house," Ethan added. "I'll have Sarah invite her over for the day. If it'll make you feel better, we can have someone stay at your place overnight—just to play it safe."

Just like that, the majority of his worries were gone. "I don't know how to thank you."

"This is what we do. We take care of our own," Ethan added.

Collin walked back in. "We're all set. I need to file a flight plan, and Reed's on the hook for a case of vodka. We'll take off out of Santa Monica. When do you want to leave?"

He glanced at his watch, calculating how long it would take to talk to Bella, make arrangements with Vinny, and head to the airport. "Does eleven work for you?"

He nodded. "Yeah, I'll get things set up and call Lyla to let her know I have to head out of town."

"I really appreciate this."

"It's what we do." Collin walked back out.

Reed gathered up his stuff. "I'm going to head back to the Palisades—go see Bella and get Vinny heading toward the airport."

"Good luck." Ethan sat behind his desk and picked up his phone. "Bella will be fine here."

"Thanks." He hurried down the hall to the elevators, glancing at his watch again when the door felt like it was taking forever to slide open. Skylar and Joey were waiting in New York. His friends here in LA were helping him out in a major way. As much as he didn't want to leave Bella for the next two days, he was ready to do whatever needed to be done to finish this thing once and for all.

"The vitamin C mask is a great addition to your regular treatment. You should see a bit of firming, and the added benefits of the antioxidants never hurt," Bella said as she applied moisturizing SPF to her client's forehead and fought to stifle yet another yawn. Typically, the spa music she played during the day soothed her. This morning, it was killing her. She needed something fun and upbeat. Maybe then she could pretend that her heart wasn't heavy or that the extra sleep she'd been able to sneak in before Reed woke her up with a cup of decaf coffee and a long hug had been enough to battle back the worst of her fatigue.

"Whatever you say. My skin has never looked better."

She smiled, always pleased when her clients were satisfied with their results. "I'm glad you're happy."

"Sweetie, I'm ecstatic. I've been seeing you for six months and I look ten years younger. I've decided I'm ready to try those laser treatments you've been talking about."

Bella wiped her hands on a towel and gently eased off the headband holding Meryl's bangs back from her face. "We can set up a consultation if you want, and I can give you a more in-depth idea of what we would be doing. I want you to be completely comfortable before we move forward."

"I told myself I would never take such drastic actions. I want to age gracefully, but spider veins are my enemy."

Grinning, Bella helped Meryl sit up, then draped her bare shoulders with a plush white robe. "There's absolutely nothing invasive about the treatments. No needles, no downtime. The lasers do all the work. We can start with one or two of your most evil veins and see what you think."

Meryl laughed. "I love that you always give me an out. No pressure—just give it a try. And I always end up loving everything you suggest."

"We can talk more, but let me step out so you can get dressed—"

Meryl shook her head. "You know I'm not interested in all of that fancy hooey and time wasting. I'm not naked, after all—got my shorts on and this towel and robe."

Bella did know, but it always seemed right to offer Meryl the option. "All right." She moved to the sink and washed her hands while Meryl stepped into the small curtained-off space to slip her clothes back on. "I'll send you home with a couple of pamphlets. There are some great before and after photos."

"I'll take them with me, but I'm ready to move forward." Meryl stepped out, fully dressed again with her white top in place. "I'll book a consultation."

"Perfect."

"No, sweetie, you're perfect. I'm just an old geezer."

Bella frowned as she dried off. "You're beautiful. Your skin's absolutely glowing."

The forty-seven-year-old shook her head. "Not like you, honey. Some of us are blessed with the whole package. I'm just glad you're willing to share your wisdom with me."

"Anytime. Come on. I'll walk you out, and we'll get you set up with that consultation and another facial." She opened the door and beamed at Reed sitting next to Lucy in the waiting area before she frowned, remembering that he wasn't supposed to be there. He'd never visited her at the office before. "Hey, you."

He stood, walking over to her. "Hey."

"Um, Meryl, will you excuse me?"

"Of course. I'll go make those appointments."

"I'll see you next time." She gestured for Reed to follow her into her workspace and closed the door. "Hi."

"Hi." He kissed her. "I'm sorry to bother you at work."

"It's okay. Is everything all right?"

He took her hands and steamed out a long breath. "I have to go to New York."

"Oh."

He tilted his wrist, looking at his watch. "In about an hour and a half."

"Oh," she said again, not looking forward to an unexpected long, quiet night alone.

He exhaled again. "Bella, I'm going to miss Abby's event tomorrow night. I won't be back until Saturday."

She barely suppressed a sigh as she stared into his apologetic eyes. Two unexpected quiet nights alone. "All right."

"I know you were looking forward to us going together."

She nodded, averting her gaze to the floor, not wanting him to see her disappointment. "I was, but maybe next time."

He lifted her chin with a gentle nudge of his finger on her jaw. "You know I wouldn't go if I didn't have to."

"I do."

"I'm so sorry, Bella. This is an awful time for me to be leaving, with the stuff going on with your dad. There's nothing I want more than to stay right here with you."

She wanted him to be here too. For so long, she'd depended on herself during tough times. It was nice having Reed to lean on. Tonight she would be walking the beach on her own when the only thing she needed right now was the comfort he brought her so easily. "I know you do."

"My shitty schedule... This will be over soon." He stroked his knuckles along her cheek, then tucked her hair behind her ear. "Things should start settling down eventually, and we can get back to the way things were when we first started dating."

She hugged him, closing her eyes and holding on, still raw and shaken after this morning's news. "That sounds really good."

He wrapped his arms tight around her. "I'm a lucky guy." He kissed the top of her head. "Not everyone would be as patient as you."

"You're worth it."

He winked as he eased back. "I'm going to call you. Tonight, tomorrow night, Saturday. We can talk for hours. It'll be like I'm lying in bed right next to you."

She sent him a wry smile. "Not quite."

He gave her a gentle jostle. "Sorta."

She grinned. "Sorta. I'm going to miss you."

"I'll miss you too. So much." He kissed her, drawing out their tender embrace with several teasing dips of his tongue.

She moaned, savoring his taste and the way his arms felt wrapped around her.

He pressed his lips to hers once more and rested his forehead against hers. "As much as I'd rather do this all day, I need to get to the airport."

She nodded. "Okay."

"Make sure you take a picture in your dress tomorrow."

"I will. Fly safe."

He kissed her again and stepped back, opening the door. "See you

Saturday."

"See you Saturday."

He paused in the doorway. "Oh, Luke is going to be staying at my place for a couple of days. He had some flooding issue or whatnot at his apartment—water damage."

"Okay."

"I'll call you tonight."

"It's a date." She watched through the window as he jogged to his truck. Then she tidied up her space, preparing for her next client. Plastering on a bright smile, she moved to the waiting room. "Mindy, it's good to see you."

Mindy stood. "It's good to see you too."

"Let's go get started." She glanced out the glass door as Reed pulled into traffic, and she buried another wave of disappointment, remembering that he was worth it.

Reed sat buckled in one of the plane's plush leather bucket seats while Collin flew them east toward their destination. He bobbed his leg up and down as he glanced out the window, then at his watch, noting that they'd been in the air only an hour when it felt like a damn century. He looked at Vinny asleep in the chair next to him and muttered a curse, debating whether or not he should tell Collin to turn the jet around. Vinny's color was way off—jaundiced—and his face was more drawn than usual. Luckily, his portable oxygen wasn't a problem for the flight, but Reed would be holding his breath for the next forty-eight hours, praying like hell that everything went according to plan. Bella would never forgive him if something happened to her dad.

Vinny opened his eyes. "I can feel you staring at me." He frowned as he sat up. "What's your problem? You look like you're about to piss your pants."

Reed unbuckled his belt and stood, walking the short aisle of the cabin. "I don't like this. I don't like that you're on this plane or that we're lying to Bella."

"We're doing this for her."

"I don't like it," he repeated. "I hate leaving her alone when I know she needs me—fucking disappointing her all the damn time." He clenched his jaw, remembering the way the light had left her eyes when he told her he was heading to New York. "I'm always apologizing for something, constantly letting her down."

"You'll make it up to her. When those bastards can't touch her, all of this will have been worth it."

He jammed his hand through his hair, knowing Vinny was right. He never would have agreed to any of this if there had been another way. But there wasn't. "You just keep yourself healthy. You're going to bed as soon as we get to the hotel—taking it easy as much as you can tomorrow. You're going to do exactly what I say."

Vinny raised his brow. "We'll see about that."

He sat down again, not bothering with his seat belt. "Just what I say, Vinny."

"Jesus, you're wound up tight."

"Damn straight. Go back to sleep. Rest." He sighed as he rested his head against the cushion and stared out at the vast blue sky. Everything was on the line for the next two days. If anything went wrong, he had no doubt he would lose Bella.

☙ Chapter Thirty-Seven ❧

Reed breathed in the earthy scent of fresh dirt as the backhoes did their digging. He watched small teams of Evidence Response Agents continue their search in the original hole Vinny had pointed out down by the creek, but it was Skylar and her crew huddled around an area seventy-five yards from where he stood that had his attention. He glanced toward the clouds threatening rain in the late afternoon sky, then tucked his chin into the collar of his warmest jacket when another nasty gust of wind blew in off the water. "Jesus, it's raw out here."

"I don't know, boss," Joey said, standing by his side in a sweatshirt and hat. "I'm thinking California living's turning you into a pansy ass."

"I guess I'm a pansy ass too, then," Collin commented, crossing his arms tighter across his chest on Reed's opposite side.

Vinny chuckled, bundled up under a half-dozen blankets in the passenger seat of the four-person ATV their small group had driven around in for hours, rolling over brush, grass, and mud in their search for potential burial sites to flag for the ground-penetrating radar teams. "I'd say their blood's thin." He chuckled again, then coughed.

"Bullshit," Reed said. "It can't be more than forty-five degrees."

"Pansy ass," Joey confirmed.

Reed let Joey's insult slide as he focused on the men and women walking their GPR machines in long, straight rows farther out in the field. One of the men stopped and shoved a red flag into the ground, signaling a probable find, then kept moving—an excellent sign in a massive area with dozens of orange markers waiting to be checked. There was no way each designated spot Vinny had pointed out was the location of a buried body, but Vinny had been instructed to let them know if anything about a particular landscape caught his attention and mark it with one of the orange flags. So far their long, cold day was paying off. Right after lunch, a body bag had been exhumed and whisked off to the lab for examination. They were still waiting for news on the findings, but things were certainly moving in the right direction.

"We sure were ballsy," Vinny said as cars rushed by on the parkway a hundred yards above, while a train moved on the tracks three hundred yards to their east.

"Arrogant's more like it," Joe said.

"For a long time, we all thought we were untouchable. Things changed eventually. When RICO happened—" He held up a finger, signaling for one minute when he began coughing again.

Reed tore his gaze away from the progress on the field, not liking the way Vinny sounded. "Are you staying warm enough?"

"Yeah."

"Let me know if you want another blanket."

"You keep piling these things on me and we'll have to worry about me smothering to death instead of catching a cold."

"You came here in reasonably decent condition. You're going home the same way."

Vinny rolled his eyes, shaking his head. "Bella would approve. You're like a damn mother hen. I sure as hell can't say you don't love my daughter."

Reed made a sound in his throat as he glanced at his watch, thinking of Bella as he'd done for much of the day. He'd slept like crap last night, barely catching more than an hour or two of decent rest. And his jaw ached from the constant clenching he couldn't seem to stop. He'd talked to her before she went to bed and this morning before work, but he wouldn't be able to relax until he dropped Vinny off in Reseda. "Just let me know if you need something."

"Sure thing."

Reed focused on Skylar's group when activity started picking up by the hole.

"We have something," she hollered, giving them two thumbs-up.

"Fuck yeah," Joey said. "Bring us up another one."

Skylar spoke to the dig coordinator, then hurried over to them, slightly breathless. "They've got another one. We're off to a great start. You should head back to the hotel. There's nothing more you can do here."

Reed shook his head. "Vinny's going, but I'm staying."

Skylar held his gaze, then looked to the sky as rain started falling. She crouched down next to Vinny and smiled. "Mr. Pescoe, I'm going to get you some footage of the areas we couldn't access today because of the mud, but I'm sending you back to the hotel for now."

"You got another one for sure?"

She nodded. "For sure. They're going to take some photographs for processing before we lose the light, and get it back to the lab. I just got news on the first body we brought up this afternoon—a bullet wound to the forehead. New York driver's license in his wallet claims he's Al Marini."

"Little Al—definitely one of Alfeo's."

"He's pretty well-preserved. There's lots of blood residue on the clothing, but they aren't sure if it's useable."

"What about a bullet?" Reed asked.

Standing again, Skylar shook her head. "No, but this is a great start."

"We were right to come," Vinny added, then started coughing, violently this time.

Reed winced, his shoulders growing tenser as he studied Vinny's paling complexion and tired eyes. Today had been a lot for everyone—and only one of them was dying. "Are you all right?" he asked, handing him a water.

Vinny nodded, wheezing with every breath. "I'm fine. This happened last night too."

"Why didn't you say something—call for me or something?"

He uncapped the water and took a sip. "What would you have done about it? Are you an MD?"

"We could have taken you to the hospital. We *are* taking you to the hospital. Your lungs—"

"Bullshit you are. You're taking me back to the hotel so I can rest for a few minutes—without you hovering over me. Stop worrying about getting in trouble with Bella for five damn seconds and do what you need to for her safety."

"We can't ignore your health, Vinny. She needs you around for as long as you can be here."

"I'll be fine. Just get me out of here."

Collin hopped into the driver's seat of the ATV where Reed had once been sitting. "I'll take him to the hotel."

Joey settled in back. "I'll go with them, boss—help them get settled in, make sure there's no trouble. Call me later."

Reed leaned close to Vinny, giving him a final eagle-eyed appraisal. "Are you sure you don't want to go to the hospital?"

"I just need to rest—maybe try some soup."

"We'll get you some ordered up," Collin assured him and drove over to their waiting van.

When they were settled in, Reed dialed Collin's number.

"Yeah?"

"If he keeps up the coughing, take him to the hospital. His lungs are probably getting worse." He would rather deal with Bella than watch something happen to Vinny because he'd been more worried about covering his ass than doing what was right for the sick man helping them.

"I'll take care of it."

"Thanks."

Joey got in the driver's seat and took off, heading toward Manhattan.

Reed rubbed at his jaw, swearing as he met Skylar's bright blue eyes.

"I had no idea you were in love with Nicoli's daughter."

"Our relationship"—he gestured between the two of them—"has always worked best on a need-to-know basis."

She grinned. "Sounds pretty serious. Is she the one?"

"Yeah, she's the one. If I can pull this off, she might decide I'm the one for her too."

"Well, you've certainly made one hell of a mess for yourself."

"I've always admired your determination to look at the bright side—really focus on the positive."

She chuckled. "If we have what we came looking for—and it looks like we just might—that seems pretty bright to me."

The dig coordinator signaled for Skylar as the team unearthed the next bag.

Reed jogged over by her side, staring at the grody plastic fully intact as it started raining harder. "Another one."

Skylar gave his knuckles a bump in celebration. "We'll have the lab get moving on this. Let's get out of here for now. They'll have to stop for tonight, but I'll be back tomorrow."

He glanced toward the parkway and another train passing by as they headed to the makeshift parking lot. "You need to watch your back. There's no way this is going unnoticed."

"I can take care of myself."

Skylar was five feet ten inches—a built blonde stunner and more than worthy boxing opponent in the ring, but she was no match for the brutality of Caparelli's men. "Be careful anyway."

"You too."

"Will do."

They made it to Skylar's government-issued car, both of them scanning the area before they left, making the long, soggy journey back toward Midtown.

"So, I'll keep you up to date on what we've got. Maybe they'll get into this bag right away and let us know what's what," she said as she drove past the hotel forty minutes later.

"No matter what, I'm taking Vinny back tomorrow. He's done all he can for us here. I want him back in LA by early afternoon at the latest."

"Agreed. We're waiting on Evidence Response and the anthropologists at this point anyway. They'll put a rush on everything, but it's still going to take time. I'll get some video of the areas the ATV couldn't get to—where Vinny thought there might be more. Hopefully you two can look that over sooner rather than later."

"Once you send it, we'll take a peek."

"I'm going to fly out and get his formal statements on record—document each murder before it's too late. I'll bring Joey since you two worked in the Caparelli trenches. Maybe Vinny's responses will spark thoughts from both of you—opportunities for more in-depth questions."

"Sounds good."

"It would be great if we have more bodies to work with—the more details we can link, the better." She pulled off to the side seven blocks from the hotel, both of them well-used to extra precautions. "I'll see you in California."

He opened his door. "Thanks for everything."

"Let's put the bastards away for good."

He smiled. "Bye."

"Bye."

He shut the door and walked up an extra block to one of his favorite coffee shops. He ordered a large hazelnut with a shot of cream and took his drink to the quiet corner, sitting by the fire as he selected Bella's number. She would like the ambiance here—warm, classy. Just like her.

"Hello?"

He smiled when he heard her voice and sank farther into his seat. "Hey. How are you?"

"Good. My last client canceled her appointment, so I'm on my way to pick up Lyla. We're heading over to Abby's for a pre-fundraiser girls' night."

"Sounds like fun."

"It's going to be. Jerrod mentioned to Abby that you and Collin left for your last-minute assignment, so she thought we should get together for dinner. I offered to do their hair and makeup."

"They'll look amazing."

"They *already* look amazing."

"You'll give them the Bella touch."

She laughed. "It's easy to add a little extra oomph to beautiful women. How are things going? How was your day?"

"Pretty good. It's cloudy and cold—raining."

"The sun's shining and it's seventy-seven here."

"Nobody likes a bragger."

She laughed again.

He felt himself grin. "I wish I was there, Bella. I wish I could walk into that fundraiser with you on my arm and know I'm with the most gorgeous woman in the room."

"Aww."

"I mean it."

"Next time."

"It seems like we're always waiting for next time."

"It's a temporary situation."

He hoped so. "I want our time back—the way it was when this whole thing between us started."

She sighed. "Me too."

He closed his eyes, wanting nothing more than to be by her side. "Have fun tonight. Dance and laugh and don't forget to take a picture in your dress."

"I can always put the dress on when you get home. Then you can take it off me."

He chuckled. "Now you're talking."

"But I'll take a picture anyway and send it to you—give you something to think about."

"You're always on my mind, Bella. Always."

"Aren't you a charmer?"

He was crazy in love. Never had he spoken to a woman the way he spoke to Bella. Giving her words was easy. Bringing her flowers was a pleasure. If only he could tell her the truth… "I should let you go. I want you concentrating on the road."

"Okay. I'm going to give Dad a call before things get too crazy."

"How's he doing?" He gripped the cup, shaking his head, forever hating this game.

"He says he's good. He actually has a little pep in his voice, so I believe him."

"That's great."

"I can't wait to see him on Sunday. I can't wait to see you tomorrow."

He glanced at his watch. "Just a few more hours."

"Mmm."

"Call me before you go to bed."

"It'll be late," she warned him.

"I'll sleep better if I know you're home and tucked in."

"Okay. I'll call you."

"Have fun."

"I will," she said. "Stay safe."

"I will. Bye."

"Bye."

He disconnected and stared at Bella's picture. They were less than twenty-four hours away from pulling this off. Standing, he tossed his cup in the trash and walked the miserable eight blocks back to the hotel, taking the elevator to the seventh floor. He knocked four times and waited.

"Yeah?"

"It's Reed."

Collin opened the door.

"How are things going in here?" He shut the door behind him and locked up.

"Okay. Vinny had a little soup and fell asleep."

"Any more coughing?"

"No. The cold air might have been irritating his throat—"

"I'm fine." Vinny sat up on the couch in the small common room in their three-bedroom suite. "Did the body come up?"

"Yeah, they pulled in another bag. They were getting it ready for transport when Skylar and I left." He looked at Collin. "We've got the all clear to go home. As soon as you can get us out of here."

"I'll take a look at the weather and get us set up."

"I'm going to meet with my informant tonight," he said to both men.

Vinny frowned. "That sounds risky."

"I'll be fine."

"Vinny and I'll stay right here." Collin took out his phone. "I'm going to file the flight plan and give Lyla a call."

"She and Bella are heading over to Abby's."

"Good. That means she's having fun." He walked off to his temporary bedroom.

"I'm going to make my call," Reed said. He grabbed the burner phone from his laptop case and dialed.

"Hello?"

"I want to meet."

"Where?"

"West 46th Street. The Coffee Shop. Ten o'clock."

"I'll be there."

He hung up and texted Joey.

Nine thirty. The Coffee Shop on West 46th.

Seconds later, Joe texted back.

Got you covered, boss.

He turned as Collin came back in. "We're good for takeoff tomorrow at nine fifteen."

"Perfect. I'm meeting my informant at ten. I'll be gone about an hour—two at the most. Joey's coming along for backup."

"We'll be good here—probably watch a movie and rest up for the flight."

He nodded. "I don't know about you, but I'm ready for some eats."

Collin grinned. "I'm always ready for food—meat."

Reed smiled. "Collin's fiancée is a vegetarian."

"Ly-Ly keeps mentioning making the leap to veganism." He shuddered. "Hopefully it's just the pregnancy talking."

Vinny laughed. "You should probably order the biggest slab on the menu."

"I'll take one of those too." Reed grabbed the room service offerings, letting his shoulders relax for the moment. Bella was with Jerrod and her friends. Vinny was holding his own. "What about you, Vinny?"

"Nothing. My appetite's gone."

"I'll get some of the wonton soup just in case you change your mind." He would browbeat him into a couple of bites the way Bella always did. That was going to have to work for the time being.

☙ CHAPTER THIRTY-EIGHT ❧

"THANK YOU." BELLA SMILED AS SHE ACCEPTED A GLASS OF champagne from the waiter's tray while he walked around Sophie McCabe's Rodeo Drive jewelry store. The music was pumping and the place packed for the swank little post-fashion-show party. Lily Brand and the Abigail Quinn Line had been successful again, raising thousands of dollars for their growing number of Stowers House locations. She sipped her drink and waved to Hailey and Alexa across the room, then fixed her ruby and silver dangle earrings when she caught a glimpse of herself in one of the mirrors hanging on the wall. She'd styled her hair in a downdo, curling her long tresses, leaving her face unframed with a clip. Her bold red dress was certainly daring with its deep V-neck and sleeveless, backless design, but she loved the way the fabric clung to her curves and its funky, irregular hemline—another genius creation by Abby Quinn herself. Now if only Reed were here to enjoy it.

She glanced around at the couples mingling, wishing he was standing by her side, but as she looked closer, she realized that several women from the Ethan Cooke Security family were also here stag. This was her world now—their world. She loved a man whose career took him away for days at a time—as Lyla's fiancé was right now, and Morgan's husband, and Alexa's. Reed was bound to miss special occasions from time to time. Right now, he seemed to be missing them all, but he would be home tomorrow. Every time he walked out the door, he risked his life to help someone else. As long as he made it back safely from New York, that would be good enough for her.

"Bella."

She turned, grinning as Jed walked her way. "Hi, stranger." She kissed his cheek when he stopped in front of her, holding a half-empty glass of champagne. "How are you?"

"Good." He nodded, stepping back, looking her up and down.

"That's quite a dress. You look beautiful."

"Thank you. And you in your tux." Jed certainly cleaned up well. He was handsome regardless of his attire—dark green eyes, short black hair, golden skin, a nice build.

He pulled at his bow tie uncomfortably. "I'm counting down the minutes until I can take this thing off."

She laughed.

"Would you like to dance?"

"Sure. That would be nice."

He took her glass and set both hers and his on a tray, then held out his arm to her.

She hooked hers through his and walked to the small designated dancing area.

"So, how are things going?" he asked as he captured her hand in his and settled his opposite arm around her waist. "We haven't talked in a couple of months."

She rested her palm against his firm shoulder and followed his lead. "Really good. Great, actually."

"Awesome. You were able to make contact with your father?"

She nodded. "I was. We've been getting to know each other again." She nibbled her lip, debating whether she wanted to tell him about Dad's health. "Unfortunately, he's sick."

Jed frowned. "I'm sorry."

"Me too, but I'm so thankful you helped me find him. He has cancer and not a lot of time left."

His frown deepened. "Bella, I'm so sorry."

"It's tough but I'm treasuring every second we have together. And that's thanks to you and all your hard work."

"I'm just glad I could help. If there's anything—"

"Can you smile for the camera?" the photographer from the *LA Times* interrupted as he stopped next to them.

"Oh." Bella stood cheek to cheek with Jed and smiled as he did.

The man snapped a picture. "Thank you. May I get your names?"

"This is Isabella Colby, and I'm Jed Hoffman," Jed offered.

The reporter wrote down their names. "Thank you." He snapped one more and walked off.

"I wonder if we'll make the paper?" he asked, wiggling his brow.

"I don't know. We'll have to take a look tomorrow morning." The song ended and Bella stepped back from his embrace. "Thank you for the dance."

"No problem. It was fun." He shoved his hands in his pockets in a gesture that reminded her so much of Reed, she couldn't help but smile. "So, we never got around to getting a drink."

Her smile dimmed as she realized this was about to turn into one of those awkward situations she hated. "Jed, I'm seeing someone."

"Shit," he said with a wince. "I didn't know."

"I'm sorry." She settled her hand on his arm. "I should have said something sooner. I just—I didn't," she finished lamely. It wasn't like she walked around randomly announcing her relationship status.

He glanced around. "Is he here?"

"No, he's on duty in New York. I'm with Reed McKinley."

"Reed?" He nodded what seemed to be his approval. "He's a great guy."

"He is." She touched his arm again. "But that doesn't mean we can't stop off for a glass of wine sometime. I just wanted you to know that I'm not single."

"How about a glass of champagne now?"

She nodded. "Sure."

He offered her his arm again and they walked toward the bar.

"I think they have beer," she said.

"Perfect. I'll grab one of those."

She chuckled. "Just another hour and you can probably lose the bow tie."

"I can't wait."

She grinned, happy that Jed was willing to be such a good sport.

Reed walked toward The Coffee Shop after backtracking several blocks, making certain that no one was following him. His guard was up again—the need to look over his shoulder constantly was back. Not even an hour after he and Collin had finished their steaks, Joey called to let them know that the Caparellis had taken out another one of their old-time men—Patrizio Caparelli's former underboss. The man had been ancient, nearly ninety years old, but they'd put a bullet in the back of his head anyway. For most of the day, Reed, Vinny, and the rest of their team had been less than a mile from the location of the latest hit. He wanted them out of New York as soon as possible.

Standing across the street from the designated meeting spot, he located his informant sitting in the back corner of the restaurant—far away from the doors and windows. Joey sat at a table several booths away, sipping at a coffee while he read a newspaper. Reed pulled his phone from his pocket and sent Joe a text.

Joey glanced up and out the window, making eye contact. He scratched his cheek, their signal that everything was clear.

He waited to cross with several pedestrians—extra insurance that he wasn't about to become a hit man's easy target with a car. Walking inside, he ordered a plain decaf, then went back to Bruno's table, studying the groups of artsy patrons and the men and women sitting in front of their laptops along the way. He took his seat, eyeing the short, stocky man who had a solid decade on him, noting the perspiration on Bruno's forehead and the tense fingers gripping his cup.

"You saw the news?" Bruno asked, gulping at his coffee.

"Yeah, I saw it." Reed sipped his own brew with little interest in the drink.

"They took out Carlo Lamberti—whacked him right on his front steps." He licked his lips as he glanced toward the door.

Reed followed his gaze. "Are you expecting company?"

"At this point, we're all expecting company. You don't know who; you don't know when." He leaned in closer. "They're cleaning house. Not even their closest confidants are safe. First Dino, now Carlo. I was supposed to meet Dino the day they whacked him," he hissed in a whisper. "Matty calls me up—says have Dino head your way." Bruno drank deep from his cup again. "He was coming to meet *me*."

"So you knew the hit was going to happen?"

He shook his head adamantly. "Do you think they were gonna tell me they were whacking Dino Asante?" Bruno wiped his hands on his jeans. "Christ, Dino went to visit Alfie at the prison when Matty couldn't make it out that way. One of the family's most trusted members and he's six feet under." He looked over his shoulder toward the windows. "They're watching everyone. Anyone who looks suspicious—breathes wrong. Anyone who had anything to do with Alfie—"

"Then you should be in the clear. You didn't come on until after he was locked up. Dino's the one who made you—brought you up through the ranks to be a captain."

"That don't mean I'm not sweatin' bullets. I was running errands for the family—bookmaking—while Alfie was acting boss. I keep trying to figure out if there's something Dino told me that would put my nuts on the block."

"Keep your guard up, and if you think of anything, make sure you tell me. I'm your shot at staying alive."

"Thanks for the advice, but I figured that one out before we sat down."

Reed took another sip. "Any word on what's going on? Any new developments?"

Bruno shook his head again. "I got nothin'. Matty's keeping us out of the loop. He wants us to make sure our earners are earning and keeping themselves undetected. No hassles with the cops. He's made it clear that if anyone decides they want to flip, they'll not only get themselves killed but their families too." He wiped at his brow. "I got a wife—two sons."

Alfeo was a brutal bastard—and smart. Becoming an informant for the Feds would get you killed, but keeping your mouth shut didn't guarantee your safety either. It was a bad time to be in the mob. Reed nodded. "What did you find out about the kid?"

"I don't know where you heard something about a kid, cause I ain't heard nothing about Nicoli having a kid."

And that's exactly the way he hoped it stayed. "What about Walter Hodds? Have you heard of him?"

He narrowed his eyes, nodding slowly. "The name sounds familiar."

"Someone broke into his place mid-February—ransacked it, tried to access his home computer."

"Huh."

"I want to know what had them so interested in a US Marshal."

Bruno sat back in the booth. "It's gonna take some time—tiptoeing's what I'm up to. Minding my own business, running the things I run. I'll see what I can get from Felipio—see if he had anything to do with it, but not till after he's had a few drinks. I'm not coming right out and asking. Guy's gonna get himself whacked if he doesn't watch it and shut his trap."

"You just make sure you get me what you can before he gets himself killed."

Bruno nodded. "I've got my ears open and my antennae up, but I want out. You need to get me out of this."

"I'll talk to my guy at the FBI. What are the other families thinking about all of this?" He made a subtle gesture of a gun with his thumb and index finger, letting Bruno know he was talking about the murders.

"They're keeping their distance—keeping quiet. Nobody trusts nobody."

Reed pulled an envelope from his jacket pocket and passed it under the table. "The amount we agreed upon."

He snatched it and tucked it in his sleeve. "I don't know if this is worth it anymore."

"This is just a measure of good faith. Your ticket to freedom is finding me something the Feds want."

"I'm working on it."

"Good." Reed stood. "I'll call you next week."

"No. I don't like that. Let me call you when I got something. I don't want to have to do any explaining."

Neither did he. The last thing he wanted was for Bella to hear his burner phone ring. "If you call me, it better be worth it—life-altering. We'll talk then." He left, making eye contact with Joey as he opened the door, then walked several blocks in the opposite direction of the hotel, finally hailing a cab ten minutes later.

His phone rang as he settled in the back—Joey's ringtone. "Yeah?"

"He left clean—no one met him afterward and he didn't make any calls."

"He's watching his steps. Watch yours too."

"Don't worry about me, boss."

"You shouldn't go back to the field." It was bad enough Skylar was now assigned there. "It's not a place you need to be."

"I'll steer clear. It was good having you back in town for a couple days. I hate seeing you go."

Right now, he felt like he couldn't get out of here fast enough. "You and Melanie should head out our way—visit for a couple weeks."

"We'll have to make that happen. Safe flight, buddy."

"Thanks." He hung up as the taxi pulled up in front of the hotel. He got out and took the elevator to his room without the information he was hoping for, but he had enough to be confident Bella was safe for now.

Bella stepped from the bathroom after a quick shower, more than ready for bed. She dropped her towel on the floor and crawled under her covers, looking at the clock. It was almost one, which meant it was nearly four in New York. She picked up her phone and hesitated, then selected Reed's number.

"Hey," he answered on the first ring, his voice deep and sleepy.

She smiled. "I debated whether or not to call."

"If you didn't call soon, I was going to call you."

She frowned. "Haven't you been sleeping?"

"I've dozed off a couple of times, but mostly I've been thinking about you."

She grinned and turned onto her side, nuzzling her cheek against the silky softness of her pillowcase. "I'm looking at your pillow right now. I wish you were lying on it."

"Tonight I'll be right next to you."

She made a sound in her throat. "That sounds perfect."

"What's on the agenda for tomorrow—or, I guess, today?"

"I'm watching Faith for a little while. We're having a play date at the Cookes' at nine."

"Sounds fun."

"I agree. But I'm looking forward to seeing you."

"Ditto that. Am I taking you out for dinner or are we staying in?"

"We're staying in. I have a dress for you to peel off me. It's hanging in the closet, waiting patiently."

He chuckled. "That's right. Did you have fun?"

"I did. A great time, actually. Jed was there, so we hung out for a while."

"I'm glad he could keep you company."

"He's a nice guy, but he's not you." She yawned. "Sorry."

"It sounds like I should let you go."

"You don't have to."

"Get some sleep, Bella."

She yawned again. "Okay."

"Is Luke still next door?"

"I'm pretty sure I saw his car. I wasn't paying all that much attention. I was more interested in a shower and getting into bed."

"I like knowing one of the guys is next door."

"I'm a big girl. I can take care of myself. Besides, I have my fierce companion snoring away just a couple feet from me."

"Right. Have fun with Faith."

"I will. See you this afternoon." She wanted to tell him she loved him, but when she finally gave him the words, she planned to be looking him in the eye. "Good night."

"Good night."

She put the phone back on the side table, shut off the light, and pulled Reed's pillow closer, breathing in the scent of the man she missed like crazy, and fell asleep.

☙ Chapter Thirty-Nine ❧

REED SAT NEXT TO VINNY IN THE PREBOARDING AREA AT TETERboro Airport, waiting for Collin to deal with the final maintenance checks for their flight. They were in Jersey—a solid hour's drive from Brooklyn and the violence in Bensonhurst—but he wanted them in the air, where he could finally relax a little bit. The ongoing rain showers were making for a chilly, overcast morning, but Collin didn't seem concerned, so he wasn't either. Soon they would be soaring well above the cloud cover, leaving the mid-Atlantic region behind. He glanced at his watch, estimating that they had another twenty minutes here on the ground. Then he looked at Vinny sipping the tea he'd forced on him, gauging his coloring, which wasn't entirely horrible, especially after yesterday's seemingly endless ATV adventure. If his instincts were right, Vinny was tired, but he was having the time of his life.

"Son of a bitch." Vinny shuddered, resting the paper cup on his thigh. "I don't know why you couldn't have gotten me a coffee like I asked."

"That's better for you." He gestured to the chamomile drink.

"Like it matters."

"It matters to your daughter." His phone started ringing, and he grinned at Bella's beautiful face filling his screen. "Speaking of."

Vinny grumbled.

"Hey, beautiful," he answered. "You're up early."

"Yeah. Lucy's bladder doesn't care much that I didn't get to bed on time."

He grinned again. "Sorry to hear that."

"I'll survive. Were you able to get some sleep?"

Mostly he'd lain awake, replaying his conversation with Bruno, hoping that his informant was going to deliver something useful for their case sooner rather than later. "A little." He looked at Vinny when he started coughing.

"You'll sleep better tonight. I'm planning on wearing you out."

Reed stood, walking to the window, distancing himself from Vinny as he continued hacking up a lung. "I appreciate your willingness to help me out like that."

She laughed. "Whatever it takes. Good grief. Who *is* that?"

He glanced over his shoulder. "Uh, just another passenger waiting to board."

"Well, they sound awful. Make sure you keep your distance. We don't want you getting sick."

He couldn't exactly tell Bella that he wasn't worried about catching what Vinny had. "Will do."

Vinny cleared his throat, giving him a thumbs-up as his coughing fit settled down.

Reed nodded, turning away.

"I thought I would let you know that I made the paper. Jed texted me a couple minutes ago."

"Oh, yeah?"

"The "Life and Style" pages," she said in a snooty tone.

He smiled. "*LA Times*?"

"But of course."

"Let's see here." He took his seat again and dug out his laptop from its case. "You don't mind if I check out the sports headlines first, do you?"

"Football scores can wait."

He chuckled as he typed in the *Times*' web address. "It's not football season."

"Oh."

The smile froze on his face as he stared at Bella and Jed grinning, standing cheek to cheek. Christ, she was an absolute stunner. And Jed didn't look half-bad himself.

"Did you find it?"

"Yeah." He read the caption. *Jed Hoffman and his date Isabella Colby enjoy a dance at Lily Brand and Abigail Quinn's annual Stowers House fundraising event.* His gaze kept wandering back to the word *date*. "You look amazing. That dress is..."

"Pretty daring."

"Incredibly sexy." Clinging red fabric and teasing glimpses of sensational breasts. "Lots of skin." And Jed had been touching her. He scanned the other pictures from the night, spotting one more of Bella standing by Abby and Sophie with Jed by her side as they all smiled in a group shot. And Jed had his arm around her naked shoulders, touching her again. "It looks like you had a great time."

"I did."

"You were easily the most beautiful woman there."

"Aw, thank you. Oh."

He frowned at the surprise in her voice. "What?"

"I didn't realize—I'm just reading the caption. Jed certainly wasn't my date."

"It's not a big deal." But he didn't like it, especially when he should have been there. He wasn't often jealous. He'd never considered himself the type, but he definitely was right now.

"It was just a dance. I told Jed I was very much taken."

"Damn straight."

She chuckled. "Well, I should go. Lucy and I have a *very* busy day of basking in our fame."

He smiled. "Enjoy it."

"We're going to start off with a bowl of cereal—or kibble, in Lucy's case. Then we're going to pick up Faith and bring her over to Sarah and Ethan's, where I'll more than likely be covered in drool and/or spit-up within the first half hour."

"Sounds impressive. You do famous well."

"I couldn't agree more. Today sounds perfect."

Collin started their way, giving him and Vinny a nod. "My flight's about to board."

"Great. I'll see you this afternoon, handsome."

"Okay. Bye." He hung up and looked at Vinny. "Are you going to be okay for the flight?"

"I'm fine. Got some of this sick-ass tea down the wrong tube." He gestured to his cup. "We can throw this out before we leave."

"Bella would want you drinking it."

"I'm pretty sure she's not here right now."

"Call her. If she tries to call you while we're in the air and can't get ahold of you, she'll head up to Reseda."

"I never call her this early."

"Make an exception. Tell her you saw her in the paper." He turned the computer Vinny's way.

Vinny raised his brow as he looked from the screen to Reed and back. "Well, well. Are you being replaced?"

His nostrils flared. "No, I'm not being replaced. They're friends."

"Looks cozy." Vinny's eyes glittered with gleeful fun as they met his.

Reed shrugged, trying to ignore Vinny's jabs. "I guess, but I doubt she'll be thinking about him when I take her to bed tonight." He barely held back his own grin when Vinny's disappeared.

"A father doesn't want to hear stuff like that."

"Call her."

"Fine. I'll call her." Vinny dialed Bella's number, mumbling something about how fathers didn't like thinking about their beautiful daughters having sex.

Reed listened to snatches of Vinny and Bella's quick conversation, staring at Bella snuggled up with Jed once more, then shut off his laptop for the long flight home.

Bella grinned as she pulled into her driveway, staring at Reed's truck parked in his own. "Reed's home."

Lucy's ears perked up.

"I know. It's pretty great, huh?" She shut off the engine and got out, hurrying around to Lucy's side to open the door.

Lucy bolted from the car and trotted up the walkway, whining when she reached the doorway.

"Give me a second, silly. You have four legs. I only have two." Chuckling, she picked up her pace, just as eager to greet Reed as their puppy. "Should we go say hi?"

Lucy wagged her tail.

"Come on, then." She tested the doorknob, found that it turned in her hand, and walked inside, grinning again when Reed crouched down in his favorite pair of jeans and a ratty sleeveless T-shirt, petting an excited Lucy.

"Hey, girl." He gave her a solid rub on her sides, accepting several kisses on his cheek. "How's my girl? Did you help Bella babysit today?"

"She played with her doggy pals Bear and Reece. She'll be comatose until Monday."

"Sounds intense." He gave Lucy another firm pat and gained his feet, staring at her. "Hi."

Her heart rate kicked up several notches, reading perfectly well the hungry desire burning in his eyes. "Hi." She let her purse fall to the floor and launched herself into his arms, wrapping her legs around his waist. "You have no idea how excited I am to see you."

He hoisted her farther up with his hands on her ass. "Probably about as excited as I am to see you." He captured her mouth, immediately playing his tongue against hers.

She whimpered, meeting him stroke for stroke. "I missed you," she gasped out as he went after her jaw and neck.

"I missed you too."

She ran her fingers through his damp hair. "Your hair's wet."

"I took a shower. Couch?"

"Wherever. Just now."

He collapsed with her onto the cushions. "Naked sex?"

"Any kind of sex." She fought with his jeans as he struggled with hers.

"I like your dresses better. Easier access."

She tugged his pants down his hips. "Babysitting in a dress doesn't typically work out very well. Let me." She freed one of her legs from the snug denim.

"You forgot your panties." He yanked them to one side. "Good thing we can work around them." He shoved himself inside her.

She moaned, absorbing the sharp rush of pleasure, and let her head fall back against the pillow. "God, I missed you."

"Forty-eight hours is practically a lifetime."

"Yes." She slid her palms under his shirt, tracing her fingers up his spine, then clutching at his shoulders, needing to touch him everywhere. "You feel so good. You always feel so good inside me."

He groaned.

Her hands wandered down to his ass, gripping his muscled cheeks, thrusting him forward. "Hard. Fast."

He clenched his jaw as his eyes flashed. "You've got it." He pumped like a madman.

She gasped as the throbbing built with every thrust, holding his gaze as heat rushed to her center, then exploded through her core. She tensed with the waves of overwhelming sensations and cried out. "Faster."

He yanked up her hips, pulling her into an arch, and pounded away, until she called his name and he erupted inside her. He collapsed forward, pressing her into the cushions as he steamed out hot, unsteady breaths next to her ear. "God, Bella. God, Bella," he said again.

She closed her eyes and smiled, trailing her fingers up his sweaty back. "That was an excellent way to say hello."

He lifted his head, smiling. "I thought I was going to peel you out of that red dress."

"Mmm." She kissed him and snagged his lower lip with her teeth. "You can. Later. After we have dinner."

He chuckled. "You are one *sexy* woman."

She grinned. "You make me feel sexy."

"That's not hard to do." His smiled dimmed as he adjusted his weight so he could brush the hair back from her forehead. "I missed you. Really missed you." He kissed her sweetly, drawing out the tender moment.

She sighed as he drew back, perfectly content in his arms. "I missed you too."

"When I'm not with you, I want to be. I shouldn't have to travel anymore for a while."

"Good." She hugged him. "I like it better when you're here."

"That makes two of us." He rested his forehead against hers. "I want you again."

"Whenever you're ready." She let her eyes flutter closed and opened them when he began to move slowly.

He smiled. "How's this?"

She smiled back. "Great. Perfect. Welcome home."

"I don't want to be anywhere else." He captured her mouth again, tenderly, clasping their fingers, taking her on another exquisite journey.

Reed pulled himself free of Bella and rolled to his back, out of breath after they'd just destroyed each other again. "I'm starting to think you're trying to kill me."

She laughed as she turned on her side and walked her fingers up his stomach, taking a couple of steadying breaths of her own. "I told you I was going to wear you out."

"Yes, you did." He tugged her against him, hooking his arm around her waist as she settled her head on his shoulder. "You're doing a hell of a job." They'd been going at it for hours, stopping for dinner on the porch and a couple of episodes of *The Office*. Then they'd taken a sexy shower and ended up in bed for the rest of the evening. He had yet to get her in and out of that little red dress, but there was always later. "Thank God tomorrow's Sunday. I'm going to need the day to recover."

She grinned, tracing his pecs. "You can sleep while I go see my dad. I still can't believe they released him without calling me first."

He'd settled Vinny in at his house right around one thirty, then headed out to the store to stock his fridge with the juices and soups he seemed to like before heading back to the Palisades. They'd decided that Vinny should call Bella at four and let her know he was home from the hospital and resting. "It sounds like they didn't need to keep him any longer. He had a little pep to him, right?"

"He did, but I still would have appreciated a call."

"Everything worked out." He kissed her forehead, choosing to focus on the fact that they were together right now instead of his latest series of lies. "I'll come with you. We'll go to Reseda together."

"You need to rest."

He shook his head. "I need to be with you."

Her eyes went soft. "How can I argue with that?" She lifted her head and kissed him. "Why don't you shut your eyes?"

He sighed, truly relaxed for the first time since early Thursday morning. "Sounds good." He pulled up the covers and tugged her closer, wanting to feel her soft skin against his. "I missed lying like this."

"Me too."

He reached up and shut off the light. "Night, Bella."

"Night."

He closed his eyes and hugged her tighter, ready to give in to exhaustion. His eyes flew open again when he heard his phone alert to a new text on the downstairs coffee table. "You know, Lucy had a lot of water before bed. Maybe I should take her out one last time."

Bella moaned her protest. "I'm sure she's fine."

Something was up. If someone was texting just shy of midnight, something was going on. "I don't want to have to get up once I'm asleep."

Bella sat up on her elbow. "I'll keep the bed warm."

"I'll be right back." He stood, grabbing fresh boxers from his drawer, not quite certain where the pair he'd been wearing earlier ended up. "Come on, Lucy. Let's go potty."

Lucy didn't move.

"See? I think she's fine."

He shook his head. "You'll both thank me later when we all sleep through the night. Come on, Lucy."

Lucy reluctantly got up and started down the hall.

"We'll be quick." He followed the sulking puppy downstairs, grabbing his phone on the way to the French doors, reading Skylar's text as he stepped outside.

Updates whenever you're ready.

He selected her number, waiting through one ring, then two as he closed the door and looked around, making sure he was alone.

"The lab boys are working late tonight," she said instead of answering with a hello. "We have some preliminaries on the two bodies we pulled in today."

They'd had another good day in the fields. The stress and worry of taking Vinny to New York had been worth it now that they were seeing results.

"Body number one had no identification, but his jewelry should make for an easy preliminary ID once we show it to potential family members. He's fairly well-preserved. His hands were severed. Gunshot wound to the forehead."

Reed leaned against the porch railing, tracking Lucy's movements in the small yard with his eyes. "To the forehead?"

"To the forehead," she confirmed. "Forensic anthropologist is calling the wound a through-and-through."

He crossed his arms, holding the phone with his shoulder. "So no bullet."

"No bullet. Unfortunately, things look pretty much the same with victim number two."

He huffed out a breath. "Damn it."

"We were able to identify him, though."

"Who is it?"

"New York license says he's Felice Dioli."

"You found Big Felice?"

"Looks like it. They'll run DNA for confirmation, but anthropology is confident it's him."

"I guess that's something."

"I have a few full days in the field, but I'm going to make Vinny those recordings either tomorrow or Monday morning at the latest."

"My week's jam-packed, so I won't be able to see him again on my own until this next weekend."

"I'm making arrangements to come out. I want Vinny thinking about Felice's murder. And Al's. Those two specifically since we have IDs. I want to go to the site of their execution and search for trace evidence. I know it's unlikely we'll find anything, but we're checking anyway."

"Makes sense. We want this as airtight as possible—no chance for Alfeo getting out of this."

"Exactly. I'm going home."

He petted Lucy as she walked by on her way up the steps to the door. "Call me if anything else comes in."

"You know I will." She hung up.

He shook his head, turning off his phone for now. He needed a solid eight hours of shut-eye. Things were moving right along—the pieces were finally falling into place. Bodies were being found. There would be video footage for Vinny to look at shortly. He smiled at Lucy waiting on him. "Ready to go in?" He locked up and they went back upstairs. Getting into bed, he pulled Bella close.

"Night," she murmured, already mostly asleep.

"Good night." He kissed the top of her head and closed his eyes, planning on sleeping like a rock now that Bella was wrapped in his arms.

☙ Chapter Forty ❧

Bella stood on the Cookes' massive deck, savoring the warm sun on her shoulders and the ocean breeze blowing through her hair. She leaned against the sturdy railing and sipped her cucumber-lemon water, smiling as she watched sweet toddlers and precious babies coexisting on a large blanket while their parents sat in chairs close by. The afternoon was practically perfect—good food, great friends, amazing weather. Now if only Reed were here. She glanced at her watch, then toward the stairs, certain that he would be walking up the steps at any moment. He was running a little behind, but that wasn't surprising on a Saturday afternoon. The traffic was probably insane.

She'd been looking forward to Ethan and Sarah's get-together for the last several days, especially after such a crazy week. Reed had technically been home, but not in quite the way she'd been expecting when he told her he wouldn't have to travel for a while. Monday he'd been out late working an all-star concert event at the Staples Center with several of his coworkers. Then Tuesday, Wednesday, and Thursday, he'd covered Tyson's overnight shifts. Finally, they'd had a little time together last night, walking the beach and snuggling up on the couch for an episode of *The Office*, but he'd fallen dead asleep before the theme song ended. He was exhausted—in need of a relaxing day exactly like this one, but this morning he'd been up and at it again, heading downtown to the office, promising to meet her at the Cookes' no later than one. It was currently one fifteen.

"Bella," Kylee called from the blanket, gesturing for Bella to come over.

Grinning, she waved to both Kylee and Olivia and started their way, always happy to chat with the Cookes' and Matthews' oldest daughters. "Hi," she said, crouching down in front of the pretty blondes.

Kylee smiled. "Me and Olivia get to come to your house sometime."

"I know." She gave her a gentle poke to the belly, then Olivia. "We're going to have fun."

"We're going to make a new friend," Olivia said, tucking her hair back as the wind played with her long golden locks.

"Yes, you are. Emilia."

"She was in a fire that burned her and made her look different, but she's still a nice girl," Kylee supplied.

"She does look different." Bella pulled her phone from the back pocket of her fitted denim capris and searched through her photos until she found one of Emilia painting Lucy's nails—a shot Emilia had no idea she'd taken—wanting the girls to understand exactly what that meant. "This is Emilia."

The girls blinked at the screen.

"She looks *very* different," Olivia said.

"She does, but she used to look a lot like you. The fire hurt her skin very badly."

"Does it make her cry?" Kylee wanted to know.

Bella nodded. "Sometimes."

The girls still stared.

"Emilia's going to be starting back to school soon. She'll be in your kindergarten class. She's going to need a lot of help letting your classmates know that even though she doesn't look quite the same, she's still a nice girl who wants to have friends just like everyone else."

"We're going to help her," Kylee said with a brisk nod.

"We'll be her friends," Olivia added.

Bella blinked as her eyes filled, touched by their easy acceptance and wonderful sense of compassion. "I know you will." She hugged them and kissed their cheeks. "You two are the best."

They grinned.

Olivia touched Bella's earring, toying with the simple silver dangle. "Will you play pretend makeup with us so we can be beautiful like you?"

How could she possibly resist? "Of course I will."

Kylee beamed as she bounced on her tiptoes. "We want you to make us look *just* like you—except we have blue eyes and yours are brown. And your hair's black."

Bella grinned. "I think we should make sure you look just like you. You should be proud of your pretty faces, but you know what's even better than that?"

"What?" the girls asked in unison.

"Your pretty hearts."

Kylee frowned. "We have pretty hearts?"

Bella nodded. "Beautiful hearts." She stood and held out her hands to them, glancing toward the stairs again. Still no Reed.

"Over here." The girls led Bella to the play table where a pink box full of beauty toys waited to be used.

Bella sat in one of the tiny chairs. "Let's see what we have here." She set up her fictitious tools and got to work, starting with their hair before she moved on to makeup. "A nice sweep of blush right here along your cheekbones." She slid the powder brush over Olivia's cheeks then Kylee's. "You girls have beautiful, healthy skin. You must drink lots of water and eat plenty of good food."

Olivia nodded. "I eat grapes and bananas, but I don't like fish." She wrinkled her nose. "Mommy says I have to try a bite whenever she makes it, but I don't like it at all."

Bella laughed. "Maybe someday you'll take a bite and decide you love it."

Olivia nodded, but doubt lingered in her eyes.

Bella grinned, completely in love. "Okay. Your hair and makeup are officially finished." She pressed a gentle hand to the top of Kylee and Olivia's matching French braids. "I think you're ready to ride your horses."

"Let's go." The girls clasped hands and made a beeline for the stairs, unhinging the baby gate and shutting it like pros before they ran to the amazing swing set in the side yard. The girls hopped on the horse-shaped double swing and rode away to wherever it was their imaginations were taking them.

"It looks like you made two little girls very happy," Jed said, offering her a hand to help her out of the child-sized chair.

"Thanks." She took it and stood, studying Jed's tough boxer's build in his olive-green T-shirt and cargo shorts. "I love kids, especially smart munchkins like those two. They always find a way to make me laugh."

Jed grinned. "They seem like they have a lot of energy."

She watched as the girls sent their horse soaring. "I imagine they sleep well at night."

He smiled again. "Is—I haven't—Reed's not here today?"

She looked at her watch, realizing the girls had occupied a huge chunk of her time. It was quarter till. "No. Not yet. He said he was coming, but he might've gotten stuck at the office with paperwork. He had a busy week." She forced a smile. "If you'll excuse me, I'm going to take care of my glass."

"Yeah, sure."

She grabbed her water off the play table and walked to the kitchen, setting her glass in the dishwasher, tempted to give Reed a call and make sure everything was okay, but she hesitated. She wasn't the type to nag or wait around on someone else, especially a man. Even if it was Reed. She was either a priority in his life or she wasn't. Right now she clearly wasn't. She frowned, pausing as she started back through the doorway, surprised by the direction her thoughts were taking. Where was this coming from? Reed was stuck at work. He had a demanding career. None of the other women seemed to have a problem with what their partners did for a living, so why did she?

She glanced around the busy deck, then down toward the lush yard. Hunter had returned from his trip and was currently pushing his son on one of the swings while Morgan caught him on the upswing and kissed his toddler toes. Jackson was back too, holding Owen and Alexa on his lap in one of the chairs. And Collin wrapped his arms around Lyla's waist, resting his hands on her budding baby belly while they chatted with Hailey and Austin. Everyone was here. Except Reed.

Her gaze landed on Jed as he helped Emma build a block tower. He wasn't even employed by Ethan, but he'd made it to the party. She looked over her shoulder at the mostly empty tray of lemon tarts she'd brought along, remembering that Reed had asked her to save him one. Ignoring the latest wave of disappointment, she turned away and walked through the kitchen and down the hall to the front door, stepping out onto the walkway. "Lucy, come on," she called.

Lucy came running with the pack of dogs following behind. Everyone had brought their four-legged friends along.

She couldn't help but smile as several adorable doggy faces stared back at her. "Sorry, guys. Just Lucy will fit." She opened the door and waited for Lucy to finagle her way into her spot. "Let's go to the beach."

Lucy whined when Mutt barked.

"We'll have fun." She turned over the ignition and drove down the long lane, stopping and waiting for the huge wrought-iron gate to open. Taking a right, she headed through the pretty neighborhoods on her way to the water and slowed as she approached the small brick and wood house that had been on the market for close to four months. She pulled up to the curb and put the car in park, studying the sweet little two-story in need of some major TLC. New windows, a new front door, paint, someone to come deal with the mountain of overgrown, ugly shrubbery. But there was something about the place that she loved. "Isn't it great?"

Lucy panted in her direction.

"This could be ours. We could—" Her phone rang—once, twice—and she swallowed, staring at Reed's gorgeous, grinning face filling her screen. She shook her head and set the phone back in the console, not interested in talking to him. He was likely calling to tell her he'd lost track of the time and he was sorry, but she didn't want to hear his apologies right now. "Come on. Let's go." She put the car in drive and eased back onto the street, eager to walk on the sand at her most favorite place.

"So, this spot here?" Reed asked, pointing at his laptop screen while they rolled through the footage Skylar had captured earlier in the week.

Vinny nodded. "There's something about the rocks and trees that make me want to say yes."

"That's good enough for me." He paused the video and smoothed out the map as the breeze caught the edges of the page. He circled the area with a blue marker. They'd been scrutinizing the Brooklyn field location for the last three hours on the shaded back porch. Vinny had been in the mood to work outdoors, and Reed hadn't argued. Later, when he met up with Bella, he wouldn't have to worry about trying to explain why he smelled like cigarette smoke, especially when he told her he was taking care of paperwork at the office. And Vinny looked like he could use the fresh air, even if he was breathing in oxygen from the portable unit tucked close by his side. His color and energy level were off today.

"Ready?" Vinny asked, holding the laptop on his stomach while he rested his head on the pillows Reed had brought out and propped up on the cheap lounger.

"Yeah, go ahead."

Vinny tapped the mouse, starting the video again.

For fifteen minutes, Reed watched Vinny stare at the screen, waiting for something else in the marshy area to catch his attention.

Vinny shook his head as the final seconds wound down. "I'm not seeing anything."

"Okay, that's it," Skylar said as her dirt-smudged face filled the screen. "I've gotten what I can, which is pretty much everywhere the ATV wasn't able to go. I hope this helps."

Reed x'ed out of the footage and sat back in his plastic chair, lacing his fingers behind his head. "I guess that's it, then." They didn't get nearly as much as he'd been hoping for—just one or two more possible locations for the GPR team to check out—but overall, they'd had a productive few hours. Thanks to Vinny's memory, Skylar had two abandoned warehouse basements to process for trace evidence in the decades-old murders of Big Felice and Little Al. They'd accomplished their video viewing objective. And Reed still had a solid ten minutes before he needed to hit the road. Not bad.

Vinny closed the laptop and handed it over. "Things seem like they're moving right along."

Reed nodded, setting the computer on the table. "Better than we could have expected. I have to admit, I wasn't crazy about taking you back to Bensonhurst, but it's paying off big-time. We've had a hell of a week." On Tuesday and Wednesday, two more bodies had been brought to the lab—both with severed hands and gunshot wounds to the forehead—but their big break had come Thursday evening, when the forensic anthropologist discovered a bullet lodged in the cracked parietal bone of their second victim. And just this morning, Skylar had called to let him know the GPR team had confirmed another gravesite.

"What will they do with that bullet they found?" Vinny wanted to know.

"They've sent it over to Firearms Examination. They'll take a look at it there. If they can link it to Alfeo's gun, he's fucked."

Vinny lifted his juice off the concrete and set it on his chest, fiddling with his straw instead of taking a drink. "Sounds good to me."

Reed glanced at his watch and sat up. "I should probably get ready to head out. Why don't I give you a hand getting back inside?"

Vinny struggled some as he sat up. "Sure."

It concerned him that Vinny hadn't given him any grief when he'd helped him get outside shortly after he arrived, nor was he now. "We'll—" His phone rang as he stood. "Hold on." He glanced at the screen. "It's Skylar."

Vinny nodded and sagged back against the pillows.

"Hello?"

"The lab's working on our latest John Doe. We've got another bullet wound to the forehead."

He walked to the edge of the porch and back. "That's great."

"We've also got a knife."

He frowned. "A knife?"

"We brought it in a couple hours ago. Evidence Response found it in the dirt after they brought up the body. It has initials engraved on the handle—A.C."

He stopped in his tracks and ran his fingers through his hair. "You're kidding."

"Do I *ever* joke about evidence?"

He huffed out a laugh. "You don't joke about much of anything."

"I'm a comedian on the inside."

He grinned. "This is great."

"I want Vinny to take a look. The body has bone trauma to the sternum and a couple of ribs, indicative of several stab wounds. The signatures appear to be a match to the knife's blade. I'm sending pictures now. I've got a couple of artifacts too. I want to see if he can identify them. There's no ID on this guy."

"Yeah. Sure." His email dinged as he opened his laptop again. He glanced at his watch and winced as he noted that he was out of time. Ten more minutes and then he would have to go. He could make up the time on the interstate.

"Did you get it?" she asked.

"Yeah." He opened the attachment, studying the rusted five-inch blade and slightly rotted wooden handle. "It's right here. I'll get back to you." He hung up and looked at Vinny lying back with his eyes closed. "Do you have a little more in you? They found a knife Skylar wants you to look at."

"A knife? Let's see it."

Reed set the computer on Vinny's stomach.

Vinny brought it closer to his face. "They found it in the body?"

"No. In the dirt close by—part of the dig site." He crossed his arms, struggling with the frustration of needing to leave, but wanting to stay to get Skylar the information she could potentially use to put another nail in Alfeo's coffin. "So, what do you think?"

"It's Alfie's. My father gave that to him. There should be initials engraved on one side—an A.C. toward the bottom."

Reed sat down in his chair, feeling the rush of triumph as Vinny's description fit the one Skylar shared. He flipped to the next picture. "Kinda like this?"

He smiled. "Exactly like that. He loved that thing—got it for his sixteenth birthday. I forgot all about it. He ended up using it on Gerry Pecoraro—one of his best friends."

"The body they found this morning has marks on the sternum and ribs. The injuries to the bones match the blade."

"I imagine they might."

"Did he kill anyone else with it?"

"No, he lost it after Gerry. We looked around for it some when Alfie realized it was gone, but we weren't sure where he'd dropped it."

Reed grabbed his notepad, writing down the information Vinny shared. "Why did Alfeo kill Gerry?"

"One night Pops got a call from my uncle. Uncle Sal said he caught Gerry getting fresh with my cousin Christina. Uncle Sal wanted him whacked, so Pop got the okay from the other bosses and gave Alfie the order to take care of it."

Reed knew the drill, had heard it several times before, but he still didn't understand. "Your brother killed one of his best friends because he was fooling around with your cousin?"

"You don't mess with a made man's family. It's disrespectful."

Reed shook his head. "So the poor bastard died because he liked a girl, messed around with her, and therefore disrespected her father?"

"Pretty much."

"How old was Christina?"

"Eighteen, nineteen—something like that. A couple years younger than Alfie."

"So, a consenting adult?"

"Disrespectful," Vinny reminded him.

Reed rubbed at the back of his neck. "That's fucked up, Vinny."

"The code is sacred—or was. Back in those days, it wasn't to be messed with. Gerry knew there were rules to follow. He could have gone through the proper channels and made something official between the two of them, but he wanted to be a weasel instead."

"So Gerry's the only one who got it with the knife?"

"He got a blast from the gun too, but Alfie went after him with the knife first. Gerry was begging and crying the whole time Alfie was trying to talk to him—pissed him off, so he jammed the blade in him a few times to shut him up. It was Alfie's first murder—his opportunity to show our father that he was ready to be a full-fledged part of the life."

"And a gun wouldn't have accomplished that?"

"A pop to the head is less personal. He was making a statement. Everybody knew Alfie was a mean son of a bitch—beat the shit out of people all the time. He wanted to be the youngest made man. He was sealing the deal by not only taking out Gerry to honor the family but also making sure it was brutal—wanted to impress my father and uncle."

Reed shook his head. "An animal."

Vinny smiled wryly. "For most of his life."

"Fucked up," Reed said again and took a deep drink of his cold coffee, needing the kick. He was running on fumes after one hell of a long week. "Does this look familiar?" he asked, moving on to the next picture, of a corroded necklace.

Vinny frowned. "Not really. It's a cross. Everybody wore one."

"So you killed by the week and prayed on Sunday?"

"Sometimes we killed on Sunday too."

Reed raised his eyebrow when Vinny spoke so matter-of-factly. "It's hard to equate you with this." He gestured to the pictures and map.

"It was my life. I grew up in it. My father had us working by the time we were seven—bookmaking, running favors, eventually collecting money."

Reed scrubbed his hand over his mouth, finding himself sympathizing with a man who had been the epitome of everything he stood against and wanted to destroy. "You didn't even get a choice."

Vinny shrugged. "Some people have their sons work in their restaurants or stores. We worked for the mob. I worshiped my big brother, but I had to work at being mean. It came natural to Pops and Alfie. I didn't think there was much wrong with what we did. It was all about family and honor. No one got hurt unless they deserved it—till we killed Elena and her little girl. That was never supposed to have happened. Women are never supposed to be involved."

"You shot a toddler."

"Not intentionally." Vinny sat up. "It was only supposed to be Giovanni. As soon as I realized Elena and the girl were in the car, I tried to stop it. Elena and I had history. She was pregnant and bleeding and begging for my help. I went to get her out of the front seat and Alfie walked up and shot her in the face."

That had been the story Nicoli Caparelli told in court. Reed had always figured it was bullshit, but now that he could see Vinny's troubled eyes, he believed that was exactly what happened. "Did you ever think about getting out—before you flipped?"

Vinny shook his head and sighed. "You know there's no way out."

"Yeah." He swallowed. "Maybe we should call it a day." He glanced at his watch and rushed to his feet. "Fuck!"

"What?"

"How the hell is it one thirty? Fuck! I need to get you inside."

"Bella?"

"I was supposed to meet her at Ethan's. I should have been there half an hour ago. Fuck." He slammed the laptop closed and dropped it in his bag, then picked up the map and notebook, shoving them in. "Let's get you settled in." He grabbed the oxygen and helped Vinny up, keeping a firm hand on his bony arm as they slowly made it to the recliner in the living room. "Do you need anything?"

"No. Go see Bella."

He hesitated, not liking the gray cast to Vinny's skin. "Let me get you some water or a juice or something."

Vinny frowned. "Go see my daughter."

Reed stood where he was.

"Get out of my house," Vinny demanded with a wave of his hand.

"Okay." He locked up behind him and ran to the truck—much like he had a week and a half ago when he'd dropped the ball and missed their cooking class. He buckled up and left Darby Avenue behind, weaving his way through Reseda traffic, waiting until he was gaining speed on the 405 before he dialed Bella. Her phone rang once, twice, five times. "Come on. Pick up."

"This is Bella. Leave a message and I'll get back to you."

"Bella, I'm coming. I'll be there as soon as I can. It looks like I'm about forty minutes out with the traffic." He hung up, not bothering to apologize. What good would it do to tell her he was sorry again? "Damn it." He slammed his palm against the steering wheel, well aware that he was destroying the most important part of his life in his attempt to assure the safety of the one person he couldn't live without. There was no doubt in his mind that Bella was blowing him off right now.

He pushed his speed to ninety, anxiously watching the miles pass in slow motion as he glanced at the clock more than a few times, hoping she might call him back. He dialed her again, swearing when she didn't pick up. "Son of a bitch." He hung up and dialed Ethan.

"I guess you didn't make it after all."

He clenched his jaw. "Can you let Bella know I'm coming? I'm ten minutes out."

"She's not here. She left a while ago."

He muttered another swear as his stomach sank, afraid that she might not let him fix things this time. "Thanks. I need to go." He tossed his phone onto the passenger seat and headed toward the water instead of the house, already knowing where he was going to find Bella. Hadn't she told him once that she went to the beach when she was mad at the world? Unfortunately, today she was pissed at him. And he couldn't blame her.

Ten minutes later, he brought the truck to an abrupt stop in a parking spot three spaces down from Bella's convertible. He got out and scanned the people walking on the sand, searching for a huge dog and beautiful woman wearing sexy capri jeans and an embroidered white cami. He found them, pulled off his sneakers and socks, and jogged out to where she waded in the surf.

She glanced up as he approached and turned away, walking in the opposite direction.

"Bella." He dropped his shoes and ran after her when she picked up her pace, quickly closing the distance between them. "Hold up," he said, snagging her by the wrist.

She whirled and yanked free of his grip, her eyes flashing with temper as they met his through the amber tint of her lenses.

"Bella—"

She looked at her watch and shook her head. "I don't want to hear your apologies."

Sighing, he backed off and shoved his hands in his pockets.

"Where *were* you?"

He noted the hurt and weariness in her tone more than anger. Not a good sign. "At work."

"Okay." She nodded. "How can I resent that? You had to work."

"Bella—"

"But I do. I do resent it." She crossed her arms, hugging herself tight. "You're gone all the time. When you're home—meaning in Los Angeles—you're so busy you're not actually here. I keep telling myself that it's okay. This is who you are; this is part of what you do. But maybe I'm not okay with it."

What could he say? How could he make this better when he had no solution? "My job's crazy right—"

She shook her head again. "You were supposed to be there. You said you would be there, Reed."

He jammed his hand through his hair. "I know."

"Three cooking classes, Abby's fundraiser, today..."

"I know," he repeated.

"Is this—" She looked down. "Do you even want this?"

He took a step closer. "What?"

"Us?"

"Yes." He settled his hands on her rigid shoulders, waiting for her to meet his gaze again, terrified that she'd had more than enough. "Yes, I want this. I want you. I love you."

She blinked as she stared at him.

He blew out another long breath, realizing just how badly he was screwing this up. "I love you so much." He pulled her against him, wrapping his arms around her, holding her tight as he kissed the top of her head. "So much, Bella."

Moments later, her arms came around him.

"You've been more than patient with me." He eased back slightly, wanting her to see that he was getting her message loud and clear. "*More* than."

"Because I love you too."

He rested his forehead against hers, absorbing the rush of relief and pleasure from her words. "I know this sucks right now. You have no idea how ready I am for this to be over."

She settled her hands on his hips. "You keep saying that. I know you mean it..."

He played his fingers through her hair. "I'm sorry."

She nodded.

"Thank you for being so patient."

"I'm trying."

"You've given me so much more than I deserve." He cupped her cheeks, still shaken after the last few minutes. "You're so much more than I deserve, Bella."

She gripped his wrists. "Don't say that. You're exactly who I want—what I need."

He wanted so badly to be the man she thought he was. "For the rest of today, I'm yours. Tomorrow too. Monday and Tuesday night if I can help it."

She shook her head and stepped out of his embrace. "I don't want the impossible. But I need more than this. Don't promise what you can't deliver."

"I can promise you today and tomorrow."

"The girls are coming tomorrow."

"I know. I'm looking forward to seeing them again."

"And I'm going to see my dad after they leave."

"I'll be right by your side."

She crossed her arms again as she sent him a small smile, her body language telling him that the air still wasn't one hundred percent clear between them.

"Come back here for a minute." He wrapped her up once more, sliding his palms down her sides. "I want for us to be okay. I need for you to know that there is *nothing* more important in my life than you."

Her shoulders finally relaxed as she settled her cheek against his chest.

He breathed her in, felt the warmth of her skin against his. "What do you want to do tonight? Anything you want."

"I don't care. I just want us to be together."

Knives, artifacts, and dead bodies were going to have to wait until Monday. The woman he adored was very much alive and in his arms. He cupped her cheeks again, stroking his thumbs along her jaw. "I love you."

She smiled. "I love you too."

He kissed her, letting his lips linger and his tongue tangle lazily with hers as the water tickled his toes. "What should we do?"

"Walk the beach. Then I want us to go home and have a normal night—the kind we used to have."

He brushed his fingers along her arms, always eager to touch her. "Dinner, TV, and ice cream."

"And maybe a shower or something."

He grinned. "That goes without saying."

She laughed. "Of course it does, but I wanted to mention it anyway."

His smile vanished as he studied her stunning face. "I want to marry you."

Her eyes grew wide.

"When we're ready for that step," he added quickly. "A while back, you asked me if it was going to be a problem if you fell in love with me. I'm telling you I see my future wrapped up in you, Bella. A house, a wedding—big or small, I really don't care—kids. That's not going to be a problem, is it?"

She beamed, clasping her fingers at the back of his neck. "That's definitely not a problem."

"Let's go home," he said, pressing another kiss to her lips, forever craving her taste. "I want to cook with you."

"What are we making?"

"Whatever you want."

"I know just the thing. I have seafood waiting in the fridge, and the man I'm crazy in love with just happens to be a master with the grill."

He grinned. "I'm glad you think so."

"I definitely do." She took his hand, lacing their fingers as they started back toward their vehicles with Lucy following behind.

☙ Chapter Forty-One ❧

Reed sat on Bella's kitchen floor, bobbing his head in time with the beat of the song playing on the stereo while Emilia painted his toenails a horrifyingly bright shade of pink.

"Your big toes are hairy," she said, doing what she could to keep the glob of paint on his toes, but the majority of the liquid dribbled down his skin despite her best efforts.

He frowned, studying his feet. "I'm a guy. They're supposed to be like that."

Emilia shrugged and absently swiped at her ponytail with the stumpy section of her arm—where her hand used to be. "Maybe Bella could use her lasers on it."

"*No*, she can't." He looked at Bella as she grinned, sitting by his side while she helped Bianca paint Lucy's nails.

"I like Reed's hairy big toes." Bella winked.

He smiled at her, giving her a gentle bump to the shoulder. Things were good between them—back to normal. They'd barely left each other's side since they talked at the beach yesterday. Last night and even today had been exactly what they both needed—a chance to have fun together the way they used to before Operation Caparelli Takedown had taken over his life.

"Reed's your boyfriend," Emilia said, glancing from Bella to Reed.

"Yes, he is."

"My aunt says you're really hot," she told Reed.

Bella laughed. "I'm sure Aunt Peggy will be *so* happy you shared that little tidbit of information."

He chuckled. "I'm definitely flattered, but I'm a one-woman kind of guy." He tugged on Bella's chin, pulling her closer and pressing a noisy kiss to her lips.

The girls giggled.

The final notes of Hailee Steinfeld's latest hit segued into a commercial for the Los Angeles Zoo. "We should go soon," Reed said. "The four of us."

"To the zoo?" Bianca asked with a frown.

Reed nodded. "Sure. Why not? But we would have to leave a certain Great Dane here," he said in a conspirator's whisper as he pointed to Lucy.

The girls giggled again.

"I would have to wear a mask," Bianca said. "Germs make me sick. It's dangerous for me to get sick."

"So we'll make sure you wear a mask."

"I don't like to go out." Emilia moved to Reed's left foot. "Everyone looks at me."

He sighed quietly, his heart breaking for the sweet kid who would always have so much to overcome. Emilia and Bianca had been in his and Bella's care for the last hour and a half, and he'd fallen in love. He fully understood why Bella volunteered her time with the children here and at the hospital. He'd had a chance to meet only two of her friends so far—and they were both bright, funny little girls who deserved all the compassion and kindness the world had to offer. "So let them look."

She stopped her painting and blinked at him. "I don't like it."

He leaned forward, picking her up under the arms, and settled her on his lap. "Let them look, Emilia."

She shook her head, staring down at the tile.

He lifted her chin. "People just need a chance to get to know you. Once they do, they'll see that what's on the outside isn't nearly as important as what's in here." He tapped his finger to her heart.

"But you're handsome like a movie star. I look like a monster."

Damn, this sucked. Emilia's bastard father had caused his daughter so much more than physical damage. "You don't look like a monster."

"I'll never look like a movie star. Even when Bella helps me with my makeup, I don't look normal."

What the hell was he supposed to say to that? "My mom and dad are responsible for the way I look. I didn't get a say one way or the other. But who I am inside is up to me."

Emilia nodded. "I like you."

"I like you too. I'm lucky Bella introduced me to a couple of *very* cool new friends." He pressed a kiss to her scarred cheek.

She smiled as much as her lips allowed.

"So, what do you say? Will you come to the zoo with me?"

She nodded and threw her arms around him.

He hugged her back, holding Bella's misty gaze as he did.

Emilia eased away, looking at him. "They're gonna take off my leg." She pointed to the bandage protecting the ulcer on a leg that was mostly scar tissue covering bone.

"They make pretty cool fake ones—prosthetics. You'll probably get around easier, and maybe it won't hurt you so much anymore. You can do all kinds of stuff with one of those things. And I'll bring you flowers while you're in the hospital."

Her eyes brightened. "You will?"

"You better believe it."

She smiled again. "I need to finish your toes before Aunt Peggy comes to pick us up."

"By all means." He lifted her, setting her back in her original spot. "Paint away." He winked at Bella, realizing she was still staring at him.

She took his hand and kissed his knuckles, then pressed his palm to her cheek, nuzzling him.

He stroked her skin and let his hand drop away as they both gave their attention back to their guests.

Bella held Reed's foot in her lap while she wiped away the flamingo-pink polish Emilia had applied lavishly to his toes. "You're a good sport."

He shrugged as he sat leaning back against the refrigerator door. "It wasn't that big a deal."

"I'm not so sure I agree." She smiled at him. "Not all men would let little girls paint their toenails and put barrettes in their hair."

He grinned. "I can undo barrettes and nail polish pretty easily—no permanent harm done to my strapping masculinity." Winking, he made his pecs dance beneath his shirt. "But those clip-on earrings Bianca kept talking about probably would have crossed the line."

She laughed, adoring the man sitting with her on the kitchen floor. "Well, I can assure you that if I hadn't already been *desperately* in love with you before today, I would have fallen hard after your little chat with Emilia."

"She's a good kid. I like her."

Her eyes watered as she remembered the way Emilia had hugged him so freely. "You're an amazing man, Reed."

"I want to track her father down and beat the shit out of him," he continued, shrugging again as he popped one of the leftover grapes from the small fruit tray she'd prepared for the girls into his mouth.

She felt herself frown, surprised by the abrupt turn their conversation had just taken. "Oh."

"It's the least the bastard deserves."

"Yes, I imagine it is."

He plucked up a cube of watermelon. "It *definitely* is. He'll get out of his prison cell eventually, but Emilia will have to deal with her scars for the rest of her life." He fed her the piece of fruit.

"Thanks," she said with her mouth full of sweet, juicy goodness.

"You're welcome."

She chewed and swallowed. "I guess I can appreciate your sense of justice—even if it's slightly violent."

Chuckling, he scooted forward and kissed her.

Holding his gaze, she touched his cheek. "I'm so glad you're mine."

He let his forehead rest against hers. "The feeling's mutual."

She pressed her lips to his, still amazed that she was so deeply loved by such a wonderful man. "You really were good for Emilia today. She doesn't trust men easily, but clearly she likes you."

"You do amazing things for these kids. I want to do my part too." He slid his fingers through her hair. "You make me a better person, Bella."

She exhaled as her heart melted.

"Something was dead inside me before we met."

She hugged him, holding on tight. "I don't even know what to say."

He wrapped his arms around her, sliding his hands up and down her back. "You don't have to say anything. I just want you to know that everything about my life has been so much better since Lucy walked through my front door."

She drew back. "This has been perfect. Today."

"And last night—and not just because the sex was phenomenal."

Flutters rushed through her belly as she thought of all the different ways Reed had driven her crazy. "It was, wasn't it?"

"Oh, *hell* yeah." He nipped and nibbled at her jaw. "That mouth of yours is pure magic." He went after her chin. "And not just because you taste so good."

She grinned, pleased that she'd driven him crazy too. "I love it when we get to be together like this—just you and me."

He tucked her hair behind her ear. "Ditto."

"But I need to go see Dad."

"I'm coming with you."

"You know you don't have to."

"I want to. Plus, I promised you Saturday *and* Sunday. Whatever's on your agenda is on mine."

"All right then." She moved, settling his foot in her lap again. "Let's get the rest of this polish off you first. We probably shouldn't leave without getting your last two toes."

"I like the way you think."

She went to work on his nails as her mind wandered back to yesterday—to Reed's declarations on the beach and her impromptu stop off at the sweet little house she loved so much. "Um, what would you say if I told you I want to go somewhere before we head up to Dad's?"

"I'd say let's do it."

She nodded, not wanting to mention exactly where she wanted to take him. Reed would more than likely give the place an automatic veto if she shared too many details, but she might be able to change his kneejerk reaction to say no if he could see their potential new home through her eyes. "I want to show you something."

"Sure." He ate a piece of pineapple. "We can do anything you want."

She struggled with her conscience, knowing that her approach was a little on the sneaky side. "It'll be quick."

"It can be whatever you want. I'm just happy to be with my girl."

She sent him a small smile and wiped off the last of the bold pink. "There." Tossing away her trash, she stood and extended her hands to him. "Ready?"

He accepted her offer of help and gained his feet. "Yeah, let's go."

She made fast work of washing the scent of the nail polish remover off her hands and went to the closet for Lucy's leash. "Lucy, let's go see Grandpa."

Lucy ran to the door.

Reed started outside, waiting for Bella to lock up as Lucy hopped in the back of the truck. "I guess she's excited to see her Grandpa Vinny today."

"I guess so." She took his hand and walked with him to the passenger side.

"I believe this is your stop." He opened her door.

"Thanks." She got in and buckled up.

He moved around to his side, stopping to shut Lucy in the back before he took his seat. "Where to?" he asked, sliding his sunglasses in place.

"Head toward Ethan's."

"You've got it." He backed out of the driveway and took a left out of their development, driving them through the posh Palisades neighborhoods. "Now what?"

"You can slow down a little. We're just about there."

He slowed, glancing around. "Where are we going?"

"There." She pointed to the house.

He frowned. "Where, Bella?"

"That house for sale."

He raised his brow as he pulled to the curb. "Huh."

She nibbled her lip as he stared. "So, what do you think?"

"I think this place looks like a money pit."

She shook her head. "You have to look past that."

He slid his gaze her way, clearly unimpressed. "This place needs a lot of work. The windows and doors. New paint. The landscaping would have to be completely redone. And that's just a starting point."

"Yes. That's all true. But think of the potential."

He killed the engine. "To go bankrupt?"

She grinned, shaking her head. "We wouldn't go bankrupt." She opened her door and got out. "Come look with me."

He sighed. "Bella."

"Live on the edge and come look with me."

He got out and walked to the driveway, kicking the toe of his flip-flop against the pitted concrete. "This would have to be resurfaced."

"Yes, but imagine sparkling new windows and thick wooden double doors." She wrapped her arms around his waist as she stood by his side. "Can you see the fresh paint and pretty pots of flowers?"

Hooking his arm around her shoulders, he narrowed his eyes. "If I try really, *really* hard."

She laughed.

"It could be nice," he conceded. "We could rip out those ugly bushes ourselves. Plant something better."

She beamed. "Exactly. Let's look at the backyard." She took his hand and pulled him around the side with Lucy following behind.

He winced, stopping abruptly as they rounded the corner. "Jesus, look at this mess. It's dirt and more overgrown bushes. This thing must be a mud pit when it rains."

"Possibilities," she whispered. "A garden. A little patch of drought-resistant grass. A sweet table and chair set with a big chunky candle in the center. Dinners and breakfasts while we sit out here. The patio's actually in good shape."

"This would take months of work."

"Some things are worth it. I can see it all in my head—what we could do. How we could make this ours. That would be our bedroom right there." She pointed to the far end of the second story. "The one with the picture windows and little deck."

He rubbed at the back of his neck. "You really want this place?"

She nodded. "I've been inside a couple of times. Three," she amended. "It's so charming. It has the most amazing curving staircase, but it needs new flooring, and the bathrooms need updating—the kitchen too."

"Bella."

"Potential." She clasped her fingers at the back of his neck as she smiled into his eyes. "So much potential."

He settled his hands on her hips. "What's the asking price?"

"It's a pretty good deal, actually, especially for around here."

He lifted his eyebrow. "And what's your idea of a pretty good deal?"

"Um, four seventy-five."

He puffed out a laugh as he rolled his eyes to the sky. "We'd spend that much on a remodel."

She shook her head. "I had Stone come with me the last time I visited. He thought maybe a hundred grand would fix most everything. And I can do a lot of the stuff he was talking about, which would cut down on the price. If we do it together, we could cut costs even more. And I'm sure Wren can give us a hand with the decorating."

He huffed out another incredulous laugh. "Isabella Colby, I love the absolute hell out of you. If I could give you everything you want, I would, but we *cannot* afford this house, renovations, and Wren too."

"Sure we can." She pressed her lips to his. "I'll just barter with her like I always do. She gets stuff at a discount or has pieces on hand that clients let her take after she redecorates. I get some of the stuff for free and pay for a lot of it in spa packages—some services for her personally and some for her VIP clientele. I do that with Abby and Sophie too. It works out well for all of us."

"That's how you decorated your place?"

"Mmm-hmm. My bedroom set and kitchen table didn't cost me a thing."

He bobbed his head. "No kidding."

"Wren has been very good to me."

He studied the house again. "This is really what you want?"

"It's nineteen hundred square feet, three bedrooms and two-and-a-half baths, which means there's a room for your boxing stuff and a guest room for now."

"And when we have kids?"

She loved the idea of raising children with Reed. "You'll go to the gym and we'll get a comfy pullout couch."

He grinned. "I have some money. Not enough. My dad left me an inheritance that I haven't touched. And I didn't do much with my NYPD paychecks except pay rent and eat."

"My mom left me an inheritance too. Sort of." She stepped back from Reed and turned toward the overgrown bushes, tracing a leaf as some of the excitement of the afternoon faded away. "I kind of sold off everything she owned after she died—furnishings, her art collections, her car, jewelry." She flicked him a glance, trying to bury the guilt of casting away the pieces of her mother's life so easily. "I didn't want any of it," she rushed on, "just the pictures of her and my dad that I have upstairs and the engagement ring he gave her."

"Okay." Reed tugged her around to face him. "What's wrong with that?"

She jerked her shoulders. "Sometimes I think that makes me a bad person."

"Not even close." He wrapped her up in a hug. "There is *nothing* about you that fits into the bad person category."

She wasn't so sure. "All of that stuff was from men—gifts or tips for...for being what she was."

"Hey." He cradled her face in his hands. "There is no shame in getting rid of stuff. Objects. You kept what was important. That's what felt right for you. You took care of you."

She nodded, forever cherishing the way he understood her so well. "It's a couple hundred thousand, and I haven't been able to bring myself to spend it—not one dime. It's just sitting in a savings account. It feels wrong—like I would somehow be benefiting from the fact that she prostituted herself."

"So let it be her last gift to you—a legacy from the woman who told you that smart, pretty girls can have it all."

She closed her eyes as they filled, completely undone by his ability to take away the shame. He always knew just what to say. "I love you."

"I love you too."

"No." She shook her head, looking at him again. "You don't understand. I love you so much. It's so big, so..." She faltered, unable to find the words. "It makes me feel like I can't breathe."

"I get it." He pressed his mouth to hers. "Perfectly."

She smiled.

Sighing, he studied the house again. "We can call the real estate agent."

She beamed. "We'll think about it for a while. You deserve the opportunity to make sure this is what *you* want."

"What if someone buys it?"

"Then it wasn't meant to be ours."

He kissed her again. "I love the way your brain works."

She hooked her arms around the back of his neck and gained her tiptoes. "But I want it to be ours," she whispered next to his ear. "I want to make a baby with you while the moon shines through our brand-new picture windows. In that room right up there."

"We'll call the agent."

She laughed her delight. "Our children are going to run around out here, Reed. I can feel it right here." She brought his hand to her heart.

He smiled. "I like that idea. A lot."

"Me too."

"How many do you want?"

"Two. I hated being an only child."

He nodded. "Two's a good number."

"A family of four in this sweet little house."

"Once things settle down, we'll make an appointment and bring Stone with us for another whirl."

"Okay." Her phone rang, bursting her bubble of sweet dreams and contentment. "It's Dad." She pressed *talk*. "We were just on our way to come visit."

The line stayed silent.

She frowned. "Dad?"

"Bella," he gasped.

She pressed her hand to her stomach as her heart rate accelerated. "Dad, what's wrong?"

"I can't—I can't—"

She gripped Reed's arm as her fear compounded. "Daddy?"

Reed took her hand. "What's wrong?"

"I don't know. Call 911 and send them to my dad's."

He nodded. "My phone's in the truck." He booked it around to the front of the house.

She followed as Lucy ran after Reed. "Daddy, can you talk to me?"

"Bella."

"Reed's calling for an ambulance. They're going to come pick you up. They're going to help you."

"Bella."

She hurried to the truck, half listening to Reed communicating with the 911 operator while she signaled for Lucy to hop in the back. "Just hang on." She slammed the gate closed and gripped the warm metal, struggling to stay calm when all she felt was helpless. "Please hang on, Daddy. Please."

He breathed in her ear.

Reed walked over, still on the line with dispatch. "They're sending someone over. Get in."

"Did you tell them he has cancer? That he gets light-headed and he's using oxygen?"

"I told them what we know."

She sat in her seat, shutting her door as Reed pulled away from the curb.

"They're coming, Daddy. They're coming."

"Buckle up, Bella," Reed said.

She absently secured her seat belt as Reed sped through the neighborhoods to the highway.

Tense moments passed, and finally there was a commotion in the background. "Ma'am?"

She clutched her phone tighter. "Yes?"

"This is Wade with Reseda Fire and Rescue. We're going to take your father to the hospital."

She closed her eyes with the rush of relief. "Thank you. Tell him I'm coming. I'll be there as soon as I can."

"I'll tell him."

"Thank you." She hung up and let her phone fall from numb fingers, staring at her lap as she sucked in several shaky breaths, surrendering to her tears. "I don't know what's wrong—why he couldn't talk to me."

Reed took her hand, pressing a firm kiss to her knuckles. "They're taking him to the hospital, and we're on our way."

"If we'd left sooner, we would almost be there." She swiped at her cheeks. "We shouldn't have gone to see the house."

"Of course we should have. Neither of us had any idea this was going to happen."

She sniffled. "I talked to him last night. He didn't sound great, but he didn't sound like...that." She started crying again.

"Hang on, Bella."

"I'm trying." She glanced behind her and gaped. "Lucy. Oh my God. I forgot about Lucy. What about Lucy?"

"I'll call my mom. She can go stay with Mom and Aunt Bonnie for a while. Their house is a couple blocks from here."

She stared at her puppy lifting her face to the breeze, oblivious to the fact that there was a crisis going on. "Do you think that'll be okay?"

He nodded and dialed. "Mom? Hey— Yeah, I'm okay. Yes, I'm still with Bella. We're good. Mom—" He shook his head, muttering a curse. "Mom, I need to drop Lucy off with you. Bella's father is having a medical emergency. He's on his way to the hospital. Thanks. We'll be over in a few minutes." He hung up. "Everything's all set."

"Okay." She wiped at her tears again, trying to pull herself together, knowing that her falling apart wasn't helping anything. "Thanks."

"No problem."

Moments later they pulled up in Aunt Bonnie's driveway.

Linda hurried outside with Bonnie following behind.

Bella got out as Reed did.

"Bella." Linda hugged her tight. "Sweetie, it's so good to see you again."

Bella held on. "I'm so sorry about this. Thank you for taking Lucy for us."

"Of course, sweetie."

Lucy walked over, wagging her tail.

Bonnie laughed. "Lucy, you're here for a visit." She bent over, showering her with hugs and kisses.

Bella relaxed where Lucy's care was concerned. She was going to be spoiled rotten for the next little while. "You have no idea how much I appreciate this."

"Honey, I think I appreciate it more. Teresa, the new part-time nurse, started a couple days ago. We're having a bit of an adjustment period. Seeing Bonnie this happy is nice."

"Hey, Mom." Reed kissed Linda's cheeks as he walked over from securing the back of the truck. "That's great about the nurse—"

"No, it's not great, young man," Aunt Bonnie stood straight, scolding with a point of her finger. "It's not great at all. A stranger in your own home is a nightmare."

Linda sighed. "We're taking things slow."

Reed rubbed at the back of his neck. "Let me know how I can help, but we should go."

"Of course, honey."

"Um, here are my keys." Bella handed them over. "I don't know if you want to take Lucy to my house. She gets two cups of food for dinner. The kibble's in the pantry. She's well-behaved. If you take her into the backyard, she'll do her business. "

"We can do that. She'll fit in the SUV." Linda wrapped her arms around Bella again. "Go take care of your father."

"Lucy's going to be just fine with us." Aunt Bonnie walked over with Lucy by her side. "She'll be worrying about you, but we're going to help keep her spirits up. I'll probably read to her for a while."

"Thank you, Aunt Bonnie."

Aunt Bonnie hugged Bella. "Your daddy's going to be just fine too. Just fine."

She nodded, unable to speak, on the verge of tears again.

"Now you take this box of tissues I brought outside for you and go see your daddy. My nephew Reed is going to take good care of you while you're gone." She gave his forearm a solid pat.

"Yes, I will. Let's get going." Reed settled his arm around Bella's waist, and they walked back to the truck.

She looked at him as she buckled up. "Please hurry. I don't know if—I don't know."

He took her hand, holding it tight. "I'm right here with you."

She nodded as Reed backed out of the driveway for the long ride to Reseda.

☙ Chapter Forty-Two ❧

Reed sat in the hospital's small family waiting room, absently flipping through a *Time* magazine while Bella leaned against the wall, clutching her arms across her chest as she stared out the window. He glanced at his watch and steamed out a long breath, as worried about Vinny as Bella was. For over two and a half hours, they'd been eagerly awaiting some sort of update on Vinny's condition. Shortly after Vinny arrived at North Medical Center, the doctors had rushed him into emergency surgery for an abdominal bleed. At this point that was the only information they knew.

He closed the magazine and tossed it on the table, then rubbed at the ache in his tense jaw. The afternoon had certainly taken one hell of a turn. Impromptu house hunting and discussions about baby making in the moonlight seemed like some distant dream now that everything was hanging in the balance. He needed Vinny to pull through this latest setback. There was still work to do. Skylar had yet to secure Vinny's video testimony the prosecution would use as a vital piece in their case against Alfeo Caparelli, but not everything was about Operation Caparelli Takedown. Reed had grown fond of Vinny over the last few weeks. Somewhere along the way, he'd stopped equating Vincent Pescoe with Nicoli Caparelli, the brutal Mafioso. Vinny was Isabella Colby's adoring father who simply wanted to assure his daughter's long-term safety.

"It's cruel leaving people to wonder and worry this way," Bella said quietly, still staring out the window. "Why won't they tell us what's going on?"

He focused on her rigid stance, listening to the pain and fear radiating from her voice as she spoke. It absolutely sucked that there was nothing he could do to make this situation better. "They'll let us know when they can."

She shook her head. "It's not enough."

"Come on over here." He hooked his finger through the belt loop on her trendy denim shorts and tugged her his way, settling her on his lap. "Sit with me for a few minutes and keep me company."

She rested her forehead against his and closed her eyes. "Why won't they tell me what's going on?"

He cradled her cheeks and stroked her skin. "Because they're focusing on your dad right now, which is exactly what we want."

She nodded as her breathing grew unsteady. "I just—I can't stop thinking about the way he sounded on the phone—how he kept saying my name. He was so weak, and there was nothing I could do to help him."

He kissed her as his heart hurt for her. "You did help him. He's here right now because of you."

She shook her head again as a tear spilled over. "Telling you to call an ambulance hardly feels like enough."

He caught one drop, then two more, wiping them away with gentle slides of his thumbs. "That's what he needed—"

"Excuse me." The doctor stepped into the room, still dressed in his surgical scrubs. "Isabella Colby?"

Bella rushed to her feet. "Yes, I'm Isabella Colby."

Reed stood, taking Bella's hand, wanting to be right by her side. It was hard to say how the next few minutes were going to go. "How's Vinny doing?"

"He's out of surgery and resting. We've been watching him closely for the last little while. He had some fairly significant intestinal bleeding."

Bella gripped Reed's hand tighter. "Why? What happened?"

"Ms. Colby, your father's health is growing quite fragile now that his cancer is in advanced stages. His liver is failing rapidly, which can cause the type of hemorrhaging we saw today. His platelet function and counts are abnormal—a condition that will only continue to deteriorate."

She swiped at her hair, tucking long locks behind her ear. "Is he going to—will he recover from this?"

"It's hard to say. He appears to be a fighter. I can say with certainty that not everyone in his condition would have survived the procedure we performed this afternoon."

"So he might be able to go home?"

"It's my opinion that hospice care would be of great benefit to you and your family during your father's final weeks. There are several facilities in the area—"

Bella shook her head. "But I want him at home with me."

"That's something you and your husband will have to discuss, but I caution you to consider the type of support your father is going to need. Another hemorrhage is by no means out of the question."

She nodded, looking at Reed.

He ignored the doctor's assumption that they were married and focused on the fact that Vinny was down to *weeks*. Months no longer appeared to be part of the equation. He already knew what needed to happen for all of their sakes. "We'll talk it over—weigh all of the pros and cons."

Bella nodded again. "Okay."

"If you'll follow me," the doctor said, "I can take you down to see your father."

Reed wrapped his arm around Bella's shoulders as the doctor walked them down the hall toward the surgical ICU.

"Your visits will need to be short. He's breathing with some oxygen support, but he should be able to talk to you if he's lucid enough. He's been in and out of it."

"Thank you, Doctor."

They walked through a door and turned, starting down another long hall of glassed-in rooms—some with curtains pulled for patient privacy while nurses sat in small cubby-like areas, keeping track of vitals on computer screens.

The doctor stopped in front of room ten. "One at a time is best."

"I'll wait right here." Reed sent Bella a small smile of support, even as his mind raced. He needed to see Vinny—to gauge whether or not Operation Caparelli Takedown was officially fucked, but that wasn't the priority right now. "Go on in."

Bella hesitated, wrapping her arms around him as her eyes filled.

He hugged her, holding on tight. "I'll be right here," he murmured for only her to hear.

She nodded against his chest. "Okay."

"I'm right here, Bella." He kissed her forehead before she stepped away.

Bella's pulse pounded as she slowly slid open the glass door to Dad's room, not quite sure what to expect. Several different machines were beeping. She stepped around the curtain offering Dad some privacy from anyone passing by, and froze, staring at the pale, sickly man lying with his eyes closed. Every time she saw him, he looked less and less like Dad and more like a very ill stranger. She took several steadying breaths, struggling to keep her emotions in check, and sat in the chair by his bed, glancing around at the dozens of tubes and wires protruding from here and there. "I'm here, Daddy," she whispered, touching his hand with gentle fingers. "The doctor said you did great—that everything went really well."

His eyes fluttered open.

She forced a smile as she gripped his fingers. "Hey there."

"Hi."

"You just got out of surgery."

"I feel like it."

"You did really well," she repeated, choosing to focus on the fact that he was still here with her instead of the doctor's devastating new time frame. Weeks.

"Is Reed with you?"

"Yes. He's waiting outside."

"I need to see him."

She frowned at his request. "Okay, I'll send him in."

"How long are they keeping me?"

Her gaze wandered to all of the intimidating medical equipment again. "For a few days."

He nodded. "And you're going to go to work and live your life."

She pressed her lips together and blinked back tears, fighting the tug of war to honor Dad's requests when she wanted to stay close. "I'm going to visit at night."

"That doesn't sound like you living your life."

"You're part of my life, Daddy. A very important part of my life." She wanted to talk to him about coming home with her, loathing the idea of hospice care, but now wasn't the time. "I want you to rest."

"I want you to go home."

"I will, but I'm coming tomorrow night—just for a little while."

"Tomorrow's a work day."

"I know."

"I'm not feeling well enough to argue."

"Then don't argue. Just say okay."

He smiled. "Okay."

She smiled back. "I'm going to let you rest. I'll see you tomorrow night." She stood and kissed his forehead. "I love you."

"I love you too."

She kissed him again, growing more afraid that one of these times might be the last. "I'll be back tomorrow."

"All right. I need Reed."

"I'm going to get him." She walked to the curtain and waved, then moved out into the hall.

Reed shoved his phone in his back pocket. "How's he doing?"

She shrugged, afraid she would cry. "Dad wants to see you."

"He does?"

She nodded.

"I'll be right back."

"Okay." She walked to the end of the hall, needing the view out the window. Typically she yearned to stay, but today the wretched hospital smell was almost more than she could stand. She clutched her arms across her chest and focused her attention on the sun sinking toward the horizon instead of the fact that in the very near future, she was going to lose Dad.

Reed walked into Vinny's room and shut the sliding door before he pushed the curtain aside. He stopped in his tracks and winced, slightly shocked by Vinny's fragile appearance.

"I thought I was a goner," he said, keeping his eyes closed.

He sat in the chair next to Vinny, studying the ghostly grayish cast to his skin. "For a few minutes, so did I."

Vinny opened his eyes, looking at Reed. "I'm running out of time. We need to finish this thing up."

Reed had texted Skylar and Joey, updating them on the current situation as soon as Bella had left his side. "You need to focus on resting and healing."

"Did they get anything back on the bullet?"

He shook his head. "Not yet. The lab boys will get to it tomorrow."

Vinny frowned. "Tomorrow?"

"It's Sunday."

"I'm dying and the lab's closed. Do they want to keep him in prison or not?"

"They're working on it. You need to focus on healing," he repeated. "Remember that Bella needs you here for a while yet. So do I."

"What's the next step?"

"Uh," he cleared his throat, "they want to transfer you to hospice."

"Bullshit."

"It's time, Vinny. I was talking to the doctor while Bella was in here with you. There's a facility in the Palisades—"

Vinny shook his head slowly. "I can't—"

"It's a couple miles from Bella's place," he continued, already knowing that Vinny would protest the Palisades location due to its proximity to Bella. "It'll be easier for us to finish this and ease Bella's mind to know you're being taken care of just down the road."

Vinny sighed.

"You need help. You're in no shape to live on your own anymore. This will keep you out of her house—from burdening her with being your constant caregiver."

"I don't like it."

"If I thought this was going to compromise her safety in any way, I wouldn't mention it. It's the best solution for all of us. Mostly for Bella. Think about Bella."

"That's all I've ever done."

Reed nodded, knowing that was the absolute truth. "When she comes to visit tomorrow, you bring it up. She still thinks you're coming home with her. If she believes hospice is what you want, she'll go along with it."

"You're sure this is right?"

He nodded. "Absolutely. I'll be able to get over to see you more often—keep you up to date on the investigation. As soon as we can get you out of here, I'll have Skylar and Joey fly in."

"Fine. I'll talk to Bella tomorrow."

Reed stood, knowing that Vinny needed to sleep. "Hang in there. We need you to pull through this."

"I'm not going anywhere until I know my little girl's safe."

"I'm counting on that."

He closed his eyes. "Go take care of my daughter."

"I'm going." He walked back out, leaving the door open as he left. He started down the hall and frowned, surprised when he didn't see Bella. He picked up his pace, eventually spotting her staring out one of the windows as he rounded the corner.

She whirled as he approached. "What did he want?"

"To make sure I'm taking care of you."

"Oh." She turned away and pushed through the door to the stairwell instead of heading for the elevators.

"Bella." He grabbed her arm.

She yanked away. "I need to get out of here." She moved faster, running down the three flights of stairs, rushing for the exit.

"Bella." He snagged her by the wrist, turning her to face him as they made it to the parking lot.

She burst into tears.

He wrapped his arms around her, holding her while she cried it out.

"He looks awful," she said with her face still pressed to his shirt.

There wasn't much use in denying what was so plainly obvious, nor did it do any good to tell her that everything was going to be okay, because where Vinny was concerned, it wasn't. He was certainly approaching the end of his life. "I talked to the doctor for a couple of minutes while you were in with your dad." He eased her back, sliding his fingers through her hair as he stared in her eyes. "They have a hospice facility in the Palisades—"

She shook her head. "I want him at home with me."

"He's not going to want that. He won't want to interrupt your life."

She sniffled, losing her composure again. "I want him to be comfortable and well-cared-for."

"He will be. The place in the Palisades is supposed to be great. We can check it out together."

"I just—I just—"

"He needs more care than either of us can offer."

She shook her head again as more tears fell.

There was no way he was letting this go until Bella was on board with having Vinny at the facility. It was one thing to have Nicoli Caparelli close to his daughter's residence; it was entirely another to make Bella an obvious target. "What happens when you're at work? What happens if I'm out of town and he needs help getting to the bathroom? He's thin, but as he gets weaker, he'll be dead weight. This is a great compromise."

She wiped at her cheeks. "Getting him into that place won't be easy. I imagine there's quite a waiting list."

"I'm going to call Ethan when we get home. His father might have some pull."

"Wren says their father is an awful man."

"He's a selfish bastard, but he's chief of staff at Los Angeles General. He'll be able to cut through some of the red tape."

She pressed her forehead to his chest and inhaled a deep breath. "I'll talk to Dad tomorrow."

He rubbed his hands up and down her back, slightly relieved that father and daughter were both going to play things his way. "Let me take you home. You can take a bath, and I'll see what Ethan can do to give us a hand while I go grab us some dinner."

"I just want to snuggle up with you and watch TV and pretend my father isn't wasting away before our eyes."

"We can do that, but we're stopping off at the deli." He nudged her back until she looked at him again. "You need to eat and take care of yourself."

She nodded. "We'll stop at the deli."

"Let's go home."

"Thank you." She kissed him. "Thank you for being everything I need."

He kissed her back. "You've got it." He opened her door. "Buckle up." Walking around to his side, he focused on all of the things that needed to fall into place, particularly Vinny's hospice care. Nothing else could happen until they had a room secured. Time was nearly up, and Reed wasn't even close to ready.

☙ Chapter Forty-Three ❧

Reed stood out of the way while the nurse helped Vinny settle into his new room at Southern California Hospice Center. He slid his hands in his pockets, glancing around at thriving potted plants, glossy hardwood floors, and pretty paintings hanging on the soothing blue walls—a major step up from Vinny's cold, sterile hospital digs.

"There you go, Vinny." Heather adjusted the oxygen tubing around Vinny's ears and stepped back. "It looks like you're all set. Can I get you anything?"

"No. Thank you."

"I'll let you and Reed enjoy your visit."

Reed smiled at the redheaded twenty-something dressed in cheerful purple scrubs. Heather had been nothing but kind since they met Vinny's transport team at the front door half an hour ago. "Thank you for everything. You've been great."

"You're welcome. Help yourself to anything in the kitchen."

"I appreciate it." He smiled again, waiting for Heather to close the door on her way out.

"It's about damn time," Vinny grumbled as he settled more comfortably on the small pile of pillows. "How hard is it to get five damn minutes alone?"

Apparently pretty tricky. They'd been trying to find a quick moment to catch up on the case for over a week, but Reed's schedule hadn't offered him many opportunities to make it up to Reseda—and Bella had been with him on the two occasions he'd made it home early enough to tag along. Last night when Bella asked him to meet Vinny's ambulance at the center due to some sort of work conflict today, he'd jumped at the chance. "That shouldn't be a problem anymore. I'll be able to get over here a lot more often."

Vinny nodded as his gaze tracked around the room. "This place is nice enough."

"Bella likes it." Her worries had been put to rest within moments of their tour last Monday evening. "How about some fresh air?"

"Sure."

He opened the French doors to the beautiful gardens. The whole facility was gorgeous—comforting and homey. Thanks to Grant Cooke, Vinny had been guaranteed a spot at the swank establishment within minutes of Ethan's phone call to his father. "Do you need a drink or anything?"

Vinny shook his head. "Don't treat me like a pansy ass. That's my daughter's job."

He smiled, even as he worried. Vinny was still incredibly pale and weak. It didn't appear that he would be rallying back from his recent surgery the way Reed had been hoping. "And she can have it."

"Have you heard from your informant?"

"No. He said he would get back to me when he had something."

"What about the bullet? Did they get any results on that?"

He sat down in the recliner and leaned back, making himself at home. "It's a match."

Vinny closed his eyes in what could only be relief. "Thank God."

"Skylar's been out processing the warehouses—Al Marini's and Felice Dioli's murder scenes."

"And?"

He shook his head. "She hasn't come up with anything."

"What about the field?"

He laced his hands behind his head and crossed his ankles. "The rain's been making it hard for them to get a whole lot done, but they'll get back to it."

"When are they coming—Joey and Skylar?"

"Tomorrow."

Vinny nodded.

"Are you up for that?"

"Yeah," he said as he pulled his blanket to his chin, struggling to keep his eyes open.

Reed exhaled a long, quiet breath, wondering if Vinny had weeks or days left in him, because weeks seemed pretty optimistic at this point. "Good. They arrive later tonight. I've made arrangements with my coworker to cover me, so we'll meet here after I know Bella's settled in at her office."

"Sounds like a good plan. Are you still looking after that girl—the one who's being followed or whatnot?"

"For now. Her parents are talking about sending her over to Europe for the summer—get her out of here for a while."

Vinny frowned. "Are you gonna go with her?"

He shook his head. "Ethan tries not to send us away for more than two weeks at a time if we have families."

"So you'll never be away from Bella for more than a couple weeks?"

"That's always the idea."

Vinny nodded again. "You've got a good boss."

"I like him." His phone rang. He reached into his back pocket and grabbed it, smiling at Bella's face filling the screen. "Hey, beautiful," he answered.

"Hi. How did everything go?"

"Great."

"Dad's all settled in?"

"Yup. He has been for a little while now—probably about half an hour. We're sitting here watching some TV and telling each other lies." He picked up the remote on the side table and turned on the television, wanting something about his visit with Vinny to be the truth.

Bella laughed. "Sounds interesting."

"I'm not hating it."

She chuckled. "I bet."

He grinned, feeling himself relax. Tomorrow this was all going to be over. Or at least, the majority of it. They were going to have Vinny's testimony on tape. Eventually Reed would have to go to New York to testify before the grand jury, but that wouldn't impact Bella in any way. He would just have to tell her he was going away on business.

"I'm heading your way now," she said. "I was thinking about stopping off at the deli. We can have dinner and visit for a while before we head home."

"Sounds great."

"I'm going to get Dad some soup. They always have chicken noodle. Do you want anything special?"

"Nah. Go ahead and surprise me."

"All right."

"Why don't I let you go so you can concentrate on the road?"

"Okay."

"See you soon."

"Reed?"

"Yeah?"

"Thanks. For meeting Dad today. For getting him into that amazing place. For everything."

"You're welcome."

"I love you."

"I love you too. I'll see you soon."

"Okay. Bye."

He hung up and shoved his phone away. "Bella's grabbing some dinner and she'll be..." He stopped, realizing Vinny was sleeping. Sitting back, he glanced at his watch, already counting down the minutes until Skylar and Joey would help him wrap up the California end of Operation Caparelli Takedown. Vinny was just barely hanging on.

Bella moaned and closed her eyes while Reed ran his fingers through her wet hair, rinsing away any remaining conditioner while they both stood beneath the shower's warm spray. "That feels good. So relaxing."

"Good." He pushed her long locks to one side and kissed the back of her neck—once, twice.

"Mmm, that's nice too."

He wrapped his arms around her waist and slid his slippery palms up her belly to her breasts. "How about this?"

She snagged her bottom lip with her teeth and purred her satisfaction, relishing the way his touch always brought heat rushing to her center. "Even better." She turned and faced him, smiling into his eyes as she settled her hands on his hips. "It's been awhile since we've done this."

"Over a week," he murmured against her lips, tracing her spine with the tips of his fingers. "Things have been a little crazy."

She shivered as goose bumps puckered her skin. "Luckily, they seem to be settling down."

He made a sound in his throat as he held her gaze.

"Thank you again for meeting Dad today. It eased my mind knowing you were going to be there when he arrived."

"You're welcome. Now that he's close, we'll both be able to get over and visit more often."

How lucky was she that she'd found a man who was willing to take on the huge and often overwhelming responsibilities of caring for an ill loved one without complaint. He'd promised to stand by her side, and he'd been there every step of the way. "I know I resisted a little at first, but you were totally right about the hospice center." She let her hands wander up the sides of his waist, then gently raked her fingernails down his abs, loving the way she could make his muscles quiver. "As much as I wish I could take care of him here, I know he's in better hands with the staff there. His room is beautiful. And the view."

"It's an amazing facility."

"Mmm. I like that Lucy gets to come too." She smiled, remembering the way Dad had laughed when their sweet puppy edged up to his bedside and kissed his cheek. Unfortunately, he was still pale and weak. It was nice that Lucy could bring him a little joy when he was feeling so poor. "And he's just minutes down the road."

"A win-win for everyone."

"It is." She swallowed, seeing the desire in Reed's eyes. "Dad's all settled in and we've had dinner. What should we do with the rest of our evening?"

"We can finish season six of *The Office* and eat ice cream, or we could go to bed."

She nodded. "Good ideas. I like option two best, but it's a little early to call it a night."

He dipped his fingers inside her. "I don't think I said anything about sleeping."

She whimpered, clutching at his shoulders as he played her.

He eased her back against the tile as he used his tongue to tease her nipples. "We could finish this right here. This works too."

She shook her head. "In the bedroom." She stroked his erection as she stood on her tiptoes and tugged on his ear with her teeth. "But tonight I get to be in charge."

He lifted his brow. "I like the way that sounds."

"You should. I'm planning on taking *very* good care of you."

He reached behind him, shutting off the water, then lifted her in his arms, moving with her to the bedroom.

She laughed. "We forgot our towels."

"We don't need them."

Reed's phone alerted him to a text as they walked by the dresser.

She snatched it up, reading the screen. "Skylar G. says they made it and everything's all set." She frowned, looking at him. "Sounds mysterious."

"Not really." He took the phone from her and tossed it into the small pile of dirty clothes. "I've been doing a little consulting on an old case she and I were both involved with."

"I see."

"I can tell you all about it." He collapsed onto the mattress and growled, attacking her neck with nibbles. "Or I can do this."

Laughing, she swatted at his back and bucked beneath him. "That tickles!"

He grinned, staring down at her. "This seems like the better option. Cop talk's boring."

"I agree." She motioned for him to reverse their positions.

He complied.

She sat up, straddling him. "Now, where were we?"

"You were going to be in charge."

She wiggled her eyebrows. "That's right."

He chuckled.

She gripped him in her hand, moving up and down. "I'm going to do all kinds of naughty things to you."

He grinned. "Who am I to stop you?" In a lightning-fast move, he had her on her back again. "Unless I get to it first."

She laughed, hooking her arms around the back of his neck. These were her favorite moments—when they spent time together, having fun. Reed told her that she'd changed his life, but he'd changed hers too. Every day was better because he was in it. "You have an unfair advantage. You're stronger and weigh more than I do. I'm totally at your mercy."

"That's true." He sank himself inside her.

She tipped her head back, crying out, as waves of pleasure careened through her body.

"Sounds like this is working for you though," he said, his breathing already growing unsteady.

She nodded, still reeling from the onslaught of sensations. "Since we're already here, how about you have a turn first, and I'll have mine next?"

He grinned, then kissed her forehead and the tip of her nose, instantly changing the mood of their lovemaking. "I just need you."

She brushed her fingers through his hair, forever amazed that Reed was hers. That this was her life. Their life. "I need you too."

"I love you."

"I love you too." She captured his mouth and moved with him, more than happy to be wrapped up in Reed's arms for a rare quiet night.

꧁ Chapter Forty-Four ꧂

Reed grabbed the large corkboard he was borrowing from Ethan Cooke Security and leaned it against the wall by Vinny's bedside. He pulled a file folder from his laptop case next and started pinning up documents and various images in a rough timeline of events—the way he'd done more times than he could count at the Brooklyn precinct. Up went pictures of Bella standing next to Dino Asante and Matty Caparelli at Luisa's grand opening event; the stack of prison letters Alfeo had written to his poor mother; a current map of the field with circles and *x*'s where corpses had been pulled from the ground; a surprisingly cool shot Skylar had taken of him, Vinny, Joey, and Collin in the four-person ATV with the skyline behind them; photographs of each of the bodies in their unzipped body bags on the anthropologist's table; and the knife. They were all parts of the whole—all parts of connecting the dots and drawing final conclusions before Vinny couldn't answer their questions anymore.

"So this is what you guys do in your cop shops." Vinny played with the straw in his water glass as he lay back against his pillows, his color slightly better than it had been yesterday. "Make posters for the walls."

Smiling, Reed added two more photos to the top—one of Nicoli Caparelli in his heyday and another of Nicoli and Alfeo caught by FBI surveillance. "It puts it out there in a nice little line—lets us all see the big picture."

Vinny sat up farther in his bed. "How are you gonna explain all this if one of the nurses walks in?"

Reed snagged a blanket and set it at the top of the board in a way that would allow him to drape the images quickly if anyone entered that they weren't expecting. "Hopefully they won't. I told them that a videographer and her assistant were coming in to capture a keepsake video."

Vinny grinned as he shook his head. "You don't miss a trick."

Not when everything was on the line. They had one shot at getting this right. "It pays to be thorough."

"I guess so." Vinny sipped his drink. "When are they coming?"

There was a knock at the door and Skylar and Joey walked in, both carrying equipment.

Reed shoved his hands in his pockets, never quite so happy to see his buddies. "How's that for an answer?"

"Hey," Skylar said to Reed as she set down the bulky case and walked over to Vinny. She was dressed in tailored gray slacks and a fitted blazer—the constant professional and hard-ass. "It's nice to see you again, Mr. Pescoe."

Vinny accepted Skylar's hand. "I thought we decided you were gonna call me Vinny."

She smiled. "I guess we did. I'll get things set up."

Vinny nodded. "Cop number two," he said to Joey as Joey shut the door.

"What's going on, Vinny?" Joey shook Vinny's hand, dressed far more casually in cargo shorts and a T-shirt.

"It's nice and spacious in here," Skylar commented as she adjusted the tripod and set the recorder in place like a pro. "Vinny, I want to get a head-on shot of you while I interview you, if that's okay."

He shrugged. "Whatever we need to do to get this done. For my daughter."

"Where's Bella today, anyway?" Joey asked as he sat down at the small table with chairs for two.

"Working until four." Reed crossed his arms and sat in the recliner, close by the board, doing his best to ignore the tension creeping up his neck. "She has an earlier day, so this needs to be wrapped up sooner rather than later." He glanced at his watch, noting that they had plenty of time to take care of business. Just a few more hours and they would have what they needed for the DA and a grand jury. After this, he got to move on with his life and stop with all the damn lying. Maybe this weekend he would surprise Bella with another visit to her dream house—with a real estate agent in tow.

"All right." Skylar framed Vinny's face in the small screen on the camera and grabbed her notes, setting them on the table close to where she stood next to Joey. "I think we're good. Let's begin. Today's date is Tuesday, May tenth, two thousand sixteen. The time is currently nine fifteen a.m. in Los Angeles, California. I'm Special Agent Skylar Grayson, interviewing state's witness Nicoli Caparelli. Please state your name and date of birth for the camera."

"My name is Vin—Nicoli Caparelli. Birthdate is August eleventh, 1952."

"Nicoli, I would like to start our interview with your early life."

Vinny nodded, sipping his water. "Okay."

"You're the youngest son of Patrizio and Isabella Caparelli?"

"Yes."

"You have a sibling four years your senior, Alfeo Caparelli. Is this correct?"

"It is."

"You grew up in New York?"

"I did. Brooklyn."

"You were a resident of Brooklyn, New York, until you relocated with the Witness Protection Program in 1989?"

He nodded again. "Yes."

"What did you do for employment before your relocation?"

"I worked for the Caparelli crime family."

"Can you attest to the fact that the Caparelli Family was and is part of La Cosa Nostra?"

"Yes. My grandfather, Sony Caparelli, was the original founder of the five families of La Cosa Nostra. The Capo Di Tutti Capi."

"Which means?"

"The boss of all bosses. He raised my father, Patrizio, to be Godfather and my older brother, Alfeo, to take over when that day finally came."

"When did you become involved with the Caparelli crime family?"

"I can't remember a time when I wasn't. I was ranked an associate as a young boy—did some bookmaking, ran money, parked cars. My father wanted Alfie and me to earn our way up the chain in the organization just like everyone else. To learn the business."

"When you mention Alfie, you're speaking of your older brother Alfeo?"

"I am."

"What part did you play later on in the organization—as you got older?"

"I was a capo for several years."

"Please explain what that means."

"Caporegime—a captain. I was a high-ranking member of the

family. I oversaw a large group of men—kept them in line, made sure they were earning for the organization."

"Would you say you had a lot of influence within the family?"

Vinny moved his head from side to side. "I would say I was well-respected—the most level-headed out of my father, brother, and me. The men liked to talk to me instead of either of them. They were less likely to get shot that way, so I would say yes."

"You mentioned keeping people in line just a moment ago. What does that mean?"

"All kinds of things," he said as he adjusted the oxygen tubing on his face.

"Did you ever commit murder?"

"Yes."

"Can you recall how many individuals you killed?"

"Six."

"You killed six men?"

He shrugged. "Death is part of the life. If you're not the one doing the killing, someone else is. If it's not you doing the whacking, you're probably about to get whacked yourself."

"Whacked? Can you explain that term for me, Mr. Caparelli?"

"To murder—kill."

"Did your brother Alfeo kill anyone?"

Vinny nodded. "Alfeo did the majority of the killing for the family. My father preferred it that way."

Reed sat back, adjusting his ball cap so that he wore it backward as he crossed his ankles on the coffee table, listening to Skylar work her way through Nicoli Caparelli's long interview.

Bella sang along with the radio as she drove toward Dad's with the top down. She bobbed her head in time with the beat blasting through the speakers, more than a little thrilled that she'd been able to cut out of work early. Her three o'clock body sculpting appointment had ended up rescheduling. Abby called at one thirty, still stuck in a meeting, unable to make their two o'clock facial. It was a rare and beautiful occasion when she was able to sneak away for a half day, and she had every intention of taking full advantage.

She'd dropped Lucy off at home and changed into her adorable new black spaghetti-strap romper. Abby had been so right when she encouraged her to grab the playful wrap-tie sandals to complement her outfit. Basically, the afternoon was off to a glorious start. A visit with Dad was first on the agenda. Maybe they could sit in the garden and soak up a little sunshine and fresh air. Then she had a few errands to run before Reed got home. She smiled, remembering her hot night with her favorite guy—and this morning too. Perhaps he would be up for a repeat performance. Maybe she would just tackle him as soon as he walked through the door. "Easy girl," she muttered and chuckled.

She slowed for the next stoplight and sat up taller when she spotted the sign for The Juice Bar. Smoothies definitely had to happen today. She flipped on her turn signal and pulled through the drive-thru, ordering two small pineapple-mango treats. Dad wasn't likely to drink much, but he would have the option if he wanted it. Joining the flow of traffic again, she drove the last two miles to the hospice center and glanced at the dashboard clock, thrilled that her new commute from door to door was right around seven minutes. She pulled into a spot by a truck that looked just like Reed's and shrugged, knowing he had a full hour left on duty with Sadie. She grabbed the tropical drinks and went inside.

"Hi, Bella."

"Hi." She smiled at Heather and kept going, not wanting to interrupt Dad's nurse as she spoke to one of the other patients' family members Bella recognized from yesterday. Moving down the hall, she paused outside of Dad's room and adjusted the cups in her hands, then knocked and turned the doorknob. "Daddy, I—" She blinked her surprise as she stepped in, glancing from Dad to Reed as he yanked his feet off the coffee table and rushed to stand, pulling a blanket over a board full of pictures.

"Bella."

She looked at Joey, then a tall, beautiful blonde standing by a video camera. "What's going on in here?"

Reed tossed his hat to the chair and jammed his fingers through his hair in the tense silence.

She realized the video camera was pointed at Dad and stepped farther inside when she was mostly certain she wanted to turn and leave. "What is this?"

"Bella, I'm Skylar Grayson."

She frowned, growing more confused by the second. "From the FBI?"

"Yes. I'm going to step out and give you a minute."

Joey stood. "Bella."

"Joey," she said quietly.

He stepped out with Skylar and shut the door.

She set the drinks down on the table and pressed her hand to her queasy stomach. "Why do I feel sick?"

Reed pulled out a chair. "Go ahead and take a seat."

She shook her head, staring into his eyes, seeing the apology there. "Just tell me what's going on."

He steamed out a breath. "It's a long story."

"Just say it."

He shoved his hands in his pockets. "Vinny and I are helping the FBI with a case."

She pressed her fingers to her temples as a headache started brewing. "I don't understand."

"We're helping the DA build a case against Alfeo Caparelli."

Why did that name sound so familiar? "Caparelli," she whispered, trying to place it as her mind raced.

"The Caparelli crime family," Reed said.

"Like Mr. Asante? I don't— Why?" She looked at Dad. "How do you know Alfeo Caparelli?"

Dad struggled to sit up farther in his bed. "He's my brother."

She gripped the chair as her pulse pounded too fast. "What?"

"I'm Nicoli Caparelli, Bella."

Her breath shuddered in and out as her world started crumbling around her. "You're Vincent Pescoe."

He shook his head. "I was in the Witness Protection Program."

Was this really happening? She looked at Reed again. "I want to see the board."

"Bella—"

"Let me see it," she snapped as her voice broke.

Reed clenched his jaw as he pulled the blanket away.

Her breath came faster as she stared at photographs of herself at Luisa's party and horrid, gruesome images of dead bodies. There was a rusted knife and a picture of Dad when he'd been younger, but it was the photograph of Dad bundled up in blankets, sitting next to Reed in an off-road vehicle with the New York skyline behind them, that was more than she could handle. "You two—you went..."

"Isabella, look at me," Dad said.

She turned her head and held his gaze.

"I've been a bad man. I've done so many things I'm not proud of.

I'm trying to fix them before I can't."

"I don't—" She looked at Reed again as a thought wiped away the rest. "How long have you known?"

He scrubbed at his jaw, holding her stare.

She blinked back tears as she feared she already knew the answer. "How long have you known?"

"I was part of the mafia life, Bella," Dad explained. "Reed is trying to help me right my wrongs."

She ignored Dad and stepped toe-to-toe with Reed. "Did you know about this the whole time? Did you know who my father was?"

His nostrils flared.

"Answer me!"

"I found out not long after we met."

Her heart shattered as she stepped back. "I have to go."

Reed took a step toward her. "Bella—"

"No." She pointed at him. "You stay away from me." She looked at Dad. "I don't even know what to say." She opened the door and collided with Joey. Shoving away from him, she hurried down the hall.

"Bella," Reed called after her.

She ran when she heard his footsteps not far behind. Picking up her pace, she sprinted to her car and got in, locking the door despite the top being down as Reed pulled on the handle.

"Bella, wait."

"Leave me alone!" Her breath hitched in and out as she jammed the key into the ignition with trembling hands and took off with a squeal of tires, pulling out onto the road while pain thundered in her head. She moved with the flow of traffic on automatic pilot, replaying the last few minutes, still trying to grasp that this was actually happening. Her father's name was Nicoli? Reed had lied? How was this real?

She blinked, realizing she was somehow pulling into her neighborhood, and came to an abrupt stop in the driveway. She got out and let herself into the house, locking the door behind her before she went upstairs and bolted for the bathroom, just making it to the toilet before she vomited.

Tears streamed down her cheeks as she gripped the seat and dry heaved, listening to Lucy whine by her side. She wanted to assure her puppy that she was all right, but nothing about her life was okay anymore.

Reed shoved his key into Bella's front doorknob and walked inside, taking the steps in twos when he didn't see her downstairs. For most of his frantic drive home, he'd been right behind her, but she blew through a traffic light as it turned red, leaving him in her dust. He was here now, and they were going to talk this through. He moved down the hall and slowed, swearing as he listened to her quiet crying echoing off the bathroom walls. This situation right here was exactly what he'd been trying to avoid all along. They'd been so close to finishing up—another ten minutes and they would have been done. Now he was terrified Bella was through with him. As she had every right to be. He stepped into the bathroom and clenched his jaw, staring at her kneeling by the toilet with Lucy by her side.

Her shoulders stiffened. "Get out."

"Please talk to me."

She flushed the toilet and stood, holding her head in her hands.

He frowned, moving closer to her, his first instinct to pull her close and make sure she was okay. "Are you having a migraine?"

She said nothing as she turned on the cold water and rinsed her mouth, then splashed water on her cheeks. Pulling the hand towel off the bar, she pressed her face into the cotton and started crying again.

He shook his head as he stared up at the ceiling, loathing himself for hurting her so badly. Things weren't supposed to have turned out this way. "Let me get you some medicine."

"I don't want you here." She rushed back to the toilet and puked again.

He grabbed the prescription bottle from the cupboard and shook a pill into his hand, then got her some water. "Here," he said as he moved to where she sat on the floor. "Take this."

She took the water and pill without looking at him and swallowed both down, then walked to her bed and lay on top of the covers. "Please go away."

She was so pale, so helpless, like the last time when this happened. But nothing was the same as it was before. "I will. Once I know you're going to be all right."

She stared up at him with devastated eyes. "How could you do this to me?"

He crouched down next to her, wanting to touch and soothe, but he knew he wasn't welcome. "I'm so sorry."

Tears trailed down her cheeks and she rolled, facing away from him—toward his pillow, where he usually slept.

"I'm sorry, Bella," he said again as he sat in the chair in the corner of the room and stared at her slim figure, listening to her breathing turn even as her pill kicked in, knocking her out. He rested his elbows on his thighs and rubbed at the back of his neck, feeling slightly nauseated himself. This wasn't over. He needed to explain and make her understand—to fix everything, but he was in for a long, hellish wait while she slept off her headache.

☙ Chapter Forty-Five ❧

BELLA WOKE IN THE DARK, BLINKING AS SHE STARED AT THE time glowing bright on her alarm clock. She frowned as she studied the play of light and shadows in her room, realizing that it was too quiet. Lucy wasn't snoring on her bed in the corner, and Reed wasn't breathing deeply by her side. She rolled, reaching for him, and sat up in a rush, panicked when she didn't find him there. "Reed," she called, then leaned back against her pillow as pieces of her day started filtering through the fog. Reed had lied to her...and Dad.

She pulled back the blanket Reed must have covered her with and heard a paper crinkle by her hip. Turning on the light, she squinted, reading his handwriting.

I have Lucy with me.

She swallowed, staring at the sentence, trying to process the gravity of his five simple words. Reed was taking care of their puppy. He'd taken care of her too. This afternoon he'd rushed home moments after her and had given her one of her pills when she'd been too sick and out of sorts to get one for herself. At some point, he'd taken off her shoes as well. That's what couples did—helped each other out when their partners were down for the count. But she and Reed weren't a couple anymore. "Oh, God," she shuddered out, pressing her hand to her heart as the pain came rushing back. Their relationship was over.

Wiping at her damp cheeks, she stood and looked out the window. His lights were on. She had to go over there, but she didn't want to. With little choice, she went downstairs and walked across the side yard, eyeing the glossy wood of his front door in the porch light. Taking a steadying breath, she fisted her hand and knocked, wishing desperately that Reed would just have left Lucy at home where she belonged.

He opened the door, dressed in ratty gym shorts, wearing one of his ball caps backward. "You're up."

She tucked her hair behind her ear, trailing her gaze down his naked chest. Her heart wasn't supposed to beat faster just from looking at him. She wasn't supposed to crave the feeling of his strong arms wrapped around her. Not after what happened today. "I just need Lucy."

He stepped back in the doorway. "Why don't you come in?"

She shook her head. "It's late."

"Please talk to me."

She tried to ignore the weariness in his eyes and hints of desperation in his voice. "I can't."

"Please, Bella. Let me explain."

She stared at him for several long seconds. "Okay. Fine." They were going to have to do this eventually. Now seemed as good a time as any. She stepped inside. "But I only have a minute."

"I'll take it." He closed the door behind her, scrutinizing her face as he stood inches away. "How are you feeling?"

How was she supposed to answer that when she could smell the soap on his skin? When she longed for everything to be exactly the way it had been only hours ago? "My headache's gone."

He nodded. "That's good."

She cleared her throat and swiped at her hair again. "Where's Lucy?"

"Sleeping on a blanket upstairs."

"Oh." She turned toward the windows and stared out as the tension radiating between them became unbearable. What now? How did this work when she loved so desperately but hurt so deeply? "I want you to tell me everything: who my father is." She turned, facing him. "Who you are."

"I'm still me, Bella."

"No." Her bottom lip trembled as she struggled to keep her emotions in check. "For months, I've been living a lie." She blinked, realizing that was hardly accurate. "My whole life."

"There are things I haven't told you while we've been together, but nothing's changed between you and me—"

"Everything's changed. *Everything*, Reed," she repeated as she crossed her arms, trying to rub them warm.

"I love you."

She shut her eyes. "Don't say that to me."

He closed the distance between them and gently gripped her shoulders. "It's true. I love you."

She lifted her chin and stepped back, terrified to let herself believe the truth she saw in his gaze. Right now, she had no idea what was real. "Who's my father?"

"Come sit down." He took her hand. "You're still pale."

She pulled away, finding his touch its own form of torture, and took a seat on his one and only barstool at the island.

"How about something to drink?"

She laced her fingers on the cool granite. "No. Thank you."

He opened the refrigerator door and took a pitcher off the empty shelf, pouring her a glass of water anyway. "This is fresh." He set it down in front of her.

"Just tell me."

He leaned back against the counter across from her and crossed his arms. "Your father's name is Nicoli Caparelli. He was born into the Caparelli crime family."

She rubbed at her temple. "I got that part."

"Maybe we should wait—"

She shook her head adamantly. "I want every word before I walk out that door."

He clenched his jaw and nodded. "Do you remember how I told you about the Caparellis being part of La Cosa Nostra?"

"Yes."

"They're the most powerful of the five families. They always have been. Your father grew up in that life. His father, Patrizio, groomed him to take his place in the organization."

"What did he do?"

"He was a capo—a captain."

She shrugged. "I don't know what that means."

"Basically he was one of the higher-ups in the organization. He had men who worked for him—reported to him, followed his orders, did business deals, and sent money up the chain to him and Patrizio. Kind of like being a manager for a big company."

She sipped her water, relieving her dry throat. "They did illegal things?"

"Most of their activities are illegal. Some are legit, but the majority aren't."

Her mind flashed back to the pictures of the dead bodies on the corkboard, and she shivered. "He—did he hurt people?"

He rubbed at the back of his neck and sighed. "Yeah, he hurt people."

She gripped her fingers tighter, terrified to ask the next question, but she needed to know. "Killed them?"

He steamed out a long breath. "Don't make me hurt you this way."

She wanted to hear him say what she couldn't allow herself to believe. "Did my dad kill people?"

He moved, leaning his forearms on the granite so they were eye-level as they looked at each other. "Yes."

She bit her bottom lip and stared at her hands, willing herself not to cry. How was this happening? How would anything ever feel right again? "He read me bedtime stories and put Hello Kitty Band-Aids on my skinned knees."

"You have to understand that in the mafia, it's kill or be killed. Literally, Bella. If the boss orders a hit and you don't comply, you die."

Her gaze flew to his. "You're defending him?"

"No. I want you to recognize that he had no choice. The lifestyle's violent—incredibly dangerous."

"There's always a choice."

He shook his head. "Not in this. He didn't take pleasure in it. Not the way his brother, Alfeo, did. Your dad did what was necessary to survive. Alfeo took dozens of lives without blinking an eye."

"Where is he? Alfeo?"

"In prison. For now. He's getting out next month. That's why Vinny and I have been working together. We're trying to make sure he stays there. He committed a lot of crimes he never paid for. He's a very dangerous man, Bella. Your father's been hiding from him for years."

"If Dad was so powerful, why is he hiding?"

"Because he turned state's evidence against the family."

"The Witness Protection Program?"

Reed nodded. "He and Alfeo had been ordered to pull off a hit on a capo who betrayed Patrizio. The capo wasn't sharing his full cut of the profits, which is pretty much a death sentence. To make matters worse, he was trying to hide. One night, they spotted him driving by and shot into the car. What your dad didn't know at the time was that the capo's entire family was with him—his pregnant wife and toddler."

She closed her eyes as she listened to a story that was so horribly insane, it sounded as if Reed were making it up. "Oh, God."

"When your dad realized what was going on, he ran over, wanting to help. The capo's wife was still alive. Elena. She had been a good friend of your dad's. As teenagers, they'd worked together at the restaurant your grandfather owned. She asked him for help—was begging him. He opened the door to get her out, and Alfeo walked over and shot her dead."

Tears trailed down her cheeks as she imagined the terror Elena must have suffered. The horror Dad must have felt. "A monster."

Reed nodded. "A monster. Vinny had enough after that. The mafia life is supposed to be about honor and respect. For the most part, the only people who are supposed to die are the ones who participate in it, but that didn't happen that night, so he decided he was finished."

"And now Alfeo wants my dad dead?"

"There's a half-million-dollar contract out on his head to this day."

She frowned as so many things finally made sense. "That's why Dad left us—why he wanted me to leave when I knocked on his door in Reseda."

"There isn't anything he wouldn't do for you. Even if it meant walking away to keep you safe."

She sat up abruptly as she realized that they'd gravitated closer together, both of them leaning farther across the counter—that she'd nearly reached for his hand. "And you knew all along."

"I did."

"Were you ever going to tell me?"

"No."

She stared at him, blinking as her eyes welled with fresh tears. "Why?"

"Because I wanted to protect you from all of this. I wanted you to be able to remember your dad differently than how you will now."

She dropped her gaze. "You had no right to decide for me."

"I had every right, Bella, because now the burden belongs to you too." He reached over and lifted her chin, holding her jaw in his hand so she had no choice but to look at him. "Don't you understand that you can never tell anyone about this? You can never confide in Abby or Wren or Julie, because your father's secrets will put them in danger. Just knowing puts you in danger."

Fear rushed into her heart as he spoke. "What do you mean?"

He let her go and paced away, then back. "Your father took every precaution possible to keep you safe, but there are rumors within the organization that Nicoli has a child. You're a potential target."

Her pulse pounded faster. "Is that why you're with me?"

"I'm with you because I love you, Bella."

She shook her head as her breath shuddered in and out. "I don't want to talk about this."

"I do."

She turned away. "I don't know what to believe anymore." She dashed at one tear, then two, fighting to keep her composure. She'd been doing so well; she wasn't about to lose it now.

He walked around to her side, standing in front of her. "I *love* you, Bella. You can believe that."

"Who are you?"

"The same guy who woke up next to you this morning."

She shook her head as she thought of him sitting in Dad's room with Joey and Skylar. "Until today, I didn't realize that there's a whole different side to you that I don't know."

He got down on his knees in front of her, resting his hands on the sides of her stool. "You know the best parts of me—who I am when I'm with you. That's who I want to be."

"I don't want to know only the best parts of you. I need to know all of you." She fisted her hands on her thighs, afraid that she might touch him. "I've told you about my past. I have no secrets. You can't say the same thing."

"There are things I'll never be able to tell you—for your safety and mine."

She sniffled. "So tell me what you can."

"All right. Where do you want me to start?"

"Wherever you want."

He took a deep breath. "I'll start with my career, I guess."

She nodded. "Okay."

"I worked on the Special Organized Crime Unit for the majority of my career with NYPD. For years, Joey and I did deep cover, trying to find ways to infiltrate and dismantle the Caparelli organization the way RICO decimated the other families. For as long as I can remember, I've wanted to keep Alfeo in his cell—to make him pay for everything he's ever done. I still do."

"Why is Alfeo so important to you?"

Clenching his jaw, he looked at the floor.

"Why?" she asked again, terribly afraid she wasn't going to like his answer.

"The Caparellis killed my family: my father, grandfather, my Uncle Mason."

She rushed to her feet at the shock of his words. "They killed your family?"

"Shot all three of them. The cops could never prove it—or wouldn't, but I know. I'm positive."

She pushed his arm off the stool and stepped away, turning her back on him as she pressed her face into her hands and burst into tears. Every time she thought she'd heard the worst, there was something far more terrible to comprehend.

He stood behind her, settling his palms on her shoulders.

She whirled. "My family killed your family?"

"I don't think of those people as your family."

"I just—I can't... If the cops couldn't figure it out, how do you know?"

He shrugged. "I just do."

"My God." She walked to the wall, sagging against it as she stared at his scars. "They almost killed you too."

He shoved his hand through his hair as he paced. "Joey and I were working with a team member who was playing both sides. At the time we had no idea. We were finally starting to make our way up the chain in the organization. We'd just slipped one of the Caparelli capos some information that benefited the organization—"

She gaped. "You *helped* them?"

"We needed their absolute trust. You can't do the type of job Joe and I did without it. Sometimes the end justifies the means."

Was that what his relationship with *her* had been about? She couldn't help but wonder as his deceptions took on an entirely different depth. "Whatever it takes to exact your revenge?"

His eyes sharpened on hers. "Not always. There are some lines I can never—would never cross."

She looked down, not so sure she believed that.

He rushed over to her. "Don't go there, Bella."

What good did it do to travel down that road—to add more pain to an already agonizing situation? "Tell me how you and Joey got shot."

He held her gaze in the strained silence.

"I need to know."

"Joe and I were invited to a big Fourth of July party put on by one of the mafia's higher-ups. The men we were working with were grateful for our tip. After the fireworks, we were ushered into cars and driven to a warehouse. Joey and I thought we were going to see a new illegal site they were operating, but they shot us instead. Joey got the worst of it—four bullets. Two to the leg and one to his shoulder and chest."

Her stomach churned as she glanced at his ugly wounds again. The shot to his chest had nearly been fatal. "What happened to the men who brought you there?"

"Joe got one of them on his way down, and I killed the other three. I'm not sorry. Joey was bleeding out on me, and I wasn't in great shape either. We had backup down the road. They got us to the hospital in time. We both had close calls, but we were lucky enough to make full recoveries."

She nodded, not quite sure what to think. He'd killed three men to save himself and his best friend. How could she fault him that?

"While I was lying in the hospital, healing, I found out our unit was being shut down. Anything that was left to be dealt with was going to be handed over to the FBI."

"Skylar."

He nodded. "Skylar. She'd spent time working in Violent Crimes—switched over to the Organized Crime Division a few years ago. We worked together a lot." He sighed. "In many ways, that night was a blessing in disguise. I realized I didn't want to play the game anymore. I'd almost lost my life and I wanted out. The need for revenge was eating me up—destroying me slowly—so I quit and came out to LA. Jerrod and Shane introduced me to Ethan, and I started working for him. I stayed with Mom and Aunt Bonnie for a while after I got back from my training in Europe. I thought I was going to go insane." He smiled absently. "So I got this place."

"You didn't know who I was when you moved in?"

"No." His gaze sharpened on hers again. "I had no idea. I was actually on the phone with Joey when I found Lucy in my living room. He'd called to tell me he overheard one of the guys from WITSEC talking about aliases Nicoli Caparelli was supposed to have used. I did some looking into it for him and eventually I found your father—right around the same time you and I started hanging around together."

She swallowed as they held each other's stare. "You—you used me."

He clenched his jaw. "From the moment I saw you, I was attracted to you. How could I not be? Look at you, Bella. You're gorgeous. But then you invited me over for dinner and a walk on the beach and cut my hair." He smiled again. "You intrigued me even when I didn't want to be. There's something about you—so real and warm. Everything I needed."

She didn't want to hear his pretty words—couldn't take it. "You used me."

"I started spending more time with you because I wanted to know what you knew about your father's old life."

"Nothing."

"I figured that out eventually. I told Joey I had my doubts as my feelings for you started growing. Something changed between us the night of Julie and Chase's wedding. When we were dancing. Do you remember?"

"Yes," she said quietly, looking away.

"I remember desperately wishing things were different. I just wanted to be with you without all of the complications. Not long after that, we slept together. I told Joey I was done with the whole thing. Then he took the pictures of you with Dino and Matty in New York."

She shook her head. "I don't understand."

"Matty's your cousin, Bella. Alfeo's son. He currently runs the Caparelli organization until Alfeo gets out of prison."

Her eyes went huge as she digested the next surprise. "*What*?"

"The photos were so damning. I tried to deny it—wanted to so badly, Bella, but I started thinking you were involved after all—"

Her breath shuddered in and out. "I didn't even know who he was until just now."

"I know. But I didn't then. After I met your dad, he cleared things up for me real fast. We started working together to keep Alfeo where he belongs so he can't ever hurt you."

"So Mr. Asante *was* part of the crime family?"

"Yeah."

"What about Luisa?"

"I don't know what she knows—probably not much."

She stared at the floor for a long time as she absorbed the washes of anger and betrayal—the constant lies. "Am I supposed to be grateful for all of this?"

"No."

She met his gaze. "How am I supposed to handle this? Am I supposed to take your hand, walk next door with you, and pretend this isn't happening?"

He rubbed at his jaw. "I don't know what to do."

"You've lied to me—"

"Bella—"

"You've *lied* to me," her voice broke. "Whatever your reasons, you've lied."

"I did. Over and over again, and I fucking *hated* it."

Her eyes watered as she heard the agony in his voice. "This life I thought we were building—"

He took her hand, cupping it between both of his. "It's still here."

She broke down and quickly shored herself back up. "How can you say that? This isn't real. Our whole foundation is a series of deceptions. You took my dying father to New York and I had *no* idea."

"We had to go."

"You made a fool out of me."

"Bella—"

"How do you expect for me to look at you and believe *anything* you say? I can't live like this. I can't wonder if my partner is looking me in the eyes and lying. Because you've done that, Reed. All this time, you've done exactly that."

He pressed her fingers to his lips. "But I don't have to anymore. Skylar's taking everything we have to the DA and grand jury. My part in this is mostly over." He stepped closer. "I want us to be together."

She shook her head. "I can't. We can't."

He cupped her cheeks. "Please don't walk away from what we have."

She tried to harden her heart, even as it shattered yet again. "What do we have, Reed?"

He stroked her skin. "I love you. You love me."

"Unfortunately, I do love you. But I won't. Eventually I won't."

He settled his forehead against hers—one of his usual tender gestures, and she started crying. "Bella, please."

Lucy walked down the stairs.

Bella eased him back with a push to his chest. "I'll be at work all day tomorrow. You can come pick up your stuff and leave the key on the table." She dashed at the tears on her cheeks. "This is over."

"Don't leave it like this."

More tears fell as she sucked in several shaky breaths, wanting to stay here with him as much as she hoped never to see him again. "I want you to stay away from me. No knocks on my door. No phone calls or texts. You go your way and I go mine."

He held her gaze another moment and stepped back. "Okay."

She turned toward the door and opened it. "Lucy, come on."

Lucy stayed where she was between them and whined.

"Come *on*, Lucy," she choked out.

Lucy followed, and Bella shut the door behind her without looking back.

Reed's phone rang in the dark while he sat at his desk, holding a glass of scotch in his hand. He'd already knocked back a solid three fingers, but alcohol never soothed him the way boxing did. The ringing stopped and started again—once, twice, three times. He picked it up, staring at Skylar's name on the screen, and seriously contemplated chucking the damn thing out the window. "What?" he answered instead.

"We landed at four thirty."

He sat back in his uncomfortable chair. "Great."

"The DA was waiting for us."

He sipped at his drink and set it down. Getting lit wasn't going to solve his problems, especially when he had to go to work in four hours. "Okay."

"He wanted the tape—brought me back to his office so he could take a look at the footage."

He scrubbed at his jaw. "You needed to tell me this in the middle of the night?"

"I didn't get a chance to edit, Reed. Bella's on the tape. The prosecution knows who she is."

He rushed to his feet. "What?" He jammed his fingers through his hair and walked to his bed and back. "What the fuck, Skylar? Why didn't you turn the damn thing off?"

"She took us all by surprise. In the moment, I was thinking more about you getting a chance to explain than hitting the *off* button."

He steamed out a breath. "Damn it."

"The footage is going into a vault. His copy and mine are encrypted. It's for his eyes only."

"But he knows. No one was supposed to know."

"Unfortunately, he does, but I made sure to play the scene back—made sure he understood that she knew nothing about any of this. Has *never* had anything to do with the Caparellis. For now, I think we're good."

"Let's hope it stays that way."

"Did you track her down?"

"I don't want to talk about it. Keep me up to date on the case." He hung up and sat back down, staring into the night.

CHAPTER FORTY-SIX

Reed rapped his knuckles against Vinny's bedroom door and walked in, pausing mid-step as he stared at Vinny's ghostly pale complexion. He exhaled a deep breath and shoved his hands in his pockets, studying the new IV catheter taped to Vinny's bony arm and the addition of several blankets to his bed. Heather had mentioned Vinny's request for pain medication during the night, but Reed hadn't been expecting such a drastic decline. "Vinny?" he whispered.

Vinny opened his eyes, making no attempt to sit up on his pillows the way he usually did.

Reed moved closer. "How's it going?"

"I'm dying. How do you think?"

"Is there anything I can do? Can I get you anything?"

Vinny shook his head. "You didn't answer my phone calls."

"No." He sat on the edge of the comfy recliner and rubbed at his tired eyes. He hadn't slept in two days—since Bella walked out on him. "I've been busy."

"You look like shit."

He *felt* like shit. Each morning, he'd gotten up and gone to work, then boxed until he almost collapsed, or ran the beach until he was forced to sit down in the sand or fall over. Nothing was easing the pain. His stomach was raw; his heart ached. Bella was done with him. "Thanks."

"Did you talk to her?"

"Yeah." He stood and started pacing. "We talked."

"And?"

"And it's over. We're through." He kicked the baseboard on his next pass. Never had he felt so helpless before. Bella walked away from him and he'd been given no other choice but to live with it. "It's fucking over."

"Give her time."

He shook his head. "I could give her a lifetime and it doesn't change the fact that I lied—that she doesn't trust me anymore." And it was killing him.

Vinny exhaled a quiet, humorless laugh. "If she won't forgive you, I guess I shouldn't hold out much hope."

His gaze whipped to Vinny's. "She hasn't been by to see you?"

Vinny shook his head, looking suddenly old and very vulnerable.

"She'll come. She loves you. She understands the situation."

Vinny struggled to reach for his cup of water and dropped his hand by his side. "We did what was right for her, but she'll never see it that way. She knows about me now. Knows what I did. Who I am."

Reed walked over and brought the straw to Vinny's dry lips. "Who you were. You haven't been that man for decades."

Vinny sipped and swallowed. "It doesn't erase the fact that I ended lives for my father's honor."

Reed set the cup down and sat again. "You've done what you can to right your wrongs. You created a stunning daughter. On her worst day, Bella's better than either one of us on our best. That counts for something."

Vinny smiled. "She's a good girl. There's nothing Kelly and I ever did more right than Bella."

"You didn't have an opportunity to stay with her for very long, but she loves you. Her best memories are of you and her mom at the house in Ohio—the gardens and bike rides in the park." Sweet family moments he and Bella were supposed to have created for their own children but never would.

Vinny nodded. "Those are my favorites too. I've thought of them a million times over the years."

No matter how horrible this was for him right now, it was so much worse for Vinny. "I bet."

Vinny adjusted his blankets. "So, what about the case? What happens now?"

"Skylar handed everything over to the DA yesterday." Telling Vinny that the DA knew about Bella wouldn't do him any good, particularly when Reed had every intention of making sure they kept her out of this entire mess. "We wait to see if he thinks there's enough evidence to bring before the grand jury while Evidence Response keeps looking for bodies in the field."

Vinny frowned. "That's it?"

He nodded. "There's no way this isn't going before the grand jury. We'll get our indictment. We've helped the prosecution build one hell of a strong case. But for now, it's a waiting game."

Vinny grumbled. "What about Bella? How do we know she'll stay safe?"

"I haven't heard anything new from my informant. No news is good news." Although he wanted something: an update on the Walter Hodds situation and his inquiries into Nicoli's kid. It had been nearly three weeks since their meeting in New York—completely unacceptable.

Vinny grumbled again. "That doesn't make me feel any better."

"I'm never going to let anything happen to Bella." He leaned closer, staring Vinny in the eyes, making sure Vinny knew he meant what he said. "No matter how things have ended between Bella and me, I promise you I'll keep her safe."

"Whether she likes it or not?"

He smiled for the first time in forty-eight hours. "Whether she likes it or not."

"You're a good man, Reed. That little girl loves you. Give her time."

He nodded, but he wasn't holding out much hope. He'd seen the finality in her eyes, heard it in her voice when she told him they were finished.

Vinny winced as he pressed his hands to his stomach.

Reed rushed to his feet. "What?"

"Nothing. I've been having some pain the past couple days. I'm tired. Dying's hard on a body."

"Do you want me to get Heather?"

"No. I just need to get some rest."

He nodded. "I'll come by tomorrow."

"You don't have to come by anymore. We've done what we needed to do."

He folded his arms. "I thought we were friends."

Vinny stared at him. "I guess we are."

"I'll see you tomorrow."

Vinny closed his eyes. "I'll see you tomorrow."

Reed walked to the door, studying Vinny. Worrying. He hoped Bella wouldn't wait too long. Vinny was running short on time.

Bella maneuvered through the heavy Thursday night traffic on her way to visit with Dad. Adam Levine's smooth voice crooned through her speakers and the wind played with her hair as she drove with the top down—a scenario sickeningly reminiscent of Tuesday afternoon, except nothing was the same. Smoothies and chats in the garden certainly weren't on the agenda. She wasn't exactly sure what to expect. All she knew was that she and Dad needed to talk.

Dad and Reed were constantly on her mind. Focusing on her job had been a chore. The last two days had easily been the hardest of her life. Never had she been so blindsided—so broken. More than once, she'd contemplated packing a bag and heading out of town with Lucy for a while—ideally to gain a little perspective, but she couldn't be certain Dad had that kind of time. They'd lost precious moments when she stayed away yesterday. She couldn't allow that to happen again today. There were plenty of issues to work out, but she wasn't about to let Dad die alone.

Slowing for her turn, she made a right and pulled into the hospice center parking lot, taking the first spot she could find. Eager to get inside, she hurried up the path and opened the door, sending the nightshift nurse a small smile as she stopped at the front desk. "Hi, Wanda."

"Good evening, Bella. Don't you look beautiful."

She smiled again, still dressed for the day in the simple black pencil skirt and fitted white top she'd pulled out of her closet this morning. "Thank you. How's Dad doing?"

"He's been in quite a bit of pain over the last twenty-four hours. Last night we inserted an IV catheter to administer some medication since he's having trouble keeping things down."

"Oh," she said quietly as waves of guilt swamped her. Dad was hurting and she hadn't been there for him.

"Heather administered another dose shortly after Reed left this afternoon."

She perked up, trying to ignore the uptick in her pulse. "Reed was here?"

"He was." Wanda grinned. "Vinny certainly enjoys his company."

"Yes, he does. They have a very special relationship." She cleared her throat and fiddled with her purse strap, not quite sure of what else to say on that subject. "Um, I'm going to go on down."

"Okay, honey. Vinny's medicine will be wearing off soon. If he starts getting uncomfortable, just let me know."

"Thank you." She turned and started down the hall, walking slowly, her nerves compounding with every step closer to the door. Taking a deep breath, she lifted her hand and gave a quick knock, then stepped inside. "Daddy?"

He opened his eyes in the dim lamplight and tried to sit up. "Bella."

"Oh, Daddy, don't. Stay lying down." She hurried over, shocked by how pale he was—by how much a mere two days had changed his appearance. "Just stay lying down," she soothed, quickly pulling over the wooden chair Joey had been sitting in on Tuesday.

He let his head rest against the pillow, wheezing with every breath. "I wasn't sure you would come back."

Her guilt compounded as she studied the man who'd been a starry-eyed little girl's hero. Once upon a time, he'd been so strong and handsome. Now he looked old and fragile. His eyes were so dull, yet radiated a staggering vulnerability that broke her heart. "Of course I was coming back." She took his hand, holding on tight as she fought to keep her voice steady. "I just needed a chance to figure things out."

"I'm so sorry about all of this." He gave her fingers a squeeze. "Every bit of it."

She bowed her head and blinked rapidly, trying but failing to keep her tears from falling.

"I'm sorry, Bella."

She nodded, unable to meet his gaze—unable to speak.

"I wish I could have done things differently. I would have given just about anything to make that possible."

"I know," she shuddered out.

"When I met your mom, I saw my shot at a normal life—at having everything I was never able to in Brooklyn."

She met his gaze. "I wish I'd known—"

He shook his head. "I didn't want you to."

She plucked a tissue from the side table and wiped her nose. "What made you leave? Why did you go?"

"I picked you up from preschool one afternoon. You were such a bright, beautiful girl, Bella. My pride and joy." He smiled. "It was a couple days before your birthday. I took you with me to get some auto parts so Mom could run errands for your party. When we got to the shop, one of the guys kept staring at me. He told me I looked like Nicoli Caparelli. You piped right up and told him that I wasn't Nicoli. My name was Vinny and you were Isabella Raine Colby. At that moment, I knew I had to go. How many more times would someone recognize me? What happened when the wrong person spotted me and I had my baby girl with me, or her mother?"

"We needed you." She held him tighter. "I needed you."

He closed his eyes. "I missed you every day, but I couldn't risk you. I couldn't drag you into witness protection with me—continually changing your name, having to leave your life behind at a moment's notice, making you a constant target. I never wanted that for you."

She sniffled, remembering Reed telling her that there wasn't anything her father wouldn't have done to keep her safe. "You were always so good to me—the best daddy any daughter could ask for."

"You made it easy. You were my sweet baby girl—always so kind. Those few years I had with you and your mother were the absolute best of my life." He kissed her knuckles. "Leaving you two was the hardest thing I ever had to do. I couldn't at first. I followed you—kept an eye on things."

She blinked as a memory flashed through her mind. "The day at the park in Kentucky. I saw you standing in the trees by the monkey bars. When I ran over to tell Mom and looked back, you were gone."

He nodded. "I left after that. I wanted to pick you up and take you with me—both of you. I almost let you see me again, but I turned and left instead." He squeezed her hand as his eyes watered.

"I'm sorry you had to go." She pressed her lips together as they trembled, collecting herself. "I wish so much that you could have stayed."

"Me too, but you had a good life. You and your mom. You had a good life."

She nodded, wanting to give him that peace, even if it wasn't entirely true. He'd sacrificed so much for her. "We had a great life, Daddy. I had a wonderful life."

"That's all I've ever wanted."

"You gave up everything."

"Because they're dangerous. The Caparellis are very, very dangerous, Bella." He tugged her closer. "They'll kill you just because you're mine. Reed's keeping an eye—"

She shook her head. "I don't want to talk about him."

"He loves you. That man loves you to the moon and back."

She looked down, pressing her hand to the pain in her heart, and began sobbing quietly, as she hadn't let herself since she shut Reed out of her life.

"Bella."

She stared at the blankets.

"Isabella." He lifted her chin. "There wasn't a single second during all of this that he wasn't thinking of you—trying to protect you and put you first."

She shook her head as she cried harder.

"There are few people I trust in this world. Maybe two. Reed's the only one I trust with you."

"I can't be with him." How could she explain how deeply his lies had wounded—how much his betrayal hurt? "I *can't*."

Dad wiped away her tears—the way he'd done numerous times when she'd been a little girl. "Maybe you can and maybe you can't. But promise me that if you're in trouble, if he ever comes to you and tells you you're in danger, you'll do what he says."

She sniffled, her rebellious streak breaking through the sorrow.

"Promise me that, Bella. *Promise* me," he said fiercely.

The desperation in his eyes made her nod. "I promise."

"He'll keep you safe. No matter how things work out between you two, I know he'll keep you safe. I need to know you're going to be okay."

"I'll be okay."

"With Reed."

"If I'm in danger," she clarified, not wanting to give Dad false hope. Clearly he wanted them to be together.

He settled back against his pillows and cringed, gripping his stomach.

She rushed to her feet. "Daddy?"

He took her hand again. "I'm running out of time, Bella. I'm running out of time here with you."

She clutched him tighter. "I'll get Wanda. She'll bring you some medicine for the pain."

He nodded. "Okay."

She bolted down the hall, overwhelmed by a sickening sense of helplessness, knowing that there was nothing she could do to make this better for him. "Dad could use something. He's really hurting."

Wanda stood. "We want to keep him as comfortable as we can."

She nodded, tucking her hair behind her ear with trembling fingers. "How much—how much longer do I have with him?"

"Oh, honey, I can't say. I just don't have that answer."

"Of course not. I'm sorry." She hurried back down to Dad and sat by his side on the mattress, settling a supportive hand on his shoulder. "Wanda's coming, Daddy."

"I want you to go home," he struggled to say as he clenched his teeth.

She shook her head. "No, I'm going to stay—"

"I want you to go. I don't want you seeing me like this. I'm just going to sleep anyway. Please, Bella. Go be with Lucy."

"Okay."

Wanda walked in and injected something into the line on Dad's arm. "Here you go, Vinny. This should kick in quick and help you rest."

"Thank you." He looked at Bella again. "I'm going to get some sleep."

She bent over and kissed his forehead—once, twice, then rested her cheek against his cool skin. "I'm just down the road if you need me."

"All right. I love you, Bella."

"I love you too." She hesitated, wanting to stay, but needed to respect his wishes. "I'll see you tomorrow. I'll be back tomorrow," she said, then rushed down the hall and outside, gulping in the fresh air as she got in her car and drove home as fast as the traffic allowed. Making quick work of letting herself into the house, she crouched down in the entryway and hugged Lucy, gripping her close as more tears fell. "Come on, Luce. I need to get out of here. I need the beach."

Lucy followed her to the car.

As Bella opened the passenger side door, she looked toward Reed's place, noting that his bike was gone and the lights were off. Sighing, she stared at his truck. There wasn't a moment in the day when she didn't miss him. Each night, she woke reaching for him. Even after everything that had happened between them, she found herself longing to hold his hand and walk by the water—to breathe him in as he held her close and let him make everything okay again.

She flinched, surprised by her wandering thoughts. "Kneejerk," she whispered as she got in and buckled up, then drove off, reminding herself that Reed didn't belong in her life anymore.

☙ Chapter Forty-Seven ❧

Reed spotted Bella's car in the hospice center parking lot as he got out of his truck and shut the door. He took a step toward the building and hesitated, debating whether it would be better to avoid her and come back after his shift or go in and check on Vinny now. "Fuck it," he muttered and hit the key fob, locking up as he went inside. Bella always went to yoga, then directly to work in the mornings. If she was here at seven a.m., something was going on. He wasn't about to drive off without making sure everything was okay first. He stopped at the front desk, smiling at Heather. "Morning."

Heather smiled back. "Good morning."

"How's Vinny doing today?"

Heather's smile faded. "He had a rough night. Wanda called Bella early this morning."

He nodded, reading between the lines easily enough. Vinny was down to his final hours. "I'm going to head down."

"Okay."

He moved down the hall and stopped outside the half-closed door, absorbing the punch of longing as he stared at Bella holding Vinny's hand while he slept. Three days. It had been three endless days since their paths had crossed. She'd pulled her hair back in a messy ponytail and wore a simple outfit of snug jeans and a white T-shirt, but she was stunning nonetheless. Fisting his hand, he rapped a quiet knock on the doorframe and stepped inside.

She turned her head, locking gazes with him.

He clenched his jaw as his heart kicked up to a wild beat. How was it that she took his breath away every single time? "Hey."

Bella swallowed. "Hey."

He absently petted Lucy as the sweet puppy walked up to his side and leaned against his leg the way she usually did. "How's he doing?"

Bella shook her head. "Not good. He's in and out of it."

She was exhausted. And hurting. The pain was radiating from her big brown eyes. "What can I do?"

She looked away, staring down at the floor. "Nothing."

Damn, this was agony, watching her go through this alone when he was right here. He walked over to her chair and crouched down, wanting to pull her against him—to comfort and hold her close, but he kept his hands to himself. "Have you had breakfast?"

"I'm not hungry."

He breathed in the scent of her shampoo as he settled on his knees in front of her, waiting for her to meet his gaze again. "You need to eat, Bella. To take care of yourself."

She blinked as tears pooled in her eyes. "I'm fine."

"No, you're not."

A tear fell. "I'll get something later."

Sighing, he stroked his knuckles along her cheek, unable to resist any longer. "Did you get any sleep?"

She snagged her bottom lip with her teeth and closed her eyes as she moved into his touch. "A little."

He opened his hand and rested his palm against her soft skin. "How much is a little?"

She eased away, pushing at his arm. "A couple hours, I think."

He gripped the edges of her chair, his assurance to himself that he wouldn't reach for her again. "Do you want me to take Lucy? I can bring her home."

She shook her head. "You never gave me back my key."

He hadn't picked up his stuff either. He wasn't ready to say things were over, even if Bella already had. "I don't know how to walk away from you. I don't know how to stop wanting you."

She exhaled a shaky breath. "I can't do this—"

"Bella," Vinny whispered.

Reed gained his feet as Bella leaned in close to Vinny.

"I'm here, Daddy."

Vinny opened his eyes. "Reed."

"I'm right here, Vinny."

"I need to talk to you."

"I'm right here," he repeated.

Bella stood as the tension between them came rushing back. "I'll be out in the hall."

Vinny waited while Bella walked out of the room. "Help me."

Reed sat in the chair Bella had abandoned, studying the frail, helpless man who had once been his enemy. "What do you need?"

"I have money for Bella. At the rental in Reseda. It's in the floorboard under the rug in my bedroom. Get it for her. Hold on to it until after the funeral. I don't want her spending it on my box for the ground."

He nodded. "I'll get it."

"The key's in the drawer over there." He tried to lift his hand.

Reed settled his arm back on the bed. "I'll find it."

"Make sure you tell her it's honest money—from my days as a mechanic and the chunk they gave me from WITSEC in the beginning."

"I'll tell her."

Vinny gripped Reed's hand. "Take care of her. Take care of my little girl. I need to know she's going to be all right."

He squeezed back, hearing the desperation in Vinny's quiet voice. "I promise I'm never going to let anything happen to Bella."

Vinny nodded. "Don't give up on her." He coughed, then winced. "She loves you." He swallowed loudly as he fought for every breath. "My brother—I'm sorry he hurt your family."

"You don't have to apologize for him. You righted your wrongs. The two of us are square."

"They could learn something from you. Honor and respect. I'm not sorry I met you, Reed."

"You're not so bad yourself."

Vinny smiled, then closed his eyes.

Reed stood, not wanting to occupy too much of Vinny's time when he didn't have much left. "I'll come by tomorrow."

Vinny opened his eyes and shook his head. "I won't be here tomorrow."

He steamed out a long breath, seeing the knowledge in Vinny's glassy eyes. Bending down, he gave him a hug. "I'll take care of her."

The heavy weight of Vinny's arm settled on his back. "I can rest easier knowing you will."

He eased away. "Good-bye, Vinny."

"Good-bye."

Reed cleared his throat and turned from the bed, brushing away the tear rolling down his cheek. Looking up, he met Bella's gaze while she watched him from the doorway. He walked to the drawer, grabbed Vinny's key, and stopped in front of her on his way out. "I'm going."

She nodded.

He started down the hall, surprised when he had to wipe at his cheeks again. Grieving the death of Nicoli Caparelli was nothing he'd ever expected.

"Reed," Bella called as he made it to the front desk.

He stopped and turned.

She hurried after him, holding his gaze as she closed the distance between them.

He automatically reached for her hands as he scrutinized the myriad emotions playing over her face—sorrow, regret. "What is it?"

"I don't—" She shook her head. "I can't be with—we can't..." She lifted his hand and cradled his palm against her cheek. "I don't want you to be sad. I don't want you to hurt."

He pulled her against him, loving her impossibly more as he wrapped her up in a tight hug and closed his eyes. Bella's intention was to offer comfort and support because she was too kind not to, but she was ripping him apart. He pressed a kiss to her forehead and let her go. "If there's anything I can do, let me know."

She nodded.

He turned and pushed through the door, noting that the clouds were starting to swallow the sun as he got in his truck. Taking his seat, he slammed his hands against the steering wheel. "Fuck!" This wasn't *right*. Things weren't supposed to have turned out this way. They loved each other, damn it. And Bella needed him. She was dealing with Vinny's last moments on her own when he'd promised to be there for her. He swore again as he yanked his phone out of his pocket and dialed Ethan.

"Hello?"

"Hey, it's Reed." He let his head settle back against the rest. "I'm at the hospice center. Vinny's more than likely not going to make it through the day."

"I'm sorry."

"I'm going to call Tyson and see if he can cover Sadie. I'll take a couple of round-the-clock shifts to make it up to him."

"We'll figure something out."

He turned over the ignition and secured his seat belt, ready to be on his way. "Vinny asked me to do something. I want to get it taken care of before the landlord rents out his place and I can't get in there anymore."

"Why don't I call Tyson for you?"

He backed out of his spot, glancing at Bella's car in the rearview mirror. "I appreciate it."

"Let me know if there's anything else you need."

"I will. Thanks." He hung up and pulled into traffic, starting east toward the 405. Pressing on the gas, he watched the miles pass, making it to Reseda in an hour's time. He eased to a stop on Darby Avenue, looking around before he got out at the curb, well aware that even as Vinny lay on his deathbed, the threats to his life were still very real. As far as the mafia was concerned, the contract was worth a payout until Nicoli Caparelli was six feet under.

He unlocked the door and stopped in the empty living room, noting that the landlord hadn't wasted any time moving Vinny's stuff out—not that there had been much. Making a quick sweep of the small place, he went back to the bedroom where the rug had once been and crouched down, trying to figure out which board hid Bella's money. He gave the slats a wiggle until he found the loose piece of wood and pried it free.

"Bingo," he muttered, lifting an old Nike shoebox out of the tight space. He opened it, whooshing out a breath as he stared at the nine-millimeter pistol and rolls of cash. "Holy shit," he whispered, picking up a bundle, realizing that there were dozens upon dozens of hundred dollar bills. There had to be half a million dollars here—easy. He grabbed the two pictures tucked along the side: one of Vinny and Bella's mother when Kelly Colby had been very young and pregnant. Vinny's eyes had been soft—in love and happy. Then he looked at sweet Bella Colby grinning her huge grin as she sat in the child's seat on the back of Vinny's bike. The happy life she'd had—the one she wanted back and actively sought. The one he could no longer offer her or be a part of.

Sighing, he set the gun on the floor then picked up the folded sheet of notebook paper taped to the inside top and opened it, reading Vinny's handwriting.

Bella,
Have a happy life. That's all I've ever wanted for you.
I love you,
Dad

He folded it closed and shut the box, then checked the safety on the weapon before shoving the Glock into the back of his jeans. He looked around the empty room, put the board back, and stood, leaving Vinny Pescoe's house for the last time.

Bella sat by Dad's bedside, listening to the soothing cricket song playing through the open French doors. She held his hand, staring at him in the dim lamplight, etching into her mind her final hours with her father while he slept. Throughout most of the evening, Wanda had been in and out of the room, checking on both her and Dad as his breathing patterns changed and the end grew nearer. She studied his sunken eyes and hollow cheeks, already mourning the short amount of time they'd had together. Memories of bike rides and bedtime stories were hardly enough. She wanted so much more. When she knocked on his door, she'd anticipated years together, not months. Dad was supposed to have walked her down the aisle and snuggled his grandbabies. They were supposed to have sat around festive holiday tables and unwrapped gifts under beautifully decorated trees, but that would never be.

She squeezed his fingers as she suddenly grew afraid, realizing she was losing her only link to the past. "Daddy," she whispered in a shuddering breath, willing him to wake up and share happy stories she could cling to long after he was gone. "You were so handsome and Mom so pretty." She smiled, thinking of the few pictures she had. "Like a fairy tale—"

Someone interrupted with a gentle knock on the door.

She turned, squashing her disappointment when Wanda stood in the doorway instead of Reed.

"I have some dinner for you, honey." Wanda held up a white bag from Bella's favorite deli. "Reed brought it by. He told me to tell you to eat it."

She closed her eyes, missing him—needing him. "Thank you."

Wanda set the paper sack on the table and walked to Bella's side, resting her hand on her shoulder. "I can give him a call if you would like. I'm sure he'll come back and sit with you."

She shook her head as she sniffled. "Reed and I—we're not seeing each other anymore."

Wanda's eyes softened with understanding. "I'm sorry to hear that."

She plucked a tissue from the box and wiped her nose. "Sometimes things don't work out."

"Maybe they will for you. I've been doing this job for almost fifteen years, and life and love still never cease to amaze me."

Bella shook her head again, certain that there would be no happy ending for her and Reed. "I don't think so."

Wanda gave her a sympathetic squeeze. "Make sure you have something to eat, honey."

She nodded. "I will."

"I'll come check on you in a little while."

"Thank you," she said, staring at the bag on the table, catching a whiff of her favorite sandwich as Wanda left. She turned away as she flashed back to her embrace with Reed this morning—when he'd wrapped her up tight the way she missed the most. She'd been helpless to do anything but hurry after him when she watched a tear roll down his cheek after he gave Dad a hug. Her family had murdered his father, grandfather, and uncle, yet he'd been nothing but wonderful to both her and her dad. Except for Reed telling her lie after lie for months on end, he was pretty much the perfect guy. Her breath trembled in and out as she shook her head, not wanting to think of him anymore.

"He loves you," Dad mumbled.

Her gaze whipped to his as she clutched his hand. "Daddy."

His face scrunched up in pain. "I'm tired, Bella."

Lucy stood from her spot close by and walked over to the bed.

"She's a good dog."

"Yes, she is."

His gaze wandered back to Bella's. "You're a good girl, Bella. You're the best thing that's ever come out of my life. I'm proud of the woman you've become."

Tears rained down her cheeks, knowing that he was saying goodbye. "I love you, Daddy." She pressed his hand to her cheek. "No matter what happened, I love you, and I'm proud of you for doing what you could to make things right. I'm so lucky to call you my dad."

He opened his trembling hand, holding his palm against her skin. "I want you to be happy—to be okay."

She tried to smile. "I will be. I am."

"Don't walk away from Reed so easy. You get only one love of your life."

Her smile crumbled into quiet crying.

"Don't cry, Bella." He groaned in pain. "Don't cry for me."

She wiped her eyes.

"I'm so tired."

"I know you are." She brushed the hair back from his forehead. "I know you are, Daddy. Close your eyes." She kissed his cheek. "You can go. I'm going to be just fine."

"Don't let Reed go, Bella," he said quietly. "I love you, Bella Boop."

"I love you too." She rested her head against the side of his hand as he held hers. "I love you, Daddy."

He breathed in and out several times in the quiet of the night before his hand went lax on hers.

She looked up, waiting for his chest to rise again, but it didn't. "Oh, Daddy. Oh, Daddy, good-bye." She kept his hand gripped in hers as she pressed her face to Lucy's neck and sobbed.

☙ Chapter Forty-Eight ❧

Reed sat at his desk, staring out into the dark through his open bedroom window. He had work to do—a couple of follow-up questions to answer for the DA. And he still needed to respond to Skylar's texts. Earlier this afternoon, Evidence Response had brought up another body. Not long after, the anthropologists found a bullet lodged in the corpse's skull. Things were moving along in New York, but he couldn't focus on the Caparellis right now. His mind was on Bella. For hours, she'd occupied his thoughts. Not a minute had passed when he hadn't wondered and worried about her. He could barely tolerate the idea of her sitting by Vinny's side alone, but that's what she seemed to want, so he'd done what he could to offer her support by dropping off a freaking turkey sandwich while her father lay on his deathbed.

He rubbed at his tense jaw and gave his attention back to the laptop. The sooner he wrapped this up, the better. He settled his fingers on home row and got to work just as his phone started ringing. Pausing mid-thought, he glanced at the screen and yanked it up when Southern California Hospice Center popped up on the readout. "Hello?"

"Reed, this is Wanda from hospice."

He sat farther up in his seat. "Hey. How's Vinny?" Although he was afraid he already knew.

"I'm sorry to say that he passed away about half an hour ago."

He closed his eyes and steamed out a breath. "How's Bella doing?"

"I think she might need you."

He clenched his jaw, wishing that were true, but the last person Bella wanted or needed was him. "I'm not so sure—" He cleared his throat. "We're not together anymore."

"Vinny made me promise to give you a call after he passed. He told me that Bella would need you and you would come."

"All right." He stood and grabbed a T-shirt from his drawer to pair with the black athletic shorts he was already wearing as he slipped his feet into his flip-flops. "I'll be right there."

"I'll see you soon."

"Okay." He ran down the stairs and snagged his keys off the counter, then hurried to his truck, making quick work of heading toward the hospice center. Vinny was gone and Bella was left to grieve on her own. Maybe that's exactly the way she wanted it, but he'd promised Vinny he would take care of her—whether she liked it or not. Probably she would ask him to leave, but he was going to make sure she was all right first.

He breezed through several green lights, then pressed on the gas when the next light turned yellow. Within minutes, he was pulling into a parking spot close to Bella's car and jogging to the door. He stepped inside and moved to the front desk.

Wanda stood from her chair, blinking as she glanced from her watch to him. "That was quick."

He slid his fingers through his hair. "We live right down the road."

"Thank you for coming, honey."

He would have been here all along if it had been up to him. "She's down with Vinny?"

"Yes. Bella told me she wanted to be alone, but I think she could use some support."

He nodded and walked down the hall, stopping in the doorway as he stared at Bella hunched in her seat, clutching Vinny's hand between both of hers while Lucy sat close by her side. He exhaled a quiet breath as he moved to her chair, crouching down next to her. "Hey, beautiful."

She looked at him with red-rimmed eyes and her nose pink. "He's gone."

"I know. Wanda called me."

Her lips trembled as tears fell. "He's getting—he's not that warm anymore. I covered him with another blanket, but..." She sucked in several shaky breaths.

"Bella," he whispered as he skimmed his fingers along her jaw. Losing Vinny was tough, but seeing her like this was heart-wrenching. "Why don't I take you home?"

She shook her head. "I want to stay."

"There's nothing more you can do for him. Let Wanda have her turn." He lifted Vinny's hand out of her gentle hold and settled his arm by his side.

"I can't leave him," she sobbed out. "I know he's not here anymore, but I can't make myself get up and leave him."

"All right," he soothed as he lifted her into his arms and grabbed her purse. "Let's go home. Come on, Lucy."

Bella nestled her face into the crook of his neck and cried quietly.

"We'll get outside and get some fresh air," he murmured next to her ear as he headed down the hall. "Thank you," he said to Wanda and walked out to his truck, settling Bella in the passenger side and buckling her belt.

"I can't go home with you."

"Yeah, you can." He wiped her cheeks. "Just for tonight." He closed her in and opened the back for Lucy. "Up you go."

Lucy hopped in without hesitation.

"Good girl." He gave her a solid pat, then got in and started home in the heavy silence, glancing Bella's way several times as she stared out her open window. She was exhausted—running on fumes and grief. "We'll get you some dinner and get you into bed."

"I just want a shower."

He had every intention of making sure she ate something before she fell asleep, but he said nothing more as he turned into their development, then pulled into her driveway shortly after.

Bella got out and walked up the path to her front door.

He let Lucy out of the back and followed, twisting his key in the lock while Bella searched through her purse for her own.

She glanced up at him, then went upstairs with her puppy following behind.

Muttering a curse, he moved into the kitchen, grabbing the makings for a sandwich as the water turned on in the master bathroom. He added Dijon mustard and turkey to the slices of whole grain bread, pulled a plate from the cupboard, and walked upstairs to the bedroom as Bella crawled onto her bed in one of her sexy camisoles.

"Thank you for driving me," she said as she sat in the center of the mattress, hooking her arms around her knees.

"You're welcome." He joined her in the middle, sitting crisscross by her side. "I made you something to eat."

"I'm not really hungry."

He lifted a half. "Try a couple of bites."

She took the sandwich and nibbled on the corner. "You don't have to stay. I'm fine."

He shook his head, watching her eyes well while she held his gaze. "You don't have to be okay tonight."

She set the sandwich down and covered her face with her hands as she started crying.

"Come here." He lifted her, settling her bottom in the empty space between his legs, and pulled her against him, holding her tight.

She rested her head on his shoulder as she returned his embrace.

"I'm sorry about your dad," he said quietly as he slid his hands up and down her back. "I'm sorry you went through that alone."

She sniffled, gripping him tighter. "I wanted more time with him. We hardly had any at all."

He let his cheek rest against her temple. "I know."

"He's not in pain anymore." She eased away enough to meet his gaze. "Do you think he's okay?"

He tucked her wet hair behind her ear. "I think he's in a perfect place."

She nodded.

He took her hand, bringing her knuckles to his lips. "What can I do, Bella? How can I help you?"

She shook her head. "I don't know. I don't think you can." More tears fell.

He wiped them away with a gentle slide of his thumb. "It's hard to do nothing when I know you're sad."

She closed her eyes as she shuddered out a breath and let her forehead rest against his.

He cupped her cheeks, stroking her soft skin. "Do you want me to take Lucy tonight so you can get some sleep?"

"No."

He pressed a chaste kiss to her lips. "Are you going to be okay?"

"Yes. Eventually." She held his gaze and returned his kiss with one of her own.

He could see the pain and vulnerability in her eyes. The desire. "Bella—"

She moved in again, capturing his mouth, nipping and nibbling as her fingers slid through his hair.

He let his eyes flutter closed, helplessly responding, letting his tongue tangle with hers as he pulled her closer and plundered.

She whimpered as her hands trailed down his biceps and up his forearms.

He took them both deeper, needing, aching as she moaned. He

wanted her. Wanted this, but not when she wasn't thinking straight. "Bella." He pulled back. "We can't do this."

Her chest heaved as she stared at him.

"I'm not going to give you another reason to hate me in the morning."

"I don't hate you." Her eyes watered as she gripped his wrists. "I don't hate you, Reed, but I can't be with you."

He clenched his jaw, refusing to accept what she was saying, but for now he was going to have to. "Let's get you into bed."

She untangled herself from his hold and moved to pull back the covers.

He got to his feet as she settled in. "I'm sorry, Bella." He crouched down by her side. "About everything."

"Why did you have to lie? Why did you have to *change* everything?"

"Because your dad and I both thought it was the right thing."

She shook her head.

He jammed his hand through his hair. Now wasn't the time for this. "Let me know if you need anything."

"I won't." She swallowed. "I won't need anything."

He got her gist easy enough and had every intention of backing off for now. She needed time and space to grieve. "You know where I am if you change your mind." He gained his feet and left when all he wanted to do was stay.

The endless night ticked slowly into day while Bella rested her head on her arm and stared at Reed's empty side of the bed. Rain poured outside her windows—the weather a perfect match for her mood. She had no more tears left to shed despite the constant ache in her chest, so the sky cried for her. She blinked her tired eyes and toyed with the edge of Reed's pillowcase, yearning to go back to Tuesday morning when she woke snuggled and happy in his arms. They'd made crazy, passionate love before they parted ways for the day, Dad had been alive, and she'd been oblivious to the truth hidden behind all of their lies.

Sighing, she rolled over and faced the wall, wishing desperately that she didn't miss Reed. There were two huge holes in her heart, but loneliness and heartbreak were no excuse to make bad decisions—

like she had hours ago when she kissed Reed and had been ready to take him to bed. It would have been easy to get lost in him—to let pleasure banish the worst of her pain, but it frightened her to know that she'd nearly let herself fall prey to the self-destructive streak that ran so strong in the Colby genes.

Somewhere along the way, Mom had succumbed to her fair share of hard knocks. She'd been completely shattered after Dad left, and slowly the woman who'd believed that smart, pretty girls could have it all drowned in her own despair.

Reed's betrayal had rocked her to her core; her life was certainly falling apart, but she refused to follow Mom's path. If she chose to, she could take Reed back and pretend that everything between them would be fine. A huge part of her wanted to get out of her bed and crawl into his, but where would that leave them in the end? Reed said he loved her and she believed him. She had no doubt that the man next door was the love of her life, but she couldn't be with someone who loved the way he did. She didn't want to spend the rest of her days second-guessing and putting up walls, waiting for him to disappoint and destroy her again.

It devastated her to know that she and Reed had no future together. Tonight had been their true end. From this point forward, there was no reason for their paths to cross except in the most casual of ways. She planned to keep her distance and make sure he did the same. If the Caparellis ever discovered her identity, she would honor her promise to Dad and take the help Reed could give, but she couldn't build a life with him. She needed to take care of herself and heal her heart the way Mom's never had. Time was the answer—lots of time until she was whole once again. "Everything's going to be all right," she mumbled as her eyes drooped closed and she rolled, pulling Reed's pillow closer, breathing him in as she finally slept.

☙ Chapter Forty-Nine ❧

Reed stood beneath his umbrella in the pouring rain, half-listening to the priest welcoming Vincent Pescoe into eternal life. Gray clouds hung low and the wind blew cool, compounding Vinny's pathetic idea of a funeral. The one-time mobster had arranged his own no-frills service: no music, flowers, or additional friends, just two people standing by his graveside to bid him a final farewell. If Reed had been aware of Vinny's meager plans, he would have stopped off for a couple of bouquets—something pretty Bella would have liked to chase away some of the gloom.

He stared at her across the simple pine casket, watching the breeze toy with the curls she'd added to her glossy hair. The basic black skirt and white cardigan she'd paired with pumps added a hint of sexy vulnerability to her looks. Even in mourning, Bella was nothing short of spectacular.

She glanced up, meeting his gaze with devastated eyes, and quickly looked down.

He fisted his hands, watching as another tear trailed down her cheek. He should have been standing by her side. They should have been coping with the loss of her father together, but they both stood alone because that's what Bella wanted.

It had been three days since they sat on her bed—three days since they'd spoken. He'd expected her to take some time to rest and regroup after Vinny's death, but every morning since her dad's passing, he'd watched her walk out to her car and head off to yoga while he drank his first cup of coffee. Last night, he'd spotted her coming home well after sunset, holding her beach hat in hand. Bella was moving on with her life without him.

He blinked, realizing the service was over when Bella walked over to Father Ludwick.

"Thank you." She smiled sadly. "This meant so much."

Father Ludwick took her hand. "May you find comfort in knowing that your father is at peace in God's Kingdom."

"I do. Thank you again for everything." She turned and started toward her car, pausing when she and Reed made eye contact again.

Reed fell into step beside her, breathing in her familiar scent. "Hey."

She quickened her pace. "Hi."

"How are you holding up?"

"Fine, thanks."

So this was what the cold shoulder from Bella felt like. Over the past week, she'd been angry and hurt, but they'd still had a strong connection. She'd still been willing to let him in. That didn't appear to be the case today. "I have something for you. From Vinny."

She faltered, then kept going. "I can't do this right now."

"Bella." He reached out, snagging her wrist, torturing himself with the feel of her soft skin.

Sighing, she stopped.

He noted she wore the bracelet her dad had given her for her birthday. "It's something he wanted you to have. He asked me to hold on to it for you. If you want to stop by, I can get it for you, or I can bring it over."

She swallowed. "I'll, um, I'll stop by. Are you going to work?"

He shook his head. "Tyson and I switched shifts. I'm covering him tonight."

She expelled another long, quiet breath, clearly uncomfortable with the idea.

"It'll only take a minute."

"All right."

"I'll see you at the house."

She nodded and walked to her car.

He stood where he was, watching her get in, collapse her umbrella, then drive off without bothering to look his way. "Son of a bitch," he muttered as he scrubbed his hand over his jaw. Bella definitely had her guard up. Clearly she'd meant what she said when she told him she wouldn't be needing anything from him. Part of him—the part that was terrified he wouldn't find a way to get her back—wanted to knock at the walls she was building up, but that wasn't what she needed right now.

He hurried to his truck and caught up to Bella on Sunset Boulevard, stopping behind her car at a red light. He glanced at the laptop bag on his passenger seat when the burner phone he kept close by started ringing. Reaching inside, he felt around until he made contact with the plastic. "Hello?"

"I talked to Felipio," Bruno said right away.

He narrowed his eyes, hearing the edginess in Bruno's words as he accelerated with the traffic again. "And?"

"And he says Dino had a little sit-down with that Hodds guy you were talking about—the Marshal."

He tightened his grip on the phone. "Why?"

"Sounds like Hodds was Nicoli's handler."

Son of a bitch. The mob sure as hell wasn't supposed to know that. "Do you know where Nicoli is?"

"No."

He slowed for the next light in the busy midmorning traffic. "Do they?"

"I didn't get a chance to ask. Matty walked into the bar where we were drinking."

He took his hand off the wheel to rub at the tense muscles in his neck before he started moving again. "What about the kid?"

"Felipio wouldn't say."

"Wouldn't say or doesn't know?"

"I'm assuming doesn't know."

"Fuck, Bruno, what the hell kind of information is this?"

"Everybody's watching everybody. I don't know who I can trust anymore. Even Felipio's watching his back—hardly drinking anymore."

Reed shook his head as he turned into the neighborhood. "Just keep digging. I'll send some money your way."

"I don't want the money. I want a deal. I want out."

"I can't get you out without something big. I've already told you that. You get me something on Matty—get me more information on Hodds and Dino—where the organization thinks Nicoli is. Some sort of official confirmation about the kid, and I'll talk to my guy on the inside."

"There's gotta be more you can do."

He wasn't doing jack shit until he knew without a doubt that Bella was in the clear. "Get me something better, Bruno. It sounds like your life depends on it. I'll put your money in the mail." He hung up and shoved the phone back in the bag as he pulled into his driveway. Four fucking weeks and he *still* had more questions than answers. He glanced Bella's way as she got out of her car. The Caparellis and New York were going to have to wait. The next few minutes belonged to the woman next door.

⸻

Bella drove home listening to the monotonous back-and-forth motion of her windshield wipers as she stopped for another traffic light. She'd been hoping for a better day for Dad—warmth and sunshine. He'd deserved both, but the rain and slight chill in the air had welcomed him to his final resting place. Despite the gloomy morning, it felt good to know he was at peace. She would always miss him and wish they'd had more time, but she found comfort in believing that Mom and Dad were finally together.

Life was supposed to get back to normal now. She was supposed to grieve and wake every morning knowing that each day was going to be a little easier than the last. She was supposed to make dates with friends, eagerly sign up for cooking classes, and love her morning yoga the way she had before everything fell apart. And the man following her home wasn't supposed to own her heart.

He'd respected her wishes, giving her plenty of space over the last three days. They hadn't seen each other since the night she kissed him on her bed. Then, an hour ago, she'd spotted him in the cemetery, walking her way through the downpour, dressed in a black suit and tie. She gripped the steering wheel tighter, remembering the way her heart had fluttered a quick beat every time she'd met his bold blue eyes over Dad's casket.

She glanced in her rearview mirror, watching Reed talking on the phone. When would she stop *aching* for him? Why couldn't she just loathe him for everything he'd done? She focused on the road again and took the turn into their development, then pulled into her driveway, steeling herself for another encounter she wasn't quite certain she was strong enough to handle.

Reed pulled into his spot next to his covered bike and got out, getting soaked.

She grabbed her umbrella and walked over to where he stood under the roof's overhang, swallowing when she realized his eyelashes were all spiky from the rain. "I can—I'll just wait here."

He shook his head. "Come on in." He moved to his door and unlocked it.

"I really don't mind waiting."

"It's pouring, and I'm not giving you your father's last gift at the front door." He walked in, not sticking around to see if she followed.

Sighing, she abandoned her umbrella by the doorframe and went inside, staring at the furniture in the living room and coffee-hued paint on the walls. The huge comfy couch he'd liked was in place on a white shag rug, and the dark, chunky TV stand held a big-screen. She felt herself frown as she glanced around at the masculine lamps, tables, and leafy plant tucked in the corner. Why did it bother her so much to see his home starting to take shape? She turned away and looked to the ceiling as he walked overhead, then toward the door, more than a little tempted to leave.

Seconds later his footsteps echoed on the steps as he hurried downstairs, carrying a box and pulling a dry T-shirt down his washboard abs. He'd changed into jeans and looked just as good now as he had minutes ago—maybe better. Her *GQ* standards were no more. She was a full-fledged fan of T-shirts and blue jeans: Reed McKinley's style. Or she had been, anyway.

Crossing her arms, she rubbed them warm with her hands. "Option three."

He frowned. "I'm sorry?"

She gestured to his homier living room. "The furniture and paint. Option three from the binder."

"Yeah. I figure I might as well get comfy since I'll be here for a while." He shrugged, staring at her as he stood in front of her.

And now she understood her negative reaction as she glanced at his furnishings again. He would be here in his condo because they no longer lived together. They wouldn't be buying the sweet little house and making babies in the moonlight. She cleared her throat as she met his gaze.

"How are you, Bella?"

"I'm hanging in there," she said quietly, seeing that there was strain in his eyes. This wasn't easy for him either. "You?"

"I'm all right."

She nodded, looking at the shoebox he held. "That's from Dad?"

He nodded.

"What is it?"

He handed it over. "Go ahead and take a look."

She took the box and whooshed out a small breath, surprised by its weight. "I didn't realize it was going to be so heavy. Thanks for holding onto this." She backed up, ready to turn toward the door.

"You might want to take a look before you go."

Something in his tone made her walk to his counter and open it there. Her eyes went huge as she stared at the rolls of money. "It's—what..." She gently pulled on the piece of paper taped to the inside of the lid and unfolded it, reading Dad's handwriting.

Bella,
Have a happy life. That's all I've ever wanted for you.
I love you,
Dad

She pressed her lips together as they started to tremble, and she gasped as she noticed the photos tucked along the sides. "Pictures," she whispered as she pulled them free, looking at Mom and Dad, skimming a gentle finger over both of their faces. "They're so beautiful. So happy."

Reed stepped closer by her side. "You can see it in their eyes."

She looked at him, then at the next photo of herself as a little girl, grinning as she sat in the seat on the back of Dad's bike. She treasured this so much more than the cash. "Where did this come from? Did he rob a bank?" It shamed her that the thought even crossed her mind, but she couldn't keep money that belonged to someone else.

"No. He wanted me to be sure to tell you every dollar of that is honest. He saved it from his years as a mechanic and his early days in WITSEC."

She frowned. "From Witness Protection?"

"They usually give witnesses enough to get started. High-caliber guys like your dad get more—lots more. It's an incentive to stay safe and follow the rules. Witnesses tend to live longer, and the Feds know they have access to them again if future cases warrant their testimony."

She looked at the picture of her dad, understanding the nostalgic portrait wasn't as simple as it seemed. "You knew him better than I did."

He shook his head. "Only about his old life—pieces of his past, but not the parts that counted the most." He pointed to the pictures she still held. "He saved the best for you, Bella. He absolutely adored you."

She blinked as her eyes watered. "He cared about you—trusted you."

"The feeling was mutual. I'm sorry he's gone."

She looked at the money again, choosing to focus on that rather than her constant sense of sadness. "There's so much."

"Probably half a million, maybe a little less—could be a little more."

She puffed out a breath, still in disbelief. "I don't know what to do with this. I can't just walk into a bank."

"Get yourself a safe deposit box—start transferring some of it over slowly and hold on to the rest of it there for now."

Planning to do so immediately, she put the pictures back and secured the lid. "Thank you."

"Be careful."

"I'm going to get a safe deposit box right away."

"I'm talking about the Caparellis, Bella. I just heard from my informant on the drive home."

She looked away, not wanting to hear about the horrible men in New York. "Do they know about me—who I am?"

"I'm not sure. At this point, probably not, but they figured out who Vinny's handler was."

She shook her head as she shrugged. "Handler?"

"The man who looked after your dad while he was in the Witness Protection Program."

Jargon she didn't want to understand—a life she wanted no part of.

"At this point, you need to be keeping your eyes open—paying attention to your surroundings."

"I am."

"If you see anything that seems off, feels off, I need to know."

She nodded, burying the stirrings of fear, and started toward the door.

"Bella." He snagged her by the hand, sliding his thumb along the sensitive skin of her wrist. "Matty's dangerous. He's not the man you met at Luisa's party."

She removed her arm from his hold, finding his touch to be too much. "I'll be careful."

"This has to be your secret."

Whether she wanted it or not. "I know."

"You'll tell me if anything seems wrong?"

"I'll tell you." She turned toward the door again.

"Wait."

She closed her eyes, not sure how much longer she could take this, and opened them as she turned to look at him.

"You're going to be okay?"

She shuddered out a breath as she saw everything she'd ever wanted staring back at her in his gaze. "Yes. I should go."

He nodded.

She yanked open the door and ran across the side yard, forgetting her umbrella in her haste to be gone—to stop wanting what she shouldn't and move on. She had money to deal with and a life to put back together. Starting now. Unlocking her door, she went inside and set the money on the entryway table, then hurried upstairs for a quick change into jeans and a dry long-sleeve top. Comfortable and finally warm, she immediately went back downstairs and walked over to her laptop, determined to take the next step. Within minutes, she was signed up for the twelve-week cooking classes she'd been putting off. Chef Paul had offered to save her spot and she was going to take it. She x'ed out of the screen, clicked on the long list of emails she'd been avoiding over the last few days, and deleted the ones that weren't important before opening the one from Wren.

Are you coming to girls' night this weekend?

She hit *reply*.

Yes, I'll be there! It's been pretty busy around here. I can't wait to see everyone and catch up.

She hesitated with her finger hovering over the *send* button, not wanting to go, not wanting to do anything, but she had every intention of going anyway. Mom had moped for weeks—for months—after Dad left them. Bella planned to do everything exactly the opposite, forever reminding herself that Mom's path was not hers. Heartbreak wasn't going to destroy her. Dad wanted her to live a full, happy life, so that's what she was going to do.

"I'll be back," she said as she walked over to Lucy and bent down, hugging her puppy and kissing her on the nose. "I have to go open a safe deposit box. Grandpa left us some money." She stood, opened the closet, and grabbed a tote bag, setting the shoebox inside before she locked up again.

Hurrying to the car, she looked up when a movement caught her eye, and watched Reed punching the heavy bag in his home gym. She got in the driver's side and took off without glancing in the rear-view mirror the way she wanted to. Today she was taking her life back even if her heart wasn't in it at all.

☙ Chapter Fifty ❧

Bella closed the front door behind Lucy and hurried to the kitchen, pulling the flourless chocolate cake she'd made off the top shelf. She grabbed a cold tote from the freezer and put the dessert inside. "I really think the ladies are going to like this one. I mean, I don't see how they couldn't. It's dark chocolate," she explained to her puppy as she glanced at the clock, wincing when she realized she was now half an hour late for girls' night. Ms. Sanderson had been extra chatty after her stretch mark reduction therapy, putting Bella even further behind than she already was. Typically, she would have had everything ready to go—plates, napkins, and plasticware waiting on the counter for a quick after-work pickup—but over the last few days, she'd found herself struggling to get out of her own way. Waking up at five to bake when she'd barely slept again last night had been its own feat. "You have no idea how sorry I am that you won't be able to have any of this. It's a crime against nature that dogs can't indulge in chocolate—particularly females."

Lucy wagged her tail as she sat by the table.

"I'll bring you a couple of treats to make up for the injustice. And plates," she whispered to herself as she headed over to the pantry, plucking up the package she'd bought at the store as her phone started ringing. "I bet they're wondering where I am." She moved quickly into the living room, frowning as she snatched her phone up off the entryway table, not recognizing the number on the screen. "Hello?"

"Bella Colby?" a woman said.

Her frown deepened as she listened to some sort of yelling and commotion in the background. "Yes, this is Bella."

"Bella, this is Teresa, Bonnie McKinley's nurse."

"Oh. Yes. Hello."

"I'm so sorry to call, but I'm having a little trouble. I can't seem to get ahold of Linda or Reed, and Bonnie's quite beside herself." Something smashed in the background. "Bonnie, calm down."

"I won't calm down. I want Bella. Call Bella."

Bella walked to the window, looking toward Reed's place, hoping he might have come home during the last few minutes, but his truck was still gone. "Teresa, why don't you put Bonnie on the phone?"

There was another large crash and the line went dead.

"Hello? Hello?" She grimaced as she looked at Lucy. "That can't be good." She called the number back and got a busy signal. "Shoot. Lucy, come on. Aunt Bonnie needs our help." She ran into the kitchen for her dessert and hurried to the car. Exchanging her sundress for shorts and her new fun, flirty top wasn't going to happen with her abrupt change of plans. "In you go, sweetie."

Lucy settled in her spot.

"Good girl." She put the tote in the trunk and headed toward the McKinleys', worrying because she had a solid ten-mile drive to tackle before she could get there. Who knew what was going on, but based on the troubling phone call, Bonnie's nurse had her hands full. Giving the gas an extra punch, she made it through several yellow lights, then sat impatiently through two red. Twenty minutes later, she pulled into the driveway and let Lucy out, then ran to the house as fast as her high heels allowed and rang the doorbell.

A petite blonde who wasn't much older than Bella opened the door. "Can I help you?"

"Teresa, I'm Bella Colby."

Teresa closed her eyes as she exhaled a quiet breath. "Thank you for coming. Bonnie's locked herself in the bathroom, and I can't get her to come out. I think I might need to call the police."

"No." She shook her head adamantly. "Let's see if we can handle this on our own." She stepped inside with Lucy and stopped dead as she stared at the shattered lamps and broken picture frames on the floor.

"Bonnie knocked them off the shelf while we were listening to the radio. "My Girl" came on, and she's been agitated ever since."

"That was special to her and her husband." Bella hurried down the hall to the bathroom and knocked. "Aunt Bonnie—"

"Go away!"

"Aunt Bonnie, it's Bella."

"Who's Bella? I don't know Bella. You're the devil, I just know it."

Bella tucked her hair behind her ear as she licked her lips, not quite sure what to do. "Aunt Bonnie, Lucy's here," she tried, shrugging as she looked at her puppy. “Speak, Lucy.”

Lucy barked.

The crying in the bathroom quieted.

“Aunt Bonnie, Lucy wants to see you. Speak again, Lucy,” Bella whispered.

Lucy barked twice.

“Lucy, is that you?”

Lucy barked again.

The lock turned and Aunt Bonnie came out with tear-streaked cheeks, but she was grinning. “Lucy, there you are.”

Lucy wagged her tail.

Aunt Bonnie laughed and petted Lucy, then gasped as she made eye contact with Bella. “Well, Bella, what on earth are you doing here, honey?”

Bella relaxed her shoulders and smiled. “Lucy and I thought we would come see you.”

Aunt Bonnie hugged her. “I'm still going to be your bridesmaid?”

She ignored the hitch in her heart and made herself smile again as she nodded, returning her embrace. “Of course you are.” She kissed her cheek. No matter how things had ended between her and Reed, she still cared for his family. “Would you like me to do your hair?” She brushed her fingers through Bonnie's disheveled locks, fixing them as best she could. “We can add some curls.”

“No, I want you to take me to the beach. We're going to go for a nice walk.”

“Oh.” Bella blinked her surprise as she looked at Teresa. “Are you up for the beach?”

“Not her.” Aunt Bonnie pointed her finger at the poor, harried nurse. “She's not going to the beach. Just you, Lucy, and me. We're the only ones going to the beach.”

“Okay,” Bella soothed her, taking Aunt Bonnie's hand. “We'll go to the beach. Just the three of us.”

“Of course we will.” She let Bella go and started down the hall. “We'll have a nice stroll. I should write a note for Mason, though. He gets worried when I leave and don't tell him where Kurt and I are going.”

Bella followed, stopping to pick Bonnie's glasses up off the floor. Bonnie could probably use a change before they left. Her cotton pants were wrinkled and there was a tear toward the bottom of her shirt, but that was the least of their problems right now. “We can leave a note."

Teresa hurried after them. "I don't think this is a good idea."

Bella glanced around at the mess. Staying here didn't seem like a better alternative. "We're going to be fine. I have my phone. You can try Linda again and let her know what's going on. We'll be gone for an hour or so." She smiled at Aunt Bonnie and slid her glasses back on her face. "You're going to have to sit in the back seat."

"That's just fine. I love that fancy little car of yours." She laughed as she looked out the window. "We'll keep the top down—just a couple of girls having our own adventure."

Tonight that sounded good—more low-key. She adored her friends, but the idea of girl talk, which would undoubtedly include relationship updates, was more than she wanted to deal with. "Do you want to leave your note?"

Aunt Bonnie frowned. "What note, honey?"

Sighing, she wrapped her arm around Bonnie's waist. "Let's go check out the water."

Bonnie hurried them along to the car and hopped in back, buckling up as Bella let Lucy in. "I'm ready."

She chuckled as she got behind the wheel. "Here we go." She drove Bonnie through the busy rush hour traffic toward her favorite spot, making certain the radio was off, even if she didn't typically listen to the oldies station. Bonnie was finally calm. She had every intention of keeping her that way.

"I just love the breeze in my hair. The sun feels so *good*. Where's Reed today?"

Bella gripped the steering wheel tighter. It looked like Reed was going to be a topic of conversation regardless of where she spent her evening. "Um, he's working."

Bonnie shook her head as she clucked her tongue. "He works too much. Linda worries about him out on those mean streets every day, pretending to be someone he's not. It's a dangerous element he deals with—dangerous."

Bella made a sound in her throat as she slowed for their turn, assuming Bonnie believed Reed was still a cop. "Here we are." She pulled into a parking space, hoping they might focus on the gorgeous hues of deep blue and stunning white sand that went on for miles. She didn't want to talk about Reed anymore. As it was, she thought about him too much no matter how hard she tried not to. "So, what do you think?"

"I think I might be in heaven."

She opened her door and let Aunt Bonnie out, keeping a cautious eye on her the way she would a small child.

Aunt Bonnie breathed deep and smiled. "I love it here."

She smiled back. "Me too. How about a walk in the sand?"

"But my shoes." Aunt Bonnie lifted up her sneakered foot.

Her mind flashed back to the first night she'd invited Reed to join her at the beach—when he'd assured her he wasn't much for sand in his socks. Everything had been so wonderful and simple. Their beginning. "We can take them off." She slipped off her pale yellow pumps and tossed them in the back seat. "Kinda like that."

Aunt Bonnie laughed. "All right." She gasped. "Lucy's run off."

Bella whirled and relaxed when she saw Lucy barking at the gulls. "She's okay. She loves to chase the birds."

"She looks like a horse."

"I've always thought a moose."

Bonnie laughed again as she nodded. "A moose."

Bella helped Aunt Bonnie take off her socks and shoes, then hooked her arm through hers as they began to walk. Breathing deep, she let the salty air and wind soothe her as the strong breeze played with her hair. "This is my happy place."

"It's nice to feel the sand on my toes."

"Yes, it is."

"I've missed you, you know. I haven't seen you for a few weeks."

"Life's been pretty crazy."

"Your father's feeling better?"

She shook her head. "He passed away. Last Friday." It still surprised her that it had only been a week.

Aunt Bonnie stopped. "That's a true shame, Bella. A true shame." She hugged her.

Bella wrapped her arms around her, holding on tight, treasuring the hug she didn't know she'd needed as her eyes watered. "Thank you."

"Oh, honey, time heals the worst of our aches."

She nodded, counting on that to be true. The last few days had been the worst of her life. Nothing felt right anymore. At some point, things *had* to get better.

"Time heals us," Aunt Bonnie repeated as she eased back and took Bella's hand. "Reed's a good boy. He'll take care of you. He's always been good to me and his mom, even when they had their falling out."

She looked at Bonnie as they started walking again. “They had a falling out?”

Aunt Bonnie nodded. “Linda didn’t want him mixed up in police work. They fought about it quite often, I’m afraid—the closer he got to leaving for college, the worse it seemed to get. There’s been a bit of a strain ever since. She didn’t want to bury her son the way she had her husband and in-laws.”

Bella studied Bonnie’s eyes, seeing that they were clear and in the present. Reed’s aunt was one hundred percent with her. “I’m sorry that happened.”

“It took a toll on us—all of us—but it hurt Kurt and Reed the most. Little boys losing their daddies when they weren’t much more than babies. Kurt’s gone now. It pains my heart, but Reed’s the one who dealt with the worst of it.”

“Why do you say that?”

“Because of the car.”

She frowned. “The car?”

“He was in the back seat. I couldn’t take it when I saw what they did in the kitchen—and I was full-grown. I can’t imagine being five.”

Aunt Bonnie wasn’t making any sense. “I’m glad you don’t have to worry about that anymore.”

“It will always be there. We’ll always remember.”

And her family—the Caparellis, whether Bella knew them or not—was responsible. Her mood started to nosedive, so she looked toward the water, watching the waves, concentrating on the serenity. “Aunt Bonnie, do you like chocolate cake?”

“Who doesn’t, honey?”

“I have one in the trunk.”

Aunt Bonnie frowned. “You do?”

Nodding, she smiled. “I do. We could have a chocolate cake picnic and watch Lucy chase the seagulls.”

“I’d like that. But then we should get home. I need to get Kurt his supper. Mason’s working late tonight, but I’ll fix him a plate for the fridge.”

She smiled sadly. Poor Aunt Bonnie. It had to be hell slipping from past to present with no control. “We’ll have a little treat and get you home in time for dinner.” She walked them to the car, cut two slices of the cake with the knife she’d brought along, and put them on paper plates. “Shoot. We have a problem.”

“What?”

"I don't have any silverware. I forgot it."

"We have fingers."

She grinned. "Yes, we do."

"And there's a whole ocean full of water where we can wash our hands afterward." Bonnie picked up her slice and bit in, leaving a mess around her mouth.

Bella laughed, following Bonnie's lead.

"Well, you're just covered in chocolate, honey."

"So are you." She leaned against the back of the car as Bonnie did.

"I'm sure glad we came."

She swallowed. "Me too." It had been a while since she'd felt warm inside. She'd filled the last seven days with yoga, work, and long walks on the beach until even Lucy was eager to head home—whatever it took to keep her mind busy. Ironically, she'd rushed to Aunt Bonnie's rescue, but Aunt Bonnie was the one who'd done the saving tonight. "We'll have to do it again."

"Of course we will, honey. Any time. You're our family. You're Reed's."

She paused as she brought the sweet treat back to her mouth, then took a huge bite, hoping to drown her misery in chocolate cake.

Bella tied her robe in place as she walked downstairs, pausing on the bottom step when someone knocked on her front door. She tensed, gripping the banister, forever spooked by the idea of the Caparellis hunting her down—especially when she was alone at night. The knock came again and she tucked her wet hair behind her ear as she made eye contact with Lucy. "Be ready to bite."

Lucy wagged her tail.

She grabbed her phone off the entryway table and moved toward the door, peeking through the side window, whooshing out a breath of relief when Wren waved at her. Smiling, she unlocked the door. "Hey, you. Come on in."

Wren stepped inside. "Hi, bestie. We missed you tonight."

"I missed you too." She closed the door, locking it, then hugged her friend. "I'm sorry I couldn't make it. Reed's aunt was having some trouble. Her nurse needed a hand." After she'd dropped Bonnie off and did what she could to help Linda soothe ruffled feathers about Terrible Teresa's impending return to the house tomorrow, she hadn't had the energy to paste on happy smiles for her friends. "Can I get you something to eat or drink?"

"No, thanks. But you can tell me what's going on with you." She blinked, smiling sweetly as she rubbed her hands up and down her belly. "I'm not leaving until you do." She sat on the arm of the love seat. "And I'm sitting right here because I can't get up by myself otherwise."

Bella grinned. "You're getting uncomfortable."

"*Mack truck* and *cow* come to mind when I think of words to describe my current state."

Bella smiled again. "You're beautiful."

"I'm ready to meet this baby and have my body back."

"Soon."

"Very soon," she said with a decisive nod. "Enough about me. Tell me about you."

Exhaling a quiet breath, Bella moved to sit on the couch. She'd known this day of explanations would come eventually; she just hadn't planned on it being right now. "What do you want me to say?"

"What's going on with you and Reed? You haven't mentioned him at yoga once in over a week—and I'm not the only one who's noticed. Plus, why is he having me decorate his place when you two pretty much live together?"

She could feel the tears coming—the emotion clogging her throat as she gripped her hands together in her lap. "We, um, we broke up."

Wren blinked. "*What*?"

She sniffled as she looked down.

"Honey, how could you not think that was worth a mention?"

She shrugged. "I guess I haven't wanted to talk about it."

"Bella." Wren gained her feet and walked over to the couch, sitting down next to her. "What happened?"

Tears fell, streaming down her cheeks. She'd tried so hard to keep her emotions in check. Not once since she'd picked up Dad's box at Reed's had she let herself cry. It was so much easier to deny the pain and pretend that it would go away eventually. "It's complicated—really, really complicated. Reed was working on an old case that ended up involving my father. He lied to me—used me."

Wren frowned as she wrapped her arm around Bella's shoulders. "Honey, I saw the two of you together at Chase and Julie's wedding. That looked pretty real to me."

"It was, I guess." She wiped her cheeks. "He says he loves me. I know he does," she corrected herself.

"Do you love him?"

She nodded and covered her face with her hands as she started crying again.

"Oh, Bella." Wren hugged her. "It's going to be okay."

She rested her head on Wren's shoulder. "I don't see how. I've never felt so awful."

"Of course you do." She gave her a supportive squeeze. "Did I tell you how I met Tucker?"

She wiped her eyes again. "Yes."

"I've given you the abridged version. Another long story short: he wasn't entirely honest with me in the beginning either. He withheld some information. I was pretty upset when I found out, but we were able to work things out."

"Did he sign up for cooking classes with you and take you out on dates with the hope that you would introduce him to your family members?"

She frowned. "No."

"Did he at any point sleep with you while he was unsure of your character or have questions about who you were as a person because your father hasn't always been an honest man?"

"Absolutely not." Wren looked out the window, glaring toward Reed's house. "Toad. I would totally knock him out if he wasn't bigger than me—and a hell of a lot stronger." She turned back to Bella. "I'll have Tucker do it."

She chuckled as she grabbed a tissue and wiped her nose. "I'm not being completely fair. There's a lot more to the story, but I can't share it with you right now." She would never be able to. "Technically, he had his reasons—pretty good reasons—but that doesn't mean I can be with him."

"Aw, sweetie." She touched her forehead to Bella's. "Do you and Lucy wanna come spend the night? You can sit up with me while baby boy here kicks my ribs. We could eat ice cream and watch movies."

"That's sweet, but I think I'll be okay."

"My ears are open whenever you need to talk."

She hugged Wren. "I know they are. You're the best." She kissed her cheek. "Thanks for coming to check on me."

"You're welcome." She eased away. "If you really love Reed and there are technicalities that are keeping me from siccing Tucker on him, maybe you guys could fix things."

She shook her head, remembering the life-altering moment when she'd walked into Dad's room and seen Reed sitting by that disgusting board—the shocking disbelief and staggering punch of pain to her heart. "I don't know how I can ever trust him again." She crumpled the tissue in her hand. "I want so much more than that. I need it."

Wren nodded.

"I thought we had everything going for us." She swallowed. "I thought he was the one I was going to spend the rest of my life with. I love him. So much." She paused when her voice grew unsteady. "But how do we build on a foundation that's mostly lies?" She wanted an answer. She wanted Wren to dispense some sort of wisdom that would make everything all right again.

"Give yourself time and see how it all settles."

She nodded.

Wren kissed Bella's cheek and stood. "I'm going to head home so Tucker can read to my belly."

She grinned, loving such a sweet idea. "He reads to your belly?"

"He's in love with our little boy, and he's only seen him in 4-D once."

Bella smiled again, happy for her friends. "You two are going to be great parents."

"The nursery's finally finished. You should come over and take a look."

"I will. Sometime next week." She walked Wren to the door. "Thank you."

"Anytime."

She watched Wren walk to her car and drive away, then closed the door, noting that Reed's lights were off and his truck was gone. They were both busy moving on with their own lives.

☙ Chapter Fifty-One ❧

Reed yawned as he drove home from dropping Sadie off with Tyson after one hell of a long night. He'd had dicey moments during his years with NYPD. More than a few times he'd risked his life for his job, but spending sixteen hours with twelve teenage girls and two softball coaches had nearly been his undoing. Never again would he listen when a dumbass bus driver assured him he knew a shortcut back to Los Angeles, especially when said shortcut took them through the desert at eleven o'clock at night where all kinds of shitty things could happen—like overheated engines in the middle of nowhere and nonexistent cell phone service to go along with it. Add a deranged stalker to the mix and you had the recipe for a fucking nightmare. Luckily, Sadie's secret admirer had decided to give him a break and not follow along on their trip.

Eventually things had settled down. After four-and-a-half hours on the dusty roadside, a kindhearted farmer had driven by in a pickup and dropped the group off at some Podunk motel. Reed had sat up until dawn on a rickety wooden chair, keeping his ears open and eyes glued to the shoddy lock on the door while Sadie and her three pals doubled up in queen-size beds and slept away in their assigned room. The three-hour drive back this morning had been its own adventure while cranky, sleep-deprived young women bitched and argued about music, food, and boys. By nine, he'd been more than ready for Tyson to take over.

He yawned again as his phone rang, then groaned as he looked at the readout. Mom. "Shit," he muttered, not in the mood for a conversation right now—particularly when he was going to have to break the news about him and Bella. "Shit," he said again as he picked up on the third ring, knowing she would just call back. "Hey, Mom."

"Hi, honey. I haven't talked to you in a while."

"I've been pretty busy." Boxing and extra shifts had been his saving grace over the last few days.

"That's why we need to catch up. Do you and Bella want to come over tonight? We'll have dinner."

He gripped the wheel tighter and shook his head. "Tonight's not going to work. I'm just getting off my shift. I haven't slept in over twenty-four hours."

"Oh, you poor thing. How about tomorrow, then?"

He rolled his tense neck as he kept his eyes on the road. "Yeah, sure."

"Make sure you tell Bella that the only thing the two of you need to bring is yourselves. I know she'll ask. She's so lovely, honey."

And this is why he'd hesitated to answer. Mom was going to be devastated, but he might as well get it over with. "Mom, Bella and I broke up over a week ago. You won't be seeing her anymore." And the idea made his already raw stomach ache even more.

"*What*? Honey, she was here last night. She didn't mention anything about it."

He frowned. "She was at the house?"

"Aunt Bonnie had a spell. Teresa couldn't get her to come out of the bathroom. Bella and Lucy came over and worked their magic. She ended up taking her to the beach, fed her chocolate cake, and brought her home. Bonnie's still talking about it."

"Huh," was his response. What else could he say? Bella had helped out his family because she was a sweetheart. He wanted it to mean something more than that, but it probably didn't.

"What happened, honey? You two were so happy. I've never seen *you* so happy."

He took his hand off the wheel to scratch his jaw. "I don't want to talk about it."

She sighed. "All right. I hope to see you for dinner."

"I'll be there."

"Bye, honey."

"Bye." He turned into the development, then into his driveway, more than ready for bed. Getting out, he glanced toward Bella's place, seeing that she was home. If things were different, he would be walking through her front door, but they weren't, so he started toward his own.

Lucy ran through the side yard, wagging her tail and barking as she stopped in front of him.

He grinned. "Hey, girl."

"Lucy!" Bella ran around the corner of the house and smacked into him, soaking them both with the full watering can she held in her hand.

"Whoa." He wrapped his arms around her to keep her from stumbling back and breathed her in.

"Sorry." She stepped away. "Sorry," she said again as she stared at his dripping shirt."

He shrugged as he tracked his gaze over her. She looked beautiful—ready for summer in her white short shorts, navy-blue tank shirt, and leather sandals. She'd slid one of those headband things in her hair, leaving her spectacular face unframed, which made her big brown eyes appear even larger. "I need to change anyway."

"I'm thinking I might have to get some sort of tie for the backyard since a certain someone keeps wandering off." She lifted her eyebrow at Lucy as she spoke.

Lucy leaned against Reed.

If only Bella was as eager to see him as her dog was. "She wants to say hi. Don't you, pretty girl?" He gave the puppy a good rub, missing Lucy as much as he did Bella—the little family the three of them had made together.

"Well, she's not supposed to run away and scare five years off my life."

He smiled, remembering a similar situation—the first night she'd invited him over for dinner.

She frowned, stepping closer. "You look tired. Really tired."

He nodded, noting that Bella's concealer wasn't doing much to cover up the dark circles under her eyes. Apparently, she wasn't sleeping any better than he was. "Rough night."

"Sadie?"

"Yeah." He scrubbed at his face. "And eleven of her closest friends. The bus broke down in the middle of nowhere while we were on our way home from a softball tournament. We just got back into town an hour ago."

A smile warmed her face.

He couldn't help but chuckle. "It sucked pretty bad."

"I can only imagine."

"I shudder to think a similar fate could be mine this summer—the student exchange program in London."

Her smile dimmed. "You're going to Europe?"

"Maybe. It would be only for a couple of weeks. We're still ironing out the details." He'd made it clear to Ethan that he wouldn't be going anywhere until he had a better idea of what the Caparellis were up to.

She looked down. "I guess I should probably get going. The girls are coming over today."

"Yeah? Make sure you tell them I say hi."

She nodded, meeting his gaze.

He swallowed, holding her stare. Clearly the easy moment they'd managed was over.

"Sorry about the water."

"It's no big deal."

"I'll, um, I'll see you around." She turned and walked off.

He stood where he was, shoving his hands in his pockets as he sighed, not quite ready to say good-bye. "Hey, Bella?"

She stopped and turned back.

"Thanks for helping out with Aunt Bonnie." He moved her way, closing the distance between them, wanting every moment he could squeeze out of this opportunity. Not being able to wake up with her every day was bad enough. Not even being able to talk to her was pure torture.

"I think she was missing Lucy."

"Chocolate cake at the ocean?"

She shrugged and sent him one of her excellent grins. "We had a good time."

"Mom says Aunt Bonnie's still talking about it."

"I like your family, Reed."

"They love you." And the tension was back just like that. "Anyway, thanks."

"You're welcome."

"Don't forget to tell the girls I say hello."

"I won't."

He nodded and walked around to his front door, stepping into his empty house when he wanted nothing more than to wrap himself up in Bella.

Bella rushed around the kitchen, making certain that everything was in place for the girls. Snacks were set on the table in their usual spot, a variety of nail polishes waited to be used on the floor, and the supplies she needed for therapeutic facials were ready in the living room. "That should be everything," she said as she leaned back against the pantry door. Now if only she could find some of her usual energy. Her butt was officially dragging after last night's gorge fest on the beach and her emotional purge in Wren's supportive arms. It was safe to say that she was teetering on the edge of true exhaustion. She'd been pushing herself hard despite her inability to sleep, doing whatever she could to ignore just how unhappy she was. After her quick run-in with Reed this morning, she felt completely wrung out. For several minutes afterward, she'd toyed with the idea of calling Emilia's aunt and rescheduling for next weekend, but she couldn't do that to two of her favorite people. This afternoon was bound to be as good for her as it would be the girls.

A car pulled up in the driveway, and she smiled when Lucy hurried to the door. "It sounds like your friends are here. Hold on a minute while I go get them." She walked outside, grinning as Emilia and Bianca got out of Aunt Peggy's new minivan. "There's my girls."

They came running. "Bella!"

She crouched down and hugged them, gripping them tight. "I've *missed* you two. How are you?"

"Good," they said in unison.

"That's great." She kissed their cheeks.

Emilia frowned as she eased back, looking around. "Where's Reed?"

She glanced toward his house. "He, uh, he has some stuff to do today."

"Oh," Emilia said as she looked down.

"Emilia made him a card," Bianca supplied.

"She did?" Bella looked at Emilia. "You did?"

She nodded.

"I'll make sure he gets it."

"Okay." But her disappointment was obvious.

"Come on. Let's go inside." She ushered the girls into the house, waiting while they showered Lucy with hugs and kisses. Sighing, she watched Emilia struggle to pet the puppy and hold the card at the same time. "Sweetie, I can take that for you."

"Thanks." Emilia handed it over and went back to loving on Lucy.

Bella started toward the kitchen, opening the folded sheet of printing paper, and stopped as she studied the crayon drawings: flowers, rainbows, and butterflies, but it was the recent picture of Emilia—scars and all—taped in the center that made her press her hand to her heart. Her eyes filled as she glanced Emilia's way, understanding just how big of a breakthrough this was for the little girl. Nibbling her lip, she looked out the window at Reed's truck parked in the driveway, then back at the sweet six-year-old who needed all the love and support she could get. "Emilia, I know Reed has a few things to do today, but we could go knock on his door if you want."

Emilia gained her feet. "We can?"

"Sure."

"Now?"

"If you want."

She smiled. "I want to."

"Okay. Let's go." She straightened her shoulders as she walked next door, bracing herself for another encounter with Reed when one today had been more than enough. He'd looked completely worn out but delicious nonetheless. "Go ahead and knock."

The girls curled their small fists and gave a couple of solid pounds, then looked at her when he didn't answer.

"Maybe try another." Bella added her own knock while the girls pounded again.

"Why isn't he coming?" Bianca wanted to know.

"He might have his music on. Sometimes he listens to it loud when he exercises. We'll come back later." She winced when Emilia's face fell. "Or we can try again right now." She tested the doorknob and smiled when she found that it turned in her hand. "Let me see if this is a good time for him. He's probably upstairs boxing." She stepped inside, realizing that the house was silent. "Come stand right here."

The girls stepped into the living room, and she shut the door, locking it, constantly thinking of the Caparellis.

"I'll be right back. Stay here."

"We'll stay here," Bianca assured.

She walked quietly up the steps, straining her ears in the quiet, listening for the shower running in the master bathroom, but she didn't hear anything as she moved down the hall. "Reed?" She peeked in his gym and kept going, stopping dead in his bedroom doorway as she stared at him lying facedown on his bed, still fully clothed in the jeans and T-shirt she'd accidentally soaked. "Oh, my God. Reed." She rushed over to him and shook his arm. "Reed—"

He rolled, yanking on her wrist, pulling her down on the bed. Before she knew what was happening, he was straddling her waist and pointing a gun in her face.

She gasped, holding her hands up as her chest heaved. "It's me. It's just me."

He blinked several times, and the fierce coldness vanished from his sleepy eyes. "Jesus." He dropped his weapon to his side. "What the hell, Bella?"

Was that Mad Dog McKinley? Was the frightening man she'd just witnessed the same guy who'd buried himself in the Caparelli trenches for seven years? "I'm—I'm sorry. I didn't..." She pressed a hand to her racing heart. "I'm sorry," she said again.

He climbed off her and set the gun on the side table as he sat next to her. "I was dead asleep." He scrubbed his hands over his face. "What's going on?"

"The girls." She sat up, wanting to stand, but she couldn't guarantee her legs would hold her just yet. "They're downstairs. Emilia made you something."

"She did?"

She nodded, itching to smooth down his spiky hair. "I can tell them this isn't a good time."

He stood, grabbing his gun. "I'll come down and see them." Walking to his closet, he grabbed a lockbox and secured his weapon, then pulled off his shirt, tossing it toward the laundry basket in the corner.

She stared at his broad shoulders and powerful chest as he walked to his drawer. Had it really been almost two weeks since she'd touched him, since he'd pressed her into the mattress with that gorgeous body of his? It didn't take much to remember his taste or the way he felt when he pushed himself deep inside her.

He grabbed another shirt and slid it on, holding her gaze. "Is everything okay?"

Nothing was okay. "Yeah." She stood, whether her legs were ready or not. "Fine." She moved down the hall and started downstairs.

"Wait." He took her hand, stopping her on the third step from the top.

"What." She turned, facing him when she was in desperate need of some space.

He moved down two stairs so they were eye-level. "Everything's been good? You haven't seen anything? I should have asked you earlier when we were outside, but..." He shook his head. "I guess I'm just tired."

"Uh, there's been nothing," she said as her gaze wandered to his firm lips before meeting his eyes again. "Nothing out of the ordinary."

He traced her skin with his thumb. "No cars lingering by the house or at work—someone you keep seeing at the beach?"

"No," she said breathlessly, wanting to pull away from his touch, but she needed to feel it more. "Do you know something? Is something going on that you're not telling me?"

"I haven't heard anything new."

"Why did you have your gun?"

"I don't know. Old habit, I guess."

Unable to take it any longer, she lifted her free hand and slid her fingers through his hair, fixing the few disheveled pieces.

"Thanks." His thumb went to work along her knuckles as they continued to stare into each other's eyes.

"I, um—" She pulled away from him before she caved to her weakness for Reed and let him kiss her. "The girls." She hurried down the stairs, panicking momentarily when she didn't see them, but then she noticed the cartoon on the television and Emilia's ponytail cascading over the arm of the couch. "I see you two have made yourselves at home."

"We like the couch," Bianca said. "It's comfy."

Reed poured himself a glass of water. "It's a good couch."

"Reed!" Both of the girls scrambled off the cushions and launched themselves at him.

He hooked an arm around their waists, cushioning the blow as the momentum of the hug sent the three of them crashing into the fridge. "Whoa. That's a whole lot of hug." He crouched down in front of them.

Bianca frowned. "You look sleepy."

He nodded. "I am. I didn't go to bed last night."

She touched the dark circles under his eyes. "How come?"

"That's part of my job sometimes."

Bella stood by the island, watching him as she thought of a teenage girl in need of his protection—of him sitting up for hours, keeping watch.

Bianca wrinkled her nose. "I don't want that job."

He grinned. "I like my job."

"I'm going to be a doctor and make it so kids don't get sick."

"Sounds like a good profession." He looked at Emilia. "What about you? What are you going to be?"

She shook her head as she shrugged. "I don't know yet."

"You have plenty of time to decide."

"I made something for you."

"Oh, yeah?" He sat down on the floor, pulling the girls onto each of his thighs. "Let's see." He took the card from Emilia. "'To Reed. Love Emilia.' We're off to a great start."

Emilia smiled.

He opened it, beaming as his eyes tracked over the page. "You made this for me?"

Emilia nodded. "What's your favorite part?"

"It's hard to choose. These are top-notch drawings, but I think your picture might be my favorite. Hold this." He gave her the piece of paper back, then hooked an arm around each of the girls' waists and stood, lifting both kids as if they weighed nothing.

They laughed.

"Here we go." He set them back down. "*This* is going on my fridge right away." He took the card back from Emilia and secured it to the refrigerator with a magnet.

"That's you and Bella." Bianca pointed to the strip of pictures from Julie and Chase's wedding. "You look silly. Except for that one. That one looks normal." She pointed to the last picture, in which they held each other close and smiled. "Are you guys gonna get married?"

"Uh..." Reed rubbed at the back of his neck. "I think we're going to take things a day at a time."

Bella crossed her arms as she laughed uncomfortably. "We should probably get going."

Emilia and Bianca looked at her.

"But I didn't tell Reed about my surgery yet."

Emilia hadn't told Bella about it either. "Go ahead."

He crouched down next to her. "You're having your surgery?"

She nodded. "They're gonna take off my leg for sure." She pointed to the dressings on another new ulcer.

"When?"

"I don't know. Soon, though."

He took Emilia's hand. "Don't forget I'm going to come see you."

"You're going to bring flowers."

He nodded. "I happen to be good at picking out pretty ones."

Bella exhaled a quiet breath. He *was* good at picking out pretty ones.

"How will you know when to come to the hospital?" Emilia asked.

"Bella's going to tell me." He glanced at her.

She stepped closer. "I'll let Reed know, honey."

"You're really going to come?"

"Definitely," he said with a decisive nod.

"Promise?"

"Try and keep me away."

She smiled before it faded. "I won't be able to come to Bella's house for a while. I'm probably going to miss you a lot."

Bella blinked, certain she couldn't take any more.

"I'll miss you too, but my truck can take me anywhere—to the hospital, to your house. Just because you can't come to Bella's doesn't mean we can't see each other. I'm going to need more pictures for my fridge. Look at all of that empty space."

Emilia smiled. "Okay."

Bella turned toward the window. How was she supposed to resist him when he was so sweet? Because he was—kind and wonderful. She would have given just about anything to make the last few months not matter—to forgive and forget—but the last few months were all they had. How many times had he looked her in the eyes and lied? How often had he given her the truth? And there was the problem: she had no idea. Turning back, she realized he was staring at her while the girls chatted about the strip of pictures on the freezer door. "We should go."

"Okay," the girls said in unison.

He held her gaze another moment before he gave his attention back to the kids. "Thanks for swinging by, ladies."

Emilia and Bianca hugged him.

He hugged them back. "I'll see you around."

Emilia held on to him after Bianca walked away. "I'll miss you."

"I'm going to see you after your surgery." He kissed her cheek. "And I love the picture."

She smiled. "You can come to Bella's with us."

He looked at Bella again. "Maybe next time. I have some stuff I need to do."

"All right."

Bella opened the door. "Thanks for letting us intrude."

"Anytime." He took her hand before she could leave as the girls started walking next door. "Come out on the bike with me tonight. Let me take you to dinner."

She shook her head, terrified she would say yes when she knew she needed to say no. "I can't."

He clenched his jaw and let her go. "Okay."

She walked out, hurrying across the yard to where the girls waited, not daring to look back. This couldn't keep happening. Her heart couldn't take any more close encounters with Reed.

The house was quiet again and the mess cleaned up after a busy few hours with the girls. They'd had a great time snacking on healthy treats, listening to music, and painting nails—the usual. Lucy was stuck with pink and purple paws for the next couple of weeks, but the zonked-out puppy didn't seem to mind too much.

Bella smiled, listening to Lucy's snoring as she pulled a tank top from the dryer and folded it, then set it on top of the machine in a neat stack. This afternoon had started out a little rocky, but for once she felt relatively steady—like she was ready to tackle her upcoming workweek with a positive state of mind. The key was to keep putting one foot in front of the other and staying busy—like she had today.

With a decisive nod, she reached into the dryer again and grabbed a T-shirt, stopping mid-fold when she realized it was one of Reed's. She frowned, glancing at the five others she'd folded without even thinking. Two weeks' worth of laundry had piled up—and apparently some of it was his. She set his shirt aside and grabbed another item, huffing out a breath when she held his gray hoodie—one of her favorite cozy items she often slipped on.

She glanced around the room, spotting his shoes tucked in the corner by the French doors and his protein powder on the counter. There were reminders of him *everywhere*—in the bathroom, bedroom, living room. It was bad enough that he hadn't come for his stuff, but no matter how hard she tried, she couldn't seem to get away from him. Last night, there'd been Aunt Bonnie and her conversation with Wren. This morning Lucy had booked it around the house to say hello. Then there was the whole thing upstairs in his room when she stopped off with the girls to deliver Emilia's card. How was this supposed to work when he lived right next door? She tossed the sweatshirt back into the dryer and slammed the door closed. "I can't do this anymore."

Lucy lifted her head.

"This isn't working." She rushed to the closet and yanked a canvas bin from the shelf, dumping out a pile of Lucy's bath items on the floor. Hurrying into the kitchen, she grabbed Reed's Ethan Cooke

Security mug and protein powders off the counter. She opened cupboards and tossed his cereals and snack crackers in as well, wanting no reminders of him left in her space. His sneakers went in next before she moved to the living room, plucking up flip-flops, a DVD, and one of his favorite pairs of sunglasses. She went for the picture frames on the shelves, pulling off the one she loved best of herself, Reed, and Lucy at the beach. She stopped, staring at their grinning faces pressed cheek to cheek, and closed her eyes as her breathing grew unsteady. "I can't do this anymore," she repeated when the panic started settling in. She was never going to stop loving him. Decades would pass, but he would always be the one.

"No," she said as she set the frame picture side down and sat on the couch. She needed to take drastic measures—make big changes. Today. She crossed her arms, giving them a gentle rub while her mind raced, trying to figure out the solution. "The house." She rushed to her feet and moved to the entryway table for her phone. "My house." She scrolled through her contacts until she found her real estate agent and dialed.

"This is Winter Williams."

"Hey, Winter. It's Bella Colby."

"Hey, Bella. How are you?"

"Good, thanks. I think I'm ready." She shook her head. "I *am* ready. I want to buy the house. It's still available?"

"As far as I know."

"Then I want it."

"You're sure?"

She nodded. "Yes. I know this is totally last-minute, but is there any way you could meet me there? I'd like to take one last look around."

"Of course. I'm probably about twenty minutes away—probably more like half an hour with the traffic."

"That's completely fine."

"All right. Let's go take a look at your house."

She beamed, feeling excited—*alive*—for the first time in nearly two weeks. "Thanks, Winter."

"I'll see you soon."

"Drive safely." She hung up and looked at Lucy. "I'm going to do it. I'm going to buy us our house."

The puppy wagged her tail on her bed, still worn out from the girls.

Her phone rang, and she frowned as Jed's number popped up

when she'd half-expected it to be Winter. "Hello?"

"Bella?"

"Hey, Jed."

"You sound like you're in good spirits."

She smiled again. "I am."

"That's great."

"I certainly don't mind it."

He chuckled. "So, I'm going to be over your way in a little while. Do you and Reed want to grab a drink?"

She rolled her eyes to the ceiling. "Reed and I aren't seeing each other anymore."

"Oh, I didn't know. I'm sorry."

"It's okay."

"How's your dad doing?"

"He passed away."

"Jesus, I'm on a roll."

She smiled. "I didn't mention it, so you couldn't possibly have known."

"I'm sorry, Bella. Really."

"It's fine."

"Do you want to meet up—just for a glass of wine or something?"

She looked at Reed's stuff and turned away, squelching any embers of guilt. They weren't together. It was perfectly acceptable for her to make plans with a friend. "Sure. Do you want to come here? I have half a chocolate cake sitting in my fridge."

"Do you have coffee?"

She looked toward the Keurig and the hazelnut brew Reed usually drank. "I do."

"Sounds good to me. What time?"

"How about seven?" She glanced at her watch. "I'm actually on my way out to look at a property I've had my eye on."

"Do you want company?"

"Sure. We can come back here afterward."

"Where are we meeting?"

She gave him the address. "I'm going to head over now. The real estate agent's still a few minutes out, but I'm eager to get the ball rolling."

"I'll see you in about ten minutes."

"Great." She hung up and went upstairs, changed into a simple red sundress, and slid on a pair of leather sandals. This was exactly what she needed: a new adventure to look forward to and a relaxing evening with a friend. She walked downstairs and into the kitchen. "I'll be back in a little while." She kissed Lucy's nose and locked up, driving toward the home she had every intention of making her own.

☙ Chapter Fifty-Two ❧

"So, you're sure about that place?" Jed asked as he forked up more chocolate cake. "This is good, by the way."

"Thanks." Bella pushed her half-eaten slice to the side and leaned back in her chair, enjoying the evening breeze while they sat in the dim glow of her porch light. "I'm absolutely sure. I've had my eye on that house for months." She smiled, thinking of it.

"If you're really going to make an offer, I think you should lowball them."

She frowned. "I don't want to lose it."

His eyebrows winged up on his handsome face. "I don't think you have to worry about that."

She grinned. "It's going to be beautiful."

He huffed out a laugh as he set down his fork. "If you say so."

She'd tried sharing her visions of what the house could be while they walked from room to room, but he hadn't been able to see the big picture the way Reed had. "I do."

"It's a steep asking price for the renovations you're going to have to put in. The roof's a mess."

Luckily, she had a huge chunk of change to work with—not that she intended to spend all of the money on the property. She was too penny-wise for that. After her new home was under contract, she planned to sit down with a financial planner and make sure Mom's and Dad's last gifts set her up for the rest of her life. "Stone and I are putting our heads together. We've already been texting back and forth."

"He's a good guy for the project. Sounds like you have it all planned out."

"I always do. Step by step. It's kinda how I live my life." She always had. Except for where Reed was concerned. He hadn't been part of the plan. Loving him was never supposed to have happened. She cleared her throat and grabbed her glass, sipping the dessert wine Jed had brought over.

"I guess the next step is to go for it, then."

She nodded. "Winter's submitting my offer first thing tomorrow morning. If they accept, Stone and I are going to draw up some preliminaries before the baby comes—stuff I can start doing on my own right away."

Jed sat back, lacing his hands behind his head. "Sounds pretty exciting."

"It is."

"When's Sophie due, anyway?"

"Any day now. Abby too."

"There's baby fever around here."

She grinned. "I love watching my friends' families grow. Family's everything."

He nodded. "I'm sorry about your dad, Bella. I wish I could've found him sooner."

She studied Jed as the crickets sang. Kind, intelligent, good-looking. But she sensed there was something more below the surface—or maybe she just counted on it after the last few weeks. She'd always been cautious, but now she wondered if everyone had an ulterior motive. "I'm glad we got the time we did—that I could be there for him in the end." She touched his hand. "That's because of you."

He covered her fingers. "Is there anything I can do? Anything you need?"

"No. Thank you, though. Right now, I'm trying to get through the days. Dad wanted me to be happy, so I'm working hard to fulfill his wish."

"That's a good way to look at it."

"Some days are harder than others." She eased her hand away from his and reached for her glass.

He looked at his watch. "It's getting pretty late. I should probably get going."

She gained her feet as he did. "Thank you for coming."

"It was fun." He sniffed the air. "What is that? I keep smelling something...good."

"It's probably the lavender." She pointed to the pot and walked to the thriving purple flowers, picking one and bringing it to his nose. "Is this it?"

He nodded. "Yeah." He took the stem from her fingers and tucked it in her hair.

She swallowed, holding his gaze, knowing he was going to kiss her as he leaned in and pressed his lips to her cheek.

He slid his fingers along her jaw and moved in again, touching his mouth to hers.

Her hands wandered to his shoulders as she closed her eyes and let him take them both deeper, waiting for the heat to engulf her, eager to be swept away, but she felt nothing more than Jed's skilled tongue teasing hers. He didn't taste like Reed; his muscles didn't feel the same under her palms. Her heart didn't pound simply from *needing* him.

He dove in once more and eased back, touching her jaw again.

She exhaled a quiet breath and shook her head, teetering on the edge of despair. Nothing about this was fair to Jed. Nothing about this was right for her. Maybe it never would be.

"Too soon," he said.

She nodded. "I'm sorry."

"Don't be." He offered her his hand. "Friends?"

She smiled, accepting, giving his fingers a warm squeeze. "Friends."

"Why don't I get out of your way?" He turned to the French doors and headed inside.

"I'm glad you came." She looked up and did a double take, standing frozen in her spot when she stared into Reed's eyes through his bedroom window. Her heart kicked up to pounding, the way she wished it had moments ago as their gazes held. She took a step toward the deck stairs, ready to sprint across the yard to tell him that the last few minutes weren't what they seemed, but she turned away instead because it didn't matter anymore—couldn't. They weren't a couple. She owed him no explanations even when she was certain she'd just wounded him. Unable to help herself, she glanced over her shoulder once more, but he was gone. Sending Jed a small smile, she followed him into the kitchen.

"Thanks for dessert."

She cleared her throat, pressing her hand to her chest, still shaken. "Uh, thanks for looking at the house with me."

"If you and Stone end up needing help with a hammer, I hope you'll let me know."

"I definitely will." She opened the front door. "Good night, Jed."

"Good night."

She watched him get in his car and waved as he drove away, then locked up, sagging against the door, staring at Reed's stuff still sitting in the corner on the floor. Tears filled her eyes as she headed upstairs, feeling torn in a way she'd never been before.

Reed's chin hit his chest for the third time as he dozed on the couch. He sat up and stretched, realizing he'd missed another twenty minutes of the action flick he'd started watching over an hour ago. Grabbing the remote, he turned off the TV and stood, hitting the lights on his way up the stairs. It was only nine thirty but he was ready for bed. After Bella and the girls left this afternoon, he hadn't been able to fall back to sleep; that didn't appear to be a problem now. Maybe he would try the movie again after he had more than a two-hour nap under his belt.

His phone started ringing in his back pocket as he walked down the hall. Smiling, he shook his head, already knowing who was on the line. He answered without bothering to glance at the readout. "Do you have an off switch?"

"I'll let you know if I ever find it," Skylar said. "They pulled another body."

"At twelve thirty in the morning?"

"No, earlier this evening. I've been busy."

He switched on the lamp by his bedside and contemplated whether his teeth would really suffer if he didn't brush for one night. "You always are."

"This one has Alfeo's MO, but there was no bullet present in the bag. License says we found Leone Picano."

He nodded. "'Lucky' Picano. Vinny said he was one of Alfeo's."

"So, how are you?"

He frowned at the abrupt change in their conversation. "Why are you asking me that? You never ask me that."

"I thought I'd give it a try. So, how are you?"

He rubbed at the back of his neck, well aware that she was checking on him. Joey had called earlier while he'd driven over to Malcoms to grab a bite to eat. "Never better."

"I *almost* believe you."

He sighed.

"Why don't you come out for a few days? Come see Joe and me. Stand on the sidelines at the field and keep me company. I'll have Evidence Response make you feel important. You can hold a clipboard or something."

He couldn't help but grin. And surprisingly, he was tempted to head to New York. "Maybe sometime. I've got stuff to do around here." Like get Bella back.

"Don't say I didn't try to help."

"I'd be happy to pretend the last few minutes never happened. I'd hate to think that you're getting soft—kinda girly."

"You're an ass, McKinley." She hung up.

Chuckling, he tossed the phone on the bed and took off his shirt as he walked toward the bathroom, deciding to brush his teeth after all. He paused mid-step when he heard voices outside and moved to the window, staring at Jed standing next to Bella on her deck as she picked a piece of lavender from the pot she'd planted weeks ago.

Jed took the flower from Bella's fingers and slid it into her hair.

"You son of a bitch," Reed whispered through clenched teeth, knowing exactly where this was going. "You bastard." He fisted his hands as Ethan's PI leaned in and kissed Bella's cheek, then captured her mouth.

He shook his head when Bella settled her hands on Jed's shoulders—not exactly pushing him away—and stabbed Reed in the heart. He knew he should close the blind—that who Bella kissed was none of his damn business anymore—but he tortured himself instead, watching the woman he loved move on with another man.

Agonizing moments passed before Bella stepped back and took Jed's hand while the two of them spoke, then Jed started inside. She looked up, her eyes widening as they locked on Reed's.

He swallowed, feeling the connection radiating between them despite what he'd just seen. Hours ago they'd stood on his stairs, touching each other, *drawn* to one another as if they had no choice. Just this afternoon she'd been fighting not to give in to him. "Fuck," he said when she turned away. "*Fuck*," he repeated, hearing the anguish in his own voice, barely able to tolerate the idea of Bella taking Jed to her bed. He grabbed his phone and dialed Skylar as he moved to the bathroom.

"I thought we were finished for the night."

He closed his eyes, resting his forehead against the doorframe. "I'm coming out. I'll be out in a couple of days."

The line stayed silent. "We'll take you out for some beers—do one of Joey's pub crawls and talk shop. The DA's always on my ass about this case. I'll deflect it off on you for a while."

She didn't try to soothe him with false promises that everything was going to be okay, yet he knew Skylar understood that he needed her. His friends had experienced losing at love because of the professions they'd chosen. "All right."

"Go to bed, Reed. Get some sleep."

"I will." Hanging up, he set the phone on the bathroom counter and walked down the hall, taking refuge in his gym instead of following Skylar's advice. He slipped on his gloves, pausing when he heard Jed's engine turn over and the vehicle drive away, but knowing Jed and Bella weren't sleeping together did little to ease his endless frustrations about where things stood between Bella and him.

He moved to the speed bag, finding his rhythm—his salvation—listening to the monotonous sound of his fist on firm leather, until he was certain that when he closed his eyes, he would finally be able to sleep.

ꟼ Chapter Fifty-Three ꟼ

Bella pushed her cart through the produce section at the local grocery store, stopping by the assortment of ripe tomatoes. She grabbed a pretty Roma and gave it a gentle squeeze, finding it to be perfect for her dinner. Tonight she was making a huge blackened chicken salad to celebrate the contract on her new house. For three days, she'd waited on pins and needles for the current owners to decide if her lowball offer was good enough. She'd followed Jed's advice with Winter's blessing and cut fifty-five thousand off the asking price—a real estate steal in the Palisades. With no other nibbles on the property, they'd accepted with one condition: they wanted a fast closing.

She smiled as she moved on to the cucumber selections, still trying to believe that this was going to happen. She was not only buying her dream home but also getting it in fifteen days instead of thirty. After dinner, she had every intention of heading over to her new place to get a head start on yanking up the God-awful shrubbery out front now that she had the official okay. Once she had that cleared away, the new windows and doors could be installed. By the end of summer, she would be living in her new home, even if it wasn't entirely finished. Her fresh start. A *real* fresh start.

A man crashed into her cart as he passed by. "Sorry about that."

"Oh, that's okay." She paused as she reached for an onion, glancing over her shoulder when she realized he'd sounded a lot like Joey—the strong New York accent. She shrugged as he kept moving toward the registers and got back to scrutinizing vegetables.

"What on earth?"

Her gaze whipped up, and she grinned as Linda and Aunt Bonnie headed her way. "Aw. Hey, you two."

"Honey, look at you out and about, doing your shopping." Aunt Bonnie enveloped her in a hug. "You're just as beautiful as always—so pretty in your sundress."

Bella returned her embrace. "Thank you. I'm grabbing some goodies for a celebratory salad. I'm buying a house."

Linda's eyes widened as Aunt Bonnie gasped.

"Congratulations, sweetie." Linda hugged her and kissed her cheek. "I was sorry to hear about your father."

"Thank you." As Bella looked at Linda, she wondered if Linda knew—if Reed had mentioned that the man who gave her life was from the same family who took her husband. "It's comforting to know he's not in pain anymore."

Linda took her hand. "I'm so sorry about you and Reed. We sure are going to miss you, sweetie."

She exhaled a quiet breath, looking down before she met Linda's gaze again. "I'll miss you too." And she truly would. For a few fleeting weeks, she'd believed she was going to be a McKinley—that she was going to be the woman to give Linda the beautiful grandbabies she so desperately wanted.

"Bella's going to come by and see us anytime she wants. Anytime. Right, honey?"

She smiled sadly, not so sure she could. She needed to cut Reed and anyone associated with him out of her life—for now. Until her heart stopped hurting every day. "I'll certainly visit," she fibbed.

"Lucy will miss us if we can't get a look at her every now and again."

"When my new house is ready for friends, I'll have you over for dinner." Surely she'd feel steadier by then.

Linda smiled. "We would love it."

"I think a night out might do Linda some good—cheer her up now that Reed's going off to New York again," Bonnie commented as she gave Linda's shoulder a supportive pat.

Bella gripped the cart handle. "Reed's going to New York?"

Worry clouded Linda's eyes. "I'm afraid so."

"Why?"

Linda shrugged as she shook her head. "I'm not quite sure. He doesn't say much about that part of his life. He knows it upsets me, but he was over for dinner Sunday night when Joey gave him a call." She sighed. "I think he's mixed up in his old police work again."

Bella made a sound in her throat, not sure what to say. From what Reed had told her, it didn't sound like he'd ever left NYPD behind. "I'm sorry to hear that."

Linda gripped Bella's hand. "I know you're not together anymore."

She swallowed. "But I'm hoping you might be able to talk him out of going—"

She shook her head. "Linda—"

"He'll listen to you. He would stay for you. I'm just—I see the news, Bella. I can't stand the idea of losing him the way I did Travis."

"Dangerous place," Bonnie added. "Mighty dangerous place for our Reed."

She looked from Bonnie to Linda—two widows who'd lost their husbands at the hands of her uncle. "Okay. I'll talk to him. When is he leaving?"

"Tomorrow."

"I'll try to catch him, but he hasn't been home much." At all. She hadn't seen him once since her gaze met his through his bedroom window Saturday night.

"He's boxing a lot and working all the time—back to his old ways."

She tried to let Linda's comment roll off her back. She didn't want to remember the day Reed had told her he'd been dead inside before they met. "I'll stop by and see if he's at the gym."

"I wouldn't ask if I didn't think you could help him."

"I'll try." She hugged Linda. "It's good seeing you." She hugged Bonnie next. "I'll have you over to the house sometime this summer."

"We can't wait." Bonnie cupped Bella's cheeks. "You take care of yourself and that wonderful dog of yours. We sure do love you, honey."

She nodded, blinking back tears as Reed's family walked away, the joy of her shopping trip completely gone. She yanked up a head of romaine, not bothering to scrutinize the lettuce before she tossed it in her cart and headed toward the checkout, trying not to be angry that she'd been put in this impossible position. Reed had made this entire mess, altering so many lives with his choice to pursue the Caparellis. He was a grown man, free to come and go to New York as he pleased. But she worried as she put her items on the belt in the express line, remembering Dad's warnings about his brutal brother. Why was Reed going? Did he plan to meet with his informant or do something equally dangerous? What if he got shot again—or worse? "Damn it," she whispered as she swiped her credit card, grabbed her bag, and left, hurrying out to her car.

She drove past their neighborhood at the height of rush hour and headed into Santa Monica, tracking down the gym she was mostly certain Reed worked out at, and slowed, taking a right into Rusty's parking lot when she spotted his truck. After getting out, she stopped at the door and lifted her chin, reminding herself that this was about Reed's safety—nothing more. They would talk, she would make him see that he needed to stay in LA, and then she would go.

Walking inside, she breathed in the not-so-pleasant odor of gym equipment and sweat as she searched for Reed among the men and a few women working out in the dingy space, feeling entirely out of place in her white sundress and cowgirl boots.

"Can I help you?"

She turned, smiling at the well-muscled black man. "Yes, I'm looking for Reed McKinley."

"He's sparring." He gestured to the two men in the ring throwing punches.

"Oh. Thanks. I'll just wait until he's finished if that's okay."

"Sure."

She walked closer to the ropes, watching Reed's muscles bunch and release with his every move. He was beautiful even as he ducked a blow, landed one in his opponent's face, then his ribs, and took one to the chin. She winced, trying to see the appeal of his favorite sport. Leaning against a close-by table, she folded her arms, waiting for him to finish, not exactly sure what she was going to say after what he'd seen on Saturday night.

Reed finished his sparring match, fist-bumping his friend Tink with their gloves still on. "That was a hell of a punch. I'm going to need to ice my jaw. Probably my eye too." He smiled, finally relaxed after a great workout.

"I'll definitely be wrapping my ribs." Tink grabbed his water bottle from the corner of the ring and paused with the nozzle at his lips. "Holy shit."

"What?" Reed turned and stared at Bella leaning against a dingy table, dressed in a devastatingly simple spaghetti-strap sundress and cowgirl boots.

"Who the hell is that?"

He didn't answer as he held her gaze and tugged off his gloves, trying to ignore the uptick in his pulse. Bella was truly the most spectacular woman he'd ever seen. She'd pulled her hair back in a barrette the way he liked best and had done something with her makeup that made her eyes even more hypnotizing than they already were. He steamed out a quiet breath, doing what he could to prepare himself for an encounter he hadn't been expecting, and went under the ropes, grabbing a towel as he hopped down and walked over to her. "Hey."

She stood straight, gripping her arms tighter across her chest. "Are you going to New York?"

He frowned, surprised by the edge in her voice. "What?"

"Are you going to New York?"

He wiped at his face, noting that there was none of the usual warmth in her gaze. Clearly this wasn't a friendly visit. "Yeah."

She adjusted her posture, standing hipshot. "Business or pleasure?"

"Bella—"

"Are you going to see your informant?"

He looked over his shoulder as he took her by the arm and walked her closer to the door. "I'm meeting up with Skylar."

She took a step away from him. "About the case?"

"For some of it, yeah." He looked around again. "Let's go outside."

She pushed through the door. "Have Joey do it. Whatever you're going for, he can do it instead."

He shook his head as they faced each other again. "Joey didn't talk to your father the way I did. He doesn't communicate with my informant."

"Don't go."

He heard the pleading in her voice, saw it in her big brown eyes. "I have to—for you, for me."

She shook her head. "I didn't ask you to go for me."

"Vinny did."

She swallowed, looking down, then met his gaze again. "I'm asking you to stay. Your mother—"

"My mother?" He took a step away this time, hardly able to believe he was hearing this. "Did she *call* you?"

"No, I saw her at the store. Don't go to New York, Reed." She settled her hand on his arm. "Stay home."

Christ, she was lethal. "You're asking for something I can't give. I need to get the hell out of here for a while—clear my head."

"So you're going to get away from me?"

He rubbed at the back of his neck as the already choking tension grew worse. "The DA's on Skylar. I can give her a hand. The only way they're going to keep Alfeo where he belongs is if the case is airtight.

One hundred percent airtight, Bella."

"You're risking too much."

He would do whatever it took to end this once and for all. "Your father's testimony, the information Joey and I gathered over the years, that's enough to be sure he never gets a chance to hurt you, or anyone else, for that matter. Murder one. Multiple counts if we can make it stick."

"What about you?"

Seeing the concern in her eyes, breathing her in, *touching* her made him want something that didn't look like it was going to happen. Saturday night had made things perfectly clear on where he stood with Bella. "What about me?"

"I care about— I don't want anything happening to you."

He didn't want to hear about how she cared. "Don't worry about it."

"Of course I'm going to worry about it. There's no need to put yourself in danger—"

"I appreciate your concern, but it's not necessary. You have your life. I have mine, right?" He heard the bitterness in his own words.

She blinked. "Reed—"

"Just go, Bella. What I do has nothing to do with you anymore. What you do has nothing to do with me." He turned, ready for another round in the ring.

"This has everything to do with me." She reached out, snatching his wrist. "Everything."

He faced her again. "You wouldn't have known anything about it if my mother hadn't told you." He pulled away from her. "Maybe I'll see you around sometime."

Hurt clouded her eyes as she turned and headed for her car.

He sighed, remembering his promise to Vinny—to take care of Bella no matter what. Even if he no longer wanted any part of it. Causing more friction between them wasn't going to solve their problems. He needed to be certain she would come to him if there was trouble. "Bella."

She ignored him as she moved faster through the parking lot.

"Wait, damn it." He jogged after her, catching up with her by her car. "Bella—"

She whirled. "I never asked for any of this!"

"I know." He couldn't make himself apologize because he hadn't asked for most of it either. "You're watching your back?"

She huffed out a humorless laugh as she rolled her eyes to the sky and shook her head. “My back is fine. I’m sure good old Uncle Alfeo doesn’t even know I exist.”

“Watch your back anyway.”

They stared at each other for several long seconds before she turned toward her car and got in.

He stood back as she tossed the Bug in reverse and pulled into traffic without bothering to look at him. “Son of a bitch,” he muttered as he walked back into the gym. He and Bella were certainly heading their separate ways.

ൽ Chapter Fifty-Four ൾ

REED REACHED INTO HIS DRAWER AND GRABBED SEVERAL T-shirts, tossing them on top of the shorts and jeans he'd already packed. He picked up the sweatshirt Bella had left on his back porch yesterday and added it to the pile. When he'd gotten home from the gym last night, he found a laundry basket full of his clothes, shoes, sunglasses, and everything else he'd brought over to her place. He glanced toward the house across the side yard as he caught a whiff of her laundry detergent and swore as he zipped his bag closed.

Over the last twenty-four hours, he'd given serious consideration to packing up all of his shit, shipping it east, and just staying in New York. He enjoyed his job with Ethan and liked the new friends he'd made. For a while, he'd loved his life, but nothing was working for him in Los Angeles anymore. The Big Apple had security firms. There were boxing rings everywhere. But Bella lived here. A huge part of him wanted to turn his back and walk away, but the part of him that couldn't fathom living the rest of his life without her was still in charge.

After yesterday, it was clear they needed some space. A few days away in Manhattan would give them both a chance to breathe. Bella would have time to work on the house Stone had mentioned she was buying, and he would have an opportunity to get his head on straight, because when he landed in LA next Tuesday, he had every intention of fighting like hell for Isabella Colby—whatever he had to do to convince her to take him back. His gorgeous next-door neighbor didn't stand a chance, because he didn't plan to play fair. Jed might have had his lips on Bella's Saturday night, but no one knew her the way he did.

"Fucker," he muttered as he shouldered his laptop case and grabbed his carry-on. With a glance at his watch, he headed downstairs, grabbing his keys off the counter as his phone started ringing.

"Hello?"

"Where are you?"

He stopped with his hand on the doorknob, immediately alerted by Skylar's tone. "At home—on my way to the airport. Why?"

"Joey just called. They pulled Bruno out of a dumpster half an hour ago."

"*What*?"

"Joe asked me to give you a call. He rushed down to the scene as soon as he heard—arrived about fifteen minutes ago. He's trying to get us more details."

"Shit." He jammed his hand through his hair. "What do we know so far?"

"They tortured him—multiple third-degree burns, gunshot wounds to the kneecaps and abdomen. I guess it's pretty bad. There was a paper with your name and number written on it shoved in his mouth along with a dead rat. His burner phone was protruding from his anus. Joe said he's missing his hands, so you can bet your ass Matty had a part in it."

"Bella." He dropped his bags and ran upstairs, taking his gun and an extra magazine from the lockbox. The Caparellis had to know he was connected to the dig going on in the Brooklyn field—that he was trying to help the Feds keep Alfeo where he belonged. "How long has he been dead?"

"They're thinking seventy-two hours, but it's probably more like five days—that's the last time his wife saw him. The body's still at the scene, so it's hard to say until the ME gets a look at him. He's pretty decomposed. The heat's gotten to him. Somebody called it in—could smell him from the street."

"If he's been missing five days, why are we just hearing about it?"

"I have no idea."

"Son of a *bitch*."

"They know you're an ex-cop, Reed—what you're all about. It's not going to be hard to trace you to your new life."

"And they've had three to five days to do it." He ran downstairs, grabbing his bags again, and booked it outside to the truck, tossing his stuff in the back before he got in and reversed from the driveway with a squeal of tires. "You can bet Bruno told them what they wanted to know—that I was looking for information about Alfeo, Dino, and Walter Hodds. About Nicoli's kid."

"You need to watch your back."

He wasn't worried about himself—just Bella. "I need to get to Bella."

"There's no way they know you're linked to his child."

"If they've been watching me, they know she's important to me. She's been with my family, to my mom's house. She stopped by the fucking gym yesterday. We argued in the parking lot for anyone to see."

"That doesn't mean they know she's Nicoli's."

"Maybe not, but how long did it take us to put the pieces together? They'll look into her because she's connected to me. It won't take Matty long to realize she's Luisa's friend. He'll think she's on my side—the law's side. You know as well as I do they'll think we sent her to Bensonhurst to spy." And the thought of what that meant for Bella made him sick. "I'll call you back after I have her with me." He hung up and dialed Bella's number as he weaved his way through the evening traffic to get to Bella's office five miles away.

Bella made a mental note of product she was running low on as she tidied her space for tomorrow's clientele. She needed to order in more of the vitamin C firming gel everyone seemed to love and the cotton pads she could never keep on the shelf, but otherwise she was in good shape—at least for the rest of this week. She shut off the music and rolled her stool closer to the treatment bed, then opened her door, stepping into the main office as a man walked past her, sending her a polite nod. She smiled, then felt herself frown as her gaze followed his path down the hall and out the door. "Who was that?" she asked Tonya as her assistant pushed her chair to her desk and grabbed her purse to leave for the day.

"Some guy here to see you—or to get more information about tattoo removal, anyway."

"Oh." Her frown returned as she looked at the door again, certain she'd seen him before. "Has he been in for something else—an appointment with Dr. Huberty?"

"No. I don't remember him. He said he has a tat on his left shoulder he wants removed. I gave him one of your new client packets, the before-and-after pamphlets—the usual stuff."

She shrugged. "Sounds good. Thanks."

"No problem." Tonya grabbed her lunchbox from her bottom

drawer. "I don't know about you, but I'm outta here."

"Yeah, I'm heading out in a minute too. I just need to put an order into the computer real quick. The vitamin C gel is a hit."

"I happen to love it myself." Tonya wiggled her brow. "My job definitely has its perks."

Bella chuckled.

"Dr. Huberty already left, so the back's all locked up."

"Perfect. I'll see you tomorrow."

"See ya." Tonya made a kissy noise at Lucy and headed out to the parking lot.

Bella sighed as she glanced at her watch, then smiled at Lucy. "Are you ready to go home?"

Lucy stood and stretched.

"What do you say we live on the edge and I put my order in tomorrow morning? We can go home for a quick dinner, then head back over to the house for a couple hours before we lose the light." She had a few blisters after clearing bushes last night, which was proving to be a bigger job than she'd expected, but that's what gloves were for. And she'd bought two pairs. "I hope you're going to leave the squirrels alone today. You're not making a very good impression on your new friends." She crouched down, giving her puppy a good rub, and laughed as she thought of the way Lucy had paced around the big tree in the backyard, waiting for her furry buddies to come back down. "I have a feeling you and that bunch are going to have a long, tenuous relationship."

Her phone rang as she stood. "Let me get that." Hurrying back to the treatment room, she hesitated, staring at Reed's gorgeous, grinning face filling her screen. She'd meant to erase her favorite shot of him—along with all of the other photos they'd taken over the last few months—but she couldn't. She wasn't ready yet. Sighing, she answered when it was probably better for both of them if she ignored his call, especially after their unpleasant little scene in the gym parking lot yesterday evening. "Hello?"

"Where are you?"

She heard the tension in his voice as she grabbed her purse and shut her door. "At the office. I'm closing up."

"Do you have Lucy with you?"

"Of course." She signaled for her puppy to follow and walked outside, locking the main entrance. "We're just about to head home."

"Stay in the building. Lock the doors. Don't get in your car."

"What? Why?"

"Skylar just called. They found my informant's body in a dumpster. They know who I am, Bella, which means they might know who you are too."

Fear washed over her as her gaze whipped around the empty parking lot. "Oh, God."

"I'm coming. I'll be there in a couple of minutes."

She shoved her key back in the door and gave a frantic twist with unsteady fingers. "Shouldn't I drive away? I'm all alone."

"*No*. Do *not* get in the car, Bella. Don't open the doors; don't turn over the ignition. They could've planted it with an explosive device."

"An explosive device?" This was real. This was really happening right now. "Come on, Lucy." She locked them back inside.

"Go in your office and shut the door. Stay away from the windows."

She booked it down the hall, locking them in her treatment room. "We're in my room."

"Stay on the phone with me."

She clutched the device in her hand as her eyes darted from the window to the door while her breath heaved in and out. "You couldn't get me off this thing if you wanted to."

"I can see your building. I'm pulling into the parking lot right now. Come on out."

"Okay." She hung up. "Let's go, Lucy." She stepped outside and locked up again while Reed waited, parked half on the curb.

"Get in," he said to Bella as he opened the gate for Lucy with the phone at his ear again. "Up, Lucy."

Lucy jumped in back as Bella closed the passenger door and fought to secure her seat belt with trembling hands.

Reed shut Lucy in and moved around to his side, taking his seat while he spoke to someone.

Bella swallowed, half listening to his conversation as she stared at the pistol shoved in the waistband of his jeans. He gunned it out into the busy evening traffic.

"...take someone with you if you want, but I need you to get my family. The Caparellis are on the radar. To Ethan's. He and the kids are out of town. Call me when you get there so I can let my mother know you're legit. Thanks, Jerrod." He dialed again, weaving his way through the cars, glancing in his mirrors several times. "Mom—Mom, I need you to let me talk. My coworker's coming to pick you and Aunt Bonnie up. Pack a few things..." He muttered a curse. "Mom, the

Caparellis found me. Everything's going to be fine. I'll explain later. When Jerrod gets there, he'll call me, and I'll call you back. Keep the doors locked. Don't open the door unless I call first. I'll see you soon." He tossed his phone down. "*Damn it.*"

Bella felt her heart's frantic beat against the side of her hand as she clutched at her seat belt. "How do they know about your family?"

"Because my guy's been dead for three to five days. By now, they know everything about me."

"But why would they hurt your mom and aunt?"

"The better question is why *wouldn't* they hurt my mom and aunt?"

She pressed her fingers to her lips, shaking her head, unable to imagine people harming two older women just because they could.

"Sorry," he said, tossing her an apologetic look. "I'm sorry, Bella."

"What are we going to do?"

"Stay at Ethan's until I can figure out exactly what's going on." He accelerated through a yellow light. "Have you seen anything funny—noticed anything that's felt off?"

She shook her head. "No."

"Think harder. Think about the last few days—a solicitor knocking on the door, someone walking in the neighborhood you didn't recognize."

"No. There's nothing." Then she remembered the man at the office and something clicked. He'd bumped into her cart. "There was a man at the office a little while ago. I saw him at the grocery store last night."

"You're sure?"

She nodded. "Mostly. I didn't get a very good look at him in the market. He was wearing a ball cap, but I remember thinking he sounded like Joey."

"Like Joey?"

"His New York accent."

Reed clenched his jaw. "What did he say?"

"He apologized for bumping my cart."

"But what did he say?"

"That's what he said. He said, 'Sorry about that.'"

"What did he say today?"

"I didn't talk to him. He asked Tonya for information about tattoo removal. He has a tattoo on his left shoulder."

"Did Tonya see it?"

"No. Or she didn't mention it, and she would have. She gave him a new client packet."

He turned into the quiet upscale neighborhoods of the Palisades. "What's in the packet?"

"Uh, standard forms for treatment, before-and-after pamphlets, a small biography of me. I like my clients to know who's treating them."

"What's in the biography?"

"Stuff about where I went to school, my certifications, my goals as a practitioner, a couple of things about Lucy—just fun, friendly mentions."

"Is there a picture of you?"

"Yes. One of me and Lucy together." She gripped her hands in her lap. "But the picture doesn't matter because they already know who I am."

"I don't know if they know you're Nicoli's, but they certainly know you're mine."

She stared at him, well-aware that neither scenario worked in her favor. "They sent that man here to hurt me."

He pulled up in front of Ethan's gate. "We're still trying to figure everything out."

But he believed so whether he said it out loud or not. "They're here to kill you."

"Let's figure everything out," he said again.

She nodded. What else could she do? "You have the code?"

"We all have a default code for emergencies."

"Is this a good idea?"

"It's the only one I've got. No one's getting in this place. Between Bear and Reece, the walls, and Ethan's sensor panels, it's not happening—or at least, we'll know about it if they find a way in." He pulled through, keeping his eyes trained on the rearview mirror while the gate slid closed. He moved down the long drive and parked.

Bella got out as Reed did and met him around back, throwing her arms around him.

"Hey," he said quietly as he wrapped her up tight, burying his face in her hair. "It's okay. Everything's going to be all right."

She burrowed closer against him, unable to stop her teeth from chattering as her whole body shook. "What about your mom and Aunt Bonnie?"

He slid his hands up and down her back. "They'll be here soon." He eased away. "Let's go inside."

She nodded when all she wanted to do was ask him to hold her in his arms again—where everything felt right despite the madness. "When will you know more?"

He let Lucy out of the back. "I'm going to call Joey and Skylar as soon as I hear from Jerrod."

"Okay."

"Later I'll go to your place and grab some—"

"No." She gripped his wrist as she thought of him going home to empty condos and being harmed as the sun sank closer to the horizon. "You can't leave me. You have to stay here where it's safe."

"We'll figure it out. Let's go inside." He wrapped his arm around her waist and walked with her to the door, using another code to gain entry.

"Come on, Lucy." They stepped into Ethan and Sarah's beautiful home and she took a deep breath, trying to believe that everything was going to be all right.

ᴄꞵ CHAPTER FIFTY-FIVE ꞵᴐ

BELLA STARED INTO THE DARK THROUGH THE HUGE PANES OF glass in the guest room, listening to the ocean's surf pounding the jagged rocks several hundred feet below. The water called to her, beckoning her to open the doors and step out onto the massive deck, but she was too afraid, even when the moon shined bright and she'd kept her bathroom light on to help brighten the space. Reed had assured her there was no way anyone could get to them here at the Cooke fortress. He'd promised her she was safe. On more than one occasion, she'd seen the state-of-the-art security panels in Ethan's home office, but she was frightened nonetheless. She glanced over her shoulder, looking across the hall toward Reed's temporary room, as uneasy with their close quarters as she was everything else going on. This wasn't how she'd planned to spend tonight or any night ever again. They weren't supposed to be living in the same space—sleeping under the same roof. Every time she thought she was taking a tiny step toward moving on, fate threw them back together.

Her new home was just down the road—a mere three blocks away. She craved to be there, pulling stubborn bushes from the earth and making progress—building something that was hers alone. Sighing, she leaned her shoulder against the glass and stared out the window again, jumping when she heard the light tap on the doorframe behind her. She turned her head, meeting Reed's gaze across the room.

"Hey."

She stood straight and folded her arms across the simple two-piece nighty she borrowed from Sarah's drawers, well aware that the silky spaghetti-strap top and matching shorts didn't do much to cover her. "Hey."

"How are you?"

She nodded. "Good."

"I brought you a sandwich since you didn't come down for dinner."

He walked to her, carrying a plate. "It's just ham on whole grain."

"Thank you."

"I added carrot sticks too." He handed her the pretty crockery and stepped back, shoving his hands in his pockets.

"Thanks," she said again and cleared her throat, swiping her hair behind her ear. The tension was back, choking the room, the moment of their warm embrace by the truck long over. Keeping a cautious distance had taken a back seat to grateful relief when they'd both been okay. "I appreciate the thought, but I'm not hungry right now."

He rocked back on his heels. "You should eat anyway."

She nodded, setting the plate on the nearby dresser. "I'll have a couple of bites later."

"You should try to eat the whole thing."

"I will." Frowning, she stepped closer and reached out, forgetting that she wasn't supposed to touch him as she brushed her fingers along his bruised jaw. "You're swollen. I didn't see it before, but it catches in the light."

"It's a little sore." He gave his jaw a testing wiggle as she dropped her hand. "Tink's got one hell of a right hook."

"I have to admit, I haven't been sure about the whole boxing thing. Then I saw you get punched in the face yesterday, and I'm certain I don't get it."

He grinned. "I guess it takes all kinds."

She returned his smile. "I guess it does." She grabbed the plate and wandered over to the bed, sitting on the edge of the mattress as she found herself relaxing in his easy company. "You really should get some ice on that."

"In a few minutes." He sat next to her, snagging one of her baby carrots. "Did you get a chance to talk to Dr. Huberty?"

She sampled a bite of ham, Dijon, and sweet honey bread and swallowed. "I told her what I could. She and Tonya are going to take care of things for the next few days."

"Good."

"Want some?" She held the half up to his lips.

"I made it for you."

"I don't mind sharing. I know you're always hungry."

He bit in and nodded. "It's good," he said over his mouthful.

"You make great sandwiches."

"Thanks." He glanced at his watch. "I didn't realize it was getting so late."

Her eyes wandered to the alarm clock. Almost eleven. "I'm not tired. I don't think I'm going to be able to sleep tonight."

"We can take a walk around the property if you want—get some fresh air."

The idea was tempting—too tempting. Nothing good could come from spending time with Reed in the moonlight. "I think I'm probably going to stay in."

He nodded, chewing another carrot.

She set down her plate as the room grew quiet again—uncomfortably so.

He steamed out a breath and rubbed at the back of his neck. "I can't stop thinking about today."

"I know." She brushed a crumb off her shorts. "It was scary."

"It was more than that." He took her hand, surprising her with the intensity in his voice. "I've never been so sick with worry. When I knew you were alone...when I couldn't get to you fast enough...I thought I was going to go crazy." He kissed her knuckles—once, twice. "I just needed to get to you."

She shuddered out a quiet sigh as heat rushed through her belly at his familiar gesture.

"I've never felt anything like that, Bella."

She held his gaze, trying not to be affected by his words and the warmth of his touch—the planes and angles of his gorgeous face in the shadows. "Why are you so easy on the eyes when you're so hard on the heart?"

"Bella—"

She pulled her hand from his and walked to the windows. "You should go. Thank you for the sandwich."

He came up behind her, settling his palms on her naked shoulders. "Please talk to me."

"There's nothing we need to say."

"We were doing okay a minute ago."

She kept silent, realizing she'd been a fool to believe that she and Reed could ever have a simple moment together; everything about them was so complicated.

"I miss you." He let his fingers trail down her skin. "I miss our conversations, laughing together, touching you—everything about us."

She shivered and her breathing grew unsteady as she laced her fingers with his, helplessly responding when he said all of the things she thought constantly.

"I want us back—to start over."

She closed her eyes before she eased away and faced him. "We can't."

"Yes, we can." He caressed her jaw as he moved into her space again, where she had no choice but to feel the heat radiating between them and breathe him in. "I love you. You love me."

"But I don't want to love you." She retreated again, bumping into the glass as tears filled her eyes. "Our relationship is broken. Beyond repair."

He shook his head. "I don't believe that. It can't be good for months—so damn good, Bella—then just be over."

She shoved her way around him, needing some space. "In this case, it can. The moment I walked into the room and saw you with my Dad, Skylar, and Joey... God," she said as she felt the shocking pain all over again. "You were supposed to be the one. You were supposed to be my normal. I was supposed to be able to depend on you, but you tell lies—damn good lies, Reed. You made me believe so *many* things that weren't true. Too many. How do I move past that?" She pressed her hands to her heart, absorbing true despair. "I'm in love with a liar, but I'm not Kelly Colby. I won't pine over you until I self-destruct. I won't make one bad decision after another because you were careless with me."

"Careless?" He gaped at her. "*Careless*? I didn't have a choice!" He paced away and back. "You act like I took pleasure in what I had to do. I lied to you, but I'm not a liar. I haven't lied to you since I've been given the choice not to."

"The result is still the same." Her voice grew louder, matching his. "We have nothing without trust. You broke that in a million different ways every single day. You broke my heart. Every time I see you, it breaks all over again."

"I'm sorry I hurt you, Bella." He captured her hands. "I'm so *damn* sorry."

She shook her head adamantly, her only armor against true regret. "It's not okay."

"What about the rest: the fun we had, the walks on the beach, our dinners on the porch, the way we were in bed? That had nothing to do with anyone but you and me. That was just the two of us, moving together, staring into each other's eyes. We didn't make that up. We couldn't."

She looked down. "That's over."

"Only because you've *said* so."

"That's right. I'm moving on. Isn't that what we're supposed to be doing? Moving on with our lives? I have mine, you have yours? Those are your words." She pointed at him. "Yours."

"What else am I supposed to say?" He kicked the side of the bed as he turned away and whirled back. "You haven't given me any damn choice."

She took her turn to pace as she looked at him, *loving* him despite everything. "I wish I could hate you. I want so badly to be able to hate you, but I can't. I've tried."

"Christ, you can be cold. There's no forgiveness?"

"I can't let you hurt me again."

"I've apologized," he shouted. "I've explained why I did what I did."

"Is that supposed to make it better?" She rushed up to him with a new wave of anger. "You could have kept things platonic. You could have—"

"I *tried*." He yanked her against him. "Don't you remember our kiss on the couch? I stopped that. But the more time we spent together... I couldn't resist you. After a while, I didn't *want* to. At some point, loving you became more important than hating the bastards that killed my family."

Their breath heaved in and out as they stared at each other.

"God." He cupped her cheeks as the anger vanished and his voice grew weary. "Do you think it didn't kill me every fucking time I looked at you and told you something that wasn't true? Do you think it didn't make me *sick* to know I was most likely destroying the one good thing I had in my life? I get that this is hard on you. But don't think for one damn second that this is any easier on me. It's not easy at all." He let her go and walked out, disappearing down the hall.

She closed her eyes, pressing her hand to her chest. How were they going to do this? How were they going to stay in this house together and not tear each other apart?

Reed sat on the front lawn, tossing tennis balls to Ethan's golden mastiffs while Lucy lay curled up by his side. His phone rang and he snatched it up, eager to focus on work instead of how bad things sucked between him and Bella. At this point, he had no idea how to fix their relationship. Maybe he couldn't, but he didn't want to think about that right now. "What do you have?" he asked Skylar. It had been hours since he'd gotten an update.

"Felipio's dead."

He paused with the ball above his head. "*What*?"

"Some club hoppers found him in a dumpster about an hour ago—a couple miles away from Bruno's scene. Joe's down there now."

"Jesus." He chucked the ball and stood, walking to his truck, too restless to stay still. "What's Joe saying?"

"That Felipio looks a lot like Bruno—minus the note in his mouth and phone up the ass, but they did find a rat."

Reed frowned. "He's not an informant—at least not mine."

"Maybe they felt like he was telling Bruno too much. It's looking like their bodies are in the same state of decomposition—more than likely killed at the same time."

He steamed out a breath, leaning against the grill. "Where's Matty during all of this?"

"In his house, lawyered up and offended that anyone would be stupid enough to question him about two murders that have nothing to do with him."

He clenched his jaw. "Sounds about right." He swung his arm in the air, swatting away a bug. "Did we figure out why Joe never got wind that Bruno was missing?"

"His wife never reported it. Her official line is she thought he was out of town."

He nodded. "Smart woman. Hopefully she'll pack up and get the hell out of there."

"What did you find out about the guy following Bella?"

"Not a damn thing other than he has dark hair, an olive complexion, a stocky build, and a strong New York accent. He may or may not have a tattoo on his left shoulder." Reed rolled his tense neck. "Bella's coworker couldn't tell me anything more than Bella did." And now that Bruno was gone, there was no one to ask whom he should be looking for.

"Keep me up to date if you get anything new."

"You know I will." He glanced toward the house when a light turned on in one of the upstairs windows.

"I talked to the DA before close of business," Skylar said, jumping topics.

He looked at his watch. Five o'clock in New York was hours ago.

"You and Joe are being subpoenaed," she continued.

"I figured as much."

"They're bringing in Isabella too."

"Bullshit." He pushed away from the truck. "The fuck they are, Skylar. You fix this."

"There's nothing I can do. I tried."

He walked down the driveway as his anger grew. "What are they thinking? Someone's after her, for Christ's sake."

"Someone's after *you*. The prosecution isn't going to back off on this because some guy bumped her cart at the grocery store and walked into her place of business. For all we know, it's a coincidence."

"Fuck that," he snapped.

"Until we can prove otherwise, you know that's what they'll say, and even if there is a threat against her, they'll still want her testimony. You're coming, aren't you?"

He tossed a look over his shoulder, realizing all three dogs were following him. "That's completely different."

"It's exactly the same. That's what the Marshals are for. Both of your protection."

He paced the width of the concrete, back and forth to the grass. "This is bullshit." He wanted Bella here behind Ethan's walls, where he had no doubt she would stay safe.

"She's Nicoli's daughter."

"And she knows nothing," he said, pointing to the air, punctuating every word. "You know she doesn't know one goddamn thing."

"The DA wants to talk to her—see that for himself."

"And if we refuse?"

"Don't be an idiot, Reed. Don't even think about blowing this whole thing and landing your ass in jail. We can keep her safe while you're here."

He swore again, well aware that there were no choices.

"The DA wants Alfeo staying right where he belongs as much as we all do," Skylar reminded him.

He doubted anyone wanted this more than he did, but he didn't bother to say so. "When is this happening?"

"Soon. I'm waiting on details. We all know we're under a time crunch. If we want to keep Alfeo behind bars during the new trial, this indictment needs to happen now. We're going to go after him with the bodies we can link to him with the most certainty and deal with the rest later."

"Fuck."

"I'm going to handle as much of this as I can—make sure the Marshals select men and women I know personally."

He stopped his pacing. "That's supposed to make me feel better?"

"It's the best I can do."

He rubbed at the back of his neck and sighed. "I know."

"I'll set up a team—"

"No." He shook his head, not liking any of this. "I want this kept quiet—all of it. You get me a date and time when he wants us to appear and I'll handle the rest. This is between you, me, and Joe."

"Reed—"

"You, me, and Joe." He hung up and shoved his phone away, ready to explode. First his knock-down-drag-out with Bella a few minutes ago and now this. "Son of a *bitch*," he said as all three dogs looked at him and wagged their tails. "This isn't the way things were supposed to happen." He let loose another long sigh and headed inside to Ethan's gym. He needed a workout to clear his head so he could think everything through. He was going to be planning their arrival and stay in New York—in and out. He knew for a fact that he wasn't dirty, and he was certain he could trust Joey and Skylar, but he couldn't be sure about anyone else.

☙ Chapter Fifty-Six ❧

Bella gripped the railing tight while she stood on the first-story deck, letting the wind dry her tears. She stared out at the water, replaying the harsh words she and Reed had tossed at one another. Wasn't it only moments ago that he'd sent her one of his sexy grins? Hadn't it been a mere two weeks since they'd laughed together and made love? She tipped her head to the stars, still trying to figure out how they'd gotten to this place where they wounded each other every time they found themselves occupying the same space.

"Bella?"

She whirled, dashing at her cheeks as Linda walked her way, wrapped in a light cotton robe. "Hi," Bella said, trying to smile.

Concern filled Linda's eyes as she stopped in front of her. "Oh, honey, look at you."

She wiped at another tear. "I'm just—I'm all right."

Linda frowned. "You don't look all right. You and Reed shouting at each other didn't sound all right."

She dropped her gaze, more than a little ashamed that she'd lost her cool to the point that she'd forgotten Reed's family was staying here too. "I'm sorry you overheard that."

"Honey, I listened to the whole thing. My room's right next door to yours."

She blinked, surprised by Linda's honesty. "Oh."

"I know that was rude of me. Reed would certainly accuse me of meddling—and I was—but it was sort of hard to walk away, particularly when I was certain the two of you had patched things up."

She huffed out a miserable laugh as she rolled her eyes to the sky. "No, we definitely didn't do that."

"Oh, sweetie." Linda settled a supportive hand on her shoulder. "Did Reed ever tell you about the night his father died?"

She wiped at a fresh tear as she shook her head. "No."

"Let's get some tissues and some of the nice cold water I spotted in the fridge." Linda wrapped her arm around Bella's waist and led her to the kitchen. "We'll have ourselves a seat and talk about it."

Bella grabbed the box of tissues on the counter and sat down while Linda poured their drinks.

"Here we go." Linda set two waters on the table and took the chair next to Bella's.

"Thank you."

"You're welcome, sweetie." She covered Bella's hand with her own. "So, what has Reed told you about his family?"

"Um, that his father was murdered." She swiped her hair behind her ear. "His grandfather and uncle too."

Linda nodded. "The night Travis died was the worst of my life. A piece of me went to his grave right along with him."

Bella reversed her hand, gripping Linda's as sympathy swamped her. She had no idea how Reed fit into her life anymore, but she couldn't imagine her world without him in it. "I'm so sorry."

"Travis was working a lot, doing deep cover. Typically, he spent tons of time with Reed, but the job was getting the better of him—started to take over as he infiltrated the mob."

Bella plucked up a tissue and froze. "You knew?"

Linda shook her head. "I had no idea what he and my father-in-law were doing at the time. I'm thankful for that, because I wouldn't have been able to function whenever he walked out the door."

"I can believe it." She wiped her nose and crumpled the tissue in her free hand.

"Reed was *very* close to Travis—to his grandfather and Uncle Mason too. We all lived within a couple blocks of one another—spent a lot of time together as a family."

"That sounds wonderful."

"It was. I miss our holiday gatherings and taking Reed and his cousin Kurt to the playground. Those two were inseparable."

"Special memories."

Linda nodded. "It was late May when we lost the men in our lives. Travis had a couple days off and decided he wanted to take Reed to a ball game for an early birthday present. The Red Sox were in town. Grandpa K. went along too. Unfortunately, they never came home."

Bella swallowed. "What happened?"

"Travis was driving them home after the game. They stopped at a red light just outside one of the parking garages. Witnesses say a couple of men stepped off the sidewalks from opposite directions, came up to the windows, and shot them."

She felt her eyes go huge as her heart stopped. "Reed was there?"

"Yes. Lying down in the back seat, covered up with a blanket. Travis had probably told him to get some sleep. He saved his son's life."

Bella pressed trembling fingers to her lips, trying to imagine a sweet little boy experiencing something so horrific. Innocence immediately lost. "I didn't—I had no idea."

"He was five. Not quite out of kindergarten. As two assassins were killing my husband and father-in-law, another two men walked into Bonnie and Mason's house and shot him right in front of her in the kitchen."

Bella fought a fresh wave of tears, consumed by the guilt of knowing she was from the family who ended lives so brutally, so uselessly. "Linda—"

Linda squeezed her fingers. "For a long time, Reed forgot about it—or put it out of his mind, is a better way to think about it, I guess. He never did say much about that night. He still doesn't."

"Do you think he remembers?"

"I have no doubt that he does."

She shook her head. She couldn't help but cry, hurting for him—the child and the man.

"As soon as the funerals were over, Reed and I moved. I was terrified the men who killed our family would come back for the rest of us, so I took him to Minnesota. When he was thirteen, we came out here to Los Angeles for a visit with Bonnie and Kurt. Kurt ended up saying some things to Reed about their fathers, and Reed soon became obsessed with figuring out why his dad died the way he did. We fought about it quite a bit as he grew older, but he was determined to find out every detail he could. Nothing gets in my son's way when he's set his mind to something."

"I've noticed."

Linda smiled. "By the time Reed was eighteen, I think he knew as much about the mafia as the men who run the organizations themselves. He was so talented in sports—a football star—but he didn't want the scholarships the Big Ten schools were throwing his way. He ended up choosing a college in the city. He was bound and determined to go to New York and right the wrongs he couldn't fix when he'd been a five-year-old hiding under a blanket."

Bella dropped her gaze, staring at the table as her heart broke all over again.

"I didn't see him much after he left. I tried making it hard on him—cut him off financially, hoping he would come back—but he made his own way. After he graduated from the police academy and moved up the ranks into the Special Crimes Unit, he started to change. For seven years, I watched him grow colder, harder, obsessed with getting justice. My son became a shell of a man. Until you." Linda lifted Bella's chin. "You brought a light back to his eyes, honey. He started smiling again. I think he realized for the first time that there was something more for him. Something better."

She shook her head. "I don't know what to say."

"Whatever has happened between the two of you, whatever truths he didn't tell you, that's real. You have a right to be angry and hurt. You have a right to your feelings of betrayal, but, honey, Reed's not a liar." She scooted closer and kissed Bella's cheek. "You're the best thing that's ever happened to him. I have no doubt that Reed loves you from the very *depths* of his soul."

Her lips trembled. "My father's family did this. I'm a Caparelli," she confessed in a rush. "I don't know any of them, but it doesn't make it any less true. They killed your family."

Linda shook her head, pulling Bella into a tight hug. "Oh, honey, Reed explained. Or at least what he could. You had nothing to do with this. Nothing at all. You're as innocent in all this as Reed. It just touched him differently because he was there that night, and you had no idea until just recently, sweetie."

She stood and walked to the counter, fiddling with a baby toy that had been left behind. "I'm so confused."

"Do you love him?"

She turned, meeting Linda's gaze. "I can't put into words how much."

"Talk to him, sweetie. When there's that much love between two people, there has to be a way to work it out."

She nodded, but she had no idea what to do.

Bella followed Metallica's blasting guitar riffs down the hall to Ethan's gym. She stopped in the doorway, watching Reed throwing a series of jabs at the heavy bag. Sweat dribbled down his muscled chest and stomach—flew off his powerful arms with every punch. She caught a glimpse of his ugly scars as she moved farther into the room and turned down the music.

He glanced her way and got back to work.

She folded her arms, clutching them tight. "You never told me you were in the car."

He stepped away from the bag and pulled off his gloves. "It never mattered."

She blinked, taken aback by his response. "How can you say that? You were just a little boy."

He grabbed a towel and wiped his face and chest. "Sympathy points. I don't want any."

She exhaled a quiet breath. "Is that what you think this is?"

He tossed down the towel and picked up his water bottle. "Pretty much."

She shook her head. "You want me to trust you. You want me to believe in you, but you leave out the most important parts."

His gaze whipped to hers—cold, edgy. "Does it matter anymore? You're with Jed now, right?"

She shook her head adamantly. "No—"

"It looked that way to me." He set down the bottle with a sharp slap and went back to the bag.

She clutched at her skin as the tension grew impossibly worse. "Jed's my friend."

He huffed out a laugh. "I guess we have different ideas of what constitutes a friend."

"That whole thing was a mistake."

"Was it? Because it looked like you were kissing him right back."

She walked closer to him, trying her best to find a way, remembering Linda's words about a love like theirs. "Do you know what I was thinking about that night? When he kissed me?"

He punched in another rapid combination. "I couldn't tell you."

"I was thinking about how he didn't taste like you. He didn't feel like you under my hands."

He tossed her a side glance as he shook his head. "You know how to mess a guy up."

Her eyes welled with tears. "I want you, Reed, but I can't have you."

"I'm right here."

"No." She pressed her fingers to her temple as her frustration grew. Why was this so *hard*? "I don't know what to *do* anymore. What am I supposed to do?" She dashed at a tear.

"I've said what I needed to say. I've apologized. You know who I am. Deep down, you know me."

She swallowed. "Do I?"

"You're the only one who does." He punched again. "I want to fight for you. I love you. I can't imagine spending another day without you, let alone the rest of my life, but maybe loving you means letting you go. Maybe me going to New York after we get this straightened out is the best thing I can do for you—for both of us. You can get on with things—build something new with someone who deserves you."

She turned away and burst into tears because she didn't want to share her life with anyone else, but how did she let go of the terror of handing him her heart again?

"Don't cry, Bella. Christ, it rips me up when you do. Especially when you won't let me fix it."

"I'm sorry. I can't help it." She took several steadying breaths and wiped at her cheeks, then turned back, facing him. "I don't know how to do this with you anymore. I don't know how I'm not supposed to feel guarded—like I need to protect myself from you. I let you into the deepest parts of me—my most shameful secrets." She paused, clearing her throat when her voice trembled again. "When I was confessing all, telling you about my mother and father, you held me close and listened. You made me feel safe—like I could tell you anything. You told me I could trust you, and I believed you. I let you into my world in a way that I've never done with anyone else, and you had an agenda the entire time."

"And you'll never know how sorry I am that our relationship wasn't just about the two of us, but it can be now."

"So I'm just supposed to flip a switch and be in that place with you?"

He jerked his shoulders as he shook his head. "I don't know anymore, Bella."

"I need time. I need some time to think and figure stuff out."

"So take it."

She nodded, intending to do just that.

"We have to go to New York."

She frowned at his rapid change of subject. "What?"

"We leave Monday morning—or at this point, we do."

"Why?"

"We're being subpoenaed to testify in front of the grand jury."

Her frown returned as she pressed her hand to her chest. "Me?"

He stopped, facing her with his hands on his hips. "I tried to keep you out of it—I'm still trying—but you're Nicoli Caparelli's daughter."

"But I don't know anything."

"I guess they want to hear you say that yourself."

She nibbled her lip, remembering their frightening afternoon. "What about the man who came to my work?"

"I'm going to talk to the DA when his office opens—"

"What about you?"

"Your father and I started this. I've lost everything that *matters* for this. The last thing I'm going to do is let Alfeo walk."

"Reed—"

"I don't want to talk about it anymore." He turned back to the bag. "You need time. We both need some space. We'll do what we can to stay out of each other's way around here."

She lifted her chin, well aware that she'd been dismissed. "I guess I'll see you Monday, then."

He stopped punching. "I said I'm going to talk to the DA."

"I'm going with you."

"Not if I can help it."

"The Caparellis have taken everything from your family. They robbed me of my father—of my mother, for that matter. If the DA thinks I can help keep my uncle in prison, then I'm going to do it. Maybe we can stop this horrible cycle right here. Maybe that's what this was supposed to have been about all along."

He clenched his jaw, steaming out a long breath through his nose. "I want you as far away from this as possible."

"I'm not going to sit back behind Ethan's walls while you risk it all."

"I started this—"

"No, they started this long before either one of us had a choice, but I have one now."

"Bella—"

"You're always so worried about my safety and protecting me. Maybe this time I can offer something that might protect you. Both of our lives are on the line, not just mine." She turned and walked off, still as confused and unsure about where she and Reed stood romantically, but she was going to do whatever she could to help take down the Caparellis.

☙ Chapter Fifty-Seven ❧

Reed opened the door to his and Bella's twenty-fifth-story hotel room, scanning the large, posh space before he let her inside. "Go ahead and take care of the lock for me," he said, keeping his hand close to the holster he wore beneath his sports coat while he did a quick sweep—opening the closet door, glancing under the bed, then pushing back the shower curtain in the bathroom. "We're good."

"Good." She set down her overnight bag and sent him a small smile as she swiped her hair behind her ear with a tense, jerky movement. "So, one bed." She gestured to their California king.

He shoved his hands in his pockets. "I was going to go for two doubles, but married couples typically share."

"I guess it would look kind of weird if we didn't."

He nodded. "We're doing our best to fly under the radar for the next few hours. Hopefully we won't even have to sleep here."

She nodded. "Do you want a particular side?"

He took off his jacket, wishing he could get rid of the damn slacks and tie too. "The usual works for me."

She set her bag beside the mattress on the left, where she typically slept. "I guess we're all set."

"Looks like it," he said, rubbing at the back of his neck.

"Great."

"Great." Christ, this was painful. They'd kept their distance over the last few days, managing to avoid each other for the most part. He'd been so busy coordinating the trip to New York with Ethan, Skylar, and Joey, he hadn't had time to focus on his personal life. Private jets, hotel reservations, assumed names, and the hundred other precautions they'd put into place were far less daunting than his and Bella's mess.

She stepped out of her black pumps. "So, when do we leave for the trial?"

"Remember, it's just a hearing—more like a meeting. You're going to talk to the DA in his private office instead of in front of the grand jury." Because he'd fought like hell to make sure it happened that way.

"Right."

He grabbed the remote and handed it to her. "We have a couple hours before Skylar picks us up. The DA's meeting with you at two so you might as well make yourself comfortable."

She nodded, flipping on the TV as she sat down on the edge of the bed and stared straight ahead.

He clenched his jaw as he pulled out the chair at the desk and took a seat. They were turning into strangers. The entire day had been pretty much the same thing—a few awkward words spoken here and there, then long stretches of hellish silence. He trailed his gaze up her trendy black slacks and spaghetti-strap polka-dot top. Stylish Bella Colby—so different from him. Maybe they just weren't meant to be together. Sighing, he scrubbed his hands over his face and walked to the window, standing to the side of the glass as he peered out at the city.

"Is it safe to look out?"

"It should be."

She stood by his side, grinning as her gaze tracked around their view of the buildings and park. "I've never been to Central Park before. It's so iconic."

She smelled so damn good. "I wish I could take you. You would love Bethesda Fountain and Bow Bridge. There's a zoo too."

"Maybe sometime."

He watched her eyes trail over his holster and stop on the gun tucked snug against his ribs. "Hey."

She met his gaze.

"This will be over soon. We're going to do what we need to do and get out of here."

She nodded.

Taking a chance, he lifted his hand and slid his fingers along her jaw. "I miss you, Bella. So much."

Her eyes went soft—the way they used to—as she pressed his palm to her cheek. "I miss you too."

He stroked her skin, wanting to capture her mouth and taste her, but he winked and stepped away instead, deciding to keep the moment easy. "Why don't we find something to watch on TV?"

"I'm probably going to freshen my makeup and do my hair in a French braid first."

"Okay."

She grabbed her bag and smiled at him before she closed herself in the bathroom.

He stared at the door and fist-pumped the air. She missed him. That was a start, but repairing their relationship was going to have to wait a little while longer. He needed to worry about getting them through the next few hours first.

Bella stabbed the last bite of her huge room service salad and laughed at Amy Schumer's latest shenanigans. She glanced at Reed sitting on his side of the bed and grinned when he burst out laughing again.

"Damn, this is funny." He picked up the remains of his cheeseburger and popped it in his mouth. "Why haven't we watched this movie before?" he asked over his mouthful.

Reed had come across *Trainwreck* on the guide while they'd waited for their lunch to arrive. For the first time in too long, they'd found a way to have a little fun together. "I guess we were too busy with *The Office*." She set down her fork and wiped her mouth with the cloth napkin. "I think we need to start branching out more."

He shook his head. "We have to finish what we started first."

She dabbed at her mouth again and cleared her throat, not quite sure how to respond to his blatant double meaning. "I don't know what to say to that."

He flashed her a smile. "Maybe we'll just let it go for now."

She smiled back as she set down her napkin. "Okay."

"Did you get enough to eat?"

"Yes, I—" She froze when someone knocked on the door.

Reed rushed off the mattress, holding a finger to his lips as he moved his right hand to his gun.

She nodded, feeling her heart pounding as she watched the light leave his eyes and Mad Dog McKinley appear. For just a moment, she'd forgotten that they were in danger—that they still had everything to lose.

"It's Skylar," a woman's voice called from the hallway.

He walked over to the door and peeked through the peephole,

then twisted the knob. “Hey.”

“Hey.” Skylar stepped inside dressed in practical heels, tailored gray slacks, and a jacket. She offered Bella a professional smile. “Ms. Colby, thank you for coming all this way.”

Ms. Colby? Bella stood, studying the gorgeous blonde, not quite certain if it was hostility she felt from Reed’s pal or if Skylar’s intense, no-bull energy was just part of the whole law enforcement package. “I’m happy I can help. I hope you’ll call me Bella.”

“Bella.” Skylar gave her a brisk nod and turned her attention to Reed. “The car Joe dropped off is parked in the garage.”

He nodded, touching his gun again before he put on his sport coat. “Let’s do this.” He looked at Bella. “Ready?”

“Um, yes.” She walked over to the desk and grabbed her purse as she slipped on her heels, trying her best to ignore her nerves.

Skylar walked out first.

Bella followed.

Reed snagged her by the hand. “Stay with me, Bella. I want you right here next to me.”

She nodded, gripping his fingers tight as they stepped into the elevator just down the hall from their room. Moments later, the door slid open in the dimly lit parking garage.

“Right over there.” Skylar walked to the Buick Regal parked half-way down the lot, hitting the key fob.

Bella moved to follow.

Reed pulled on her hand, keeping her next to him as he held open the elevator. “Hold on.”

She frowned. “What are we doing?”

“Waiting.”

“For what?”

“Just wait right here.”

Skylar got in and turned over the engine.

“Okay,” he said.

Bella’s stomach roiled as she realized they’d been waiting to see if Skylar blew up—the explosive devices Reed had mentioned the day he told her not to get in her vehicle because the Caparellis could have rigged it with a bomb.

He opened the back door. “Go ahead and get in.”

She let go of his hand and slid in, more than a little relieved when he took the seat next to her.

“Looks good,” he said as he glanced around.

Skylar accelerated, keeping a fast pace as they wound their way up three stories to street level and into afternoon traffic.

Bella gripped her hands together as she looked out at the pedestrians making their way around the city on the sunny New York afternoon. She'd always found urban living fascinating—particularly the Big Apple—but today she craved to be anywhere else as the sickening tension filling the car made her head hurt. She glanced down at Reed's hand resting next to her leg and grabbed it.

He met her gaze and laced their fingers, giving her a gentle squeeze. "We're doing fine," he said quietly.

Then why did he look like he was ready to kick some serious ass? But she nodded anyway, holding his intense stare as they made their way to the Brooklyn Bridge.

"We're okay," he reassured her again.

She nodded a second time, wanting the moment back in the hotel room when he'd grinned at her and been the Reed McKinley she'd fallen in love with. That sweet, funny man had been absent for days. She'd gotten a firsthand glimpse of who Reed had once been during their stay at the Cookes': unapproachable, unreadable—a million miles away even when they'd sat across from each other at the dinner table.

"Trust me," he whispered.

When it came to her heart, she was trying; when it came to her safety, she didn't hesitate. She settled her free hand over their intertwined fingers, telling him so with her gesture.

Eventually, Skylar took a right by the courthouse and pulled into another parking garage, taking them down into a tunnel-like area before she stopped by a door where Joey waited.

"Let's go," Reed said as Skylar got out and opened Bella's door. Skylar then gained entry into the building with the swipe of a card and a punch of a code into a keypad.

"Everything looks good," Joey said as he settled in the driver's seat and took off.

Reed wrapped his arm around Bella's waist and ushered her up three flights of stairs, down a long hall, and into a small room with benches, a two-door access, and a bathroom.

Moments later a woman walked in—another no-nonsense type in a power suit. "Special Agent Grayson."

Skylar gave the brunette fortysomething a brisk nod. "ADA Gardenbaum."

Bella watched the professional exchange, growing more uncomfortable by the second. Did these women ever *smile*?

"Mr. McKinley, Ms. Colby, I'm Assistant DA Sally Gardenbaum." Her lips curved slightly. "Ms. Colby, the DA will be ready for you shortly."

"Okay. Thank you."

The assistant DA walked back out, leaving the three of them to wait.

Bella blew out a long breath as she paced back and forth. "I think I'm going to use the restroom." She closed the door most of the way and crossed her arms as she stared at the colorful panes of privacy glass decorating the window, doing her best to steady her racing heartbeat.

"Bella?" Reed gave a quick knock and stuck his head in. "Are you okay?"

She turned. "I don't know why I'm so nervous."

He stepped in, closing the door behind him. "Today's pretty informal—not that big of a deal."

She frowned. "You're not nervous. Why aren't you nervous?"

"Because I used to do this all the time, and the DA can move forward with the case whether the jury agrees with his decision to prosecute or not."

"Right." She blew out another breath. "Of course." She pressed her hand to her stomach.

"Hey." He captured her by the elbow and pulled her close, letting his forehead rest against hers as he locked his wrists behind her waist. "Relax."

Closing her eyes, she hesitated before she settled her hands on his powerful arms, allowing herself the luxury of taking the comfort he offered. "It's just—I know how important this is."

"And you're going to do great. The DA wants to ask you a few questions. Answer as honestly you can and let him handle the rest."

She nodded. "Thank you."

"You're welcome."

She eased away enough to straighten his collar and adjust his tie, forever thinking of Linda's powerful words Wednesday night. If Reed was willing to fight for them, then she wanted to try too. Despite the reason for their visit to New York, this was the first time anything had felt right since she'd told him their relationship was over. Standing here, touching him, and talking eased her in a way nothing else could. "You look handsome today. Your tie matches your eyes."

He held her gaze. "Thanks."

"You know, I used to think neckties and slacks were pretty sexy."

"You don't anymore?"

She shrugged. "I kind of have a thing for blue jeans and athletic shorts."

They grinned at each other.

Skylar knocked and opened the door. "The DA's ready."

Bella met Skylar's steely stare, noting the hints of disapproval. Interesting.

Reed lifted her chin with a gentle finger under her jaw. "Should we go get this over with?"

"Yes."

"Come on." He walked next to her as the assistant DA caught up with them in the hall.

"Right this way. Elliot's eager to get started. Mr. McKinley, we'll be calling you directly after Ms. Colby is finished."

He nodded. "Thanks."

They stepped into an office decorated in burgundy leather and dark wood. A tall, thin man with strawberry blond hair stood. "Ms. Colby, it's good to see you. I'm District Attorney Elliott Moore."

She shook his hand. "Hello."

"Mr. McKinley." The DA extended his hand to Reed as well.

"It's nice to see you again, DA Moore."

A short woman with pretty hazel eyes walked in with a tray of bottled waters as Reed and Bella took their seats in front of the DA's desk. "Here you go. Let me know if you need anything else."

"Thank you, Shawna. If you'll just close the door on your way out, I think we're all set."

Shawna smiled and left.

The DA sat down, glancing at his watch before he met Bella's gaze. "We'll get started right away. I'm going to ask you some questions. All I need you to do is provide me with an honest answer."

She nodded, taking a long, steadying breath. "Okay."

He picked up his pen as the assistant DA did the same in the chair next to his. "Ms. Colby, can you please state your full name?"

"Yes, my name is Isabella Raine Colby."

"You're the daughter of Nicoli Caparelli?"

"Yes, although I knew my father by a different name."

"Your father was a participant in Witness Protection?"

She nodded. "But it's only recently that I was made aware of that."

He scribbled a note on his yellow legal pad. "You didn't know your father was part of the Witness Protection Program?"

She shook her head. "No."

"When did you find out?"

"Um, just about three weeks ago. I stumbled upon him making a recording for the FBI—or you, I guess." She cleared her throat as she glanced at Reed.

"Ms. Colby, as we move forward, I would like to refer to your father as Nicoli to keep his alias protected and you safe."

She nodded. "All right."

"Nicoli helped raise you?"

"Until I was five. He left a few days before my fifth birthday."

"Can you tell me more about that?"

She gripped her hands in her lap, realizing that today was going to be not only nerve-wracking but also painful. "My father shared with me that he had been recognized and thought it safest to leave my mother and me behind. He didn't want us living the life that's required of someone in the program. One night, he told me he had to go and was gone the next morning."

The DA added another note to his sheet. "Thank you."

Bella went on to answer question after question about her time with Dad as a little girl, sharing the few pathetic details she could remember before they moved on to discuss their relationship from the moment she knocked on his door in Reseda until his death.

The DA sat back in his chair and laced his fingers. "Tell me what you know about Alfeo Caparelli."

"Not much. Just that he's the head of the Caparelli crime family, he's in prison, and he's a terrible, dangerous man."

"Would you say you're afraid of your uncle?"

"As I said, I don't know him. I can only go by the stories I've heard—the facts that I've read in the news or that Reed or my father have shared—but I'm certainly afraid of any man who would kill his brother if he had the chance and murdered a pregnant woman in cold blood. My father was very much afraid for me."

The DA sat up again. "Thank you, Ms. Colby."

"You're welcome."

He flipped the pages of his notebook closed. "I think that's all I need."

She frowned. "That's it?"

"Yes."

"What's next? Will I go before the grand jury?"

"No, but I appreciate you flying all the way in from California."

"But I want to help. I must have told you something that might be helpful."

"You gave me a glimpse into Nicoli Caparelli—one I haven't seen before."

"Maybe that would be beneficial to the trial."

"Ms. Colby, our goal is *always* to protect our witnesses. Although I'm grateful for your time, I didn't find anything particularly compelling about your testimony—certainly nothing that warrants the risks of exposing your identity on the witness stand. The Caparellis are extremely dangerous. I would like to keep you away from that."

But Reed still had to risk it all. "Thank you," she said again and stood, walking into the hall, fairly certain she couldn't have failed her father or Reed more than she just did.

Reed followed, pulling her back into the room where Skylar waited. "You did a good job."

She shook her head. "I'm sorry."

He frowned, taking her hands and tugging her into the corner with him. "Why are you apologizing?"

"I wanted to do more. I wanted to help you."

"All I've ever wanted is to keep you out of this whole damn mess."

"But—"

"I'm glad they won't use you. I'm *glad*, Bella." He squeezed her fingers. "I would have fought him—gone above his head if he had made any other decision."

She felt her shoulders stiffen.

"I need you safe." He pressed a gentle kiss to her forehead. "There's nothing more important than your safety."

"What about yours?"

"I'm going to be fine."

She held his stare, not quite so sure.

The interior door opened to a large conference-type room, and the assistant DA walked in. "We're ready for you, Mr. McKinley."

"Thank you." He gave Bella his attention. "Stay here with Skylar. I'll be back as soon as I can."

"Okay."

He walked out with the assistant DA, and Bella looked at Skylar. "I guess we're stuck here for a while."

Skylar glanced up from her phone mid-text. "You might as well take a seat."

She stayed on her feet, not loving Skylar's tone. "You don't like me much, do you?"

Skylar lifted a perfectly sculpted eyebrow, holding her stare. "Reed deserves to be happy. You make him happy and I'll like you just fine."

She settled her purse more securely on her shoulder, refusing to be intimidated by the woman across the room. "Our relationship is complicated, but we're trying to figure things out."

"Good." Skylar's phone rang. "Special Agent Grayson." She held up a finger to Bella, signaling for one minute, and walked into the hall.

Bella sighed and rolled her eyes to the ceiling, never a big fan of drama, but she couldn't blame Reed's friend for looking out for him. His buddies were protective. How could she fault them for that? She sat down and pulled out her phone to check her email, then glanced up when she heard the voices in the room where Reed had disappeared. Standing, she walked to the door that had been left ajar and caught her bottom lip between her teeth as she opened it further to peek in, watching Reed while he sat in a chair across from a group of individuals at a conference table.

"Please state your name for the grand jury," DA Moore said.

"My name is Reed McKinley."

"Mr. McKinley, please share with us your background."

"I'm a former undercover officer with NYPD. I worked deep cover in the Special Organized Crime Unit infiltrating the Caparelli crime family for seven years."

"If the group can focus their attention on the screen, please. Many of the images you're about to see are quite graphic," the DA warned as the lights were dimmed and a picture appeared on the projector.

Bella moved closer to the crack, staring at a light-colored sedan with blood spattered around broken glass, realizing they were crime scene photographs.

"Mr. McKinley, you have more than just a law enforcement connection to the Caparelli crime family, correct?"

"Yes, I do."

"Do you recognize this photograph?"

"Yes. That's a crime scene photo from May twenty-sixth, 1989."

"Mr. McKinley, how old were you in May of 1989?"

"Five—nearly six."

A picture of a small boy wrapped in a blanket, clinging to a police officer, filled the screen. The image shattered Bella's heart, but she couldn't tear her gaze away from the child's terrified blue eyes—Reed's eyes.

"Mr. McKinley, do you know who that child is?"

"Yes. That's me."

"You're five in this picture?"

"Yes."

"Can you describe what's going on in this photograph, please?"

"I was being taken away from my family car. My father and grandfather had been assassinated minutes before. The officer carrying me found me in the back seat."

Another gruesome picture appeared—so much blood and two male bodies slumped in seats.

Bella pressed her hand to her mouth, wanting to look away, but she made herself watch Reed's worst moments play out in a horrific slide show.

"Tell us about this picture please, Mr. McKinley. I'm sorry if this is tough."

He nodded. "The driver is my father with a fatal gunshot wound to the left temple, and the passenger is my grandfather, also with a fatal gunshot wound to the right temple."

"And you were in the back of the car at the time of the murders?"

"Yes. I was lying down when my family was killed."

"Hiding under a blanket?"

He shook his head. "No."

DA Moore moved back to his table, flipping through several sheets of paper. "The police report says you were hiding under the blanket."

"I hid after I saw what happened to my dad and grandpa. If you'll return to the picture where the officer is holding me, you'll see that I have blood and brain matter in my hair, which corroborates my memories."

The projector moved to the previous slide, and there was indeed blood and brain matter in the sweet little boy's hair—on his cheeks.

Bella shook her head, unable to hold back her tears. "You poor baby," she whispered.

"Your father was a police officer?"

"Yes. A detective with NYPD. He'd moved over to the Special Organized Crime Unit a year before his death."

And your grandfather?"

"He was a Senior Special Agent with the Federal Bureau of Investigation. My father and grandfather were working as a father/son unit as part of their cover while they infiltrated the Caparelli crime family."

"There was another murder the night your father and grandfather were killed." A new picture appeared of a man lying dead—shot in the head and staring blankly by a kitchen stove. "Can you tell us who this man is, Mr. McKinley?"

"That's my Uncle Mason. My father's brother. He was murdered in front of his wife at their home."

"He was also an NYPD officer, correct?"

"Yes."

"What part did he play in the Caparelli investigation?"

"None whatsoever. He was a beat cop for fifteen years before his death."

"On the night of your family's massacre, it was reported that you heard the men approaching the car, saying something about Alfeo Caparelli."

"Yes. I heard the man by my father's door say 'This is from Alfie' before he shot my father."

"Alfeo Caparelli shot your father?"

"No. Alfeo Caparelli's hit team shot my father on Alfeo Caparelli's orders."

"That's a strong statement—a damning accusation."

"It's a fact."

"Then why was Alfeo Caparelli never charged with the capital murders of three law enforcement officers, Mr. McKinley?"

"I was interviewed by the police on several different occasions after my family's murders. I spoke of Alfeo Caparelli at the scene but never mentioned him again after. The authorities were unable to move forward with charges without stronger evidence."

"Yet you remember the incident you've described as fact?"

He nodded. "Absolutely."

"Mr. McKinley, you were very young at the time. Not even out of kindergarten."

"Yes."

"Isn't it possible that your memories have become inaccurate over time? Perhaps *skewed* is a better word."

He shook his head. "That night is something I'll never forget. Can't forget. I remember it like a dream, but the dream has stayed one hundred percent consistent for nearly twenty-six years."

"Thank you, Mr. McKinley." The projector moved on to new slides dated from last year as the DA fast-forwarded to the July night Reed was shot.

Bella wiped her cheeks, watching Reed patiently explaining photos of his and Joey's post-surgery wounds, pictures of evidence markers placed next to their pools of blood at the warehouse crime scene, and another photograph of him and Joe sitting side by side in wheelchairs, holding IV poles while giving the camera thumbs-up. He'd been through hell. Reed had lived through unimaginable tragedies and violence, yet he was an amazing man. He had every right to be angry and bitter, but he regularly brought the woman he loved flowers and befriended disfigured little girls. He'd helped care for a cancer-stricken man he easily could have hated.

She moved to one of the benches and sat down, having seen more than enough finally to understand. Reed had lied to her so many times, but he'd done so to save her—and maybe himself in the process. *Something was dead inside me before we met.* She closed her eyes, remembering the cozy moment on her kitchen floor when they'd been caught up in each other—when they'd been happy and nothing else mattered. All this time, she'd needed Reed to be her normal, but he needed her to be his normal too—a chance to start over and leave the past behind. She finally got that she couldn't save him from the Caparellis, but they could save each other from the aftermath and build a beautiful life.

She looked up when Skylar walked into the room and shut the door.

Skylar frowned. "Are you okay?"

She nodded, but she wasn't. Nothing would be okay again until she could talk to Reed and make things right.

☙ Chapter Fifty-Eight ❧

Bella waited for Reed to unlock their hotel room door and walked inside.

"Go ahead and get the lock," he said as he shut them in for the night and followed the same procedure he had earlier in the afternoon—looking in the closet, under the bed, and in the bathroom.

She secured the deadbolt and threw the latch in place for good measure, then slipped off her shoes, wiggling her toes as she set down her purse. The ride back from the courthouse had been long and quiet. Reed hadn't said much—just held her hand as they made their way through the city.

He walked out of the bathroom, rubbing at his jaw, then the back of his neck—telltale signs that he was edgy after a long day. "Everything looks fine."

But he didn't. She studied his eyes, seeing the strain he tried to hide. "Good."

"Joe's bringing us dinner in about an hour." He took off his jacket and holster, hanging both on the back of the desk chair. "We'll figure out how we're going to work things tomorrow since I have to go back—"

Unable to take it any longer, she closed the distance between them and wrapped him up in a hug. Dinner and tomorrow didn't matter right now.

"Whoa." He returned her embrace, gripping her tight.

She closed her eyes, settling her cheek on his firm chest, and breathed him in.

He rested his chin on top of her head. "What's all this?"

She burrowed closer. "You have every right to be horrible, but you're not."

He eased her back. "What's going on, Bella?"

Her eyes filled as she held his gaze, swamped by a wave of love, hurting for him. "You tried to tell me. And your mom tried to tell me. Aunt Bonnie and even my dad too, but today I saw everything for myself, and I'm so sorry."

He slid his thumbs along her cheeks, catching her tears. "Don't cry."

She sniffled, shaking her head. "I'm not. Truly. I'm just—I'm sorry."

He frowned. "I'm not sure what we're talking about here."

"I saw the pictures. I heard what you lived through. The door was open to the grand jury room, and I eavesdropped when Skylar left—"

His frown deepened. "Skylar left you?"

She shook her head. "She was in the hall. I was fine. That doesn't matter anyway. I saw, Reed. You were so little. Those photographs broke my heart."

"We all live with stuff."

"Not stuff like that."

He clenched his jaw. "You didn't have it easy growing up either."

"My childhood was certainly different, but my worst day *never* compared to yours." Her eyes welled again.

"It was a long time ago."

"But you carry it with you. You said so yourself. You can never forget it. I can see it in your eyes right now—the pain today caused you."

He stepped away, jamming his fingers through his hair. "I don't want to talk about it."

"I do." She took his hand, stopping him from turning away. "I want all of you, Reed. The triumphs and tragedies. The good and the bad. Your faults and virtues. Everything that makes you who you are. I need you to trust me."

"I do."

She brought his knuckles to her cheek, nuzzling him. "I want for you to be able to tell me anything and everything the way I can you. That's the only way this is going to work."

His eyes sharpened on hers. "What are you saying right now?"

"I'm saying I love you and I've been so wrong."

He cradled her face. "Bella—"

She gripped his wrists. "The lies and secrets hurt me so badly—"

"I never wanted to hurt you. Through all of this, I never, *ever* wanted to hurt you."

She nodded. "I know. I understand that now. I think I've understood that all along..." She took a deep breath. "I'm still scared, but I'm more afraid of being without you. I don't want to live without you."

He kissed her, diving deep and groaning as he plundered.

She moaned, standing on her tiptoes and wrapping her arms around the back of his neck as she savored the bold taste of him and the way her body molded so perfectly to his. This was what it felt like to be warm again—to be whole.

"I want to start over," he said, pressing kisses to her chin and jaw. "Let's go back to the beginning and do this right—the way I wish we could have all along."

She loosened his tie, pulling it off. "But I love so much of who we are—of what we already have."

He gently pulled the elastic from her hair and freed her long locks from her braid. "So we'll tweak the couple of parts that need a little maintenance."

"I like that idea." She went after the buttons on his shirt. "I guess if we're starting over, we'll need a first date."

He grinned. "If I could walk out the door with you right now, I would. I'd bring you to the park, but we're going to have to wait until all of this is over."

"We can do the park next time." She snagged his ear, nipping and tugging with her teeth. "I guess you'll just have to take me to bed. We'll live on the edge and pretend I'm easy. Tonight you're hitting a home run and you didn't even buy me dinner first."

He laughed, sending his hands on a journey down her back and over her ass. "I'm not really into easy chicks."

She kissed his neck. "We're pretending, remember?"

"I don't have to pretend that I'm into you." He made quick work of ridding her of her top and slacks.

"Perfect." She sent his shirt to the floor, cruising her palms over hot flesh. "I've missed touching you. I never want to stop touching you."

He closed his eyes, steaming out a long breath.

She trailed her mouth over his pecs as she tugged on his belt, then his snap, pushing his pants past his hips.

"Lie down with me." He walked her backward to the bed and settled himself on top of her. "I want to make out with you for a while."

She grinned, relishing his weight pushing her into the mattress. "I can live with that."

He stared into her eyes as the setting sun played with the light in the room. "I've been so afraid this was never going to happen again. I know we have a lot of work to do—issues to find our way through—but I need you to know how much I love you." He kissed the tip of her nose. "I'm so in love with you, Bella."

Flutters rushed through her belly as she smiled. "I love you too. So much." She pulled his face down to hers and kissed him, letting the moment draw out.

He touched her, sliding his fingers along her waist, up her stomach, and finally he took off her bra.

She moaned, shivering as he traced her sensitive peaks with his thumbs, then his tongue. "I want to be with you," she whispered.

He rose on his knees and pulled off her panties, then made quick work of taking off his boxers. "You're sure this is what you want?"

She nodded, opening her arms to him, welcoming him back to her.

He settled himself between her legs and captured her mouth as he buried himself inside her.

She whimpered, savoring the way he filled her.

He moved slowly—torturously so. "God, Bella, you feel so good."

She wrapped her arms around him and then her legs, pushing him deeper, certain she could never be close enough.

He kept his pace steady, staring into her eyes.

"I need you." She gripped his shoulders, rocking her hips, feeling herself building. "I need you," she shuddered out.

He took her hands, lacing their fingers and pushing their arms beneath the pillows. "I want to come with you. Wait for me."

She nodded, moving with him, urging him to follow her to the edge as she listened to his breathing grow unsteady. "I need to—I'm ready. I'm ready," she said.

He arrowed deeper and she gasped, crying out as he captured her mouth and fell over the cliff with her.

Reed fought to catch his breath as he stared into Bella's eyes, still trying to wrap his mind around the reality that they were actually lying here together again. Finally, he was holding her and touching her the way he'd yearned to since she walked out on him three long weeks ago. "How are you?"

"Great. Excellent, in fact." She grinned, tracing his ears. "Have I ever mentioned that you're an amazing lover?"

He smiled back, sliding his fingers through her hair. "Not straight out."

"You're very good in bed." She nipped his chin.

"Thanks, but I think it's because of my partner. We make a pretty good team."

"Yes, we do."

"Plus you're smokin' hot, which gets me all worked up..."

She laughed.

Grinning again, he brought her palm to his lips, kissing her—once, twice—before he studied her healing blisters. "Something's telling me you got these beauties working on the new house—maybe pulling up the ugly bushes out front?"

She chuckled. "Good guess."

He rolled them so they lay on their sides, facing each other. "Are you going to let me give you a hand with the rest?"

"Yes."

"Are you going to let me sign my name next to yours on the mortgage?"

She nodded. "Mmm-hmm."

He hooked his arm around her waist and pulled her closer. "I've been so damn miserable without you."

She pressed her lips to his. "I missed you every day. I woke up reaching for you almost every night."

He rested his forehead against hers. "I never want— I need for us to work. I can't imagine spending another minute without you."

She played her fingers along the back of his neck. "I need for you to let me in. All the way in, Reed. No more secrets."

He closed his eyes and nodded, knowing she was right—that she deserved all of him, even when what she asked for wasn't easy. "Today sucked." He opened his eyes, staring into hers. "Bad."

She stroked his cheek. "I'm sorry."

"I hate remembering. I hate having to take it all back out again. More than anything, I hate that they died like that."

Compassion filled her gaze. "How can I help you? What can I do?"

"Just be here."

"I'm right here." She took his hand, settling it against her heart. "I'm not going anywhere."

He exhaled a quiet breath with a sense of relief he'd never known before. For decades, he'd shouldered the burdens of witnessing violent death and the painful aftermath alone, but Bella was offering to carry some of the load—the way he would for her without a second thought. "I miss my Dad—all of them."

"Your mom said you were close."

He nodded. "He saved my life that night. He told me to lie down right before we pulled out of the parking garage. I remember him saying that if I didn't get some sleep, I'd be too tired for our donut trip and my favorite cartoons the next morning. We always watched Bugs Bunny together."

She blinked as her eyes grew damp. "Sounds pretty special."

"I like remembering that part. I could do without the rest."

"I bet." She kissed him, clutching his hand tight in hers. "If you remember everything so clearly, why didn't you mention Alfeo to the police after your initial interview?"

"Because I saw the terror in my mom's eyes the first time I did."

"Oh, Reed." She wrapped her arm around him and held on.

Returning her embrace, he rolled so she lay on top of him and breathed in her shampoo as her hair cascaded around them. "I want this to be over. I don't want to have to think about it anymore."

She slid her long locks behind her ears and settled her arms on his chest as they looked in each other's eyes. "You can put it away tomorrow."

He shook his head. "Until the trial."

"And then it's finished."

He nodded. "I just want to laugh with you and walk on the beach. I haven't had ice cream since you left."

"Aww." Her eyes went soft and dewy. "Aww," she repeated, nuzzling his cheek with hers.

He let his fingers trail up and down her spine. "The last three weeks have been hell. I don't ever want to hurt you again. I will because I'm human and I'll make mistakes, but not like I did. I'm so sorry I hurt you, Bella."

"I know you are. We're going to be okay."

"The way I see it, we hit a bump in the road—a crater—but we're strong enough to work through it."

"Of course."

"And I'm pretty much the best damn thing that's ever happened to you." He rolled on top of her. "*And* if I haven't mentioned it lately, I'm absolutely crazy in love with you." He growled and nipped at her neck.

She laughed, settling her hands on his shoulders. "I want to take things slow for a little while."

He sent her a wry smile. "We're naked and I'm hard again. We're buying a house."

She grinned. "I mean the other stuff: living together while we're fixing up the house. I need for us to go slow until we've found our footing again."

"Whatever you want."

"I just want it to be right."

"It's right. You and me are exactly right. Let me show you." He pushed himself into her and took her on a fast-paced journey. Flesh slapped against flesh as he yanked her hips high and pounded, watching stunned pleasure play over her face as he brought her up fast and hard. He covered her mouth with his, swallowing her long, loud scream as he came on a loud moan of his own and collapsed on top of her.

"Oh, my God," she panted out. "Oh, my God."

His cell phone rang as he gasped for air. "Man, that's bad timing," he heaved out against her neck. "But I should probably get it." He reached over the edge of the bed and grabbed his phone from his pants pocket. "Hello?"

"I can't cover you tomorrow morning," Skylar said.

He rolled off Bella and lay back against the pillows, still trying to catch his breath as he pulled her against his side. "Why?"

"Because they're taking me off the Caparellis and moving me to some new task force in fucking Los Angeles."

He frowned. "Since when?"

"Since I got back to the office an hour ago and Special Agent in Charge said we're meeting in the morning to discuss details."

"I guess we're going to be neighbors."

She spouted off a few inventive expletives about what Special Agent in Charge could do with his dick.

He winced and sat up when Bella's eyes went wide as she looked from him to the phone and grinned. "All right, then. So it sounds like Joey's on the hook for tomorrow."

"I talked to the DA. The room where we waited today is going to be occupied by another witness. We can't use that space."

He rubbed at the back of his neck, already knowing where this was going. "We stick together. No exceptions. Bella stays with me."

"We can keep her at the hotel—"

"Nope."

"I can get a couple of Marshals—"

He shook his head. "Not good enough."

"Reed—"

"Not good enough," he repeated, heating up. "Make something work or we'll be on the plane back to LA tonight."

"You've been subpoenaed. You don't have a choice—"

"We all have choices. The DA wants my testimony, so he'll find a way to make sure Bella can be at the courthouse with me."

"I'll call you back." She hung up.

He tossed the phone down and sat back, scrubbing at his face. "Son of a bitch."

"I can stay here."

"No, you can't." He had every intention of sitting his ass in the grand jury chair tomorrow and finishing this, but Bella was going to be there too, where he could make sure she was safe. "They're playing this my way or losing their witness." His phone rang again. "Hello?"

"The DA says we can put Bella in one of the judges' chambers while you're finishing up. Mathison is in Aruba this week, so his room is free."

"With Joey."

"You'll have to talk to him when he brings you your dinner."

He looked at his watch, realizing Joe would be there in less than fifteen minutes.

"Bella's going to be fine. She'll be on the second floor—almost right below the grand jury room. The DA's thinking he needs you for another hour—two, tops."

He sighed, wanting Bella in the room right next to his like she had been today, but this was a reasonable concession. "Sounds good."

"Reed."

"Yeah?"

"I like her. I like her for you."

He smiled. "Thanks."

"Let me know what you and Joe work out. I'll be there as soon as my meeting's over. We'll get you back to the airport together."

"I'll call you later." He hung up and looked at Bella.

"I can stay here."

He shook his head. "You and Joey are going to hang out in Judge Mathison's chambers while I testify. It should be an in-and-out, pretty quick deal. We can go home afterward."

"To Ethan's?"

"For now—until we get stuff figured out." Which wasn't going to be a fast process. This was never going to end for them until they found a way to take care of the Caparellis. *All* of the Caparellis.

She sighed, plucking at the comforter. "I want to get back to working on my new home—our new home."

"I know."

She crawled into his lap and hooked her legs around his waist, framing his face between her hands. "Our new home, Reed."

He kissed her. "Ours." He glanced at his watch again. "I *really* hate to say it, but we should probably get dressed. Joe's going to be here any minute."

"I'm going to go take a quick shower." She kissed him again, trailing her fingers down his chest and stomach. "I'll be thinking about how I wish you were joining me."

He groaned as he nibbled her shoulder. "That's not nice."

She grinned. "Maybe we can pick up right here later."

He cupped her breasts. "Are you sure? Because I thought we were taking things slow."

She whimpered, tracing his lips with her tongue. "Not too slow."

He gripped her ass, ready to devour her all over again. Joey could wait in the hall. "We're going to be good, Bella. This is going to be good."

She nodded. "Yes, it is. Now let's get dressed."

꧁ Chapter Fifty-Nine ꧂

Bella took another bite of her cream cheese-slathered bagel while she sat across from Joey at the small table in Judge Mathison's second-story chambers. She'd been slightly surprised by the homey atmosphere when they walked into the pretty space over an hour ago—comfy couches, stylish accent lamps, pictures of family, and numerous leafy plants set around the large windows, soaking up the bright morning sunshine. She wiped her fingers on the paper napkin in her lap, then set down the next card in her pile while she and Joey played war.

"Ah, here we go." Joey smiled his triumph when they both drew a seven. "Set down three and make your fourth lousy."

She put down her three cards and flipped the fourth, laughing when she won and Joey swore.

"It's your lucky day." He gestured to his dwindling pile.

"I guess so." She looked at her watch, then pulled in her take, adding it to her deck.

"Getting antsy?"

She shrugged. "A little."

He peeked at his own watch. "I can't imagine it'll be all that much longer. Sounds like the DA covered a lot of ground yesterday."

"I'm just ready to go home. I miss Lucy."

"I'm sure you do. That's a hell of a dog you've got." He took a *huge* bite of his third bagel. "So, tell me more about this house you mentioned last night," he said over his mouthful. "We didn't have time for much more than shop talk before I had to go."

She blinked and looked down, trying to disguise a smile as she grabbed her cell phone from her back pocket. She'd never known anyone quite like Reed's best friend. He was big, loud, and more than a little rough around the edges, but adorable nonetheless. "It needs a lot of work." She scrolled through her photos, finding the series of pictures she'd taken, and handed him her phone. "It's certainly a work in progress."

Joe frowned as he swiped at the screen several times. "Huh."

She grinned. "That's exactly what Reed said when I brought him by to check out the place."

He scratched at his beard. "Kinda looks like a money pit."

She threw her head back and laughed, clasping her hands together. "You two *definitely* think alike." She took the phone back and studied the last picture she'd snapped on Tuesday night—the one where she'd ripped up another three ugly bushes. Snagging her bottom lip with her teeth, she barely suppressed a giddy sigh. That was theirs—hers and Reed's. Or it would be very soon. They were together again. They'd spent the night making each other absolutely *crazy*. "It's going to be beautiful when we finish it. I can see it so clearly."

He went after another bite of his midmorning snack. "I'll have to take your word for it."

She slid her phone back in her jeans pocket. "You and Mel will have to come stay with us."

"Count on it." Joe set down another card as she did and pushed his losing hand her way. "I'm glad you and Reed were able to work things out. Nobody deserves to be happy more than my buddy." He pointed to the ceiling. Reed sat somewhere on the third story above them.

"After seeing all of you in my dad's room...I needed a little time to figure things out."

"Sounds like it worked out in the end, right?"

She nodded.

"He's different now, you know. I can hear it when we talk on the phone. I can see it when I look at him."

She swiped her hair behind her ear, not quite sure she knew what Joey was implying. "He's just—he's Reed."

"No, he's not," he said, shaking his head. "Not even close, but it's a good thing. Mad Dog's lost his edge."

She frowned. "I don't want him to lose his edge. He still has a dangerous job."

"He'll be all right." He narrowed his eyes as he contemplated. "I'm talking about the emotional armor he needed to survive out here. He doesn't need that anymore, especially now that he has you. Reed's got himself a brand-new life—a great one."

"Thank you."

They played a few more hands, Bella winning most. "Have you

ever considered trying something different?"

He laughed, shaking his head. "Being a cop runs in my blood. Four generations. I can't imagine doing anything other than what I do now."

"Sounds like you're happy."

"I am. I'm gonna propose to Mel next month on her birthday."

Bella paused with her next card as her heart went soft. "That's wonderful, Joey."

He nodded. "When you've got a good apple, it's smart to keep her around." He winked, then rushed to his feet in a lightening move, drawing his gun and aiming, when the interior door to the judge's chambers creaked slowly open. He moved to the right, blocking Bella from whatever waited on the other side of the mahogany wood.

DA Moore's secretary stepped in, gasped, and stumbled back with the tray of bottled waters she held.

Bella hurried to her feet. "Oh, my gosh. It's okay. Shawna, right?"

The woman bobbed her head as she stared at the weapon pointed at her. "Yes. I'm sorry. I just—Elliott said you were down—I thought you might like something to drink."

Bella walked over, her black pumps slapping on the hardwood floor in her haste to take the tray. Joey lowered his weapon but didn't put it away. "Thank you so much for thinking of us."

She nodded again and stepped out. "I'm sorry."

Bella smiled reassuringly. "It's okay."

"Jesus." Joey shoved his gun back in his holster. "What the fuck was that?"

"She just brought us some water." Bella set the tray on the judge's desk with less than steady hands.

"No one's supposed to know we're here. And who opens a door like that, anyway?"

"I think she had to because of the tray." Bella grabbed their drinks, leaving the plate of pastries behind, and sat down, exhaling a shaky breath while her heart pounded a wild beat.

Joey walked over to the door and locked it, then sat back down. "Sorry about that."

"It's okay."

"You wanna finish our game or do something different? It looks like the judge has got himself a TV."

"Uh, how about you finish telling me about your plans for Mel."

He smiled. "If you want to hear them."

"Of course I do." She handed him one of the bottled waters. "I'm a sucker for romance."

He grinned. "You're all right, Bella."

She beamed. "Thank you."

"So, I'm thinking I'm gonna take her away for the weekend—rent us a place up in Vermont or something."

"What about going to a bed-and-breakfast?"

He nodded, pointing at her. "Perfect. A fucking bed-and-breakfast. Why didn't I think of that?"

She chuckled, wondering if it was possible for Joey to go a full thirty minutes without dropping an f-bomb.

"I'll take her out for dinner. Maybe I can pay someone to put a whole bunch of flowers in the room—light some candles for when we get back—and I'll ask her."

"That sounds lovely. Mel's a very lucky woman." And she meant it. Joe was Reed's brother in all the ways that mattered, so he was hers now too.

"She's a—" Joey froze when they heard a thump in the main hallway and someone test the locked doorknob.

Bella rushed to her feet as Joey did. "Who's that?"

He took out his gun and his eyes changed, turning from friendly to deadly in a blink like Reed's had yesterday. "Lock yourself in the bathroom."

She shook her head, reaching out her hand to him. "What about you?"

"Lock yourself in the bathroom, Bella. Go."

She turned to do what Joey said when both doors burst open with a sharp crack. Two men wearing janitorial outfits and dark gray caps rushed in from opposite sides, firing shots in four quick metallic clicks at Joey before he could get one off. Bella stared in horror as Joey jerked and fell back, breaking the table and solid wood chair with his impact. Turning, she ran for the bathroom and slammed the door, fumbling with the lock, then grabbed her phone and found Reed's number. She listened to the incessant ringing as she gasped for each breath and tucked herself in the corner by the toilet. "Come on. Come *on*," she shuddered out as tears poured down her cheeks. The door burst open and she screamed. "Help!"

"Shut up." The man walked over and smacked her over the head with the pistol he'd used to kill Joey.

She felt a wretched pain radiate through her temple, then nothing else.

Reed occupied the same uncomfortable chair he'd sat in yesterday afternoon as he glanced at his watch—like he'd done several times over the last half hour. The DA's endless questions were hitting the ninety-minute mark and he was getting restless. Typically he would have applauded DA Moore's thoroughness—especially when they were talking about garnering an indictment for Alfeo Caparelli—but today he just wanted to get the hell out of there. He rubbed at his jaw and bobbed his leg up and down, fighting the urge to stand up and leave. For the last several minutes, he'd been unable to shake the feeling that something was wrong. It was tempting to grab his cell phone and send off a quick text—just to make sure things were going well—but he folded his hands on the table instead, struggling to pay attention.

Everything was fine. Joe and Bella were locked in the judge's chambers just downstairs. If he had to guess, Joe was stuffing his face full of bagels and sharing stories about the good old days Reed was never going to be able to live down. Yet even as he tried to convince himself that all was good, something felt off.

"...Mr. McKinley for your testimony today."

He blinked, realizing the DA was talking to him. "I'm sorry. Can you repeat that?"

"I said thank you for your testimony today."

"You're welcome." He sent the group of men and women sitting around the conference table a small smile as he stood, then walked out into the main hallway. Finally. Now they could go home. He started toward the elevators and grabbed his phone from his pocket, realizing that Bella had tried to get ahold of him eighteen minutes ago.

"Hey," Skylar called to him from behind.

He paused, glancing over his shoulder as she jogged his way wearing one of her typical tailored suit-and-heel combinations.

"I'm here. I made it," she said, slightly out of breath as she sidled up next to him.

"Hey." He dialed Bella's number back and brought the phone to his ear, absently listening to it ringing as he hit the button for the elevator. "So, are you a California chick now?"

Skylar flared her nostrils. "Apparently so, but I don't want to talk about it."

"You can have my place since—"

"This is Bella. Leave a message and I'll get back to you."

His blood ran cold and the hair stood up on the back of his neck when he heard her voicemail instead of Bella herself. Something was wrong. "Call Joe." He booked it to the stairwell and shoved through the door, running down the stairs.

Skylar followed with the phone at her ear. "What the hell's going on?"

"She's not answering. She should be answering."

"I'm getting Joe's voicemail."

"They've got her. I can feel it." And the idea made him ill.

"We don't know that."

"They're not *answering*." He pushed through the door to the second floor and sprinted down the long, quiet hall to Judge Mathison's chambers, noting that the old mahogany door was splintered and half-closed. "Oh, God. Oh, God," he repeated, instantly living a thousand nightmares. Clenching his jaw, he drew his gun as Skylar did the same.

She met his gaze and immediately moved to take her stance by the side of the doorway.

Nodding, he kicked open the door and rushed in with Skylar covering him. He stopped, staring at the broken table and chair as Joey groaned and attempted to gain all fours while blood poured down the left side of his face. "Oh, Christ. *Fuck*! Bella!" Reed hurried into the bathroom, noting another splintered door and the two drops of blood on the white tile. "Where is she?" He moved over to Joey in three quick strides and crouched down. "Where is she, Joe? How long have you been out?"

Joey groaned again, losing his balance, and fell back on his ass. "Fuckin' pricks were dressed like janitors."

"How many?"

"Two."

"How long ago do you think?"

"I don't know. Twenty minutes—twenty-five? Damn, the room's spinning."

"Perimeter's clear," Skylar said as she came back in from the opposite hallway and shoved her gun away while still holding her phone to her ear. She crouched down and grabbed a wad of napkins from the bagel bag, then pressed them to Joey's nasty head wound. "Don't try to stand up. The ambulance is coming. What have we got?"

Joey blinked several times. "Uh, two white males wearing gray caps and janitor's clothing. Got off four shots—wet suppressors."

"Two white males, janitor's clothing and gray caps," Skylar repeated to someone on the other end of the line as she settled Joe's hand over the saturated napkins and gained her feet. "I'm going to look at security footage and see what they've got there. More police are on the way. What's Bella wearing today?"

Reed jammed his hand through his hair, commanding himself to think. "Uh, blue jeans, black heels, and a white elastic-y tank top thing."

Skylar nodded. "We're going to get her back." She hurried off, shouting orders as her high heels echoed her frantic pace down the hall.

Reed wanted to run after her, to go wherever he would find Bella, but at this point, he had no idea where that was. He focused on Joe and the next step, allowing himself to slip into the cool, detached place that had served him well for ten years. He needed to gather details and follow the clues; that was the only way he was ever going to hold Bella again. "What the hell happened?"

"Cards." Joey gestured to the upended table and deck scattered around the floor. "We were playing and talking about me proposing to Mel. There was a noise in the hall, then someone testing the doorknob. I told her to get in the bathroom. She was headed that way when the fuckers barged in and shot me in the chest. Lost my balance from the impact and hit my fucking head on the way down. Lights out." Wincing, he rubbed at his chest where his vest had saved his life. "Broke some ribs, I think."

"You didn't hear or see anything after you fell?"

"Lights out," he repeated with a shake of his head as he tried to stand. "We need to get her back."

Reed pressed his hand to Joey's shoulder. "You need to stay down before you hurt yourself even more."

"Matty's got her."

"Of course he does." He stood, unable to be still any longer as the fear tried to sneak beneath his carefully composed armor. "Now we have to figure out where." He scrubbed at his face with unsteady hands. "He's going to torture her, Joe—like he did Bruno. He's not going to make it quick."

"Don't focus on that." Joey turned his head and puked, moaning as he heaved. “Shit. My fuckin’ *ribs*.”

Skylar hurried back in with the paramedics following.

“Concussion and possible broken ribs,” Reed said to the medical team, then gave his attention to Skylar. Joe was talking and breathing, so he would worry about him later.

“The cameras are out in this wing and down in the east alleyway. The surveillance crew started experiencing technical difficulties about thirty minutes ago, but we were able to roll through some footage out by the parking garage and found two men climbing out of a black Cadillac CTS wearing janitor’s clothing and gray hats. We’ve got some people in Transportation looking at the traffic cams, seeing if they can track them down. We know the vehicle took a right out by the garage. We’ll see if they can pick up their route from there.”

He nodded.

“One of the security guards just talked to a woman who witnessed two men in similar dress pushing a large recycling cart to the elevator a few minutes ago. The cart was found in the alley.” She touched his arm. “There was some blood residue, Reed.”

He rubbed at the back of his neck, not wanting to hear any more—not wanting for any of this to be real. But it was. Bella was hurt and he couldn’t help her. “This is an inside job. Someone told them we were here—how to get around and make this happen.”

“And we’ll find them, but let’s get Bella first.”

He nodded again, pacing back and forth, certain he would lose his mind simply from feeling helpless. “No one heard anything in the surrounding rooms?”

She shook her head. “At this point, we can’t find anyone. The judge’s assistant is on vacation, and the boiler room is directly below us. We’re working on getting Bella’s phone carrier to ping her cell phone.”

He clenched his jaw, looking to the ceiling. “That could take hours with all the red tape. We don’t have hours.” He glanced at his watch. Fifteen, maybe twenty minutes had passed since they’d run into the judge’s chambers, yet it felt like a lifetime. They needed every second they could get. Matty wasn’t going to spare his cousin any pain. If anything, he would be more brutal.

Skylar’s phone rang. “Yeah.” She nodded, looking at Reed. “Okay. That’s great. Excellent. Thanks.” She hung up.

“What?” he asked, refusing to get his hopes up.

“They’ve spotted the Cadillac on the parkway—found it on various traffic cameras throughout the city and have been able to trace its path. Footage shows the vehicle took exit 4 about five minutes ago. They lost them there, but we have a place to start."

Which wasn't nearly good enough. "She could be anywhere."

"They've issued a city-wide BOLO. Everyone's watching for her. They're moving in to swarm the area."

He didn't want the backup—they were risking some dirty asshole tipping off the Caparellis—but they couldn't do this alone.

"That's down by Cropsey, Eighty-Sixth, and Bath Ave," Joe said as the paramedics hoisted up the gurney. "Old stomping ground."

"Let's go." Reed booked it out of the room and down a flight of stairs, following Skylar to her car. He knew Bensonhurst like the back of his hand, but they were still miles from where they needed to be.

"Buckle up," Skylar said as she pulled out with a squeal of tires and her lights blazing.

He watched the speedometer, fisting his hands on his lap as Skylar weaved her way in and out of traffic.

"I'm going to cut across here. It's faster." She took a sharp, last-minute right.

He moved with her turn. "Do whatever. Just get us there." His phone rang, and he swore when it was Joe's ringtone instead of Bella. He wanted nothing more than to hear her voice—for her to tell him that she'd gotten away and she was okay. "What the hell, Joe? You need to go to the hospital."

"I'm heading there now."

"So what are—"

"She thought about me. When the shit was hitting the fan and I told her to go hide in the bathroom, she reached out for me. I'm going to help you find her even if it's from the fucking ambulance."

He clenched his jaw, watching Skylar push her speed to ninety when they hit the parkway. "I can't lose her. I just got her back."

"I know. We gotta get in his head," Joe continued. "We gotta put on our sadistic bastard thinking caps and figure out Matty's plan."

Reed put Joey on speaker for Skylar to hear too. "We know Matty has Nicoli's daughter. If Matty hasn't figured that out yet, he knows he has a rat." And both were a punishing death sentence.

"Let's assume the worst," Joey said. "Let's go with the theory that Matty knows Bella's Nicoli's. They went to a lot of trouble for this, took a lot of risks to grab a snitch. So it makes sense to follow the path that he knows who she is."

Joe was one hundred percent right, but Reed didn't like it.

"What's your gut telling you?" Skylar asked as she took exit 4, following the twist in the road around to Bay Eighth Street, and shut off her lights. "It's never wrong."

If he'd listened to his instincts thirty minutes ago, he might have been able to stop this entire thing from happening. He shook his head. "I don't know."

Skylar took a right on Bath Avenue as a police cruiser moved their way, going as slowly as Skylar.

Reed watched the cop shake his head and felt the rush of panic, no longer able to fight back the waves of terror. He reached for the door handle, needing to run, to sprint and yell for Bella until she answered. "I don't know where she is. I don't *know*." He jammed his fingers through his hair as his heart pounded and his breath rushed in and out. "He's hurting her. He's hurting her and I can barely stand it."

"Get it together, boss," Joey snapped. "She needs you to keep it together. Focus on who they are. On what you know. No one knows these bastards better than you do. You've been studying them since you were a kid. What's Matty thinking?"

"I'm turning onto Bay Forty-Sixth Street and making a left on Cropsey," Skylar said for Joey's benefit.

"Cropsey Avenue. Nicoli and Alfeo's old turf," Joey reminded him. "They ran that area for decades. Patrizio's restaurant. Dino's pawn shop. The bowling alley."

Reed racked his brain, trying to remember the numerous locations Vinny had mentioned he and Alfeo had hung out at while Skylar drove them past Patrizio Caparelli's long-ago pizza place. He stared out at the area he knew well, the place where he'd spent seven years of his life with Joey, trying to infiltrate the worst of the worst. Which spot held the most meaning? Where would Alfeo want to give his little brother the finger? Because that's exactly what this was about. "Elena."

Skylar looked at him.

Reed came to attention as he stared farther down the road. "Elena. They killed Elena the next block up—the beginning of the end. Nicoli's breaking point. Alfeo's endgame after Nicoli turned him in."

"That's good, boss. That's real good."

"Matty wouldn't be able to help himself. He would go for something symbolic." He blew out a trembling breath as the realization brought about a new wave of bone-chilling fear. "He definitely knows

Bella is Nicoli's daughter. Speed up and go around the block. The old warehouse over there." He pointed to his left. "That's the bar Nicoli and Alfeo walked out of the night they spotted the capo they were contracted to kill." His gaze wandered to the area across from it—the huge brick building. "Maybe there." He unbuckled his seat belt and touched his gun.

Skylar drove by. "Possible lookout car to my left."

Reed subtly looked that way and spotted two men sitting in a car, eating sandwiches. "Go up a block and come around. We'll head to the back. This warehouse was the Caparellis'."

They turned again, and Skylar slowed as they passed the building. "There," she said, hitting the brakes. "The car parked all the way in the back. By the farthest loading dock."

"You got the place?" Joe wanted to know.

He leaned closer to Skylar's side, scrutinizing the vehicle he could barely see with the chain-link fence and graffiti-riddled trailers scattered around the abandoned lot. "Looks like it."

"This place is huge. We need to wait for backup."

Reed shook his head. "No."

Skylar drove down another block and parked. "We can't go in alone."

He opened the door, glancing at his watch. "Call it in, but I'm not waiting. I'm not sitting out here while they hurt her more."

"Let me know when you have her back," Joe said. "You'll get her back, Reed."

"Thanks." He hung up.

Skylar dialed and checked her gun as she got out. "I guess we're going in together."

"Let's finish this." They started down the block at a steady pace when all he wanted to do was run.

☙ Chapter Sixty ❧

Bella whimpered as she opened her eyes and stared at the rusted metal desk across the dim, dusty room. Blinking, she glanced around at a wall of dirty interior windows and old papers littering the scarred wood floor. She moved to press her hand to the pounding in her head, but her hands were immobilized behind her back. Panic surged through her foggy brain as she tried to stand and quickly realized she was tied down to a chair. "What? Where am I?" And then she remembered, going instantly still. The man in the judge's bathroom had hit her, and now she was here.

"You're up."

She whipped her head to her left, immediately regretting her fast movement when her vision blurred. She swallowed another rush of fear, staring at Matty Caparelli closing a door behind him.

"Cousin Isabella." He grinned as he approached her, wearing Italian loafers and a two-thousand-dollar suit.

She tugged on her wrists and fought to move her legs, finding whatever was holding her in place to be too strong to budge.

He stopped in front of her, crossing his arms and shaking his head. "What? You don't have anything to say to your own family?"

"Please let me go."

"A dreamer with a nasty head wound." He bent close and gripped her chin between his fingers, holding her gaze. "You have his eyes. Caparelli eyes. Why didn't I realize that sooner?" He gave her jaw another painful squeeze. "So where *is* Nicoli?"

She blinked, fighting back tears, refusing to cry. "He passed away."

He smirked and let her go. "Your loyalty rests with the wrong people, cousin."

Her lips trembled, and she hated that a tear slipped down her cheek. "He died of cancer two-and-a-half weeks ago."

"Okay." He gave her cheek a series of small, nasty slaps, making her head throb with each jarring movement. "My condolences, then. Uncle Nicky. Pop says I liked him." He shrugged. "I liked you too, at Luisa's party." He walked away and took a seat behind the rusted desk. "But I don't like you anymore, Isabella. You're a rat just like your old man."

Another man walked into the room, and her eyes went huge.

Matty chuckled. "Does he look familiar? I think you two bumped into each other at the grocery store, or maybe you remember him from your office. Tony, go ahead and cut her free. Isabella and I are gonna have ourselves a little sit-down."

The stocky man walked over and cut the zip tie from around her wrists, then her ankles. "Get up," he said as he yanked her to her feet and dragged her more than guided her to the chair across from Matty's.

Matty sat back and laced his fingers on his stomach. "So, Cousin Isabella, tell me what it is you're doing here in New York."

She lifted her chin. "I'm sightseeing."

He grinned. "Brave."

She swallowed, refusing to reply.

"So you were sightseeing at the courthouse?" He pulled her cell phone out of his pocket. "With him." He turned the screen so she could see one of her pictures of Reed.

Again she said nothing as terror clogged her throat.

He raised his brow, turned the phone, and swiped through the other images. "You and the cop have a thing. Got yourselves a big, ugly dog and an even uglier house." He set the phone down with a slap. "I don't like cops." He shrugged. "Grew up that way, but I especially hate this cop." He gestured to the phone. "You know he's gonna pay, right? Cause he's a nosy pig. Asking Bruno questions he had no business asking."

"I don't know who Bruno is," she said, watching his eyes glitter.

"Bruno *was* a fucking rat and your boyfriend's bitch." He sat back again, lacing his fingers. "Bruno shared some interesting facts with me before he died from unfortunate circumstances. I was quite intrigued by Detective Reed McKinley's fascination with Nicoli Caparelli and his inquiries into whether Uncle Nicky had a kid. Imagine my surprise when Tony did a little investigating and I realized that Detective McKinley's neighbor was Isabella Colby—Luisa's very good friend."

She swallowed. "Luisa doesn't know anything. I don't know anything."

"We're keeping an eye on Luisa for a while. Her pops was loyal to the family, so she'll probably live. I'm afraid I can't say the same for you."

She narrowed her eyes even as her pulse quickened to a sickeningly fast beat.

"You are fearless, aren't you? A Caparelli trait." He pulled a gun from the holster on his hip. "But fearlessness isn't always smart. Sometimes fearlessness can be deadly." He pointed the gun between her eyes. "You know what I mean?"

Her breath hitched in and out as she trembled in her chair. She wanted to run or at least try to fight for her life, but there was nowhere to go—no one to help her overpower two men twice her size. "So you're just going to kill me?"

"I am." He rested his finger on the trigger. "I don't like liars. And you're a liar, Beautiful Bella. Your story about sightseeing at the courthouse just isn't adding up for me."

Bella closed her eyes as several tears fell, thinking of Reed while she waited for the end.

Matty laughed. "You don't think I'm going to make it that easy, do you? Usually it's a pop to the back of the head. Quick. Painless. But that won't be your fate."

She opened her eyes, staring into the nasty, hard depths of her cousin's.

"Your Uncle Alfeo wants your death to be painful." He reached over and captured her hand, holding it in his. "Long and drawn out. Uncle Nicky's gone, so you're gonna have to take a little something for him too. Sins of the father, I think the saying goes." In a quick move, he tugged her forward by the wrist and slammed the butt of the gun down on top of her hand.

She cried out as heat and agony radiated through her bones. Whimpering, she yanked away and cradled her injury against her chest.

"Hurts?" He reached across the table, snatching her by the arm and set her hand back on the table.

She struggled, trying to pull away. "Please don't. Please."

He gentled his grip. "What do you take me for, cousin, an animal?" He held her gaze and slammed the heavy weight down twice more, his lips pressing firm with the effort he put into the assault.

She screamed, fighting to free herself as black spots filled her vision.

"Ouch." Matty sucked in a breath through his teeth and shook his head mournfully. "I think that might be broken. It's unfortunate for you that your Uncle Alfeo insisted we draw this out. I'm gonna do something like that to your arms and legs, probably your knees. Maybe your ribs." He stood, walked around the desk, and jerked her head back so she was forced to look up at him as he loomed over her. "Beautiful skin." He stroked a finger along her cheek. "I'm a little embarrassed to admit that I had a few lustful thoughts about you when we sat down at Luisa's shindig." He grabbed a square of sandpaper off the dirty desk. "When you were there trying to gather information for the Feds."

She stared at the fine grit, terrified of what he would do with it. "I didn't know who you were."

He grinned. "You're good. I almost believe you." He rubbed the rough texture along her cheek in punishing circles. "Almost. Let's exfoliate. That's what they call it, right?"

"Stop!" She tried to fight him off as the friction burned and scraped her skin. "Please stop!"

"When I'm done with you, they'll have no idea who you are—no fingerprints or identifying features. Just another Jane Doe in the morgue." He added more pressure while she continued to do what she could to evade the worst of his abuse. "I don't like feeling like a fool, Isabella. Sightseeing at the courthouse?" He stopped his scrubbing.

More tears fell as she sobbed quietly.

"Tell me what you were doing there today."

She looked down. "Taking a tour." Telling the truth would spare her nothing, but maybe she could protect Reed to some degree.

"She's a tough one, Tony. Good thing Shawna was able to clue us in."

She blinked. "Shawna? The district attorney's secretary?"

Matty grinned. "And Tony's girl." He laughed. "Tony, you got your knife on you?"

"I do." Tony pulled it from his pocket and handed it over.

"You turned on your Uncle Alfeo." He flipped the blade up and traced the knife along her neck. "What did my pops ever do to you?"

She shied away. "Please don't."

He tilted her head farther back and brought the blade to her jaw. She gasped as she felt the nick and warmth.

"Should I go all the way across now or later?"

"You won't get away with this," she choked out over her tears.

"I get away with everything. We own this city, Isabella. That's the privilege and honor of being a Caparelli. That's our *legacy*. You were robbed of family, of that honor, because your father was a vile, Fed-flipping pig. A snitch! The ultimate betrayal." He nicked her again. "If Uncle Nicky had remembered his place, I would have made it my duty to defend you. To look after you. No one messes with Caparelli women. But that's not how it worked out." He smeared his palm in her blood, showing her his crimson fingers. "Your blood. My blood. *Our* blood. You're an insult to—"

There was a loud crash somewhere beyond the door.

Matty came to attention as Tony did. "Go check it out."

Tony drew his gun and opened the door to the long, dark hallway and left.

Minutes passed in silence as Bella stared at the knife Matty had set on the desk when he reached for his pistol.

"Tony?" Matty called as his gaze darted around the room. "Hey, Tony," he yelled again and moved to the door, opening it enough to peer out.

Bella licked her lips and snagged the knife, settling it beneath her leg as her heart raced. The odds of wounding Matty and Tony enough to get away weren't in her favor, especially when she had only one hand to work with. She glanced down at her swollen, bruised knuckles she kept elevated at her chest and tried to ignore the excruciating pain. Right now, she needed to focus on getting the heck out of there. She opened her mouth to get Matty's attention and ideally make him come closer, but Tony came back.

"Where the fuck have you been?"

"We should go look around together. I think we got rats in the building."

Matty looked at Bella. "Tie her back up."

"I only got one tie left. One of the smaller ones."

"So use it!"

Tony came over and yanked on her injured hand, securing it to the chair.

She cried out as he fastened the thin plastic around her wrist and pulled on the tie until it bit into her skin. "It's too tight."

Tony smiled cruelly. "Then we know you'll stay put."

"Hurry up." Matty pointed the gun at Bella. "This is your lucky day.

You might end up with that pop to the back of the head after all." He waited for Tony and shut the door behind them.

She sat perfectly still, training her ears, listening for any noises in the hallway, but it was impossible to hear anything past the solid metal. Grabbing the knife with trembling fingers, she pushed the button on the handle and flinched when the nasty blade swung up into place. Wasting no time, she went after the plastic with firm downward strokes while she pulled and tugged on her trapped arm. Tears streamed down her face and she whimpered as true terror and agony spurred her closer to the finish line. "Come on. Come on," she gasped out and yanked hard, snapping the stubborn tie.

"Okay." She rushed to her feet for a better look through the filthy windows and gripped the chair, blinking away another wave of dizziness as she stared out at the massive warehouse space one story below. Rows upon rows of sectioned-off twelve-foot-high pallets and huge garage doors at the back that had to lead outside. She trailed her gaze over the old metal staircase and access door located somewhere beyond the room she was currently stuck in and moved to the door Matty and Tony disappeared through.

She pocketed the knife and took off her heels, leaving them behind, then twisted the doorknob, peeking out into the shadows. It was now or never. She could try to get away and possibly live or she could stand here and wait to die. Going for it, she hurried down the hall to the next door and opened it, never quite so happy to see a flight of stairs. Glancing over her shoulder one last time, she quietly closed herself in the enormous space and ran down the steps, making her way into the pallet stacks, hurrying left then right, hoping to get lost in the maze. She focused on the light shining in through the windows toward the back of the football-field-size room and kept going, stopping only when a door creaked open and footsteps echoed on the staircase behind her.

"Isabella, get out here!" Matty hollered. "Tony, go check the offices."

She froze, backing up against one of the boards, fighting to steady her breathing so she could listen to the path of his approach but her heart pounded too hard.

"Don't draw this out, cousin."

She glanced right as his voice carried from that direction and moved left, keeping her focus on the windows ahead. She stopped abruptly, startled by several loud pops somewhere outside. Gunshots. She pressed her hand to her heaving chest as she struggled with a fresh wave of tears. Reed was here. They'd found her. Now she needed to survive long enough to make it to safety. Joey wasn't going to have died in vain.

She took a step and paused, ducking when Matty passed two rows to her right. Holding her breath, she watched him disappear through the thin slats in the old wood and counted to ten, then took off, moving farther away to the left. Her head throbbed as she constantly looked around, waiting for their paths to cross. Minutes ticked by in eerie silence—or maybe it was hours—as she made her way closer to the doors, zigzagging. She moved to change rows yet again and stopped dead when another movement farther ahead caught her attention. "Skylar," she whispered, watching her disappear around another wall of pallets.

Relief quickly vanished into horror when she realized Skylar was headed right into Matty's path. "No. Oh, no." She ran in the opposite direction—away from the promise of safety, frantic to save Reed's friend. "I'm over here, you bastard!"

He laughed and started back, the slap of his leather soles announcing that he wasn't all that far away.

Sprinting toward the stairs, she glanced over her shoulder and ducked into another row as he moved closer. She barely stifled a scream when an arm reached out and snagged her around the waist, yanking her into the next aisle. She met Reed's bold blue eyes as he brought his finger to his lips, then pushed her behind him.

There was no time for joy or hugs. Suddenly the room was silent again. The hunter still hunted.

"You're going to wish you'd kept heading toward the exit," Matty yelled. "You know I'm going to find you eventually."

Reed nudged her backward with his shoulder, signaling for her to move behind the next wall as Matty inched his way closer. Reed raised his gun in two hands and rested his index finger on the trigger in a stance she'd seen a million times in the movies. He bumped her again, edging her to the middle of the stack. Their surroundings grew ominously quiet.

They heard a noise to their right and Reed pivoted, firing twice.

Bella screamed, covering her ears in reflex as she watched Matty jerk from the impact of the bullets hitting him in his chest and neck and the gun he'd aimed their way fly from his hand. She stared into his eyes—Caparelli eyes—before he stumbled back and crashed into the wall of pallets, then fell to the ground.

Reed continued to hold him at gunpoint and kicked Matty's pistol out of his reach, even as Matty stared blankly at the ceiling.

Bella screamed again when another shot echoed somewhere in the room.

"McKinley," Skylar yelled.

"Yeah?"

"I'm headed your way." Skylar ran to them with her gun still ready to fire. "You're okay?"

He nodded. "Fine."

"I dropped one. Shot to the head." She grabbed her phone and dialed a number. "Two down in the warehouse. Hostage recovered. Give us a minute to get out of here." She gave Reed her attention again. "They're sweeping the building now."

He nodded, keeping his weapon in hand as he turned, staring at Bella.

She started crying and hurried into his arms.

"Bella." He held her tight, pressing a long kiss to her uninjured cheek. "God, Bella." He kissed her again.

She sobbed now, shaking uncontrollably. "I didn't think I was going to see you again."

He stroked her hair and ran his arm up and down her back. "I'm right here."

"I'm so sorry about Joey."

"He's okay."

She drew away enough to meet his gaze. "He's okay?"

"He's got a concussion and broken ribs."

Her relief was huge, bringing on another wave of tears.

"It's all right. Everything's all right now." He tracked his gaze over her face with concern radiating in his eyes. "Look at you. Look what he did to you."

"I think my hand might be broken."

"Keep us covered," he said to Skylar as he shoved his weapon away and picked Bella up. "Tell them to get us an ambulance."

"We're coming out the back entrance," Skylar relayed. "Have paramedics ready."

"Let's get out of here." He kissed her again. "Keep your head down. Bury your face right against my neck. The press has to be on this by now. I don't want anyone seeing you."

She nodded, clinging to him, breathing him in, feeling his tough body protecting hers as they left the building, walking out into the chaos of flashing lights, police vehicles, and dozens of men and women swarming the scene while helicopters flew overhead. “I want to go home.”

“We’re going to the hospital first.” He stepped up into the back of the ambulance and sat down on the bed, refusing to let her go.

She gripped him tighter, realizing he was shaking too. “You saved me.”

He tucked her hair behind her ear. “I wasn’t leaving without you.”

The doors closed, and they were whisked off to the emergency room.

☙ Chapter Sixty-One ❧

REED BACKED UP ALONGSIDE THE HOUSE AND STOPPED JUST BEfore the truck's tires could roll over the new sod they were still babying. He killed the engine and got out, dropping the gate for Lucy. "Down you go, Luce."

Lucy wasted no time booking it over to the huge tree in the corner of the yard where she spent most of her time circling the trunk, waiting for her new friends to tease her mercilessly from the tall branches above.

Chuckling, he shook his head and grabbed Bella's presents from the bed. Their new home was mostly finished. The construction crews had packed up and rolled out over a week ago. Now it was time for a few finishing touches. He walked past the pretty patio space where he and Bella had eaten their lunch earlier and set down the bushes he'd purchased at the local nursery, scanning the planting instructions when he typically would have guessed. But some things were worth an extra couple of minutes—and this was one of them. He reached for the shovel and stopped when his phone alerted him to a text. Snagging his phone from his pocket, he read Skylar's text.

Transfer's complete.

He nodded, instinctively glancing east in the direction of Alfeo Caparelli's tiny, isolated prison cell at the Federal Supermax in Colorado. No one had been more surprised than Reed when La Cosa Nostra's most notorious boss pled guilty to the multiple charges brought against him. Thanks to Vincent Pescoe's excellent memory and damning videotaped testimony, his older brother would spend the rest of his life right where he belonged. With Matty dead and the internal executions of the organization's most influential men, the Caparelli crime family was finished—and Bella's identity was safe.

DA Morris's secretary would serve some time for aiding and abetting the mob, and after Skylar's interrogation room "chat" with the terrified woman, Reed had no doubt Secretary Shawna would keep Bella's identity to herself. He tossed his gaze to the bright blue sky on the gorgeous California afternoon, certain that Vinny was looking down with a smile. His phone dinged again, bringing him back to attention and another text from Skylar.

Tell Bella I'll pick up dessert at the store. The cookies are a bust. Now that the fire department's gone, I'm going to work for a while.

I'll let her know, he replied, grinning as he shoved his phone away. Skylar was all moved in at his old place—and she *sucked* in the kitchen. Twice in the last six weeks, fire trucks had rolled up to her front door. Apparently, three times now. And Bella had only given her two basic cooking lessons.

He picked up the shovel and started digging, loving that his biggest worry was Skylar burning down her house. Even his assignment with Sadie was wrapping up with a promising break in her stalking case. He stomped his work boot down on the blade and stopped, listening to the birdsong in the quiet neighborhood while he stared at the glistening windows and solid wooden doors on his and Bella's new place, still in awe that this was his life. A stunning woman tinkering around inside, an adorable dog pacing back and forth by the tree, and this amazing home they got to call their own. "Not too shabby," he muttered and got back to his task, eager to finish up and guide Bella outside to show her the latest surprise he knew she was going to love.

Bella glided her roller over the final patch of wall space still in need of pale yellow paint and grinned. She went after the spot again for good measure and stepped back, scrutinizing the way the color she and Reed had finally selected played so well with the pretty crown molding and beautiful bamboo flooring in the sunny dining room. "Absolutely perfect."

Tomorrow the new rug would arrive. Then they could accept delivery for the gorgeous maple table-and-chair set she and Wren had picked out weeks ago. She set the roller back on the tray, imagining that Linda and Aunt Bonnie were going to be impressed with the progress—not that they hadn't stopped by yesterday and multiple times during the last month and a half. And neither she nor Reed had minded. They had welcomed all the help they could get with their new place, especially when her cast wasn't going anywhere for at least another fourteen days.

She glanced at the pale purple plaster encasing her hand and dismissed the minor annoyance. She was alive, and thanks to the miracle work of Dr. Huberty and a few corrective laser treatments, her face had healed without any permanent scaring. But she didn't want to think about that. Today was too wonderful to focus on a time she wished to forget. Instead, she gave her attention to the boxes in the living room and the new curtain rods that needed hanging.

Lucy sent up a frantic din in the backyard, and Bella rolled her eyes. "Those poor *squirrels*." Chuckling, she walked through the kitchen and outside, stopping on the patio when she spotted Reed sitting back on his haunches while he worked on something in the corner. "What are you doing over there, handsome?"

He looked over his shoulder. "This is where the garden's going, right?"

"Yes, but I thought we were waiting until next year to start that project."

"We are. But that doesn't mean we can't add a couple of touches right now."

Curious, she headed his way.

He glanced over his shoulder again. "Hold up there, nosy. Turn around before you ruin the surprise."

Laughing, she turned away. "I'm not sure I can handle the suspense."

"Give it your best shot." He brushed off his hands with a couple of solid claps and walked to stand in front of her, locking his wrists around her waist. "Hey, beautiful."

She smiled, loving that he wore his ball cap backward with his T-shirt and jeans. "You're back from running your errands."

"I am."

"Where'd you go?"

He grinned. "Here and there."

"No clues?"

He shook his head. "Nope."

She nipped his chin. "That's not very nice."

He pulled her closer. "What have you been up to for the last little while?"

She hooked her arms around the back of his neck. "I finished the dining room."

"Oh, yeah?"

"Mmm-hmm." She stroked her fingers along his skin. "We're almost finished. I can hardly believe it."

"The place looks amazing. You were right."

She looked back at the pretty pots of verbena and new landscaping complimenting the creamy almond exterior paint and pressure-washed brick. "I love that we did this together—you and me and all of our family and friends."

"Speaking of friends, Skylar wanted me to let you know that she's picking up dessert at the store."

She laughed. "The cookies didn't work out?"

He shook his head. "The fire department stopped by again."

She threw her head back, laughing harder. "I'm not ready to give up on her yet." She nuzzled her cheek against his chest, forever treasuring his masculine scent. "Emilia's aunt called while you were gone. The girls are beside themselves with excitement about the barbecue next weekend, but Aunt Peggy's worried about Emilia's wheelchair."

He shrugged. "I'm not. We'll make it work."

"That's what I said." She kissed him. "Apparently Emilia's still sleeping with the teddy bear you brought her. And they had to dry the bouquet. It's in a vase on the dresser by her bed."

He grinned. "What can I say? I've got an eye for flowers."

She smiled, thinking of the pretty carnations on their new granite countertop in the kitchen. "Yes, you do."

"So, Joe and Mel decided they're going to fly in after all. He sent me a text while I was out."

She beamed, thrilled that they were going to have a full house for their first party. "It'll be great."

"Tell me that after we listen to him bitch about his ribs for forty-eight hours straight. Even Mel's starting to lose her patience, and that woman's a saint."

"We can put up with it. He helped save my life."

Some of the joy left his eyes. "Alfeo made the transfer to Colorado today."

"Good, but I don't want to talk about him. I'll be happy never to think of him."

"So, we won't."

"Sounds good."

"How about we move things along to your surprise?"

She fluttered her lashes. "Yes, please."

"Close your eyes."

She did.

He turned her around and guided her forward. "Ready?"

She nodded. "Definitely."

He took her hand, lacing their fingers. "Okay."

She opened her eyes and pressed her cast to her chest as her heart melted. "Reed. Raspberry bushes."

He gave her fingers a squeeze. "Raspberry bushes."

She threw her arms around him. "I *love* them."

"The woman at the nursery says they'll need a couple years to grow before we'll have enough for jam, but I figure we have to start somewhere."

"You're the best." She stood on her tiptoes and pressed a noisy kiss to his lips. "I love you so much."

He played his fingers through her hair. "I love you too."

She sighed. "We have raspberry bushes."

"And strawberry plants." He gestured to the items still in the back of the truck.

"Strawberries too?"

"I thought we could add to the tradition. I want our kids growing up remembering that they helped their mom and dad make raspberry *and* strawberry jam."

She blinked as her eyes filled, constantly thankful that this wonderful man was her partner. "I love that idea."

He hooked his thumbs through the loops on her short shorts. "Tonight's our first night in the new house."

She wiggled her brow. "I know."

"I was thinking that after Skylar heads home, we could take the bike over to the beach."

"Mmm. Yes."

"You know, when I looked at the calendar this morning, I noticed that the moon's supposed to be full tonight." He glanced up to their new bedroom windows.

She snagged her lip with her teeth, understanding exactly what he was suggesting. "I'm still on the pill."

"So maybe you stop taking it and we'll start practicing for the next moon."

Her heart pounded with joy. "Really?"

He nodded. "And since we're about to get serious about baby-making, we should probably get married."

"Reed," she whispered as a tear rolled down her cheek.

He rested his forehead against hers. "I want to marry you, Bella. Nothing about my life has been the same since you walked into it. I'm ready for weddings and kids running around in the yard—our future. Everything. As long as I get to share all of it with you."

"Yes. Let's get married. Let's make babies."

He cradled her cheeks in his palms and kissed her, taking her deeper with gentle glides of his tongue. "What do you say we head upstairs?"

"I thought you'd never ask."

"Come on, Lucy." He picked Bella up and walked toward their new home. "So, how much notice would we have to give if we wanted to cancel dinner with a good friend?"

She grinned as she stared into his bold blue gaze, letting Lucy in before she locked them inside. "I think if we called right now, we'd be okay."

"Consider it done." He hustled up the curved staircase to the master bedroom and kicked the door closed. "We can do dinner tomorrow. I'm planning on snacking on you tonight." He growled, nipping at her neck, as they collapsed onto the bed and he pressed her into the mattress.

Her laughter echoed through the big, beautiful room while the sun shined bright through their brand-new picture windows.

The End

Thank you!

Hi there!

Thank you for reading *Deceiving Bella*. What did you think of Reed and Bella's story? Did you love it, like it, or maybe even hate it? Honest reviews are vital to authors. Please consider taking a moment to share your thoughts on Amazon, Goodreads, or the vendor you purchased the book from. Thank you!

I'll see you again soon when we catch up with another installment of the *Bodyguards of L.A. County* series.

Until next time,

~Cate

Also By Cate Beauman

Bodyguards of L.A. County Series

Morgan's Hunter

Falling For Sarah

Hailey's Truth

Forever Alexa

Waiting For Wren

Justice For Abby

Saving Sophie

Reagan's Redemption

Answers For Julie

Finding Lyla

About The Author

Cate Beauman is the author of the international best-selling series *The Bodyguards of L.A. County*. She currently lives in North Carolina with her husband, two boys, and their Saint Bernards, Bear and Jack.

www.catebeauman.com
www.facebook.com/CateBeauman
www.goodreads.com/catebeauman
Follow Cate on Twitter: @CateBeauman

Made in the USA
Lexington, KY
13 June 2018